The Portable

HARLEM
RENAISSANCE
READER

The Portable

HARLEM
RENAISSANCE
READER

Edited and with an Introduction by

DAVID LEVERING LEWIS

VIKING

VIKING
Published by the Penguin Group
Penguin Books USA Inc., 375 Hudson Street,
New York, New York 10014, U.S.A.
Penguin Books Ltd, 27 Wrights Lane,
London W8 5TZ, England
Penguin Books Australia Ltd, Ringwood,
Victoria, Australia
Penguin Books Canada Ltd, 10 Alcorn Avenue,
Toronto, Ontario, Canada M4V 3B2
Penguin Books (N.Z.) Ltd, 182-190 Wairau Road,
Auckland 10, New Zealand

Penguin Books Ltd, Registered Offices:
Harmondsworth, Middlesex, England

First published in 1994 by Viking Penguin,
a division of Penguin Books USA Inc.

1   3   5   7   9   10   8   6   4   2

Pages 764–766 constitute an extension of this copyright page.

LIBRARY OF CONGRESS CATALOGING IN PUBLICATION DATA
The Portable Harlem Renaissance reader/edited and with an
introduction by David L. Lewis.
p.   cm.
ISBN 0-670-84510-8
1. American literature—Afro-American authors.   2. Afro-Americans—
Literary collections.   3. American literature—New York (N.Y.)
4. American literature—20th century.   5. Harlem Renaissance.
I. Lewis, David L.
PS153.N5P67   1994
810.8'089073—dc20   93-30233

Printed in the United States of America
Set in Sabon

To Enid, Eugene, Gretta,
Johnnetta, Niara, Norman,
Preston, Richard, Timothy &
The Class of '56,
with Special Thanks to Esme Bhan

CONTENTS

INTRODUCTION

THE HARLEM RENAISSANCE was a somewhat forced phenomenon, a cultural nationalism of the parlor, institutionally encouraged and directed by leaders of the national civil rights establishment for the paramount purpose of improving race relations in a time of extreme national backlash, caused in large part by economic gains won by Afro-Americans during the Great War. W. E. B. Du Bois labeled this mobilizing elite the "Talented Tenth" in a seminal 1903 essay. He fleshed out the concept that same year in "The Advance Guard of the Race," a piece in *Booklover's Magazine* in which he identified the poet Paul Laurence Dunbar, the novelist Charles W. Chesnutt, and the painter Henry O. Tanner, among a small number of other well-educated professionals, as representatives of this class. The Talented Tenth formulated and propagated a new ideology of racial assertiveness that was to be embraced by the physicians, dentists, educators, preachers, businesspeople, lawyers, and morticians who comprised the bulk of the African American affluent and influential—some ten thousand men and women out of a total population in 1920 of more than ten million. (In 1917, traditionally cited as the natal year of the Harlem Renaissance, there were 2,132 African Americans in colleges and universities, probably no more than fifty of them attending "white" institutions.)

It was, then, the minuscule vanguard of a minority—a fraction of 0.1 percent of the racial total—that jump-started the New Negro Arts Movement, using as its vehicles the National Association for the Advancement of Colored People (NAACP) and the National Urban League (NUL), and their respective publications, *The Crisis* and *Opportunity* magazine. The Harlem Renaissance was not, as some students have maintained, all-inclusive of the early twentieth-century African American urban experience. Not everything that happened between 1917 and 1935 was a Renaissance happening. The potent mass movement founded and led by the charismatic Marcus Garvey was to the Renaissance what nineteenth-century populism was to progressive reform: a parallel but socially different force related primarily through dialectical confrontation. Equally different from the institutional ethos and purpose of the Renaissance was the Black Church. If the leading intellectual of the race, Du Bois, publicly denigrated the personnel and preachings of the Black Church, his animadversions were merely more forthright than those of other New Negro notables James Weldon Johnson, Charles S. Johnson, Jessie Redmon Fauset, Alain Locke, and Walter Francis White. An occasional minister (such as the father of poet Countee Cullen) or exceptional Garveyites (such as Yale-Harvard man William H. Ferris) might move in both worlds, but black evangelism and its cultist manifestations, such as Black Zionism, represented emotional and cultural retrogression in the eyes of the principal actors in the Renaissance.

When Du Bois wrote a few years after the beginning of the New Negro movement in arts and letters that "until the art of the black folk compels recognition they will not be rated as human," he, like most of his Renaissance peers, fully intended to exclude the blues of Bessie Smith and the jazz of "King" Oliver. Spirituals sung like *Lieder* by the disciplined Hall Johnson Choir—and, better yet, *Lieder* sung by conservatory-trained Roland Hayes, 1924 recipient of the NAACP's prestigious Spingarn Medal—were deemed appropriate musical forms to present to mainstream America. The deans of the Renaissance were entirely content to leave discovery and celebration of Bessie, Clara, Trixie, and various other blues-singing Smiths to white music critic Carl Van Vechten's effusions in *Vanity Fair*. When the visiting Russian film director Sergei Eisenstein enthused about new black musicals, Charles S. Johnson and Alain Locke expressed mild consternation in their interview in *Opportunity* magazine. As board members of the Pace Phonograph Company, Du Bois, James Weldon Johnson, and others banned "funky" artists from the Black Swan list of recordings, thereby contributing to the demise of the African American–owned firm. But the wild Broadway success of Miller and Lyles's musical *Shuffle Along* (which helped to popularize the Charleston) or Florence Mills's *Blackbirds* revue flouted such artistic fastidiousness.

The very centrality of music in black life, as well as of black musical stereotypes in white minds, caused popular musical forms to impinge inescapably on Renaissance high culture. Eventually, the Renaissance deans made a virtue out of necessity; they applauded the concert-hall ragtime of "Big Jim" Europe and the "educated" jazz of Atlanta University graduate and big-band leader Fletcher Henderson, and took to hiring Duke Ellington or Cab Calloway as drawing cards for fund-raising socials. Still, their relationship to music remained beset by paradox. New York ragtime, with its "Jelly Roll" Morton strides and Joplinesque elegance, had as much in common with Chicago jazz as Mozart did with "Fats" Waller.

Although the emergence of the Harlem Renaissance seems much more sudden and dramatic in retrospect than the historic reality, its institutional elaboration was, in fact, relatively quick. Because so little fiction or poetry had been produced by African Americans in the years immediately prior to the Harlem Renaissance, the appearance of a dozen or more poets and novelists and essayists seemed all the more striking and improbable. Death from tuberculosis had silenced poet-novelist Dunbar in 1906, and poor royalties had done the same for novelist Chesnutt after publication the previous year of *The Colonel's Dream*. Since then, no more than five African Americans had published significant works of fiction and verse. There had been *Pointing the Way* in 1908, a flawed, fascinating civil rights novel by the Baptist preacher Sutton Griggs. Three years later, Du Bois's sweeping sociological allegory *The Quest of the Silver Fleece* appeared. The following year came James Weldon Johnson's well-crafted *The Autobiography of an Ex-Colored Man*, but the author felt compelled to disguise his racial identity. A ten-year silence fell afterward, finally to be broken in 1922 by Claude McKay's *Harlem Shadows*, the first book of poetry since Dunbar.

Altogether, the Harlem Renaissance evolved through three stages. The first phase, ending in 1923 with the publication of Jean Toomer's unique prose poem *Cane*, was deeply influenced by white artists and writers—Bohemians and Revolutionaries—fascinated for a variety of reasons with the life of black people. The second phase, from early 1924 to mid-1926, was presided over by the Civil Rights Establishment of the NUL and the NAACP, a period of interracial collaboration between Zora Neale Hurston's "Negrotarian" whites and the African American Talented Tenth. The last phase, from mid-1926 to the Harlem Riot of March 1935, was

increasingly dominated by the African American artists themselves—the "Niggerati," in Hurston's pungent phrase. The movement, then, was above all literary and self-consciously an enterprise
of high culture well into its middle years. When Charles S. Johnson,
new editor of *Opportunity,* sent invitations to some dozen young
and mostly unknown African American poets and writers to attend
a celebration at Manhattan's Civic Club of the sudden outpouring
of "Negro" writing, on March 21, 1924, the Renaissance shifted
into high gear. "A group of the younger writers, which includes
Eric Walrond, Jessie Fauset, Gwendolyn Bennett, Countee Cullen,
Langston Hughes, Alain Locke, and some others," would be present, Johnson promised each invitee. All told, in addition to the
"younger writers," some fifty persons were expected: "Eugene
O'Neill, H. L. Mencken, Oswald Garrison Villard, Mary Johnston,
Zona Gale, Robert Morss Lovett, Carl Van Doren, Ridgely Torrence, and about twenty more of this type. I think you might find
this group interesting enough to draw you away for a few hours
from your work on your next book," Johnson wrote almost coyly
to the recently published Jean Toomer.

Although both Toomer and Langston Hughes were absent in
Europe, approximately 110 celebrants and honorees assembled
that evening; included among them were Du Bois, James Weldon
Johnson, and the young NAACP officer Walter Francis White,
whose energies as a literary entrepreneur would soon excel even
Charles Johnson's. Locke, a professor of philosophy at Howard
University and the first African American Rhodes scholar, served
as Civic Club master of ceremonies. Fauset, the literary editor of
The Crisis and a Phi Beta Kappa graduate of Cornell University,
enjoyed the distinction of having written the second fictional work
and first novel of the Renaissance, *There Is Confusion,* just released
by Horace Liveright. Liveright, who was present, rose to praise
Fauset as well as Toomer, whose prose poem *Cane* his firm had
published in 1923. Speeches followed pell mell—Du Bois, James
Weldon Johnson, Fauset. White called attention to the next Renaissance novel—his own, *The Fire in the Flint,* shortly forthcoming
from Knopf. Albert Barnes, the crusty Philadelphia pharmaceutical
millionaire and art collector, described the decisive impact of African art on modern art. Poets and poems were commended—
Hughes, Cullen, and Georgia Douglas Johnson of Washington,
D.C., with Gwendolyn Bennett's stilted yet appropriate "To Us-
ward" punctuating the evening: "We claim no part with racial

dearth,/We want to sing the songs of birth!" Charles Johnson wrote the vastly competent Ethel Ray Nance, his future secretary, of his enormous gratification that Paul Kellogg, editor of the influential *Survey Graphic,* had proposed that evening to place a special number of his magazine "at the service of representatives of the group."

Two compelling messages emerged from the Civic Club gathering: Du Bois's that the literature of apology and the denial to his generation of its authentic voice were now ending; Van Doren's that African American artists were developing at a uniquely propitious moment. They were "in a remarkable strategic position with reference to the new literary age which seems to be impending," Van Doren predicted. "What American literature decidedly needs at this moment," he continued, "is color, music, gusto, the free expression of gay or desperate moods. If the Negroes are not in a position to contribute these items," Van Doren could not imagine who else could. The African American had indisputably moved to the center of Mainstream imagination with the end of the Great War, a development nurtured in the chrysalis of the Lost Generation—Greenwich Village Bohemia. Ready conversance with the essentials of Freud and Marx became the measure of serious conversation in MacDougal Street coffeehouses, Albert Boni's Washington Square Book Shop, or the Hotel Brevoort's restaurant, where Floyd Dell, Robert Minor, Matthew Josephson, Max Eastman, and other *enragés* denounced the social system, the Great War to which it had ineluctably led, and the soul-dead world created in its aftermath, with McKay and Toomer, two of the Renaissance's first stars, participating. The first issue of Randolph Bourne's *Seven Arts* (November 1916)—which featured, among others of the "Lyrical Left," Waldo Frank, James Oppenheim, Robert Frost, Paul Rosenfeld, Van Wyck Brooks, and the French intellectual Romain Rolland—professed contempt for "the people who actually run things" in America. Waldo Frank, Toomer's bosom friend and literary mentor, foresaw a revolutionary new America emerging "out of our terrifying welter or steel and scarlet." The Marxist radicals (John Reed, Floyd Dell, Helen Keller, Max Eastman) associated with *Masses* and its successor magazine, *Liberator,* edited by Max and Crystal Eastman, were theoretically much more oriented to politics. The inaugural March 1918 issue of *Liberator* announced that they would "fight for the ownership and control of industry by the workers."

Among the Lyrical Left writers gathered around *Broom, S4N,* and *Seven Arts,* and the political radicals associated with *Liberator,* there was a shared reaction against the ruling Anglo-Saxon cultural paradigm. Bourne's concept of a "trans-national" America, democratically respectful of its ethnic, racial, and religious constitutents, complemented Du Bois's earlier concept of divided racial identity in *The Souls of Black Folk.* From such conceptions, the Village's discovery of Harlem followed both logically and, more compellingly, psychologically, for if the factory, campus, office, and corporation were dehumanizing, stultifying, or predatory, the African American, largely excluded because of race from all of the above, was a perfect symbol of cultural innocence and regeneration. He was perceived as an integral, indispensable part of the hoped-for design, somehow destined to aid in the reclamation of a diseased, dessicated civilization.

Public annunciation of the rediscovered Negro came in the fall of 1917 with Emily Hapgood's production at the old Garden Street Theatre of three one-act plays by her husband, Ridgely Torrence. *The Rider of Dreams, Simon the Cyrenian,* and *Granny Maumee* were considered daring because the casts were black and the parts were dignified. The drama critic from *Theatre Magazine* enthused of one lead player that "nobody who saw Opal Cooper—and heard him as the dreamer, Madison Sparrow—will ever forget the lift his performance gave." Du Bois commended the playwright by letter, and James Weldon Johnson excitedly wrote his friend, the African American literary critic Benjamin Brawley, that *The Smart Set*'s Jean Nathan "spoke most highly about the work of these colored performers." From this watershed flowed a number of dramatic productions, musicals, and several successful novels by whites—yet also, with great significance, *Shuffle Along,* a cathartic musical by the African Americans Aubry Lyles and Flournoy Miller. Theodore Dreiser grappled with the explosive subject of lynching in his 1918 short story "Nigger Jeff." Two years later, the magnetic African American actor Charles Gilpin energized O'Neill's *Emperor Jones* in the 150-seat theater in a MacDougal Street brownstone taken over by the Provincetown Players.

The year 1921 brought *Shuffle Along* to the 63rd Street Theatre, with music, lyrics, choreography, cast, and production uniquely in African American hands, and composer Eubie Blake's "I'm Just Wild About Harry" and "Love Will Find a Way" entered the list of all-time favorites. Mary Hoyt Wiborg's *Taboo* was produced that year, with a green Paul Robeson making his theatrical debut. Clement Wood's 1922 sociological novel *Nigger* sympathetically tracked a beleaguered African American family from slavery through the Great War into urban adversity. *Emperor Jones* (revived in 1922 with Robeson in the lead part) showed civilization's pretentions being mocked by forces from the dark subconscious. That same year T. S. Stribling's *Birthright* appeared, a novel remarkable for its effort to portray an African American male protagonist of superior education (a Harvard-educated physician) martyred for his ideals after returning to the South. "Jean Le Negre," the black character in e. e. cummings's *The Enormous Room* (1922), was another Noble Savage paradigm observed through a Freudian prism.

But Village artists and intellectuals were aware and unhappy that they were theorizing about Afro-America and spinning out African American fictional characters in a vacuum—that they knew almost nothing firsthand about these subjects. Sherwood Anderson's June 1922 letter to H. L. Mencken spoke for much of the Lost Generation: "Damn it, man, if I could really get inside the niggers and write about them with some intelligence, I'd be willing to be hanged later and perhaps would be." Anderson's prayers were answered almost immediately when he chanced to read a Jean Toomer short story in *Double-Dealer* magazine. With the novelist's assistance, Toomer's stories began to appear in the magazines of the Lyrical Left and the Marxists, in *Dial, S4N, Broom,* and *Liberator.* Anderson's 1925 novel *Dark Laughter* bore unmistakable signs of indebtedness to Toomer, whose work, Anderson readily admitted, had given him a true insight into the cultural energies that could be harnessed to pull America back from the abyss of fatal materialism. Celebrity in the Village brought Toomer into Waldo Frank's circle, and with it criticism from Toomer about the omission of African Americans from Frank's sprawling work *Our America.* After a trip with Toomer to South Carolina in the fall of 1922, Frank published *Holiday* the following year, a somewhat overwrought treatment of the struggle between the two races in the South, "each of which . . . needs what the other possesses."

Claude McKay, whose volume of poetry *Harlem Shadows* (1922) made him a Village celebrity (he lived in Gay Street, then entirely inhabited by nonwhites), found his niche among the *Liberator* group, where he soon became co-editor of the magazine with Michael Gold. The Eastmans saw the Jamaican poet as the kind of writer who would deepen the magazine's proletarian voice. McKay increased the circulation of *Liberator* to sixty thousand, published the first poetry of e. e. cummings (over Gold's objections), introduced Garvey's Universal Negro Improvement Association (UNIA), and generally treated the readership to experimentation that had little to do with proletarian literature. "It was much easier to talk about real proletarians writing masterpieces than to find such masterpieces," McKay told the Eastmans and the exasperated hard-line Marxist Gold. Soon all manner of Harlem radicals began meeting, at McKay's invitation, in West 13th Street, while the Eastmans fretted about Justice Department surveillance. Richard B. Moore, Cyril Briggs, Otto Huiswood, Grace Campbell, W. A. Domingo, inter alia, represented Harlem movements ranging from Garvey's UNIA and Briggs's African Blood Brotherhood to the CPUSA with Huiswood and Campbell. McKay also attempted to bring the Village to Harlem, in one memorable sortie taking Eastman and another Villager to Ned's, his favorite Harlem cabaret. Ned, notoriously anti-white, expelled them.

This was part of the background to the Talented Tenth's abrupt, enthusiastic, and programmatic embrace of arts and letters after the First World War. With white Broadway audiences flocking to O'Neill plays and shrieking with delight at *Liza*, *Runnin' Wild*, and other imitations of *Shuffle Along*, Charles Johnson and James Weldon Johnson, Du Bois, Fauset, White, Locke, and others saw a unique opportunity to tap into the American mainstream. Harlem, the Negro Capital of the World, filled up with successful bootleggers and racketeers, political and religious charlatans, cults of exotic character ("Black Jews"), street-corner pundits and health practitioners (Hubert Harrison, "Black Herman"), beauty culturists and distinguished professionals (Madame C. J. Walker, Louis T. Wright), religious and civil rights notables (Reverends Cullen and Powell, Du Bois, Johnson, White), and hard-pressed, hardworking families determined to make decent lives for their children. Memories of the nightspots in "The Jungle" (133rd Street), of Bill "Bojangles" Robinson demonstrating his footwork on Lenox Avenue, of raucous shows at the Lafayette that gave Florenz Ziegfeld some of his ideas, of the Tree of Hope outside Connie's Inn where musicians gathered as at a labor exchange, have been vividly set down by Arthur P. Davis, Regina Andrews, Arna Bontemps, and Langston Hughes.

If they were adroit, African American civil rights officials and intellectuals believed they stood a fair chance of succeeding in re-shaping the images and repackaging the messages out of which Mainstream racial behavior emerged. Bohemia and the Lost Generation suggested to the Talented Tenth the new approach to the old problem of race relations, but their shared premise about art and society obscured the diametrically opposite conclusions white and black intellectuals and artists drew from them. Harold Stearns's Lost Generation *revoltés* were lost in the sense that they professed to have no wish to find themselves in a materialistic, mammon-mad, homogenizing America. Locke's New Negroes very much wanted full acceptance by Mainstream America, even if some, like Du Bois, McKay, and the future *enfant terrible* of the Renaissance, Wallace Thurman, might have immediately exercised the privilege of rejecting it. For the whites, art was the means to change society before they would accept it. For the blacks, art was the means to change society in order to be accepted into it. For this reason, many of the Harlem intellectuals found the white vogue in Afro-Americana troubling, although they usually feigned enthusiasm about the new dramatic and literary themes. Despite the insensitivity, burlesquing, and calumny, however, the Talented Tenth convinced itself that the civil rights dividends were potentially greater than the liabilities. Benjamin Brawley put this potential straightforwardly to James Weldon Johnson: "We have a tremendous opportunity to boost the NAACP, letters, and art, and anything else that calls attention to our development along the higher lines."

Brawley knew that he was preaching to the converted. Johnson's preface to his best-selling anthology *The Book of American Negro Poetry* (1922) proclaimed that nothing could "do more to change the mental attitude and raise his status than a demonstration of intellectual parity by the Negro through his production of literature and art." Putting T. S. Stribling's *Birthright* down, an impressed Jessie Fauset nevertheless felt that she and her peers could do better. "We reasoned," she recalled later, " 'Here is an audience waiting to hear the truth about us. Let us who are better qualified to present that truth than any white writer, try to do so.' " The result was *There Is Confusion*, her novel about genteel life among Philadelphia's aristocrats of color. Similarly troubled by *Birthright* and other two-dimensional or symbolically gross representations of African American life, Walter White complained loudly to H. L. Mencken, who finally silenced him with the challenge "Why don't you do the right kind of novel? You could do it, and it would create a sensation." White did. And the sensation turned out to be *The Fire in the Flint* (1924), the second novel of the Renaissance, which he wrote in less than a month in a borrowed country house in the Berkshires. Meanwhile, Langston Hughes, whose genius (like that of Toomer's) had been immediately recognized by Fauset, published several poems in *The Crisis* that would later appear in the collection *The Weary Blues*. The euphonious "The Negro Speaks of Rivers" (dedicated to Du Bois) ran in *The Crisis* in 1921. With the appearance of McKay's *Harlem Shadows* and Toomer's *Cane* the next year, 1923, the African American officers of the NAACP and the NUL saw how a theory could be put into action. The young New York University prodigy Countee Cullen, already published in *The Crisis* and *Opportunity,* had his Mainstream breakthrough in 1923 in *Harper's* and *Century* magazines. Two years later, with Carl Sandburg as one of the three judges, Cullen won the prestigious Witter Bynner poetry prize. Meanwhile, Paul Kellogg's *Survey Graphic* project moved apace under the editorship of Locke.

Two preconditions made this unprecedented mobilization of talent and group support in the service of a racial arts-and-letters movement more than a conceit in the minds of a handful of leaders: demography and repression. The Great Black Migration from the rural South to the industrial North produced the metropolitan dynamism undergirding the Renaissance. The Red Summer of 1919, a period of socialist agitation and conservative backlash following the Russian Revolution, produced the trauma that led to the cultural sublimation of civil rights. In pressure-cooker fashion, the increase in its African American population caused Harlem to pulsate as it pushed its racial boundaries south below 135th Street to Central Park and north beyond 139th ("Strivers' Row"). In the first flush of Harlem's realization and of general African American exuberance, the Red Summer of 1919 had a cruelly decompressing impact upon Harlem and Afro-America in general. Charleston, South Carolina, erupted in riot in May, followed by Longview, Texas, in July, and Washington, D.C., later in the month. Chicago exploded on July 27. Lynchings of returning African American soldiers and expulsion of African American workers from unions abounded. In the North, the white working classes struck out against perceived and manipulated threats to job security and unionism from blacks streaming north. In Helena, Arkansas, where a pogrom was unleashed against black farmers organizing a cotton cooperative, and outside Atlanta, where the Ku Klux Klan was reconstituted, the message of the white South to African Americans was that the racial *status quo ante bellum* was on again with a vengeance. Twenty-six race riots in towns, cities, and counties swept across the nation all the way to Nebraska. The "race problem" became definitively an American dilemma in the summer of 1919, and no longer a remote complexity in the exotic South.

The term "New Negro" entered the vocabulary in reaction to the Red Summer, along with McKay's poetic catechism—"Like men we'll face the murderous, cowardly pack/Pressed to the wall, dying, but fighting back!" There was a groundswell of support for Marcus Garvey's UNIA. Until his 1924 imprisonment for mail fraud, the Jamaican immigrant's message of African Zionism, anti-integrationism, working-class assertiveness, and Bookerite business enterprise increasingly threatened the hegemony of the Talented Tenth and its major organizations, the NAACP and NUL, among people of color in America (much of Garvey's support came from the West Indians). "Garvey," wrote Mary White Ovington, one of the NAACP's white founders, "was the first Negro in the United States to capture the imagination of the masses." *The Negro World*, Garvey's multilingual newspaper, circulated throughout Latin America and the African empires of Britain and France. Locke spoke for the alarmed "respectable" civil rights leadership when he wrote, in his introductory remarks to the special issue of *Survey Graphic*, that, although "the thinking Negro has shifted a little to the left with the world trend," black separatism (Locke clearly had Garveyism in mind) "cannot be—even if it were desirable." Although the movement was its own worst enemy, the Talented Tenth was pleased to help the Justice Department speed its demise.

No less an apostle of high culture than Du Bois, initially a Renaissance enthusiast, vividly expressed the farfetched nature of the arts-and-letters movement as early as 1926: "How is it that an organization of this kind [the NAACP] can turn aside to talk about art? After all, what have we who are slaves and black to do with art?" It was the brilliant insight of the men and women associated with the NAACP and NUL that, although the road to the ballot box, the union hall, the decent neighborhood, and the office was blocked, there were two untried paths that had not been barred, in large part because of their very implausibility, as well as irrelevancy to most Americans: arts and letters. They saw the small cracks in the wall of racism that could, they anticipated, be widened through the production of exemplary racial images in collaboration with liberal white philanthropy, the robust culture industry primarily located in New York, and artists from white Bohemia (like themselves marginal and in tension with the status quo). If, in retrospect, then, the New Negro Arts Movement has been interpreted as a natural phase in the cultural evolution of another American group, as a band in the literary continuum running from New England, Knickerbocker New York, Hoosier Indiana, to the Village's Bohemia, to East Side Yiddish drama and fiction, and then on to the Southern Agrarians, such an interpretation sacrifices causation to appearance. Instead, the Renaissance represented much less an evolutionary part of a common experience than it did a generation-skipping phenomenon in which a vanguard of the Talented Tenth elite recruited, organized, subventioned, and guided an unevenly endowed cohort of artists and writers to make statements that advanced a certain conception of the race, a cohort of men and women most of whom would never have imagined the possibility of artistic and literary careers.

Toomer, McKay, Hughes, and Cullen possessed the rare ability combined with personal eccentricity that defined the artist, but the Renaissance not only needed more like them but a large cast of supporters and extras. American dropouts heading for seminars in garrets and cafés in Paris were invariably white and descended from an older gentry displaced by new moneyed elites. Charles Johnson and his allies were able to make the critical Renaissance mass possible. Johnson assembled files on prospective recruits throughout the country, going so far as to cajole Aaron Douglas, the artist from Kansas, and others into coming to Harlem, where a network manned by his secretary, Ethel Ray Nance, and her friends Regina Anderson and Louella Tucker (assisted by gifted Trinidadian short-story writer Eric Walrond) looked after them until a salary or a fellowship was secured. White, the very self-important assistant secretary of the NAACP, urged Paul Robeson to abandon law for an acting career, encouraged Nella Larsen to follow his own example as a novelist, and passed the hat for artist Hale Woodruff. Fauset continued to discover and publish short stories and verse, such as those of Wallace Thurman and Arna Bontemps. Shortly after the Civic Club evening, both the NAACP and the NUL announced the creation of annual awards ceremonies bearing the titles of their respective publications, *Crisis* and *Opportunity*.

The award of the first *Opportunity* prizes came in May 1925 in an elaborate ceremony at the Fifth Avenue Restaurant with some three hundred participants. Twenty-four distinguished judges (among them Carl Van Doren, Zona Gale, Eugene O'Neill, James Weldon Johnson, and Van Wyck Brooks) had ruled on the worthiness of entries in five categories. The awards ceremony was interracial, but white capital and influence were crucial to success, and the white presence, in the beginning, was pervasive, setting the outer boundaries for what was creatively normative. Money to start the *Crisis* prizes had come from Amy Spingarn, an accomplished artist and poet, and wife of Joel Spingarn, chairman of the NAACP's board of directors. The wife of the influential attorney, Fisk University trustee, and Urban League Board chairman, L. Hollingsworth Wood, had made a similar contribution to initiate the *Opportunity* prizes. These were the whites Zora Neal Hurston, one of the first *Opportunity* prizewinners, memorably dubbed "Negrotarians." There were several categories: Political Negrotarians like progressive journalist Ray Stannard Baker, and maverick socialist types associated with *Modern Quarterly* (V. F. Calverton, Max Eastman, Lewis Mumford, Scott Nearing); salon Negrotarians like Robert Chanler, Charles Studin, Carl and Fania (Marinoff) Van Vechten, and Eleanor Wylie, for whom the Harlem artists were more exotics than talents. They were kindred spirits to Lost Generation Negrotarians, drawn to Harlem on their way to Paris by a need for personal nourishment and confirmation of a vision of cultural health, in which their romantic or revolutionary perceptions of African American vitality played a key role—Anderson, O'Neill, Georgia O'Keefe, Zona Gale, Waldo Frank, Louise Bryant, Sinclair Lewis, Hart Crane. The commercial Negrotarians like the Knopfs, the Gershwins, Rowena Jelliffe, Horace Liveright, V. F. Calverton, and Sol Hurok scouted and mined Afro-American like prospectors.

The May 1925 *Opportunity* gala showcased the steadily augmenting talent in the Renaissance—what Hurston characterized as the "Niggerati." Two laureates, Cullen and Hughes, had already won notice beyond Harlem. The latter had engineered "discovery" as a Washington, D.C., bellhop by placing dinner and three poems on Vachel Lindsay's hotel table. Some prizewinners were barely to be heard from again: Joseph Cotter, G. D. Lipscomb, Warren Mac-

Donald, Fidelia Ripley. Others, like John Matheus (first prize in the short-story category) and Frank Horne (honorable mention in short-story writing), fell short of first-rank standing in the Renaissance. Most of those whose talent had staying power were introduced that night: E. Franklin Frazier, who won the first prize for an essay on social equality; Sterling Brown, who took second prize for an essay on the singer Roland Hayes; Hurston, awarded second prize for a short story, "Spunk"; and Eric Walrond, third-prize winner for his short story "Voodoo's Revenge." James Weldon Johnson read the poem that took first prize, "The Weary Blues," Langston Hughes's turning-point poem, combining the gift of a superior artist and the enduring, music-encased spirit of the black migrant. Comments from Negrotarian judges ranged from O'Neill's advice to "be yourselves," to novelist Edna Worthley Underwood's exultant anticipation of a "new epoch in American letters," and Clement Wood's judgment that the general standard "was higher than such contests usually bring out."

The measures of Charles S. Johnson's success were the announcement of a second *Opportunity* contest to be underwritten by Harlem "businessman" (and numbers king) Caspar Holstein, former *Times* music critic Carl Van Vechten's enthusiasm over Hughes and subsequent arranging of a contract with Knopf for Hughes's first volume of poetry, and, one week after the awards ceremony, a prediction by the New York *Herald Tribune* that the country was "on the edge, if not already in the midst of, what might not improperly be called a Negro renaissance"—thereby giving the movement its name. Priming the public for the Fifth Avenue Restaurant occasion, the special edition of *Survey Graphic*, "Harlem: Mecca of the New Negro," edited by Locke, had reached an unprecedented 42,000 readers in March 1926. The ideology of cultural nationalism at the heart of the Renaissance was crisply delineated in Locke's opening essay, "Harlem," stating that, "without pretense to their political significance, Harlem has the same role to play for the New Negro as Dublin has had for the New Ireland or Prague for the New Czechoslovakia." A vast racial formation was under way in the relocation of the peasant masses ("they stir, they move, they are more than physically restless"), the editor announced. "The challenge of the new intellectuals among them is clear enough." The migrating peasants from the South were the soil out of which all success must come, but soil must be tilled, and the Howard University philosopher reserved that task exclusively for the Talented Tenth in liaison with its Mainstream analogues—in the "carefully maintained contacts of the enlightened minorities of both race groups." There was little amiss about America that interracial elitism could not set right, Locke and the others believed. Despite historic discrimination and the Red Summer, the Rhodes scholar assured readers that the increasing radicalism among African Americans was superficial. At year's end, Albert and Charles Boni published Locke's *The New Negro*, an expanded and polished edition of the poetry and prose from the *Opportunity* contest and the special *Survey Graphic*.

The course of American letters was unchanged by the offerings in *The New Negro*. Still, it carried several memorable works, such as the short story "The South Lingers On" by Brown University and Howard Medical School graduate Rudolph Fisher; the acid poem "White House(s)" and the euphonic "The Tropics in New York" by McKay, now in European self-exile; and several poetic vignettes from Toomer's *Cane*. Hughes's "Jazzonia," previously published in *The Crisis,* was so poignant as to be almost tactile as it described "six long-headed jazzers" playing while a dancing woman "lifts high a dress of silken gold." In "Heritage," a poem previously unpublished, Cullen outdid himself in his grandest (if not his best) effort with its famous refrain, "What is Africa to me." The book carried the distinctive silhouette drawings and Egyptian-influenced motifs by Aaron Douglas, whose work was to become the artistic signature of the Renaissance. With thirty-four African American contributors (four were white), Locke's work included most of the Renaissance regulars. The notable omissions from *The New Negro* were Asa Randolph, George Schuyler, and Wallace Thurman. These were the gifted men and women who were to show by example what the potential of some African Americans could be and who proposed to lead their people into an era of opportunity and justice.

By virtue of their symbolic achievements and their adroit collaboration with the philanthropic and reform-minded Mainstream, their augmenting influence would ameliorate the socioeconomic conditions of their race over time and from the top downward. Slowly but surely, they would promote an era of opportunity and justice. It was a Talented Tenth conceit, Schuyler snorted in Asa Randolph's *Messenger* magazine, worthy of a "high priest of the intellectual snobbocracy," and he awarded Locke the magazine's "elegantly embossed and beautifully lacquered dill pickle." Yet it seemed to work, for although the objective conditions confronting most African Americans in Harlem and elsewhere were deteriorating, optimism remained high. Harlem recoiled from Garveyism and socialism to applaud Phi Beta Kappa poets, university-trained painters, concertizing musicians, and novel-writing officers of civil rights organizations. "Everywhere we heard the sighs of wonder, amazement and sometimes admiration when it was whispered or announced that here was one of the 'New Negroes,' " Bontemps recalled.

By summer of 1926, Renaissance titles included *Cane* (1923), *There Is Confusion* (1924), *Fire in the Flint* (1924), *Flight* (1926), McKay's *Harlem Shadows* (1922), Cullen's *Color* poetry volume (1924), and *The Weary Blues* volume of poetry (1926). The second *Opportunity* awards banquet, April 1926, was another artistic and interracial success. Playwright Joseph Cotter was honored again, as was Hurston, for a short story. Bontemps, a California-educated poet struggling in Harlem, won first prize for "Golgotha Is a Mountain," and Dorothy West, a Bostonian aspiring to make a name in fiction, made her debut, as did essayist Arthur Fauset, Jessie's able brother. The William E. Harmon Foundation transferred its attention at the beginning of 1926 from student loans and blind children to the Renaissance, announcing seven annual prizes for literature, music, fine arts, industry, science, education, and race relations, with George Edmund Haynes, African American official in the Federal Council of Churches, and Locke as chief advisors. That same year, the publishers Boni & Liveright offered a thousand-dollar prize for the "best novel on Negro life" by an African American. Casper Holstein contributed one thousand dollars that year to endow *Opportunity* prizes. Van Vechten made a smaller contribution to the same cause. Amy Spingarn provided six hundred dollars toward the *Crisis* awards. Otto Kanh underwrote two years in France for the young artist Hale Woodruff. There were Louis Rodman Wanamaker prizes in music composition.

The third *Opportunity* awards dinner was a vintage one for poetry, with entries by Bontemps, Sterling Brown, Hughes, Helene Johnson, and Jonathan H. Brooks. In praising their general high quality, the white literary critic Robert T. Kerlin added the revealing comment that their effect would be "hostile to lynching and to jim-crowing." Eric Walrond's lush, impressionistic collection of short stories *Tropic Death* appeared from Boni & Liveright at the end of 1926, the most probing exploration of the psychology of cultural underdevelopment since Toomer's *Cane*. If *Cane* recaptured in a string of glowing vignettes (most of them about women) the sunset beauty and agony of a preindustrial culture, *Tropic Death* did much the same for the Antilles. Hughes's second volume of poetry, *Fine Clothes to the Jew* (1927), spiritedly portrayed the city life of ordinary men and women who had traded the hardscrabble of farming for the hardscrabble of domestic work and odd jobs. Hughes scanned the low-down pursuits of "Bad Man," "Ruby Brown," and "Beale Street" and shocked Brawley and other Talented Tenth elders with the bawdy "Red Silk Stockings." "Put on yo red silk stockings,/Black gal," it began, urging the protagonist to show herself to white boys. It ended wickedly with "An' tomorrow's chile'll/Be a high yaller."

A veritable Ministry of Culture now presided over Afro-America. McKay, viewing the scene from abroad, spoke derisively of the artistic and literary autocracy of "that NAACP crowd." The Ministry mounted a movable feast to which the anointed were invited, sometimes to Walter and Gladys White's apartment at 409 Edgecombe Avenue, where they might share cocktails with Sinclair Lewis or Mencken; often (after 1928) to the famous 136th Street "Dark Tower" salon maintained by beauty culture heiress A'Lelia Walker, where guests might include Sir Osbert Sitwell, the Crown Prince of Sweden, or Lady Mountbatten; and very frequently to the home of Carl and Fania Van Vechten, to imbibe the host's sidecars and listen to Robeson sing or Jim Johnson recite from "God's Trombones" or George Gershwin play the piano. Meanwhile, Harlem's appeal to white revellers inspired the young physician Rudolph Fisher to write "The Caucasian Storms Harlem," a satiric piece in the August 1927 *American Mercury*.

The third phase of the Harlem Renaissance began even as the second had only just gotten under way. The second phase (1924 to mid-1926) was dominated by the officialdom of the two major civil rights organizations, with its ideology of civil rights advancement of African Americans through the creation and mobilization of an artistic-literary movement. Its essence was summed up in blunt declarations by Du Bois that he didn't care "a damn for any art that is not used for propaganda" or in exalted formulations by Locke that the New Negro was "an augury of a new democracy in American culture." The third phase of the Renaissance, from mid-1926 to the end of 1934, was marked by rebellion against the Civil Rights Establishment on the part of many of the artists and writers whom that Establishment had assembled and promoted. Three publications during 1926 formed a watershed between the genteel and the demotic Renaissance. Hughes's "The Negro Artist and the Racial Mountain," which appeared in the June 1926 issue of *The Nation,* served as manifesto of the breakaway from the arts-and-letters party line. Van Vechten's *Nigger Heaven*, released by Knopf that August, drove much of literate Afro-America into a dichotomy of approval and apoplexy over "authentic" versus "proper" cultural expression. Wallace Thurman's *Fire!!*, available in November, assembled the rebels for a major assault against the Civil Rights Ministry of Culture.

Hughes's turning-point essay had been provoked by Schuyler's essay in *The Nation*, "The Negro-Art Hokum," ridiculing "eager apostles from Greenwich Village, Harlem, and environs" who made claims for a special African American artistic vision distinct from that of white Americans. "The Aframerican is merely a lamp-blacked Anglo-Saxon," Schuyler had sneered. In a famous peroration, Hughes answered that he and his fellow artists intended to express their "individual dark-skinned selves without fear or shame. If white people are pleased we are glad. . . . If colored people are pleased we are glad. If they are not, their displeasure doesn't matter either." There was considerable African American displeasure; and it was complex. Much of the condemnation of the license for expression Hughes, Thurman, Hurston, and other artists arrogated to themselves was generational or puritanical, and usually both. "Vulgarity has been mistaken for art," Brawley spluttered after leafing the pages of the new magazine *Fire!!*, which contained among other shockers Richard Bruce Nugent's extravagantly homoerotic short story "Smoke, Lillies and Jade!" Du Bois was said to be deeply aggrieved.

But much of the condemnation stemmed from racial sensitivity, from sheer mortification at seeing uneducated, crude, and scrappy black men and women depicted without tinsel and soap. Thurman and associate editors John Davis, Aaron Douglas, Gwendolyn Bennett, Arthur Huff Fauset, Hughes, Hurston, and Nugent took the Renaissance out of the parlor, the editorial office, and the banquet room. With African motifs by Douglas and Nordic-featured African Americans with exaggeratedly kinky hair by Nugent; poems to an elevator boy by Hughes; a taste for the jungle by Edward Silvera; short stories about prostitution ("Cordelia the Crude") by Thurman, gender conflict between black men and women at the bottom of the economy ("Sweat") by Hurston, and a burly boxer's hatred of white people ("Wedding Day") by Gwendolyn Bennett; a short play about pigment complexes within the race (*Color Struck*) by Hurston—the focus shifted to Locke's "peasant matrix," to the sorrows and joys of those outside the Talented Tenth. "Let the blare of Negro jazz bands and the bellowing voice of Bessie Smith . . . penetrate the closed ears of the colored near-intellectuals," Hughes exhorted in "The Negro Artists and the Racial Mountain."

Carl Van Vechten's influence decidedly complicated the reactions of otherwise worldly critics like Du Bois, Fauset, Locke, and Cullen. While the novel's title alone enraged many Harlemites who felt their trust and hospitality betrayed, the deeper objections of the sophisticated to *Nigger Heaven* lay in its message that the Talented Tenth's preoccupation with cultural improvement was a misguided affectation that would cost the race its vitality. It was the "archaic Negroes" who were at ease in their skins and capable of action, Van Vechten's characters demonstrated. Significantly, although Du Bois and Fauset found themselves in the majority among the Renaissance leadership (ordinary Harlemites burned Van Vechten in effigy at 135th Street and Lenox Avenue), Charles Johnson, James Weldon Johnson, Schuyler, White, and Hughes praised the novel's sociological verve and veracity and the service they believed it rendered to race relations.

The younger artists embraced Van Vechten's fiction as a worthy model because of its ribald iconoclasm and iteration that the future of African American arts and letters lay in the culture of the working poor and even of the underclass—in bottom-up drama, fiction, music, and poetry, and painting. Regularly convening at the notorious "267 House," the brownstone an indulgent landlady provided Thurman rent-free on 136th Street (alternately known as "Niggerati Manor"), the group that came to produce *Fire!!* saw art not as politics by other means—civil rights between covers or from a stage or an easel—but as an expression of the intrinsic conditions most men and women of African descent were experiencing. They spoke of the need "for a truly Negroid note," for empathy with "those elements within the race which are still too potent for easy assimilation," and they openly mocked the premise of the Civil Rights Establishment that (as a Hughes character says in *The Ways of White Folks*) "art would break down color lines, art would save the race and prevent lynchings! Bunk!" Finally, like creative agents in society from time immemorial, they were impelled to insult their patrons and to defy conventions.

To put the Renaissance back on track, Du Bois sponsored a symposium in late 1926, "The Criteria of Negro Art," inviting a spectrum of views about the appropriate course the arts should take. His unhappiness was readily apparent, both with the overly literary tendencies of Locke and with the bottom-up school of Hughes and Thurman. The great danger was that politics were dropping out of the Renaissance, that the movement was turning into an evasion, sedulously encouraged by certain whites. "They are whispering, 'Here is a way out. Here is the real solution to the color problem. The recognition accorded Cullen, Hughes, Fauset, White and others shows there is no real color line,' " Du Bois charged. He then announced that *Crisis* literary prizes would henceforth be reserved for works encouraging "general knowledge of banking and insurance in modern life and specific knowledge of what American Negroes are doing in these fields." Walter White's own effort to sustain the civil-rights-by-copyright strategy was the ambitious novel *Flight*, edited by his friend Sinclair Lewis and released by Knopf in 1926. Kind critics found White's novel (a tale of near-white African Americans of unusual culture and professional accomplishment who prove their moral superiority to their oppressors) somewhat flat. The reissue the following year of *The Autobiography of an Ex–Colored Man* (with Johnson's authorship finally acknowledged) and publication of a volume of Cullen poetry, *Copper Sun*, continued the tradition of genteel, exemplary letters. In a further effort to restore direction, Du Bois's *Dark Princess* appeared in 1928 from Harcourt, Brace, a large, serious novel in which the "problem of the twentieth century" is taken in charge by a Talented Tenth International whose prime mover is a princess from India. But the momentum stayed firmly with the rebels.

Although Thurman's magazine died after one issue, respectable Afro-America was unable to ignore the novel that embodied the values of the Niggerati—the first Renaissance best-seller by a black author—McKay's *Home to Harlem*, released by Harper & Brothers in spring 1928. Its milieu is wholly plebeian. The protagonist, Jake, is a Lenox Avenue Noble Savage who demonstrates (in marked contrast to the book-reading Ray) the superiority of the Negro mind uncorrupted by European learning. *Home to Harlem* finally shattered the enforced literary code of the Civil Rights Establishment. Du Bois confessed to feeling "distinctly like needing a bath" after reading McKay's novel about the "debauched tenth." Rudolph Fisher's *The Walls of Jericho*, appearing that year from Knopf, was a brilliant, deftly executed satire which upset Du Bois as much as it heartened Thurman. Fisher, a successful Harlem physician with solid Talented Tenth family credentials, satirized the NAACP, the Negrotarians, Harlem high society, and easily recognized Renaissance notables, while entering convincingly into the world of the working classes, organized crime, and romance across classes.

Charles Johnson, preparing to leave the editorship of *Opportunity* for a professorship in sociology at Fisk University, now encouraged the young rebels. Renaissance artists were "now less self-conscious, less interested in proving that they are just like white poeple. . . . Relief from the stifling consciousness of being a problem has brought a certain superiority" to the Harlem Renaissance, Johnson asserted. Meanwhile, McKay's and Fisher's fiction inspired the Niggerati to publish an improved version of *Fire!!*. The magazine, *Harlem*, appeared in November 1928. Editor Thurman announced portentously, "The time has now come when the Negro artist can be his true self and pander to the stupidities of no one, either white or black." While Brawley, Du Bois, and Fauset continued to grimace, *Harlem* benefitted from significant defections. It won the collaboration of Locke and White, and lasted two issues. Roy de Coverly, George W. Little, and Schuyler signed on, and Hughes contributed one of the finest short stories, based on his travels down the West Coast of Africa—"Luani of the Jungles," a polished genre piece on the seductions of the civilized and the primitive.

The other Renaissance novel that year from Knopf, Nella Larsen's *Quicksand*, achieved the distinction of being praised by Du Bois, Locke, and Hughes. Larsen claimed to have been the daughter of a Danish mother and an African American father from the Danish Virgin Islands. In fact, her father was probably a chauffeur who lived in New York; and Larsen was probably born in New York, rather than in Chicago as she claimed. Trained in the sciences at Fisk, she never pursued further studies, as has been reported, at the University of Copenhagen. She would remain something of a mystery woman, helped in her career by Van Vechten and White but somehow always receding, and finally disappearing altogether from the Harlem scene. *Quicksand* was a triumph of vivid yet economic writing and rich allegory. Its very modern heroine experiences misfortunes and ultimate destruction from causes that are both racial and individual. She is not a tragic mulatto but a mulatto who is tragic for reasons that are both sociological and existential. Helga Crane, Larsen's protagonist, was the Virginia Slim of Renaissance fiction. If there were reviews (*Crisis, New Republic, New York Times*) that were as laudatory about Fauset's *Plum Bun*, also a 1928 release, they were primarily due to the novel's engrossing reconstruction of rarefied, upper-class African American life in Philadelphia, rather than to special literary merit. Angela Murray (Angele, in her white persona), the heroine of Fauset's second novel, was the Gibson Girl of Renaissance fiction. *Plum Bun* continued the second phase of the Renaissance, as did Cullen's second volume of poetry, published in 1929, *The Black Christ*. Ostensibly about a lynching, the lengthy title poem lost its way in mysticism, paganism, and religious remorse. The volume also lost the sympathies of most reviewers.

Thurman's *The Blacker the Berry*, published by Macaulay in early 1929, although talky and awkward in spots (Thurman had hoped to write the Great African American Novel), was a breakthrough novel. The reviewer for the Chicago *Defender* enthused, "Here at last is the book for which I have been waiting, and for which you have been waiting." Hughes praised it as a "gorgeous book," mischieveously writing Thurman that it would embarrass those who bestowed the "seal-of-high-and-holy approval of Harmon awards." The Ministry of Culture found the novel distinctly distasteful, *Opportunity* judging *The Blacker the Berry* to be fatally flawed by "immaturity and gaucherie." For the first time in African American fiction, color prejudice within the race was the central theme of a novel. Emma Lou, its heroine (like the author very dark and conventionally unattractive), is obsessed with respectability as well as tortured by her pigment, for Thurman makes the point on every page that Afro-America's aesthetic and spiritual center resides in the unaffected, unblended, noisome common folk and the liberated, unconventional artists. With the unprecedented Broadway success of *Harlem*, Thurman's sensationalized romp through the underside of Harlem, the triumph of Niggerati aesthetics over Civil Rights arts and letters was impressively confirmed. Another equally sharp smell of reality irritated Establishment nostrils that same year, with the publication of McKay's second novel, *Banjo*, appearing only weeks after *The Blacker the Berry*. "The Negroes are writing against themselves," lamented the reviewer for the *Am-*

sterdam News. Set among the human flotsam and jetsam of Marseilles and West Africa, the message of McKay's novel was again that European civilization was inimical to Africans everywhere.

The stock market collapsed, but reverberations from the Harlem Renaissance seemed stronger than ever. Larsen's second novel, *Passing*, appeared. Its theme, like Fauset's, was the burden of mixed racial ancestry. But, although *Passing* was less successful than *Quicksand*, Larsen's novel again evaded the trap of writing another tragic-mulatto novel by opposing the richness of African American life to the material advantages afforded by the option of "passing." In February 1930, Marc Connelly's dramatization of Roark Bradford's book of short stories opened on Broadway as *The Green Pastures.* The Hall Johnson Choir sang in it, Richard Harrison played "De Lawd," and scores of Harlemites found parts during 557 performances at the Mansfield Theatre, and then on tour across the country. The demanding young critic and Howard University professor of English Sterling Brown pronounced the play a "miracle." After *The Green Pastures* came *Not Without Laughter*, Hughes's glowing novel from Knopf. Financed by Charlotte Osgood Mason (the often tyrannical bestower of artistic largesse nicknamed "Godmother") and Amy Spingarn, Hughes had resumed his college education at Lincoln University and completed *Not Without Laughter* his senior year. The beleaguered family at the center of the novel represents Afro-America in transition in white America. Hughes's young male protagonist learns that proving his equality means affirming his distinctive racial qualities. Not only Locke admired *Not Without Laughter*; the *New Masses* reviewer embraced it as "our novel." The Ministry of Culture decreed Hughes worthy of the Harmon gold medal for 1930. The year ended with Schuyler's ribald, sprawling satire *Black No More*, an unsparing demolition of every personality and institution in Afro-America. Little wonder that Locke titled his retrospective piece in the February 1931 *Opportunity* "The Year of Grace."

Depression notwithstanding, the health of the Renaissance appeared to be more robust than ever. The first Rosenwald fellowships for African Americans had been secured largely due to James Weldon Johnson's influence the previous year. Since 1928, advised by Locke, the Harmon Foundation had mounted an annual traveling exhibition of drawings, paintings, and sculpture by African Americans. The 1930 participants introduced the generally unsuspected talent and genius of Palmer Hayden, William H. Johnson,

Archibald Motley, Jr., James A. Porter, and Laura Wheeler Waring in painting. Sargent Johnson, Elizabeth Prophet, and Augusta Savage were the outstanding sculptors of the show. Both Aaron Douglas and Romare Bearden came to feel that the standards of the foundation were somewhat indulgent and, therefore, injurious to many young artists, which was undoubtedly true even though the 1931 Harmon Travelling Exhibition of the Work of Negro Artists was seen by more than 150,000 people.

Superficially, Harlem itself appeared to be in fair health well into 1931. James Weldon Johnson's celebration of the community's strengths, *Black Manhattan*, was published near the end of 1930. "Harlem is still in the process of making," the book proclaimed, and the author's confidence in the power of the "recent literary and artistic emergence" to ameliorate race relations was unshaken. In Johnson's Harlem, redcaps and cooks cheered when Renaissance talents won Guggenheim and Rosenwald fellowships; they rushed to newsstands whenever the *American Mercury* or *New Republic* mentioned activities above Central Park. It was much too easy for Talented Tenth notables like Johnson, White, and Locke not to notice in the second year of the Great Depression that, for the great majority of the population, Harlem was in the process of unmaking. Still, there was a definite prefiguration of Harlem's mortality when A'Lelia Walker suddenly died in August 1931, a doleful occurrence shortly followed by the sale of Villa Lewaro, her Hudson mansion, at public auction. By the end of 1929, African Americans lived in the five-hundred block of Edgecombe Avenue, known as "Sugar Hill." The famous "409" overlooking the Polo Grounds was home at one time or another to the Du Boises, the Fishers, and the Whites. Below Sugar Hill was the five-acre Rockefeller-financed Dunbar Apartments complex, its 511 units fully occupied in mid-1928. The Dunbar eventually became home for the Du Boises, E. Simms Campbell (illustrator and cartoonist), Fletcher Henderson, the A. Philip Randolphs, Leigh Whipper (actor), and (briefly) Paul and Essie Robeson. The complex published its own weekly bulletin, the *Dunbar News*, an even more valuable record of Talented Tenth activities during the Renaissance than the *Inter-State Tattler*.

The 1931 *Report on Negro Housing*, presented to President Hoover, was a document starkly in contrast to the optimism found in *Black Manhattan*. Nearly 50 percent of Harlem's families would be unemployed by the end of 1932. The syphilis rate was nine times higher than white Manhattan's; the tuberculosis rate was five times greater; pneumonia and typhoid were twice that of whites. Two African American mothers and two babies died for every white mother and child. Harlem General Hospital, the single public facility, served 200,000 African Americans with 273 beds. A Harlem family paid twice as much of their income for rent as a white family. Meanwhile, median family income in Harlem dropped 43.6 percent by 1932. The ending of Prohibition would devastate scores of marginal speakeasies, as well as prove fatal to theaters like the Lafayette. Connie's Inn would eventually migrate downtown. Until then, however, the clubs in "The Jungle" (133rd Street)—Bamville, Connor's, Clam House, Nest Club—and elsewhere (Pod's and Jerry's, Smalls' Paradise) continued to do a land-office business. With the repeal of the Eighteenth Amendment, honorary Harlemites like Van Vechten sobered up and turned to other pursuits. Locke's letters to Charlotte Osgood Mason turned increasingly pessimistic in the winter of 1931. In June 1932, he perked up a bit to praise the choral ballet presented at the Eastman School of Music—*Sahdji*, with music by William Grant Still and scenario by Nugent, but most of Locke's news was distinctly downbeat. The writing partnership of two of his protégés, Hughes and Hurston, their material needs underwritten in a New Jersey township by "Godmother" Charlotte Mason, collapsed in acrimonious dispute. Each claimed principal authorship of the only dramatic comedy written during the Renaissance, *Mule Bone*, a three-act folk play unperformed (as a result of the dispute) until 1991. Locke took the side of Hurston, undermining the tie of affection between Godmother and Hughes and effectively ending his relationship with the latter. The part played in this controversy by their brilliant secretary, Louise Thompson, the strong-willed, estranged wife of Wallace Thurman, remains murky, but it seems clear that Thompson's Marxism had a deep influence on Hughes in the aftermath of his painful breakup with Godmother, Locke, and Hurston.

In any case, beginning with "Advertisement for the Waldorf-Astoria" published in the December 1931 *New Masses*, Hughes's poetry became markedly political. "Elderly Race Leaders" and "Goodbye Christ," as well as the play "Scottsboro, Limited," were irreverent, staccato offerings to the coming triumph of the proletariat. The poet's departure in June 1932 for Moscow, along with Louise Thompson, Mollie Lewis, Henry Moon, Loren Miller, Theodore Poston, and thirteen others, ostensibly to act in a Soviet

film about American race relations, *Black and White*, symbolized
the shift in patronage and accompanying politicization of Renaissance artists. *One Way to Heaven*, Cullen's first novel, badly
flawed and clearly influenced by *Nigger Heaven*, appeared in 1932,
but it seemed already a baroque anachronism with its knife-
wielding Lotharios and elaborately educated types. An impatient
Du Bois, already deeply alienated from the Renaissance, called for
a second Amenia Conference to radicalize the movement's ideology
and renew its personnel. Jessie Fauset remained oblivious to the
profound artistic and political changes under way. Her final novel,
Comedy: American Style (1933), was technically much the same
as *Plum Bun*. Her subject, once again, was skin pigment and the
neuroses of those who had just enough of it to spend their lives
obsessed by it. James Weldon Johnson's autobiography, *Along
This Way*, an elegantly written review of his sui generis public
career as archetypal renaissance man in both meanings of the
word, was the publishing event of the year. McKay's final novel
also appeared that year. He worried familiar themes, but *Banana
Bottom* represented a philosophical advance over *Home to Harlem*
and *Banjo* in its reconciliation through the protagonist, Bita Plant,
of the previously destructive tension in McKay between the natural
and the artificial—soul and civilization.

The publication at the beginning of 1932 of Thurman's last
novel, *Infants of the Spring*, had already announced the end of the
Harlem Renaissance. The action of Thurman's novel is in the ideas
of the characters, in their incessant talk about themselves, Booker
T. Washington, Du Bois, racism, and the destiny of the race. Its
prose is generally disappointing, but the ending is conceptually
poignant. Paul Arbian (Richard Bruce Nugent) commits suicide in
a full tub of water, which splashes over and obliterates the pages
of Arbian's unfinished novel on the bathroom floor. A still legible
page, however, contains this paragraph, which was, in effect, an
epitaph:

> He had drawn a distorted, inky black
> skyscraper, modeled after Niggerati Manor,
> and on which were focused an array of
> blindingly white beams of light. The
> foundation of this building was composed
> of crumbling stone. At first glance it
> could be ascertained that the skyscraper

> would soon crumple and fall, leaving the
> dominating white lights in full possession
> of the sky.

The literary energies of the Renaissance finally slumped. McKay returned to Harlem in February 1934 after a twelve-year sojourn abroad, but his creative powers were spent. The last novel of the movement, Hurston's beautifully written *Jonah's Gourd Vine*, went on sale in May 1934. Charles Johnson, James Weldon Johnson, and Locke applauded Hurston's allegorical story of her immediate family (especially her father) and the mores of an African American town in Florida called Eatonville. Fisher and Thurman could have been expected to continue to write, but their fates were sealed by professional carelessness. Thurman died a few days before Christmas 1934, soon after his return from an abortive Hollywood film project. Ignoring his physician's strictures, he hemorrhaged after drinking to excess while hosting a party in the infamous house at 267 West 136th Street. Four days later, Fisher expired from intestinal cancer caused by repeated exposure to his own X-ray equipment.

Locke's *New Negro* anthology had been crucial to the formation of the Renaissance. As the movement ran down, another anthology, English heiress Nancy Cunard's *Negro*, far more massive in scope, recharged the Renaissance for a brief period, enlisting the contributions of most of the principals (though McKay and Walrond refused, and Toomer no longer acknowledged his African American roots), and captured its essence in the manner of expert taxidermy. A grieving Locke wrote Charlotte Mason from Howard University, "It is hard to see the collapse of things you have labored to raise on a sound base."

Arthur Fauset, Jessie's perceptive brother, attempted to explain the collapse to Locke and the readers of *Opportunity* at the beginning of 1934. He foresaw "a socio-political-economic setback from which it may take decades to recover." The Renaissance had left the race unprepared, Fauset charged, because of its unrealistic belief "that social and economic recognition will be inevitable when once the race has produced a sufficiently large number of persons who have properly qualified themselves in the arts." Du Bois had not only turned his back on the movement, he had left the NAACP and Harlem for a university professorship in Atlanta after an enormous row over civil rights policy. Marxism had begun to exercise a decided appeal for him, but as the 1933 essay "Marxism and the Negro Problem" had made abundantly clear, Du Bois ruled out collaboration with American Marxists because they were much too racist. James Weldon Johnson's philosophical *tour d'horizon* appearing in 1934, *Negro Americans, What Now?*, asked precisely the question of the decade. Most Harlemites were certain that the riot exploding on the evening of March 19, 1935, taking three lives and costing two million dollars in property damage, was not an answer. By then, the Works Progress Administration (WPA) had become the major patron of African American artists and writers. Writers William Attaway, Ralph Ellison, Margaret Walker, Richard Wright, and Frank Yerby would emerge under its aegis, as would painters Romare Bearden, Jacob Lawrence, Charles Sebree, Lois Maillou Jones, and Charles White. The Communist Party was another patron, notably for Richard Wright, whose 1937 essay "Blueprint for Negro Writing" would materially contribute to the premise of Hughes's "The Negro Artist and the Racial Mountain." For thousands of ordinary Harlemites who had looked to Garvey's UNIA for inspiration, then to the Renaissance, there was now Father Divine and his "heavens."

In the ensuing years, much was renounced, more was lost or forgotten, yet the Renaissance, however artificial and overreaching, left a positive mark. Locke's *New Negro* anthology featured thirty of the movement's thirty-five stars. They and a small number of less gifted collaborators generated twenty-six novels, ten volumes of poetry, five Broadway plays, countless essays and short stories, three performed ballets and concerti, and a considerable output of canvas and sculpture. If the achievement was less than the titanic expectations of the Ministry of Culture, it was an arts-and-letters legacy, nevertheless, of which a beleaguered and belittled Afro-America could be proud, and by which it could be sustained. If more by osmosis than conscious attention, Mainstream America was also richer for the color, emotion, humanity, and cautionary vision produced by Harlem during its Golden Age.

"If I had supposed that all Negroes were illiterate brutes, I might be astonished to discover that they can write good third rate poetry, readable and unreadable magazine fiction," wrote one contemporary white Marxist passing flinty judgment upon the Renaissance. Nevertheless there were many white Americans—perhaps the majority—who found the African American artistic and literary ferment of the period wholly unexpected and little short of incredible. If the judgment of the Marxist observer soon became a commonplace, it was because the Harlem Renaissance demonstrated—finally, irrefutably, during slightly more than a decade—the considerable creative capacities of the best and brightest of a disadvantaged racial minority.

CHRONOLOGY

1917   Ridgely Torrence and Emily Hapgood present three one-act plays—*The Rider of Dreams, Simon the Cyrenean*, and *Granny Maumee*—with all-black casts at the Provincetown Playhouse.

1917–1923   Phase One: The Bohemian Renaissance

1919   The Red Summer. McKay's poem "If We Must Die" published.

1920   Production of Eugene O'Neill's *The Emperor Jones*, starring Charles Gilpin. Marcus Garvey's First International Convention of the Negro Peoples of the World held at Madison Square Garden in August–September.

1922   Miller and Lyles's musical *Shuffle Along* staged on Broadway. Publication of Claude McKay's volume of poetry *Harlem Shadows*, James Weldon Johnson's *Book of American Negro Poetry*, and T. S. Stribling's novel *Birthright*.

1923   Toomer's *Cane* published by Boni & Liveright.

1924–1926   Phase Two: The Talented Tenth Renaissance

1924   Jessie Redmon Fauset's novel *There Is Confusion* published by Boni & Liveright. Walter Francis White's novel *The Fire in the Flint* published by Alfred A. Knopf. In March, Charles S. Johnson sends out his invitations to the Civic Club.

1925   Countee Cullen's first volume of poetry, *Color*, pub-
            lished by Harper & Brothers. First *Opportunity*
            Awards banquet held in May.

1926–1935   Phase Three: The Negro Renaissance

1926   Special issue of *Survey Graphic* published in March,
            edited by Alain Locke and featuring the work of Har-
            lem artists. Langston Hughes's volume of poetry *The
            Weary Blues* published by Knopf. Eric Walrond's
            story collection *Tropic Death* published by Boni &
            Liveright. Second *Opportunity* Awards banquet held
            in April. Alain Locke's anthology *The New Negro*
            published by Albert and Charles Boni. In June, Lang-
            ston Hughes's "The Negro Artist and the Racial
            Mountain" and George Schuyler's "The Negro-Art
            Hokum" appear in *The Nation*. Carl Van Vechten's
            novel *Nigger Heaven* and Walter White's *Flight* both
            published by Knopf. In November, Wallace Thurman
            edits and publishes the one issue of *Fire!!*

1927   Langston Hughes's second volume of poetry, *Fine
            Clothes to the Jew*, published by Knopf. Countee Cul-
            len's second poetry collection, *Copper Sun*, published
            by Harper.

1928   In March, Nella Larsen's novel *Quicksand* published
            by Knopf and Claude McKay's novel *Home to Harlem*
            published by Harper. Rudolph Fisher's *The Walls of
            Jericho* published by Knopf. W. E. B. Du Bois's second
            novel, *Dark Princess*, published by Harcourt, Brace.
            Wallace Thurman edits and publishes *Harlem*, the suc-
            cessor to *Fire!!*, in November.

1929   In January, Jessie Fauset's *Plum Bun* published by
            Frederick A. Stokes. Wallace Thurman's novel *The
            Blacker the Berry* . . . published by Macaulay in
            March. Nella Larsen's second novel, *Passing*, pub-
            lished by Knopf in May. Claude McKay's *Banjo: A
            Story Without a Plot* published by Harper. Countee
            Cullen's volume of poetry *The Black Christ* published
            by Harper. The Great Depression begins with stock
            market crash in October.

1930   Marc Connelly's drama *The Green Pastures* opens on Broadway in February. Langston Hughes's novel *Not Without Laughter* published by Knopf.

1931   George Schuyler's satirical novel *Black No More* published by Macaulay in January. James Weldon Johnson's history *Black Manhattan* published by Knopf. A'Lelia Walker, the millionaire daughter of Madame C. J. Walker, dies in August. Arna Bontemps's novel *God Sends Sunday* published by Harcourt, Brace. Jessie Fauset's *The Chinaberry Tree* published by Stokes.

1932   Publication of Wallace Thurman's second novel, *Infants of the Spring*, in February. Rudolph Fisher's *The Conjure-Man Dies* published by Covici, Friede. Countee Cullen's novel *One Way to Heaven* published by Harper. In June, twenty-two Americans sail for the Soviet Union to take roles in *Black and White*, the Meschrabpom film about racial segregation in the American South.

1933   Claude McKay's second novel, *Banana Bottom*, published by Harper. Jessie Fauset's last novel, *Comedy: American Style*, published by Stokes. James Weldon Johnson's autobiographical *Along This Way* published by Knopf.

1934   Zora Neale Hurston's first novel, *Jonah's Gourd Vine*, published by Lippincott in May. Langston Hughes's story collection *The Ways of White Folks* published by Knopf in June. Rudolph Fisher and Wallace Thurman die in December.

1935   The Harlem Riot on March 19 marks the end of the Renaissance.

1936   Arna Bontemps's novel *Black Thunder* published by Macmillan.

The Portable

HARLEM RENAISSANCE READER

PART I

ESSAYS AND MEMOIRS

W. E. B. DU BOIS

From Du Bois's "Returning Soldiers" to Johnson's Black Manhattan, *the two themes of these several entries are militancy and migration. Inspired by the Great War, men and women of African descent asserted their rights to civil and social equality. With the influx of European labor cut off by the war and conditions in the South (boll weevil infestation, upsurge in lynchings) becoming more oppressive, a massive, accelerating relocation of African Americans took place from rural regions to Northern industrial centers, accompanied by significant infusions of peoples from the West Indies (see Carter G. Woodson, "The Migration of the Talented Tenth," and W. A. Domingo, "Gift of the Black Tropics"). The confluence of this new sense of collective self and the movement from Southern farms and towns and from the Antilles to the metropolitan centers of the North provided the conditions for the Harlem Renaissance. Mary White Ovington captured the broad appeal of the messianic Jamaican Marcus Garvey. James Weldon Johnson described Harlem as a slice of America—no different from any burgeoning community except in the skin color of most of its citizens: "Harlem talks American, reads American, thinks American."*

RETURNING SOLDIERS

WE ARE RETURNING from war! *The Crisis* and tens of thousands of black men were drafted into a great struggle. For bleeding France and what she means and has meant and will mean to us and humanity and against the threat of German race arrogance, we fought gladly and to the last drop of blood; for America and her highest ideals, we fought in far-off hope; for the dominant southern oligarchy entrenched in Washington, we fought in bitter resignation. For the America that represents and gloats in lynching, disfranchisement, caste, brutality and devilish insult—for this, in the hateful upturning and mixing of things, we were forced by vindictive fate to fight, also.

But today we return! We return from the slavery of uniform which the world's madness demanded us to don to the freedom of civil garb. We stand again to look America squarely in the face and call a spade a spade. We sing: This country of ours, despite all its better souls have done and dreamed, is yet a shameful land.

It *lynches*.

And lynching is barbarism of a degree of contemptible nastiness unparalleled in human history. Yet for fifty years we have lynched two Negroes a week, and we have kept this up right through the war.

It *disfranchises* its own citizens.

Disfranchisement is the deliberate theft and robbery of the only protection of poor against rich and black against white. The land that disfranchises its citizens and calls itself a democracy lies and knows it lies.

It encourages *ignorance*.

It has never really tried to educate the Negro. A dominant minority does not want Negroes educated. It wants servants, dogs, whores and monkeys. And when this land allows a reactionary group by its stolen political power to force as many black folk into these categories as it possibly can, it cries in contemptible hypocrisy: "They threaten us with degeneracy; they cannot be educated."

It *steals* from us.

It organizes industry to cheat us. It cheats us out of our land; it cheats us out of our labor. It confiscates our savings. It reduces our wages. It raises our rent. It steals our profit. It taxes us without representation. It keeps us consistently and universally poor, and then feeds us on charity and derides our poverty.

It *insults* us.

It has organized a nation-wide and latterly a world-wide propaganda of deliberate and continuous insult and defamation of black blood wherever found. It decrees that it shall not be possible in travel nor residence, work nor play, education nor instruction for a black man to exist without tacit or open acknowledgement of his inferiority to the dirtiest white dog. And it looks upon any attempt to question or even discuss this dogma as arrogance, unwarranted assumption and treason.

This is the country to which we Soldiers of Democracy return. This is the fatherland for which we fought! But it is *our* fatherland. It was right for us to fight. The faults of *our* country are *our* faults. Under similar circumstances, we would fight again. But by the God of Heaven, we are cowards and jackasses if now that that war is over, we do not marshal every ounce of our brain and brawn to fight a sterner, longer, more unbending battle against the forces of hell in our own land.

We *return*.

We *return from fighting*.

We *return fighting*.

Make way for Democracy! We saved it in France, and by the Great Jehovah, we will save it in the United States of America, or know the reason why.

CARTER G. WOODSON

THE MIGRATION OF THE TALENTED TENTH

WHAT CLASSES THEN have migrated? In the first place, the Negro politicians, who, after the restoration of Bourbon rule in the South, found themselves thrown out of office and often humiliated and impoverished, had to find some way out of the difficulty. Some few have been relieved by sympathetic leaders of the Republican party, who secured for them federal appointments in Washington. These appointments when sometimes paying lucrative salaries have been given as a reward to those Negroes who, although dethroned in the South, remain in touch with the remnant of the Republican party there and control the delegates to the national conventions nominating candidates for President. Many Negroes of this class have settled in Washington. In some cases, the observer witnesses the pitiable scene of a man once a prominent public functionary in the South now serving in Washington as a messenger or a clerk.

The well-established blacks, however, have not been so easily induced to go. The Negroes in business in the South have usually been loath to leave their people among whom they can acquire property, whereas, if they go to the North, they have merely political freedom with no assurance of an opportunity in the economic world. But not a few of these have given themselves up to unrelenting toil with a view to accumulating sufficient wealth to move North and live thereafter on the income from their investments. Many of this class now spend some of their time in the North to educate their children. But they do not like to have these children who have been under refining influences return to the South to suffer the humiliation which during the last generation has been growing more and more aggravating. Endeavoring to carry out their policy of keeping the Negro down, southerners too often carefully plan to humiliate the progressive and intelligent blacks and in some cases form mobs to drive them out, as they are bad examples for that class of Negroes whom they desire to keep as menials.

There are also the migrating educated Negroes. They have studied history, law and economics and well understand what it is to get the rights guaranteed them by the constitution. The more they know the more discontented they become. They cannot speak out for what they want. No one is likely to second such a protest, not even the Negroes themselves, so generally have they been intimidated. The more outspoken they become, moreover, the more necessary is it for them to leave, for they thereby destroy their chances to earn a livelihood. White men in control of the public schools of the South see to it that the subserviency of the Negro teachers employed be certified beforehand. They dare not complain too much about equipment and salaries even if the per capita appropriation for the education of the Negroes be one fourth of that for the whites.

In the higher institutions of learning, especially the State schools, it is exceptional to find a principal who has the confidence of the Negroes. The Negroes will openly assert that he is in the pay of the reactionary whites, whose purpose is to keep the Negro down; and the incumbent himself will tell his board of regents how much he is opposed by the Negroes because he labors for the interests of the white race. Out of such sycophancy it is easily explained why our State schools have been so ineffective as to necessitate the sending of the Negro youth to private institutions maintained by northern philanthropy. Yet if an outspoken Negro happens to be an instructor in a private school conducted by educators from the North, he has to be careful about contending for a square deal; for, if the head of his institution does not suggest to him to proceed conservatively, the mob will dispose of the complainant. Physicians, lawyers and preachers who are not so economically dependent as teachers can exercise no more freedom of speech in the midst of this triumphant rule of the lawless.

A large number of educated Negroes, therefore, have on account of these conditions been compelled to leave the South. Finding in the North, however, practically nothing in their line to do, because of the proscription by race prejudice and trades unions, many of them lead the life of menials, serving as waiters, porters, butlers and chauffeurs. While in Chicago, not long ago, the writer was in the office of a graduate of a colored southern college, who was showing his former teacher the picture of his class. In accounting for his classmates in the various walks of life, he reported that more than one third of them were settled to the occupation of Pullman porters.

The largest number of Negroes who have gone North during this period, however, belong to the intelligent laboring class. Some of them have become discontented for the very same reasons that the higher classes have tired of oppression in the South, but the larger number of them have gone North to improve their economic condition. Most of these have migrated to the large cities in the East and Northwest, such as Philadelphia, New York, Indianapolis, Pittsburgh, Cleveland, Columbus, Detroit and Chicago. To understand this problem in its urban aspects the accompanying diagram showing the increase in the Negro population of northern cities during the first decade of this century will be helpful.

Some of these Negroes have migrated after careful consideration; others have just happened to go north as wanderers; and a still larger number on the many excursions to the cities conducted by railroads during the summer months. Sometimes one excursion brings to Chicago two or three thousand Negroes, two thirds of whom never go back. They do not often follow the higher pursuits of labor in the North but they earn more money than they have been accustomed to earn in the South. They are attracted also by the liberal attitude of some whites, which, although not that of social equality, gives the Negroes a liberty in northern centers which leads them to think that they are citizens of the country.

This shifting in the population has had an unusually significant effect on the black belt. Frederick Douglass advised the Negroes in 1879 to remain in the South where they would be in sufficiently large numbers to have political power, but they have gradually scattered from the black belt so as to diminish greatly their chances ever to become the political force they formerly were in this country. The Negroes once had this possibility in South Carolina, Georgia, Alabama, Mississippi and Louisiana and, had the process of Africanization prior to the Civil War had a few decades longer to do its work, there would not have been any doubt as to the ultimate preponderance of the Negroes in those commonwealths. The tendencies of the black population according to the censuses of the United States and especially that of 1910, however, show that the chances for the control of these State governments by Negroes no longer exist except in South Carolina and Mississippi. It has been predicted, therefore, that, if the same tendencies continue for the next fifty years, there will be even few counties in which the Negroes will be in a majority. All of the Southern States except Arkansas showed a proportionate increase of the white population over that of the black between 1900 and 1910, while West Virginia and Oklahoma with relatively small numbers of blacks showed, for reasons stated elsewhere, an increase in the Negro population. Thus we see coming to pass something like the proposed plan of Jefferson and other statesmen who a hundred years ago advocated the expansion of slavery to lessen the evil of the institution by distributing its burdens.

The migration of intelligent blacks, however, has been attended with several handicaps to the race. The large part of the black population is in the South and there it will stay for decades to come. The southern Negroes, therefore, have been robbed of their due part of the talented tenth. The educated blacks have had no constituency in the North and, consequently, have been unable to realize their sweetest dreams of the land of the free. In their new home the enlightened Negro must live with his light under a bushel. Those left behind in the South soon despair of seeing a brighter day and yield to the yoke. In the places of the leaders who were wont to speak for their people, the whites have raised up Negroes who accept favors offered them on the condition that their lips be sealed up forever on the rights of the Negro.

This emigration too has left the Negro subject to other evils. There are many first-class Negro business men in the South, but although there were once progressive men of color, who endeavored to protect the blacks from being plundered by white sharks and harpies there have arisen numerous unscrupulous Negroes who have for a part of the proceeds from such jobbery associated themselves with ill-designing white men to dupe illiterate Negroes. This trickery is brought into play in marketing their crops, selling them supplies, or purchasing their property. To carry out this iniquitous plan the persons concerned have the protection of the law, for while Negroes in general are imposed upon, those engaged in robbing them have no cause to fear.

W. A. DOMINGO

GIFT OF THE BLACK TROPICS

FROM 1920 to 1923 the foreign-born Negro population of the United States was increased nearly 40 per cent through the entry of 30,849 Africans (black). In 1921 the high-water mark of 9,873 was registered. This increase was not permanent, for in 1923 there was an exit of 1,525 against an entry of 7,554. If the 20 per cent that left that year is an index of the proportion leaving annually, it is safe to estimate a net increase of about 24,000 between 1920 and 1923. If the newcomers are distributed throughout the country in the same proportion as their predecessors, the present foreign-born Negro population of Harlem is about 35,000. These people are, therefore, a formidable minority whose presence cannot be ignored or discounted. It is this large body of foreign-born who contribute those qualities that make New York so unlike Pittsburgh, Washington, Chicago and other cities with large aggregations of American Negroes.

The largest number come from the British West Indies and are attracted to America mainly by economic reasons: though considerable numbers of the younger generation come for the purposes of education. The next largest group consists of Spanish-speaking Negroes from Latin America. Distinct because of their language, and sufficiently numerous to maintain themselves as a cultural unit, the Spanish element has but little contact with the English-speaking majority. For the most part they keep to themselves and follow in the main certain definite occupational lines. A smaller group, French-speaking, have emigrated from Haiti and the French West Indies. There are also a few Africans, a batch of voluntary pilgrims over the old track of the slave-traders.

Among the English-speaking West Indian population of Harlem are some 8,000 natives of the American Virgin Islands. A considerable part of these people were forced to migrate to the mainland as a consequence of the operation of the Volstead Act which destroyed the lucrative rum industry and helped to reduce the number of foreign vessels that used to call at the former free port of Charlotte Amelia for various stores. Despite their long Danish connection these people are culturally and linguistically English, rather than Danish. Unlike the British Negroes in New York, the Virgin Islanders take an intelligent and aggressive interest in the affairs of their former home, and are organized to co-operate with their brothers there who are valiantly struggling to substitute civil government for the present naval administration of the islands.

To the average American Negro, all English-speaking black foreigners are West Indians, and by that is usually meant British subjects. There is a general assumption that there is everything in common among West Indians, though nothing can be further from the truth. West Indians regard themselves as Antiguans or Jamaicans as the case might be, and a glance at the map will quickly reveal the physical obstacles that militate against homogeneity of population; separations of many sorts, geographical, political and cultural tend everywhere to make and crystallize local characteristics.

This undiscriminating attitude on the part of native Negroes, as well as the friction generated from contact between the two groups, has created an artificial and defensive unity among the islanders which reveals itself in an instinctive closing of their ranks when attacked by outsiders; but among themselves organization along insular lines is the general rule. Their social grouping, however, does not follow insular precedents. Social gradation is determined in the islands by family connections, education, wealth and position. As each island is a complete society in itself, Negroes occupy from the lowliest to the most exalted positions. The barrier separating the colored aristocrat from the laboring class of the same color is as difficult to surmount as a similar barrier between Englishmen. Most of the islanders in New York are from the middle, artisan and laboring classes. Arriving in a country whose every influence is calculated to democratize their race and destroy the distinctions they had been accustomed to, even those West Indians whose stations in life have been of the lowest soon lose whatever servility they brought with them. In its place they substitute all of the self-assertiveness of the classes they formerly paid deference to.

West Indians have been coming to the United States for over a century. The part they have played in Negro progress is conceded to be important. As early as 1827 a Jamaican, John Brown Russwurm, one of the founders of Liberia, was the first colored man to be graduated from an American college and to publish a newspaper in this country; sixteen years later his fellow countryman, Peter Ogden, organized in New York City the first Odd-Fellows Lodge for Negroes. Prior to the Civil War, West Indian contribution to American Negro life was so great that Dr. W. E. B. Du Bois, in his *Souls of Black Folk*, credits them with main responsibility for the manhood program presented by the race in the early decades of the last century. Indicative of their tendency to blaze new paths is the achievement of John W. A. Shaw of Antigua who, in the early '90's of the last century, passed the civil service tests and became deputy commissioner of taxes for the County of Queens.

It is probably not realized, indeed, to what extent West Indian Negroes have contributed to the wealth, power and prestige of the United States. Major-General Goethals, chief engineer and builder of the Panama Canal, has testified in glowing language to the fact that when all other labor was tried and failed it was the black men of the Caribbean whose intelligence, skill, muscle and endurance made the union of the Pacific and the Atlantic a reality.

Coming to the United States from countries in which they had experienced no legalized social or occupational disabilities, West Indians very naturally have found it difficult to adapt themselves to the tasks that are, by custom, reserved for Negroes in the North. Skilled at various trades and having a contempt for body service and menial work, many of the immigrants apply for positions that the average American Negro has been schooled to regard as restricted to white men only, with the result that through their persistence and doggedness in fighting white labor, West Indians have in many cases been pioneers and shock troops to open a way for Negroes into new fields of employment.

This freedom from spiritual inertia characterizes the women no less than the men, for it is largely through them that the occupational field has been broadened for colored women in New York. By their determination, sometimes reinforced by a dexterous use of their hatpins, these women have made it possible for members of their race to enter the needle trades freely.

It is safe to say that West Indian representation in the skilled trades is relatively large; this is also true of the professions, especially medicine and dentistry. Like the Jew, they are forever launching out in business, and such retail businesses as are in the hands of Negroes in Harlem are largely in the control of the foreign-born. While American Negroes predominate in forms of business like barber shops and pool rooms in which there is no competition from white men, West Indians turn their efforts almost invariably to fields like grocery stores, tailor shops, jewelry stores and fruit vending in which they meet the fiercest kind of competition. In some of these fields they are the pioneers or the only surviving competitors of white business concerns. In more ambitious business enterprises like real estate and insurance they are relatively numerous. The only Casino and moving picture theatre operated by Negroes in Harlem is in the hands of a native of one of the small islands. On Seventh Avenue a West Indian woman conducts a millinery store that would be a credit to Fifth Avenue.

The analogy between the West Indian and the Jew may be carried farther; they are both ambitious, eager for education, willing to engage in business, argumentative, aggressive and possessed of great proselytizing zeal for any cause they espouse. West Indians are great contenders for their rights and because of their respect for law are inclined to be litigious. In addition, they are, as a whole, home-loving, hard-working and frugal. Like their English exemplars they are fond of sport, lack a sense of humor (yet the greatest black comedian of America, Bert Williams, was from the Bahamas) and are very serious and intense in their attitude toward life. They save their earnings and are mindful of their folk in the homeland, as the volume of business of the Money Order and Postal Savings Departments of College Station Post Office will attest.

Ten years ago it was possible to distinguish the West Indian in Harlem, especially during the summer months. Accustomed to wearing cool, light-colored garments in the tropics, he would stroll along Lenox Avenue on a hot day resplendent in white shoes and flannel pants, the butt of many a jest from his American brothers who, to-day, have adopted the styles that they formerly derided. This trait of non-conformity manifested by the foreign-born has irritated American Negroes, who resent the implied self-sufficiency, and as a result there is a considerable amount of prejudice against West Indians. It is claimed that they are proud and arrogant; that they think themselves superior to the natives. And although educated Negroes of New York are loudest in publicly decrying the hostility between the two groups, it is nevertheless true that feelings against West Indians are strongest among members of that class. This is explainable on the ground of professional jealousy and competition for leadership. As the islanders press forward and upward they meet the same kind of opposition from the native Negro that the Jew and other ambitious white aliens receive from white Americans. Naturalized West Indians have found from experience that American Negroes are reluctant to concede them the right to political leadership even when qualified intellectually. Unlike their American brothers, the islanders are free from those traditions that bind them to any party and, as a consequence, are independent to the point of being radical. Indeed, it is they who largely compose the few political and economic radicals in Harlem; without them the genuinely radical movement among New York Negroes would be unworthy of attention.

There is a diametrical difference between American and West Indian Negroes in their worship. While large sections of the former are inclined to indulge in displays of emotionalism that border on hysteria, the latter, in their Wesleyan Methodist and Baptist churches maintain in the face of the assumption that people from the tropics are necessarily emotional, all the punctilious emotional restraint characteristic of their English background. In religious radicalism the foreign-born are again pioneers and propagandists. The only modernist church among the thousands of Negroes in New York (and perhaps the country) is led by a West Indian, Rev. E. Ethelred Brown, an ordained Unitarian minister, and is largely supported by his fellow islanders.

In facing the problem of race prejudice, foreign-born Negroes, and West Indians in particular, are forced to undergo considerable adjustment. Forming a racial majority in their own countries and not being accustomed to discrimination expressly felt as racial, they rebel against the "color line" as they find it in America. For while color and caste lines tend to converge in the islands, it is nevertheless true that because of the ratio of population, historical background and traditions of rebellions before and since their emancipation, West Indians of color do not have their activities, social, occupational and otherwise, determined by their race. Color plays a part but it is not the prime determinant of advancement; hence, the deep feeling of resentment when the "color line," legal or customary, is met and found to be a barrier to individual progress. For this reason the West Indian has thrown himself whole-heartedly into the fight against lynching, discrimination and the other disabilities from which Negroes in America suffer.

It must be remembered that the foreign-born black men and women, more so even than other groups of immigrants, are the hardiest and most venturesome of their folk. They were dissatisfied at home, and it is to be expected that they would not be altogether satisfied with limitation of opportunity here when they have staked so much to gain enlargement of opportunity. They do not suffer from the local anesthesia of custom and pride which makes otherwise intolerable situations bearable for the home-staying majorities.

Just as the West Indian has been a sort of leaven in the American loaf, so the American Negro is beginning to play a reciprocal rôle in the life of the foreign Negro communities, as for instance, the recent championing of the rights of Haiti and Liberia and the Virgin Islands, as well as the growing resentment at the treatment of natives in the African colonial dependencies. This world-wide reaction of the darker races to their common as well as local grievances is one of the most significant facts of recent development. Exchange of views and sympathy, extension and co-operation of race organizations beyond American boundaries, principally in terms of economic and educational projects, but also to a limited extent in political affairs, are bound to develop on a considerable scale in the near future. Formerly, ties have been almost solely through the medium of church missionary enterprises.

It has been asserted that the movement headed by the most-advertised of all West Indians, Marcus Garvey, absentee "president" of the continent of Africa, represents the attempt of West Indian peasants to solve the American race problem. This is no more true than it would be to say that the editorial attitude of *The Crisis* during the war reflected the spirit of American Negroes respecting their grievances or that the late Booker T. Washington successfully delimited the educational aspirations of his people. The support given Garvey by a certain type of his countrymen is partly explained by their group reaction to attacks made upon him because of his nationality. On the other hand, the earliest and most persistent exposures of Garvey's multitudinous schemes were initiated by West Indians in New York like Cyril Briggs and the writer.

Prejudice against West Indians is in direct ratio to their number; hence its strength in New York where they are heavily concentrated. It is not unlike the hostility between Englishmen and

Americans of the same racial stock. It is to be expected that the feeling will always be more or less present between the immigrant and the native born. However it does not extend to the children of the two groups, as they are subject to the same environment and develop identity of speech and psychology. Then, too, there has been an appreciable amount of intermarriage, especially between foreign-born men and native women. Not to be ignored is the fact that congestion in Harlem has forced both groups to be less discriminating in accepting lodgers, thus making for reconciling contacts.

The outstanding contribution of West Indians to American Negro life is the insistent assertion of their manhood in an environment that demands too much servility and unprotesting acquiescence from men of African blood. This unwillingness to conform and be standardized, to accept tamely an inferior status and abdicate their humanity, finds an open expression in the activities of the foreign-born Negro in America.

Their dominant characteristic is that of blazing new paths, breaking the bonds that would fetter the feet of a virile people— a spirit eloquently expressed in the defiant lines of the Jamaican poet, Claude McKay:

> Like men we'll face the murderous, cowardly pack,
> Pressed to the wall, dying, but fighting back.

MARCUS GARVEY

AFRICA FOR THE AFRICANS

FOR FIVE YEARS the Universal Negro Improvement Association has been advocating the cause of Africa for the Africans—that is, that the Negro peoples of the world should concentrate upon the object of building up for themselves a great nation in Africa.

When we started our propaganda toward this end several of the so-called intellectual Negroes who have been bamboozling the race for over half a century said that we were crazy, that the Negro peoples of the western world were not interested in Africa and could not live in Africa. One editor and leader went so far as to say at his so-called Pan-African Congress that American Negroes could not live in Africa, because the climate was too hot. All kinds of arguments have been adduced by these Negro intellectuals against the colonization of Africa by the black race. Some said that the black man would ultimately work out his existence alongside of the white man in countries founded and established by the latter. Therefore, it was not necessary for Negroes to seek an independent nationality of their own. The old time stories of "African fever," "African bad climate," "African mosquitos," "African savages," have been repeated by these "brainless intellectuals" of ours as a scare against our people in America and the West Indies taking a kindly interest in the new program of building a racial empire of our own in our Motherland. Now that years have rolled by and the Universal Negro Improvement Association has made the circuit of the world with its propaganda, we find eminent statesmen and leaders of the white race coming out boldly advocating the cause of colonizing Africa with the Negroes of the western world. A year ago Senator MacCullum of the Mississippi Legislature introduced a resolution in the House for the purpose of petitioning the Congress of the United States of America and the President to use their good influence in securing from the Allies sufficient territory in Africa in liquidation of the war debt, which territory should be used for the establishing of an independent nation for American Negroes. About the same time Senator France of Maryland gave expression to a similar desire in the Senate of the United States. During a speech on the "Soldiers' Bonus." He said: "We owe a big debt to Africa and one which we have too long ignored. I need not enlarge upon our peculiar interest in the obligation to the people of Africa. Thousands of Americans have for years been contributing to the missionary work which has been carried out by the noble men and women who have been sent out in that field by the churches of America."

This reveals a real change on the part of prominent statesmen in their attitude on the African question. Then comes another suggestion from Germany, for which Dr. Heinrich Schnee, a former Governor of German East Africa, is author. This German statesman suggests in an interview given out in Berlin, and published in New York, that America takes over the mandatories of Great Britain and France in Africa for the colonization of American Negroes. Speaking on the matter, he says, "As regards the attempt to colonize Africa with the surplus American colored population, this would in a long way settle the vexed problem, and under the plan such as Senator France has outlined, might enable France and Great Britain to discharge their duties to the United States, and simultaneously ease the burden of German reparations which is paralyzing economic life."

With expressions as above quoted from prominent world statesmen, and from the demands made by such men as Senators France and McCullum, it is clear that the question of African nationality is not a far-fetched one, but is as reasonable and feasible as was the idea of an American nationality.

A "Program" at Last

I trust that the Negro peoples of the world are now convinced that the work of the Universal Negro Improvement Association is not a visionary one, but very practical, and that it is not so far fetched, but can be realized in a short while if the entire race will only co-operate and work toward the desired end. Now that the work of our organization has started to bear fruit we find that some of these "doubting Thomases" of three and four years ago are endeavoring to mix themselves up with the popular idea of rehabilitating Africa in the interest of the Negro. They are now advancing spurious "programs" and in a short while will endeavor to force themselves upon the public as advocates and leaders of the African idea.

It is felt that those who have followed the career of the Universal Negro Improvement Association will not allow themselves to be deceived by these Negro opportunists who have always sought to live off the ideas of other people.

THE DREAM OF A NEGRO EMPIRE

It is only a question of a few more years when Africa will be completely colonized by Negroes, as Europe is by the white race. What we want is an independent African nationality, and if America is to help the Negro peoples of the world establish such a nationality, then we welcome the assistance.

It is hoped that when the time comes for American and West Indian Negroes to settle in Africa, they will realize their responsibility and their duty. It will not be to go to Africa for the purpose of exercising an over-lordship over the natives, but it shall be the purpose of the Universal Negro Improvement Association to have established in Africa that brotherly co-operation which will make the interests of the African native and the American and West Indian Negro one and the same, that is to say, we shall enter into a common partnership to build up Africa in the interests of our race.

ONENESS OF INTERESTS

Everybody knows that there is absolutely no difference between the native African and the American and West Indian Negroes, in that we are descendants from one common family stock. It is only a matter of accident that we have been divided and kept apart for over three hundred years, but it is felt that when the time has come for us to get back together, we shall do so in the spirit of brotherly love, and any Negro who expects that he will be assisted here, there or anywhere by the Universal Negro Improvement Association to exercise a haughty superiority over the fellows of his own race, makes a tremendous mistake. Such men had better remain where they are and not attempt to become in any way interested in the higher development of Africa.

The Negro has had enough of the vaunted practice of race superiority as inflicted upon him by others, therefore he is not prepared to tolerate a similar assumption on the part of his own people. In America and the West Indies, we have Negroes who believe themselves so much above their fellows as to cause them to think that any readjustment in the affairs of the race should be placed in their hands for them to exercise a kind of an autocratic and despotic control as others have done to us for centuries. Again I say, it would be advisable for such Negroes to take their hands and minds off the now popular idea of colonizing Africa in the interest of the Negro race, because their being identified with this new program will not in any way help us because of the existing feeling among Negroes everywhere not to tolerate the infliction of race or class superiority upon them, as is the desire of the self-appointed and self-created race leadership that we have been having for the last fifty years.

THE BASIS OF AN AFRICAN ARISTOCRACY

The masses of Negroes in America, the West Indies, South and Central America are in sympathetic accord with the aspirations of the native Africans. We desire to help them build up Africa as a Negro Empire, where every black man, whether he was born in Africa or in the Western world, will have the opportunity to develop on his own lines under the protection of the most favorable democratic institutions.

It will be useless, as before stated, for bombastic Negroes to leave America and the West Indies to go to Africa, thinking that they will have privileged positions to inflict upon the race that bastard aristocracy that they have tried to maintain in this Western world at the expense of the masses. Africa shall develop an aristocracy of its own, but it shall be based upon service and loyalty to race. Let all Negroes work toward that end. I feel that it is only a question of a few more years before our program will be accepted not only by the few statesmen of America who are now interested in it, but by the strong statesmen of the world, as the only solution to the great race problem. There is no other way to avoid the threatening war of the races that is bound to engulf all mankind, which has been prophesied by the world's greatest thinkers; there is no better method than by apportioning every race to its own habitat.

The time has really come for the Asiatics to govern themselves in Asia, as the Europeans are in Europe and the Western world, so also is it wise for the Africans to govern themselves at home, and thereby bring peace and satisfaction to the entire human family.

THE FUTURE AS I SEE IT

It comes to the individual, the race, the nation, once in a life-time to decide upon the course to be pursued as a career. The hour has now struck for the individual Negro as well as the entire race to decide the course that will be pursued in the interest of our own liberty.

We who make up the Universal Negro Improvement Association have decided that we shall go forward, upward and onward toward the great goal of human liberty. We have determined among ourselves that all barriers placed in the way of our progress must be removed, must be cleared away for we desire to see the light of a brighter day.

THE NEGRO IS READY

The Universal Negro Improvement Association for five years has been proclaiming to the world the readiness of the Negro to carve out a pathway for himself in the course of life. Men of other races and nations have become alarmed at this attitude of the Negro in his desire to do things for himself and by himself. This alarm has become so universal that organizations have been brought into being here, there and everywhere for the purpose of deterring and obstructing this forward move of our race. Propaganda has been waged here, there and everywhere for the purpose of misinterpreting the intention of this organization; some have said that this organization seeks to create discord and discontent among the races; some say we are organized for the purpose of hating other people. Every sensible, sane and honest-minded person knows that the Universal Negro Improvement Association has no such intention. We are organized for the absolute purpose of bettering our condition, industrially, commercially, socially, religiously and politically. We are organized not to hate other men, but to lift ourselves, and to demand respect of all humanity. We have a program that we believe to be righteous; we believe it to be just, and we have made up our minds to lay down ourselves on the altar of sacrifice for the realization of this great hope of ours, based upon the foundation of righteousness. We declare to the world that Africa must be free, that the entire Negro race must be emancipated from industrial bondage, peonage and serfdom; we make no compromise, we make no apology in this our declaration. We do not desire to create offense on the part of other races, but we are determined that we shall be heard, that we shall be given the rights to which we are entitled.

THE PROPAGANDA OF OUR ENEMIES

For the purpose of creating doubts about the work of the Universal Negro Improvement Association, many attempts have been made to cast shadow and gloom over our work. They have even written the most uncharitable things about our organization; they have spoken so unkindly of our effort, but what do we care? They spoke unkindly and uncharitably about all the reform movements that have helped in the betterment of humanity. They maligned the great movement of the Christian religion; they maligned the great liberation movements of America, of France, of England, of Russia; can we expect, then, to escape being maligned in this, our desire for the liberation of Africa and the freedom of four hundred million Negroes of the world?

We have unscrupulous men and organizations working in opposition to us. Some trying to capitalize the new spirit that has come to the Negro to make profit out of it to their own selfish benefit; some are trying to set back the Negro from seeing the hope of his own liberty, and thereby poisoning our people's mind against the motives of our organization; but every sensible far-seeing Negro in this enlightened age knows what propaganda means. It is the medium of discrediting that which you are opposed to, so that the propaganda of our enemies will be of little avail as soon as we are rendered able to carry to our peoples scattered throughout the world the true message of our great organization.

"CROCODILES" AS FRIENDS

Men of the Negro race, let me say to you that a greater future is in store for us; we have no cause to lose hope, to become faint-hearted. We must realize that upon ourselves depend our destiny, our future; we must carve out that future, that destiny, and we who make up the Universal Negro Improvement Association have pledged ourselves that nothing in the world shall stand in our way, nothing in the world shall discourage us, but opposition shall make us work harder, shall bring us closer together so that as one man the millions of us will march on toward that goal that we have set for ourselves. The new Negro shall not be deceived. The new Negro refuses to take advice from anyone who has not felt with him, and suffered with him. We have suffered for three hundred years, therefore we feel that the time has come when only those who have suffered with us can interpret our feelings and our spirit. It takes the slave to interpret the feelings of the slave; it takes the unfortunate man to interpret the spirit of his unfortunate brother; and so it takes the suffering Negro to interpret the spirit of his comrade. It is strange that so many people are interested in the Negro now, willing to advise him how to act, and what organizations he should join, yet nobody was interested in the Negro to the extent of not making him a slave for two hundred and fifty years, reducing him to industrial peonage and serfdom after he was freed; it is strange that the same people can be so interested in the Negro now, as to tell him what organization he should follow and what leader he should support.

Whilst we are bordering on a future of brighter things, we are also at our danger period, when we must either accept the right philosophy, or go down by following deceptive propaganda which has hemmed us in for many centuries.

DECEIVING THE PEOPLE

There is many a leader of our race who tells us that everything is well, and that all things will work out themselves and that a better day is coming. Yes, all of us know that a better day is coming; we all know that one day we will go home to Paradise, but whilst we are hoping by our Christian virtues to have an entry into Paradise we also realize that we are living on earth, and that the things that are practiced in Paradise are not practiced here. You have to treat this world as the world treats you; we are living in a temporal, material age, an age of activity, an age of racial, national selfishness. What else can you expect but to give back to the world what the world gives to you, and we are calling upon the four hundred million Negroes of the world to take a decided stand, a determined stand, that we shall occupy a firm position; that position shall be an emancipated race and a free nation of our own. We are determined that we shall have a free country; we are determined that we shall have a flag; we are determined that we shall have a government second to none in the world.

An Eye for an Eye

Men may spurn the idea, they may scoff at it; the metropolitan press of this country may deride us; yes, white men may laugh at the idea of Negroes talking about government; but let me tell you there is going to be a government, and let me say to you also that whatsoever you give, in like measure it shall be returned to you. The world is sinful, and therefore man believes in the doctrine of an eye for an eye, a tooth for a tooth. Everybody believes that revenge is God's, but at the same time we are men, and revenge sometimes springs up, even in the most Christian heart.

Why should man write down a history that will react against him? Why should man perpetrate deeds of wickedness upon his brother which will return to him in like measure? Yes, the Germans maltreated the French in the Franco-Prussian war of 1870, but the French got even with the Germans in 1918. It is history, and history will repeat itself. Beat the Negro, brutalize the Negro, kill the Negro, burn the Negro, imprison the Negro, scoff at the Negro, deride the Negro, it may come back to you one of these fine days, because the supreme destiny of man is in the hands of God. God is no respecter of persons, whether that person be white, yellow or black. Today the one race is up, tomorrow it has fallen; today the Negro seems to be the footstool of the other races and nations of the world; tomorrow the Negro may occupy the highest rung of the great human ladder.

But, when we come to consider the history of man, was not the Negro a power, was he not great once? Yes, honest students of history can recall the day when Egypt, Ethiopia and Timbuctoo towered in their civilizations, towered above Europe, towered above Asia. When Europe was inhabited by a race of cannibals, a race of savages, naked men, heathens and pagans, Africa was peopled with a race of cultured black men, who were masters in art, science and literature; men who were cultured and refined; men who, it was said, were like the gods. Even the great poets of old sang in beautiful sonnets of the delight it afforded the gods to be in companionship with the Ethiopians. Why, then, should we lose hope? Black men, you were once great; you shall be great again. Lose not courage, lose not faith, go forward. The thing to do is to get organized; keep separated and you will be exploited, you will be robbed, you will be killed. Get organized, and you will compel the world to respect you. If the world fails to give you consideration, because you are black men, because you are Negroes, four hundred millions of you shall, through organization, shake the pillars of the universe and bring down creation, even as Samson brought down the temple upon his head and upon the heads of the Philistines.

AN INSPIRING VISION

So Negroes, I say, through the Universal Negro Improvement Association, that there is much to live for. I have a vision of the future, and I see before me a picture of a redeemed Africa, with her dotted cities, with her beautiful civilization, with her millions of happy children, going to and fro. Why should I lose hope, why should I give up and take a back place in this age of progress? Remember that you are men, that God created you Lords of this creation. Lift up yourselves, men, take yourselves out of the mire and hitch your hopes to the stars; yes, rise as high as the very stars themselves. Let no man pull you down, let no man destroy your ambition, because man is but your companion, your equal; man is your brother; he is not your lord; he is not your sovereign master.

We of the Universal Negro Improvement Association feel happy; we are cheerful. Let them connive to destroy us; let them organize to destroy us; we shall fight the more. Ask me personally the cause of my success, and I say opposition; oppose me, and I fight the more, and if you want to find out the sterling worth of the Negro, oppose him, and under the leadership of the Universal Negro Improvement Association he shall fight his way to victory, and in the days to come, and I believe not far distant, Africa shall reflect a splendid demonstration of the worth of the Negro, of the determination of the Negro, to set himself free and to establish a government of his own.

LIBERTY HALL
EMANCIPATION DAY SPEECH

Fifty-nine years ago Abraham Lincoln signed the Emancipation Proclamation declaring four million Negroes in this country free. Several years prior to that Queen Victoria of England signed the Emancipation Proclamation that set at liberty hundreds of thousands of West Indian Negro slaves.

West Indian Negroes celebrate their emancipation on the first day of August of every year. The American Negroes celebrate their emancipation on the first of January of every year. Tonight we are here to celebrate the emancipation of the slaves in this country.

We are the descendants of the men and women who suffered in this country for two hundred and fifty years under that barbarous, that brutal institution known as slavery. You who have not lost trace of your history will recall the fact that over three hundred years ago your fore-bears were taken from the great Continent of Africa and brought here for the purpose of using them as slaves. Without mercy, without any sympathy they worked our fore-bears. They suffered, they bled, they died. But with their sufferings, with their blood, which they shed in their death, they had a hope that one day their posterity would be free, and we are assembled here tonight as the children of their hope.

I trust each and every one of you therefore will realize that you have a duty which is incumbent upon you; a duty that you must perform, because our fore-bears who suffered, who bled, who died had hopes that are not yet completely realized. They hoped that we as their children would be free, but they also hoped that their country from whence they came would also be free to their children, their grand-children and great grand-children at some future time. It is for the freedom of that country—that Motherland of ours—that four and a half million Negroes, as members of the Universal Negro Improvement Association, are laboring today.

This race of ours gave civilization, gave art, gave science; gave literature to the world. But it has been the way with races and nations. The one race stands out prominently in the one century or in the one age; and in another century or age it passes off the stage of action, and another race takes its place. The Negro once occupied a high position in the world, scientifically, artistically and commercially, but in the balancing of the great scale of evolution, we lost our place and some one, other than ourselves occupies the stand we once held.

God never intended that man should enslave his fellow, and the price of such a sin or such a violation of Heaven's law must be paid by every one. As for me, because of the blessed past, because of the history that I know, so long as there is within me the breath of life and the spirit of God, I shall struggle on and urge others of our race to struggle on to see that justice is done to the black peoples of the world. Yes, we appreciate the sorrows of the past, and we are going to work in the present that the sorrows of our generation shall not be perpetuated in the future. On the contrary, we shall strive that by our labors, succeeding generations of our own shall call us blessed, even as we call the generation of the past blessed today. And they indeed were blest. They were blest with a patience not yet known to man. A patience that enabled them to endure the tortures and the sufferings of slavery for two hundred and fifty years. Why? Was it because they loved slavery so? No. It was because they loved this generation more. Isn't it wonderful? Transcendent? What then are you going to do to show your appreciation of this love, what gratitude are you going to manifest in return for what they have done for you? As for me, knowing the sufferings of my fore-fathers I shall give back to Africa that liberty that she once enjoyed hundreds of years ago, before her own sons and daughters were taken from her shores and brought in chains to this Western World.

No better gift can I give in honor of the memory of the love of my fore-parents for me, and in gratitude of the sufferings they endured that I might be free; no grander gift can I bear to the sacred memory of the generation past than a free and a redeemed Africa—a monument for all eternity—for all times.

As by the action of the world, as by the conduct of all the races and nations it is apparent that not one of them has the sense of justice, the sense of love, the sense of equity, the sense of charity, that would make men happy, and make God satisfied. It is apparent that it is left to the Negro to play such a part in human affairs—for when we look to the Anglo-Saxon we see him full of greed, avarice, no mercy, no love, no charity. We go from the white man to the yellow man, and we see the same unenviable characteristics in the Japanese. Therefore we must believe that the Psalmist had great hopes of this race of ours when he prophesied

"Princes shall come out of Egypt and Ethiopia shall stretch forth her hands unto God"

If humanity is regarded as made up of the children of God and God loves all humanity (we all know that) then God will be more pleased with that race that protects all humanity than with the race that outrages the children of God.

And so tonight we celebrate this anniversary of our emancipation, we do it not with regret, on the contrary we do it with an abiding confidence, a hope and faith in ourselves and in our God. And the faith that we have is a faith that will ultimately take us back to that ancient place, that ancient position that we once occupied, when Ethiopia was in her glory.

MARY WHITE OVINGTON

ON MARCUS GARVEY

GARVEY WAS BORN in the year 1887 at St. Anne's Parish, Jamaica, British West Indies. His place in this island was that of a member of an inferior race, one of the black masses ruled by a few whites. Between the black and the white were the mulattoes, or "colored," who enjoyed greater privileges, social and economic, than the black. The boy Marcus was educated at public and private schools, and at sixteen was taught the printer's trade. He supported himself at this work for some years, and brought out a paper of his own. He managed to visit England, where at London he studied evenings in the University and met interesting people. Among them was Duse Mahomad Effendi, editor of the *African and Oriental Review*. Effendi spoke of him afterwards as an excellent talker, but lazy. Garvey travelled on the continent, where he was a careful observer, and on the ship returning to America, met a passenger recently from Africa, who recited tales of the cruelty practised upon the natives. He cruised in the West Indies, worked at ports in Central America, and saw everywhere the exploitation of the black man. Black Jamaicans, his countrymen, were piling up millions of profits for the great companies that employed them, and yet they themselves remained in poverty.

"Poverty is a hellish state to be in," he wrote later, "it is no virtue, it is a crime."

There grew in his mind, from his European observations and from his intimate knowledge of conditions in the Caribbean, the conviction that a race could not attain permanent wealth and power in a land that was not its own. The government would always be prejudiced against it. If the master race increased in numbers, the servant race would be left to starve. This, he felt, was not

a trait peculiar to the whites, but was shared by all people. Therefore, the only hope for Negro advancement was a return to Africa,
where with native blacks, the American Negro, led by Marcus Garvey, would build up a civilization equal to any in the world.

It took two trips to the United States to win for Garvey even
the slightest foothold. He endured many hardships, and was cold
and hungry his first winter in New York. A few beans, a can of
sardines, a banana or two, insufficient clothing—these seemed a
poor exchange for the beauty and warmth of Jamaica. But Garvey
held his ground and slowly gained support. His ideas appealed at
first to the West Indian rather than to the American Negro, and
he has been accused, with some justice, of setting black against
mulatto. One of his most important converts was the West Indian,
Hubert Harrison, at one time a socialist, who had won fame by
his brilliant, witty street speeches. It was not, however, until Garvey was able to acquire the *Negro World,* an inconspicuous colored sheet, that his real success began. With a newspaper of his
own, he could spread his propaganda throughout the States.

He had two plans—first, propaganda, preaching the doctrine
of a return to Africa; second, a commercial enterprise, a triangular
steamship company, that should ply between the United States, the
West Indies, and Africa. He spoke of Africa vaguely, but he seemed
to have in mind the South and West coast. Here American Negroes,
aided by natives, should get a foothold, and from this point of
vantage would form a Negro super-government, of which Garvey
would be the head. This super-government would control the four
hundred million of the Negro race as the Pope from the Vatican
controlled the Catholics of the world. The two immediate steps
then necessary were the spread of the gospel of African freedom
and the operation of the Black Star Line.

The Black Star Line! Whatever the Garvey movement lacked
in practicality it made up in poesy. The name of the new line of
steamships, soon to be advertised in the *Negro World,* fired the
imagination of the American Negro. Donations for the enterprise
poured in. Garvey received them as donations, but a disobliging
district attorney insisted that money for a business enterprise could
not be received in this casual way, to be used without accounting
as the recipient might see fit. The Black Star Line must be incorporated. This was done. The line was capitalized at ten million
dollars and two million dollars' worth of stock was offered for
sale. As the stock began to sell, the company proceeded to liquidate

its debts acquired prior to incorporation—an illegal proceeding. Business training had not been a part of Marcus Garvey's education.

Other business enterprises were started—laundries, a factory or two, and Liberty Hall, an immense auditorium, was purchased. The movement was christened the Universal Negro Improvement Association. It received its greatest impetus when, in the fall of 1919, a crank fired four times at Garvey as he was about to go to a Black Star Line meeting. He was wounded and partly crippled for life, but bandaged and limping he entered Liberty Hall. The enthusiasm was prodigious. Men and women went wild. Their leader became a martyr, a saint. Stock was lavishly subscribed, and Garvey's popularity assured.

In the winter of 1919 and the spring of 1920, half a million dollars' worth of Black Star stock was sold to the Negroes. In one college alone in Louisiana, students raised seven thousand dollars. No white man might become a stockholder or a member of the U.N.I.A. In many places no white man might be admitted to a Garvey meeting. This was a black man's job. And all over the United States, on the pleasant farms of Virginia, in the cabins of the cotton belt, in the city homes of the Pacific coast, throughout the Negro quarters of the Middle West, wherever black men and women were gathered in numbers, word was spread of the new organization that would bring freedom to all, and of the line of steamships that would soon ply between America and the Motherland.

White people, when they heard of the movement, either laughed or applauded. Despite the very real popularity of Negro labor among many employers, white Americans look with favor upon the departure of the black man, and with him his problem, from the United States. *The World's Work* printed a long and highly entertaining article on Marcus Garvey. Newspapers enjoyed giving him publicity, and the prestige of the Black Star Line and the Universal Negro Improvement Association grew each month.

The majority of the educated Negroes stood aloof, not feeling they could praise, not wishing to blame. "They either think I am crazy," Garvey said, "or they do what is far worse, ignore me." But some gathered to his side, among them William Ferris, scholar and lecturer, to whom he gave high honor, and Noah Thompson of Los Angeles, a prominent citizen whose endorsement gave Garvey prestige on the coast. Leaders were found to head the movement in various sections and it gained in numbers not only in this country, but in the West Indies.

Students of African tribal life say that a Negro government tends to despotism. This was true with the United Negro Improvement Association. At the head was His Excellency, His Highness, the Provisional President of Africa. Then came the knights—only a few of these—Knight-Commanders of the Distinguished Order of Ethiopia, Knight-Commanders of the Sublime Order of the Nile. There were lesser nobles, and there were commoners. There were Black Cross nurses, and there was the great African Army. The colors of the new movement were Black, Red, and Green. "Black for our race," as His Excellency said, in his regal robes of these colors, "Red for our blood, and Green for our hope." The old fraternal orders with their regalia paled before this new organization. It appealed to the love of beauty, of color so keen in the African, and it also aroused his self-respect and pride. The sweeper in the subway, the elevator boy eternally carrying fat office men and perky girls up and down a shaft, knew that when night came he might march with the African Army and bear a wonderful banner to be raised some day in a distant, beautiful land. Liberty Hall rang at night with songs of battle and victory.

The Second International Convention was held in August, 1921. It lasted for a month. Delegates came, not only from the states and larger cities of the Union, but also from Cuba, Haiti, the West Indies, Central and South America. They came from Canada, from Europe, from Australia, from Abyssinia, from Liberia. An immense meeting took place in Madison Square Garden, the largest auditorium in New York. A procession formed at Liberty Hall that for gold braid and brass buttons surpassed anything Harlem had seen. Garvey led on his horse, robed in the colors of United Africa. Following him came the knights and nobles; then the grand, resplendent Army. Banners waved bearing victorious slogans: "Africa Must Be Free." "The Negro fought in Europe, he can fight in Africa." "Africa a Nation, One and Indivisible." "Garvey, The Man of the Hour." Best of all, trumpets blared, and drums beat their magnificent music.

This convention marked the height of Garvey's power, but it also marked the beginning of his downfall. Of oratory there was plenty. The auditors were told by Africa's president that day by day they were writing a new history, recounting new deeds of valor. But the Universal Negro Improvement Association was a business concern and the delegates wanted a careful financial statement. Especially they wanted to see the Black Star Line ships. Three had been bought, they knew, the *Yarmouth,* the *Maceo,* and the *Shadyside.* A fourth, the *Phyllis Wheatley,* was advertised weekly in the *Negro World.* It was a noble ship, equipped with all modern improvements, formerly the *Orion,* purchased by the Black Star Line from the United States Shipping Board. According to the advertisement the vessel would run to Havana, Cuba, St. Kitts, Barbados, Trinidad, Demerara, Dakar, and Monrovia. The date of sailing had been frequently postponed, but the advertisement continued to appear in the *Negro World.* Where, then, was the ship?

JAMES WELDON JOHNSON

FROM *BLACK MANHATTAN*

WITH THOUSANDS OF NEGROES pouring into Harlem month by
month, two things happened: first, a sheer physical pressure for
room was set up that was irresistible; second, old residents and
new-comers got work as fast as they could take it, at wages never
dreamed of, so there was now plenty of money for renting and
buying. And the Negro in Harlem did, contrary to all the burlesque
notions about what Negroes do when they get hold of money, take
advantage of the low prices of property and begin to buy. Buying
property became a contagious fever. It became a part of the gospel
preached in the churches. It seems that generations of the experience of an extremely precarious foothold on the land of Manhattan
Island flared up into a conscious determination never to let that
condition return. So they turned the money from their new-found
prosperity into property. All classes bought. It was not an unknown thing for a coloured washerwoman to walk into a
real-estate office and lay down several thousand dollars on a house.
There was Mrs. Mary Dean, known as "Pig Foot Mary" because
of her high reputation in the business of preparing and selling that
particular delicacy, so popular in Harlem. She paid $42,000 for a
five-story apartment house at the corner of Seventh Avenue and
One Hundred and Thirty-seventh Street, which was sold later to a
coloured undertaker for $72,000. The Equitable Life Assurance
Company held vacant for quite a while a block of 106 model private houses, designed by Stanford White, which the company had
been obliged to take over following the hegira of the whites from
Harlem. When they were put on the market, they were promptly
bought by Negroes at an aggregate price of about two million dollars. John E. Nail, a coloured real-estate dealer of Harlem who is

a member of the Real Estate Board of New York and an appraisal authority, states that Negroes own and control Harlem real property worth, at a conservative estimate, between fifty and sixty million dollars. Relatively, these figures are amazing. Twenty years ago barely a half-dozen coloured individuals owned land on Manhattan. Down to fifteen years ago the amount that Negroes had acquired in Harlem was by comparison negligible. Today a very large part of the property in Harlem occupied by Negroes is owned by Negroes.

It should be noted that Harlem was taken over without violence. In some of the large Northern cities where the same sort of expansion of the Negro population was going on, there was not only strong antagonism on the part of whites, but physical expression of it. In Chicago, Cleveland, and other cities houses bought and moved into by Negroes were bombed. In Chicago a church bought by a coloured congregation was badly damaged by bombs. In other cities several formerly white churches which had been taken over by coloured congregations were bombed. In Detroit, mobs undertook to evict Negroes from houses bought by them in white neighbourhoods. The mob drove vans up to one house just purchased and moved into by a coloured physician, ordered him out, loaded all his goods into the vans, and carted them back to his old residence. These arrogated functions of the mob reached a climax in the celebrated Sweet case. A mob gathered in the evening round a house in a white neighbourhood which Dr. O. H. Sweet, a coloured physician, had bought and moved into the day before. When the situation reached a critical point, shots fired from within the house killed one person in the crowd and seriously wounded another. Dr. Sweet, his wife, and eight others, relatives and friends, who were in the house at the time, were indicted and tried for murder in the first degree. They were defended in two long trials by the National Association for the Advancement of Colored People, through Clarence Darrow and Arthur Garfield Hays, assisted by several local attorneys, and were acquitted. This was the tragic end of eviction by mob in Detroit.

Although there was bitter feeling in Harlem during the fifteen years of struggle the Negro went through in getting a foothold on the land, there was never any demonstration of violence that could be called serious. Not since the riot of 1900 has New York witnessed, except for minor incidents, any inter-racial disturbances. Not even in the memorable summer of 1919—that summer when the stoutest-hearted Negroes felt terror and dismay; when the race got the worst backwash of the war, and the Ku Klux Klan was in the ascendant; when almost simultaneously there were riots in Chicago and in Longview, Texas; in Omaha and in Phillips County, Arkansas; and hundreds of Negroes, chased through the streets or hunted down through the swamps, were beaten and killed; when in the national capital an anti-Negro mob held sway for three days, in which time six persons were killed and scores severely beaten— not even during this period of massacre did New York, with more than a hundred thousand Negroes grouped together in Harlem, lose its equanimity. . . .

At any rate, there is no longer any apparent feeling against the occupancy of Harlem by Negroes. Within the past five years the colony has expanded to the south, the north, and the west. It has gone down Seventh Avenue from One Hundred and Twenty-seventh Street to Central Park at One Hundred and Tenth Street. It has climbed upwards between Eighth Avenue and the Harlem River from One Hundred and Forty-fifth Street to One Hundred and Fifty-fifth. It has spread to the west and occupies the heights of Coogan's Bluff, overlooking Colonial Park. And to the east and west of this solid Negro area, there is a fringe where the population is mixed, white and coloured. This expansion of the past five years has taken place without any physical opposition, or even any considerable outbreak of antagonistic public sentiment.

The question inevitably arises: Will the Negroes of Harlem be able to hold it? Will they not be driven still farther northward? Residents of Manhattan, regardless of race, have been driven out when they lay in the path of business and greatly increased land values. Harlem lies in the direction that path must take; so there is little probability that Negroes will always hold it as a residential section. But this is to be considered: the Negro's situation in Harlem is without precedent in all his history in New York; never before has he been so securely anchored, never before has he owned the land, never before has he had so well established a community life. It is probable that land through the heart of Harlem will some day so increase in value that Negroes may not be able to hold it—although it is quite as probable that there will be some Negroes able to take full advantage of the increased values —and will be forced to make a move. But the next move, when it comes, will be unlike the others. It will not be a move made solely at the behest of someone else; it will be more in the nature of a bargain. Nor will it be a move in which the Negro will carry with him only his household goods and utensils; he will move at a financial profit to himself. But at the present time such a move is nowhere in sight.

On December 15, 1919 John Drinkwater's *Abraham Lincoln* had its American *première* at the Cort Theatre in New York, and Charles Gilpin, formerly with both the Lincoln and the Lafayette companies, was drafted to create the role of the Rev. William Custis, a Negro preacher who goes to the White House for a conference at the request of Lincoln, this conference between the President and the black man constituting one of the strongest and most touching scenes in the play. The character of Custis was intended by the playwright to be a representation of Frederick Douglass. Drinkwater in writing the play had largely followed Lord Charnwood's life of Abraham Lincoln, in which Douglass is erroneously set down as "a well-known Negro preacher." The playwright also made the error of putting Custis's lines into dialect. He may, as a dramatist, have done this intentionally to heighten the character effect; or he may, as an Englishman, have done it through unfamiliarity with all the facts. In either case, the dialect was such as no American Negro would ever use. It was a slightly darkened pidgin-English or the form of speech a big Indian chief would be supposed to employ in talking with the Great White Father at Washington. However, Gilpin was a success in the role.

Meanwhile Eugene O'Neill was experimenting with the dramatic possibilities of the Negro both as material and as exponent. He had written a one-act play, *The Moon of the Caribbees,* in which the scene was laid aboard a ship lying in a West Indian harbour, and the characters were members of the ship's crew and Negro natives of the island. The play was produced at the Provincetown Playhouse, New York, in 1918, with a white cast. He had also written a one-act tragedy, *The Dreamy Kid,* in which all of the four characters were Negroes. *The Dreamy Kid* was produced at the Provincetown Playhouse, October 31, 1919, with a Negro cast and with Harold Simmelkjaer—who, despite the Dutch name, is a Negro—in the title-role. This play was later revived with Frank Wilson as the Dreamy Kid. In the season of 1919–20 Butler Davenport's Bramhall Players produced at their playhouse in East Twenty-seventh Street a play called *Justice* with a mixed cast. Frank Wilson and Rose McClendon played important parts.

None of these efforts, so far as the Negro is concerned, evoked more than mildly favourable comment. But on November 3, 1920 O'Neill's *The Emperor Jones* was produced at the Provincetown Playhouse, with Charles Gilpin in the title-role, and another important page in the history of the Negro in the theatre was written. The next morning Gilpin was famous. The power of his acting was enthusiastically and universally acclaimed. Indeed, the sheer physical feat of sustaining the part—the whole play is scarcely more than a continuous monologue spoken by the principal character— demanded admiration. The Drama League voted him to be one of the ten persons who had done most for the American theatre during the year; and some of the readers of these pages will recall the almost national crisis that was brought on as a consequence of this action. As was the custom, the Drama League gave a dinner in honour of the ten persons chosen; and, as seemed quite natural to do, invited Mr. Gilpin. Thereupon there broke out a controversy that divided the Drama League, the theatrical profession, the press, and the public. Pressure was brought to have the invitation withdrawn, but those responsible for it stood firm. Then the pressure was centred upon Mr. Gilpin to induce him not to attend the dinner. The amount of noise and heat made, and of serious effort expended, was worthy of a weightier matter than the question of a dinner with a coloured man present as a guest. This incident occurred only ten years ago, but already it has an archaic character. It is doubtful if a similar incident today could provoke such a degree of asininity. Mr. Gilpin attended the dinner.

By his work in *The Emperor Jones* Gilpin reached the highest point of achievement on the legitimate stage that had yet been attained by a Negro in America. But it was by no sudden flight; it was by a long, hard struggle. Before being dined by the Drama League as one of those who had done most for the American theatre, he had travelled with small road shows playing one-night stands, been stranded more than once, been compelled to go back to work at his trade as a printer, been a member of a minstrel show, worked in a barber-shop, joined a street fair company, gone out with a concert company, tried being a trainer of prize-fighters, sung with a company of jubilee singers, worked as an elevator-boy and switch-board operator in an apartment house on Riverside Drive, been a railroad porter, played vaudeville, held a job as a janitor, and hesitated greatly about giving it up. His real theatrical career can be traced from Williams and Walker's company to Gus Hill's *Smart Set,* to the Pekin stock-company, to the Anita Bush

Players at the Lincoln in Harlem, to the Lafayette Players, to John Drinkwater's *Abraham Lincoln,* and to *The Emperor Jones.* Mr. Gilpin was awarded the Spingarn Medal in 1920. He died May 6, 1930. . . .

In the summer of 1921 along came *Shuffle Along,* and all New York flocked to the Sixty-third Street Theatre to hear the most joyous singing and see the most exhilarating dancing to be found on any stage in the city. *Shuffle Along* was a record-breaking, epoch-making musical comedy. Some of its tunes—"I'm Just Wild about Harry," "Gipsy Blues," "Love Will Find a Way," "I'm Cravin' for That Kind of Love," "In Honeysuckle Time," "Bandana Days," and "Shuffle Along"—went round the world. It would be difficult to name another musical comedy with so many song hits as *Shuffle Along* had. Its dances furnished new material for hundreds of dancing performers. *Shuffle Along* was cast in the form of the best Williams and Walker, Cole and Johnson tradition; but the music did not hark back at all; it was up to the minute. There was, however, one other respect in which it did hark back; it was written and produced, as well as performed, by Negroes. Four men—F. E. Miller, Aubrey Lyles, Eubie Blake, and Noble Sissle—combined their talents and their means to bring it about. Their talents were many, but their means were limited, and they had no easy time.

They organized the show in New York and took it on a short out-of-town try-out, with Broadway as their goal. It was booked for an opening at the Howard Theatre, a coloured theatre in Washington. When the company assembled at the Pennsylvania Station, it was found that they did not have quite enough money for transportation, and there had to be quick scurrying round to raise the necessary funds. Such an ominous situation could not well be concealed, and there were misgivings and mutterings among the company. After all the tickets were secured, it took considerable persuasion to induce some of its members to go so far away from New York on such slim expectations.

They played two successful weeks at the Howard Theatre and so had enough money to move to Philadelphia, where they were booked to play the Dunbar Theatre, another coloured house. Broadway, their goal, looked quite distant even from Philadelphia. The managers, seeking to make sure of getting the company to New York, suggested to the owner of the Dunbar Theatre that it would be a good investment for him to take a half-interest in the show for one thousand dollars, but he couldn't see it that way. They played two smashing weeks at the Dunbar and brought the company intact into New York, but, as they expressed it, on a shoe-string. They went into the Sixty-third Street Theatre, which had been dark for some time; it was pretty far uptown for Broadway audiences. Within a few weeks *Shuffle Along* made the Sixty-third Street Theatre one of the best-known houses in town and made it necessary for the Traffic Department to declare Sixty-third Street a one-way thoroughfare. *Shuffle Along* played New York for over a year and played on the road for two years longer. It was a remarkable aggregation. There was a chorus of pretty girls that danced marvellously. The comedians were Miller and Lyles, and a funny black-face pair they were. Their burlesque of two ignorant Negroes going into "big business" and opening a grocery-store was a never-failing producer of side-shaking laughter. There was a quartet, the Four Harmony Kings, that gave a fresh demonstration of the close harmony and barber-shop chords that are the chief characteristics of Negro quartets. There was Lottie Gee, jauntiest of *ingénues,* and Gertrude Saunders, most bubbling of comediennes. There was Noble Sissle with his take-it-from-me style of singing, and there was Eubie Blake with his amazing jazz piano-playing. And it was in *Shuffle Along* that Florence Mills, that incomparable little star, first twinkled on Broadway.

Shuffle Along pre-empted and held New York's interest in Negro theatricals for a year. In the fall of 1921 another venture was made, when Irving C. Miller, a brother of the Miller of *Shuffle Along,* produced *Put and Take,* a musical comedy, at Town Hall (New York). *Put and Take,* by all ordinary standards, was a good show, but it was overshadowed by the great vogue of *Shuffle Along.* In the spring of 1923 Irving C. Miller had better success with *Liza,* a tuneful and very fast dancing show that he produced at a downtown theatre.

In the fall Miller and Lyles came out with a new play, *Runnin' Wild,* and opened at the Colonial Theatre, on upper Broadway, on October 29. The old combination had been broken. Miller and Lyles had remained together; Sissle and Blake had formed a separate partnership, and Florence Mills was lost to both sides; she was heading a revue at the Plantation, a downtown night-club. Notwithstanding, *Runnin' Wild,* even in the inevitable comparison with its predecessor, was a splendid show. It had a successful run of eight months at the Colonial. *Runnin' Wild* would have been notable if for no other reason than that it made use of the "Charleston," a Negro dance creation which up to that time had been known only to Negroes; thereby introducing it to New York, America, and the world. The music for the dance was written by Jimmie Johnson, the composer of the musical score of the piece. The Charleston achieved a popularity second only to the tango, also a Negro dance creation, originating in Cuba, transplanted to the Argentine, thence to the world via Paris. There is a claim that Irving C. Miller first introduced the Charleston on the stage in his *Liza;* even so, it was *Runnin' Wild* that started the dance on its world-encircling course. When Miller and Lyles introduced the dance in their show, they did not depend wholly upon their extraordinarily good jazz band for the accompaniment; they went straight back to primitive Negro music and had the major part of the chorus supplement the band by beating out the time with hand-clapping and foot-patting. The effect was electrical. Such a demonstration of beating out complex rhythms had never before been seen on a stage in New York. However, Irving C. Miller may indisputably claim that in his show *Dinah,* produced the next year at the Lafayette Theatre, he was the first to put another Negro dance, the "Black Bottom," on the stage. The "Black Bottom" gained a popularity which was only little less than that of the Charleston.

The Sissle and Blake show of this same year was *Chocolate Dandies*. In comparison with *Runnin' Wild,* its greatest lack lay in the fact that it had no comedians who approached the class of Miller and Lyles. But *Chocolate Dandies* did have Johnny Hudgins, and in the chorus a girl who showed herself to be a comedienne of the first order. Her name was Josephine Baker.

On May 7, 1923 there was witnessed at the Frazee Theatre what was the most ambitious attempt Negroes had yet made in the legitimate theatre in New York. The Ethiopian Art Players, organized by Raymond O'Neil and Mrs. Sherwood Anderson, presented Oscar Wilde's *Salome;* an original interpretation of Shakespere's *The Comedy of Errors;* and *The Chip Woman's Fortune,* a one-act Negro play by Willis Richardson. The acting of Evelyn Preer in the role of Salome, and her beauty, received high and well-deserved praise from the critics; and the work of Sidney Kirkpatrick, Laura Bowman, Charles Olden, and Lionel Monagas, all formerly of the Lafayette Players, won commendation. But the only play on the bill that was fully approved was *The Chip Woman's*

Fortune. Some of the critics said frankly that however well Negroes might play "white" classics like *Salome* and *The Comedy of Errors,* it was doubtful if they could be so interesting as they would be in Negro plays, if they could be interesting at all. The Ethiopian Art Players had run up against one of the curious factors in the problem of race, against the paradox which makes it quite seemly for a white person to represent a Negro on the stage, but a violation of some inner code for a Negro to represent a white person. This, it seems, is certain: if they had put into a well-written play of Negro life the same degree of talent and skill they did put into *Salome* and *The Comedy of Errors,* they would have achieved an overwhelming success. But it appears that at the time no such play was available for them. Beginning June 4, the company played for a week at the Lafayette in Harlem. . . .

But on May 15, 1924 Eugene O'Neill produced at the Provincetown Playhouse a Negro play that made New York and the rest of the country sit up and take notice. The play was *All God's Chillun Got Wings.* The cast was a mixed one, with Paul Robeson in the principal role, playing opposite Mary Blair, a white actress. Public excitement about this play did not wait for the opening in the theatre, but started fully three months before; that is, as soon as it was seen through the publication of the play in the *American Mercury* that the two chief characters were a coloured boy and a white girl, and that the boy falls in love with the girl and marries her. When it was learned that the play was to be produced in a New York theatre with a coloured and a white performer in these two roles, a controversy began in the newspapers of the city that quickly spread; and articles, editorials, and interviews filled columns upon columns in periodicals throughout the country. The discussion in the press was, as might be expected, more bitter than it had been in the incident of the Drama League dinner to Charles Gilpin. The New York *American* and the *Morning Telegraph* went further than other New York publications. For weeks they carried glaring headlines and inciting articles. They appeared to be seeking to provoke violence in order to stop the play.

The New York *American* on March 18, eight weeks before the opening, carried an article headed: "Riots Feared From Drama—'All God's Chillun' Direct Bid for Disorders, the View of George G. Battle—Thinks City Should Act." In the article George Gordon Battle was quoted as saying: "The production of such a play will be most unfortunate. If the Provincetown Players and Mr.

O'Neill refuse to bow before public opinion, the city officials should take action to ban it from the stage." In the same article Mrs. W. J. Arnold, "a founder of the Daughters of the Confederacy," was quoted as saying: "The scene where Miss Blair is called upon to kiss and fondle a Negro's hand is going too far, even for the stage. The play may be produced above the Mason and Dixie [*sic*] line, but Mr. O'Neill will not get the friendly reception he had when he sent 'Emperor Jones' his other coloured play into the South. The play should be banned by the authorities, because it will be impossible for it to do otherwise than stir up ill feeling between the races."

An issue of the Hearst publication said editorially:

> Gentlemen who are engaged in producing plays should not make it any harder for their friends to protect them from censorship. They should not put on plays which are, or threaten to become, enemies of the public peace; they should not dramatize dynamite, because, while helping the box office, it may blow up the business.
>
> We refer to the play in which a white woman marries a black man and at the end of the play, after going crazy, stoops and kisses the Negro's hand.
>
> It is hard to imagine a more nauseating and inflammable situation, and in many communities the failure of the audience to scrap the play and mutilate the players would be regarded as a token of public anemia.

It would be still harder to imagine yellower journalism than this, or why a thing that has happened more than once in actual life should be regarded as so utterly beyond conception as a theatrical situation.

The opening night came, the theatre was crowded—the attacks had served as publicity—there was some feeling of tenseness on the part of the audience and a great deal on the part of the performers, but the play proceeded without any sign of antagonistic demonstration, without even a hiss or a boo. None of the appeals to prejudice, hate, and fear had had the intended effect. The pressure brought on Mayor Hylan and the Police Department got no further result than the refusal of permission to allow a group of children to appear in the opening scene. The public at large failed to be moved to any sense of impending danger to either the white or the black race because of this play. The outcome of the whole business proved that the rabid newspapers were not expressing public sentiment, but were striving to stir up a public sentiment.

All God's Chillun Got Wings did not prove to be another *Emperor Jones*. One sound reason why it did not was because it was not so good a play. It was dramatic enough, but the incidents did not link up along the inevitable line that the spectator was made to feel he must follow. It may be that as the play began to grow, Mr. O'Neill became afraid of it. At any rate, he side-stepped the logical question and let his heroine go crazy; thus shifting the question from that of a coloured man living with a white wife to that of a man living with a crazy woman; from which shift, so far as this particular play was concerned, nothing at all could be demonstrated. The play, as a play, did not please white people, and, on the other hand, it failed to please coloured people. Mr. O'Neill, perhaps in concession to public sentiment, made the white girl who is willing to marry the black student, and whom he is glad to get, about as lost as he could well make her. Coloured people not only did not consider this as any compliment to the race, but regarded it as absolutely contrary to the essential truth. However, the play ran for several weeks, and Paul Robeson increased his reputation by the restraint, sincerity, and dignity with which he acted a difficult role.

Mr. Robeson's reputation is now international. He played the leading Negro character in the London production of *Show Boat*. He played the title role in a successful revival of *The Emperor Jones* in Berlin early in 1930. And it has been announced that he will play Othello in a production to be made of Shakspere's immortal tragedy at the Savoy Theatre, London, in May 1930.

Perhaps it was now time for New York again to sing and dance and laugh with the Negro on the stage; and it soon had the opportunity. On October 29, 1924, exactly one year after the opening of *Runnin' Wild*, Florence Mills came to the Broadhurst Theatre in *Dixie to Broadway*, and New York had its first Negro revue. For the Florence Mills show broke away entirely from the established traditions of Negro musical comedy. Indeed, it had to, because she was the star; and the traditions called for a show built around two male comedians, usually of the black-face type. The revue was actually an enlarged edition of the one in which Miss Mills had been appearing at the Plantation. It was also the same revue that had been played in London the season before under the title of *Dover to Dixie* with her as the star. On the night of the production of *Dixie to Broadway* New York not only found itself with a novelty in the form of a Negro revue, but also discovered that it had a new artist of positive genius in the person of Florence Mills. She had made a name in *Shuffle Along,* but in *Dixie to Broadway* she was recognized for her full worth.

ALAIN LOCKE

HARLEM WAS PERCEIVED by its inhabitants as a world entire unto itself, the cradle of a culture that would perform much the same role, proclaimed Alain Locke, as Dublin and Prague had performed in the creation of the new Ireland and new Czechoslovakia. Yet Harlem was also said to be distinctive only the better to make its contribution to the American whole. "Separate as it may be in color and substance," Locke announced confidently in The New Negro, *"the culture of the Negro is of a pattern integral with the times and with its cultural setting." Thus, its music was distinctive (Rogers on jazz), its very existence a source of creative exploration (Robeson on O'Neill), its future the recapitulation and fulfillment of glories in the distant African past (Schomburg), and, in the words of Elise Johnson McDougald, its "progressive and privileged groups of Negro women," like Harlem's Talented Tenth men, inspired by the finest American ideals of personal character and social mobility.*

THE NEW NEGRO

IN THE LAST DECADE something beyond the watch and guard of statistics has happened in the life of the American Negro and the three norns who have traditionally presided over the Negro problem have a changeling in their laps. The Sociologist, the Philanthropist, the Race-leader are not unaware of the New Negro, but they are at a loss to account for him. He simply cannot be swathed in their formulae. For the younger generation is vibrant with a new psychology; the new spirit is awake in the masses, and under the very eyes of the professional observers is transforming what has been a perennial problem into the progressive phases of contemporary Negro life.

Could such a metamorphosis have taken place as suddenly as it has appeared to? The answer is no; not because the New Negro is not here, but because the Old Negro had long become more of a myth than a man. The Old Negro, we must remember, was a creature of moral debate and historical controversy. His has been a stock figure perpetuated as an historical fiction partly in innocent sentimentalism, partly in deliberate reactionism. The Negro himself has contributed his share to this through a sort of protective social mimicry forced upon him by the adverse circumstances of dependence. So for generations in the mind of America, the Negro has been more of a formula than a human being—a something to be argued about, condemned or defended, to be "kept down," or "in his place," or "helped up," to be worried with or worried over, harassed or patronized, a social bogey or a social burden. The thinking Negro even has been induced to share this same general attitude, to focus his attention on controversial issues, to see himself in the distorted perspective of a social problem. His shadow, so to speak, has been more real to him than his personality. Through having had to appeal from the unjust stereotypes of his oppressors and traducers to those of his liberators, friends and benefactors he has had to subscribe to the traditional positions from which his case has been viewed. Little true social or self-understanding has or could come from such a situation.

But while the minds of most of us, black and white, have thus burrowed in the trenches of the Civil War and Reconstruction, the actual march of development has simply flanked these positions, necessitating a sudden reorientation of view. We have not been watching in the right direction; set North and South on a sectional axis, we have not noticed the East till the sun has us blinking. . . .

There is, of course, a warrantably comfortable feeling in being on the right side of the country's professed ideals. We realize that we cannot be undone without America's undoing. It is within the gamut of this attitude that the thinking Negro faces America, but with variations of mood that are if anything more significant than the attitude itself. Sometimes we have it taken with the defiant ironic challenge of McKay:

> Mine is the future grinding down to-day
> Like a great landslip moving to the sea,

> Bearing its freight of débris far away
> Where the green hungry waters restlessly
> Heave mammoth pyramids, and break and roar
> Their eerie challenge to the crumbling shore.

Sometimes, perhaps more frequently as yet, it is taken in the fervent and almost filial appeal and counsel of Weldon Johnson's:

> O Southland, dear Southland!
> Then why do you still cling
> To an idle age and a musty page,
> To a dead and useless thing?

But between defiance and appeal, midway almost between cynicism and hope, the prevailing mind stands in the mood of the same author's *To America*, an attitude of sober query and stoical challenge:

> How would you have us, as we are?
>   Or sinking 'neath the load we bear,
> Our eyes fixed forward on a star,
>   Or gazing empty at despair?
>
> Rising or falling? Men or things?
>   With dragging pace or footsteps fleet?
> Strong, willing sinews in your wings,
>   Or tightening chains about your feet?

More and more, however, an intelligent realization of the great discrepancy between the American social creed and the American social practice forces upon the Negro the taking of the moral advantage that is his. Only the steadying and sobering effect of a truly characteristic gentleness of spirit prevents the rapid rise of a definite cynicism and counter-hate and a defiant superiority feeling. Human as this reaction would be, the majority still deprecate its advent, and would gladly see it forestalled by the speedy amelioration of its causes. We wish our race pride to be a healthier, more positive achievement than a feeling based upon a realization of the shortcomings of others. But all paths toward the attainment of a sound social attitude have been difficult; only a relatively few enlightened minds have been able as the phrase puts it "to rise above" prejudice. The ordinary man has had until recently only a hard choice between the alternatives of supine and humiliating submission and stimulating but hurtful counter-prejudice. Fortunately from some inner, desperate resourcefulness has recently sprung up the simple expedient of fighting prejudice by mental passive resistance, in other words by trying to ignore it. For the few, this manna may perhaps be effective, but the masses cannot thrive upon it.

Fortunately there are constructive channels opening out into which the balked social feelings of the American Negro can flow freely.

Without them there would be much more pressure and danger than there is. These compensating interests are racial but in a new and enlarged way. One is the consciousness of acting as the advance-guard of the African peoples in their contact with Twentieth Century civilization; the other, the sense of a mission of rehabilitating the race in world esteem from that loss of prestige for which the fate and conditions of slavery have so largely been responsible. Harlem, as we shall see, is the center of both these movements; she is the home of the Negro's "Zionism." The pulse of the Negro world has begun to beat in Harlem. A Negro newspaper carrying news material in English, French and Spanish, gathered from all quarters of America, the West Indies and Africa has maintained itself in Harlem for over five years. Two important magazines, both edited from New York, maintain their news and circulation consistently on a cosmopolitan scale. Under American auspices and backing, three pan-African congresses have been held abroad for the discussion of common interests, colonial questions and the future co-operative development of Africa. In terms of the race question as a world problem, the Negro mind has leapt, so to speak, upon the parapets of prejudice and extended its cramped horizons. In so doing it has linked up with the growing group consciousness of the dark-peoples and is gradually learning their common interests. As one of our writers has recently put it: "It is imperative that we understand the white world in its relations to the non-white world." As with the Jew, persecution is making the Negro international.

As a world phenomenon this wider race consciousness is a different thing from the much asserted rising tide of color. Its inevitable causes are not of our making. The consequences are not necessarily damaging to the best interests of civilization. Whether it actually brings into being new Armadas of conflict or argosies of cultural exchange and enlightenment can only be decided by the attitude of the dominant races in an era of critical change. With the American Negro, his new internationalism is primarily an effort to recapture contact with the scattered peoples of African derivation. Garveyism may be a transient, if spectacular, phenomenon, but the possible rôle of the American Negro in the future development of Africa is one of the most constructive and universally helpful missions that any modern people can lay claim to.

Constructive participation in such causes cannot help giving the Negro valuable group incentives, as well as increased prestige at home and abroad. Our greatest rehabilitation may possibly come through such channels, but for the present, more immediate hope rests in the revaluation by white and black alike of the Negro in terms of his artistic endowments and cultural contributions, past and prospective. It must be increasingly recognized that the Negro has already made very substantial contributions, not only in his folk-art, music especially, which has always found appreciation, but in larger, though humbler and less acknowledged ways. For generations the Negro has been the peasant matrix of that section of America which has most undervalued him, and here he has contributed not only materially in labor and in social patience, but spiritually as well. The South has unconsciously absorbed the gift of his folk-temperament. In less than half a generation it will be easier to recognize this, but the fact remains that a leaven of humor, sentiment, imagination and tropic nonchalance has gone into the making of the South from a humble, unacknowledged source. A second crop of the Negro's gifts promises still more largely. He now becomes a conscious contributor and lays aside the status of a beneficiary and ward for that of a collaborator and participant in American civilization. The great social gain in this is the releasing of our talented group from the arid fields of controversy and debate to the productive fields of creative expression. The especially cultural recognition they win should in turn prove the key to that revaluation of the Negro which must precede or accompany any considerable further betterment of race relationships. But whatever the general effect, the present generation will have added the motives of self-expression and spiritual development to the old and still unfinished task of making material headway and progress. No one who understandingly faces the situation with its substantial accomplishment or views the new scene with its still more abundant promise can be entirely without hope. And certainly, if in our lifetime the Negro should not be able to celebrate his full initiation into American democracy, he can at least, on the warrant of these things, celebrate the attainment of a significant and satisfying new phase of group development, and with it a spiritual Coming of Age.

JOEL A. ROGERS

JAZZ AT HOME

In its elementals, jazz has always existed. It is in the Indian war-dance, the Highland fling, the Irish jig, the Cossack dance, the Spanish fandango, the Brazilian *maxixe*, the dance of the whirling dervish, the hula hula of the South Seas, the *danse du vêntre* of the Orient, the *carmagnole* of the French Revolution, the strains of Gypsy music, and the ragtime of the Negro. Jazz proper, however, is something more than all these. It is a release of all the suppressed emotions at once, a blowing off of the lid, as it were. It is hilarity expressing itself through pandemonium; musical fireworks.

The direct predecessor of jazz is ragtime. That both are ata-vistically African there is little doubt, but to what extent it is difficult to determine. In its barbaric rhythm and exuberance there is something of the bamboula, a wild, abandoned dance of the West African and the Haytian Negro, so stirringly described by the anonymous author of *Untrodden Fields of Anthropology*, or of the *ganza* ceremony so brilliantly depicted in Maran's *Batouala*. But jazz time is faster and more complex than African music. With its cowbells, auto horns, calliopes, rattles, dinner gongs, kitchen utensils, cymbals, screams, crashes, clankings and monotonous rhythm it bears all the marks of a nerve-strung, strident, mechanized civilization. It is a thing of the jungles—modern man-made jungles.

The earliest jazz-makers were the itinerant piano players who would wander up and down the Mississippi from saloon to saloon, from dive to dive. Seated at the piano with a carefree air that a king might envy, their box-back coats flowing over the stool, their Stetsons pulled well over their eyes, and cigars at an angle of forty-five degrees, they would "whip the ivories" to marvelous chords and hidden racy, joyous meanings, evoking the intense delight of their hearers who would smother them at the close with huzzas and whiskey. Often wholly illiterate, these humble troubadours knowing nothing of written music or composition, but with minds like cameras, would listen to the rude improvisations of the dock laborers and the railroad gangs and reproduce them, reflecting perfectly the sentiments and the longings of these humble folk. The improvised bands at Negro dances in the South, or the little boys with their harmonicas and jews'-harps, each one putting his own individuality into the air, played also no inconsiderable part in its evolution. "Poverty," says J. A. Jackson of the *Billboard*, "compelled improvised instruments. Bones, tambourines, make-shift string instruments, tin can and hollow wood effects, all now utilized as musical novelties, were among early Negroes the product of necessity. When these were not available 'patting juba' prevailed. Present-day 'Charleston' is but a variation of this. Its early expression was the 'patting' for the buck dance."

The origin of the present jazz craze is interesting. More cities claim its birthplace than claimed Homer dead. New Orleans, San Francisco, Memphis, Chicago, all assert the honor is theirs. Jazz, as it is to-day, seems to have come into being this way, however: W. C. Handy, a Negro, having digested the airs of the itinerant musicians referred to, evolved the first classic, *Memphis Blues*. Then came Jasbo Brown, a reckless musician of a Negro cabaret in Chicago, who played this and other blues, blowing his own extravagant moods and risqué interpretations into them, while hilarious with gin. To give further meanings to his veiled allusions he would make the trombone "talk" by putting a derby hat and later a tin can at its mouth. The delighted patrons would shout, "More, Jasbo. More, Jas, more." And so the name originated.

As to the jazz dance itself: at this time Shelton Brooks, a Negro comedian, invented a new "strut," called "Walkin' the Dog." Jasbo's anarchic airs found in this strut a soul mate. Then as a result of their union came "The Texas Tommy," the highest point of brilliant, acrobatic execution and nifty foot-work so far evolved in jazz dancing. The latest of these dance is the "Charleston," which has brought something really new to the dance step. The "Charleston" calls for activity of the whole body. One characteristic is a fantastic fling of the leg from the hip downwards. The dance ends in what is known as the "camel-walk"—in reality a gorilla-like shamble—and finishes with a peculiar hop like that of the Indian war dance. Imagine one suffering from a fit of rhythmic ague and you have the effect precisely.

The cleverest "Charleston" dancers perhaps are urchins of five and six who may be seen any time on the streets of Harlem keeping time with their hands, and surrounded by admiring crowds. But put it on a well-set stage, danced by a bobbed-hair chorus, and you have an effect that reminds you of the abandon of the Furies. And so Broadway studies Harlem. Not all of the visitors of the twenty or more well-attended cabarets of Harlem are idle pleasure seekers or underworld devotees. Many are serious artists, actors and producers seeing something new, some suggestion to be taken, too often a pallid imitation, to Broadway's lights and stars.

This makes it difficult to say whether jazz is more characteristic of the Negro or of contemporary America. As is shown, it is of Negro origin plus the influence of the American environment. It is Negro-American. Jazz proper, however in idiom—rhythmic, musical and pantomimic—thoroughly American Negro; it is his spiritual picture on that lighter comedy side, just as the spirituals are the picture on the tragedy side. The two are poles apart, but the former is by no means to be despised and it is just as characteristically the product of the peculiar and unique experience of the Negro in this country. The African Negro hasn't it, and the Caucasian never could have invented it. Once achieved, it is common property, and jazz has absorbed the national spirit, that tremendous spirit of go, the nervousness, lack of conventionality and boisterous good-nature characteristic of the American, white or black, as compared with the more rigid formal natures of the Englishman or German.

But there still remains something elusive about jazz that few, if any of the white artists, have been able to capture. The Negro is admittedly its best expositor. That elusive something, for lack of a better name, I'll call Negro rhythm. The average Negro, particularly of the lower classes, puts rhythm into whatever he does, whether it be shining shoes or carrying a basket on the head to market as the Jamaican women do. Some years ago while wandering in Cincinnati I happened upon a Negro revival meeting at its height. The majority present were women, a goodly few of whom were white. Under the influence of the "spirit" the sisters would come forward and strut—much of jazz enters where it would be least expected. The Negro women had the perfect jazz abandon, while the white ones moved lamely and woodenly. This same lack of spontaneity is evident to a degree in the cultivated and inhibited Negro.

In its playing technique, jazz is similarly original and spontaneous. The performance of the Negro musicians is much imitated, but seldom equaled. Lieutenant Europe, leader of the famous band of the "Fifteenth New York Regiment," said that the bandmaster of the Garde Republicaine, amazed at his jazz effects, could not believe without demonstration that his band had not used special instruments. Jazz has a virtuoso technique all its own: its best performers, singers and players, lift it far above the level of mere "trick" or mechanical effects. Abbie Mitchell, Ethel Waters, and Florence Mills; the Blues singers, Clara, Mamie, and Bessie Smith; Eubie Blake, the pianist; "Buddy" Gilmore, the drummer, and "Bill" Robinson, the pantomimic dancer—to mention merely an illustrative few—are inimitable artists, with an inventive, improvising skill that defies imitation. And those who know their work most intimately trace its uniqueness without exception to the folk-roots of their artistry.

Musically jazz has a great future. It is rapidly being sublimated. In the more famous jazz orchestras like those of Will Marion Cook, Paul Whiteman, Sissle and Blake, Sam Stewart, Fletcher Henderson, Vincent Lopez and the Clef Club units, there are none of the vulgarities and crudities of the lowly origin or the only too prevalent cheap imitations. The pioneer work in the artistic development of jazz was done by Negro artists; it was the lead of the so-called "syncopated orchestras" of Tyers and Will Marion Cook, the former playing for the Castles of dancing fame, and the latter touring as a concertizing orchestra in the great American centers and abroad. Because of the difficulties of financial backing, these expert combinations have had to yield ground to white orchestras of the type of the Paul Whiteman and Vincent Lopez organizations that are now demonstrating the finer possibilities of jazz music. "Jazz," says Serge Koussevitzky, the new conductor of the Boston Symphony, "is an important contribution to modern musical literature. It has an epochal significance—it is not superficial, it is fundamental. Jazz comes from the soil, where all music has its beginning." And Leopold Stokowski says more extendedly of it:

"Jazz has come to stay because it is an expression of the times, of the breathless, energetic, superactive times in which we are living, it is useless to fight against it.

Already its new vigor, its new vitality is beginning to manifest itself. . . . America's contribution to the music of the past will have the same revivifying effect as the injection of new, and in the larger sense, vulgar blood into dying aristocracy. Music will then be vulgarized in the best sense of the word, and enter more and more into the daily lives of people. . . . The Negro musicians of America are playing a great part in this change. They have an open mind, and unbiased outlook. They are not hampered by conventions or traditions, and with their new ideas, their constant experiment, they are causing new blood to flow in the veins of music. The jazz players make their instruments do entirely new things, things finished musicians are taught to avoid. They are pathfinders into new realms."

And thus it has come about that serious modernist music and musicians, most notably and avowedly in the work of the French modernists Auric, Satie and Darius Milhaud, have become the confessed debtors of American Negro jazz. With the same nonchalance and impudence with which it left the levee and the dive to stride like an upstart conqueror, almost overnight, into the grand salon, jazz now begins its conquest of musical Parnassus.

Whatever the ultimate result of the attempt to raise jazz from the mob-level upon which it originated, its true home is still its original cradle, the none too respectable cabaret. And here we have the seamy side to the story. Here we have some of the charm of Bohemia, but much more of the demoralization of vice. Its rash spirit is in Grey's popular song, *Runnin' Wild*:

> Runnin' wild; lost control
> Runnin' wild; mighty bold,
> Feelin' gay and reckless too
> Carefree all the time; never blue
> Always goin' I don't know where
> Always showin' that I don't care
> Don' love nobody, it ain't worth while
> All alone; runnin' wild.

Jazz reached the height of its vogue at a time when minds were reacting from the horrors and strain of war. Humanity welcomed it because in its fresh joyousness men found a temporary forget-fulness, infinitely less harmful than drugs or alcohol. It is partly for some such reasons that it dominates the amusement life of America to-day. No one can sensibly condone its excesses or min-imize its social danger if uncontrolled; all culture is built upon inhibitions and control. But it is doubtful whether the "jazz-hounds" of high and low estate would use their time to better advantage. In all probability their tastes would find some equally morbid, mischievous vent. Jazz, it is needless to say, will remain a recreation for the industrious and a dissipater of energy for the frivolous, a tonic for the strong and a poison for the weak.

For the Negro himself, jazz is both more and less dangerous than for the white—less, in that he is nervously more in tune with it; more, in that at his average level of economic development his amusement life is more open to the forces of social vice. The cab-aret of better type provides a certain Bohemianism for the Negro intellectual, the artist and the well-to-do. But the average thing is too much the substitute for the saloon and the wayside inn. The tired longshoreman, the porter, the housemaid and the poor ele-vator boy in search of recreation, seeking in jazz the tonic for weary nerves and muscles, are only too apt to find the bootlegger, the gambler and the demi-monde who have come there for victims and to escape the eyes of the police.

Yet in spite of its present vices and vulgarizations, its sex in-formalities, its morally anarchic spirit, jazz has a popular mission to perform. Joy, after all, has a physical basis. Those who laugh and dance and sing are better off even in their vices than those who do not. Moreover, jazz with its mocking disregard for for-mality is a leveller and makes for democracy. The jazz spirit, being primitive, demands more frankness and sincerity. Just as it already has done in art and music, so eventually in human relations and social manners, it will no doubt have the effect of putting more reality in life by taking some of the needless artificiality out. . . . Naturalness finds the artificial in conduct ridiculous. "Cervantes smiled Spain's chivalry away," said Byron. And so this new spirit of joy and spontaneity may itself play the rôle of reformer. Where at present it vulgarizes, with more wholesome growth in the future, it may on the contrary truly democratize. At all events, jazz is rejuvenation, a recharging of the batteries of civilization with prim-itive new vigor. It has come to stay, and they are wise, who instead of protesting against it, try to lift and divert it into nobler channels.

PAUL ROBESON

REFLECTIONS ON O'NEILL'S PLAYS

ALL THIS SEEMS so very strange to me—writing about the theatre. If, three years ago, someone had told me that I would be telling of my reactions as an actor I would have laughed indulgently. Even now the whole chain of events has a distinct dream-like quality. To have had the opportunity to appear in two of the finest plays of America's most distinguished playwright is a good fortune that to me seems hardly credible. Of course I am very, very happy. And with these things there has come a great love of the theatre, which I am sure will always hold me fast.

In retrospect all the excitement about "All God's Chillun" seems rather amusing, but at the time of the play's production, it caused many an anxious moment. All concerned were absolutely amazed at the ridiculous critical reaction. The play meant anything and everything from segregated schools to various phases of inter-marriage.

To me the most important pre-production development, was an opportunity to play the "Emperor Jones," due to an enforced postponement. This is undoubtedly one of "*the* great plays"—a true classic of the drama, American or otherwise. I recall how mar-velously it was played by Mr. Gilpin some years back. And the greatest praise I could have received was the expression of some that my performance was in some wise comparable to Mr. Gilpin's.

And what a great part is "Brutus Jones." His is the exultant tragedy of the disintegration of a human soul. How we suffer as we see him in the depths of the forest re-living all the sins of his past—experiencing all the woes and wrongs of his people—throw-ing off one by one the layers of civilization until he returns to the primitive soil from which he (racially) came. And yet we exult when we realize that here was a man who in the midst of all his trouble fought to the end and finally died in the "'eighth of style anyway."

In "All God's Chillun" we have the struggle of a man and woman, both fine struggling human beings, against forces they could not control,—indeed, scarcely comprehend—accentuated by the almost Christ-like spiritual force of the Negro husband,—a play of great strength and beautiful spirit, mocking all petty prejudice, emphasizing the humanness, and in Mr. O'Neill's words, "the oneness" of mankind.

I now come to perhaps the main point of my discussion. Any number of people have said to me: "I trust that now you will get a truly heroic and noble role, one portraying the finest type of Negro." I honestly believe that perhaps never will I portray a nobler type than "Jim Harris" or a more heroically tragic figure than "Brutus Jones, Emperor," not excepting "Othello."

The Negro is only a medium in the creation of a work of the greatest artistic merit. The fact that he is a Negro Pullman Porter is of little moment. How else account for the success of the play in Paris, Berlin, Copenhagen, Moscow and other places on the Continent. Those people never heard of a Negro porter. Jones's emotions are not primarily Negro, but human.

Objections to "All God's Chillun" are rather well known. Most of them have been so foolish that to attempt to answer them is to waste time. The best answer is that audiences that came to scoff went away in tears, moved by a sincere and terrifically tragic drama.

The reactions to these two plays among Negroes but point out one of the most serious drawbacks to the development of a true Negro dramatic literature. We are too self-conscious, too afraid of showing all phases of our life,—especially those phases which are of greatest dramatic value. The great mass of our group discourage any member who has the courage to fight these petty prejudices.

I am still being damned all over the place for playing in "All God's Chillun." It annoys me very little when I realize that those who object most strenuously know mostly nothing of the play and who in any event know little of the theatre and have no right to judge a playwright of O'Neill's talents.

I have met and talked with Mr. O'Neill. If ever there was a broad, liberal-minded man, he is one. He has had Negro friends and appreciated them for their true worth. He would be the last to cast any slur on the colored people.

Of course I have just begun. I do feel there is a great future on the serious dramatic stage. Direction and training will do much to guide any natural ability one may possess. At Provincetown I was privileged to be under the direction of Mr. James Light. I'm sure even he thought I was rather hopeless at first. I know I did. But he was patient and painstaking, and any success I may have achieved I owe in great measure to Mr. Light. I sincerely hope I shall have the benefit of his splendid guidance in the future.

What lies ahead I do not know. I am sure that there will come Negro playwrights of great power and I trust I shall have some part in interpreting that most interesting and much needed addition to the drama of America.

ARTHUR A. SCHOMBURG

THE NEGRO DIGS UP HIS PAST

THE AMERICAN NEGRO must remake his past in order to make his future. Though it is orthodox to think of America as the one country where it is unnecessary to have a past, what is a luxury for the nation as a whole becomes a prime social necessity for the Negro. For him, a group tradition must supply compensation for persecution, and pride of race the antidote for prejudice. History must restore what slavery took away, for it is the social damage of slavery that the present generations must repair and offset. So among the rising democratic millions we find the Negro thinking more collectively, more retrospectively than the rest, and apt out of the very pressure of the present to become the most enthusiastic antiquarian of them all.

Vindicating evidences of individual achievement have as a matter of fact been gathered and treasured for over a century: Abbé Gregoire's liberal-minded book on Negro notables in 1808 was the pioneer effort; it has been followed at intervals by less known and often less discriminating compendiums of exceptional men and women of African stock. But this sort of thing was on the whole pathetically over-corrective, ridiculously over-laudatory; it was apologetics turned into biography. A true historical sense develops slowly and with difficulty under such circumstances. But to-day, even if for the ultimate purpose of group justification, history has become less a matter of argument and more a matter of record. There is the definite desire and determination to have a history, well documented, widely known at least within race circles, and administered as a stimulating and inspiring tradition for the coming generations.

Gradually as the study of the Negro's past has come out of

the vagaries of rhetoric and propaganda and become systematic and scientific, three outstanding conclusions have been established:

First, that the Negro has been throughout the centuries of controversy an active collaborator, and often a pioneer, in the struggle for his own freedom and advancement. This is true to a degree which makes it the more surprising that it has not been recognized earlier.

Second, that by virtue of their being regarded as something "exceptional," even by friends and well-wishers, Negroes of attainment and genius have been unfairly disassociated from the group, and group credit lost accordingly.

Third, that the remote racial origins of the Negro, far from being what the race and the world have been given to understand, offer a record of credible group achievement when scientifically viewed, and more important still, that they are of vital general interest because of their bearing upon the beginnings and early development of human culture.

With such crucial truths to document and establish, an ounce of fact is worth a pound of controversy. So the Negro historian to-day digs under the spot where his predecessor stood and argued. Not long ago, the Public Library of Harlem housed a special exhibition of books, pamphlets, prints and old engravings, that simply said, to skeptic and believer alike, to scholar and school-child, to proud black and astonished white, "Here is the evidence." Assembled from the rapidly growing collections of the leading Negro book-collectors and research societies, there were in these cases, materials not only for the first true writing of Negro history, but for the rewriting of many important paragraphs of our common American history. Slow though it be, historical truth is no exception to the proverb.

Here among the rarities of early Negro Americana was Jupiter Hammon's Address to the Negroes of the State of New York, edition of 1787, with the first American Negro poet's famous "If we should ever get to Heaven, we shall find nobody to reproach us for being black, or for being slaves." Here was Phyllis Wheatley's Mss. poem of 1767 addressed to the students of Harvard, her spirited encomiums upon George Washington and the Revolutionary Cause, and John Marrant's St. John's Day eulogy to the "Brothers of African Lodge No. 459" delivered at Boston in 1789. Here too were Lemuel Haynes' Vermont commentaries on the American Revolution and his learned sermons to his white congregation in

Rutland, Vermont, and the sermons of the year 1808 by the Rev. Absalom Jones of St. Thomas Church, Philadelphia, and Peter Williams of St. Philip's, New York, pioneer Episcopal rectors who spoke out in daring and influential ways on the Abolition of the Slave Trade. Such things and many others are more than mere items of curiosity: they educate any receptive mind.

Reinforcing these were still rarer items of Africana and foreign Negro interest, the volumes of Juan Latino, the best Latinist of Spain in the reign of Philip V, incumbent of the chair of Poetry at the University of Granada, and author of Poems printed there in 1573 and a book on the Escurial published 1576; the Latin and Dutch treatises of Jacobus Eliza Capitein, a native of West Coast Africa and graduate of the University of Leyden, Gustavus Vassa's celebrated autobiography that supplied so much of the evidence in 1796 for Granville Sharpe's attack on slavery in the British colonies, Julien Raymond's Paris exposé of the disabilities of the free people of color in the then (1791) French colony of Hayti, and Baron de Vastey's *Cry of the Fatherland*, the famous polemic by the secretary of Christophe that precipitated the Haytian struggle for independence. The cumulative effect of such evidences of scholarship and moral prowess is too weighty to be dismissed as exceptional.

But weightier surely than any evidence of individual talent and scholarship could ever be, is the evidence of important collaboration and significant pioneer initiative in social service and reform, in the efforts toward race emancipation, colonization and race betterment. From neglected and rust-spotted pages comes testimony to the black men and women who stood shoulder to shoulder in courage and zeal, and often on a parity of intelligence and talent, with their notable white benefactors. There was the already cited work of Vassa that aided so materially the efforts of Granville Sharpe, the record of Paul Cuffee, the Negro colonization pioneer, associated so importantly with the establishment of Sierra Leone as a British colony for the occupancy of free people of color in West Africa; the dramatic and history-making exposé of John Baptist Phillips, African graduate of Edinburgh, who compelled through Lord Bathurst in 1824 the enforcement of the articles of capitulation guaranteeing freedom to the blacks of Trinidad. There is the record of the pioneer colonization project of Rev. Daniel Coker in conducting a voyage of ninety expatriates to West Africa in 1820, of the missionary efforts of Samuel Crowther in Sierra

Leone, first Anglican bishop of his diocese, and that of the work of John Russwurm, a leader in the work and foundation of the American Colonization Society.

When we consider the facts, certain chapters of American history will have to be reopened. Just as black men were influential factors in the campaign against the slave trade, so they were among the earliest instigators of the abolition movement. Indeed there was a dangerous calm between the agitation for the suppression of the slave trade and the beginning of the campaign for emancipation. During that interval colored men were very influential in arousing the attention of public men who in turn aroused the conscience of the country. Continuously between 1808 and 1845, men like Prince Saunders, Peter Williams, Absalom Jones, Nathaniel Paul, and Bishops Varick and Richard Allen, the founders of the two wings of African Methodism, spoke out with force and initiative, and men like Denmark Vesey (1822), David Walker (1828) and Nat Turner (1831) advocated and organized schemes for direct action. This culminated in the generally ignored but important conventions of Free People of Color in New York, Philadelphia and other centers, whose platforms and efforts are to the Negro of as great significance as the nationally cherished memories of Faneuil and Independence Halls. Then with Abolition comes the better documented and more recognized collaboration of Samuel R. Ward, William Wells Brown, Henry Highland Garnett, Martin Delaney, Harriet Tubman, Sojourner Truth, and Frederick Douglass with their great colleagues, Tappan, Phillips, Sumner, Mott, Stowe and Garrison.

But even this latter group who came within the limelight of national and international notice, and thus into open comparison with the best minds of their generation, the public too often regards as a group of inspired illiterates, eloquent echoes of their Abolitionist sponsors. For a true estimate of their ability and scholarship, however, one must go with the antiquarian to the files of the *Anglo-African Magazine*, where page by page comparisons may be made. Their writings show Douglass, McCune Smith, Wells Brown, Delaney, Wilmot Blyden and Alexander Crummell to have been as scholarly and versatile as any of the noted publicists with whom they were associated. All of them labored internationally in the cause of their fellows; to Scotland, England, France, Germany and Africa, they carried their brilliant offensive of debate and propaganda, and with this came instance upon instance of signal foreign recognition, from academic, scientific, public and official sources. Delaney's *Principia of Ethnology* won public reception from learned societies, Pennington's discourses an honorary doctorate from Heidelberg, Wells Brown's three year mission the entrée of the salons of London and Paris, and the tours of Frederick Douglass, receptions second only to Henry Ward Beecher's.

After this great era of public interest and discussion, it was Alexander Crummell, who, with the reaction already setting in, first organized Negro brains defensively through the founding of the American Negro Academy in 1897 at Washington. A New York boy whose zeal for education had suffered a rude shock when refused admission to the Episcopal Seminary by Bishop Onderdonk, he had been befriended by John Jay and sent to Cambridge University, England, for his education and ordination. On his return, he was beset with the idea of promoting race scholarship, and the Academy was the final result. It has continued ever since to be one of the bulwarks of our intellectual life, though unfortunately its members have had to spend too much of their energy and effort answering detractors and disproving popular fallacies. Only gradually have the men of this group been able to work toward pure scholarship. Taking a slightly different start, The Negro Society for Historical Research was later organized in New York, and has succeeded in stimulating the collection from all parts of the world of books and documents dealing with the Negro. It has also brought together for the first time co-operatively in a single society African, West Indian and Afro-American scholars. Direct offshoots of this same effort are the extensive private collections of Henry P. Slaughter of Washington, the Rev. Charles D. Martin of Harlem, of Arthur Schomburg of Brooklyn, and of the late John E. Bruce, who was the enthusiastic and far-seeing pioneer of this movement. Finally and more recently, the Association for the Study of Negro Life and History has extended these efforts into a scientific research project of great achievement and promise. Under the direction of Dr. Carter G. Woodson, it has continuously maintained for nine years the publication of the learned quarterly, *The Journal of Negro History,* and with the assistance and recognition of two large educational foundations has maintained research and published valuable monographs in Negro history. Almost keeping pace with the work of scholarship has been the effort to popularize the results, and to place before Negro youth in the schools the true story of race vicissitude, struggle and accomplishment. So that quite largely now the ambition of Negro youth can be nourished on its own milk.

Such work is a far cry from the puerile controversy and petty braggadocio with which the effort for race history first started. But a general as well as a racial lesson has been learned. We seem lately to have come at last to realize what the truly scientific attitude requires, and to see that the race issue has been a plague on both our historical houses, and that history cannot be properly written with either bias or counter-bias. The blatant Caucasian racialist with his theories and assumptions of race superiority and dominance has in turn bred his Ethiopian counterpart—the rash and rabid amateur who has glibly tried to prove half of the world's geniuses to have been Negroes and to trace the pedigree of nineteenth century Americans from the Queen of Sheba. But fortunately to-day there is on both sides of a really common cause less of the sand of controversy and more of the dust of digging.

Of course, a racial motive remains—legitimately compatible with scientific method and aim. The work our race students now regard as important, they undertake very naturally to overcome in part certain handicaps of disparagement and omission too wellknown to particularize. But they do so not merely that we may not wrongfully be deprived of the spiritual nourishment of our cultural past, but also that the full story of human collaboration and interdependence may be told and realized. Especially is this likely to be the effect of the latest and most fascinating of all the attempts to open up the closed Negro past, namely the important study of African cultural origins and sources. The bigotry of civilization which is the taproot of intellectual prejudice begins far back and must be corrected at its source. Fundamentally it has come about from that depreciation of Africa which has sprung up from ignorance of her true rôle and position in human history and the early development of culture. The Negro has been a man without a history because he has been considered a man without a worthy culture. But a new notion of the cultural attainment and potentialities of the African stocks has recently come about, partly through the corrective influence of the more scientific study of African institutions and early cultural history, partly through growing appreciation of the skill and beauty and in many cases the historical priority of the African native crafts, and finally through the signal recognition which first in France and Germany, but now very generally, the astonishing art of the African sculptures has received. Into these fascinating new vistas, with limited horizons lifting in all directions, the mind of the Negro has leapt forward faster than the slow clearings of scholarship will yet safely permit. But there is no doubt that here is a field full of the most intriguing and inspiring possibilities. Already the Negro sees himself against a reclaimed background, in a perspective that will give pride and self-respect ample scope, and make history yield for him the same values that the treasured past of any people affords.

ELISE JOHNSON MCDOUGALD

THE TASK OF NEGRO WOMANHOOD

THROUGHOUT THE YEARS of history, woman has been the weather-vane, the indicator, showing in which direction the wind of destiny blows. Her status and development have augured now calm and stability, now swift currents of progress. What then is to be said of the Negro woman of to-day, whose problems are of such import to her race?

A study of her contributions to any one community, throughout America, would illuminate the pathway being trod by her people. There is, however, an advantage in focusing upon the women of Harlem—modern city in the world's metropolis. Here, more than anywhere else, the Negro woman is free from the cruder handicaps of primitive household hardships and the grosser forms of sex and race subjugation. Here, she has considerable opportunity to measure her powers in the intellectual and industrial fields of the great city. The questions naturally arise: "What are her difficulties?" and, "How is she solving them?"

To answer these questions, one must have in mind not any one Negro woman, but rather a colorful pageant of individuals, each differently endowed. Like the red and yellow of the tiger-lily, the skin of one is brilliant against the star-lit darkness of a racial sister. From grace to strength, they vary in infinite degree, with traces of the race's history left in physical and mental outline on each. With a discerning mind, one catches the multiform charm, beauty and character of Negro women, and grasps the fact that their problems cannot be thought of in mass.

Because only a few have caught this vision, even in New York, the general attitude of mind causes the Negro woman serious difficulty. She is conscious that what is left of chivalry is not directed toward her. She realizes that the ideals of beauty, built up in the fine arts, have excluded her almost entirely. Instead, the grotesque Aunt Jemimas of the street-car advertisements, proclaim only an ability to serve, without grace of loveliness. Nor does the drama catch her finest spirit. She is most often used to provoke the mirthless laugh of ridicule; or to portray feminine viciousness or vulgarity not peculiar to Negroes. This is the shadow over her. To a race naturally sunny comes the twilight of self-doubt and a sense of personal inferiority. It cannot be denied that these are potent and detrimental influences, though not generally recognized because they are in the realm of the mental and spiritual. More apparent are the economic handicaps which follow her recent entrance into industry. It is conceded that she has special difficulties because of the poor working conditions and low wages of her men. It is not surprising that only the most determined women forge ahead to results other than mere survival. To the gifted, the zest of meeting a challenge is a compensating factor which often brings success. The few who do prove their mettle, stimulate one to a closer study of how this achievement is won under contemporary conditions.

Better to visualize the Negro woman at her job, our vision of a host of individuals must once more resolve itself into groups on the basis of activity. First, comes a very small leisure group—the wives and daughters of men who are in business, in the professions and a few well-paid personal service occupations. Second, a most active and progressive group, the women in business and the professions. Third, the many women in the trades and industry. Fourth, a group weighty in numbers struggling on in domestic service, with an even less fortunate fringe of casual workers, fluctuating with the economic temper of the times.

The first is a pleasing group to see. It is picked for outward beauty by Negro men with much the same feeling as other Americans of the same economic class. Keeping their women free to preside over the family, these women are affected by the problems of every wife and mother, but touched only faintly by their race's hardships. They do share acutely in the prevailing difficulty of finding competent household help. Negro wives find Negro maids unwilling generally to work in their own neighborhoods, for various reasons. They do not wish to work where there is a possibility of acquaintances coming into contact with them while they serve and they still harbor the misconception that Negroes of any station are unable to pay as much as persons of the other race. It is in these homes of comparative ease that we find the polite activities of social exclusiveness. The luxuries of well-appointed homes, modest motors, tennis, golf and country clubs, trips to Europe and California, make for social standing. The problem confronting the refined Negro family is to know others of the same achievement. The search for kindred spirits gradually grows less difficult; in the past it led to the custom of visiting all the large cities in order to know similar groups of cultured Negro people. In recent years, the more serious minded Negro woman's visit to Europe has been extended from months to years for the purpose of study and travel. The European success which meets this type of ambition is instanced in the conferring of the doctorate in philosophy upon a Negro woman, Dr. Anna J. Cooper, at the last commencement of the Sorbonne, Paris. Similarly, a score of Negro women are sojourning abroad in various countries for the spiritual relief and cultural stimulation afforded there.

A spirit of stress and struggles characterizes the second two groups. These women of business, profession and trade are the hub of the wheel of progress. Their burden is twofold. Many are wives and mothers whose husbands are insufficiently paid, or who have succumbed to social maladjustment and have abandoned their families. An appalling number are widows. They face the great problem of leaving home each day and at the same time trying to rear children in their spare time—this, too, in neighborhoods where rents are large, standards of dress and recreation high and costly, and social danger on the increase. One cannot resist the temptation to pause for a moment and pay tribute to these Negro mothers. And to call attention to the service she is rendering to the nation, in her struggle against great odds to educate and care for one group of the country's children. If the mothers of the race should ever be honored by state or federal legislation, the artist's imagination will find a more inspiring subject in the modern Negro mother—self-directed but as loyal and tender as the much extolled, yet pitiable black mammy of slavery days.

The great commercial life of New York City is only slightly touched by the Negro woman, of our second group. Negro business men offer her most of their work, but their number is limited. Outside of this field in Negro offices, custom is once more against her, and competition is keen for all. However, Negro girls are training and some are holding exceptional jobs. One of the professors in a New York college has had a young colored woman as secretary for the past three or four years. Another holds the head clerical position in an organization where reliable handling of detail and a sense of business ethics are essential. Quietly these women prove their worth, so that when a vacancy exists and there is a call, it is difficult to find even one competent colored secretary who is not employed. As a result of the opportunity in clerical work in the educational system of New York City, a number have qualified for such positions, one having been recently appointed to the office of a high school. In other departments, the civil service in New York City is no longer free from discrimination. The casual personal interview, that tenacious and retrogressive practice introduced into the federal administration during the World War, has spread and often nullifies the Negro woman's success in written tests. The successful young woman cited above was three times "turned down" as undesirable on the basis of the personal interview. In the great mercantile houses, the many young Negro girls who might be well suited to sales positions are barred from all but menial positions. Even so, one Negro woman, beginning as a uniformed maid in the shoe department of one of the largest stores, has pulled herself up to the position of "head of stock." One of the most prosperous monthly magazines of national circulation has for the head of its news service a Negro woman who rose from the position of stenographer. Her duties involve attendance upon staff conferences, executive supervision of her staff of white office workers, broadcasting and journalism of the highest order.

Yet in spite of the claims of justice and proved efficiency, telephone and insurance companies and other corporations which receive considerable patronage from Negroes deny them proportionate employment. Fortunately this is an era of changing customs. There is hope that a less selfish racial attitude will prevail. It is a heartening fact that there is an increasing number of Americans who will lend a hand in the game fight of the worthy.

Throughout the South, where businesses for Negro patronage are under the control of Negroes to a large extent, there are already many opportunities for Negro women. But, because of the nerve strain and spiritual drain of hostile social conditions in that section, Negro women are turning away from opportunities there to find a freer and fuller life in the North.

In the less crowded professional vocations, the outlook is more cheerful. In these fields, the Negro woman is dependent largely upon herself and her own race for work. In the legal, dental and medical professions, successful women practitioners have usually worked their way through college and are "managing" on the small fees that can be received from an under-paid public.

Social conditions in America are hardest upon the Negro because he is lowest in the economic scale. The tendency to force the Negro downward, gives rise to serious social problems and to a consequent demand for trained college women in the profession of social work. The need has been met with a response from young college women, anxious to devote their education and lives toward helping the submerged classes. Much of the social work has been pioneer in nature; the pay has been small, with little possibility of advancement. For, even in work among Negroes, the better paying positions are reserved for whites. The Negro college woman is doing her bit at a sacrifice, along such lines as these: as probation officers, investigators and police women in the correctional departments of the city; as Big Sisters attached to the Children's Court; as field workers and visitors for relief organizations, missions and churches; as secretaries for traveller's aid societies; in the many organizations devoted to preventative and educational medicine; in clinics and hospitals and as boys' and girls' welfare workers in recreation and industry.

In the profession of nursing, there are over three hundred in New York City. In the dark blue linen uniform of Henry Street Visiting Nurse Service, the Negro woman can be seen hurrying earnestly from house to house on her round of free relief to the needy. Again, she is in many other branches of public health nursing, in the public schools, milk stations and diet kitchens. The Negro woman is in the wards of two of the large city hospitals and clinics. After a score of years of service in one such institution, a Negro woman became superintendent of nurses in the war emergency. Deposed after the armistice, though eminently satisfactory, she retained connection with the training school as lecturer, for the inspiration she could be to "her girls." The growing need for the executive nurse is being successfully met as instanced by the supervisors in day nurseries and private sanitariums, financed and operated in Harlem entirely by Negroes. Throughout the South there is a clear and anxious call to nurses to carry the gospel of hygiene to the rural sections and to minister to the suffering not reached by organizations already in the communities. One social worker, in New York City, though a teacher by profession, is head of an organization whose program is to raise money for the payment of nurses to do the work described above. In other centers, West and South, the professional Negro nurse is supplanting the untrained woman attendant of former years.

In New York City, nearly three hundred women share in the good conditions obtaining there in the teaching profession. They measure up to the high pedagogical requirements of the city and state law, and are increasingly leaders in the community. In a city where the schools are not segregated, she is meeting with success among white as well as colored children in positions ranging from clerk in the elementary school on up through the graded ranks of teachers in the lower grades, of special subjects in the higher grades, in the junior high schools and in the senior high schools. One Negro woman is assistant principal in an elementary school where the other assistant and the principal are white men and the majority of the teachers white. Another Negro woman serves in the capacity of visiting teacher to several schools, calling upon both white and colored families and experiencing no difficulty in making social adjustments. Still another Negro woman is a vocational counsellor under the Board of Education, in a junior high school. She is advising children of both races as to future courses of study to pursue and as to the vocations in which tests prove them to be apt. This position, the result of pioneer work by another Negro woman, is unique in the school system of New York. . . .

With all these forces at work, true sex equality has not been approximated. The ratio of opportunity in the sex, social, economic and political spheres is about that which exists between white men and women. In the large, I would say that the Negro woman is the cultural equal of her man because she is generally kept in school longer. Negro boys, like white boys, are usually put to work to subsidize the family income. The growing economic independence of Negro working women is causing her to rebel against the domineering family attitude of the cruder working-class husband. The masses of Negro men are engaged in menial occupations throughout the working day. Their baffled and suppressed desires to determine their economic life are manifested in overbearing domination at home. Working mothers are unable to instill different ideals in the sons. Conditions change slowly. Nevertheless, education and opportunity are modifying the spirit of the younger Negro men. Trained in modern schools of thought, they begin to show a wholesome attitude of fellowship and freedom for their women. The challenge to young Negro womanhood is to see clearly this trend and grasp the proffered comradeship with sincerity. In this matter of sex equality, Negro women have contributed few outstanding militants, a notable instance being the historic Sojourner Truth. On the whole the Negro woman's feminist efforts are directed chiefly toward the realization of the equality of the races, the sex struggle assuming the subordinate place.

Obsessed with difficulties which might well compel individualism, the Negro woman has engaged in a considerable amount of organized action to meet group needs. She has evolved a federation of her clubs, embracing between eight and ten thousand women in New York state alone. The state federation is a part of the National Association of Colored Women, which, calling together the women from all parts of the country, engages itself in enterprises of general race interest. The national organization of colored women is now firmly established, and under the presidency of Mrs. Bethune is about to strive for conspicuous goals.

In New York City, many associations exist for social betterment, financed and operated by Negro women. One makes child welfare its name and special concern. Others, like the Utility Club, Utopia Neighborhood, Debutantes' League, Sempre Fidelius, etc., raise funds for old folks' homes, a shelter for delinquent girls and fresh-air camps for children. The Colored Women's Branch of the Y. W. C. A. and the women's organizations in the many churches as well as the beneficial lodges and associations, care for the needs of their members.

On the other hand, the educational welfare of the coming generation has become the chief concern of the national sororities of Negro college women. The first to be organized in the country, the *Alpha Kappa Alpha,* has a systematized, a continuous program of educational and vocational guidance for students of the high schools and colleges. The work of Lambda Chapter, which covers New York City and its suburbs, has been most effective in carrying out the national program. Each year, it gathers together between one and two hundred such students and gives the girls a chance to hear the life stories of Negro women, successful in various fields of endeavor. Recently a trained nurse told how, starting in the same schools as they, she had risen to the executive position in the Harlem Health Information Bureau. A commercial artist showed how real talent had overcome the color line. The graduate physician was a living example of the modern opportunities in the newer fields of medicine open to women. The vocations, as outlets for the creative instinct, became attractive under the persuasion of the musician, the dressmaker and the decorator. A recent graduate outlined her plans for meeting the many difficulties encountered in establishing a dental office and in building up a practice. A journalist spun the fascinating tale of her years of experience. The *Delta Sigma Theta* Sorority (national in scope) works along similar lines. Alpha Beta Chapter of New York City, during the current year, presented a young art student with a scholarship of $1,000 for study abroad. In such ways as these are the progressive and privileged groups of Negro women expressing their community and race consciousness.

We find the Negro woman, figuratively struck in the face daily by contempt from the world about her. Within her soul, she knows little of peace and happiness. But through it all, she is courageously standing erect, developing within herself the moral strength to rise above and conquer false attitudes. She is maintaining her natural beauty and charm and improving her mind and opportunity. She is measuring up to the needs of her family, community and race, and radiating a hope throughout the land.

The wind of the race's destiny stirs more briskly because of her striving.

LANGSTON HUGHES

THE SUCCESS OF THE HARLEM ARTS MOVEMENT *led to concern and controversy about the whirligig of interracial socializing and the uses and abuses of instant celebrity. Langston Hughes enjoyed the company of the Manhattan swells, culture mavens, and Negrotarian philanthropists, but he missed none of the humor, hypocrisy, and complexity of the "vogue," and captured the dilemmas of patronage and the fallacies of promoting civil rights through the arts in ironic and often hilarious prose montages ("When the Negro Was in Vogue," etc.). There was wide agreement that the Renaissance presented a unique opportunity for African Americans. But for what? Hughes's "Negro Artist and the Racial Mountain" spoke for many of the younger artists determined to put artistic exploration before the politics of sponsorship—painters, poets, and playwrights, musicians, novelists, and sculptors who renounced "representative" aesthetic criteria in order to capture the essence of the black folk. To which George Schuyler replied that the whole debate was misconceived because the premise that African American culture, plumbed to its depths, would be revealed as different from "Anglo-Saxon" was simply fraudulent (Schuyler, "The Negro-Art Hokum"). W. E. B. Du Bois alerted the leadership of the race and the creative talents within to the grave dangers of allowing the arts movement to become an autonomous force, a seductive evasion and well-funded illusion in which the unglamorous, brutal struggle for the ballot, education, jobs, and housing became a subordinate goal. The siren song of false allies asked, "What is the use of your fighting and complaining; do the great thing and the reward is there" (Du Bois, "Criteria of Negro Art").*

FROM *THE BIG SEA*

WHEN THE NEGRO WAS IN VOGUE

THE 1920's were the years of Manhattan's black Renaissance. It began with *Shuffle Along, Running Wild,* and the Charleston. Perhaps some people would say even with *The Emperor Jones,* Charles Gilpin, and the tom-toms at the Provincetown. But certainly it was the musical revue, *Shuffle Along,* that gave a scintillating send-off to that Negro vogue in Manhattan, which reached its peak just before the crash of 1929, the crash that sent Negroes, white folks, and all rolling down the hill toward the Works Progress Administration.

Shuffle Along was a honey of a show. Swift, bright, funny, rollicking, and gay, with a dozen danceable, singable tunes. Besides, look who were in it: The now famous choir director, Hall Johnson, and the composer, William Grant Still, were a part of the orchestra. Eubie Blake and Noble Sissle wrote the music and played and acted in the show. Miller and Lyles were the comics. Florence Mills skyrocketed to fame in the second act. Trixie Smith sang "He May Be Your Man But He Comes to See Me Sometimes." And Caterina Jarboro, now a European prima donna, and the internationally celebrated Josephine Baker were merely in the chorus. Everybody was in the audience—including me. People came back to see it innumerable times. It was always packed.

To see *Shuffle Along* was the main reason I wanted to go to Columbia. When I saw it, I was thrilled and delighted. From then on I was in the gallery of the Cort Theatre every time I got a chance. That year, too, I saw Katharine Cornell in *A Bill of Divorcement,* Margaret Wycherly in *The Verge,* Maugham's *The Circle* with Mrs. Leslie Carter, and the Theatre Guild production of Kaiser's *From Morn Till Midnight.* But I remember *Shuffle Along* best of all. It gave just the proper push—a pre-Charleston kick—to that Negro vogue of the 20's, that spread to books, African sculpture, music, and dancing.

Put down the 1920's for the rise of Roland Hayes, who packed Carnegie Hall, the rise of Paul Robeson in New York and London, of Florence Mills over two continents, of Rose McClendon in Broadway parts that never measured up to her, the booming voice of Bessie Smith and the low moan of Clara on thousands of records, and the rise of that grand comedienne of song, Ethel Waters, singing: "Charlie's elected now! He's in right for sure!" Put down the 1920's for Louis Armstrong and Gladys Bentley and Josephine Baker.

White people began to come to Harlem in droves. For several years they packed the expensive Cotton Club on Lenox Avenue. But I was never there, because the Cotton Club was a Jim Crow club for gangsters and monied whites. They were not cordial to Negro patronage, unless you were a celebrity like Bojangles. So Harlem Negroes did not like the Cotton Club and never appreciated its Jim Crow policy in the very heart of their dark community. Nor did ordinary Negroes like the growing influx of whites toward Harlem after sundown, flooding the little cabarets and bars where formerly only colored people laughed and sang, and where now the strangers were given the best ringside tables to sit and stare at the Negro customers—like amusing animals in a zoo.

The Negroes said: "We can't go downtown and sit and stare at you in your clubs. You won't even let us in your clubs." But they didn't say it out loud—for Negroes are practically never rude to white people. So thousands of whites came to Harlem night after night, thinking the Negroes loved to have them there, and firmly believing that all Harlemites left their houses at sundown to sing and dance in cabarets, because most of the whites saw nothing but the cabarets, not the houses.

Some of the owners of Harlem clubs, delighted at the flood of white patronage, made the grievous error of barring their own race, after the manner of the famous Cotton Club. But most of these quickly lost business and folded up, because they failed to realize that a large part of the Harlem attraction for downtown New Yorkers lay in simply watching the colored customers amuse themselves. And the smaller clubs, of course, had no big floor shows or a name band like the Cotton Club, where Duke Ellington usually held forth, so, without black patronage, they were not amusing at all.

Some of the small clubs, however, had people like Gladys Bentley, who was something worth discovering in those days, before she got famous, acquired an accompanist, specially written material, and conscious vulgarity. But for two or three amazing years, Miss Bentley sat, and played a big piano all night long, literally all night, without stopping—singing songs like "The St. James Infirmary," from ten in the evening until dawn, with scarcely a break between the notes, sliding from one song to another, with a powerful and continuous underbeat of jungle rhythm. Miss Bentley was an amazing exhibition of musical energy—a large, dark, masculine lady, whose feet pounded the floor while her fingers pounded the keyboard—a perfect piece of African sculpture, animated by her own rhythm.

But when the place where she played became too well known, she began to sing with an accompanist, became a star, moved to a larger place, then downtown, and is now in Hollywood. The old magic of the woman and the piano and the night and the rhythm being one is gone. But everything goes, one way or another. The '20's are gone and lots of fine things in Harlem night life have disappeared like snow in the sun—since it became utterly commercial, planned for the downtown tourist trade, and therefore dull.

The lindy-hoppers at the Savoy even began to practise acrobatic routines, and to do absurd things for the entertainment of the whites, that probably never would have entered their heads to attempt merely for their own effortless amusement. Some of the lindy-hoppers had cards printed with their names on them and became dance professors teaching the tourists. Then Harlem nights became show nights for the Nordics.

Some critics say that that is what happened to certain Negro writers, too—that they ceased to write to amuse themselves and began to write to amuse and entertain white people, and in so doing distorted and over-colored their material, and left out a great many things they thought would offend their American brothers of a lighter complexion. Maybe—since Negroes have writer-racketeers, as has any other race. But I have known almost all of them, and most of the good ones have tried to be honest, write honestly, and express their world as they saw it.

All of us know that the gay and sparkling life of the so-called Negro Renaissance of the '20's was not so gay and sparkling beneath the surface as it looked. Carl Van Vechten, in the character of Byron in *Nigger Heaven*, captured some of the bitterness and frustration of literary Harlem that Wallace Thurman later so effectively poured into his *Infants of the Spring*—the only novel by a Negro about that fantastic period when Harlem was in vogue.

It was a period when, at almost every Harlem upper-crust dance or party, one would be introduced to various distinguished white celebrities there as guests. It was a period when almost any

Harlem Negro of any social importance at all would be likely to say casually: "As I was remarking the other day to Heywood—," meaning Heywood Broun. Or: "As I said to George—," referring to George Gershwin. It was a period when local and visiting royalty were not at all uncommon in Harlem. And when the parties of A'Lelia Walker, the Negro heiress, were filled with guests whose names would turn any Nordic social climber green with envy. It was a period when Harold Jackman, a handsome young Harlem school teacher of modest means, calmly announced one day that he was sailing for the Riviera for a fortnight, to attend Princess Murat's yachting party. It was a period when Charleston preachers opened up shouting churches as sideshows for white tourists. It was a period when at least one charming colored chorus girl, amber enough to pass for a Latin American, was living in a pent house, with all her bills paid by a gentleman whose name was banker's magic on Wall Street. It was a period when every season there was at least one hit play on Broadway acted by a Negro cast. And when books by Negro authors were being published with much greater frequency and much more publicity than ever before or since in history. It was a period when white writers wrote about Negroes more successfully (commercially speaking) than Negroes did about themselves. It was the period (God help us!) when Ethel Barrymore appeared in blackface in *Scarlet Sister Mary!* It was the period when the Negro was in vogue.

I was there. I had a swell time while it lasted. But I thought it wouldn't last long. (I remember the vogue for things Russian, the season the Chauve-Souris first came to town.) For how could a large and enthusiastic number of people be crazy about Negroes forever? But some Harlemites thought the millennium had come. They thought the race problem had at last been solved through Art plus Gladys Bentley. They were sure the New Negro would lead a new life from then on in green pastures of tolerance created by Countee Cullen, Ethel Waters, Claude McKay, Duke Ellington, Bojangles, and Alain Locke.

I don't know what made any Negroes think that—except that they were mostly intellectuals doing the thinking. The ordinary Negroes hadn't heard of the Negro Renaissance. And if they had, it hadn't raised their wages any. As for all those white folks in the speakeasies and night clubs of Harlem—well, maybe a colored man could find *some* place to have a drink that the tourists hadn't yet discovered.

HARLEM LITERATI

THE SUMMER OF 1926, I lived in a rooming house on 137th Street, where Wallace Thurman and Harcourt Tynes also lived. Thurman was then managing editor of the *Messenger*, a Negro magazine that had a curious career. It began by being very radical, racial, and socialistic, just after the war. I believe it received a grant from the Garland Fund in its early days. Then it later became a kind of Negro society magazine and a plugger for Negro business, with photographs of prominent colored ladies and their nice homes in it. A. Phillip Randolph, now President of the Brotherhood of Sleeping Car Porters, Chandler Owen, and George S. Schuyler were connected with it. Schuyler's editorials, à la Mencken, were the most interesting things in the magazine, verbal brickbats that said sometimes one thing, sometimes another, but always vigorously. I asked Thurman what kind of magazine the *Messenger* was, and he said it reflected the policy of whoever paid off best at the time.

Anyway, the *Messenger* bought my first short stories. They paid me ten dollars a story. Wallace Thurman wrote me that they were very bad stories, but better than any others they could find, so he published them.

Thurman had recently come from California to New York. He was a strangely brilliant black boy, who had read everything, and whose critical mind could find something wrong with everything he read. I have no critical mind, so I usually either like a book or don't. But I am not capable of liking a book and then finding a million things wrong with it, too—as Thurman was capable of doing.

Thurman had read so many books because he could read eleven lines at a time. He would get from the library a great pile of volumes that would have taken me a year to read. But he would go through them in less than a week, and be able to discuss each one at great length with anybody. That was why, I suppose, he was later given a job as a reader at Macaulay's—the only Negro reader, so far as I know, to be employed by any of the larger publishing firms.

Later Thurman became a ghost writer for *True Story*, and other publications, writing under all sorts of fantastic names, like Ethel Belle Mandrake or Patrick Casey. He did Irish and Jewish and Catholic "true confessions." He collaborated with William Jordan Rapp on plays and novels. Later he ghosted books. In fact, this quite dark young Negro is said to have written *Men, Women, and Checks*.

Wallace Thurman wanted to be a great writer, but none of his own work ever made him happy. *The Blacker the Berry*, his first book, was an important novel on a subject little dwelt upon in Negro fiction—the plight of the very dark Negro woman, who encounters in some communities a double wall of color prejudice within and without the race. His play, *Harlem*, considerably distorted for box office purposes, was, nevertheless, a compelling study—and the only one in the theater—of the impact of Harlem on a Negro family fresh from the South. And his *Infants of the Spring*, a superb and bitter study of the bohemian fringe of Harlem's literary and artistic life, is a compelling book.

But none of these things pleased Wallace Thurman. He wanted to be a *very* great writer, like Gorki or Thomas Mann, and he felt that he was merely a journalistic writer. His critical mind, comparing his pages to the thousands of other pages he had read, by Proust, Melville, Tolstoy, Galsworthy, Dostoyevski, Henry James, Sainte-Beuve, Taine, Anatole France, found his own pages vastly wanting. So he contented himself by writing a great deal for money, laughing bitterly at his fabulously concocted "true stories," creating two bad motion pictures of the "Adults Only" type for Hollywood, drinking more and more gin, and then threatening to jump out of windows at people's parties and kill himself.

During the summer of 1926, Wallace Thurman, Zora Neale Hurston, Aaron Douglas, John P. Davis, Bruce Nugent, Gwendolyn Bennett, and I decided to publish "a Negro quarterly of the arts" to be called *Fire*—the idea being that it would burn up a lot of the old, dead conventional Negro-white ideas of the past, *épater le bourgeois* into a realization of the existence of the younger Negro writers and artists, and provide us with an outlet for publication not available in the limited pages of the small Negro magazines then existing, the *Crisis, Opportunity*, and the *Messenger*—the first two being house organs of inter-racial organizations, and the latter being God knows what.

Sweltering summer evenings we met to plan *Fire*. Each of the seven of us agreed to give fifty dollars to finance the first issue. Thurman was to edit it, John P. Davis to handle the business end, and Bruce Nugent to take charge of distribution. The rest of us were to serve as an editorial board to collect material, contribute our own work, and act in any useful way that we could. For artists and writers, we got along fine and there were no quarrels. But October came before we were ready to go to press. I had to return to Lincoln, John Davis to Law School at Harvard, Zora Hurston to her studies at Barnard, from whence she went about Harlem with an anthropologist's ruler, measuring heads for Franz Boas.

Only three of the seven had contributed their fifty dollars, but the others faithfully promised to send theirs out of tuition checks, wages, or begging. Thurman went on with the work of preparing the magazine. He got a printer. He planned the layout. It had to be on good paper, he said, worthy of the drawings of Aaron Douglas. It had to have beautiful type, worthy of the first Negro art quarterly. It had to be what we seven young Negroes dreamed our magazine would be—so in the end it cost almost a thousand dollars, and nobody could pay the bills.

I don't know how Thurman persuaded the printer to let us have all the copies to distribute, but he did. I think Alain Locke, among others, signed notes guaranteeing payments. But since Thurman was the only one of the seven of us with a regular job, for the next three or four years his checks were constantly being attached and his income seized to pay for *Fire*. And whenever I sold a poem, mine went there, too—to *Fire*.

None of the older Negro intellectuals would have anything to do with *Fire*. Dr. Du Bois in the *Crisis* roasted it. The Negro press called it all sorts of bad names, largely because of a green and purple story by Bruce Nugent, in the Oscar Wilde tradition, which we had included. Rean Graves, the critic for the *Baltimore Afro-American*, began his review by saying: "I have just tossed the first issue of *Fire* into the fire." Commenting upon various of our contributors, he said: "Aaron Douglas who, in spite of himself and the meaningless grotesqueness of his creations, has gained a reputation as an artist, is permitted to spoil three perfectly good pages and a cover with his pen and ink hudge pudge. Countee Cullen has written a beautiful poem in his 'From a Dark Tower,' but tries his best to obscure the thought in superfluous sentences. Langston Hughes displays his usual ability to say nothing in many words."

So *Fire* had plenty of cold water thrown on it by the colored critics. The white critics (except for an excellent editorial in the *Bookman* for November, 1926) scarcely noticed it at all. We had no way of getting it distributed to bookstands or news stands. Bruce Nugent took it around New York on foot and some of the Greenwich Village bookshops put it on display, and sold it for us.

But then Bruce, who had no job, would collect the money and, on account of salary, eat it up before he got back to Harlem.

Finally, irony of ironies, several hundred copies of *Fire* were stored in the basement of an apartment where an actual fire occurred and the bulk of the whole issue was burned up. Even after that Thurman had to go on paying the printer.

Now *Fire* is a collector's item, and very difficult to get, being mostly ashes.

That taught me a lesson about little magazines. But since white folks had them, we Negroes thought we could have one, too. But we didn't have the money.

Wallace Thurman laughed a long bitter laugh. He was a strange kind of fellow, who liked to drink gin, but *didn't* like to drink gin; who liked being a Negro, but felt it a great handicap; who adored bohemianism, but thought it wrong to be a bohemian. He liked to waste a lot of time, but he always felt guilty wasting time. He loathed crowds, yet he hated to be alone. He almost always felt bad, yet he didn't write poetry.

Once I told him if I could feel as bad as he did *all* the time, I would surely produce wonderful books. But he said you had to know how to *write*, as well as how to feel bad. I said I didn't have to know how to feel bad, because, every so often, the blues just naturally overtook me, like a blind beggar with an old guitar:

> You don't know,
> You don't know my mind—
> When you see me laughin',
> I'm laughin' to keep from cryin'.

About the future of Negro literature Thurman was very pessimistic. He thought the Negro vogue had made us all too conscious of ourselves, had flattered and spoiled us, and had provided too many easy opportunities for some of us to drink gin and more gin, on which he thought we would always be drunk. With his bitter sense of humor, he called the Harlem literati, the "niggerati."

Of this "niggerati," Zora Neale Hurston was certainly the most amusing. Only to reach a wider audience, need she ever write books—because she is a perfect book of entertainment in herself. In her youth she was always getting scholarships and things from wealthy white people, some of whom simply paid her just to sit around and represent the Negro race for them, she did it in such a racy fashion. She was full of side-splitting anecdotes, humorous tales, and tragicomic stories, remembered out of her life in the South as a daughter of a travelling minister of God. She could make you laugh one minute and cry the next. To many of her white friends, no doubt, she was a perfect "darkie," in the nice meaning they give the term—that is a naïve, childlike, sweet, humorous, and highly colored Negro.

But Miss Hurston was clever, too—a student who didn't let college give her a broad *a* and who had great scorn for all pretensions, academic or otherwise. That is why she was such a fine folklore collector, able to go among the people and never act as if she had been to school at all. Almost nobody else could stop the average Harlemite on Lenox Avenue and measure his head with a strange-looking, anthropological device and not get bawled out for the attempt, except Zora, who used to stop anyone whose head looked interesting, and measure it.

When Miss Hurston graduated from Barnard she took an apartment in West 66th Street near the park, in that row of Negro houses there. She moved in with no furniture at all and no money, but in a few days friends had given her everything, from decorative silver birds, perched atop the linen cabinet, down to a footstool. And on Saturday night, to christen the place, she had a *hand*-chicken dinner, since she had forgotten to say she needed forks.

She seemed to know almost everybody in New York. She had been a secretary to Fannie Hurst, and had met dozens of celebrities whose friendship she retained. Yet she was always having terrific ups-and-downs about money. She tells this story on herself, about needing a nickel to go downtown one day and wondering where on earth she would get it. As she approached the subway, she was stopped by a blind beggar holding out his cup.

"Please help the blind! Help the blind! A nickel for the blind!"

"I need money worse than you today," said Miss Hurston, taking five cents out of his cup. "Lend me this! Next time, I'll give it back." And she went on downtown.

Harlem was like a great magnet for the Negro intellectual, pulling him from everywhere. Or perhaps the magnet was New York—but once in New York, he had to live in Harlem, for rooms were hardly to be found elsewhere unless one could pass for white or Mexican or Eurasian and perhaps live in the Village—which always seemed to me a very arty locale, in spite of the many real artists and writers who lived there. Only a few of the New Negroes lived in the Village, Harlem being their real stamping ground.

The wittiest of these New Negroes of Harlem, whose tongue

was flavored with the sharpest and saltiest humor, was Rudolph Fisher, whose stories appeared in the *Atlantic Monthly*. His novel, *Walls of Jericho*, captures but slightly the raciness of his own conversation. He was a young medical doctor and X-ray specialist, who always frightened me a little, because he could think of the most incisively clever things to say—and I could never think of anything to answer. He and Alain Locke together were great for intellectual wise-cracking. The two would fling big and witty words about with such swift and punning innuendo that an ordinary mortal just sat and looked wary for fear of being caught in a net of witticisms beyond his cultural ken. I used to wish I could talk like Rudolph Fisher. Besides being a good writer, he was an excellent singer, and had sung with Paul Robeson during their college days. But I guess Fisher was too brilliant and too talented to stay long on this earth. During the same week, in December, 1934, he and Wallace Thurman both died.

Thurman died of tuberculosis in the charity ward at Bellevue Hospital, having just flown back to New York from Hollywood.

PARTIES

In those days of the late 1920's, there were a great many parties, in Harlem and out, to which various members of the New Negro group were invited. These parties, when given by important Harlemites (or Carl Van Vechten) were reported in full in the society pages of the Harlem press, but best in the sparkling Harlemese of Geraldyn Dismond who wrote for the *Interstate Tattler*. On one of Taylor Gordon's fiestas she reports as follows:

> What a crowd! All classes and colors met face to face, ultra aristocrats, Bourgeois, Communists, Park Avenuers galore, bookers, publishers, Broadway celebs, and Harlemites giving each other the once over. The social revolution was on. And yes, Lady Nancy Cunard was there all in black (she would) with 12 of her grand bracelets. . . . And was the entertainment on the up and up! Into swell dance music was injected African drums that played havoc with blood pressure. Jimmy Daniels sang his gigolo hits. Gus Simons, the Harlem crooner, made the River Stay Away From His Door and Taylor himself

brought out everything from "Hot Dog" to "Bravo" when he made high C.

A'Lelia Walker was the then great Harlem party giver, although Mrs. Bernia Austin fell but little behind. And at the Seventh Avenue apartment of Jessie Fauset, literary soirées with much poetry and but little to drink were the order of the day. The same was true of Lillian Alexander's, where the older intellectuals gathered.

A'Lelia Walker, however, big-hearted, night-dark, hair-straightening heiress, made no pretense at being intellectual or exclusive. At her "at homes" Negro poets and Negro number bankers mingled with downtown poets and seat-on-the-stock-exchange racketeers. Countee Cullen would be there and Witter Bynner, Muriel Draper and Nora Holt, Andy Razaf and Taylor Gordon. And a good time was had by all.

A'Lelia Walker had an apartment that held perhaps a hundred people. She would usually issue several hundred invitations to each party. Unless you went early there was no possible way of getting in. Her parties were as crowded as the New York subway at the rush hour—entrance, lobby, steps, hallway, and apartment a milling crush of guests, with everybody seeming to enjoy the crowding. Once, some royal personage arrived, a Scandinavian prince, I believe, but his equerry saw no way of getting him through the crowded entrance hall and into the party, so word was sent in to A'Lelia Walker that His Highness, the Prince, was waiting without. A'Lelia sent word back that she saw no way of getting His Highness in, either, nor could she herself get out through the crowd to greet him. But she offered to send refreshments downstairs to the Prince's car.

A'Lelia Walker was a gorgeous dark Amazon, in a silver turban. She had a town house in New York (also an apartment where she preferred to live) and a country mansion at Irvington-on-the-Hudson, with pipe organ programs each morning to awaken her guests gently. Her mother made a great fortune from the Madame Walker Hair Straightening Process, which had worked wonders on unruly Negro hair in the early nineteen hundreds—and which continues to work wonders today. The daughter used much of that money for fun. A'Lelia Walker was the joy-goddess of Harlem's 1920's.

She had been very much in love with her first husband, from

whom she was divorced. Once at one of her parties she began to cry about him. She retired to her boudoir and wept. Some of her friends went in to comfort her, and found her clutching a memento of their broken romance.

"The only thing I have left that he gave me," she sobbed, "it's all I have left of him!"

It was a gold shoehorn.

When A'Lelia Walker died in 1931, she had a grand funeral. It was by invitation only. But, just as for her parties, a great many more invitations had been issued than the small but exclusive Seventh Avenue funeral parlor could provide for. Hours before the funeral, the street in front of the undertaker's chapel was crowded. The doors were not opened until the cortège arrived—and the cortège was late. When it came, there were almost enough family mourners, attendants, and honorary pallbearers in the procession to fill the room; as well as the representatives of the various Walker beauty parlors throughout the country. And there were still hundreds of friends outside, waving their white, engraved invitations aloft in the vain hope of entering.

Once the last honorary pallbearers had marched in, there was a great crush at the doors. Muriel Draper, Rita Romilly, Mrs. Roy Sheldon, and I were among the fortunate few who achieved an entrance.

We were startled to find De Lawd standing over A'Lelia's casket. It was a truly amazing illusion. At that time *The Green Pastures* was at the height of its fame, and there stood De Lawd in the person of Rev. E. Clayton Powell, a Harlem minister, who looked exactly like Richard B. Harrison in the famous role in the play. He had the same white hair and kind face, and was later offered the part of De Lawd in the film version of the drama. Now, he stood there motionless in the dim light behind the silver casket of A'Lelia Walker.

Soft music played and it was very solemn. When we were seated and the chapel became dead silent, De Lawd said: "The Four Bon Bons will now sing."

A night club quartette that had often performed at A'Lelia's parties arose and sang for her. They sang Noel Coward's "I'll See You Again," and they swung it slightly, as she might have liked it. It was a grand funeral and very much like a party. Mrs. Mary McCleod Bethune spoke in that great deep voice of hers, as only she can speak. She recalled the poor mother of A'Lelia Walker in old clothes, who had labored to bring the gift of beauty to Negro womanhood, and had taught them the care of their skin and their hair, and had built up a great business and a great fortune to the pride and glory of the Negro race—and then had given it all to her daughter, A'Lelia.

Then a poem of mine was read by Edward Perry, "To A'Lelia." And after that the girls from the various Walker beauty shops throughout America brought their flowers and laid them on the bier.

That was really the end of the gay times of the New Negro era in Harlem, the period that had begun to reach its end when the crash came in 1929 and the white people had much less money to spend on themselves, and practically none to spend on Negroes, for the depression brought everybody down a peg or two. And the Negroes had but few pegs to fall.

But in those pre-crash days there were parties and parties. At the novelist, Jessie Fauset's, parties there was always quite a different atmosphere from that at most other Harlem good-time gatherings. At Miss Fauset's, a good time was shared by talking literature and reading poetry aloud and perhaps enjoying some conversation in French. White people were seldom present there unless they were very distinguished white people, because Jessie Fauset did not feel like opening her home to mere sightseers, or faddists momentarily in love with Negro life. At her house one would usually meet editors and students, writers and social workers, and serious people who liked books and the British Museum, and had perhaps been to Florence. (Italy, not Alabama.)

I remember, one night at her home there was a gathering in honor of Salvador de Madariaga, the Spanish diplomat and savant, which somehow became a rather self-conscious gathering, with all the Harlem writers called upon to recite their poems and speak their pieces. But afterwards, Charles S. Johnson and I invited Mr. Madariaga to Small's Paradise where we had a "ball" until the dawn came up and forced us from the club.

In those days, 409 Edgecombe, Harlem's tallest and most exclusive apartment house, was quite a party center. The Walter Whites and the Aaron Douglases, among others, lived and entertained there. Walter White was a jovial and cultured host, with a sprightly mind, and an apartment overlooking the Hudson. He had the most beautiful wife in Harlem, and they were always hospitable to hungry literati like me.

At the Aaron Douglases', although he was a painter, more young writers were found than painters. Usually everybody would chip in and go dutch on the refreshments, calling down to the nearest bootlegger for a bottle of whatever it was that was drunk in those days, when labels made no difference at all in the liquid content—Scotch, bourbon, rye, and gin being the same except for coloring matter.

Arna Bontemps, poet and coming novelist, quiet and scholarly, looking like a young edition of Dr. Du Bois, was the mysterious member of the Harlem literati, in that we knew he had recently married, but none of us had ever seen his wife. All the writers wondered who she was and what she looked like. He never brought her with him to any of the parties, so she remained the mystery of the New Negro Renaissance. But I went with him once to his apartment to meet her, and found her a shy and charming girl, holding a golden baby on her lap. A year or two later there was another golden baby. And every time I went away to Haiti or Mexico or Europe and came back, there would be a new golden baby, each prettier than the last—so that was why the literati never saw Mrs. Bontemps.

Toward the end of the New Negro era, E. Simms Campbell came to Harlem from St. Louis, and began to try to sell cartoons to the *New Yorker*. My first memory of him is at a party at Gwendolyn Bennett's on Long Island. In the midst of the party, the young lady Mr. Campbell had brought, Constance Willis, whom he later married, began to put on her hat and coat and gloves. The hostess asked her if she was going home. She said: "No, only taking Elmer outside to straighten him out." What indiscretion he had committed at the party I never knew, perhaps flirting with some other girl, or taking a drink too many. But when we looked out, there was Constance giving Elmer an all-around talking-to on the sidewalk. And she must have straightened him out, because he was a very nice young man at parties ever after.

At the James Weldon Johnson parties and gumbo suppers, one met solid people like Clarence and Mrs. Darrow. At the Dr. Alexander's, you met the upper crust Negro intellectuals like Dr. Du Bois. At Wallace Thurman's, you met the bohemians of both Harlem and the Village. And in the gin mills and speakeasies and night clubs between 125th and 145th, Eighth Avenue and Lenox, you met everybody from Buddy de Silva to Theodore Dreiser, Ann Pennington to the first Mrs. Eugene O'Neill. In the days when Harlem was in vogue, Amanda Randolph was at the Alhambra, Jimmy Walker was mayor of New York, and Louise sang at the old New World.

THE NEGRO ARTIST AND
THE RACIAL MOUNTAIN

ONE OF THE MOST PROMISING of the young Negro poets said to me once, "I want to be a poet—not a Negro poet," meaning, I believe, "I want to write like a white poet"; meaning subconsciously, "I would like to be a white poet"; meaning behind that, "I would like to be white." And I was sorry the young man said that, for no great poet has ever been afraid of being himself. And I doubted then that, with his desire to run away spiritually from his race, this boy would ever be a great poet. But this is the mountain standing in the way of any true Negro art in America—this urge within the race toward whiteness, the desire to pour racial individuality into the mold of American standardization, and to be as little Negro and as much American as possible.

But let us look at the immediate background of this young poet. His family is of what I suppose one would call the Negro middle class: people who are by no means rich yet never uncomfortable nor hungry—smug, contented, respectable folk, members of the Baptist church. The father goes to work every morning. He is a chief steward at a large white club. The mother sometimes does fancy sewing or supervises parties for the rich families of the town. The children go to a mixed school. In the home they read white papers and magazines. And the mother often says "Don't be like niggers" when the children are bad. A frequent phrase from the father is, "Look how well a white man does things." And so the word white comes to be unconsciously a symbol of all virtues. It holds for the children beauty, morality, and money. The whisper of "I want to be white" runs silently through their minds. This young poet's home is, I believe, a fairly typical home of the colored middle class. One sees immediately how difficult it would be for an artist born in such a home to interest himself in interpreting the beauty of his own people. He is never taught to see that beauty. He is taught rather not to see it, or if he does, to be ashamed of it when it is not according to Caucasian patterns.

For racial culture the home of a self-styled "high-class" Negro has nothing better to offer. Instead there will perhaps be more aping of things white than in a less cultured or less wealthy home. The father is perhaps a doctor, lawyer, landowner, or politician. The mother may be a social worker, or a teacher, or she may do nothing and have a maid. Father is often dark but he has usually married the lightest woman he could find. The family attend a fashionable church where few really colored faces are to be found. And they themselves draw a color line. In the North they go to white theatres and white movies. And in the South they have at least two cars and house "like white folks." Nordic manners, Nordic faces, Nordic hair, Nordic art (if any), and an Episcopal heaven. A very high mountain indeed for the would-be racial artist to climb in order to discover himself and his people.

But then there are the low-down folks, the so-called common element, and they are the majority—may the Lord be praised! The people who have their hip of gin on Saturday nights and are not too important to themselves or the community, or too well fed, or too learned to watch the lazy world go round. They live on Seventh Street in Washington or State Street in Chicago and they do not particularly care whether they are like white folks or anybody else. Their joy runs, bang! into ecstasy. Their religion soars to a shout. Work maybe a little today, rest a little tomorrow. Play awhile. Sing awhile. O, let's dance! These common people are not afraid of spirituals, as for a long time their more intellectual brethren were, and jazz is their child. They furnish a wealth of colorful, distinctive material for any artist because they still hold their own individuality in the face of American standardizations. And perhaps these common people will give to the world its truly great Negro artist, the one who is not afraid to be himself. Whereas the better-class Negro would tell the artist what to do, the people at least let him alone when he does appear. And they are not ashamed of him— if they know he exists at all. And they accept what beauty is their own without question.

Certainly there is, for the American Negro artist who can escape the restrictions the more advanced among his own group would put upon him, a great field of unused material ready for his art. Without going outside his race, and even among the better classes with their "white" culture and conscious American manners, but still Negro enough to be different, there is sufficient matter to furnish a black artist with a lifetime of creative work. And when he chooses to touch on the relations between Negroes and whites in this country with their innumerable overtones and undertones surely, and especially for literature and the drama, there is an inexhaustible supply of themes at hand. To these the Negro artist can give his racial individuality, his heritage of rhythm and warmth, and his incongruous humor that so often, as in the Blues, becomes ironic laughter mixed with tears. But let us look again at the mountain.

A prominent Negro clubwoman in Philadelphia paid eleven dollars to hear Raquel Meller sing Andalusian popular songs. But she told me a few weeks before she would not think of going to hear "that woman," Clara Smith, a great black artist, sing Negro folksongs. And many an upper-class Negro church, even now, would not dream of employing a spiritual in its services. The drab melodies in white folks' hymnbooks are much to be preferred. "We want to worship the Lord correctly and quietly. We don't believe in 'shouting.' Let's be dull like the Nordics," they say, in effect.

The road for the serious black artist, then, who would produce a racial art is most certainly rocky and the mountain is high. Until recently he received almost no encouragement for his work from either white or colored people. The fine novels of Chesnutt go out of print with neither race noticing their passing. The quaint charm and humor of Dunbar's dialect verse brought to him, in his day, largely the same kind of encouragement one would give a sideshow freak (A colored man writing poetry! How odd!) or a clown (How amusing!).

The present vogue in things Negro, although it may do as much harm as good for the budding colored artist, has at least done this: it has brought him forcibly to the attention of his own people among whom for so long, unless the other race had noticed him beforehand, he was a prophet with little honor. I understand that Charles Gilpin acted for years in Negro theatres without any special acclaim from his own, but when Broadway gave him eight curtain calls, Negroes, too, began to beat a tin pan in his honor. I know a young colored writer, a manual worker by day, who had been writing well for the colored magazines for some years, but it was not until he recently broke into the white publications and his first book was accepted by a prominent New York publisher that the "best" Negroes in his city took the trouble to discover that he lived there. Then almost immediately they decided to give a grand dinner for him. But the society ladies were careful to whisper to his mother that perhaps she'd better not come. They were not sure she would have an evening gown.

The Negro artist works against an undertow of sharp criticism and misunderstanding from his own group and unintentional bribes from the whites. "Oh, be respectable, write about nice people, show how good we are," say the Negroes. "Be stereotyped, don't go too far, don't shatter our illusions about you, don't amuse us too seriously. We will pay you," say the whites. Both would have told Jean Toomer not to write *Cane*. The colored people did not praise it. The white people did not buy it. Most of the colored people who did read *Cane* hate it. They are afraid of it. Although the critics gave it good reviews the public remained indifferent. Yet (excepting the work of Du Bois) *Cane* contains the finest prose written by a Negro in America. And like the singing of Robeson, it is truly racial.

But in spite of the Nordicized Negro intelligentsia and the desires of some white editors we have an honest American Negro literature already with us. Now I await the rise of the Negro theatre. Our folk music, having achieved world-wide fame, offers itself to the genius of the great individual American composer who is to come. And within the next decade I expect to see the work of a growing school of colored artists who paint and model the beauty of dark faces and create with new technique the expressions of their own soul-world. And the Negro dancers who will dance like flame and the singers who will continue to carry our songs to all who listen—they will be with us in even greater numbers tomorrow.

Most of my own poems are racial in theme and treatment, derived from the life I know. In many of them I try to grasp and hold some of the meanings and rhythms of jazz. I am as sincere as I know how to be in these poems and yet after every reading I answer questions like these from my own people: Do you think Negroes should always write about Negroes? I wish you wouldn't read some of your poems to white folks. How do you find anything interesting in a place like a cabaret? Why do you write about black people? You aren't black. What makes you do so many jazz poems?

But jazz to me is one of the inherent expressions of Negro life in America; the eternal tom-tom beating in the Negro soul—the tom-tom of revolt against weariness in a white world, a world of subway trains, and work, work, work; the tom-tom of joy and laughter, and pain swallowed in a smile. Yet the Philadelphia club-woman is ashamed to say that her race created it and she does not like me to write about it. The old subconscious "white is best" runs through her mind. Years of study under white teachers, a lifetime of white books, pictures, and papers, and white manners, morals, and Puritan standards made her dislike the spirituals. And now she turns up her nose at jazz and all its manifestations—likewise almost everything else distinctly racial. She doesn't care for the Winold Reiss portraits of Negroes because they are "too Negro." She does not want a true picture of herself from anybody. She wants the artist to flatter her, to make the white world believe that all Negroes are as smug and as near white in soul as she wants to be. But, to my mind, it is the duty of the younger Negro artist, if he accepts any duties at all from outsiders, to change through the force of his art that old whispering "I want to be white," hidden in the aspirations of his people, to "Why should I want to be white? I am a Negro—and beautiful?

So I am ashamed for the black poet who says, "I want to be a poet, not a Negro poet," as though his own racial world were not as interesting as any other world. I am ashamed, too, for the colored artist who runs from the painting of Negro faces to the painting of sunsets after the manner of the academicians because he fears the strange un-whiteness of his own features. An artist must be free to choose what he does, certainly, but he must also never be afraid to do what he might choose.

Let the blare of Negro jazz bands and the bellowing voice of Bessie Smith singing Blues penetrate the closed ears of the colored near-intellectual until they listen and perhaps understand. Let Paul Robeson singing "Water Boy," and Rudolph Fisher writing about the streets of Harlem, and Jean Toomer holding the heart of Georgia in his hands, and Aaron Douglas drawing strange black fantasies cause the smug Negro middle class to turn from their white, respectable, ordinary books and papers to catch a glimmer of their own beauty. We younger Negro artists who create now intend to express our individual dark-skinned selves without fear or shame. If white people are pleased we are glad. If they are not, it doesn't matter. We know we are beautiful. And ugly too. The tom-tom cries and the tom-tom laughs colored people are pleased we are glad. If they are not, their displeasure doesn't matter either. We build our temples for tomorrow, strong as we know how, and we stand on top of the mountain, free within ourselves.

GEORGE S. SCHUYLER

THE NEGRO-ART HOKUM

NEGRO ART "made in America" is as non-existent as the widely advertised profundity of Cal Coolidge, the "seven years of progress" of Mayor Hylan, or the reported sophistication of New Yorkers. Negro art there has been, is, and will be among the numerous black nations of Africa; but to suggest the possibility of any such development among the ten million colored people in this republic is self-evident foolishness. Eager apostles from Greenwich Village, Harlem, and environs proclaimed a great renaissance of Negro art just around the corner waiting to be ushered on the scene by those whose hobby is taking races, nations, peoples, and movements under their wing. New art forms expressing the "peculiar" psychology of the Negro were about to flood the market. In short, the art of Homo Africanus was about to electrify the waiting world. Skeptics patiently waited. They still wait.

True, from dark-skinned sources have come those slave songs based on Protestant hymns and Biblical texts known as the spirituals, work songs and secular songs of sorrow and tough luck known as the blues, that outgrowth of rag-time known as jazz (in the development of which whites have assisted), and the Charleston, an eccentric dance invented by the gamins around the public market-place in Charleston, S.C. No one can or does deny this. But these are contributions of a caste in a certain section of the country. They are foreign to Northern Negroes, West Indian Negroes, and African Negroes. They are no more expressive or characteristic of the Negro race than the music and dancing of the Appalachian highlanders or the Dalmatian peasantry are expressive or characteristic of the Caucasian race. If one wishes to speak of the musical contributions of the peasantry of the South, very well. Any group under similar circumstances would have produced something similar. It is merely a coincidence that this peasant class happens to be of a darker hue than the other inhabitants of the land. One recalls the remarkable likeness of the minor strains of the Russian mujiks to those of the Southern Negro.

As for the literature, painting, and sculpture of Aframericans —such as there is—it is identical in kind with the literature, painting, and sculpture of white Americans: that is, it shows more or less evidence of European influence. In the field of drama little of any merit has been written by and about Negroes that could not have been written by whites. The dean of the Aframerican literati is W. E. B. Du Bois, a product of Harvard and German universities; the foremost Aframerican sculptor is Meta Warwick Fuller, a graduate of leading American art schools and former student of Rodin; while the most noted Aframerican painter, Henry Ossawa Tanner, is dean of American painters in Paris and has been decorated by the French Government. Now the work of these artists is no more "expressive of the Negro soul"—as the gushers put it—than are the scribblings of Octavus Cohen or Hugh Wiley.

This, of course, is easily understood if one stops to realize that the Aframerican is merely a lampblacked Anglo-Saxon. If the European immigrant after two or three generations of exposure to our schools, politics, advertising, moral crusades, and restaurants becomes indistinguishable from the mass of Americans of the older stock (despite the influence of the foreign-language press), how much truer must it be of the sons of Ham who have been subjected to what the uplifters call Americanism for the last three hundred years. Aside from his color, which ranges from very dark brown to pink, your American Negro is just plain American. Negroes and whites from the same localities in this country talk, think, and act about the same. Because a few writers with a paucity of themes have seized upon imbecilities of the Negro rustics and clowns and palmed them off as authentic and characteristic Aframerican behavior, the common notion that the black American is so "different" from his white neighbor has gained wide currency. The mere mention of the word "Negro" conjures up in the average white American's mind a composite stereotype of Bert Williams, Aunt Jemima, Uncle Tom, Jack Johnson, Florian Slappey, and the various monstrosities scrawled by the cartoonists. Your average Aframerican no more resembles this stereotype than the average American resembles a composite of Andy Gump, Jim Jeffries, and a cartoon by Rube Goldberg.

Again, the Africamerican is subject to the same economic and social forces that mold the actions and thoughts of the white Americans. He is not living in a different world as some whites and a few Negroes would have us believe. When the jangling of his Connecticut alarm clock gets him out of his Grand Rapids bed to a breakfast similar to that eaten by his white brother across the street; when he toils at the same or similar work in mills, mines, factories, and commerce alongside the descendants of Spartacus, Robin Hood, and Eric the Red; when he wears similar clothing and speaks the same language with the same degree of perfection; when he reads the same Bible and belongs to the Baptist, Methodist, Episcopal, or Catholic church; when his fraternal affiliations also include the Elks, Masons, and Knights of Pythias; when he gets the same or similar schooling, lives in the same kind of houses, owns the same makes of cars (or rides in them), and nightly sees the same Hollywood version of life on the screen; when he smokes the same brands of tobacco, and avidly peruses the same puerile periodicals; in short, when he responds to the same political, social, moral, and economic stimuli in precisely the same manner as his white neighbor, it is sheer nonsense to talk about "racial differences" as between the American black man and the American white man. Glance over a Negro newspaper (it is printed in good Americanese) and you will find the usual quota of crime news, scandal, personals, and uplift to be found in the average white newspaper—which, by the way, is more widely read by the Negroes than is the Negro press. In order to satisfy the cravings of an inferiority complex engendered by the colorphobia of the mob, the readers of the Negro newspapers are given a slight dash of racialistic seasoning. In the homes of the black and white Americans of the same cultural and economic level one finds similar furniture, literature, and conversation. How, then, can the black American be expected to produce art and literature dissimilar to that of the white American?

Consider Coleridge-Taylor, Edward Wilmot Blyden, and Claude McKay, the Englishmen; Pushkin, the Russian; Bridgewater, the Pole; Antar, the Arabian; Latino, the Spaniard; Dumas, *père* and *fils*, the Frenchmen; and Paul Laurence Dunbar, Charles W. Chesnutt, and James Weldon Johnson, the Americans. All Negroes; yet their work shows the impress of nationality rather than race. They all reveal the psychology and culture of their environment—their color is incidental. Why should Negro artists of America vary from the national artistic norm when Negro artists in other countries have not done so? If we can foresee what kind of white citizens will inhabit this neck of the woods in the next generation by studying the sort of education and environment the children are exposed to now, it should not be difficult to reason that the adults of today are what they are because of the education and environment they were exposed to a generation ago. And that education and environment were about the same for blacks and whites. One contemplates the popularity of the Negro-art hokum and murmurs, "How come?"

This nonsense is probably the last stand of the old myth palmed off by Negrophobists for all these many years, and recently rehashed by the sainted Harding, that there are "fundamental, eternal, and inescapable differences" between white and black Americans. That there are Negroes who will lend this myth a helping hand need occasion no surprise. It has been broadcast all over the world by the vociferous scions of slaveholders, "scientists" like Madison Grant and Lothrop Stoddard, and the patriots who flood the treasury of the Ku Klux Klan; and is believed, even today, by the majority of free, white citizens. On this baseless premise, so flattering to the white mob, that the blackamoor is inferior and fundamentally different, is erected the postulate that he must needs be peculiar; and when he attempts to portray life through the medium of art, it must of necessity be a peculiar art. While such reasoning may seem conclusive to the majority of Americans, it must be rejected with a loud guffaw by intelligent people.

W. E. B. DU BOIS

CRITERIA OF NEGRO ART

THE QUESTION COMES NEXT as to the interpretation of these new stirrings, of this new spirit: Of what is the colored artist capable? We have had on the part of both colored and white people singular unanimity of judgment in the past. Colored people have said: "This work must be inferior because it comes from colored people." White people have said: "It is inferior because it is done by colored people." But today there is coming to both the realization that the work of the black man is not always inferior. Interesting stories come to us. A professor in the University of Chicago read to a class that had studied literature a passage of poetry and asked them to guess the author. They guessed a goodly company from Shelley and Robert Browning down to Tennyson and Masefield. The author was Countee Cullen. Or again the English critic John Drinkwater went down to a Southern seminary, one of the sort which finishes young white women of the South. The students sat with their wooden faces while he tried to get some response out of them. Finally he said, "Name me some of your Southern poets." They hesitated. He said finally, "I'll start out with your best: Paul Laurence Dunbar!"

With the growing recognition of Negro artists in spite of the severe handicaps, one comforting thing is occurring to both white and black. They are whispering, "Here is a way out. Here is the real solution of the color problem. The recognition accorded Cullen, Hughes, Fauset, White and others shows there is no real color line. Keep quiet! Don't complain! Work! All will be well!"

I will not say that already this chorus amounts to a conspiracy. Perhaps I am naturally too suspicious. But I will say that there are today a surprising number of white people who are getting great satisfaction out of these younger Negro writers because they think it is going to stop agitation of the Negro question. They say, "What is the use of your fighting and complaining; do the great thing and the reward is there." And many colored people are all too eager to follow this advice; especially those who weary of the eternal struggle along the color line, who are afraid to fight and to whom the money of philanthropists and the alluring publicity are subtle and deadly bribes. They say, "What is the use of fighting? Why not show simply what we deserve and let the reward come to us?"

And it is right here that the National Association for the Advancement of Colored People comes upon the field, comes with its great call to a new battle, a new fight and new things to fight before the old things are wholly won; and to say that the beauty of truth and freedom which shall some day be our heritage and the heritage of all civilized men is not in our hands yet and that we ourselves must not fail to realize.

There is in New York tonight a black woman molding clay by herself in a little bare room, because there is not a single school of sculpture in New York where she is welcome. Surely there are doors she might burst through, but when God makes a sculptor He does not always make the pushing sort of person who beats his way through doors thrust in his face. This girl is working her hands off to get out of this country so that she can get some sort of training.

There was Richard Brown. If he had been white he would have been alive today instead of dead of neglect. Many helped him when he asked but he was not the kind of boy that always asks. He was simply one who made colors sing.

There is a colored woman in Chicago who is a great musician. She thought she would like to study at Fontainebleau this summer where Walter Damrosch and a score of leaders of art have an American school of music. But the application blank of this school says: "I am a white American and I apply for admission to the school."

We can go on the stage; we can be just as funny as white Americans wish us to be; we can play all the sordid parts that America likes to assign to Negroes; but for anything else there is still small place for us.

And so I might go on. But let me sum up with this: Suppose the only Negro who survived some centuries hence was the Negro painted by white Americans in the novels and essays they have written. What would people in a hundred years say of black Americans? Now turn it around. Suppose you were to write a story and put in it the kind of people you know and like and imagine. You might get it published and you might not. And the "might not" is still far bigger than the "might." The white publishers catering to white folk would say, "It is not interesting"—to white folk, naturally not. They want Uncle Toms, Topsies, good "darkies" and clowns. I have in my office a story with all the earmarks of truth. A young man says that he started out to write and had his stories accepted. Then he began to write about the things he knew best about, that is, about his own people. He submitted a story to a magazine which said, "We are sorry, but we cannot take it." "I sat down and revised my story, changing the color of the characters and the locale and sent it under an assumed name with a change of address and it was accepted by the same magazine that had refused it, the editor promising to take anything else I might send in providing it was good enough."

We have, to be sure, a few recognized and successful Negro artists; but they are not all those fit to survive or even a good minority. They are but the remnants of that ability and genius among us whom the accidents of education and opportunity have raised on the tidal waves of chance. We black folk are not altogether peculiar in this. After all, in the world at large, it is only the accident, the remnant, that gets the chance to make the most of itself; but if this is true of the white world it is infinitely more true of the colored world. It is not simply the great clear tenor of Roland Hayes that opened the ears of America. We have had many voices of all kinds as fine as his and America was and is as deaf as she was for years to him. Then a foreign land heard Hayes and put its imprint on him and immediately America with all its imitative snobbery woke up. We approved Hayes because London, Paris, and Berlin approved him and not simply because he was a great singer.

Thus it is the bounden duty of black America to begin this great work of the creation of beauty, of the preservation of beauty, of the realization of beauty, and we must use in this work all the methods that men have used before. And what have been the tools of the artist in times gone by? First of all, he has used the truth—not for the sake of truth, not as a scientist seeking truth, but as one upon whom truth eternally thrusts itself as the highest hand-maid of imagination, as the one great vehicle of universal understanding. Again artists have used goodness—goodness in all its aspects of justice, honor, and right—not for sake of an ethical sanction but as the one true method of gaining sympathy and human interest.

The apostle of beauty thus becomes the apostle of truth and right not by choice but by inner and outer compulsion. Free he is but his freedom is ever bounded by truth and justice; and slavery only dogs him when he is denied the right to tell the truth or recognize an ideal of justice.

Thus all art is propaganda and ever must be, despite the wailing of the purists. I stand in utter shamelessness and say that whatever art I have for writing has been used always for propaganda for gaining the right of black folk to love and enjoy. I do not care a damn for any art that is not used for propaganda. But I do care when propaganda is confined to one side while the other is stripped and silent.

In New York we have two plays: "White Cargo" and "Congo." In "White Cargo" there is a fallen woman. She is black. In "Congo" the fallen woman is white. In "White Cargo" the black woman goes down further and further and in "Congo" the white woman begins with degradation but in the end is one of the angels of the Lord.

You know the current magazine story: a young white man goes down to Central America and the most beautiful colored woman there falls in love with him. She crawls across the whole isthmus to get to him. The white man says nobly, "No." He goes back to his white sweetheart in New York.

In such cases, it is not the positive propaganda of people who believe white blood divine, infallible, and holy to which I object. It is the denial of a similar right of propaganda to those who believe black blood human, lovable, and inspired with new ideals for the world. White artists themselves suffer from this narrowing of their field. They cry for freedom in dealing with Negroes because they have so little freedom in dealing with whites. Du-Bose Heywood writes "Porgy" and writes beautifully of the black Charleston underworld. But why does he do this? Because he cannot do a similar thing for the white people of Charleston, or they would drum him out of town. The only chance he had to tell the truth of pitiful human degradation was to tell it of colored people. I should not be surprised if Octavius Roy Cohen had approached the *Saturday Evening Post* and asked permission to write about a different kind of colored folk than the monstrosities he has created; but if he has, the *Post* has replied, "No. You are getting paid to write about the kind of colored people you are writing about."

In other words, the white public today demands from its artists, literary and pictorial, racial pre-judgment which deliberately distorts truth and justice, as far as colored races are concerned, and it will pay for no other.

On the other hand, the young and slowly growing black public still wants its prophets almost equally unfree. We are bound by all sorts of customs that have come down as second-hand soul clothes of white patrons. We are ashamed of sex and we lower our eyes when people will talk of it. Our religion holds us in superstition. Our worst side has been so shamelessly emphasized that we are denying we have or ever had a worst side. In all sorts of ways we are hemmed in and our new young artists have got to fight their way to freedom.

The ultimate judge has got to be you and you have got to build yourselves up into that wide judgment, that catholicity of temper which is going to enable the artist to have his widest chance for freedom. We can afford the truth. White folk today cannot. As it is now we are handing everything over to a white jury. If a colored man wants to publish a book, he has got to get a white publisher and a white newspaper to say it is great; and then you and I say so. We must come to the place where the work of art when it appears is reviewed and acclaimed by our own free and unfettered judgment. And we are going to have a real and valuable and eternal judgment only as we make ourselves free of mind, proud of body and just of soul to all men.

And then do you know what will be said? It is already saying. Just as soon as true art emerges; just as soon as the black artist appears, someone touches the race on the shoulder and says, "He did that because he was an American, not because he was a Negro; he was born here; he was trained here; he is not a Negro—what is a Negro anyhow? He is just human; it is the kind of thing you ought to expect."

I do not doubt that the ultimate art coming from black folk is going to be just as beautiful, and beautiful largely in the same ways, as the art that comes from white folk, or yellow, or red; but the point today is that until the art of the black folk compels recognition they will not be rated as human. And when through art they compel recognition then let the world discover if it will that their art is as new as it is old and as old as new.

I had a classmate once who did three beautiful things and died. One of them was a story of a folk who found fire and then went wandering in the gloom of night seeking again the stars they had once known and lost; suddenly out of blackness they looked up and there loomed the heavens; and what was it that they said? They raised a mighty cry: "It is the stars, it is the ancient stars, it is the young and everlasting stars!"

CRITIQUES OF CARL VAN VECHTEN'S
NIGGER HEAVEN

W. E. B. DU BOIS

CARL VAN VECHTEN'S "Nigger Heaven" is a blow in the face. It is an affront to the hospitality of black folk and to the intelligence of white. First, as to its title: my objection is based on no provincial dislike of the nickname. "Nigger" is an English word of wide use and definite connotation. As employed by Conrad, Sheldon, Allen, and even Firbanks, its use was justifiable. But the phrase, "Nigger Heaven," as applied to Harlem, is a misnomer. "Nigger Heaven," does not mean, as Van Vechten once or twice intimates (pages 15, 199) a haven for Negroes—a city of refuge for dark and tired souls; it means, in common parlance, a nasty, sordid corner into which black folk are herded, and yet a place which they in crass ignorance are fools enough to enjoy. Harlem is no such place as that, and no one knows this better than Carl Van Vechten.

But after all, a title is only a title, and a book must be judged eventually by its fidelity to truth and its artistic merit. I find this novel neither truthful nor artistic. It is not a true picture of Harlem life, even allowing for some justifiable impressionistic exaggeration. It is a caricature. It is worse than untruth because it is a mass of half-truths. Probably sometime and somewhere in Harlem every incident of the book has happened; and yet the resultant picture built out of these parts is ludicrously out of focus and undeniably misleading.

The author counts among his friends numbers of Negroes of all classes. He is an authority on dives and cabarets. But he masses this knowledge without rule or reason and seeks to express all of Harlem life in its cabarets. To him the black cabaret is Harlem; around it all his characters gravitate. Here is their stage of action. Such a theory of Harlem is nonsense. The overwhelming majority of black folk there never go to cabarets. The average colored man in Harlem is an everyday laborer, attending church, lodge and movie and is as conservative and as conventional as ordinary working folk everywhere.

Something they have which is racial, something distinctively Negroid can be found; but it is expressed by subtle, almost delicate nuance, and not by the wildly barbaric drunken orgy in whose details Van Vechten revels. There is laughter, color, and spontaneity at Harlem's core, but in the current cabaret, financed and supported largely by white New York, this core is so overlaid and enwrapped with cheaper stuff that no one but a fool could mistake it for the genuine exhibition of the spirit of the people.

To all this the author has a right to reply that even if the title is an unhappy catch-phrase for penny purposes and his picture of truth untruthful, his book has a right to be judged primarily as a work of art. Does it please? Does it entertain? Is it a good and human story? In my opinion it is not, and I am one who likes stories and I do not insist that they be written solely for my point of view. "Nigger Heaven" is to me an astonishing and wearisome hodgepodge of laboriously stated facts, quotations, and expressions, illuminated here and there with something that comes near to being nothing but cheap melodrama. Real human feelings are laughed at. Love is degraded. The love of Byron and Mary is stark cruelty and that of Lasca and Byron is simply nasty. Compare this slum picture with Porgy. In his degradation Porgy is human and interesting. But in "Nigger Heaven" there is not a single loveable character. There is scarcely a generous impulse or a beautiful ideal. The characters are singularly wooden and inhuman. Van Vechten is not the great artist who with remorseless scalpel probes the awful depths of life. To him there are no depths. It is the surface mud he slops about in. His women's bodies have no souls; no children palpitate upon his hands; he has never looked upon his dead with bitter tears. Life to him is just one damned orgy after another, with hate, hurt, gin and sadism.

Both Langston Hughes and Carl Van Vechten know Harlem cabarets; but it is Hughes who whispers:

One said he heard the jazz band sob
When the little dawn was grey.

Van Vechten never heard a sob in a cabaret. All he hears is noise and brawling. Again and again with singular lack of invention he reverts to the same climax of two creatures tearing and scratching over "mah man"; lost souls who once had women's bodies; and to Van Vechten this spells comedy, not tragedy.

I seem to see that Mr. Van Vechten began a good tale with the promising figure of Anatol, but that he keeps turning aside to write in from his notebook every fact he has heard about Negroes and their problems; singularly irrelevant quotations, Haitian history, Chesnutt's novels, race-poetry, "blues" written by white folk. Into this mass he drops characters which are in most cases thin disguises; and those who know the originals have only to compare their life and this death, to realize the failure in truth and human interest. The final climax is an utterly senseless murder which appears without preparation or reason from the clouds.

I cannot for the life of me see in this work either sincerity or art, deep thought, or truthful industry. It seems to me that Mr. Van Vechten tried to do something bizarre and he certainly succeeded. I read "Nigger Heaven" and read it through because I had to. But I advise others who are impelled by a sense of duty or curiosity to drop the book gently in the grate and try the *Police Gazette*.

JAMES WELDON JOHNSON

THE TWO BOOKS about Harlem that were most widely read and discussed were Carl Van Vechten's *Nigger Heaven*, and Claude McKay's *Home to Harlem*. Mr. Van Vechten's novel ran through a score of editions, was published in most of the important foreign languages, and aroused something of a national controversy. For directly opposite reasons, there were objections to the book by white and colored people. White objectors declared that the story was a Van Vechten fantasy; that they could not be expected to believe that there were intelligent, well-to-do Negroes in Harlem who lived their lives on the cultural level he described, or a fast set that gave at least a very good imitation of life in sophisticated white circles. Negro objectors declared that the book was a libel on the race, that the dissolute life and characters depicted by the author were non-existent. Both classes of objectors were wrong, but their points of view can be understood. Negro readers of the book who knew anything knew that dissolute modes of life and dissolute characters existed in Harlem; their objections were really based upon chagrin and resentment at the disclosures to a white public. Yet, Mr. McKay's book dealt with low levels of life, a lustier life, it is true, than the dissolute modes depicted by Mr. Van Vechten, but entirely unrelieved by any brighter lights; furthermore, Mr. McKay made no attempt to hold in check or disguise his abiding contempt for the Negro bourgeoisie and "upper class." Still, *Home to Harlem* met with no such criticism from Negroes as did *Nigger Heaven*. The lusty primitive life in *Home to Harlem* was based on truth, as were the dissolute modes of life in *Nigger Heaven*; but Mr. Van Vechten was the first well-known American novelist to include in a story a cultured Negro class without making it burlesque or without implying reservations and apologies.

Most of the Negroes who condemned *Nigger Heaven* did not read it; they were stopped by the title. I don't think they would now be so sensitive about it; as the race progresses it will become less and less susceptible to hurts from such causes. Whatever the colored people thought about *Nigger Heaven*, speaking of the author as a man antagonistic to the race was entirely unwarranted. Carl Van Vechten had a warm interest in colored people before he ever saw Harlem. In the early days of the Negro literary and artistic movement, no one in the country did more to forward it than he accomplished in frequent magazine articles and by his many personal efforts in behalf of individual Negro writers and artists. Indeed, his regard for Negroes as a race is so close to being an affectionate one, that he is constantly joked about it by his most intimate friends. His most highly prized caricature of himself is one done by Covarrubias in black-face, and presented to him on his birthday. Mr. Van Vechten's birthday, that of young Alfred Knopf, and mine fall on the same day of the same month. For four or five years we have been celebrating them jointly, together with a small group of friends. Last summer we celebrated at the country place of the Knopfs. In a conversation that Blanche Knopf, Lawrence Langner, and I were carrying on, something about the responsibility for children came up. Mr. Van Vechten interrupted Mrs. Knopf with an opinion of his own on the subject, to which she retorted, "Carl, you don't know anything about it, because you are not a parent." Mr. Van Vechten responded with, "You're mistaken; I am the father of four sons." And Alfred Knopf flashed out, "If you are, they must be the four Mills Brothers." Mr. Van Vechten joined in the outburst of laughter. From the first, my belief has held that *Nigger Heaven* is a fine novel.

RUDOLPH FISHER

RETURNING TO HARLEM from his medical residency at Howard University's Freedman General Hospital in Washington, D.C., Rudolph Fisher was struck by the popularity his favorite clubs were enjoying among Downtown whites. "The Caucasian Storms Harlem," his ribald piece in the August 1927 American Mercury, *was widely read and the source of considerable amusement among Harlemites. Fisher had already come to the enthusiastic attention of such Renaissance principals as Walter White, executive secretary of the NAACP, and Charles S. Johnson of* Opportunity *with a more sociological essay in the February 1925 issue of* Atlantic Monthly, *the engagingly written "City of Refuge." Fisher's medical practice was a success, but he clearly felt the itch to write, and Walter White, taking the measure of his considerable literary talent, encouraged Fisher and used his influence with his own publisher, Alfred A. Knopf, in his behalf.*

THE CAUCASIAN STORMS HARLEM

I

IT MIGHT NOT have been such a jolt had my five years' absence from Harlem been spent otherwise. But the study of medicine includes no courses in cabareting; and, anyway, the Negro cabarets in Washington, where I studied, are all uncompromisingly black. Accordingly I was entirely unprepared for what I found when I returned to Harlem recently.

I remembered one place especially where my own crowd used to hold forth; and, hoping to find some old-timers there still, I sought it out one midnight. The old, familiar plunkety-plunk welcomed me from below as I entered. I descended the same old narrow stairs, came into the same smoke-misty basement, and found myself a chair at one of the ancient white-porcelain, mirror-smooth tables. I drew a deep breath and looked about, seeking familiar faces. "What a lot of 'fays!" I thought, as I noticed the number of white guests. Presently I grew puzzled and began to stare, then I gaped—and gasped. I found myself wondering if this was the right place—if, indeed, this was Harlem at all. I suddenly became aware that, except for the waiters and members of the orchestra, I was the only Negro in the place.

After a while I left it and wandered about in a daze from night-club to night-club. I tried the Nest, Small's, Connie's Inn, the Capitol, Happy's, the Cotton Club. There was no mistake; my discovery was real and was repeatedly confirmed. No wonder my old crowd was not to be found in any of them. The best of Harlem's black cabarets have changed their names and turned white.

Such a discovery renders a moment's recollection irresistible. As irresistible as were the cabarets themselves to me seven or eight years ago. Just out of college in a town where cabarets were something only read about. A year of graduate work ahead. A Summer of rest at hand. Cabarets. Cabarets night after night, and one after another. There was no cover-charge then, and a fifteen-cent bottle of Whistle lasted an hour. It was just after the war—the heroes were home—cabarets were the thing.

How the Lybia prospered in those happy days! It was the gathering place of the swellest Harlem set: if you didn't go to the Lybia, why, my dear, you just didn't belong. The people you saw at church in the morning you met at the Lybia at night. What romance in those war-tinged days and nights! Officers from Camp Upton, with pretty maids from Brooklyn! Gay lieutenants, handsome captains—all whirling the lively onestep. Poor non-coms completely ignored; what sensible girl wanted a corporal or even a sergeant? That white, old-fashioned house, standing alone in 138th street, near the corner of Seventh avenue—doomed to be torn down a few months thence—how it shook with the dancing and laughter of the dark merry crowds!

But the first place really popular with my friends was a Chinese restaurant in 136th street, which had been known as Hayne's

Café and then became the Oriental. It occupied an entire house of
three stories, and had carpeted floors and a quiet, superior air.
There was excellent food and incredibly good tea and two unusual
entertainers: a Cuban girl, who could so vary popular airs that
they sounded like real music, and a slender little "brown" with a
voice of silver and a way of singing a song that made you forget
your food. One could dance in the Oriental if one liked, but one
danced to a piano only, and wound one's way between linen-clad
tables over velvety, noiseless floors.

Here we gathered: Fritz Pollard, All-American halfback, selling Negro stock to prosperous Negro physicians; Henry Creamer
and Turner Layton, who had written "After You've Gone" and a
dozen more songs, and were going to write "Strut, Miss Lizzie;"
Paul Robeson, All-American end, on the point of tackling law,
quite unaware that the stage would intervene; Preacher Harry
Bragg, Harvard Jimmie MacLendon and half a dozen others. Here
at a little table, just inside the door, Bert Williams had supper every
night, and afterward sometimes joined us upstairs and sang songs
with us and lampooned the Actors' Equity Association, which had
barred him because of his color. Never did white guests come to
the Oriental except as guests of Negroes. But the manager soon
was stricken with a psychosis of some sort, became a black Jew,
grew himself a bushy, square-cut beard, donned a skull-cap and
abandoned the Oriental. And so we were robbed of our favorite
resort, and thereafter became mere rounders.

II

Such places, those real Negro cabarets that we met in the course
of our rounds! There was Edmonds' in Fifth avenue at 130th street.
It was a sure-enough honky-tonk, occupying the cellar of a saloon.
It was the social center of what was then, and still is, Negro Harlem's kitchen. Here a tall brown-skin girl, unmistakably the one
guaranteed in the song to make a preacher lay his Bible down,
used to sing and dance her own peculiar numbers, vesting them
with her own originality. She was known simply as Ethel, and was
a genuine drawing-card. She knew her importance, too. Other girls
wore themselves ragged trying to rise above the inattentive din of
conversation, and soon, literally, yelled themselves hoarse; eventually they lost whatever music there was in their voices and ac-

quired that familiar throaty roughness which is so frequent among blues singers, and which, though admired as characteristically African, is as a matter of fact nothing but a form of chronic laryngitis. Other girls did these things, but not Ethel. She took it easy. She would stride with great leisure and self-assurance to the center of the floor, stand there with a half-contemptuous nonchalance, and wait. All would become silent at once. Then she'd begin her song, genuine blues, which, for all their humorous lines, emanated tragedy and heartbreak:

> Woke up this mawnin'
> The day was dawnin'
> And I was sad and blue, so blue, Lord—
> Didn' have nobody
> To tell my troubles to—

It was Ethel who first made popular the song, "Tryin' to Teach My Good Man Right from Wrong," in the slow, meditative measures in which she complained:

> I'm gettin' sick and tired of my railroad man
> I'm gettin' sick and tired of my railroad man—
> Can't get him when I want him—
> I get him when I can.

It wasn't long before this song-bird escaped her dingy cage. Her name is a vaudeville attraction now, and she uses it all—Ethel Waters. Is there anyone who hasn't heard her sing "Shake That Thing!"?

A second place was Connor's in 135th street near Lenox avenue. It was livelier, less languidly sensuous, and easier to breathe in than Edmonds'. Like the latter, it was in a basement, reached by the typical narrow, headlong stairway. One of the girls there specialized in the Jelly-Roll song, and mad habitués used to fling petitions of greenbacks at her feet—pretty nimble feet they were, too—when she sang that she loved 'em but she had to turn 'em down. Over in a corner a group of 'fays would huddle and grin and think they were having a wild time. Slumming. But they were still very few in those days.

And there was the Oriental, which borrowed the name that the former Hayne's Café had abandoned. This was beyond Lenox avenue on the south side of 135th street. An upstairs place, it was nevertheless as dingy as any of the cellars, and the music fairly fought its way through the babble and smoke to one's ears, suffering in transit weird and incredible distortion. The prize pet here was a slim, little lad, unbelievably black beneath his high-brown powder, wearing a Mexican bandit costume with a bright-colored head-dress and sash. I see him now, poor kid, in all his glory, shimmying for enraptured women, who marveled at the perfect control of his voluntary abdominal tremors. He used to let the women reach out and put their hands on his sash to palpate those tremors—for a quarter.

Finally, there was the Garden of Joy, an open-air cabaret between 138th and 139th streets in Seventh avenue, occupying a plateau high above the sidewalk—a large, well-laid, smooth wooden floor with tables and chairs and a tinny orchestra, all covered by a propped-up roof, that resembled an enormous lampshade, directing bright light downward and outward. Not far away the Abyssinian Church used to hold its Summer camp-meetings in a great round circus-tent. Night after night there would arise the mingled strains of blues and spirituals, those peculiarly Negro forms of song, the one secular and the other religious, but both born of wretchedness in travail, both with their soarings of exultation and sinkings of despair. I used to wonder if God, hearing them both, found any real distinction.

There were the Lybia, then, and Hayne's, Connor's, the Oriental, Edmonds' and the Garden of Joy, each distinctive, standing for a type, some living up to their names, others living down to them, but all predominantly black. Regularly I made the rounds among these places and saw only incidental white people. I have seen them occasionally in numbers, but such parties were out on a lark. They weren't in their natural habitat and they often weren't any too comfortable.

But what of Barron's, you say? Certainly they were at home there. Yes, I know about Barron's. I have been turned away from Barron's because I was too dark to be welcome. I have been a member of a group that was told, "No more room," when we could see plenty of room. Negroes were never actually wanted in Barron's save to work. Dark skins were always discouraged or barred. In short, the fact about Barron's was this: it simply wasn't a Negro cabaret; it was a cabaret run by Negroes for whites. It wasn't even on the lists of those who lived in Harlem—they'd no more think of going there than of going to the Winter Garden Roof. But these other places were Negro through and through. Negroes supported them, not merely in now-and-then parties, but steadily, night after night.

III

Now, however, the situation is reversed. It is I who go occasionally and white people who go night after night. Time and again, since I've returned to live in Harlem, I've been one of a party of four Negroes who went to this or that Harlem cabaret, and on each occasion we've been the only Negro guests in the place. The managers don't hesitate to say that it is upon these predominant white patrons that they depend for success. These places therefore are no longer mine but theirs. Not that I'm barred, any more than they were seven or eight years ago. Once known, I'm even welcome, just as some of them used to be. But the complexion of the place is theirs, not mine. I? Why, I am actually stared at, I frequently feel uncomfortable and out of place, and when I go out on the floor to dance I am lost in a sea of white faces. As another observer has put it to me since, time was when white people went to Negro cabarets to see how Negroes acted; now Negroes go to these same cabarets to see how white people act. Negro clubs have recently taken to hiring a place outright for a presumably Negro party; and even then a goodly percentage of the invited guests are white.

One hurries to account for this change of complexion as a reaction to the Negro invasion of Broadway not long since. One remembers "Shuffle Along" of four years ago, the first Negro piece in the downtown district for many a moon. One says, "Oh yes, Negroes took their stuff to the whites and won attention and praise, and now the whites are seeking this stuff out on its native soil." Maybe. So I myself thought at first. But one looks for something of oppositeness in a genuine reaction. One would rather expect the reaction to the Negro invasion of Broadway to be apathy. One would expect that the same thing repeated under different names or in imitative fragments would meet with colder and colder reception, and finally with none at all.

A little recollection will show that just what one would expect was what happened. Remember "Shuffle Along's" successors: "Put and Take," "Liza," "Strut Miss Lizzie," "Runnin' Wild," and the others? True, none was so good as "Shuffle Along," but surely they didn't deserve all the roasting they got. "Liza" flared but briefly, during a holiday season. "Put and Take" was a loss, "Strut Miss Lizzie" strutted about two weeks, and the humor of "Runnin Wild" was derided as Neo-Pleistocene. Here was reaction for you —wholesale withdrawal of favor. One can hardly conclude that such withdrawal culminated in the present swamping of Negro cabarets. People so sick of a thing would hardly go out of their way to find it.

And they *are* sick of it—in quantity at least. Only one Negro entertainment has survived this reaction of apathy in any permanent fashion. This is the series of revues built around the personality of Florence Mills. Without that bright live personality the Broadway district would have been swept clean last season of all-Negro bills. Here is a girl who has triumphed over a hundred obstacles. Month after month she played obscure, unnoticed rôles with obscure, unknown dark companies. She was playing such a minor part in "Shuffle Along" when the departure of Gertrude Saunders, the craziest blues-singer on earth, unexpectedly gave her the spotlight. Florence Mills cleaned up. She cleaned up so thoroughly that the same public which grew weary of "Shuffle Along" and sick of its successors still had an eager ear for her. They have yet, and she neither wearies nor disappoints them. An impatient Broadway audience awaits her return from Paris, where she and the inimitable Josephine Baker have been vying with each other as sensations. She is now in London on the way home, but London won't release her; the enthusiasm over her exceeds anything in the memory of the oldest reviewers.

Florence Mills, moreover, is admired by her own people too, because, far from going to her head, her success has not made her forgetful. Not long ago, the rumor goes, she made a fabulous amount of money in the Florida real-estate boom, and what do you suppose she plans to do with it? Build herself an Italian villa somewhere up the Hudson? Not at all. She plans to build a first-rate Negro theatre in Harlem.

But that's Florence Mills. Others have encountered indifference. In vain has Eddie Hunter, for instance, tried for a first-class Broadway showing, despite the fact that he himself has a new kind of Negro-comedian character to portray—the wise darkey, the "bizthniss man," the "fly" rascal who gets away with murder, a character who amuses by making a goat of others instead of by making a goat of himself. They say that some dozen Negro shows have met with similar denials. Yet the same people, presumably, whose spokesmen render these decisions flood Harlem night after night and literally crowd me off the dancing-floor. If this is a reaction, it is a reaction to a reaction, a swinging back of the pendulum from apathy toward interest. Maybe so. The cabarets may present only those special Negro features which have a particular and peculiar appeal, leaving out the high-yaller display that is merely feebly imitative. But a reaction to a reaction—that's differential calculus.

AARON DOUGLAS CHATS ABOUT
THE HARLEM RENAISSANCE

AARON DOUGLAS'S CAREER *was a classic illustration of the meld of civil rights and the arts. Charles S. Johnson, editor of Opportunity, recruited Douglas from a Kansas City high-school teaching position to serve as the painter of the movement. After a period of tutelage under Winold Reiss, Douglas produced for books and magazines canvases, murals, and illustrations distinguished by geometrical motifs depicting the progress from antiquity to modern times of African peoples. Like Hughes, Douglas was drawn into the patronage empire of "Godmother," the formidable Charlotte Osgood Mason. His close association with the hugely influential Johnson, as well as his considerable talent, enabled him to obtain a fellowship at the Barnes Foundation, another for study in Paris, and eventually the chairmanship of the art department of Fisk University. Douglas and his wife, Alta, knew everyone involved in the Harlem Renaissance, black and white, interesting and influential, destitute and deviant. Their Harlem apartment was one of the principal gathering spots. "Aaron Douglas Chats about the Harlem Renaissance," excerpted from a tape-recorded interview with Leslie Collins, professor of English at Fisk, is a memoir both analytically and anecdotally rich—a candid assessment of the era by the distinguished artist at the end of his career.*

LESLIE COLLINS: Mr. Douglas, as a participant in the Harlem Renaissance, what would you say was the best moment of the times, the most memorable?

AARON DOUGLAS: Well, that isn't easy to say. There are *so many* things that I had seen for the first time, so many impressions I was getting. One was that of seeing a big city that was entirely black, from beginning to end you were impressed by the fact that black people were in charge of things and here was a black city and here was a situation that was eventually to be the center for the great in American Culture.

COLLINS: What was the Renaissance to you? How would you define it?

DOUGLAS: It was a cultural experience; in a sense, a sort of spiritual experience. Actually it was difficult to put your hands on it, because it wasn't something that the people actually understood as *really* a thing of great importance; they had the feeling that something was going on and we acknowledged that this perhaps was something unique and destined in American black-white relationships, this touched upon the experience of black people in America, but to get hold of anything particular is difficult to realize—to achieve. So, it was only later that you had the feeling that here was something of importance to us and something that had the possibility of being a base for greater development in the future.

COLLINS: What of the man on the streets? Was he aware of anything on the way, any spiritual value being pursued by a person such as yourself, Arna Bontemps, and, earlier, James Weldon Johnson and in the Renaissance through his *God's Trombones*? Did he feel that all of you were part of a literary scheme or literary mood?

DOUGLAS: I doubt that that is true. My feeling is that the man in the street actually had no thoughts upon this thing as being a matter of importance to black and white, that it was a matter of cultural importance. As a matter of fact, if you had asked him about culture, he would have been hard-put to explain it at all, certainly to explain the black man's part in it. But he was a part of it, although he didn't understand this thing—he did not actually, consciously make a contribution; he made his contribution in an unconscious way. He was the thing on which and around which this whole idea was developed. And from that standpoint it seems to me his contribution is greater than if he had attempted consciously to make a contribution. The inner thing that came from him that some were able to understand and some of us, I believe, consciously understood (we who understand that sort of thing)—and that's the thing that made it unique, in my estimation.

COLLINS: Then the Harlemite, the man on the street, was an unconscious participant, was he not?

DOUGLAS: Yes, he was a participant. He didn't put his hands on anything. He didn't mold anything, excepting the thing was being emitted, something was coming out of him which the various artists responded to, could get hold of and make something that was later known as the Harlem Renaissance.

COLLINS: What, then, is your response to those critics who from the long view of the 60's and 70's say that those blacks who participated in the Harlem Renaissance were special beings enjoying white patronage, doll-like creatures who were manipulated and maneuvered?

DOUGLAS: To the contrary. Participants never felt like that, I do not think. Of course, I personally never felt that was true. One aspect is certain and I think we might as well acknowledge it that there were certain white people at that time that came in contact with blacks and helped make it possible for them to reach a level from which they could create, but it was *not* something dictated by white culture. It stemmed from Black culture. We were constantly working on this innate blackness at that time that made this whole thing important and unique. And in no way do I think that we should have any feeling of being talked down to or talked into things that they had no share in, that is to say, were given certain things and were simply manipulated and so on. I think that there's no reason that idea should be maintained.

COLLINS: In your estimation, how did *The Crisis* differ from *Opportunity* as a medium for the expression of younger Black authors and artists such as yourself? You were an active participant in the Renaissance with your sketches, with your illustrations for a number of dramatic moments such as James Weldon Johnson's *The Creation,* which through the years has been a beloved piece of literature both for its verse and illustrations. What, first of all, is your feeling about *The Crisis*? Did it make a different kind of offer to you as an artist than *Opportunity* did? I'm thinking now that *The Crisis* was under the aegis of Du Bois and *Opportunity* under the editorship of Charles S. Johnson.

DOUGLAS: Well, this idea might have emerged in other fields of art, but the field of plastic art was in a unique position in that there was almost no background; we had no tradition. Everything was done . . . almost for the first time, let us say, and we were so hungry at that time for something that was specifically black that they were perfectly willing to accept almost anything. I say that because as I look back at the things that I produced, it was so readily received and cheerfully received. You wonder how they could have done it! I look at it and wonder how I could have done it. And next, could there have been a group to receive it, who were willing to receive it? And although the illustrations were definitely very primitive, very unskillful, the certain drawings that I did at that time were received and I was encouraged and I went on from that to other things.

COLLINS: Then *The Crisis* as the official journal of the NAACP was no different to you than *Opportunity* magazine was as the official organ of the Urban League?

DOUGLAS: Not really . . . They never refused anything that I did. They accepted it; they put it forward. As a matter of fact, Du Bois once carried my name on *The Crisis* as the art editor. I'm sure he had his tongue in his cheek, but he was willing to do that, you see. And I've always been grateful to him for it, because it increased my motivation. I was encouraged to go on feeling that I should some day really become *worthy* of that sort of thing. My feeling was that I should go on and be worthy of the distinction that Dr. Du Bois conferred upon me.

COLLINS: Then you are saying that Dr. Du Bois *did* exert an influence on you?

DOUGLAS: In sponsorship, yes. If he hadn't done anything else, even that, what he had meant to me, for a young person reading his editorials way back when I was at an early age in the beginning of high school—beautiful things . . . the inspiration from those things was enough to make me realize the importance of any kind of association with this man.

COLLINS: Was he ever critical of you as an artist? Did he ever suggest a political angle that you might have emphasized graphically?

DOUGLAS: Yes.

COLLINS: At the beginning point of your career and earlier as a young boy spiritually and philosophically?

DOUGLAS: Yes. Yes. Tremendously.

COLLINS: Now, what about Charles S. Johnson, as editor of *Opportunity*? . . . Do you suppose he was endowed especially to help in a first step or that he was just singularly endowed with a certain kind of intuitive ingenuity to spot talent?

DOUGLAS: I suppose the both. I suppose he was, of course, a man of broad vision. But specifically, he understood how to make the way, how to indicate the next step for many of these young people at that time and make it possible for them to go on to other things.

COLLINS: In other words, he established contacts?

DOUGLAS: Yes, that's it. For instance, I met Carl Van Vechten through Charles Johnson. I met Dorothy Barnes and I went on to the Barnes Foundation through Dr. Johnson. As a matter of fact, many years passed before I was out of the real influence of Dr. Johnson. . . .

COLLINS: What are your recollections of James Weldon Johnson at this time? So many of the analysts and the critics refer to him as an "elder stateman" of the Renaissance. Were you aware very deeply of his presence as an associate or as an acquaintance in this period?

DOUGLAS: Yes, naturally you knew his earlier life and his association with the stage and that sort of thing and you've read about his work with the NAACP and he had done marvelous work and was a national figure in that respect. But then this artistic aspect of it is something that was coming on. He was a man of great culture and one that was quite capable of inspiring younger men to go on in this field and to attempt to do something *worthy* of the opportunities and worthy of those who had gone before them or those who are actively engaged in this work.

COLLINS: Were you conscious of his seeming lifetime creed that the Negro had a genius, that the Black man in America possessed a genius and that he had been and was responding to that genius?

DOUGLAS: Unconsciously, I must have been. Unconsciously. I don't remember now that attitude, that idea in respect to Johnson as I was in respect to Du Bois. Yet, Johnson had been actively working in the field much more so than Du Bois, because Du Bois was a scientist. His work was in sociology, history, and so on and so on, but Johnson had been actively engaged in the creative side of Negro life in the theater, in music, and so. And when he met me in the hall one day and asked me if I would . . . like to undertake some illustrations for [Johnson's book of poems *God's Trombones*], I was, of course, totally pleased. . . . And so I accepted the challenge and went on to do the sort of thing that we see, which didn't please me at the *time*. It was the best that I could do, I suppose, with the time I had, with the development I had. But I had the feeling that eventually I would be able to do something much more adequate with the material because I was and I am very much impressed with the enormous power, spiritual power that's behind Negro life and it's . . . if it can be mined, it's a gold mine if you can write or draw it. . . .

COLLINS: What was his response to your illustrations?

DOUGLAS: He was very enthusiastic about them. Apparently, it was just the sort of thing he wanted. He urged me to go on with the rest of them when I finished one of them and I went on to finish the work.

COLLINS: Well, you created a graphic phasing of the black man, did you not, that became rather a signature of yours?

DOUGLAS: Yes. There's a certain artistic pattern that I follow . . . I used the Egyptian form, that is to say, the head was in perspective in a profile flat view, the body, shoulders down to the waist turned half way, the legs were done also from the side and the feet were also done in a broad perspective. . . . The only thing that I did that was not specifically taken from the Egyptians was an eye . . . so you saw it in three dimensions. I avoided the three dimension and that's another thing that made it sort of unique artistically. . . .

COLLINS: One of the interpreters of the new impulse of the time was Dr. Alain Locke, who, it is said, phased the period the Negro Renaissance or Harlem Renaissance. . . . I was wondering if you as a young artist had come in contact with Dr. Locke and if you were aware of *his* being cognizant of your own contributions?

DOUGLAS: Well, I think so very much. I was sort of the fair-headed boy for this reason, not because the work was, I suppose, so important (they couldn't have known that), but I was the first one to give this thing something of a Negro content. They had the feeling this isn't something that was done by a caucasian person. This is a black person. Here at last it is a black person doing this thing. He isn't criticizing his people; he isn't placing them in a situation that they would not normally *have*; he isn't trying to exalt them and you would see that in many of these things. I was very careful to associate my figures so that they looked like the working people, see. You would not confuse them with the aspiring middle-upper-class, not that I had any antagonism, but that I felt that here is the essence of this Negro thing, here among these people. So I tried to keep it there with simple devices, such as giving the clothing, any clothing, giving—sometimes giving it ragged edges, you know, so as to keep the thing realistic. . . .

COLLINS: How did Wallace Thurman organize you and Langston Hughes and Zora Neale Hurston? What did he say to you about *Fire!!* in order to get it started, in order to get you writing and drawing to produce this magazine? Both of you had no money and you knew it to be rather an adventure that in a measure became a misadventure, but did anything deter you at all? Were you always this enthusiastic?

DOUGLAS: Oh, yes. Oh certainly. We were so enthusiastic that we forgot that there was such a thing as . . . these things were run with money. And that we knew what we wanted. We wanted a magazine to express our ideas, to set forth our ideas. . . . Putting out a magazine was, well, just *fantastic,* I mean fantastic that we could only put out the whole of Negro life. We could only put out two magazines that I know of. Two or three. The *Messenger,* of course, the labor was so definitely behind the *Messenger.* I suppose the money that went into that was so definitely *there.* That, everybody could see. And *The Crisis, Opportunity,* but that's for the whole of Negro life,—two or three little magazines. And we, just a little bunch of us, were daring enough to come forth with a thing like that. It was outrageous, outlandish and everything else for us to do that.

COLLINS: But nevertheless stimulating.

DOUGLAS: Oh, well, certainly we thought that was the greatest thing.

COLLINS: Why *Fire!!?*

DOUGLAS: Well, I guess it was the uninhibited spirit that is behind life. I suppose that is what we meant by that. I don't remember it ever being *spelled out!* But certainly that must have been the feeling behind it. . . .

COLLINS: And that experience was one of the memorable moments for you in the Harlem Renaissance?

DOUGLAS: Oh, yes. Of course, I had previously seen these things done in *Opportunity* magazine. In *The Crisis* magazine which I had been with almost a year or more. These things had come out. Some good, some serviceable, and some of them never should have been produced, but they grabbed them up and published them. As I say, I look at these things and wonder if they could have been any use to anybody, but I wasn't their editor then. They were happy to have these things. Sure, there were other artists. There were plenty good artists, but they didn't have this feeling. . . .

COLLINS: Today, the black college student is extraordinarily fascinated by the Renaissance and its people, its time. . . . Have you any explanation for their excitement by the period?

DOUGLAS: I think so. I think they were excited because they found that at that time almost fifty years ago here were some people doing the things that they were interested in doing. That as a matter of fact their function was to pick this thing up and go on with it. We only got it started. We only lit the flame. We only set fire to this thing. But it's their business to take it, magnify it and to carry it on. I think that's the thing that excited them. And the thing that I've always tried to talk to them to infuse in them the feeling not that they were second in this thing, but it was their responsibility first to understand it—and then to take it all. The need is *greater* for them almost than it was for us in the very beginning. Their struggle and their work and their work and their achievement—it *can* be greater as we (struggle through the years) up till now. Here we are, fifty years after—being remembered is something! How many others have been remembered? But here we are. If they take this thing and go on with it, they can be *far* more . . . have a greater place in this thing than what ours was at the very beginning. That's the thing that I'll always try to make them conscious of.

COLLINS: One of the most pleasant aspects of these extraordinary times of Black assertion is the evident joy that these students take in the Douglas Murals in the Old Fisk Library. . . . Won't you review the story of how the University entered into the contract with you to decorate the walls of the Library with murals?

DOUGLAS: It was in 1929 and my wife and I were on our way to Kansas. I was going back after about ten or twelve years away from home. I considered myself sort of a success at that time. I had a contract in my pocket for the book illustrations for Van Vechten's book *Nigger Heaven,* and I was doing a number of jackets. I think I was doing book-jackets for Claude

McKay at that time, which was about to be published and I was sort of walking on air. Before I got to Topeka, I got a telegram from Dr. Charles S. Johnson, saying that Dr. [Thomas Elsa] Jones was interested in some murals for Fisk University. . . . Well, to make a long story short, I talked with Dr. Jones. We got the idea. . . . After we drew up a contract, I asked for a certain amount. They couldn't quite see that amount, but we finally ended upon a price that was considerably lower, but it was considerably higher than anything I had ever dreamed of. We went on with that. The contract was signed. When school was out, Dr. Jones said to me, "Look, Mr. Douglas, we have a place up in Canada and I'm going up there with my family for the summer. Now, if you and Mrs. Douglas want to stay here at the Heritage House for the summer, you can have the whole run of the place. And you don't have to pay any rent." It worked out *beautifully*.

Well, anyway, I had my cartoons all ready for the commencement of the work, when everyone was interested, you see. The builders, the people who had to do with the inner part of the Library, the architect and so on, they were all interested in what I was going to do. So some of them, of course, thought I was going to fall on my face and I was too, but I went right on. I was fortunate enough that summer to get some graduates . . . and I had Mr. Edward Harleston who was really our finest portrait painter. He trained under Van Voston and had done a picture of DuPont for the Wilmington people and is now in the state capitol down there, but he was more or less free for that summer. I wrote him and asked if he'd come over and help me. He's the only trained person I had to work with. The other fellows were just fellows who'd never had a brush in their hands. I said, well, you don't have to know anything, just go on and I'll show you. So with these five people we started. . . .

As I said, they expected me to fall on my face, but I had this one single artist and he took charge of the work. I said Mr. Harleston, you just sort of guide this thing. That left me free again. I would come in the mornings, go over and get things started. I had to show Mr. Harleston what I wanted him to do and the whole thing just went along like clockwork. . . .

COLLINS: Then Charles S. Johnson was instrumental in your getting the commission?

DOUGLAS: Oh, definitely so.

COLLINS: And the murals were completed in what year?

DOUGLAS: The summer of 1930 and then up till October 1. Finished in October.

COLLINS: What was in your mind as you formulated thematic plans for the murals, arriving at the mythological motif in several spots and the African element in others?

DOUGLAS: Well, the main part of it was designed as a sort of panorama of the development of Black people in this hemisphere, in the new world. I began in Africa. On the one wall I began with the African life, the animal life and so on, the pyramids in Egypt, and so on, and so on. Then picking it up over on the other side, I have the slave situation and then the emancipation and freedom, and so on. Then I used Fisk as the model or the pattern of the Fisk University as represented by Jubilee Hall. I put in the sun, the rising sun and across that I had a series of graduates from the various facilities of the various sciences and literature and so on as they moved across the walls. But that was the idea from Africa to America to the slave situation, freedom and so on. Now on the other side, on the other walls I used two things: one, the Spiritual as being important or revelant to Negro life and on the other side, the south wall, I used laboring aspects of work. I was thinking of labor has been one of the most important aspects of our development. . . . It isn't grand, but it is important and it is a thing that we should be proud of, because we have that part of our life that has gone into the building of America. Not only of ourselves, but in the building of American life. And it's very worthy. We should always keep that in mind.

ALBERT C. BARNES

ALBERT BARNES WAS CONVINCED that African Americans had unique artistic powers to contribute to the nation: "The white man in the mass cannot compete with the Negro in spiritual endowment." Alain Locke shared Barnes's expectation that his race would make a singular contribution in the arts, but not because he saw contemporary African Americans as possessing "a primitive nature upon which a white man's education has never been harnessed," as Barnes did. Rather, it was precisely because African American artists were such an integral part of the society that had continually tried to exclude them, Locke believed, that they brought to their creations a special angle of vision. Locke's notes for the 1932 Travelling Exhibition of the Work of Negro Artists, after 1928 an annual exposition sponsored by the Harmon Foundation, were typical of the Civil Rights Establishment's ready applause of public exposure of African American artists, with only secondary concern for the quality of their products. Romare Bearden, then barely more than a precocious teenager, showed a professional artist's awareness of the dangers to painters and sculptors whose careers were too rapidly promoted by white patrons enthralled by a mystique of African American uniqueness.

NEGRO ART AND AMERICA

THAT THERE SHOULD HAVE DEVELOPED a distinctively Negro art in America was natural and inevitable. A primitive race, transported into an Anglo-Saxon environment and held in subjection to that fundamentally alien influence, was bound to undergo the soul-stirring experiences which always find their expression in great art. The contributions of the American Negro to art are representative because they come from the hearts of the masses of a people held together by like yearnings and stirred by the same causes. It is a sound art because it comes from a primitive nature upon which a white man's education has never been harnessed. It is a great art because it embodies the Negroes' individual traits and reflects their suffering, aspirations and joys during a long period of acute oppression and distress.

The most important element to be considered is the psychological complexion of the Negro as he inherited it from his primitive ancestors and which he maintains to this day. The outstanding characteristics are his tremendous emotional endowment, his luxuriant and free imagination and a truly great power of individual expression. He has in superlative measure that fire and light which, coming from within, bathes his whole world, colors his images and impels him to expression. The Negro is a poet by birth. In the masses, that poetry expresses itself in religion which acquires a distinction by extraordinary fervor, by simple and picturesque rituals and by a surrender to emotion so complete that ecstasy, amounting to automatisms, is the rule when he worships in groups. The outburst may be started by any unlettered person provided with the average Negro's normal endowment of eloquence and vivid imagery. It begins with a song or a wail which spreads like fire and soon becomes a spectacle of a harmony of rhythmic movement and rhythmic sound unequalled in the ceremonies of any other race. Poetry is religion brought down to earth and it is of the essence of the Negro soul. He carries it with him always and everywhere; he lives it in the field, the shop, the factory. His daily habits of thought, speech and movement are flavored with the picturesque, the rhythmic, the euphonious.

The white man in the mass cannot compete with the Negro in spiritual endowment. Many centuries of civilization have attenuated his original gifts and have made his mind dominate his spirit. He has wandered too far from the elementary human needs and their easy means of natural satisfaction. The deep and satisfying harmony which the soul requires no longer arises from the incidents of daily life. The requirements for practical efficiency in a world alien to his spirit have worn thin his religion and devitalized his art. His art and his life are no longer one and the same as they were in primitive man. Art has become exotic, a thing apart, an indulgence, a something to be possessed. When art is real and vital it effects the harmony between ourselves and nature which means happiness. Modern life has forced art into being a mere adherent upon the practical affairs of life which offer it no sustenance. The result has been that hopeless confusion of values which mistakes sentimentalism and irrational day-dreaming for art.

The Negro has kept nearer to the ideal of man's harmony with nature and that, his blessing, has made him a vagrant in our arid, practical American life. But his art is so deeply rooted in his nature that it has thrived in a foreign soil where the traditions and practices tend to stamp out and starve out both the plant and its flowers. It has lived because it was an achievement, not an indulgence. It has been his happiness through that mere self-expression which is its own immediate and rich reward. Its power converted adverse material conditions into nutriment for his soul and it made a new world in which his soul has been free. Adversity has always been his lot but he converted it into a thing of beauty in his songs. When he was the abject, down-trodden slave, he burst forth into songs which constitute America's only great music—the spirituals. These wild chants are the natural, naive, untutored, spontaneous utterance of the suffering, yearning, prayerful human soul. In their mighty roll there is a nobility truly superb. Idea and emotion are fused in an art which ranks with the Psalms and the songs of Zion in their compelling, universal appeal.

The emancipation of the Negro slave in America gave him only a nominal freedom. Like all other human beings he is a creature of habits which tie him to his past; equally set are his white brothers' habits toward him. The relationship of master and slave has changed but little in the sixty years of freedom. He is still a slave to the ignorance, the prejudice, the cruelty which were the fate of his forefathers. To-day he has not yet found a place of equality in the social, educational or industrial world of the white man. But he has the same singing soul as the ancestors who created the single form of great art which America can claim as her own. Of the tremendous growth and prosperity achieved by America since emancipation day, the Negro has had scarcely a pittance. The changed times did, however, give him an opportunity to develop and strengthen the native, indomitable courage and the keen powers of mind which were not suspected during the days of slavery. The character of his song changed under the new civilization and his mental and moral stature now stands measurement with those of the white man of equal educational and civilizing opportunities. That growth he owes chiefly to his own efforts; the attendant strife has left unspoiled his native gift of song. We have in his poetry and music a true, infallible record of what the struggle has meant to his inner life. It is art of which America can well be proud.

The renascence of Negro art is one of the events of our age which no seeker for beauty can afford to overlook. It is as characteristically Negro as are the primitive African sculptures. As art forms, each bears comparison with the great art expressions of any race or civilization. In both ancient and modern Negro art we find a faithful expression of a people and of an epoch in the world's evolution.

The Negro renascence dates from about 1895 when two men, Paul Laurence Dunbar and Booker T. Washington, began to attract the world's attention. Dunbar was a poet, Washington an educator in the practical business of life. They lived in widely-distant parts of America, each working independently of the other. The leavening power of each upon the Negro spirit was tremendous; each fitted into and reinforced the other; their combined influences brought to birth a new epoch for the American Negro. Washington showed that by a new kind of education the Negro could attain to an economic condition that enables him to preserve his identity, free his soul and make himself an important factor in American life. Dunbar revealed the virgin field which the Negro's own talents and conditions of life offered for creating new forms of beauty. The race became self-conscious and pride of race supplanted the bitter wail of unjust persecution. The Negro saw and followed the path that was to lead him out of the wilderness and back to his own heritage through the means of his own endowments. Many new poets were discovered, while education had a tremendous quickening. The yield to art was a new expression of Negro genius in a form of poetry which connoisseurs place in the class reserved for the disciplined art of all races. Intellect and culture of a high order became the goals for which they fought, and with a marked degree of success.

Only through bitter and long travail has Negro poetry attained to its present high level as an art form and the struggle has produced much writing which, while less perfect in form, is no less important as poetry. We find nursery rhymes, dances, love-songs, pæans of joy, lamentations, all revealing unerringly the spirit of the race in its varied contacts with life. There has grown a fine tradition which is fundamentally Negro in character. Every phase of that growth in alien surroundings is marked with reflections of the multitudinous vicissitudes that cumbered the path from slavery to culture. Each record is loaded with feeling, powerfully expressed in uniquely Negro forms. The old chants, known as spirituals, were pure soul, their sadness untouched by vindictiveness. After the release from slavery, bitterness crept into their songs. Later, as times changed, we find self-assertion, lofty aspirations and only a scattered cry for vengeance. As he grew in culture, there came expressions of the deep consolation of resignation which is born of the wisdom that the Negro race is its own, all-sufficient justification. Naturally, sadness is the note most often struck; but the frequently-expressed joy, blithesome, carefree, overflowing joy, reveals what an enviable creature the Negro is in his happy moods. No less evident is that native understanding and wisdom which—from the homely and crude expressions of their slaves, to the scholarly and cultured contributions of to-day—we know go with the Negro's endowment. The black scholar, seer, sage, prophet sings his message; that explains why the Negro tradition is so rich and is so firmly implanted in the soul of the race.

The Negro tradition has been slow in forming but it rests upon the firmest of foundations. Their great men and women of the past—Wheatley, Sojourner Truth, Douglass, Dunbar, Washington—have each laid a personal and imperishable stone in that foundation. A host of living Negroes, better educated and unalterably faithful to their race, are still building, and each with some human value which is an added guarantee that the tradition will be strengthened and made serviceable for the new era that is sure to come when more of the principles of humanity and rationality become the white man's guides. Many living Negroes—Du Bois, Cotter, Grimke, Braithwaite, Burleigh, the Johnsons, McKay, Dett, Locke, Hayes, and many others—know the Negro soul and lead it to richer fields by their own ideals of culture, art and citizenship. It is a healthy development, free from that pseudo-culture which stifles the soul and misses rational happiness as the goal of human life. Through the compelling powers of his poetry and music the American Negro is revealing to the rest of the world the essential oneness of all human beings.

The cultured white race owes to the soul-expressions of its black brother too many moments of happiness not to acknowledge ungrudgingly the significant fact that what the Negro has achieved is of tremendous civilizing value. We see that in certain qualities of soul essential to happiness our own endowment is comparatively deficient. We have to acknowledge not only that our civilization has done practically nothing to help the Negro create his art but that our unjust oppression has been powerless to prevent the black man from realizing in a rich measure the expressions of his own rare gifts. We have begun to imagine that a better education and a greater social and economic equality for the Negro might produce something of true importance for a richer and fuller American life. The unlettered black singers have taught us to live music that rakes our souls and gives us moments of exquisite joy. The later Negro has made us feel the majesty of Nature, the ineffable peace of the woods and the great open spaces. He has shown us that the events of our every-day American life contain for him a poetry, rhythm and charm which we ourselves had never discovered. Through him we have seen the pathos, comedy, affection, joy of his own daily life, unified into humorous dialect verse or perfected sonnet that is a work of exquisite art. He has taught us to respect the sheer manly greatness of the fiber which has kept his inward light burning with an effulgence that shines through the darkness in which we have tried to keep him. All these visions, and more, he has revealed to us. His insight into realities has been given to us in vivid images loaded with poignancy and passion. His message has been lyrical, rhythmic, colorful. In short, the elements of beauty he has controlled to the ends of art.

This mystic whom we have treated as a vagrant has proved his possession of a power to create out of his own soul and our own America, moving beauty of an individual character whose existence we never knew. We are beginning to recognize that what the Negro singers and sages have said is only what the ordinary Negro feels and thinks, in his own measure, every day of his life. We have paid more attention to that everyday Negro and have been surprised to learn that nearly all of his activities are shot through and through with music and poetry. When we take to heart the obvious fact that what our prosaic civilization needs most is precisely the poetry which the average Negro actually lives, it is incredible that we should not offer the consideration which we have consistently denied to him. If at that time, he is the simple, ingenuous, forgiving, good-natured, wise and obliging person that he has been in the past, he may consent to form a working alliance with us for the development of a richer American civilization to which he will contribute his full share.

ALAIN LOCKE

THE NEGRO TAKES HIS PLACE
IN AMERICAN ART

THERE ARE, I take it, three objectives to the movement in Negro
art of which this fifth Harmon Exhibition of the Work of Negro
Artists is an integral part, and to which, in the years of its activity,
it has made and is making a formative and important contribution.
One is the encouragement of the Negro artist; another, the development of Negro art; and a third is the promotion of the Negro
theme and subject as a vital phase of the artistic expression of
American life. Six years ago the share of Negro subject material in
the field of American fine art was negligible; little, if anything, was
being done for the encouragement of the Negro artist as such, and
many thought that there was some implied restriction and arbitrary
limitation of the Negro artist in the program of Negro art as "racial self-expression." Yet in the short intervening space of time,
practically each of these situations has been reversed in a spurt of
accumulative and perfectly compatible development.

As a net result not only is the Negro and his art more definitely
upon the artistic map, but the Negro theme and subject is coming
increasingly to the fore in the general field of art interest, as any
analysis of today's art exhibitions will show if compared with similar exhibitions of even five years ago. Some day, it is to be hoped,
an exhibition of contemporary American art dealing with the Negro theme and subject, irrespective of the racial affiliation of the
artists, will be sponsored and that it will show a remarkable development in increased emphasis, deepened interest, and reveal mature mastery and understanding of the general handling of the
Negro theme in painting, sculpture and the graphic arts—a development parallel to the remarkable growth of the Negro artist
which these Harmon exhibits have so unmistakably shown.

We may well pause for a moment to consider the causes of this advance and to estimate briefly its gains. A few years back there were Negro artists, but little or no Negro art. Most of our artists subscribed to the creed that racialism in art was an unwarranted restriction, but they either avoided racial subjects or treated them gingerly in what I used to call "Nordic transcriptions." As a result, contrasted with the vital self-expression in poetry, fiction, drama and music, there was almost nothing representative or racial in the field of the fine arts. While the poets, playwrights, writers and musicians were in the sunlight and warmth of a proud and positive race-consciousness, our artists were still for the most part in an eclipse of chilly doubt and disparagement.

Why? I think mainly because social prejudice had seized on the stigma of color and racial feature, and the Negro artist was a sensitive victim of this negative color-consciousness and it sinhibitions. Sad as was the plight of Negro art in his hands, as long as the Negro artist was in this general frame of mind, his whole expression was to some extent weak and apologetic in conception and spirit, because it was bound to be derivative, indirect and falsely sophisticated.

As the Negro subject has become more popular with the Negro artist, a steadily maturing firmness and originality in the handling of non-racial subjects have been a noteworthy and, I think, a not unconnected accompaniment. In 1929 a young Negro painter, with a creditable prize record at one of the great national schools of art, refused an invitation to exhibit in a special showing of Negro artists. He very seriously, and at that time perhaps pardonably, preferred to try for recognition "as a painter, not as a Negro painter." After an award of a fellowship for foreign study on his technical merits and promise, he was in two years' time exhibiting in the successor of the show he first refused to join, six paintings—five of them studies of race types, and one perhaps the most striking color study of a pure blood type that I have ever seen from the brush of an American artist, black or white.

It is of still greater significance that this artist's conversion of attitude seems to have occurred primarily or entirely on artistic and technical rather than sentimental or sociological grounds. Welcome as is the very real and vital racialism that is now stirring in the world of the Negro artist, it is artistically important as a sign of aesthetic objectivity and independence, and thus a double emancipation from apologetic timidity and academic imitation. We are now able to see that Negro art does not restrict the Negro artist to growth in his own soil exclusively, but only to express himself in originality and unhampered sincerity.

In fact, the relation of the Negro artist to his subject matter is not so very different from the relation of his white fellow artist to the same material, with the possible exception and advantage of closer psychological contact and understanding. It is important local color material, or provincial or national subject matter to both, and the development of the theme in contemporary American art is more and more demonstrating this.

We must soon begin, now, the frank and objective comparison of the work of the outstanding Negro artists with that of men like William Benton, James Chapin, Julius Bloch, Covarrubias, Orozco, Maurice Sterne, William McFee—to name some of the outstanding few who have notably touched the Negro subject in their art—no matter how bold or temporarily disparaging the contrast. The rapid mastery of his provincial handicaps by the Negro artist makes parity hopeful and eventually certain. There was a time, and not so far back, that the white American artist was in a no better relative position when compared with the more mature schools and traditions of European art. Every successive showing of Negro artists seems to bring Negro and white American artists closer together in this common interest in the promotion of Negro art and over the common denominator of contemporary American art expression.

One other denominator suggested by the inclusion of a Negro artist from Cuba in this exhibition is that of an interest, far from academic, in uniting for purposes of comparison the work of Negroes separated by differences of cultural background and artistic tradition. The inclusion of the interesting sculpture of Teodoro Ramos Blanco makes another interesting beginning in the stimulating influence that has emanated from these shows. Its logical extension will certainly bring together the little known but increasing contemporary art work of the native African. I have no doubt that each segment of Negro expression will show more in common with its own immediate art background; but the question of distinctive racial idiom or aptitude is purely theoretical and academic until such broad scale comparisons can actually be made.

In last analysis we should not expect art to answer or solve our sociological or anthropological questions. We must judge, create and consume it largely in terms of its universal values. But no art idiom, however universal, grows in a cultural vacuum; each, however great, always has some rootage and flavor of a particular soil and personality. And just as it has been a critical necessity to foster the development of a national character in the American art of our time, by the very same logic and often by the very same means, it has been reasonable and necessary to promote and quicken the racial motive and inspiration of the hitherto isolated and disparaged Negro artist. The day may soon come, however, when he will need no special encouragement and no particular apologetic brief. It is good both for him and for American art that he is so rapidly reaching maturity.

ROMARE BEARDEN

THE NEGRO ARTIST AND MODERN ART

FOR THE MOMENT, let us look back into the beginnings of modern art. It is really nothing new, merely an expression projected through new forms, more akin to the spirit of the times. Fundamentally the artist is influenced by the age in which he lives. Then for the artist to express an age that is characterized by machinery, skyscrapers, radios, and the generally quickened cadences of modern life, it follows naturally that he will break from many of the outmoded academic practices of the past. In fact every great movement that has changed the ideals and customs of life, has occasioned a change in the accepted expression of that age.

Modern art has passed through many different stages. There have been the periods of the Impressionists, the Post Impressionists, the Cubists, the Futurists, and hosts of other movements of lesser importance. Even though the use of these forms is on the decline, the impression they made in art circles is still evident. They are commendable in the fact that they substituted for mere photographic realism, a search for inner truths.

Modern art has borrowed heavily from Negro sculpture. This form of African art had been done hundreds of years ago by primitive people. It was unearthed by archaeologists and brought to the continent. During the past twenty-five years it has enjoyed a deserved recognition among art lovers. Artists have been amazed at the fine surface qualities of the sculpture, the vitality of the work, and the unsurpassed ability of the artists to create such significant forms. Of great importance has been the fact that the African would distort his figures, if by so doing he could achieve a more expressive form. This is one of the cardinal principles of the modern artist.

It is interesting to contrast the bold way in which the African sculptor approached his work, with the timidity of the Negro artist of today. His work is at best hackneyed and uninspired, and only mere rehashings from the work of any artist that might have influenced him. They have looked at nothing with their own eyes— seemingly content to use borrowed forms. They have evolved nothing original or native like the spiritual, or jazz music.

Many of the Negro artists argue that it is almost impossible for them to evolve such a sculpture. They say that since the Negro is becoming so amalgamated with the white race, and has accepted the white man's civilization he must progress along those lines. Even if this is true, they are certainly not taking advantage of the Negro scene. The Negro in his various environments in America, holds a great variety of rich experiences for the genuine artists. One can imagine what men like Daumier, Grosz, and Cruickshanks might have done with a locale like Harlem, with all its vitality and tempo. Instead of the Negro artist will proudly exhibit his "Scandinavian Landscape," a locale that is entirely alien to him. This will of course impress the uninitiated, who through some feeling of inferiority toward their own subject matter, only require that a work of art have some sort of foreign stamp to make it acceptable.

I admit that at the present time it is almost impossible for the Negro artist not to be influenced by the work of other men. Practically all the great artists have accepted the influence of others. But the difference lies in the fact that the artist with vision, sees his material, chooses, changes, and by integrating what he has learned with his own experiences, finally molds something distinctly personal. Two of the foremost artists of today are the Mexicans, Rivera and Orozco. If we study the work of these two men, it is evident that they were influenced by the continental masters. Nevertheless their art is highly original, and steeped in the tradition and environment of Mexico. It might be noted here that the best work of these men was done in Mexico, of Mexican subject matter. It is not necessary for the artist to go to foreign surroundings in order to secure material for his artistic expression. Rembrandt painted the ordinary Dutch people about him, but he presented human emotions in such a way that their appeal was universal.

Several other factors hinder the development of the Negro artist. First, we have no valid standard of criticism; secondly, foundations and societies which supposedly encourage Negro artists really hinder them; thirdly, the Negro artist has no definite ideology or social philosophy.

Art should be understood and loved by the people. It should

arouse and stimulate their creative impulses. Such is the role of art, and this in itself constitutes one of the Negro artist's chief problems. The best art has been produced in those countries where the public most loved and cherished it. In the days of the Renaissance the towns-folk would often hold huge parades to celebrate an artist's successful completion of a painting. We need some standard of criticism then, not only to stimulate the artist, but also to raise the cultural level of the people. It is well known that the critical writings of men like Herder, Schlegel, Taine, and the system of Marxian dialectics, were as important to the development of literature as any writer.

I am not sure just what form this system of criticism will take, but I am sure that the Negro artist will have to revise his conception of art. No one can doubt that the Negro is possessed of remarkable gifts of imagination and intuition. When he has learned to harness his great gifts of rythmn and pours it into his art—his chance of creating something individual will be heightened. At present it seems that by a slow study of rules and formulas the Negro artist is attempting to do something with his intellect, which he has not felt emotionally. In consequence he has given us poor echoes of the work of white artists—and nothing of himself.

It is gratifying to note that many of the white critics have realized the deficiencies of the Negro artists. I quote from a review of the last Harmon exhibition, by Malcolm Vaughan, in the New York *American:* "But in the field of painting and sculpture, they appear peculiarly backward, indeed so inept as to suggest that painting and sculpture are to them alien channels of expression." I quote from another review of the same exhibition, that appeared in the New York Times:

"Such racial aspects as may once have figured have virtually disappeared, so far as some of the work is concerned. Some of the artists, accomplished technicians, are seen to have slipped into grooves of one sort or another. There is the painter of the Cezannesque still life, there is the painter of the Gauginesque nudes, and there are those who have learned various 'dated' modernist tricks."

There are quite a few foundations that sponsor exhibitions of the work of Negro artists. However praise-worthy may have been the spirit of the founders the effect upon the Negro artist has been disastrous. Take for instance the Harmon Foundation. Its attitude from the beginning has been of a coddling and patronizing nature.

It has encouraged the artist to exhibit long before he has mastered the technical equipment of his medium. By its choice of the type of work it favors, it has allowed the Negro artist to accept standards that are both artificial and corrupt.

It is time for the Negro artist to stop making excuses for his work. If he must exhibit let it be in exhibitions of the caliber of "The Carnegie Exposition." Here among the best artists of the world his work will stand or fall according to its merits. A concrete example of the accepted attitude towards the Negro artist recently occurred in California where an exhibition coupled the work of Negro artists with that of the blind. It is obvious that in this case there is definitely created a dual standard of appraisal.

The other day I ran into a fellow with whom I had studied under George Grosz, at the "Art Students' League." I asked him how his work was coming. He told me that he had done no real work for about six months.

"You know, Howard," he said, "I sort of ran into a blind alley with my work; I felt that it definitely lacked something. This is because I didn't have anything worthwhile to say. So I stopped drawing. Now I go down to the meetings of The Marine and Industrial Workers' Union. I have entered whole-heartedly in their movement."

We talked about Orozco, who had lost his arm in the revolutionary struggle in Mexico. No wonder he depicted the persecution of the underclass Mexicans so vividly—it had all been a harrowing reality for him.

So it must be with the Negro artist—he must not be content with merely recording a scene as a machine. He must enter whole-heartedly into the situation which he wishes to convey. The artist must be the medium through which humanity expresses itself. In this sense the greatest artists have faced the realities of life, and have been profoundly social.

I don't mean by this that the Negro artist should confine himself only to such scenes as lynchings, or policemen clubbing workers. From an ordinary still life painting by such a master as Chardin we can get as penetrating an insight into eighteenth century life, as from a drawing by Hogarth of a street-walker. If it is the race question, the social struggle, or whatever else that needs expression, it is to that the artist must surrender himself. An intense, eager devotion to present day life, to study it, to help relieve it, this is the calling of the Negro artist.

ZORA NEALE HURSTON

WHEN LANGSTON HUGHES DECLARED in "The Negro Artist and the Racial Mountain" that the younger artists were determined to "express our individual dark-skinned selves without fear or shame," he might have had Zora Neale Hurston in mind. Hurston was a brilliant student at Howard, Barnard, and Columbia. Another of Charles Johnson's protégées, she became Fannie Hurst's secretary and traveling companion (serving as a rich source for Hurst's stereotypical characters in Imitation of Life) while at Barnard. She pursued graduate studies in anthropology under Franz Boas with such promise that she seemed bound for a professional career. Although an opportunist and something of a chameleon, she remained psychologically anchored in her rural, peasant past. She was easy in her skin, whether she was attending a Harlem rent party, an Urban League benefit, sitting devotedly at the feet of "Godmother," or studying voodoo practices in Louisiana. Her first novel, Jonah's Gourd Vine (1934), like her play Color Struck and her prize-winning short stories "Spunk" and "Sweat," showcased husky men, rambunctious women, and southern mores distinctly at odds with Talented Tenth values. These following excerpts from Dust Tracks on a Road, her autobiography, follow Hurston from Eatonville, Florida, to Washington, Manhattan, Harlem, and success as a novelist.

FROM DUST TRACKS ON A ROAD

NOW AS EVERYONE KNOWS, Howard University is the capstone of Negro education in the world. There gather Negro money, beauty, and prestige. It is to the Negro what Harvard is to the whites. They say the same thing about a Howard man that they do about Harvard—you can tell a Howard man as far as you can see him, but you can't tell him much. He listens to the doings of other Negro schools and their graduates with bored tolerance. Not only is the scholastic rating at Howard high, but tea is poured in the manner!

I had heard all about the swank fraternities and sororities and the clothes and everything, and I knew I could never make it. I told Mae that.

"You can come and live at our house, Zora," Bernice offered. At the time, her parents were living in Washington, and Bernice and Gwendolyn were in the boarding department at Morgan. "I'll ask Mama the next time she comes over. Then you won't have any room and board to pay. We'll all get together and rustle you up a job to make your tuition."

So that summer I moved on to Washington and got a job. First, as a waitress in the exclusive Cosmos Club downtown, and later as a manicurist in the G Street shop of Mr. George Robinson. He is a Negro who has a chain of white barber shops in downtown Washington. I managed to scrape together money for my first quarter's tuition, and went up to register.

Lo and behold, there was Dwight Holmes sitting up there at Howard! He saved my spirits again. I was short of money, and Morgan did not have the class-A rating that it now has. There was trouble for me and I was just about to give up and call it a day when I had a talk with Dwight Holmes. He encouraged me all he could, and so I stuck and made up all of those hours I needed.

I shall never forget my first college assembly, sitting there in the chapel of that great university. I was so exalted that I said to the spirit of Howard, "You have taken me in. I am a tiny bit of your greatness. I swear to you that I shall never make you ashamed of me."

It did not wear off. Every time I sat there as part and parcel of things, looking up there at the platform crowded with faculty members, the music, the hundreds of students about me, it would come down on me again. When on Mondays we ended the service by singing Alma Mater, I felt just as if it were the Star Spangled Banner:

> Reared against the eastern sky
> Proudly there on hill-top high

Up above the lake so blue
Stands Old Howard brave and true.
There she stands for truth and right,
Sending forth her rays of light,
Clad in robes of majesty
Old Howard! We sing of thee.

My soul stood on tiptoe and stretched up to take in all that it meant. So I was careful to do my classwork and be worthy to stand there under the shadow of the hovering spirit of Howard. I felt the ladder under my feet.

Mr. Robinson arranged for me to come to work at 3:30 every afternoon and work until 8:30. In that way, I was able to support myself. Soon, most of the customers knew I was a student, and tipped me accordingly. I averaged twelve to fifteen dollars a week.

Mr. Robinson's 1410 G Street shop was frequented by bankers, Senators, Cabinet Members, Congressmen, and gentlemen of the Press. The National Press Club was one block down the same street, the Treasury Building was one block up the street and the White House not far away.

I learned things from holding the hands of men like that. The talk was of world affairs, national happenings, personalities, the latest quips from the cloakrooms of Congress and such things. I heard many things from the White House and the Senate before they appeared in print. They probably were bursting to talk to somebody, and I was safe. If I told, nobody would have believed me anyway. Besides, I was much flattered by being told and warned not to repeat what I had heard. Sometimes a Senator, a banker, a newspaper correspondent attached to the White House would all be sitting around my table at one time. While I worked on one, the others waited, and they all talked. Sometimes they concentrated on teasing me. At other times they talked about what had happened, or what they reasoned was bound to happen. Intimate stories about personalities, their secret love affairs, cloakroom retorts, and the like. Soon they took me for granted and would say, "Zora knows how to keep a secret. She's all right." Now, I know that my discretion really didn't matter. They were relieving their pent-up feelings where it could do no harm.

Some of them meant more to me than others because they paid me more attention. Frederick William Wile, White House correspondent, used to talk to me at times quite seriously about life and opportunities and things like that. He had seen three presidents come and go. He had traveled with them, to say nothing of his other traveling to and fro upon the earth. He had read extensively. Sometimes he would be full of stories and cracks, but at other times he would talk to me quite seriously about attitudes, points of view, why one man was great and another a mere facile politician, and so on.

There were other prominent members of the press who would sit and talk longer than it took me to do their hands. One of them, knowing that certain others sat around and talked, wrote out questions two or three times for me to ask and tell him what was said. Each time the questions were answered, but I was told to keep that under my hat, and so I had to turn around and lie and say the man didn't tell me. I never realized how serious it was until he offered me twenty-five dollars to ask a certain Southern Congressman something and let him know as quickly as possible. He sent out and bought me a quart of French ice cream to bind the bargain. The man came in on his regular time, which was next day, and in his soft voice, began to tell me how important it was to be honorable at all times and to be trustworthy. How could I ask him then? Besides, he was an excellent Greek scholar and translated my entire lesson for me, which was from Xenophon's *Cyropædeia*, and talked at length on the ancient Greeks and Persians. The news man was all right. He had to get his information the best way he could, but, for me, it would have been terrible to do that nice man like that. I told the reporter how it was and he understood and never asked me again.

Mr. Johns, a pressman, big, slow, with his eternal walking-stick, was always looking for a laugh. Logan, our head-porter, was his regular meat. Logan had a long head, so flat on each side that it looked like it had been pressed between two planks. His toes turned in and his answers were funny.

One day, while shining Mr. Johns's shoes, he told him what a fighter he was. He really was tough when he got mad, according to himself. According to Logan, Logan was mean! Just couldn't help it. He had Indian blood in him. Just mean and strong. When he straightened out his African soup-bone (arm), something was just bound to fall. If a man didn't fall when *he* hit him, he went around behind him to see what was propping him up. Yassuh! Mr. Johns listened at Logan and smiled. He egged him on to tell more of his powers. The very next day Mr. Johns came in and announced that they had a bear up at Keith's theater, and they needed somebody to wrestle with him. There was good money in it for the man who would come right forward and wrestle with that bear, and knowing that Logan needed money and that he was fearless, he had put Logan's name down. He liked Logan too well to let him get cheated out of such a swell chance to get rich and famous. All Logan needed to do was to go to the theater and tell them that Mr. Johns sent him.

"Naw sir, Mr. Johns," Logan said, "I ain't wrestling no bear. Naw sir!"

"But Logan, you told me—everybody in here heard you—that when you get mad, you go bear-hunting with your fist. You don't even have to hunt this bear. He's right up there on the corner waiting for you. You can't let me down like this. I've already told the man you would be glad to wrestle his old bear!"

"How big is dat bear, Mister Johns?"

"Oh, he is just a full-grown bear, Logan. Nothing to worry about at all. He wouldn't weigh more than two hundred pounds at the outside. Soft snap for a man like you, and you weigh about that yourself, Logan."

"Naw sir! Not no big bear like that. Naw sir!"

"Well, Logan, what kind of a bear would you consider? You just tell me, and I'll fix it up with the man."

"Git me a little bitty baby bear, Mr. Johns, 'bout three months old. Dats de kind of bear I wants to wrestle wid. Yassuh!"

An incident happened that made me realize how theories go by the board when a person's livelihood is threatened. A man, a Negro, came into the shop one afternoon and sank down in Banks's chair. Banks was the manager and had the first chair by the door. It was so surprising that for a minute Banks just looked at him and never said a word. Finally, he found his tongue and asked, "What do you want?"

"Hair-cut and shave," the man said belligerently.

"But you can't get no hair-cut and shave here. Mr. Robinson has a fine shop for Negroes on U Street near Fifteenth," Banks told him.

"I know it, but I want one here. The Constitution of the United States—"

But by that time, Banks had him by the arm. Not roughly but he was helping him out of his chair, nevertheless.

"I don't know how to cut your hair," Banks objected. "I was trained on straight hair. Nobody in here knows how."

"Oh, don't hand me that stuff!" the crusader snarled. "Don't be such an Uncle Tom."

"Run on, fellow. You can't get waited on in here."

"I'll stay right here until I do. I know my rights. Things like this have got to be broken up. I'll get waited on all right, or sue the place."

"Go ahead and sue," Banks retorted. "Go on uptown, and get your hair cut, man. Don't be so hardheaded for nothing."

"I'm getting waited on right here!"

"You're next, Mr. Powell," Banks said to a waiting customer. "Sorry, mister, but you better go on uptown."

"But I have a right to be waited on wherever I please," the Negro said, and started towards Updyke's chair which was being emptied. Updyke whirled his chair around so that he could not sit down and stepped in front of it. "Don't you touch *my* chair!" Updyke glared. "Go on about your business."

But instead of going, he made to get into the chair by force.

"Don't argue with him! Throw him out of here!" somebody in the back cried. And in a minute, barbers, customers all lathered and hair half cut, and porters, were all helping to throw the Negro out.

The rush carried him way out into the middle of G Street and flung him down. He tried to lie there and be a martyr, but the roar of oncoming cars made him jump up and scurry off. We never heard any more about it. I did not participate in the mêlée, but I wanted him thrown out, too. My business was threatened.

It was only that night in bed that I analyzed the whole thing and realized that I was giving sanction to Jim Crow, which theoretically, I was supposed to resist. But here were ten Negro barbers, three porters and two manicurists all stirred up at the threat of our living through loss of patronage. Nobody thought it out at the moment. It was an instinctive thing. That was the first time it was called to my attention that self-interest rides over all sorts of lines. I have seen the same thing happen hundreds of times since, and now I understand it. One sees it breaking over racial, national, religious and class lines. Anglo-Saxon against Anglo-Saxon, Jew against Jew, Negro against Negro, and all sorts of combinations of the three against other combinations of the three. Offhand, you might say that we fifteen Negroes should have felt the racial thing and served him. He was one of us. Perhaps it would have been a beautiful thing if Banks had turned to the shop crowded with customers and announced that this man was going to be served like everybody else even at the risk of losing their patronage, with all of the other employees lined up in the center of the floor shouting, "So say we all!" It would have been a stirring gesture, and made the headlines for a day. Then we could all have gone home to our unpaid rents and bills and things like that. I could leave school and begin my wanderings again. The "militant" Negro who would have been the cause of it all, would have perched on the smuddled-up wreck of things and crowed. Nobody ever found out who or what he was. Perhaps he did what he did on the spur of the moment, not realizing that serving him would have ruined Mr. Robinson, another Negro who had got what he had the hard way. For not only would the G Street shop have been forced to close, but the F Street shop and all of his other six downtown shops. Wrecking George Robinson like that on a "race" angle would have been ironic tragedy. He always helped out any Negro who was trying to do anything progressive as far as he was able. He had no education himself, but he was for it. He would give any Howard University student a job in his shops if they could qualify, even if it was only a few hours a week.

So I do not know what was the ultimate right in this case. I do know how I felt at the time. There is always something fiendish and loathsome about a person who threatens to deprive you of your way of making a living. That is just human-like, I reckon.

At the University, I got on well both in class-work and the matter of making friends. I could take in but so many social affairs because I had to work, and then I had to study my lessons after work hours at night, and I was carrying a heavy program.

The teacher who most influenced me was Dr. Lorenzo Dow Turner, head of the English department. He was tall, lean, with a head of wavy black hair above his thin, æsthetic, tan-colored face. He was a Harvard man and knew his subject. His delivery was soft and restrained. The fact that he looked to be in his late twenties or early thirties at most made the girls conscious of shiny noses before they entered his classroom.

Listening to him, I decided that I must be an English teacher and lean over my desk and discourse on the eighteenth-century poets, and explain the roots of the modern novel. Children just getting born were going to hear about Addison, Poe, DeQuincey, Steele, Coleridge, Keats and Shelley from me, leaning nonchalantly over my desk. Defoe, Burns, Swift, Milton and Scott were going to be sympathetically, but adequately explained, with just that suspicion of a smile now and then before I returned to my notes.

The man who seemed to me to be most overpowering was E. C. Williams, Librarian and head of the Romance Language department. He was cosmopolitan and world-traveled. His wit was instant and subtle. He was so inaccessible in a way, too. He told me once that a flirtation with a co-ed was to him like playing with a teething-ring. He liked smart, sophisticated women. He used to lunch every day with E. D. Davis, head of the Greek and German department. Davis was just the antithesis of Williams, so shy, in the Charles S. Johnson manner, in spite of his erudition. They would invite me to come along and would pay for my milk and pie. Williams did most of the talking. I put in something now and then. Davis sat and smiled. Professor Williams egged me on to kiss him. He said that Davis would throw a fit, and he wanted to be present to see it. He whispered that Davis liked to have me around, but from what he ever said, I couldn't notice. When I was sick, Professor Davis came to see me and brought an arm-load of roses, but he sat there half an hour and scarcely said a word. He just sat there and smiled now and then.

All in all, I did a year and a half of work at Howard University. I would have done the two full years, but I was out on account of illness, and by the time that was over, I did not have the money for my tuition.

I joined the Zeta Phi Beta Sorority, took part in all the literary activities on the campus, and made The Stylus, the small literary society on the hill. I named the student paper *The Hill Top*. The Stylus was limited to nineteen members, two of them being faculty members. Dr. Alain Leroy Locke was the presiding genius and we had very interesting meetings.

My joining The Stylus influenced my later moves. On account of a short story which I wrote for The Stylus, Charles S. Johnson, who was just then founding *Opportunity Magazine,* wrote to me for material. He explained that he was writing to all of the Negro colleges with the idea of introducing new writers and new material to the public. I sent on *Drenched in Light* and he published it. Later, he published my second story *Spunk*. He wrote me a kind letter and said something about New York. So, beginning to feel the urge to write, I wanted to be in New York.

This move on the part of Dr. Johnson was the root of the so-called Negro Renaissance. It was his work, and only his hush-mouth nature has caused it to be attributed to many others. The success of *Opportunity* Award dinners was news. Later on, the best of this material was collected in a book called *The New Negro* and edited by Dr. Alain Locke, but it was the same material, for the most part, gathered and published by Dr. Charles Spurgeon Johnson, now of the Department of Social Sciences, Fisk University, Nashville.

Being out of school for lack of funds, and wanting to be in New York, I decided to go there and try to get back in school in that city. So the first week of January, 1925, found me in New York with $1.50, no job, no friends, and a lot of hope.

The Charles Johnsons befriended me as best they could. I could always find something to eat out at their house. Mrs. Johnson would give me carfare and encouragement. I came to worship them really.

So I came to New York through *Opportunity,* and through *Opportunity* to Barnard. I won a prize for a short story at the first Award dinner, May 1, 1925, and Fannie Hurst offered me a job as her secretary, and Annie Nathan Meyer offered to get me a scholarship to Barnard. My record was good enough, and I entered Barnard in the fall, graduating in 1928.

I have no lurid tales to tell of race discrimination at Barnard. I made a few friends in the first few days. Eleanor Beer, who lived on the next chair to me in Economics, was the first. She was a New York girl with a sumptuous home down in West 71st Street, near the Hudson. She invited me down often, and her mother set out to brush me up on good manners. I learned a lot of things from them. They were well traveled and cosmopolitan. I found out about forks, who entered a room first, sat down first, and who offered to shake hands. A great deal more of material like that. These people are still lying very close to my heart. I was invited to Eleanor's wedding when she married Enzo de Chetalat, a Swiss mining engineer, but I was down in Florida at the time. So I sent her a hat-box full of orange blossoms for the occasion, so she could know how I felt.

The Social Register crowd at Barnard soon took me up, and I became Barnard's sacred black cow. If you had not had lunch with me, you had not shot from taw. I was secretary to Fannie Hurst and living at her 67th Street duplex apartment, so things were going very well with me.

Because my work was top-heavy with English, Political Science, History and Geology, my adviser at Barnard recommended Fine Arts, Economics, and Anthropology for cultural reasons. I started in under Dr. Gladys Reichard, had a term paper called to the attention of Dr. Franz Boas and thereby gave up my dream of leaning over a desk and explaining Addison and Steele to the sprouting generations.

I began to treasure up the words of Dr. Reichard, Dr. Ruth Benedict, and Dr. Boas, the king of kings.

That man can make people work the hardest with just a look or a word, than anyone else in creation. He is idolized by everybody who takes his orders. We all call him Papa, too. One day, I burst into his office and asked for "Papa Franz" and his secretary gave me a look and told me I had better not let him hear me say that. Of course, I knew better, but at a social gathering of the Department of Anthropology at his house a few nights later, I brought it up.

"Of course, Zora is my daughter. Certainly!" he said with a smile. "Just one of my missteps, that's all." The sabre cut on his cheek, which it is said he got in a duel at Heidelberg, lifted in a smile.

Away from his office, Dr. Boas is full of youth and fun, and abhors dull, stodgy arguments. Get to the point is his idea. Don't raise a point which you cannot defend. He wants facts, not guesses, and he can pin you down so expertly that you soon lose the habit of talking all over your face. Either that, or you leave off Anthropology.

I had the same feeling at Barnard that I did at Howard, only more so. I felt that I was highly privileged and determined to make the most of it. I did not resolve to be a grind, however, to show the white folks that I had brains. I took it for granted that they knew that. Else, why was I at Barnard? Not everyone who cries, "Lord! Lord!" can enter those sacred iron gates. In her high scholastic standards, equipment, the quality of her student-body and graduates, Barnard has a right to the first line of Alma Mater. "Beside the waters of the Hudson, Our Alma Mater stands serene!" Dean Gildersleeve has that certain touch. We know there are women's colleges that are older, but not better ones.

So I set out to maintain a good average, take part in whatever went on, and just be a part of the college like everybody else. I graduated with a *B* record, and I am entirely satisfied.

Mrs. Meyer, who was the moving spirit in founding the college and who is still a trustee, did nobly by me in getting me in. No matter what I might do for her, I would still be in her debt.

Two weeks before I graduated from Barnard, Dr. Boas sent

for me and told me that he had arranged a fellowship for me. I was to go south and collect Negro folklore. Shortly before that, I had been admitted to the American Folk-Lore Society. Later, while I was in the field, I was invited to become a member of the American Ethnological Society, and shortly after the American Anthropological Society.

Booker T. Washington said once that you must not judge a man by the heights to which he has risen, but by the depths from which he came. So to me these honors meant something, insignificant as they might appear to the world. It was a long step for the waif of Eatonville. From the depth of my inner heart I appreciated the fact that the world had not been altogether unkind to Mama's child.

While in the field, I drove to Memphis, and had a beautiful reconciliation with Bob, my oldest brother, and his family. We had not seen each other since I ran off to be a lady's maid. He said that it had taken him a long time to realize what I was getting at. He regretted deeply that he had not been of more service to me on the way. My father had been killed in an automobile accident during my first year at Morgan, and Bob talked to me about his last days. In reality, my father was the baby of the family. With my mother gone and nobody to guide him, life had not hurt him, but it had turned him loose to hurt himself. He had been miserable over the dispersion of his children when he came to realize that it was so. We were all so sorry for him, instead of feeling bitter as might have been expected. Old Maker had left out the steering gear when He gave Papa his talents.

In Memphis, my brother Ben was doing well as a pharmacist and owner of the East Memphis Drug Store. Between his dogs, his wife, his store, and his car, he was quite the laughing, witty person and I was glad that he was. We talked about Clifford Joel, who had become, and still is, principal of the Negro High School in Decatur, Alabama, and I told him about seeing John in Jacksonville, Florida, where he was doing well with his market. I had the latest news for them on Everett, Mama's baby child, in the Post Office in Brooklyn, New York. Dick, the lovable, the irresponsible, was having a high-heel time up and down the east coast of the United States. He had never cared about school, but he had developed into a chef cook and could always take care of himself. Sarah was struggling along with a husband for whom we all wished a short sickness and a quick funeral.

It was a most happy interval for me. I drove back to New Orleans to my work in a glowing aura. I felt the warm embrace of kin and kind for the first time since the night after my mother's funeral, when we had huddled about the organ all sodden and bewildered, with the walls of our home suddenly blown down. On September 18th, that house had been a hovering home. September 19th, it had turned into a bleak place of desolation with unknown dangers creeping upon us from unseen quarters that made of us a whimpering huddle, though then we could not see why. But now, that was all over. We could touch each other in the spirit if not in the flesh.

While I was in the research field in 1929, the idea of "Jonah's Gourd Vine" came to me. I had written a few short stories, but the idea of attempting a book seemed so big, that I gazed at it in the quiet of the night, but hid it away from even myself in daylight.

For one thing, it seemed off-key. What I wanted to tell was a story about a man, and from what I had read and heard, Negroes were supposed to write about the Race Problem. I was and am thoroughly sick of the subject. My interest lies in what makes a man or a woman do such-and-so, regardless of his color. It seemed to me that the human beings I met reacted pretty much the same to the same stimuli. Different idioms, yes. Circumstances and conditions having power to influence, yes. Inherent difference, no. But I said to myself that that was not what was expected of me, so I was afraid to tell a story the way I wanted, or rather the way the story told itself to me. So I went on that way for three years.

Something else held my attention for a while. As I told you before, I had been pitched head-foremost into the Baptist Church when I was born. I had heard the singing, the preaching and the prayers. They were a part of me. But on the concert stage, I always heard songs called spirituals sung and applauded as Negro music, and I wondered what would happen if a white audience ever heard a real spiritual. To me, what the Negroes did in Macedonia Baptist Church was finer than anything that any trained composer had done to the folk-songs.

I had collected a mass of work-songs, blues and spirituals in the course of my years of research. After offering them to two Negro composers and having them refused on the ground that white audiences would not listen to anything but highly arranged spirituals, I decided to see if that was true. I doubted it because I had seen groups of white people in my father's church as early as I could remember. They had come to hear the singing, and certainly there was no distinguished composer in Zion Hope Baptist Church. The congregation just got hold of the tune and arranged as they went along as the spirit moved them. And any musician, I don't care if he stayed at a conservatory until his teeth were gone and he smelled like old-folks, could never even approach what those untrained singers could do. LET THE PEOPLE SING, was and is my motto, and finally I resolved to see what would happen.

So on money I had borrowed, I put on a show at the John Golden Theater on January 10, 1932, and tried out my theory. The performance was well received by both the audience and the critics. Because I know that music without motion is not natural with my people, I did not have the singers stand in a stiff group and reach for the high note. I told them to just imagine that they were in Macedonia and go ahead. One critic said that he did not believe that the concert was rehearsed, it looked so natural. I had dramatized a working day on a railroad camp, from the shack-rouser waking up the camp at dawn until the primitive dance in the deep woods at night.

While I did not lose any money, I did not make much. But I am satisfied that I proved my point. I have seen the effects of that concert in all the Negro singing groups since then. Primitive Negro dancing has been given tremendous impetus. Work-songs have taken on. In that performance I introduced West Indian songs and dances and they have come to take an important place in America. I am not upset by the fact that others have made something out of the things I pointed out. Rather I am glad if I have called any beauty to the attention of those who can use it.

In May, 1932, the depression did away with money for research so far as I was concerned. So I took my nerve in my hand and decided to try to write the story I had been carrying around in me. Back in my native village, I wrote first "Mules and Men." That is, I edited the huge mass of material I had, arranged it in some sequence and laid it aside. It was published after my first novel. Mr. Robert Wunsch and Dr. John Rice were both on the faculty at Rollins College, at Winter Park, which is three miles from Eatonville. Dr. Edwin Osgood Grover, Dr. Hamilton Holt, President of Rollins, together with Rice and Wunsch, were interested in me. I gave three folk concerts at the college under their urging.

Then I wrote a short story, "The Gilded Six-Bits," which Bob Wunsch read to his class in creative writing before he sent it off to *Story Magazine*. Thus I came to know Martha Foley and her husband, Whit Burnett, the editors of *Story*. They bought the story and it was published in the August issue, 1933. They never told me, but it is my belief that they did some missionary work among publishers in my behalf, because four publishers wrote me and asked if I had anything of book-length. One of the editors of the J. B. Lippincott Company was among these. He wrote a gentle-like letter and so I was not afraid of him. Exposing my efforts did not seem so rash to me after reading his letter. I wrote him and said that I was writing a book. Mind you, not the first word was on paper when I wrote him that letter. But the very next week I moved up to Sanford where I was not so much at home as at Eatonville, and could concentrate more and sat down to write "Jonah's Gourd Vine."

I rented a house with a bed and stove in it for $1.50 a week. I paid two weeks and then my money ran out. My cousin, Willie Lee Hurston, was working and making $3.50 per week, and she always gave me the fifty cents to buy groceries with. In about three months, I finished the book. The problem of getting it typed was then upon me. Municipal Judge S. A. B. Wilkinson asked his secretary, Mildred Knight, if she would not do it for me and wait on the money. I explained to her that the book might not even be taken by Lippincott. I had been working on a hope. She took the manuscript home with her and read it. Then she offered to type it for me. She said, "It is going to be accepted, all right. I'll type it. Even if the first publisher does not take it, somebody will." So between them, they bought the paper and carbon and the book was typed.

I took it down to the American Express office to mail it and found that it cost $1.83 cents to mail, and I did not have it. So I went to see Mrs. John Leonardi, a most capable woman lawyer, and wife of the County Prosecutor. She did not have the money at the moment, but she was the treasurer of the local Daughter Elks. She "borrowed" $2.00 from the treasury and gave it to me to mail my book. That was on October 3, 1933. On October 16th, I had an acceptance by wire.

CLAUDE MCKAY

CLAUDE MCKAY HAD NO EQUAL *as a poet except Langston Hughes. His novels were not especially well crafted, but they were searingly realistic in the mold of Zola, presenting the world of beach bums, studs, women of easy virtue, and frugal Pullman porters—and no white people or distinguished leaders of the race at all.* Home to Harlem *(1928), the first best-seller by an African American novelist, was a fulfillment of Hughes's manifesto and of the aesthetic credo of the Renaissance group around Wallace Thurman and Richard Bruce Nugent that had produced* Fire!!, *the socially and sexually shocking magazine whose one issue appeared in 1926. McKay was a Renaissance sojourner, in it but not of it, an acid critic of the Talented Tenth orchestrators of the New Negro Arts Movement and of the movement's bourgeois goals. A Jamaican descended from a line of prosperous peasant property holders, McKay experienced and reciprocated the condescension many black Americans of that time visited upon West Indians.*

Harlem Shadows *(1922), McKay's first book of poetry, was one of the catalysts of the Renaissance. Like Jean Toomer, McKay had made his literary debut in Greenwich Village's Bohemia, where he became co-editor, with Michael Gold, of* Liberator *magazine and the confidant of Max and Crystal Eastman. Eventually disenchanted with both white and black artistic and intellectual circles in America, McKay spent the years 1922 to 1934 wandering from Russia through France and Spain to North Africa. These two excerpts from his autobiography,* A Long Way from Home, *offer a range of acidulous, incisive assessments of the Harlem Renaissance from various compass points and psychological distances.*

FROM *A LONG WAY FROM HOME*

THE HARLEM INTELLIGENTSIA

I HAD DEPARTED from America just after achieving some notoriety as a poet, and before I had become acquainted with the Negro intellectuals. When I got the job of assistant editor on *The Liberator,* Hubert Harrison, the Harlem streetcorner lecturer and agitator, came down to Fourteenth Street to offer his congratulations.

I introduced him to Robert Minor, who was interested in the activities of the advanced Negro radicals. Harrison suggested a little meeting that would include the rest of the black Reds. It was arranged to take place at the *Liberator* office, and besides Harrison there were Grace Campbell, one of the pioneer Negro members of the Socialist Party; Richard Moore and W. A. Domingo, who edited *The Emancipator,* a radical Harlem weekly; Cyril Briggs, the founder of the African Blood Brotherhood and editor of the monthly magazine, *The Crusader;* Mr. Fanning, who owned the only Negro cigar store in Harlem; and one Otto Huiswood, who hailed from Curaçao, the birthplace of Daniel Deleon. Perhaps there were others whom I don't remember. The real object of the meeting, I think, was to discuss the possibility of making the Garvey Back-to-Africa Movement (officially called the Universal Negro Improvement Association) more class-conscious.

I remember that just as we ended our discussion, Max Eastman unexpectedly popped in to see how the *Liberator* office was running. Jokingly he said: "Ah, you conspirators," and everybody laughed except Robert Minor. Minor had recently renounced his anarchism for Communism and he was as austere-looking as a gaunt Spanish priest.

It was interesting to meet also some of the more conservative Negro leaders, such as the officials of the National Association for the Advancement of Colored People. Dr. W. E. B. Du Bois, the author of *The Souls of Black Folk* and editor of *The Crisis,* had me to luncheon at the Civic Club. Of Dr. Du Bois I knew nothing until I came to America. It was a white woman, my English teacher at the Kansas State College, who mentioned *The Souls of Black Folk* to me, I think. I found it in the public library in Topeka. The book shook me like an earthquake. Dr Du Bois stands on a pedestal illuminated in my mind. And the light that shines there comes from my first reading of *The Souls of Black Folk* and also from the *Crisis* editorial, "Returning Soldiers," which he published when he returned from Europe in the spring of 1919.

Yet meeting Du Bois was something of a personal disappointment. He seemed possessed of a cold, acid hauteur of spirit, which is not lessened even when he vouchsafes a smile. Negroes say that Dr. Du Bois is naturally unfriendly and selfish. I did not feel any magnetism in his personality. But I do in his writings, which is more important. Du Bois is a great passionate polemic, and America should honor and exalt him even if it disagrees with his views. For his passion is genuine, and contemporary polemics is so destitute of the pure flame of passion that the nation should be proud of a man who has made of it a great art.

Walter White, the present secretary of the National Association for the Advancement of Colored People, possessed a charming personality, ingratiating as a Y. M. C. A. secretary. One felt a strange, even comic, feeling at the sound of his name and the sight of his extremely white complexion while hearing him described as a Negro.

The White stories of passing white among the crackers were delightful. To me the most delectable was one illustrating the finger-nail theory of telling a near-white from a pure-white. White was traveling on a train on his way to investigate a lynching in the South. The cracker said, "There are many yaller niggers who look white, but I can tell them every time."

"Can you really?" Walter White asked.

"Oh sure, just by looking at their finger nails." And taking White's hand, he said, "Now if you had nigger blood, it would show here on your half-moons."

That story excited me by its paradox as much as had the name and complexion of Walter White. It seemed altogether fantastic that whites in the South should call him a "nigger" and whites in the North, a Negro. It violates my feeling of words as pictures conveying color and meaning. For whenever I am in Walter White's company my eyes compose him and my emotions respond exactly as they do in the case of any friendly so-called "white" man. When a white person speaks of Walter White as a Negro, as if that made him a being physically different from a white, I get a weird and impish feeling of the unreality of phenomena. And when a colored person refers to Walter White as colored, in a tone that implies him to be physically different from and inferior to the "pure" white person, I feel that life is sublimely funny. For to me a type like Walter White is Negroid simply because he closely identifies himself with the Negro group—just as a Teuton becomes a Moslem if he embraces Islam. White is whiter than many Europeans—even biologically. I cannot see the difference in the way that most of the whites and most of the blacks seem to see it. Perhaps what is reality for them is fantasy for me.

James Weldon Johnson, song writer, poet, journalist, diplomat and professor, was my favorite among the N. A. A. C. P. officials. I liked his poise, suavity, diplomacy and gentlemanliness. His career reveals surprises of achievement and reads like a success story. When a Negro makes an honorable fight for a decent living and succeeds, I think all Negroes should feel proud. Perhaps a day will come when, under a different social set-up, competent Negroes will be summoned like other Americans to serve their country in diplomatic posts. When that time comes Negroes may proudly cite as a precedent the record of James Weldon Johnson, Negro pioneer of the American diplomatic service, who performed his duties conscientiously and efficiently under unusually difficult conditions.

Jessie Fauset was assistant editor of *The Crisis* when I met her. She very generously assisted at the Harlem evening of one of our *Liberator* prayer meetings and was the one fine feature of a bad show. She was prim, pretty and well-dressed, and talked fluently and intelligently. All the radicals liked her, although in her social viewpoint she was away over on the other side of the fence. She belonged to that closed decorous circle of Negro society, which consists of persons who live proudly like the better class of conventional whites, except that they do so on much less money. To give a concrete idea of their status one might compare them to the expropriated and defeated Russian intelligentsia in exile.

Miss Fauset has written many novels about the people in her circle. Some white and some black critics consider these people not interesting enough to write about. I think all people are interesting to write about. It depends on the writer's ability to bring them out alive. Could there be a more commendable prescription for the souls of colored Americans than the bitter black imitation of white life? Not a Fannie Hurst syrup-and-pancake hash, but the real meat.

But Miss Fauset is prim and dainty as a primrose, and her novels are quite as fastidious and precious. Primroses are pretty. I remember the primroses where I lived in Morocco, that lovely melancholy land of autumn and summer and mysterious veiled brown women. When the primroses spread themselves across the barren hillsides before the sudden summer blazed over the hot land, I often thought of Jessie Fauset and her novels.

What Mary White Ovington, the godmother of the N.A.A.C.P., thought of me was more piquant to me perhaps than to herself. Her personality radiated a quiet silver shaft of white charm which is lovely when it's real. She was gracious, almost sweet, when she dropped in on *The Liberator*. But as I listened to her talking in a gentle subjective way I realized that she was emphatic as a seal and possessed of a resolute will.

She told me about her reaction to Booker T. Washington, the officially recognized national leader of the Negroes. Miss Ovington had visited Tuskegee informally. Booker T. Washington had disregarded her, apparently under the impression that she was a poor-white social worker. When he was informed that she originated from a family of high-ups, he became obsequious to her. But she responded coldly. By her austere abolitionist standard she had already taken the measure of the universally popular and idolized Negroid leader.

I repeated the story to my friend Hubert Harrison. He exploded in his large sugary black African way, which sounded like the rustling of dry bamboo leaves agitated by the wind. Hubert Harrison had himself criticized the Negro policy of Booker T. Washington in powerful volcanic English, and subsequently, by some mysterious grapevine chicanery, he had lost his little government job. He joined the Socialist Party. He left it. And finally came to the conclusion that out of the purgatory of their own social confusion, Negroes would sooner or later have to develop their own leaders, independent of white control.

Harrison had a personal resentment against the N.A.A.C.P., and nick-named it the "National Association for the Advancement of Certain People." His sense of humor was ebony hard, and he remarked that it was exciting to think that the N.A.A.C.P. was the progeny of black snobbery and white pride, and had developed into a great organization, with Du Bois like a wasp in Booker Washington's hide until the day of his death.

And now that I was legging limpingly along with the intellectual gang, Harlem for me did not hold quite the same thrill and glamor as before. Where formerly in saloons and cabarets and along the streets I received impressions like arrows piercing my nerves and distilled poetry from them, now I was often pointed out as an author. I lost the rare feeling of a vagabond feeding upon secret music singing in me.

I was invited to meetings in Harlem. I had to sit on a platform and pretend to enjoy being introduced and praised. I had to respond pleasantly. Hubert Harrison said that I owed it to my race. Standing up like an actor to repeat my poems and kindle them with second-hand emotions. For it was not so easy to light up within me again the spontaneous flames of original creative efforts for expectant audiences. Poets and novelists should let good actors perform for them.

Once I was invited to the Harlem Eclectic Club by its president, William Service Bell. Mr. Bell was a cultivated artistic New England Negro, who personally was very nice. He was precious as a jewel. The Eclectic Club turned out in rich array to hear me: ladies and gentlemen in *tenue de rigueur*. I had no dress suit to wear, and so, a little nervous, I stood on the platform and humbly said my pieces.

What the Eclectics thought of my poems I never heard. But what they thought of me I did. They were affronted that I did not put on a dress suit to appear before them. They thought I intended to insult their elegance because I was a radical.

The idea that I am an enemy of polite Negro society is fixed in the mind of the Negro élite. But the idea is wrong. I have never had the slightest desire to insult Harlem society or Negro society anywhere, because I happen not to be of it. But ever since I had to tog myself out in a dress suit every evening when I worked as a butler, I have abhorred that damnable uniform. God only knows why it was invented. My esthetic sense must be pretty bad, for I can find no beauty in it, either for white or colored persons. I admire women in bright evening clothes. But men! Blacks in stiff-starched white façades and black uniforms like a flock of crows, imagining they are elegant—oh no!

THE NEW NEGRO IN PARIS

I FINISHED MY NATIVE HOLIDAY in Marrakesh. In Casablanca I found a huge pile of mail awaiting me. The handsomest thing was a fat envelope from a New York bank containing a gold-lettered pocket book. The pocket book enclosed my first grand from the sale of *Home to Harlem*.

There were stacks of clippings with criticisms of my novel; praise from the white press, harsh censure from the colored press. And a lot of letters from new admirers and old friends and associates and loves. One letter in particular took my attention. It was from James Weldon Johnson, inviting me to return to America to participate in the Negro renaissance movement. He promised to do his part to facilitate my return if there were any difficulty. And he did. . . .

But the resentment of the Negro intelligentsia against *Home to Harlem* was so general, bitter and violent that I was hesitant about returning to the great Black Belt. I had learned very little about the ways of the Harlem élite during the years I lived there. When I left the railroad and the companionship of the common blacks, my intellectual contacts were limited mainly to white radicals and bohemians. I was well aware that if I returned to Harlem I wouldn't be going back to the *milieu* of railroad men, from whom I had drifted far out of touch. Nor could I go back among radical whites and try to rekindle the flames of an old enthusiasm. I knew that if I did return I would have to find a new orientation among the Negro intelligentsia.

One friend in Harlem had written that Negroes were traveling abroad *en masse* that spring and summer and that the élite would be camping in Paris. I thought that it might be less unpleasant to meet the advance guard of the Negro intelligentsia in Paris. And so, laying aside my experiment in wearing bags, bournous and tarboosh, I started out. . . .

After the strong dazzling colors of Morocco, Paris that spring appeared something like the melody of larks chanting over a gray field. It was over three years since I had seen the metropolis. At that time it had a political and financial trouble hanging heavy round its neck. Now it was better, with its head up and a lot of money in every hand. I saw many copies of my book, *Banjo*, decorating a shop window in the Avenue de l'Opéra and I was disappointed in myself that I could not work up to feeling a thrill such as I imagine an author should feel.

I took a fling at the cabarets in Montparnasse and Montmartre, and I was very happy to meet again a French West Indian girl whom I knew as a *bonne* in Nice when I was a valet. We ate some good dinners together and saw the excellent French productions of

Rose Marie and *Show Boat* and danced a little at the Bal Negre and at Bricktop's Harlem hang-out in Montmartre.

I found Louise Bryant in Paris. It was our first meeting since she took my manuscript to New York in the summer of 1926. The meeting was a nerve-tearing ordeal. About two years previously she had written of a strange illness and of doctors who gave her only six months to live and of her determination to live a long time longer than that. She had undergone radical treatment. The last time I had seen her she was plump and buxom. Now she was shrunken and thin and fragile like a dried-up reed. Her pretty face had fallen like a mummy's and nothing was left of her startling attractiveness but her eyebrows.

She embarrassed me by continually saying: "Claude, you won't even look at me." Her conversation was pitched in a nervous hysterical key and the burden was "male conceit." I told her that the female was largely responsible for "male conceit." Often when I had seen her before she had been encircled by a following of admirably created young admirers of the collegiate type. Now she was always with an ugly-mugged woman. This woman was like an apparition of a male impersonator, who was never off the stage. She had a trick way of holding her shoulders and her hands like a gangster and simulating a hard-boiled accent. A witty Frenchman pronounced her a *Sappho-manqué*. The phrase sounded like a desecration of the great glamorous name of Sappho. I wondered why (there being so many attractive women in the world) Louise Bryant should have chosen such a companion. And I thought that it was probably because of the overflow of pity pouring out of her impulsive Irish heart.

I remembered "Aftermath," the beautiful poem which she sent us for publication in *The Liberator* after John Reed died. Now it seemed of greater significance:

AFTERMATH

Dear, they are singing your praises,
Now you are gone.
But only I saw your going,
I . . . alone . . . in the dawn.

Dear, they are weeping about you,
Now you are dead,

And they've placed a granite stone
Over your darling head.

I cannot cry any more,
Too burning deep is my grief . . .
I dance through my spendthrift days
Like a fallen leaf.

Faster and faster I whirl
Toward the end of my days.
Dear, I am drunken with sadness
And lost down strange ways.

If only the dance could finish
Like a flash in the sky . . . Oh, soon,
If only a storm could come shouting—
Hurl me past stars and moon.

And I thought if I could not look frankly with admiration at Louise Bryant's face, I could always turn to the permanently lovely poem which she had created.

I had spruced myself up a bit to meet the colored élite. Observing that the Madrileños were well-tailored, I had a couple of suits made in Madrid, and chose a hat there. In Paris I added shoes and shirts and ties and gloves to my wardrobe.

The cream of Harlem was in Paris. There was the full cast of *Blackbirds* (with Adelaide Hall starring in the place of Florence Mills), just as fascinating a group off the stage as they were extraordinary on the stage. The *Porgy* actors had come over from London. There was an army of school teachers and nurses. There were Negro Communists going to and returning from Russia. There were Negro students from London and Scotland and Berlin and the French universities. There were presidents and professors of the best Negro colleges. And there were painters and writers and poets, of whom the most outstanding was Countee Cullen.

I met Professor Alain Locke. He had published *The Anthology of the New Negro* in 1925 and he was the animator of the movement as well as the originator of the phrase "Negro renaissance." Commenting upon my appearance, Dr. Locke said, "Why, you are wearing the same kind of gloves as I am!" "Yes," I said, "but my hand is heavier than yours." Dr. Locke was extremely nice and invited me to dinner with President Hope of Atlanta University. The dinner was at one of the most expensive restaurants in the *grands boulevards*. President Hope, who was even more Nordic-looking than Walter White, was very affable and said I did not look like the boxer-type drawings of me which were reproduced with the reviews of *Home to Harlem*. President Hope hoped that I would visit his university when I returned to America.

There had been an interesting metamorphosis in Dr. Locke. When we met for the first time in Berlin in 1923, he took me for a promenade in the Tiergarten. And walking down the row, with the statues of the Prussian kings supported by the famous philosophers and poets and composers on either side, he remarked to me that he thought those statues the finest ideal and expression of the plastic arts in the world. The remark was amusing, for it was just a short while before that I had walked through the same row with George Grosz, who had described the statues as "the sugar-candy art of Germany." When I showed Dr. Locke George Grosz's book of drawings, *Ecce Homo*, he recoiled from their brutal realism. (Dr. Locke is a Philadelphia blue-black blood, a Rhodes scholar and graduate of Oxford University, and I have heard him described as the most refined Negro in America).

So it was interesting now to discover that Dr. Locke had become the leading Negro authority on African Negro sculpture. I felt that there was so much more affinity between the art of George Grosz and African sculpture than between the Tiergarten insipid idealization of Nordic kings and artists and the transcending realism of the African artists.

Yet I must admit that although Dr. Locke seemed a perfect symbol of the Aframerican rococo in his personality as much as in his prose style, he was doing his utmost to appreciate the new Negro that he had uncovered. He had brought the best examples of their work together in a pioneer book. But from the indication of his appreciations it was evident that he could not lead a Negro renaissance. His introductory remarks were all so weakly winding round and round and getting nowhere. Probably this results from a kink in Dr. Locke's artistic outlook, perhaps due to its effete European academic quality.

When he published his *Anthology of the New Negro*, he put in a number of my poems, including one which was originally entitled "The White House." My title was symbolic, not meaning specifically the private homes of white people, but more the vast modern edifice of American Industry from which Negroes were effectively barred as a group. I cannot convey here my amazement and chagrin when Dr. Locke arbitrarily changed the title of my poem to "White Houses" and printed it in his anthology, without consulting me. I protested against the act, calling Dr. Locke's attention to the fact that my poem had been published under the original title of "The White House" in *The Liberator*. He replied that he had changed the title for political reasons, as it might be implied that the title meant the White House in Washington, and that that could be made an issue against my returning to America.

I wrote him saying that the idea that my poem had reference to the official residence of the President of the United States was ridiculous; and that, whether I was permitted to return to America or not, I did not want the title changed, and would prefer the omission of the poem. For his title "White Houses" was misleading. It changed the whole symbolic intent and meaning of the poem, making it appear as if the burning ambition of the black malcontent was to enter white houses in general. I said that there were many white folks' houses I would not choose to enter, and that, as a fanatical advocate of personal freedom, I hoped that all human beings would always have the right to decide whom they wanted to have enter their houses.

But Dr. Locke high-handedly used his substitute title of "White Houses" in all the editions of his anthology. I couldn't imagine such a man as the leader of a renaissance, when his artistic outlook was so reactionary.

The Negroid élite was not so formidable to meet after all. The financial success of my novel had helped soften hard feelings in some quarters. A lovely lady from Harlem expressed the views of many. Said she: "Why all this nigger-row if a colored writer can exploit his own people and make money and a name? White writers have been exploiting us long enough without any credit to our race. It is silly for the Negro critics to holler to God about *Home to Harlem* as if the social life of the characters is anything like that of the respectable class of Negroes. The people in *Home to Harlem* are our low-down Negroes and we respectable Negroes ought to be proud that we are not like them and be grateful to you for giving us a real picture of Negroes whose lives we know little about on the inside." I felt completely vindicated.

My agent in Paris gave a big party for the cast of *Blackbirds*, to which the lovely lady and other members of the black élite were invited. Adelaide Hall was the animating spirit of the *Blackbirds*. They gave some exhibition numbers, and we all turned loose and had a grand gay time together, dancing and drinking champagne. The French guests (there were some chic ones) said it was the best party of the season. And in tipsy accents some of the Harlem élite admonished me against writing a *Home-to-Harlem* book about *them*.

Thus I won over most of the Negro intelligentsia in Paris, excepting the leading journalist and traveler who remained intransigent. Besides Negro news, the journalist specialized in digging up obscure and Amazing Facts for the edification of the colored people. In these "Facts" Beethoven is proved to be a Negro because he was dark and gloomy; also the Jewish people are proved to have been originally a Negro people!

The journalist was writing and working his way through Paris. Nancy Cunard's *Negro Anthology* describes him as a guide and quoted him as saying he had observed, in the flesh market of Paris, that white southerners preferred colored trade, while Negro leaders preferred white trade. Returning to New York, he gave lectures "for men only" on the peepholes in the walls of Paris.

The journalist was a bitter critic of *Home to Harlem*, declaring it was obscene. I have often wondered if it is possible to establish a really intelligent standard to determine obscenity—a standard by which one could actually measure the obscene act and define the obscene thought. I have done lots of menial work and have no snobbery about common labor. I remember that in Marseilles and other places in Europe I was sometimes approached and offered a considerable remuneration to act as a guide or procurer or do other sordid things. While I was working as a model in Paris a handsome Italian model brought me an offer to work as an occasional attendant in a special *bains de vapeur*. The Italian said that he made good extra money working there. Now, although I needed more money to live, it was impossible for me to make myself do such things. The French say "*On fait ce qu'on peut.*" I could not. The very idea of the thing turned me dead cold. My individual morale was all I possessed. I felt that if I sacrificed it to make a little extra money, I would become personally obscene. I would soon be utterly unable to make that easy money. I preferred a menial job.

Yet I don't think I would call another man obscene who could do what I was asked to do without having any personal feeling of revulsion against it. And if an artistic person had or was familiar with such sordid experiences of life and could transmute them into literary or any other art form, I could not imagine that his performance or his thought was obscene.

The Negro journalist argued violently against me. He insisted that I had exploited Negroes to please the white reading public. He said that the white public would not read good Negro books because of race prejudice; that he himself had written a "good" book which had not sold. I said that Negro writers, instead of indulging in whining and self-pity, should aim at reaching the reading public in general or creating a special Negro public; that Negroes had plenty of money to spend on books if books were sold to them.

I said I knew the chances for a black writer and a white writer were not equal, even if both were of the same caliber. The white writer had certain avenues, social and financial, which opened to carry him along to success, avenues which were closed to the black. Nevertheless I believed that the Negro writer also had a chance, even though a limited one, with the great American reading public. I thought that if a Negro writer were sincere in creating a plausible Negro tale—if a Negro character were made credible and human in his special environment with a little of the virtues and the vices that are common to the human species—he would obtain some recognition and appreciation. For Negro writers are not alone in competing with heavy handicaps. They have allies among some of the white writers and artists, who are fighting formalism and classicism, crusading for new forms and ideas against the dead weight of the old.

But the journalist was loudly positive that it was easy for a Negro writer to make a sensational success as a writer by "betraying" his race to the white public. So many of the Negro elite love to mouth that phrase about "betraying the race"! As if the Negro group had special secrets which should not be divulged to the other groups. I said I did not think the Negro could be betrayed by any real work of art. If the Negro were betrayed in any place it was perhaps in that Negro press, by which the journalist was syndicated, with its voracious black appetite for yellow journalism.

Thereupon the journalist declared that he would prove that it was easy for a Negro to write the "nigger stuff" the whites wanted of him and make a success of it. He revealed that he was planning a novel for white consumption; that, indeed, he had already written some of it. He was aiming at going over to the white market. He was going to stop writing for Negroes, who gave him so little support, although he had devoted his life to the betterment of the Negro.

I was eager to see him prove his thesis. For he was expressing the point of view of the majority of the colored élite, who maintain that Negroes in the arts can win success by clowning only, because that is all the whites expect and will accept of them. So although I disliked his type of mind, I promised to help him, I was so keen about the result of his experiment. I introduced him to my agent in Paris, and my agent introduced him to a publisher in New York.

Our Negro journalist is very yellow and looks like a *métèque* in France, without attracting undue attention. Yet besides his "Amazing Facts" about Negroes he has written in important magazines, stressing the practical nonexistence of color prejudice in Europe and blaming Negroes for such as exists! Also he wrote in a white magazine about Africa and the color problem under a nom de plume which gave no indication of the writer's origin.

He might have thought that as he had "passed white" a little in complexion and in journalism, it would be just as easy "passing white" as a creative writer. Well, the Negro journalist deliberately wrote his novel as a "white" novelist—or as he imagined a white man would write. But the sensational white novel by a Negro has not yet found its publisher.

The last time I heard about him, he was again a Negro in Ethiopia, interviewing Haile Selassie and reporting the white rape of Ethiopia from an African point of view for the American Negro press.

Nigger Heaven, the Harlem novel of Carl Van Vechten, also was much discussed. I met some of Mr. Van Vechten's Negro friends, who were not seeing him any more because of his book. I felt flattered that they did not mind seeing me! Yet most of them agreed that *Nigger Heaven* was broadly based upon the fact of contemporary high life in Harlem. Some of them said that Harlemites should thank their stars that *Nigger Heaven* had soft-pedaled some of the actually wilder Harlem scenes. While the conventional Negro moralists gave the book a hostile reception because of its hectic bohemianism, the leaders of the Negro intelligentsia showed a marked liking for it. In comparing it with *Home to Harlem*, James Weldon Johnson said that I had shown a contempt for the Negro bourgeoisie. But I could not be contemptuous of a Negro bourgeoisie which simply does not exist as a class or a group in America. Because I made the protagonist of my novel a lusty black worker, it does not follow that I am unsympathetic to a refined or wealthy Negro.

My attitude toward *Nigger Heaven* was quite different from that of its Negro friends and foes. I was more interested in the implications of the book. It puzzled me a little that the author, who is generally regarded as a discoverer and sponsor of promising young Negro writers, gave Lascar, the ruthless Negro prostitute, the victory over Byron, the young Negro writer, whom he left, when the novel ends, in the hands of the police, destined perhaps for the death house in Sing Sing.

Carl Van Vechten also was in Paris in the summer of 1929. I had been warned by a white non-admirer of Mr. Van Vechten that I would not like him because he patronized Negroes in a subtle way, to which the Harlem élite were blind because they were just learning sophistication! I thought it would be a new experience to meet a white who was subtly patronizing to a black; the majority of them were so naïvely crude about it. But I found Mr. Van Vechten not a bit patronizing, and quite all right. It was neither his fault nor mine if my reaction was negative.

One of Mr. Van Vechten's Harlem sheiks introduced us after midnight at the Café de la Paix. Mr. Van Vechten was a heavy drinker at that time, but I was not drinking liquor. I had recently suffered from a cerebral trouble and a specialist had warned me against drinking, even wine. And when a French doctor forbids wine, one ought to heed. When we met at that late hour at the celebrated rendezvous of the world's cosmopolites, Mr. Van Vechten was full and funny. He said, "What will you take?" I took a soft drink and I could feel that Mr. Van Vechten was shocked.

I am afraid that as a soft drinker I bored him. The white author and the black author of books about Harlem could not find much of anything to make conversation. The market trucks were rolling by loaded with vegetables for Les Halles, and suddenly Mr. Van Vechten, pointing to a truck-load of huge carrots, exclaimed, "How I would like to have all of them!" Perhaps carrots were more interesting than conversation. But I did not feel in any way carroty. I don't know whether my looks betrayed any disapproval. Really

I hadn't the slightest objection to Mr. Van Vechten's enthusiasm for the truck driver's raw carrots, though I prefer carrots *en casserole avec poulet cocotte*. But he excused himself to go to the men's room and never came back. So, after waiting a considerable time, I paid the bill with some *Home to Harlem* money and walked in the company of the early dawn (which is delicious in Paris) back to the Rue Jean-Jacques Rousseau.

Mr. Van Vechten's sheik friend was very upset. He was a precious, hesitating sheik and very nervous about that introduction, wondering if it would take. I said that all was okay. But upon returning to New York he sent me a message from Mr. Van Vechten. The message said that Mr. Van Vechten was sorry for not returning, but he was so high that, after leaving us, he discovered himself running along the avenue after a truck load of carrots.

Among the Negro intelligentsia in Paris there was an interesting group of story-tellers, poets and painters. Some had received grants from foundations to continue work abroad; some were being helped by private individuals; and all were more or less identified with the Negro renaissance. It was illuminating to exchange ideas with them. I was an older man and not regarded as a member of the renaissance, but more as a forerunner. Indeed, some of them had aired their resentment of my intrusion from abroad into the renaissance set-up. They had thought that I had committed literary suicide because I went to Russia.

For my part I was deeply stirred by the idea of a real Negro renaissance. The Arabian cultural renaissance and the great European renaissance had provided some of my most fascinating reading. The Russian literary renaissance and also the Irish had absorbed my interest. My idea of a renaissance was one of talented persons of an ethnic or national group working individually or collectively in a common purpose and creating things that would be typical of their group.

I was surprised when I discovered that many of the talented Negroes regarded their renaissance more as an uplift organization and a vehicle to accelerate the pace and progress of smart Negro society. It was interesting to note how sharply at variance their artistic outlook was from that of the modernistic white groups that took a significant interest in Negro literature and art. The Negroes were under the delusion that when a lady from Park Avenue or from Fifth Avenue, or a titled European, became interested in Negro art and invited Negro artists to her home, that was a token of

Negroes breaking into upper-class white society. I don't think that it ever occurred to them that perhaps such white individuals were searching for a social and artistic significance in Negro art which they could not find in their own society, and that the radical nature and subject of their interest operated against the possibility of their introducing Negroes further than their own particular homes in coveted white society.

Also, among the Negro artists there was much of that Uncle Tom attitude which works like Satan against the idea of a coherent and purposeful Negro group. Each one wanted to be the first Negro, the one Negro, and the only Negro *for the whites* instead of for their group. Because an unusual number of them were receiving grants to do creative work, they actually and naïvely believed that Negro artists as a group would always be treated differently from white artists and be protected by powerful white patrons.

Some of them even expressed the opinion that Negro art would solve the centuries-old social problem of the Negro. That idea was vaguely hinted by Dr. Locke in his introduction to *The New Negro*. Dr. Locke's essay is a remarkable chocolate *soufflé* of art and politics, with not an ingredient of information inside.

They were nearly all Harlem-conscious, in a curious synthetic way, it seemed to me—not because they were aware of Harlem's intrinsic values as a unique and popular Negro quarter, but apparently because white folks had discovered black magic there. I understood more clearly why there had been so much genteel-Negro hostility to my *Home to Harlem* and to Langston Hughes's primitive Negro poems.

I wondered after all whether it would be better for me to return to the new *milieu* of Harlem. Much as all my sympathy was with the Negro group and the idea of a Negro renaissance, I doubted if going back to Harlem would be an advantage. I had done my best Harlem stuff when I was abroad, seeing it from a long perspective. I thought it might be better to leave Harlem to the artists who were on the spot, to give them their chance to produce something better than *Home to Harlem*. I thought that I might as well go back to Africa.

E. FRANKLIN FRAZIER

Edward Franklin Frazier's 1928 essay in the socialist monthly Modern Quarterly *was the seed of his classic monograph published in the United States many years later as* Black Bourgeoisie *(1957). Frazier's Baltimore family background and academic training at Howard and the University of Chicago certified him as a superior member of the Talented Tenth. He was an early* Opportunity *prizewinner, and Du Bois and Charles Johnson advanced his scholarship in sociology. If McKay denigrated the significance of the Harlem Renaissance from the perspective of an outsider, Frazier exposed its deficiencies from the vantage point of one of its presumed agents: "The New Negro Movement functions in the third dimension of culture; but so far it knows nothing of the other two dimensions—Work and Wealth."*

LA BOURGEOISIE NOIRE

RADICALS ARE CONSTANTLY asking the question: Why does the Negro, the man farthest down in the economic as well as social scale, steadily refuse to ally himself with the radical groups in America? On the other hand, his failure so far to show sympathy to any extent with the class which *à priori* would appear to be his natural allies has brought praise from certain quarters. Southern white papers when inclined to indulge in sentimental encomiums about the Negro cite his immunity to radical doctrines as one of his most praiseworthy characteristics. Negro orators and, until lately, Negro publications, in pleading for the Negro's claim to equitable treatment, have never failed to boast of the Negro's undying devotion to the present economic order. Those white who are always attempting to explain the Negro's social behavior in terms of hereditary qualities have declared that the Negro's temperament is hostile to radical doctrines. But the answer to what is a seeming anomaly to many is to be found in the whole social background of the Negro. One need not attribute it to any peculiar virtue (according as one regards virtue) or seek an explanation in such an incalculable factor as racial temperament.

The first mistake of those who think that the Negro of all groups in America should be in revolt against the present system is that they regard the Negro group as homogeneous. As a matter of fact, the Negro group is highly differentiated, with about the same range of interests as the whites. It is very well for white and black radicals to quote statistics to show that ninety-eight per cent of the Negroes are workers and should seek release from their economic slavery; but as a matter of fact ninety-eight per cent of the Negroes do not regard themselves as in economic slavery. Class differentiation among Negroes is reflected in their church organizations, educational institutions, private clubs, and the whole range of social life. Although these class distinctions may rest upon what would seem to outsiders flimsy and inconsequential matters, they are the social realities of Negro life, and no amount of reasoning can rid his mind of them. Recently we were informed in Dr. Herskovits' book on the Negro that color is the basis of social distinctions. To an outsider or a superficial observer this would seem true; but when one probes the tissue of the Negro's social life he finds that the Negro reacts to the same illusions that feed the vanity of white men.

What are some of the marks of distinctions which make it impossible to treat the Negro group as a homogeneous mass? They are chiefly property, education, and blood or family. If those possessing these marks of distinctions are generally mulattoes, it is because the free Negro class who first acquired these things as well as a family tradition were of mixed blood. The church in Charleston, South Carolina, which was reputed not to admit blacks did not open its doors to nameless mulatto nobodies. Not only has the distinction of blood given certain Negro groups a feeling of superiority over other Negroes, but it has made them feel superior to "poor whites." The Negro's feeling of superiority to "poor whites" who do not bear in their veins "aristocratic" blood has always created a barrier to any real sympathy between the two classes. Race consciousness to be sure has constantly effaced class feeling among Negroes. Therefore we hear on every hand Negro capitalists supporting the right of the Negro worker to organize—against white capitalists, of course. Nevertheless class consciousness has never been absent.

The Negro's attitude towards economic values has been determined by his economic position in American life. First of all, in the plantation system the Negro has found his adjustment to our economic system. The plantation system is based essentially upon enforced labor. Since emancipation the Negro has been a landless peasant without the tradition of the European peasant which binds the latter to the soil. Landownership remained relatively stationery from 1910 to 1920; while the number of landless workers increased. If this class of black workers were to espouse doctrines which aimed to change their economic status, they would be the most revolutionary group in America. From ignorant peasants who are ignorant in a fundamental sense in that they have no body of traditions even, we cannot expect revolutionary doctrines. They will continue a mobile group; while the white landlords through peonage and other forms of force will continue to hold them to the land.

Another factor of consequence in the Negro's economic life is the fact of the large number of Negroes in domestic service. One psychologist has sought to attribute this fact to the strength of the "instinct of submission" in the Negro. But it has represented an adjustment to the American environment. Nevertheless, it has left its mark on the Negro's character. To this is due the fact that he has taken over many values which have made him appear ridiculous and at the same time have robbed him of self-respect and self-reliance. This group is no more to be expected to embrace radical doctrines than the same class was expected to join slave insurrections, concerning which Denmark Vesey warned his followers: "Don't mention it to those waiting men who receive presents of old coats, etc., from their masters, or they'll betray us."

Even this brief consideration of the social situation which has determined the Negro's attitudes towards values in American life will afford a background for our discussion of the seeming anomaly which he presents to many spectators. We shall attempt to show that, while to most observers the Negro shows an apparent indifference to changing his status, this is in fact a very real and insistent stimulus to his struggles. The Negro can only envisage those things which have meaning for him. *The radical doctrines appeal chiefly to the industrial workers, and the Negro has only begun to enter industry.* For Negroes to enter industries which are usually in the cities and escape the confinement of the plantation, they have realized a dream that is as far beyond their former condition as the New Economic Order is beyond the present condition of the wage earner. It has often been observed that the Negro subscribes to all the canons of consumption as the owning class in the present system. Even here we find the same struggle to realize a status that he can envisage and has a meaning for him. Once the Negro struggled for a literary education because he regarded it as the earmark of freedom. The relatively segregated life which the Negro lives makes him struggle to realize the values which give status within his group. An automobile, a home, a position as a teacher, or membership in a fraternity may confer a distinction in removing the possessor from an inferior social status, that could never be appreciated by one who is a stranger to Negro life. An outsider may wonder why a downtrodden, poor, despised people seem so indifferent about entering a struggle that is aimed to give all men an equal status. But if they could enter the minds of Negroes they would find that in the world in which they live they are not downtrodden and despised, but enjoy various forms of distinction.

An interesting episode in the life of the Negro which shows to what extent he is wedded to bourgeois ideals is the present attempt of the Pullman porters to organize. Some people have very superficially regarded this movement as a gesture in the direction of economic radicalism. But anyone who is intimately acquainted with the psychology of the Negro group, especially the porters, know that this is far from true. One who is connected with the white labor movement showed a better insight through his remark to the writer that the porters showed little working class psychology and showed a disposition to use their organization to enjoy the amenities of bourgeois social life. The Pullman porters do not show any disposition to overthrow bourgeois values. In fact, for years this group was better situated economically than most Negroes and carried over into their lives as far as possible the behavior patterns which are current in the middle class. In some places they regarded themselves as a sort of aristocracy, and as a colored woman said in one of their meetings recently, "Only an educated gentleman with culture could be a Pullman porter." The advent of a large and consequential professional and business class among Negroes has relegated the Pullman porters to a lower status economically as well as otherwise. Collective bargaining will help them to continue in a role in the colored group which is more in harmony with their conception of their relative status in their group. It is far from the idea of the Pullman porters to tear down the present economic order, and hardly any of them would confess any spiritual kinship with the "poor whites." The Pullman porters are emerging, on the other hand, as an aristocratic laboring group just as the Railroad Brotherhoods have done.

The Negro's lack of sympathy with the white working class is based on more than the feeling of superiority. In the South, especially, the caste system which is based on color, determines the behavior of the white working class. If the Negro has fatuously claimed spiritual kinship with the white bourgeois, the white working class has taken over the tradition of the slave-holding aristocracy. When white labor in the South attempts to treat with black labor, the inferior status of the latter must be conceded in practice and in theory. Moreover, white labor in the South not only has used every form of trickery to drive the Negro out of the ranks of skilled labor, but it has resorted to legislation to accomplish its aims. Experience, dating from before the Civil War, with the white group, has helped to form the attitude of Negro towards white labor as well as traditional prejudices.[1]

In the February number of the *Southern Workman,* there appears an article in which the psychology of the Negro is portrayed as follows. The discovery is made by a white business in Chicago:

> "The average working class Negro in Chicago earns $22 a week. His wife sends her children to the Day Nursery or leaves them with relatives or friends, and she supplements the family income by from $10 to $15 or more per week. The average white man of the same class earns $33 per week and keeps his wife at home. This colored man will rent a $65 per month apartment and buy a $50 suit of clothes while the white man will occupy a $30 per month apartment and buy a $25 suit of clothes. This av-

[1] E. Franklin Frazier: "The Negro in the Industrial South." *The Nation*, Vol. 125, pp. 32–38.

erage white man will come into our store to buy furniture
and about $300 will be the limit of his estimated pur-
chase, while the colored man will undertake a thousand
dollar purchase without the least thought about meeting
the payments from his small income."

To the writer of the article the company's new policy in using
colored salesmen is a wonderful opportunity for colored men to
learn the furniture business. The furniture company is going to
make Negroes better citizens, according to the author of the article,
by encouraging them to have better homes. This situation represents not only the extent to which the average Negro has swallowed middle class standards but the attitude of the upper class
Negro towards the same values.

There is much talk at the present time about the New Negro.
He is generally thought of as the creative artist who is giving expression to all the stored-up æsthetic emotion of the race. Negro
in Art Week has come to take its place beside, above, or below the
other three hundred and fifty-two weeks in the American year. But
the public is little aware of the Negro business man who regards
himself as a new phenomenon. While the New Negro who is expressing himself in art promises in the words of one of his chief
exponents not to compete with the white man either politically or
economically, the Negro business man seeks the salvation of the
race in economic enterprise. In the former case there is either an
acceptance of the present system or an ignoring of the economic
realities of life. In the case of the latter there is an acceptance of
the gospel of economic success. Sometimes the New Negro of the
artistic type calls the New Negro business man a Babbitt, while
the latter calls the former a mystic. But the Negro business man is
winning out, for he is dealing with economic realities. He can boast
of the fact that he is independent of white support, while the Negro
artist still seeks it. One Negro insurance company in a rather cyn-
ical acceptance of the charge of Babbittry begins a large advertisement in a Negro magazine in the words of George F. Babbitt.

A perusal of Negro newspapers will convince anyone that the
Negro group does not regard itself as outcasts without status. One
cannot appeal to them by telling them that they have nothing to
lose but their chains. The chains which Negroes have known in
the South were not figurative. Negro newspapers are a good index
of the extent to which middle-class ideals have captured the imag-

ination of Negroes. In one newspaper there is a column devoted to What Society Is Wearing. In this column the apparel of those who are socially prominent is described in detail. The parties, the cars, the homes, and the jewelry of the elite find a place in all of these papers. In fact, there is no demand on the part of Negro leaders to tear down social distinctions and create a society of equals. As the writer heard a colored editor tell a white man recently, "the white people draw the line at the wrong point and put all of us in the same class."

Negro schools in the South furnish an example of the influence of middle-class ideals which make Negroes appear in a ridiculous light. These schools give annually a public performance. Instead of giving plays such as Paul Green's folk plays of Negro life, they give fashion shows which have been popularized to boost sales. Negro students appear in all kinds of gorgeous costumes which are worn by the leisured middle class. One more often gets the impression that he has seen a Mardi Gras rather than an exhibition of correct apparel.

Even the most ardent radical cannot expect the Negro to hold himself aloof from the struggle for economic competence and only dream of his escape from his subordinate economic status in the overthrow of the present system. A Negro business man who gets out of the white man's kitchen or dining room rightly regards himself as escaping from economic slavery. Probably he will maintain himself by exploiting the Negro who remains in the kitchen, but he can always find consolation in the feeling, that if he did not exploit him a white man would. But in seeking escape from economic subordination, the Negro has generally envisaged himself as a captain of industry. In regard to group efficiency he has shown no concern. For example, a group isolated to the extent of the Negro in America could have developed cooperative enterprises. There has been no attempt in schools or otherwise to teach or encourage this type of economic organization. The ideal of the rich man has been held up to him. More than one Negro business has been wrecked because of this predatory view of economic activity.

Many of those who criticize the Negro for selecting certain values out of American life overlook the fact that the primary struggle on his part has been to acquire a culture. In spite of the efforts of those who would have him dig up his African past, the Negro is a stranger to African culture. The manner in which he has taken over the American culture has never been studied in

intimate enough detail to make it comprehensible. The educated
class among Negroes has been the forerunners in this process. Except perhaps through the church the economic basis of the civilized
classes among Negroes has not been within the group. Although
today the growing professional and business classes are finding
support among Negroes, the upper classes are subsidized chiefly
from without. To some outsiders such a situation makes the Negro
intellectual appear as merely an employee of the white group. At
times the emasculating effect of Negro men appearing in the role
of mere entertainers for the whites has appeared in all its tragic
reality. But the creation of this educated class of Negroes has made
possible the civilization of the Negro. It may seem conceivable to
some that the Negro could have contended on the ground of abstract right for unlimited participation in American life on the basis
of individual efficiency; but the Negro had to deal with realities. It
is strange that today one expects this very class which represents
the most civilized group to be in revolt against the system by which
it was created, rather than the group of leaders who have sprung
from the soil of Negro culture.

Here we are brought face to face with a fundamental dilemma
of Negro life. Dean Miller at Howard University once expressed
this dilemma aphoristically, namely, that the Negro pays for what
he wants and begs for what he needs. The Negro pays, on the
whole, for his church, his lodges and fraternities, and his automobile, but he begs for his education. Even the radical movement
which had vogue a few years back was subsidized by the white
radical group. It did not spring out of any general movement
among Negroes towards radical doctrines. Moreover, black radicals theorized about the small number of Negroes who had entered
industry from the security of New York City; but none ever undertook to enter the South and teach the landless peasants any type
of self-help. What began as the organ of the struggling working
masses became the mouthpiece of Negro capitalists. The New Negro group which has shown a new orientation towards Negro life
and the values which are supposed to spring from Negro life has
restricted itself to the purely cultural in the narrow sense.

In this article the writer has attempted to set forth the social
forces which have caused the Negro to have his present attitude
towards the values in American life. From even this cursory glance
at Negro life we are able to see to what extent bourgeois ideals are
implanted in the Negro's mind. We are able to see that the Negro

group is a highly differentiated group with various interests, and that it is far from sound to view the group as a homogeneous group of outcasts. There has come upon the stage a group which represents a nationalistic movement. This movement is divorced from any program of economic reconstruction. It is unlike the Garvey movement in that Garvey through schemes—phantastic to be sure—united his nationalistic aims with an economic program. This new movement differs from the program of Booker Washington which sought to place the culture of the Negro upon a sound basis by making him an efficient industrial worker. Nor does it openly ally itself with those leaders who condemn the organization of the Pullman porters and advise Negroes to pursue an opportunistic course with capitalism. It looks askance at the new rising class of black capitalism while it basks in the sun of white capitalism. It enjoys the congenial company of white radicals while shunning association with black radicals. The New Negro Movement functions in the third dimension of culture; but so far it knows nothing of the other two dimensions—Work and Wealth.

LOUISE THOMPSON PATTERSON

FOR LOUISE THOMPSON PATTERSON, international communism held the promise of a world transformed beyond racism. Her experiences as a teacher in the South and as one of Locke and Godmother's rejects eventually led Louise Thompson into the ranks of the Communist Party (after divorcing Wallace Thurman, she married one of the African American stalwarts of the Party, William Patterson). In 1932, the Soviet film company Meschrabpom announced its intention to make a movie about white supremacy in the Southern United States, Black and White, *using African American actors and singers. Louise Patterson sailed away from the Great Depression for the USSR in June 1932 with Langston Hughes, poet Dorothy West, journalist Theodore Poston, and eighteen other men and women more or less active in the Harlem Renaissance, all to become movie actors.*

WITH LANGSTON HUGHES IN THE USSR

IT WAS JUNE 14, 1932. Boarding the North German Lloyd's largest steamship, the Europa, at its Brooklyn pier came some twenty-two young Negroes. For most of them it was their first voyage. The last to arrive, after all the many well-wishers had been put ashore, was Langston Hughes, loaded down with a huge assortment of baggage including a typewriter, record player and a big box of jazz records. Where were they all going and why? And therein lies a story that before the year ended would become international news.

It all started with an invitation from the Meschrabpom Film Corporation in Moscow for a group of Negroes to come to Russia to make a film titled *Black and White*. A prominent committee of sponsors was formed in New York and the invitation widely publicized. From every part of the country came inquiries and then volunteers for the trip willing to pay their own fare to Leningrad which was the only specification made by the film company. (At that time the one-way fare all the way to Leningrad was only ninety dollars.) Langston was reached out in California where he was on a lecture tour and invited to come along as script writer. He accepted. Interrupting his tour, joined by two other volunteers from Berkeley and Los Angeles, he traveled in his Ford across the continent, stopping only for food, to get to New York for the June 14 takeoff.

The six days of sea travel passed quickly for this gay group of young adventurers. It was for the most of them a glorious opportunity to travel and see the world, and particularly Russia, the land of the Bolsheviki, so much in the news. During the crossing many first class passengers found their way to our third class deck curious to see what this group of young men and women looked like, for the news quickly got around the ship about us. Among them were Ralph Bunche, Alain Locke and Jay Lovestone. The traditional night-before-landing parties found some of our group down to their last dollar after imbibing much champagne. Landing in Bremerhaven, Germany, we went by boat-train to Berlin where hotel accommodations were provided at company expense. We were scheduled to go by train the next day to Stettin for the Baltic trip to Leningrad. What cash still remained in the pockets of these young travelers went for a night on the town. The hotel was near a railroad station. The streets were swarming with prostitutes who would walk up in broad daylight to any of the young men and try to take them away from any of the young women of our party with whom they were walking. Panderers and purveyors of pornographic pictures hung around every corner. These sights brought home to some of us the depth of misery and despair that was the Berlin of 1932 on the eve of Hitler's takeover.

The next morning, leaving most of the group to get themselves together after a hectic night, as well as get together all our one-hundred pieces of luggage and take them to the train for Stettin, Langston and one or two others went with me to the Soviet Consulate for the necessary visas. We understood from Meschrabpom that they would be waiting for us to pick up. Here is where our woes began. Nobody in the Consulate knew anything about our coming, or so they said. There were no visas. Nothing could be done until they could reach Moscow. What a dilemma! By this time it was approaching noon and the boat-train was scheduled to leave at one o'clock. If we did not reach Stettin before the Baltic steamer took off we would be on our own in Berlin, for the boat company would no longer be responsible for us. So, sending one of us from the Consulate to the train station, the rest of us concentrated on trying to get the Consulate to move with greater speed. The prospect of seeing twenty-two young Negroes adrift in Berlin with scarcely a dollar between them made our hair stand on end. We just might have to do some panhandling ourselves!

After much pleading, cajoling and threats, telephone calls back and forth to Moscow, the visas were authorized. Down to the station we flew to find a sad, tired lot of young people sitting on duffle bags, boxes and suitcases they had thrown off the train when our messenger brought them the sad news of no visas. Another train was quickly assembled, we were hustled inside, bags, boxes, duffles tossed through windows and off to Stettin we went. We found the ship waiting for us, along with much of our baggage which never got off the first train.

The trip up the Baltic Sea gave us time to recoup from the tension and turmoil of those days. Most of us had two "firsts" to enjoy now: the "white nights" where one stood on deck at midnight reading a book by the northern lights. And the "smorgasbord," eating so much of these delightful appetizers that when the waitresses brought us the main course of the dinner we had no more room in our stomachs.

Landing in Helsinki, Finland, we took leave of our Baltic ship and after a night in that very clean but, to me, cold-looking city we boarded the train for Leningrad. As we stepped down into the station of that historic city we were met by a brass band, and wondered what notables on our train they had come to greet. We did not have to wait long to find out when the last one of our party stepped from the train, we found ourselves surrounded and welcomed. And so began this strange new experience for all of us, of warm greetings, affectionate receptions, every manner of courtesy, which led one of our number to comment from time to time as we traveled about, "Now when I get back to the good ole USA and *insignificance. . . .*"

Finally another night's train ride and Moscow. Although we all had sleeping compartments many of us stayed up all night in the passageway, too excited to sleep. Meschrabpom Film representatives met us in Leningrad and escorted us to our Moscow abode for the next weeks, the Grand Hotel where a huge banquet table was set with what for Russians were their finest delicacies—caviar, sturgeon and other cold dishes—but for young Americans used to ham and eggs, pancakes, sausage and grits this cold fare for breakfast was rather unusual.

The first meeting of the group in the Meschrabpom Film Studio brought surprise to both sides. It was hard for the Russians to believe they were facing twenty-two Negroes—for we were of all color shades from mulatto to black. Then we didn't square with their concept of working class folk, for we were students, writers, professionals and white collar workers who first saw the inside of a steel mill or any factory in the USSR. There were but two of our group with any professional stage experience and they were to find out quickly that most of the group knew no Negro folk songs, some could not carry a tune nor dance a step.

Our surprise was to find out that after all our hurrying and scurrying to get to Moscow before the end of June, they were not ready to start the picture, had not even decided upon a location for shooting it, and had a Russian script which had to be translated to English for Langston to work with it, which would take two or three weeks. When Langston finally got the translation he had this to say about it in *I Wonder As I Wander*:

"At first I was astonished at what I read. Then I laughed until I cried. And I wasn't crying really because the script was in places so mistaken and so funny. I was crying because the writer meant well, but knew so little about his subject. . . . Although the scenario concerned America, it was written by a famous Russian writer *who had never been in America*. At that time only a very few books about contemporary Negro life in our country had been translated into Russian. These the scenarist had studied, and from them he had put together what he thought was a highly dramatic story of labor and race relations in the United States. But the end result was a script improbable to the point of ludicrousness."

While the debate went on as to what to do about a scenario, for Langston finally convinced them at Meschrabpom that nothing could be done with the present one, the group became acquainted with Moscow, in various ways. Although they were not yet at work (except Langston), the film company lived up to its contract of four hundred rubles a month to each person with a hotel room and a book for the foreign workers store. Purchases could be made in this store for many foodstuffs and delicacies not available to the Soviet people and not at black market prices. 1932 was not a good year in the USSR. There was famine in various parts of the vast land, and, to make the Five Year Plan possible, all the Soviet people had but the barest necessities. We were not aware of this for most of us had more money to spend than we had ever had in our young lives. Most of it was spent in having good times—wining, dancing and dining at the Hotel Metropol, parties, and of course there was always the theatre.

I have had many occasions to wonder at the great generosity of the Soviet people. Realizing that foreigners who come to their country may have different standards of living, they make available to them many things not available to their own people. Yet I have never experienced any resentment on the part of the people about this preferential treatment. Wherever we went as a group, or in pairs, the Russians would push us to the front of the queue line for a bus or ticket, or offer us seats in a crowded streetcar. For all of us who experienced discrimination based on color in our own land, it was strange to find our color a badge of honor, our key to the city, so to speak.

But all play and no work, even with plenty of money and the "key to the city," can grow boring to young adventure seekers and some incidents began to develop that were embarrassing to most of us. Meschrabpom Studio proposed that we all go to Odessa, take a cruise down the Black Sea and then come back to a location where the shooting of the picture would begin. However, after our relaxing journey to Batum and back we were met in Odessa by a Meschrabpom director with the information that *Black and White* had been cancelled. We also learned that our group had become "world news" because of stories sent out by American correspondents always on the alert for sensational ways to attack the USSR. We returned to Moscow to find excited cables from relatives and friends who read of our being stranded and destitute while we had been cruising deluxe on the scenic Black Sea coast, wining and dining in Odessa's beautiful Londres Hotel, and still receiving four hundred rubles a month from Meschrabpom.

Division in the group, which had been growing between those who took the USSR only as a pleasure jaunt, and others who, while not Communists, wanted to learn about how a socialist system worked and how its people lived, now took sharp form. Group meetings took place all day and every day for over a week with arguments about the reasons for the cancellation of the film. Those following the lead of the anti-Soviet foreign correspondents stated that it was a betrayal of the Negro people of the world and a concession to the Americans in exchange for diplomatic recognition. The majority of the group followed the leadership of Langston that it was impossible to make a good film without a good scenario nor was there the possibility of getting one in the conceivable future. Two statements were prepared setting forth the two positions in the group. Eighteen signed the statement prepared by Langston and Loren Miller who had come from California with him in the Ford. Four signed the statement prepared by the group accusing the Soviet Union of betraying the black people of the world. Both were taken to the American correspondent who had sent out the first story of "Uncle Tom's Cabin" being adrift in Russia. The statement of the four went out by first cable; the statement of the eighteen was rejected as "not news."

So came to an end the *Black and White* episode but not the stories about it. They crop up from time to time when anti-Soviet baiters want to take a pot shot at the USSR. The latest I have read is by Homer Smith in his scurrilous book *Black Man in Red Russia*. Smith came from Minnesota to join the *Black and White* troupe in New York, although he denies it in his book. He writes of having "met" us when we arrived in Moscow, although why he found it necessary to disclaim his association seems irrelevant to his diatribe, except to lessen even more its credibility.

In the aftermath of the end of *Black and White*, those who accused the Soviet Union as a betrayer of black folk quickly departed. The others accepted the invitation of the theatrical section of the Soviet trade unions to tour the country and chose Central Asia where the people are colored and were colonials under the Czar. This was a thrilling experience for all of us to see new nations arising out of centuries of illiteracy, poverty and even nomad life to the world of collective farm, modern silk factories, schools, homes and nurseries. There was enough left of the old to contrast with new being born; to see camels and airplanes; automatic cotton pickers and primitive plows; women in "paranja" (the garment covering the entire body with an ugly horsehair veil) and young women with bobbed hair and short dresses; mud or felt-covered huts and modern apartments.

For the group it was an exciting ten-day trip. For Langston it was the beginning of many months of intensive contact and study of the customs, culture and economy of the Turkoman, Tadjik and Uzbek peoples. Whether driving through the hot, dusty Turkoman desert in an old jalopy, sharing a tea bowl with Uzbeks in a chaikhanna, wandering the streets of Samarkand and Old Bokhara (cities whose civilizations date back to B.C.), or visiting new factories and collective farms in Tashkent, Langston got to know the people of the land. Often he had no interpreter and some times he was among people who did not know Russian, a smattering of which he had picked up. "However," he says in *I Wonder As I Wander*, "when the ear gives up and intuition takes over, some sort of understanding develops instinctively."

Langston returned to Moscow from his Central Asian experiences to spend many more months there as guest of the Writers Union, meeting many writers of the USSR and others who came from afar. "And dozens of English and American tourists coming and going, most of them sympathetic liberals friendly to 'the Soviet experiment'—but many of them unsympathetic when they departed, and others entirely shorn of any illusions they might have had as to man's ability to make himself over into a new unselfish image through communism. . . . I think most idealists expected too much of Russia in too short a time. The Soviet Union was then only fifteen years old. . . ."

Harking back to his Central Asia experience, Langston continues: "Maybe my having gone to Central Asia gave me a broader viewpoint on Soviet achievements. In Turkestan the new setup was only eight years old, dating from 1924—yet there they had already come from almost complete illiteracy to schools for *all* the children, from ancient feudal serfdom to wages and work for all, from veils and harems and marriage marts to women treated like human beings and not chattels, and from Jim Crow cars to a complete lack of segregation—all in less than a decade.

"Maybe the fact that I was colored, too, made a difference. All the tourists I saw in the Soviet Union except John Hope were white. Most of the other travelers, such as the technicians and writers I saw there were white, too. Just as the dirt in Central Asia upset Koestler [Arthur], so it upset me. Dirt without Jim Crow was bad—but dirt *with Jim Crow, for me,* would have been infinitely worse. In the old days, Koestler and I could not have stayed in the same hotels together in Turkestan, nor ridden in the same railway compartments. My segregated compartment would have been dirtier. As a white man before the revolution Koestler could have ridden first-class—but not I. Koestler perhaps could not understand why I did not complain as often as he did, nor why I was not quite so impatient with the maid who refused to set our bags over the doorsill in Bokhara. Koestler had never lived as a Negro anywhere. Even with dirt, there was freedom for a Turkoman to sit in Ashkabad's dusty park and not see the old signs FOR EUROPEANS ONLY that formerly kept him out. Even with eternal grime and continued famines, racial freedom was sweeter than the lack of it. . . . After all, I suppose, how anything is seen depends on whose eyes look at it."

CLAUDE MCKAY

THE HARLEM RENAISSANCE WOUND DOWN ever more rapidly with the onset of the Great Depression. Money for annual prizes dried up along with publishers' contracts and much of the nightlife associated with prohibition, repealed in 1933 by the Twenty-first Amendment. The "vogue of the Negro" expired on Broadway. The deaths in late 1934 of two of the most gifted writers of the Renaissance, Rudolph Fisher and Wallace Thurman, amounted to the virtual end. The Harlem Riot a few months later, memorably described by the returning Claude McKay in The Nation *("Harlem Runs Wild"), was the final punctuation mark.*

HARLEM RUNS WILD

DOCILE HARLEM went on a rampage last week, smashing stores and looting them and piling up destruction of thousands of dollars worth of goods. But the mass riot in Harlem was not a race riot. A few whites were jostled by colored people in the melee, but there was no manifest hostility between colored and white as such. All night until dawn on the Tuesday of the outbreak white persons, singly and in groups, walked the streets of Harlem without being molested. The action of the police was commendable in the highest degree. The looting was brazen and daring, but the police were restrained. In extreme cases, when they fired, it was into the air. Their restraint saved Harlem from becoming a shambles.

The outbreak was spontaneous. It was directed against the stores exclusively. One Hundred and Twenty-fifth Street is Harlem's main street and the theatrical and shopping center of the colored thousands. Anything that starts there will flash through Harlem as quick as lightning. The alleged beating of a kid caught stealing a trifle in one of the stores merely served to explode the smoldering discontent of the colored people against the Harlem merchants.

It would be too sweeping to assert that radicals incited the Harlem mass to riot and pillage. The Young Liberators seized an opportune moment, but the explosion on Tuesday was not the result of Communist propaganda. There were, indeed, months of propaganda in it. But the propagandists are eager to dissociate themselves from Communists. Proudly they declare that they have agitated only in the American constitutional way for fair play for colored Harlem.

Colored people all over the world are notoriously the most exploitable material, and colored Harlem is no exception. The population is gullible to an extreme. And apparently the people are exploited so flagrantly because they invite and take it. It is their gullibility that gives to Harlem so much of its charm, its air of insouciance and gaiety. But the facade of the Harlem masses' happy-go-lucky and hand-to-mouth existence has been badly broken by the Depression. A considerable part of the population can no longer cling even to the hand-to-mouth margin.

Wherever an ethnologically related group of people is exploited by others, the exploiters often operate on the principle of granting certain concessions as sops. In Harlem the exploiting group is overwhelmingly white. And it gives no sops. And so for the past two years colored agitators have exhorted the colored consumers to organize and demand of the white merchants a new deal: that they should employ Negroes as clerks in the colored community. These agitators are crude men, theoretically. They have little understanding of and little interest in the American labor movement, even from the most conservative trade-union angle. They address their audience mainly on the streets. Their following is not so big as that of the cultists and occultists. But it is far larger than that of the Communists.

One of the agitators is outstanding and picturesque. He dresses in turban and gorgeous robe. He has a bigger following than his rivals. He calls himself Sufi Abdul Hamid. His organization is the Negro Industrial and Clerical Alliance. It was the first to start picketing the stores of Harlem demanding clerical employment for colored persons. Sufi Hamid achieved a little success. A few of the smaller Harlem stores engaged colored clerks. But on 125th Street the merchants steadfastly refused to employ colored clerical help. The time came when the Negro Industrial and Clerical Alliance felt strong enough to picket the big stores on 125th Street. At first the movement got scant sympathy from influential Negroes and the Harlem intelligentsia as a whole. Physically and mentally, Sufi Hamid is a different type. He does not belong. And moreover he used to excoriate the colored newspapers, pointing out that they would not support his demands on the bigger Harlem stores because they were carrying the stores' little ads.

Harlem was excited by the continued picketing and the resultant "incidents." Sufi Hamid won his first big support last spring when one of the most popular young men in Harlem, the Reverend Adam Clayton Powell, Jr., assistant pastor of the Abyssinian Church—the largest in Harlem—went on the picket line on 125th Street. This gesture set all Harlem talking and thinking and made the headlines of the local newspapers. It prompted the formation of a Citizens' League for Fair Play. The league was endorsed and supported by sixty-two organizations, among which were eighteen of the leading churches of Harlem. And at last the local press conceded some support.

One of the big stores capitulated and took on a number of colored clerks. The picketing of other stores was continued. And soon business was not so good as it used to be on 125th Street.

In the midst of the campaign Sufi Hamid was arrested. Sometime before his arrest a committee of Jewish Minute Men had visited the Mayor and complained about an anti-Semitic movement among the colored people and the activities of a black Hitler in Harlem. The *Day* and the *Bulletin,* Jewish newspapers, devoted columns to the Harlem Hitler and anti-Semitism among Negroes. The articles were translated and printed in the Harlem newspapers under big headlines denouncing the black Hitler and his work.

On October 13 of last year Sufi Hamid was brought before the courts charged with disorderly conduct and using invective against the Jews. The witnesses against him were the chairman of the Minute Men and other persons more or less connected with the merchants. After hearing the evidence and defense, the judge decided that the evidence was biased and discharged Sufi Hamid. Meanwhile Sufi Hamid had withdrawn from the Citizens' League for Fair Play. He had to move from his headquarters and his immediate following was greatly diminished. An all-white Harlem Merchants' Association came into existence. Dissension divided the Citizens' League; the prominent members denounced Sufi Hamid and his organization.

In an interview last October Sufi Hamid told me that he had never styled himself the black Hitler. He said that once when he visited a store to ask for the employment of colored clerks, the proprietor remarked, "We are fighting Hitler in Germany." Sufi said that he replied, "We are fighting Hitler in Harlem." He went on to say that although he was a Moslem he had never entertained any prejudices against Jews as Jews. He was an Egyptian and in Egypt the relations between Moslem and Jew were happier than in any other country. He was opposed to Hitlerism, for he had read Hitler's book, *Mein Kampf*, and knew Hitler's attitude and ideas about all colored peoples. Sufi Hamid said that the merchants of Harlem spread the rumor of anti-Semitism among the colored people because they did not want to face the issue of giving them a square deal.

The Citizens' League continued picketing, and some stores capitulated. But the Leaguers began quarreling among themselves as to whether the clerks employed should be light-skinned or dark-skinned. Meanwhile the united white Harlem Merchants' Association was fighting back. In November the picketing committee was enjoined from picketing by Supreme Court Justice Samuel Rosenman. The court ruled that the Citizen's League was not a labor organization. It was the first time that such a case had come before the courts of New York. The chairman of the picketing committee remarked that "the decision would make trouble in Harlem."

One by one the colored clerks who had been employed in 125th Street stores lost their places. When inquiries were made as to the cause, the managements gave the excuse of slack business. The clerks had no organization behind them. Of the grapevine intrigue and treachery that contributed to the debacle of the movement, who can give the facts? They are as obscure and inscrutable as the composite mind of the Negro race itself. So the masses of Harlem remain disunited and helpless, while their would-be leaders wrangle and scheme and denounce one another to the whites. Each one is ambitious to wear the piebald mantle of Marcus Garvey.

On Tuesday the crowds went crazy like the remnants of a defeated, abandoned, and hungry army. Their rioting was the gesture of despair of a bewildered, baffled, and disillusioned people.

RICHARD WRIGHT

Hughes's "Negro Artist" Manifesto had summoned the younger artists to look for authenticity in the common folk of the race. Richard Wright's "Blueprint for Negro Writing" exhorted them to lead the common people to an authentic and politically active conception of self through art that empowered. The art of the Harlem Renaissance was worthy of "French poodles who do clever tricks," Wright declared. Virtually standing Locke's "Foreword" in The New Negro *on its head, he called for new creative energies that exploited the Black Church and Black folklore in order to create a national consciousness. "They must accept the concept of nationalism because, in order to transcend it, they must possess and understand it." Wright understood this conception of nationalism to be the essential precondition of a valid Marxist aesthetic: "The ideological unity of Negro writers and the alliance of that unity with all the progressive ideas of our day is the primary prerequisite for collective work."*

BLUEPRINT FOR NEGRO WRITING

1) THE ROLE OF NEGRO WRITING: TWO DEFINITIONS

GENERALLY SPEAKING, Negro writing in the past has been confined to humble novels, poems, and plays, prim and decorous ambassadors who went a-begging to white America. They entered the Court of American Public Opinion dressed in the knee-pants of servility, curtsying to show that the Negro was not inferior, that he was human, and that he had a life comparable to that of other people. For the most part these artistic ambassadors were received as though they were French poodles who do clever tricks.

White America never offered these Negro writers any serious criticism. The mere fact that a Negro could write was astonishing. Nor was there any deep concern on the part of white America with the role Negro writing should play in American culture; and the role it did play grew out of accident rather than intent or design. Either it crept in through the kitchen in the form of jokes; or it was the fruits of that foul soil which was the result of a liaison between inferiority-complexed Negro "geniuses" and burnt-out white Bohemians with money.

On the other hand, these often technically brilliant performances by Negro writers were looked upon by the majority of literate Negroes as something to be proud of. At best, Negro writing has been something external to the lives of educated Negroes themselves. That the productions of their writers should have been something of a guide in their daily living is a matter which seems never to have been raised seriously.

Under these conditions Negro writing assumed two general aspects: 1) It became a sort of conspicuous ornamentation, the hallmark of "achievement." 2) It became the voice of the educated Negro pleading with white America for justice.

Rarely was the best of this writing addressed to the Negro himself, his needs, his sufferings, his aspirations. Through misdirection, Negro writers have been far better to others than they have been to themselves. And the mere recognition of this places the whole question of Negro writing in a new light and raises a doubt as to the validity of its present direction.

2) THE MINORITY OUTLOOK

Somewhere in his writings Lenin makes the observation that oppressed minorities often reflect the techniques of the bourgeoisie more brilliantly than some sections of the bourgeoisie themselves. The psychological importance of this becomes meaningful when it is recalled that oppressed minorities, and especially the petty bourgeois sections of oppressed minorities, strive to assimilate the virtues of the bourgeoisie in the assumption that by doing so they can lift themselves into a higher social sphere. But not only among the oppressed petty bourgeoisie does this occur. The workers of a minority people, chafing under exploitation, forge organizational forms of struggle to better their lot. Lacking the handicaps of false ambition and property, they have access to a wide social vision and a deep social consciousness. They display a greater freedom and initiative in pushing their claims upon civilization than even do the petty bourgeoisie. Their organizations show greater strength, adaptability, and efficiency than any other group or class in society.

That Negro workers, propelled by the harsh conditions of their lives, have demonstrated this consciousness and mobility for economic and political action there can be no doubt. But has this consciousness been reflected in the work of Negro writers to the same degree as it has in the Negro workers' struggle to free Herndon and the Scottsboro Boys, in the drive toward unionism, in the fight against lynching? Have they as creative writers taken advantage of their unique minority position?

The answer decidedly is *no*. Negro writers have lagged sadly, and as time passes the gap widens between them and their people.

How can this hiatus be bridged? How can the enervating effects of this long standing split be eliminated?

In presenting questions of this sort an attitude of self-consciousness and self-criticism is far more likely to be a fruitful point of departure than a mere recounting of past achievements. An emphasis upon tendency and experiment, a view of society as something becoming rather than as something fixed and admired is the one which points the way for Negro writers to stand shoulder to shoulder with Negro workers in mood and outlook.

3) A WHOLE CULTURE

There is, however, a culture of the Negro which is his and has been addressed to him; a culture which has, for good or ill, helped to clarify his consciousness and create emotional attitudes which are conducive to action. This culture has stemmed mainly from two sources: 1) the Negro church; 2) and the folklore of the Negro people.

It was through the portals of the church that the American Negro first entered the shrine of western culture. Living under slave conditions of life, bereft of his African heritage, the Negroes' struggle for religion on the plantations between 1820–60 assumed the form of a struggle for human rights. It remained a relatively revolutionary struggle until religion began to serve as an antidote for suffering and denial. But even today there are millions of American Negroes whose only sense of a whole universe, whose only relation to society and man, and whose only guide to personal dignity comes through the archaic morphology of Christian salvation.

It was, however, in a folklore moulded out of rigorous and inhuman conditions of life that the Negro achieved his most indigenous and complete expression. Blues, spirituals, and folk tales recounted from mouth to mouth; the whispered words of a black mother to her black daughter on the ways of men; the confidential wisdom of a black father to his black son; the swapping of sex experiences on street corners from boy to boy in the deepest vernacular; work songs sung under blazing suns—all these formed the channels through which the racial wisdom flowed.

One would have thought that Negro writers in the last century of striving at expression would have continued and deepened this folk tradition, would have tried to create a more intimate and yet a more profoundly social system of artistic communication between them and their people. But the illusion that they could escape through individual achievement the harsh lot of their race swung Negro writers away from any such path. Two separate cultures sprang up: one for the Negro masses, unwritten and unrecognized; and the other for the sons and daughters of a rising Negro bourgeoisie, parasitic and mannered.

Today the question is: Shall Negro writing be for the Negro masses, moulding the lives and consciousness of those masses toward new goals, or shall it continue begging the question of the Negroes' humanity?

4) THE PROBLEM OF NATIONALISM IN NEGRO WRITING

In stressing the difference between the role Negro writing failed to play in the lives of the Negro people, and the role it should play in the future if it is to serve its historic function; in pointing out the fact that Negro writing has been addressed in the main to a small white audience rather than to a Negro one, it should be stated that no attempt is being made here to propagate a specious and blatant nationalism. Yet the nationalist character of the Negro people is unmistakable. Psychologically this nationalism is reflected in the whole of Negro culture, and especially in folklore.

In the absence of fixed and nourishing forms of culture, the Negro has a folklore which embodies the memories and hopes of his struggle for freedom. Not yet caught in paint or stone, and as yet but feebly depicted in the poem and novel, the Negroes' most powerful images of hope and despair still remain in the fluid state of daily speech. How many John Henrys have lived and died on the lips of these black people? How many mythical heroes in embryo have been allowed to perish for lack of husbanding by alert intelligence?

Negro folklore contains, in a measure that puts to shame more deliberate forms of Negro expression, the collective sense of Negro life in America. Let those who shy at the nationalist implications of Negro life look at this body of folklore, living and powerful, which rose out of a unified sense of a common life and a common fate. Here are those vital beginnings of a recognition of value in life as it is *lived,* a recognition that marks the emergence of a new culture in the shell of the old. And at the moment this process starts, at the moment when a people begin to realize a *meaning* in their suffering, the civilization that engenders that suffering is doomed.

The nationalist aspects of Negro life are as sharply manifest in the social institutions of Negro people as in folklore. There is a Negro church, a Negro press, a Negro social world, a Negro sporting world, a Negro business world, a Negro school system, Negro professions; in short, a Negro way of life in America. The Negro people did not ask for this, and deep down, though they express themselves through their institutions and adhere to this special way of life, they do not want it now. This special existence was forced upon them from without by lynch rope, bayonet and mob rule. They accepted these negative conditions with the inevitability of a tree which must live or perish in whatever soil it finds itself.

The few crumbs of American civilization which the Negro has got from the tables of capitalism have been through these segregated channels. Many Negro institutions are cowardly and incompetent; but they are all that the Negro has. And, in the main, any move, whether for progress or reaction, must come through these institutions for the simple reason that all other channels are closed. Negro writers who seek to mould or influence the consciousness of the Negro people must address their messages to them through the ideologies and attitudes fostered in this warping way of life.

5) THE BASIS AND MEANING OF NATIONALISM IN NEGRO WRITING

The social institutions of the Negro are imprisoned in the Jim Crow political system of the South, and this Jim Crow political system is in turn built upon a plantation-feudal economy. Hence, it can be seen that the emotional expression of group-feeling which puzzles so many whites and leads them to deplore what they call "black chauvinism" is not a morbidly inherent trait of the Negro, but rather the reflex expression of a life whose roots are imbedded deeply in Southern soil.

Negro writers must accept the nationalist implications of their lives, not in order to encourage them, but in order to change and transcend them. They must accept the concept of nationalism because, in order to transcend it, they must *possess* and *understand* it. And a nationalist spirit in Negro writing means a nationalism carrying the highest possible pitch of social consciousness. It means a nationalism that knows its origins, its limitations; that is aware of the dangers of its position; that knows its ultimate aims are unrealizable within the framework of capitalist America; a nationalism whose reason for being lies in the simple fact of self-possession and in the consciousness of the interdependence of people in modern society.

For purposes of creative expression it means that the Negro writer must realize within the area of his own personal experience those impulses which, when prefigured in terms of broad social movements, constitute the stuff of nationalism.

For Negro writers even more so than for Negro politicians, nationalism is a bewildering and vexing question, the full ramifications of which cannot be dealt with here. But among Negro workers and the Negro middle class the spirit of nationalism is rife in a hundred devious forms; and a simple literary realism which seeks to depict the lives of these people devoid of wider social connotations, devoid of the revolutionary significance of these nationalist tendencies, must of necessity do a rank injustice to the Negro people and alienate their possible allies in the struggle for freedom.

6) SOCIAL CONSCIOUSNESS AND RESPONSIBILITY

The Negro writer who seeks to function within his race as a purposeful agent has a serious responsibility. In order to do justice to his subject matter, in order to depict Negro life in all of its manifold and intricate relationships, a deep, informed, and complex consciousness is necessary; a consciousness which draws for its strength upon the fluid lore of a great people, and moulds this lore with the concepts that move and direct the forces of history today.

With the gradual decline of the moral authority of the Negro church, and with the increasing irresolution which is paralyzing Negro middle class leadership, a new role is devolving upon the Negro writer. He is being called upon to do no less than create values by which his race is to struggle, live and die.

By his ability to fuse and make articulate the experiences of men, because his writing possesses the potential cunning to steal into the inmost recesses of the human heart, because he can create the myths and symbols that inspire a faith in life, he may expect either to be consigned to oblivion, or to be recognized for the valued agent he is.

This raises the question of the personality of the writer. It means that in the lives of Negro writers must be found those materials and experiences which will create a meaningful picture of the world today. Many young writers have grown to believe that a Marxist analysis of society presents such a picture. It creates a picture which, when placed before the eyes of the writer, should unify his personality, organize his emotions, buttress him with a tense and obdurate will to change the world.

And, in turn, this changed world will dialectically change the writer. Hence, it is through a Marxist conception of reality and society that the maximum degree of freedom in thought and feeling can be gained for the Negro writer. Further, this dramatic Marxist vision, when consciously grasped, endows the writer with a sense of dignity which no other vision can give. Ultimately, it restores to the writer his lost heritage, that is, his role as a creator of the world in which he lives, and as a creator of himself.

Yet, for the Negro writer, Marxism is but the starting point. No theory of life can take the place of life. After Marxism has laid bare the skeleton of society, there remains the task of the writer to plant flesh upon those bones out of his will to live. He may, with disgust and revulsion, say *no* and depict the horrors of capitalism encroaching upon the human being. Or he may, with hope and passion, say *yes* and depict the faint stirrings of a new and emerging life. But in whatever social voice he chooses to speak, whether positive or negative, there should always be heard or *over*-heard his faith, his necessity, his judgment.

His vision need not be simple or rendered in primer-like terms; for the life of the Negro people is not simple. The presentation of their lives should be simple, yes; but all the complexity, the strangeness, the magic wonder of life that plays like a bright sheen over the most sordid existence, should be there. To borrow a phrase from the Russians, it should have a *complex simplicity*. Eliot, Stein, Joyce, Proust, Hemingway, and Anderson; Gorky, Barbusse, Nexo, and Jack London no less than the folklore of the Negro himself should form the heritage of the Negro writer. Every iota of gain in human thought and sensibility should be ready grist for his mill, no matter how far-fetched they may seem in their immediate implications.

7) THE PROBLEM OF PERSPECTIVE

What vision must Negro writers have before their eyes in order to feel the impelling necessity for an about face? What angle of vision can show them all the forces of modern society in process, all the lines of economic development converging toward a distant point of hope? Must they believe in some "ism"?

They may feel that only dupes believe in "isms"; they feel with some measure of justification that another commitment means only another disillusionment. But anyone destitute of a theory about the meaning, structure and direction of modern society is a lost victim in a world he cannot understand or control.

But even if Negro writers found themselves through some "ism," how would that influence their writing? Are they being called upon to "preach"? To be "salesmen"? To "prostitute" their writing? Must they "sully" themselves? Must they write "propaganda"?

No; it is a question of awareness, of consciousness; it is, above all, a question of perspective.

Perspective is that part of a poem, novel, or play which a writer never puts directly upon paper. It is that fixed point in intellectual space where a writer stands to view the struggles, hopes, and sufferings of his people. There are times when he may stand too close and the result is a blurred vision. Or he may stand too far away and the result is a neglect of important things.

Of all the problems faced by writers who as a whole have never allied themselves with world movements, perspective is the most difficult of achievement. At its best, perspective is a pre-conscious assumption, something which a writer takes for granted, something which he wins through his living.

A Spanish writer recently spoke of living in the heights of one's time. Surely, perspective means just *that*.

It means that a Negro writer must learn to view the life of a Negro living in New York's Harlem or Chicago's South Side with the consciousness that one-sixth of the earth surface belongs to the working class. It means that a Negro writer must create in his readers' minds a relationship between a Negro woman hoeing cotton in the South and the men who loll in swivel chairs in Wall Street and take the fruits of her toil.

Perspective for Negro writers will come when they have looked and brooded so hard and long upon the harsh lot of their race and compared it with the hopes and struggles of minority peoples everywhere that the cold facts have begun to tell them something.

8) THE PROBLEM OF THEME

This does not mean that a Negro writer's sole concern must be with rendering the social scene; but if his conception of the life of his people is broad and deep enough, if the sense of the *whole* life he is seeking is vivid and strong in him, then his writing will embrace all those social, political, and economic forms under which the life of his people is manifest.

In speaking of theme one must necessarily be general and abstract; the temperament of each writer moulds and colors the world he sees. Negro life may be approached from a thousand angles, with no limit to technical and stylistic freedom.

Negro writers spring from a family, a clan, a class, and a nation; and the social units in which they are bound have a story, a record. Sense of theme will emerge in Negro writing when Negro writers try to fix this story about some pole of meaning, remembering as they do so that in the creative process meaning proceeds *equally* as much from the contemplation of the subject matter as from the hopes and apprehensions that rage in the heart of the writer.

Reduced to its simplest and most general terms, theme for Negro writers will rise from understanding the meaning of their being transplanted from a "savage" to a "civilized" culture in all of its social, political, economic, and emotional implications. It means that Negro writers must have in their consciousness the foreshortened picture of the *whole,* nourishing culture from which they were torn in Africa, and of the long, complex (and for the most part, unconscious) struggle to regain in some form and under alien conditions of life a *whole* culture again.

It is not only this picture they must have, but also a knowledge of the social and emotional milieu that gives it tone and solidity of detail. Theme for Negro writers will emerge when they have begun to feel the meaning of the history of their race as though they in one life time had lived it themselves throughout all the long centuries.

9) AUTONOMY OF CRAFT

For the Negro writer to depict this new reality requires a greater discipline and consciousness than was necessary for the so-called Harlem school of expression. Not only is the subject matter dealt with far more meaningful and complex, but the new role of the writer is qualitatively different. The Negro writers' new position demands a sharper definition of the status of his craft, and a sharper emphasis upon its functional autonomy.

Negro writers should seek through the medium of their craft to play as meaningful a role in the affairs of men as do other professionals. But if their writing is demanded to perform the social office of other professions, then the autonomy of craft is lost and writing detrimentally fused with other interests. The limitations of the craft constitute some of its greatest virtues. If the sensory vehicle of imaginative writing is required to carry too great a load of didactic material, the artistic sense is submerged.

The relationship between reality and the artistic image is not always direct and simple. The imaginative conception of a historical period will not be a carbon copy of reality. Image and emotion possess a logic of their own. A vulgarized simplicity constitutes the greatest danger in tracing the reciprocal interplay between the writer and his environment.

Writing has its professional autonomy; it should complement other professions, but it should not supplant them or be swamped by them.

10) THE NECESSITY FOR COLLECTIVE WORK

It goes without saying that these things cannot be gained by Negro writers if their present mode of isolated writing and living continues. This isolation exists *among* Negro writers as well as *between* Negro and white writers. The Negro writers' lack of thorough integration with the American scene, their lack of a clear realization among themselves of their possible role, have bred generation after generation of embittered and defeated literati.

Barred for decades from the theater and publishing houses, Negro writers have been *made* to feel a sense of difference. So deep has this white-hot iron of exclusion been burnt into their hearts that thousands have all but lost the desire to become identified with American civilization. The Negro writers' acceptance of this enforced isolation and their attempt to justify it is but a defense-reflex of the whole special way of life which has been rammed down their throats.

This problem, by its very nature, is one which must be approached contemporaneously from *two* points of view. The ideological unity of Negro writers and the alliance of that unity with all the progressive ideas of our day is the primary prerequisite for collective work. On the shoulders of white writers and Negro writers alike rest the responsibility of ending this mistrust and isolation.

By placing cultural health above narrow sectional prejudices, liberal writers of all races can help to break the stony soil of aggrandizement out of which the stunted plants of Negro nationalism grow. And, simultaneously, Negro writers can help to weed out these choking growths of reactionary nationalism and replace them with hardier and sturdier types.

These tasks are imperative in light of the fact that we live in a time when the majority of the most basic assumptions of life can no longer be taken for granted. Tradition is no longer a guide. The world has grown huge and cold. Surely this is the moment to ask questions, to theorize, to speculate, to wonder out of what materials can a human world be built.

Each step along this unknown path should be taken with thought, care, self-consciousness, and deliberation. When Negro writers think they have arrived at something which smacks of truth, humanity, they should want to test it with others, feel it with a degree of passion and strength that will enable them to communicate it to millions who are groping like themselves.

Writers faced with such tasks can have no possible time for malice or jealousy. The conditions for the growth of each writer depend too much upon the good work of other writers. Every first rate novel, poem, or play lifts the level of consciousness higher.

CHARLES S. JOHNSON

THIRTY YEARS AFTER the first Opportunity-sponsored gathering in 1924, Charles S. Johnson, the principal architect of the Harlem Renaissance, assessed its purpose and achievements in an essay contributed to a symposium at Howard University—"The Negro Renaissance and Its Significance"—a document of remarkable insight.

THE NEGRO RENAISSANCE AND ITS SIGNIFICANCE

THERE IS A DOUBLE PRESUMPTUOUSNESS about this presentation: It is not only a sort of history, constructed in large part from memory; but it is presented as history in the presence of rigid and exacting historians who regard the proper and unchallengeable enlightenment of future generations as their sacred trust.

There are, however, some compensating factors for this boldness: We are, in a sense, memorializing Alain Locke, an important maker of history who is himself inadequately recorded. And while some of the fragments of memory and experience may be compounded with a prejudiced aura of friendship, this fact itself from a collateral contemporary may have some value.

As a sociologist rather than an historian, it is expected that particular events would be viewed in the light of broader social processes, thus offering greater illumination to what has come to be recognized as a dramatic period in our national history.

American Negroes in the 1920's were just a little more than

a half century on their rugged course to citizenship. This period was the comet's tail of a great cultural ferment in the nation, the "melting pot" era, a period of the ascendancy of unbridled free enterprise, of the open beginnings of class struggle and new and feeble mutterings of self-conscious labor; of muckrakers and social settlements, of the open and unabashed acceptance of "inferior and superior races and civilizations." Likewise, the era just preceding the 1920's was a period of the sullen and frustrated gropings of the agrarian and culturally sterile South, in its "colonial" dependence upon the industrial North. It had been left in indifference to settle its problem of democracy in its own way.

In the wake of Reconstruction in the South there had been for the Negro, almost total political disfranchisement, economic disinheritance, denial of, or rigid limitation of, educational opportunity, complete racial segregation, with a gaudy racial philosophy to defend it, cultural isolation with its bitter fruit of inner personal poison, followed by mass migrations and revolt, and the tortuous struggle to slough off the heavy handicaps in order to achieve more completely a new freedom.

These were a part of the backdrop of what we have called the "Negro Renaissance," that sudden and altogether phenomenal outburst of emotional expression, unmatched by any comparable period in American or Negro American history.

It is well to point out that this was not a crisis and trauma affecting only the Negroes. It was fundamentally and initially a national problem.

James Weldon Johnson, who, with W. E. B. Du Bois emerged in the period just preceding the epochal 1920's, recognized this relationship and said this:

A good part of white America frequently asks the question, "What shall we do with the Negro?" In asking the question it completely ignores the fact that the Negro is doing something with himself, and also the equally important fact that the Negro all the while is doing something with America.

Before Johnson there had been only a few Negroes capable of articulating the inner emotional turmoil of the race in full consciousness of its role in a nation that was itself in great stress. Frederick Douglass had been a powerful oratorical force for the abolition of slavery, convincing to a sector of the nation in his own superiority as a person. Booker T. Washington had been a social strategist, speaking to the nation from the heavy racial miasma of the deep South, with wise words of economic counsel and even wiser words of tactical racial strategy. He parried the blows of the skeptical ones and the demagogues, who spoke hopelessly and menacingly of the destiny of the millions of ex-slaves in the South, still very largely unlettered and sought the armistice of tolerance during a vital period of regional gestation, as he negotiated with the industrial strength and benevolence of the North that was in being and the industrial dreams of the South, as yet unrealized.

W. E. B. Du Bois, brilliant, highly cultured, and racially sensitive, wrote with such bitter contempt for the American racial system that his flaming truths were invariably regarded as incendiary. He got attention but scant acceptance. And there was the poet Paul Laurence Dunbar who, like Booker T. Washington, came at a dark period, when with the release of the white working classes the independent struggle of Negroes for existence had become almost overwhelming in its severity. Dunbar caught the picture of the Negro in his pathetic and contagiously humorous moods and invested him with a new humanity. He embellished a stereotype and made likeable, in a homely way, the simple, joyous creature that was the mass Southern Negro, with the soft musical dialect and infectious rhythm. William Dean Howells, in an article in *Harper's Magazine*, hailed Dunbar as the first Negro to feel Negro life esthetically and express it lyrically. But in his candid moments, Dunbar confessed to Johnson that he resorted to dialect verse to gain a hearing and then nothing but his dialect verse would be accepted. He never got to the things he really wanted to do.

The acceptability of Dunbar's verse inspired many followers, including, for a brief spell, Johnson himself. The period of Johnson, however, was one that permitted bolder exploration and he turned forthrightly to poetry of race-consciousness. They were poems both of revelation and of protest. William Stanley Braithwaite was able to say of him that he brought the first intellectual substance to the context of poetry by Negroes, and a craftsmanship more precise and balanced than that of Dunbar. His Negro sermons symbolized the transition from the folk idiom to conscious artistic expression. In naive, non-dialect speech, they blend the rich imagery of the uneducated Negro minister with the finished skill of a cultured Negro poet. In a curiously fascinating way both style and content bespoke the meeting and parting of the old and new in Negro life in America.

The commentators even farther removed from today will be able to define more clearly the influence of these social and economic forces shortly after World War I, moving beneath the new mind of Negroes, which burst forth with freshness and vigor in an artistic "awakening." The first startlingly authentic note was sounded by Claude McKay, a Jamaican Negro living in America. If his was a note of protest it came clear and unquivering. But it was more than a protest note; it was one of stoical defiance which held behind it a spirit magnificent and glowing. One poem, "If We Must Die," written at the most acute point of the industrialization of Negroes when sudden mass contact in the Northern states was flaming into riots, voiced for Negroes, where it did not itself create, a mood of stubborn defiance. It was reprinted in practically every Negro newspaper, and quoted wherever its audacious lines could be remembered. But McKay could also write lyrics utterly divorced from these singing daggers. "Spring in New Hampshire" is one of them. He discovered Harlem and found a language of beauty for his own world of color.

> Her voice was like the sound of blended flutes
> Blown by black players on a picnic day.

Jean Toomer flashed like a meteor across the sky, then sank from view. But in the brilliant moment of his flight he illuminated the forefield of this new Negro literature. *Cane*, a collection of verse and stories, appeared about two years ahead of its sustaining public mood. It was significantly a return of the son to the Southland, to the stark, natural beauties of its life and soil, a life deep and strong, and a virgin soil.

More than artist, he was an experimentalist, and this last quality carried him away from what was, perhaps, the most astonishingly brilliant beginning of any Negro writer of his generation.

With Countee Cullen came a new generation of Negro singers. Claude McKay had brought a strange geographical background to the American scene which enabled him to escape a measure of the peculiar social heritage of the American Negro which similarly lacked the impedimenta of an inhibiting tradition. He relied upon nothing but his own sure competence and art; one month found three literary magazines carrying his verse simultaneously, a distinction not to be spurned by any young poet. Then came his first volume, *Color*. He brought an uncannily sudden maturity and classic sweep, a swift grace and an inescapable beauty of style and meaning. The spirit of the transplanted African moved through his music to a new definition—relating itself boldly to its past and present.

> Lord, not for what I saw in flesh or bone
> Of fairer men; not raised on faith alone;
> Lord, I will live persuaded by mine own.
> I cannot play the recreant to these;
> My spirit has come home, that sailed the doubtful seas.

He spoke, not for himself alone, but for the confident generation out of which he came. White gods were put aside and in their place arose the graces of a race he knew.

> Her walk is like the replica
> Of some barbaric dance
> Wherein the soul of Africa
> Is winged with arrogance.

and again:

> That brown girl's swagger gives a twitch
> To beauty like a queen.

No brief quotations can describe this power, this questioning of life and even God; the swift arrow thrusts of irony curiously mingled with admiration; the self-reliance and bold pride of race; the thorough repudiation of the double standard of literary judgment. He may have marvelled "at this curious thing to make a poet black and bid him sing," but in his *Heritage* he voiced the half-religious, half-challenging spirit of an awakened generation. "He will be remembered," said the *Manchester Guardian*, "as one who contributed to his age some of its loveliest lyric poetry."

Langston Hughes, at twenty-four, had published two volumes of verse. No Negro writer so completely symbolizes the new emancipation of the Negro mind. His was a poetry of gorgeous colors, of restless brooding, of melancholy, of disillusionment:

> We should have a land of sun
> Of gorgeous sun,
> And a land of fragrant water
> Where the twilight
> Is a soft bandana handkerchief
> And not this land where life is cold.

Always there is, in his writing, a wistful undertone, a quiet sadness. That is why, perhaps, he could speak so tenderly of the broken lives of prostitutes, the inner weariness of painted "jazz-hounds" and the tragic emptiness beneath the glamour and noise of Harlem cabarets. His first volume, *The Weary Blues*, contained many moods; the second, *Fine Clothes to the Jew*, marked a final frank turning to the folk life of the Negro, a striving to catch and give back to the world the strange music of the unlettered Negro —his "Blues." If Cullen gave a classic beauty to the emotions of the race, Hughes gave a warm glow of meaning to their lives.

I return again more comfortably to my role as a sociologist in recording this period following the deep and disrupting crisis of a world war, with its uprooting of customs and people in which there developed two movements with clashing ideologies. There was reassertion with vigor of the old and shaken racial theories, with "racial purity clubs," intelligence tests "proving" the unchangeable inferiority of the Negro and other darker peoples, Congressional restrictions of immigration according to rigid racial formulas, race riots, dark foreboding prophecies of the over-running of the white race by the dark and unenlightened hordes from Asia and Africa, in Lothrop Stoddard's *Rising Tide of Color*.

These were only reflections of the new forces set loose in the world and finding expression in such mutterings as "India for the Indians," "A Free Ireland," self-determination for the smaller countries of the world.

For the just-emerging Negro who had freed himself geographically at least, there was much frustration. Perhaps the most dramatic phase of this was the Garvey movement. Here were hundreds of thousands of Negroes who had reached the promised land of the North and found it a bitter Canaan. Having nowhere else to seek haven in America their dreams turned to Africa under the powerful stimulation of the master dream-maker from the West Indies, Marcus Garvey. They would find haven in their ancestral homeland, and be free from the insults and restrictions of this nation and England, on their chance for greatness. Provisionally there were created Dukes of the Nile, Princesses of Ethiopia, Lords of the Sudan, for the weary and frustrated people whose phantom freedom in the North was as empty as their explicit subordination in the South.

Of this desperate and pathetic mass fantasy I find an editorial note in *Opportunity Magazine* in 1923 in a mood of brooding concern for the present and apprehension for the future:

> It is a symbol, a symptom, and another name for the new psychology of the American Negro peasantry—for the surge of race consciousness felt by Negroes throughout the world, the intelligent as well as the ignorant.

> It is a black version of that same one hundred per cent mania that now afflicts white America, that emboldens the prophets of a Nordic blood renaissance, that picked up and carried the cry of self-determination for all people, India for the Indians, A Free Ireland.

> The sources of this discontent must be remedied effectively and now, or the accumulating energy and unrest, blocked off from its dreams, will take another direction. Perhaps this also will be harmless, but who knows.

To this note of 1923 might be added the observation of what is happening in the Asian-African Conference in Bandung in 1955; what happened in this long interval to make it possible for twenty-nine nations that in 1923 were only muttering against colonial imperialism and now are speaking as free and independent nations collectively to preserve the peace and security of the world.

It was out of forces of such magnitude that the voices of the Negro Renaissance made themselves heard and felt. It was a period, not only of the quivering search for freedom but of a cultural, if not a social and racial emancipation. It was unabashedly self-conscious and race-conscious. But it was race-consciousness with an extraordinary facet in that it had virtues that could be incorporated into the cultural bloodstream of the nation.

This was the period of the discovery by these culturally emancipated Negroes of the unique esthetic values of African art, of beauty in things dark, a period of harkening for the whispers of greatness from a remote African past. This was the period of Kelly

Miller's Sanhedrin to reassess the lost values and build upon newly-found strengths. It was the period of the reaching out of arms for other dark arms of the same ancestry from other parts of the world in a Pan-African Conference.

Significantly, Dr. W. E. B. Du Bois made his first talk after returning from the Pan-African Conference of 1923 at the first *Opportunity Magazine* dinner, sponsoring the fledgling writers of the new and lively generation of the 1920's.

The person recognized as the Dean of this youthful group was Alain Locke. A brilliant analyst trained in philosophy, and an esthete with a flair for art as well as letters, he gave encouragement and guidance to these young writers as an older practitioner too sure of his craft to be discouraged by failure of full acceptance in the publishing media of the period.

Perhaps this is the point at which to add a previously unwritten note to the history of the period. The importance of the *Crisis Magazine* and *Opportunity Magazine* was that of providing an outlet for young Negro writers and scholars whose work was not acceptable to other established media because it could not be believed to be of standard quality despite the superior quality of much of it. What was necessary was a revolution and a revelation sufficient in intensity to disturb the age-old customary cynicisms. This function became associated with *Opportunity Magazine*.

Alain Locke recognized the role and possibility of this organ for creating such a revolution and associated himself with it, first as a reviewer and appraiser of various literary and sociological efforts and later as a contributor of major articles. As a by-product of his acquaintance with France, England and Germany through frequent visits, he wrote articles on current issues affecting Negroes from the perspective of Europe: "The Black Watch on the Rhine" (1921), "Apropos of Africa" (1924) and "Back Stage on European Imperialism" (1925). These articles were of such mature sophistication and insight that *Opportunity* offered to share their publication with the *Survey Magazine* to get a larger reading public. This magazine not only published the articles jointly with *Opportunity* but requested special ones for the *Survey* readers. Thus began an important relationship with the editor of the *Survey* and *Survey Graphic*.

The first *Opportunity* contest had Alain Locke's enthusiastic support and assistance. It was a dual venture in faith: faith in the creative potential of this generation in its new cultural freedom;

and faith in the confidence of the nation's superior mentalities and literary creators. Both were justified. Locke's mellow maturity and esthetic sophistication were the warrant of confidence in the possibilities of these youth as well as the concrete evidence of accomplishment. The American scholars and writers who stretched out their arms to welcome these youthful aspirants to cultural equality were, without exception, the intellectual and spiritual leaders of the nation's cultural life and aspirations. They served as judges in these contests and in this role gave priceless assistance to this first and vital step in cultural integration. They were such great figures of American literary history as Van Wyck Brooks, Carl Van Doren, Eugene O'Neill, James Weldon Johnson, Paul Kellogg, Fannie Hurst, Robert Benchley, Zona Gale, Dorothy Canfield Fisher, Witter Bynner, W. E. B. Du Bois, Alexander Woollcott, John Macy, John Dewey, Carl Van Vechten, John Farrar and others.

They not only judged the poetry, essays, short stories and plays, but lent a supporting hand to their development in the best literary traditions.

At the first *Opportunity* dinner at the Civic Club in New York, Alain Locke was as a matter of course and appropriateness, moderator. It happens that this was one of the most significant and dramatic of the announcements of the renaissance. It marked the first public appearance of young creative writers in the company of the greatest of the nation's creative writers and philosophers. Out of this meeting came some of the first publications in the best publication tradition.

I cannot refrain from quoting briefly a poem read at this dinner by Gwendolyn Bennett:

TO USWARD

> And some of us have songs to sing
> Of purple heat and fires
> And some of us are solemn grown
> With pitiful desires;
> And there are those who feel the pull
> Of seas beneath the skies;
> And some there be who want to croon
> Of Negro lullabies.
> We claim no part with racial dearth
> We want to sing the songs of birth.

And so we stand like ginger jars,
Like ginger jars bound round
With dust and age;
Like jars of ginger we are sealed
By nature's heritage.
But let us break the seal of years
With pungent thrusts of song
For there is joy in long dried tears
For whetted passions of a throng.

For specific identification, it should be noted that Frederick Allen of *Harper's Magazine* made a bid for Countee Cullen's poems for publication as soon as he had finished reading them at this *Opportunity* dinner; and Paul Kellogg of the *Survey* sought to carry the entire evening's readings in an issue of the magazine. This fumbling idea lead to the standard volume of the period, *The New Negro*.

Winold Reiss, a German artist of extraordinary skill in pictorial interpretation had just completed some drawings for the *Survey* of Sea Island Negroes. The publishers Boni and Boni who were interested in a book of Winold Reiss' drawings decided to carry the literary content along with the pictures. This literary content had been carried first in the *Survey Graphic* in a special issue under the editorship of Alain Locke. As a book it became *The New Negro*, also edited by Locke, and expanded from the special issue of the *Survey Graphic* to the proportions that now make brilliant history.

The impetus to publication backed by the first recognition of creative work in the best literary tradition, swept in many if not most of the budding writers of this period, in a fever of history-making expression.

Removed by two generations from slavery and in a new cultural environment, these Negro writers were less self-conscious and less interested in proving that they were just like white people; in their excursions into the fields of letters and art, they seemed to care less about what white people thought, or were likely to think, than about themselves and what they had to say. Relief from the stifling consciousness of being a problem had brought a certain superiority to it. There was more candor, even in discussions of themselves about weaknesses, and on the very sound reasoning that unless you are truthful about your faults, you will not be believed when you speak about your virtues. The emancipation of these writers gave them freedom to return to the dynamic folk motives. Carl Van Doren, in commenting upon this material said:

> If the reality of Negro life is itself dramatic there are, of course, still other elements, particularly the emotional power, with which Negroes live—or at least to me they seem to live. What American literature needs at this moment is color, music, gusto, the free expression of gay, or desperate moods. If the Negroes are not in a position to contribute these items, I do not know which Americans are.

As a rough cultural yardstick of the continuing repercussions of the period called the Renaissance, I have looked up the record of the youthful writers and commentators of this period for evidences of their effect upon the present state of the American culture.

An anthology called *Ebony and Topaz* carried about twenty young Negro writers, previously unknown to the great and critical public. Of those still living Langston Hughes and Sterling Brown are established poets, Arna Bontemps is a major novelist, having left his poetry with his youth; Aaron Douglas is one of the country's best-known artists; Zora Neale Hurston is a writer-anthropologist; Allison Davis is a distinguished psychologist and Abram Harris an equally distinguished economist, and both are on the faculty of the University of Chicago. Ira Reid heads the Department of Sociology at Haverford; Frank Horne is a national housing official. E. Franklin Frazier is one of the nation's most notable sociologists and a former president of the American Sociological Society, George Schuyler is a well-known columnist and John P. Davis is publisher of *Our World Magazine*.

There are others, of course, but the important thing is to show some end result of the striving.

As master of ceremonies for the first *Opportunity* dinner Alain Locke had this to say about these young spirits being launched on their careers: "They sense within their group—a spiritual wealth which if they can properly expound, will be ample for a new judgment and re-appraisal of the race."

Whether or not there has been a reappraisal of the race over these past thirty years rests with our estimates of the contributions of those who began their careers in the 1920's. It is my opinion that the great fire and enthusiasm of the earlier period, and the creative dynamism of self-conscious racial expression are no longer present. They have faded with the changed status of Negroes in American life.

With the disappearance of many of the barriers to participation in the general culture the intense race-consciousness has been translated into contributions within the accepted national standards of the special professional fields.

One of Goethe's commentators referred to his literary art as the practice of living and pointed out that his life was as much worth studying as his work. Goethe in one of his diaries said:

> People who are always harping on the value of experience tend to forget that experience is only the one-half of experience. The secret of creative living consists in relating the rough and tumble of our contact with the world outside ourselves to the work which our minds put in on this stuff of experience. The full value of experience is in seeing the significance of what has happened. Without this awareness we do not really live. Life lives us.

This, it seems to me, is the essence of the shift in Negro life and Negro appraisals of life.

The infectious race-conscious movement of the period of the "Renaissance" has been transmitted into less race-conscious scholarship. The historical research of John Hope Franklin, Benjamin Quarles and Rayford Logan appears as aspects of American history even though the subject matter may be Negroes. Similarly the sociological writing of E. Franklin Frazier, Ira de A. Reid, and Oliver Cox is in the broader context of the American society. Frank Yerby's romantic novels are best sellers and deal only incidentally with Negroes, if at all.

The most recent books by Negro authors, interestingly enough, are travel studies of other lands and people. Saunders Redding and Carl Rowan have written about India, Richard Wright and Era Belle Thompson about Africa. Meanwhile the kind of writing done by American Negroes in the 1920's is reflected in the books today by Peter Abrahams of South Africa and George Lamming of Trinidad, in the British West Indies.

In 1923 Franklin Frazier who was one of the first *Opportunity* prize winners with a bold essay on "Social Equality and the Negro" had this to say:

> The accomplishment of a consciously built-up culture will depend upon leaders with a vision and understanding of cultural processes. Nevertheless, spiritual and intellectual emancipation of the Negro awaits the building of a Negro university, supported by Negro educators, who have imbibed the best that civilization can offer, where its savants can add to human knowledge and promulgate those values which are to inspire and motivate Negroes as a cultural group.

We have in this present period, and out of the matrix of the Renaissance period, scholars who know the cultural process, and savants who have imbibed the best that civilization can offer and can and are aiding human knowledge, within the context, not of a special culture group, but of the national society and world civilization.

PART II

POETRY

GWENDOLYN BENNETT

THERE WAS GREAT VARIETY *in Harlem Renaissance poetry, as well as extremes in quality. Mae Cowdery, Joseph Cotter, Sr., Joseph Cotter, Jr., Fenton Johnson, and Helene Johnson were much admired during the early years but were soon largely forgotten. Their poetry was usually more interesting, edifying, or poignant for the sentiments or ideas expressed than for creative or appealing composition. The younger Cotter's "Sonnet to Negro Soldiers," which appeared in his* The Band of Gideon and Other Lyrics *(1918), was one of the most popular and powerful works produced during a life that was tragically brief (1895–1919). Du Bois featured it in the special* Crisis *"Soldiers' Number" for June of that year. Born in Boston in 1907, Helene Johnson's poetry was influenced by Whitman and sometimes distinguished by venturesome forays into colloquialisms, as in the popular "Bottled" (in the May 1927 issue of* Vanity Fair*), and into mild eroticism, as in "Sonnet to a Negro in Harlem" (awarded the* Opportunity *contest's fourth prize in 1928).*

SONG

> I am weaving a song of waters,
> Shaken from firm, brown limbs,
> Or heads thrown back in irreverent mirth.
> My song has the lush sweetness
> Of moist, dark lips
> Where hymns keep company

With old forgotten banjo songs.
Abandon tells you
That I sing the heart of a race
While sadness whispers
That I am the cry of a soul. . . .

A-shoutin' in de ole camp-meetin' place,
A-strummin' o' de ole banjo.
Singin' in de moonlight,
Sobbin' in de dark.
Singin', sobbin', strummin' slow . . .
Singin' slow; sobbin' low.
Strummin', strummin', strummin' slow. . . .

Words are bright bugles
That make the shining for my song,
And mothers hold brown babes
To dark, warm breasts
To make my singing sad.

A dancing girl with swaying hips
Sets mad the queen in a harlot's eye.
    Praying slave
    Jazz band after
    Breaking heart
    To the time of laughter. . . .
Clinking chains and minstrelsy
Are welded fast with melody.
    A praying slave
    With a jazz band after . . .
    Singin' slow, sobbin' low.
Sun-baked lips will kiss the earth.
Throats of bronze will burst with mirth.
    Sing a little faster,
    Sing a little faster!
    Sing!

HATRED

I shall hate you
Like a dart of singing steel
Shot through still air
At even-tide.
Or solemnly
As pines are sober
When they stand etched
Against the sky.
Hating you shall be a game
Played with cool hands
And slim fingers.
Your heart will yearn
For the lonely splendor
Of the pine tree;
While rekindled fires
In my eyes
Shall wound you like swift arrows.
Memory will lay its hands
Upon your breast
And you will understand
My hatred.

ARNA BONTEMPS

ARNA BONTEMPS, *Langston Hughes's closest friend and occasional collaborator, was not a prolific poet. He arrived in Harlem at the beginning of the Renaissance's second phase. Although an excellent craftsman, he did not strive for the special effects of Hughes, the mannered irony and ennui of Countee Cullen, or the demotic modes of Claude McKay and Sterling Brown. Bontemps's moderately brooding perspective was fully in keeping with the circumspection of the Talented Tenth literary canon. "The Day-Breakers" appeared in Locke's* The New Negro, *while the popular and stately "Golgotha Is a Mountain" took the Alexander Pushkin first prize in the 1926* Opportunity *contest.*

THE DAY-BREAKERS

> We are not come to wage a strife
>   With swords upon this hill,
> It is not wise to waste the life
>   Against a stubborn will.
> Yet would we die as some have done.
> Beating a way for the rising sun.

GOLGOTHA IS A MOUNTAIN

Golgatha is a mountain, a purple mound
Almost out of sight.

One night they hanged two thieves there,
And another man.
Some women wept heavily that night;
Their tears are flowing still. They have made a river;
Once it covered me.
Then the people went away and left Golgotha
Deserted.
Oh, I've seen many mountains:
Pale purple mountains melting in the evening mists and blurring
    on the borders of the sky.
I climbed old Shasta and chilled my hands in its summer snows.
I rested in the shadow of Popocatepetl and it whispered to me of
    daring prowess.
I looked upon the Pyranees and felt the zest of warm exotic
    nights.
I slept at the foot of Fujiyama and dreamed of legend and of
    death.
And I've seen other mountains rising from the wistful moors like
    the breasts of a slender maiden.
Who knows the mystery of mountains!
Some of them are awful, others are just lonely.

Italy has its Rome and California has San Francisco,
All covered with mountains.
Some think these mountains grew
Like ant hills
Or sand dunes.
That might be so—
I wonder what started them all!
Babylon is a mountain
And so is Nineval,
With grass growing on them;
Palaces and hanging gardens started them.
I wonder what is under the hills
In Mexico
And Japan!
There are mountains in Africa too.
Treasure is buried there:
Gold and precious stones
And moulded glory.
Lush grass is growing there
Sinking before the wind.

Black men are bowing.
Naked in that grass
Digging with their fingers.
I am one of them:
Those mountains should be ours.
It would be great
To touch the pieces of glory with our hands.
These mute unhappy hills,
Bowed down with broken backs,
Speak often one to another:
"A day is as a year," they cry,
"And a thousand years as one day.
We watched the caravan
That bore our queen to the courts of Solomon;
And when the first slave traders came
We bowed our heads.
Oh, Brothers, it is not long!
Dust shall yet devour the stones
But we shall be here when they are gone."
Mountains are rising all around me.
Some are so small they are not seen;
Others are large.
All of them get big in time and people forget
What started them at first.
Oh the world is covered with mountains!
Beneath each one there is something buried:
Some pile of wreckage that started it there.
Mountains are lonely and some are awful.

One day I will crumble.
They'll cover my heap with dirt and that will make a mountain.
I think it will be Golgotha.

STERLING BROWN

STERLING BROWN'S VOLUME OF POETRY Southern Road *came in 1932, near the end of the Harlem Renaissance. Alain Locke believed that if anything could have prolonged the Renaissance it was the naturalistic force and quality of Brown's poems. In the title poem of his collection and in "Long Gone" and "Ma Rainey," Brown strove, far more than even Langston Hughes, to erase the gap between the creative artist and the folk. Emotion, milieu, and language were fused together so consummately as to make Brown's portrayals of the hard life of the common man and woman the most authentic, hard-boiled, and fatalistic of the Renaissance.*

Brown's "Long Gone" captured the robust, peripatetic ideal of lovemaking held by a vast number of black males born into and permanently trapped at the bottom of the labor scale: "I laks yo' kin' of lovin,/Ain't never caught you wrong,/But it jes' ain' nachal/ Fo to stay here long." In the epic "Remembering Nat Turner," the voice of a roving African American from this century recounts the great slave rebellion through the blurred anecdotal impressions of black and white people encountered along the route taken by Turner in 1831. Brown endeavored to present the heroic futility of people at the bottom, ceaselessly struggling against every manner of racial barrier.

SOUTHERN ROAD

Swing dat hammer—hunh—
Steady, bo';

Swing dat hammer—hunh—
Steady, bo';
Ain't no rush, bebby,
Long ways to go.

Burner tore his—hunh—
Black heart away;
Burner tore his—hunh—
Black heart away;
Got me life, bebby,
An' a day.

Gal's on Fifth Street—hunh—
Son done gone;
Gal's on Fifth Street—hunh—
Son done gone;
Wife's in de ward, bebby,
Babe's not bo'n.

My ole man died—hunh—
Cussin' me;
My ole man died—hunh—
Cussin' me;
Ole lady rocks, bebby,
Huh misery.

Doubleshackled—hunh—
Guard behin';
Doubleshackled—hunh—
Guard behin';
Ball an' chain, bebby,
On my min'.

White man tells me—hunh—
Damn yo' soul;
White man tells me—hunh—
Damn yo' soul;
Got no need, bebby,
To be tole.

Chain gang nevah—hunh—
Let me go;
Chain gang nevah—hunh—
Let me go;
Po' los' boy, bebby,
Evahmo'. . . .

ODYSSEY OF BIG BOY

Lemme be wid Casey Jones,
   Lemme be wid Stagolee,
Lemme be wid such like men
   When Death takes hol' on me,
      When Death takes hol' on me. . . .

Done skinned as a boy in Kentucky hills,
   Druv steel dere as a man,
Done stripped tobacco in Virginia fiel's
   Alongst de River Dan,
      Alongst de River Dan;

Done mined de coal in West Virginia,
   Liked dat job jes' fine,
Till a load o' slate curved roun' my head,
   Won't work in no mo' mine,
      Won't work in no mo' mine;

Done shocked de corn in Marylan',
   In Georgia done cut cane,
Done planted rice in South Caline,
   But won't do dat again,
      Do dat no mo' again.

Been roustabout in Memphis,
   Dockhand in Baltimore,
Done smashed up freight on Norfolk wharves,
   A fust class stevedore,
      A fust class stevedore. . . .

Done slung hash yonder in de North
    On de ole Fall River Line,
Done busted suds in li'l New York,
    Which ain't no work o' mine—
        Lawd, ain't no work o' mine.

Done worked and loafed on such like jobs,
    Seen what dey is to see,
Done had my time wid a pint on my hip
    An' a sweet gal on my knee,
        Sweet mommer on my knee:

Had stovepipe blond in Macon,
    Yaller gal in Marylan',
In Richmond had a choklit brown,
    Called me huh monkey man—
        Huh big fool monkey man.

Had two fair browns in Arkansaw
    And three in Tennessee,
Had Creole gal in New Orleans,
    Sho Gawd did two time me—
        Lawd two time, fo' time me—

But best gal what I evah had
    Done put it over dem,
A gal in Southwest Washington
    At Four'n half and M—
        Four'n half and M. . . .

Done took my livin' as it came,
    Done grabbed my joy, done risked my life;
Train done caught me on de trestle,
    Man done caught me wid his wife,
        His doggone purty wife. . . .

I done had my women,
    I done had my fun;
Cain't do much complainin'
    When my jag is done,
        Lawd, Lawd, my jag is done.

An' all dat Big Boy axes
  When time comes fo' to go,
Lemme be wid John Henry, steel drivin' man,
  Lemme be wid old Jazzbo,
    Lemme be wid ole Jazzbo. . . .

FRANKIE AND JOHNNY

Oh Frankie and Johnny were lovers
Oh Lordy how they did love!
           OLD BALLAD

Frankie was a halfwit, Johnny was a nigger,
  Frankie liked to pain poor creatures as a little 'un,
Kept a crazy love of torment when she got bigger,
  Johnny had to slave it and never had much fun.

Frankie liked to pull wings off of living butterflies,
  Frankie liked to cut long angleworms in half,
Frankie liked to whip curs and listen to their drawn out cries,
  Frankie liked to shy stones at the brindle calf.

Frankie took her pappy's lunch week-days to the sawmill,
  Her pappy, red-faced cracker, with a cracker's thirst,
Beat her skinny body and reviled the hateful imbecile,
  She screamed at every blow he struck, but tittered when he
    curst.

Frankie had to cut through Johnny's field of sugar corn
  Used to wave at Johnny, who didn't *pay no min'*—
Had had to work like fifty from the day that he was born,
  And wan't no cracker hussy gonna put his work behind—.

But everyday Frankie swung along the cornfield lane,
  And one day Johnny helped her partly through the wood,
Once he had dropped his plow lines, he dropped them many
    times again—
  Though his mother didn't know it, else she'd have whipped
    him good.

Frankie and Johnny were lovers; oh Lordy how they did love!
  But one day Frankie's pappy by a big log laid him low,
To find out what his crazy Frankie had been speaking of;
  He found that what his gal had muttered was exactly so.

Frankie, she was spindly limbed with corn silk on her crazy
      head,
  Johnny was a nigger, who never had much fun—
They swung up Johnny on a tree, and filled his swinging hide
      with lead,
  And Frankie yowled hilariously when the thing was done.

MA RAINEY

I

When Ma Rainey
Comes to town,
Folks from anyplace
Miles aroun',
From Cape Girardeau,
Poplar Bluff,
Flocks in to hear
Ma do her stuff;
Comes flivverin' in,
Or ridin' mules,
Or packed in trains,
Picknickin' fools. . . .
That's what it's like,
Fo' miles on down,
To New Orleans delta
An' Mobile town,
When Ma hits
Anywheres aroun'.

II

Dey comes to hear Ma Rainey from de little river settlements,
From blackbottom cornrows and from lumber camps;
Dey stumble in de hall, jes a-laughin' an' a-cacklin',
Cheerin' lak roarin' water, lak wind in river swamps.

An' some jokers keeps deir laughs a-goin' in de crowded aisles,
An' some folks sits dere waitin' wid deir aches an' miseries,
Till Ma comes out before dem, a-smilin' gold-toofed smiles
An' Long Boy ripples minors on de black an' yellow keys.

III

O Ma Rainey,
Sing yo' song;
Now you's back
Whah you belong,
Git way inside us,
Keep us strong. . . .
O Ma Rainey,
Li'l an' low;
Sing us 'bout de hard luck
Roun' our do';
Sing us 'bout de lonesome road
We mus' go. . . .

IV

I talked to a fellow, an' the fellow say,
"She jes' catch hold of us, somekindaway.
She sang Backwater Blues one day:

> *'It rained fo' days an' de skies was dark as night,*
> *Trouble taken place in de lowlands at night.*

> *'Thundered an' lightened an' the storm begin to roll*
> *Thousan's of people ain't got no place to go.*

'*Den I went an' stood upon some high ol' lonesome hill,*
An' looked down on the place where I used to live.'

An' den de folks, dey natchally bowed dey heads an' cried,
Bowed dey heavy heads, shet dey moufs up tight an' cried,
An' Ma lef' de stage, an' followed some de folks outside."

Dere wasn't much more de fellow say:
She jes' gits hold of us dataway.

LONG GONE

> I laks yo' kin' of lovin',
>   Ain't never caught you wrong,
> But it jes' ain' nachal
>   Fo' to stay here long;
>
> It jes' ain' nachal
>   Fo' a railroad man,
> With a itch fo' travelin'
>   He cain't understan'. . . .
>
> I looks at de rails,
>   An' I looks at de ties,
> An' I hears an ole freight
>   Puffin' up de rise,
>
> An' at nights on my pallet,
>   When all is still,
> I listens fo' de empties
>   Bumpin' up de hill;
>
> When I oughta be quiet,
>   I is got a itch
> Fo' to hear de whistle blow
>   Fo' de crossin' or de switch,
>
> An' I knows de time's a-nearin'
>   When I got to ride,

Though it's homelike and happy
  At yo' side.

You is done all you could do
  To make me stay;
'Tain't no fault of yours I'se leavin'—
  I'se jes dataway.

I is got to see some people
  I ain't never seen,
Gotta highball thu some country
  Whah I never been.

I don't know which way I'm travelin'—
  Far or near,
All I knows fo' certain is
  I cain't stay here.

Ain't no call at all, sweet woman,
  Fo' to carry on—
Jes' my name and jes' my habit
  To be Long Gone. . . .

GEORGIE GRIMES

Georgie Grimes, with a red suitcase,
  Sloshes onward through the rain,
Georgie Grimes, with a fear behind him,
  Will not come back again.

Georgie remembers hot words, lies,
  The knife, and a pool of blood,
And suddenly her staring eyes,
  With their light gone out for good.

Georgie mutters over and over,
  Stumbling through the soggy clay,
"No livin' woman got de right
  To do no man dat way."

REMEMBERING NAT TURNER

We saw a bloody sunset over Courtland, once Jerusalem,
As we followed the trail that old Nat took
When he came out of Cross Keys down upon Jerusalem,
In his angry stab for freedom a hundred years ago.
The land was quiet, and the mist was rising,
Out of the woods and the Nottaway swamp,
Over Southampton the still night fell,
As we rode down to Cross Keys where the march began.

When we got to Cross Keys, they could tell us little of him,
The Negroes had only the faintest recollections:
    "I ain't been here so long, I come from up roun' Newsome;
    Yassah, a town a few miles up de road,
    The old folks who coulda told you is all dead an' gone.
    I heard something, sometime; I doan jis remember what.
    'Pears lak I heard that name somewheres or other.
    So he fought to be free. Well. You doan say."

And old white woman recalled exactly
How Nat crept down the steps, axe in his hand,
After murdering a woman and child in bed,
"Right in this house at the head of these stairs."
(In a house built long after Nat was dead.)
She pointed to a brick store where Nat was captured,
(Nat was taken in a swamp, three miles away)
With his men around him, shooting from the windows
(She was thinking of Harper's Ferry and old John Brown).
She cackled as she told how they riddled Nat with bullets
(Nat was tried and hanged at Courtland, ten miles away)
She wanted to know why folks would come miles
Just to ask about an old nigger fool.
    "Ain't no slavery no more, things is going all right,
    Pervided thar's a good goober market this year.
    We had a sign post here with printing on it,
    But it rotted in the hole and thar it lays;
    And the nigger tenants split the marker for kindling.
    Things is all right, naow, ain't no trouble with the niggers.
    Why they make this big to-do over Nat?"

As we drove from Cross Keys back to Courtland,
Along the way that Nat came down from Jerusalem,
A watery moon was high in the cloud-filled heavens,
The same moon he dreaded a hundred years ago.
The tree they hanged Nat on is long gone to ashes,
The trees he dodged behind have rotted in the swamps.

The bus for Miami and the trucks boomed by,
And touring cars, their heavy tires snarling on the pavement.

MAE COWDERY

Mae Cowdery's "The Young Voice Cries" was a proto-feminist appeal, dedicated to Alice Dunbar Nelson, a lesbian, a poet, and a remarkable feminist.

THE YOUNG VOICE CRIES

To Alice Dunbar Nelson

> Can you not hear us?
> Or are you deaf
> To our pleading . . .
> Can you not see us?
> Or are you blind
> To our weeping . . .
> We yearn to hear
> The beauty of truth
> From your lips.
> As rain drips
> From trees
> On the budding flowers
> 'Neath its feet.
> We look to see
> The naked loveliness
> Of things . . . thru your eyes
> A barren cliff . . . made
> A crimson rise

Of earth's breast
Against the sky!

But
We must be the roots
Of the tree
And push up alone
Thru earth
Rocky with prejudice
And foul with smirking
Horrors . . .
Until at last
We thrust our rough virile
Bodies into the sun
And lift verdant arms in prayer
That we might drip soft rain
On the budding flowers
'Neath our feet.

And when we look
To see the naked loveliness
Of things
There is only a barren cliff
Veiled in ugly mists
Of dogmas and fear.
But we will send our singing into
The wind . . . and blow the mists away
That those who still are in the valley
May see it . . . A crimson rise
Of earth's breast against the sky!

O! You who bore us in pain and joy
To whom God entrusted our souls . . .
Be not deaf to our pleading
Nor blind to our silent weeping!
Look not down in frowning anger!
Else tired of futile tears . . .
We blaze a new path into depths you
Cannot enter . . . and only from afar
Will you see the naked loveliness of things

And the simple beauty of truth
To which time has blinded and defended you!

The young voice cries
For the pagan loveliness.
Of a moon
For the brazen beauty
Of a jazz song . . .
The young voice
Is hushed
In silent prayer
At beauty's shrine . . .

JOSEPH S. COTTER

THE WAYSIDE WELL

A fancy halts my feet at the way-side well.
It is not to drink, for they say the water is brackish.
It is not to tryst, for a heart at the mile's-end beckons me on.
It is not to rest, for what feet could be weary when a heart at
    the mile's-end keeps time with their tread?
It is not to muse, for the heart at the mile's-end is food for
    my being.
I will question the well for my secret by dropping a pebble
    into it.
Ah, it is dry.
Strike lightning to the road, my feet, for hearts are like wells.
    You may not know they are dry 'til you question their
    depths.
Fancies clog the way to heaven, and saints miss their crowns.

COUNTEE CULLEN

MUCH OF THE MAINSTREAM *reading public expected Renaissance poets to write about jungles, gamey sexual passions, and the psychic woe of being black. Countee Cullen's lyrical poetry was capable of satisfying all of these stereotypes and projections, as in the beautifully evocative-of-Africa "Heritage," the homoerotic "To a Brown Boy" (with Langston Hughes in mind), "Tableau," the deeply morbid "Nothing Endures," and "Requiescam."*

"Harlem Wine" and "From the Dark Tower" (which gave Harlem hostess A'Lelia Walker's famous salon its name) were quintessential Harlem Renaissance poems in their extolling of African American creative energies balked or discounted because of racial discrimination. Cullen achieved an irony in his racial poems that was at once elegant and adamantine, as in "For a Lady I Know" and "Incident." The other chord he often sounded in his "race" poetry was that of alienation, of being the perspicacious outsider in his own land and culture, as in "Heritage," "Yet Do I Marvel" ("Yet do I marvel at this curious thing:/To make a poet black, and bid him sing!"), and "To France." "Two Poets," from Cullen's long, ambitious poem The Black Christ, *was a poignant blending of ennui and sexual destiny.*

FOR A LADY I KNOW

She even thinks that up in heaven
Her class lies late and snores,

> While poor black cherubs rise at seven
> To do celestial chores.

INCIDENT
For Eric Walrond

> Once riding in old Baltimore,
>   Heart-filled, head-filled with glee,
> I saw a Baltimorean
>   Keep looking straight at me.
>
> Now I was eight and very small,
>   And he was no whit bigger,
> And so I smiled, but he poked out
>   His tongue, and called me, "Nigger."
>
> I saw the whole of Baltimore
>   From May until December;
> Of all the things that happened there
>   That's all that I remember.

HARLEM WINE

> This is not water running here,
> These thick rebellious streams
> That hurtle flesh and bone past fear
> Down alleyways of dreams.
>
> This is a wine that must flow on
> Not caring how or where,
> So it has ways to flow upon
> Where song is in the air.
>
> So it can woo an artful flute
> With loose, elastic lips,

Its measurement of joy compute
With blithe, ecstatic hips.

YET DO I MARVEL

I doubt not God is good, well-meaning, kind,
And did He stoop to quibble could tell why
The little buried mole continues blind,
Why flesh that mirrors Him must some day die,
Make plain the reason tortured Tantalus
Is baited by the fickle fruit, declare
If merely brute caprice dooms Sisyphus
To struggle up a never-ending stair.
Inscrutable His ways are, and immune
To catechism by a mind too strewn
With petty cares to slightly understand
What awful brain compels His awful hand.
Yet do I marvel at this curious thing:
To make a poet black, and bid him sing!

HERITAGE

What is Africa to me:
Copper sun or scarlet sea,
Jungle star or jungle track,
Strong bronzed men, or regal black
Women from whose loins I sprang
When the birds of Eden sang?
One three centuries removed
From the scenes his fathers loved,
Spicy grove, cinnamon tree,
What is Africa to me?
So I lie, who all day long
Want no sound except the song
Sung by wild barbaric birds
Goading massive jungle herds,
Juggernauts of flesh that pass

Trampling tall defiant grass
Where young forest lovers lie,
Plighting troth beneath the sky.
So I lie, who always hear,
Though I cram against my ear
Both my thumbs, and keep them there,
Great drums throbbing through the air.
So I lie, whose fount of pride,
Dear distress, and joy allied,
Is my somber flesh and skin,
With the dark blood dammed within
Like great pulsing tides of wine
That, I fear, must burst the fine
Channels of the chafing net
Where they surge and foam and fret.

Africa? A book one thumbs
Listlessly, till slumber comes.
Unremembered are her bats
Circling through the night, her cats
Crouching in the river reeds,
Stalking gentle flesh that feeds
By the river brink; no more
Does the bugle-throated roar
Cry that monarch claws have leapt
From the scabbards where they slept.
Silver snakes that once a year
Doff the lovely coats you wear,
Seek no covert in your fear
Lest a mortal eye should see;
What's your nakedness to me?
Here no leprous flowers rear
Fierce corollas in the air;
Here no bodies sleek and wet,
Dripping mingled rain and sweat,
Tread the savage measures of
Jungle boys and girls in love.
What is last year's snow to me,
Last year's anything? The tree
Budding yearly must forget
How its past arose or set—

Bough and blossom, flower, fruit,
Even what shy bird with mute
Wonder at her travail there,
Meekly labored in its hair.
One three centuries removed
From the scenes his fathers loved,
Spicy grove, cinnamon tree,
What is Africa to me?

So I lie, who find no peace
Night or day, no slight release
From the unremittent beat
Made by cruel padded feet
Walking through my body's street.
Up and down they go, and back,
Treading out a jungle track.
So I lie, who never quite
Safely sleep from rain at night—
I can never rest at all
When the rain begins to fall;
Like a soul gone mad with pain
I must match its weird refrain;
Ever must I twist and squirm,
Writhing like a baited worm,
While its primal measures drip
Through my body, crying, "Strip!
Doff this new exuberance.
Come and dance the Lover's Dance!"
In an old remembered way
Rain works on me night and day.

Quaint, outlandish heathen gods
Black men fashion out of rods,
Clay, and brittle bits of stone,
In a likeness like their own,
My conversion came high-priced;
I belong to Jesus Christ,
Preacher of humility;
Heathen gods are naught to me.

Father, Son, and Holy Ghost,
So I make an idle boast;

Jesus of the twice-turned cheek,
Lamb of God, although I speak
With my mouth thus, in my heart
Do I play a double part.
Ever at Thy glowing altar
Must my heart grow sick and falter,
Wishing He I served were black,
Thinking then it would not lack
Precedent of pain to guide it,
Let who would or might deride it;
Surely then this flesh would know
Yours had borne a kindred woe.
Lord, I fashion dark gods, too,
Daring even to give You
Dark despairing features where,
Crowned with dark rebellious hair,
Patience wavers just so much as
Mortal grief compels, while touches
Quick and hot, of anger, rise
To smitten cheek and weary eyes.
Lord, forgive me if my need
Sometimes shapes a human creed.

All day long and all night through,
One thing only must I do:
Quench my pride and cool my blood,
Lest I perish in the flood.
Lest a hidden ember set
Timber that I thought was wet
Burning like the dryest flax,
Melting like the merest wax,
Lest the grave restore its dead.
Not yet has my heart or head
In the least way realized
They and I are civilized.

FROM THE DARK TOWER

We shall not always plant while others reap
The golden increment of bursting fruit,

Not always countenance, abject and mute,
That lesser men should hold their brothers cheap;
Not everlastingly while others sleep
Shall we beguile their limbs with mellow flute,
Not always bend to some more subtle brute;
We were not made eternally to weep.

The night whose sable breast relieves the stark
White stars is no less lovely, being dark;
And there are buds that cannot bloom at all
In light, but crumple, piteous, and fall;
So in the dark we hide the heart that bleeds,
And wait, and tend our agonizing seeds.

TO A BROWN BOY

That brown girl's swagger gives a twitch
    To beauty like a queen;
Lad, never dam your body's itch
    When loveliness is seen.

For there is ample room for bliss
    In pride in clean, brown limbs,
And lips know better how to kiss
    Than how to raise white hymns.

And when your body's death gives birth
    To soil for spring to crown,
Men will not ask if that rare earth
    Was white flesh once, or brown.

TABLEAU

Locked arm in arm they cross the way,
The black boy and the white,
The golden splendor of the day,
The sable pride of night.

From lowered blinds the dark folk stare,
And here the fair folk talk,
Indignant that these two should dare
In unison to walk.

Oblivious to look and word
They pass, and see no wonder
That lightning brilliant as a sword
Should blaze the path of thunder.

SATURDAY'S CHILD

Some are teethed on a silver spoon,
With the stars strung for a rattle;
I cut my teeth as the black racoon—
For implements of battle.

Some are swaddled in silk and down,
And heralded by a star;
They swathed my limbs in a sackcloth gown
On a night that was black as tar.

For some, godfather and goddame
The opulent fairies be;
Dame Poverty gave me my name,
And Pain godfathered me.

For I was born on Saturday—
"Bad time for planting seed,"
Was all my father had to say,
And, "One mouth more to feed."

Death cut the strings that gave me life,
And handed me to Sorrow,
The only kind of middle wife
My folks could beg or borrow.

TWO POETS

"How could a woman love him; love, or wed?"
And thinking only of his tuneless face
And arms that held no hint of skill or grace,
They shook a slow, commiserative head
To see him amble by; but still they fed
Their wilting hearts on his, were fired to race
Once more, and panting at life's deadly pace,
They drank as wine the blood-in-song he shed.

TO FRANCE

I have a dream of where (when I grow old,
Having no further joy to take in lip
Or limb, a graybeard caching from the cold
The frail indignity of age) some ship
Might bear my creaking, unhinged bones
Trailing remembrance as a tattered cloak,
And beach me glad, though on their sharpest stones
Among a fair and kindly folk.

There might I only breathe my latest days,
With those rich accents falling on my ear
That most have made me feel that freedom's rays
Still have a shrine where they may leap and sear,—
Though I were palsied there, or halt, or blind,
So I were there, I think I should not mind.

NOTHING ENDURES

Nothing endures,
Not even love,
Though the warm heart purrs
Of the length thereof.

Though beauty wax,
Yet shall it wane;
Time lays a tax
On the subtlest brain.

Let the blood riot,
Give it its will;
It shall grow quiet,
It shall grow still.

Nirvana gapes
For all things given;
Nothing escapes,
Love not even.

REQUIESCAM

I am for sleeping and forgetting
    All that has gone before;
I am for lying still and letting
    Who will beat at my door;
I would my life's cold sun were setting
    To rise for me no more.

WARING CUNEY

WARING CUNEY, Edward Silvera, and, as often as not, Countee Cullen specialized in themes that were seen as exotic, decadent, or despairing.

THE DEATH BED

All the time they were praying
He watched the shadow of a tree
Flicker on the wall.

There is no need of prayer,
He said,
No need at all.

The kin-folk thought it strange
That he should ask them from a dying bed.
But they left all in a row
And it seemed to ease him
To see them go.

There were some who kept on praying
In a room across the hall
And some who listened to the breeze
That made the shadows waver
On the wall.

He tried his nerve
On a song he knew
And made an empty note
That might have come,
From a bird's harsh throat.

And all the time it worried him
That they were in there praying
And all the time he wondered
What it was they could be saying.

JESSIE REDMON FAUSET

JESSIE FAUSET was better known as a novelist. Her "La Vie C'est la Vie" (with Du Bois in mind) was illustrative of the refined sentiments she and the first cohort of Renaissance writers went to considerable lengths to convey.

LA VIE C'EST LA VIE

On summer afternoons I sit
Quiescent by you in the park,
And idly watch the sunbeams gild
And tint the ash-trees' bark.

Or else I watch the squirrels frisk
And chaffer in the grassy lane;
And all the while I mark your voice
Breaking with love and pain.

I know a woman who would give
Her chance of heaven to take my place;
To see the love-light in your eyes,
The love-glow on your face!

And there's a man whose lightest word
Can set my chilly blood afire;
Fulfillment of his least behest
Defines my life's desire.

But he will none of me, nor I
Of you. Nor you of her. 'Tis said
The world is full of jests like these.—
I wish that I were dead.

DEAD FIRES

If this is peace, this dead and leaden thing,
    Then better far the hateful fret, the sting,
Better the wound forever seeking balm
    Than this gray calm!

Is this pain's surcease? Better far the ache,
    The long-drawn dreary day, the night's white wake,
Better the choking sigh, the sobbing breath
    Than passion's death!

LANGSTON HUGHES

LANGSTON HUGHES, *the most popular poet of the Harlem Renaissance, was, with Claude McKay, also its finest. His early verse, Whitmanesque and agreeably didactic, admirably expressed the sentiments of the Talented Tenth. A delighted Jessie Fauset, literary editor of* The Crisis, *published "The Negro Speaks of Rivers" and suggested that Hughes dedicate it to Du Bois. "America," awarded third prize in the first* Opportunity *contest of 1925, was a paean to the melting pot—"Little dark baby,/Little Jew baby,/Little outcast,/America is seeking the stars." The racial romanticism of such early poems as "Dream Variation" also pleased the architects of the Renaissance.*

But Hughes had even then begun to explore the milieux of the honky-tonk disdained by most "representative Negroes." He excelled at improvisation and authentic portrayal of the lives of ordinary people—simple folk. The revolutionary "Weary Blues," which took first prize in 1925 and was read aloud by James Weldon Johnson at the Opportunity *banquet, had jazz built into the beat. "Jazzonia" placed its readers "in a whirling cabaret/Six long-headed jazzers play." The direct, declaratory lines of "Negro," "Mulatto," and "Elevator Boy"—"I am a Negro:/Black as the night is black"—seemed to be spoken by the titular subjects. "Life for me ain't been no crystal stair" is the mother's memorable sigh in "Mother to Son." The publication in 1926 of his first book of poetry,* The Weary Blues, *established Hughes as the "poet laureate" of the New Negro Arts Movement.*

When Hughes's second book of poetry, Fine Clothes to the Jew, *appeared in 1927, many of the orchestrators of the Renaissance were deeply pained. It contained poems such as "Ruby*

Brown" and "Red Silk Stockings," which they considered to be in exceedingly bad taste. By the end of the Harlem Renaissance, Hughes's strong flirtation with Marxism caused custodians of Talented Tenth virtues to despair as his iconoclastic, antireligious, and anticapitalist poems appeared in left-wing reviews like Race *and* New Masses, *of which "Advertisement for the Waldorf-Astoria" was perhaps the most effective.*

THE NEGRO SPEAKS OF RIVERS

I've known rivers:
I've known rivers ancient as the world and older than the flow
    of human blood in human veins.

My soul has grown deep like the rivers.

I bathed in the Euphrates when dawns were young.
I built my hut near the Congo and it lulled me to sleep.
I looked upon the Nile and raised the pyramids above it.
I heard the singing of the Mississippi when Abe Lincoln went
    down to New Orleans, and I've seen its muddy bosom turn
    all golden in the sunset.

I've known rivers:
Ancient, dusky rivers.

My soul has grown deep like rivers.

I, TOO

I, too, sing America.

I am the darker brother.
They send me to eat in the kitchen
When company comes.
But I laugh,

And eat well,
And grow strong.

To-morrow
I'll sit at the table
When company comes
Nobody 'll dare
Say to me,
"Eat in the kitchen"
Then.

Besides, they'll see how beautiful I am
And be ashamed,—

I, too, am America.

AMERICA

Little dark baby,
Little Jew baby,
Little outcast,
America is seeking the stars,
America is seeking tomorrow.
You are America.
I am America
America—the dream,
America—the vision.
America—the star-seeking I.
Out of yesterday
The chains of slavery;
Out of yesterday,
The ghettos of Europe;
Out of yesterday,
The poverty and pain of the old, old world,
The building and struggle of this new one,
We come
You and I,
Seeking the stars.
You and I,

You of the blue eyes
And the blond hair,
I of the dark eyes
And the crinkly hair.
You and I
Offering hands
Being brothers,
Being one,
Being America.
You and I.
And I?
Who am I?
You know me:
I am Crispus Attucks at the Boston Tea Party;
Jimmy Jones in the ranks of the last black troops marching
     for democracy.
I am Sojourner Truth preaching and praying for the goodness
     of this wide, wide land;
Today's black mother bearing tomorrow's America.
Who am I?
You know me,
Dream of my dreams,
I am America.
I am America seeking the stars.
America—
Hoping, praying,
Fighting, dreaming.
Knowing
There are stains
On the beauty of my democracy,
I want to be clean.
I want to grovel
No longer in the mire.
I want to reach always
After stars.
Who am I?
I am the ghetto child,
I am the dark baby,
I am you
And the blond tomorrow
And yet

I am my one sole self,
America seeking the stars.

THE WEARY BLUES

Droning a drowsy syncopated tune,
Rocking back and forth to a mellow croon,
        I heard a Negro play.
Down on Lenox Avenue the other night
By the pale dull pallor of an old gas light
        He did a lazy sway . . .
        He did a lazy sway . . .
To the tune o' those Weary Blues.
With his ebony hands on each ivory key
He made that poor piano moan with melody.
        O Blues!
Swaying to and fro on his rickety stool
He played that sad raggy tune like a musical fool.
        Sweet Blues!
Coming from a black man's soul.
        O Blues!

In a deep song voice with a melancholy tone
I heard that Negro sing, that old piano moan—
        "Ain't got nobody in all this world,
        Ain't got nobody but ma self.
        I's gwine to quit ma frownin'
        And put ma troubles on the shelf."
Thump, thump, thump, went his foot on the floor.
He played a few chords then he sang some more—
        "I got the Weary Blues
        And I can't be satisfied.
        Got the Weary Blues
        And can't be satisfied—
        I ain't happy no mo'
        And I wish that I had died."
And far into the night he crooned that tune.
The stars went out and so did the moon.

The singer stopped playing and went to bed
While the Weary Blues echoed through his head.
He slept like a rock or a man that's dead.

JAZZONIA

Oh, silver tree!
Oh, shining rivers of the soul!

In a Harlem cabaret
Six long-headed jazzers play.
A dancing girl whose eyes are bold
Lifts high a dress of silken gold.

Oh, singing tree!
Oh, shining rivers of the soul!

Were Eve's eyes
In the first garden
Just a bit too bold?
Was Cleopatra gorgeous
In a gown of gold?

Oh, shining tree!
Oh, silver rivers of the soul!

In a whirling cabaret
Six long-headed jazzers play.

MOTHER TO SON

Well, son, I'll tell you:
Life for me ain't been no crystal stair.
It's had tacks in it,
And splinters,
And boards torn up,
And places with no carpet on the floor—

Bare.
But all the time
I'se been a-climbin' on,
And reachin' landin's,
And turnin' corners,
And sometimes goin' in the dark
Where there ain't been no light.
So boy, don't you turn back.
Don't you set down on the steps

NEGRO

I am a Negro:
    Black as the night is black,
    Black like the depths of my Africa.

I've been a slave:
    Caesar told me to keep his door-steps clean.
    I brushed the boots of Washington.

I've been a worker:
    Under my hand the pyramids arose.
    I made mortar for the Woolworth Building.

I've been a singer:
    All the way from Africa to Georgia
    I carried my sorrow songs.
    I made ragtime.

MULATTO

Because I am the white man's son—his own,
Bearing his bastard birth-mark on my face,
I will dispute his title to his throne,
Forever fight him for my rightful place.
There is a searing hate within my soul,
A hate that only kin can feel for kin,
A hate that makes me vigorous and whole,

And spurs me on increasingly to win.
Because I am my cruel father's child,
My love of justice stirs me up to hate,
A warring Ishmaelite, unreconciled,
When falls the hour I shall not hesitate
Into my father's heart to plunge the knife
To gain the utmost freedom that is life.

ELEVATOR BOY

I got a job now
Runnin' an elevator
In the Dennison Hotel in Jersey,
Job aint no good though.
No money around.
    Jobs are just chances
    Like everything else.
    Maybe a little luck now,
    Maybe not.
    Maybe a good job sometimes:
    Step out o' the barrel, boy.
Two new suits an'
A woman to sleep with.
    Maybe no luck for a long time.
    Only the elevators
    Goin' up an' down,
    Up an' down,
    Or somebody else's shoes
    To shine,
    Or greasy pots in a dirty kitchen.
I been runnin' this
Elevator too long.
Guess I'll quit now.

RED SILK STOCKINGS

Put on yo' red silk stockings,
Black gal.

Go out an' let de white boys
Look at yo' legs.

Ain't nothin' to do for you, nohow.
Round this town.—
You's too pretty.
Put on yo' red silk stockings, gal,
An' tomorrow's chile'll
Be a high yaller.

Go out an' let de white boys
Look at yo' legs.

RUBY BROWN

She was young and beautiful
And golden like the sunshine
That warmed her body.
And because she was colored
Mayville had no place to offer her,
Nor fuel for the clean flame of joy
That tried to burn within her soul.

One day,
Sitting on old Mrs. Latham's back porch
Polishing the silver,
She asked herself two questions
And they ran something like this:
What can a colored girl do
On the money from a white woman's kitchen?
And ain't there any joy in this town?

Now the streets down by the river
Know more about this pretty Ruby Brown.

ELDERLY RACE LEADERS

Wisdom reduced to the personal equation:
Life is a system of half-truths and lies,
 Opportunistic, convenient evasion
   Elderly,
   Famous,
   Very well-paid,
  They clutch at the egg
   Their master's
   Goose laid:
   $$$$$$$$
   $$$$$$$
   $$$$$$
   $$$$$

DREAM VARIATION

To fling my arms wide
In some place of the sun,
To whirl and to dance
Till the bright day is done.
Then rest at cool evening
Beneath a tall tree
While night comes gently
Dark like me.
That is my dream.
To fling my arms wide
In the face of the sun.
Dance! Whirl! Whirl!
Till the quick day is done.
Rest at pale evening,
A tall, slim tree,
Night coming tenderly
Black like me.

GOODBYE, CHRIST

Listen, Christ,
You did alright in your day, I reckon—
But that day's gone now.
They ghosted you up a swell story, too,
Called it Bible—
But it's dead now.
The popes and the preachers've
Made too much money from it.
They've sold you to too many

Kings, generals, robbers, and killers—
Even to the Tzar and the Cossacks,
Even to Rockefeller's Church,
Even to THE SATURDAY EVENING POST.
You ain't no good no more.
They've pawned you
Till you've done wore out.

Goodbye,
Christ Jesus Lord God Jehova,

Beat it on away from here now.
Make way for a new guy with no religion at all—
A real guy named
Marx Communist Lenin Peasant Stalin Worker ME—

I said, ME!

Go ahead on now,
You're getting in the way of things, Lord.
And please take Saint Ghandi with you when you go,
And Saint Pope Pius,
And Saint Aimee McPherson,
And big black Saint Becton
Of the Consecrated Dime.
Move!

Don't be so slow about movin'!
The world is mine from now on—
And nobody's gonna sell ME
To a king, or a general,
Or a millionaire.

ADVERTISEMENT FOR THE
WALDORF-ASTORIA

Fine living à la carte!

LISTEN, HUNGRY ONES!

Look! See what *Vanity Fair* says about the new Waldorf-Astoria:
"All the luxuries of private home . . ."
Now, won't that be charming when the last flophouse has turned
you down this winter?
Furthermore:
"It is far beyond anything hitherto attempted in the hotel world.
. . ." It cost twenty-eight million dollars. The famous Oscar
Tschirky is in charge of banqueting. Alexandre Gastaud is
chef. It will be a distinguished background for society.
So when you've got no place else to go, homeless and hungry ones,
choose the Waldorf as a background for your rags—
(Or do you still consider the subway after midnight good enough?)

ROOMERS

Take a room at the new Waldorf, you down-and-outers—sleepers
in charity's flop-houses where God pulls a long face, and you
have to pray to get a bed.
They serve swell board at the Waldorf-Astoria. Look at this menu,
will you:

GUMBO CREOLE
CRABMEAT IN CASSOLETTE
BOILED BRISKET OF BEEF
SMALL ONIONS IN CREAM

WATERCRESS SALAD
PEACH MELBA

Have luncheon there this afternoon, all you jobless.
    Why not?
Dine with some of the men and women who got rich off of your
    labor, who clip coupons with clean white fingers because your
    hands dug coal, drilled stone, sewed garments, poured steel to
    let other people draw dividends and live easy.
(Or haven't you had enough yet of the soup-lines and the bitter
    bread of charity?)
Walk through Peacock Alley tonight before dinner, and get warm,
    anyway. You've got nothing else to do.

EVICTED FAMILIES

All you families put out in the street:
    Apartments in the Towers are only $10,000 a year. (Three
    rooms and two baths.) Move in there until times get good,
    and you can do better. $10,000 and $1.00 are about the same
    to you, aren't they?
Who cares about money with a wife and kids homeless, and no-
    body in the family working? Wouldn't a duplex high above
    the street be grand, with a view of the richest city in the world
    at your nose?
"A lease, if you prefer, or an arrangement terminable at will."

NEGROES

Oh, Lawd, I done forgot Harlem!
Say, you colored folks, hungry a long time in 135th Street—they
    got swell music at the Waldorf-Astoria. It sure is a mighty nice
    place to shake hips in, too. There's dancing after supper in a
    big warm room. It's cold as hell on Lenox Avenue. All you've
    had all day is a cup of coffee. Your pawnshop overcoat's a
    ragged banner on your hungry frame. You know, downtown
    folks are just crazy about Paul Robeson! Maybe they'll like
    you, too, black mob from Harlem. Drop in at the Waldorf
    this afternoon for tea. Stay to dinner. Give Park Avenue a lot

of darkie color—free for nothing! Ask the Junior Leaguers to
sing a spiritual for you. They probably know 'em better than
you do—and their lips won't be so chapped with cold after
they step out of their closed cars in the undercover driveways.
   Hallelujah! Undercover driveways!
   Ma soul's a witness for de Waldorf-Astoria!
(A thousand nigger section-hands keep the roadbeds smooth, so
   investments in railroads pay ladies with diamond necklaces
   staring at Cert murals.)
   Thank God A-mighty!
(And a million niggers bend their backs on rubber plantations, for
   rich behinds to ride on thick tires to the Theatre Guild to-
   night.)
   Ma soul's a witness!
(And here we stand, shivering in the cold, in Harlem.)
   Glory be to God—
   De Waldorf-Astoria's open!

EVERYBODY

So get proud and rare back; everybody! The new Waldorf-Astoria's
   open!
(Special siding for private cars from the railroad yards.)
   You ain't been there yet?
(A thousand miles of carpet and a million bathrooms.)
   What's the matter?
You haven't seen the ads in the papers? Didn't you get a card?
   Don't you know they specialize in American cooking?
   Ankle on down to 49th Street at Park Avenue. Get up off that
   subway bench tonight with the evening *POST* for cover!
   Come on out o' that flop-house! Stop shivering your guts out
   all day on street corners under the El.
Jesus, ain't you tired yet?

CHRISTMAS CARD

Hail Mary, Mother of God!
   the new Christ child of the Revolution's about to be born.
(Kick hard, red baby, in the bitter womb of the mob.)

Somebody, put an ad in *Vanity Fair* quick!
Call Oscar of the Waldorf—for Christ's sake!
     It's almost Christmas, and that little girl—turned whore be-
     cause her belly was too hungry to stand it anymore—wants a
     nice clean bed for the Immaculate Conception.
Listen. Mary, Mother of God, wrap your new born babe in the
     red flag of Revolution: the Waldorf-Astoria's the best manger
     we've got. For reservations: Telephone EL. 5-3000.

FENTON JOHNSON

FENTON JOHNSON, among the earliest of the Renaissance poets, sometimes wrote as a modern pessimist, expressing a sense of futility that was rarely heard in poetry by African Americans. His "Children of the Sun" expresses a resolute, still aspiring Johnson, while "The Banjo Player" is simply ironic mischief.

CHILDREN OF THE SUN

We are children of the sun,
        Rising sun!
Weaving Southern destiny,
Waiting for the mighty hour
When our Shiloh shall appear
With the flaming sword of right,
With the steel of brotherhood,
And emboss in crimson die
Liberty! Fraternity!

We are the star-dust folk,
        Striving folk!
Sorrow songs have lulled to rest;
Seething passions wrought through wrongs,
Led us where the moon rays dip
In the night of dull despair,
Showed us where the star gleams shine,

And the mystic symbols glow—
Liberty! Fraternity!

We have come through cloud and mist,
    Mighty men!
Dusk has kissed our sleep-born eyes,
Reared for us a mystic throne
In the splendor of the skies,
That shall always be for us,
Children of the Nazarene,
Children who shall ever sing
Liberty! Fraternity!

THE BANJO PLAYER

There is music in me, the music of a peasant people.
I wander through the levee, picking my banjo and singing my
    songs of the cabin and the field. At the Last Chance Saloon
    I am as welcome as the violets in March; there is always
    food and drink for me there, and the dimes of those who
    love honest music. Behind the railroad tracks the little
    children clap their hands and love me as they love Kris
    Kringle.
But I fear that I am a failure. Last night a woman called me a
    troubadour.
What is a troubadour?

GEORGIA DOUGLAS JOHNSON

GEORGIA DOUGLAS JOHNSON'S POEMS seemed to sigh and often verged on the cloying, as in the case of "I Want to Die While You Love Me," which nevertheless managed to convey an affecting sorrow. Johnson, widely acclaimed as the first African American female poet of the twentieth century, persevered at her craft year after year, while maintaining a famous salon in Washington that was frequented by Du Bois, Fauset, Hughes, Locke, Toomer, and most of the lights of the Renaissance.

LET ME NOT LOSE MY DREAM

Let me not lose my dream, e'en though I scan the veil
    with eyes unseeing through their glaze of tears,
Let me not falter, though the rungs of fortune perish
    as I fare above the tumult, praying purer air,
Let me not lose the vision, gird me, Powers that toss
    the worlds, I pray!
Hold me, and guard, lest anguish tear my dreams
    away!

OLD BLACK MEN

They have dreamed as young men dream
Of glory, love and power;
They have hoped as youth will hope
Of life's sun-minted hour.

They have seen as others saw
Their bubbles burst in air,
They have learned to live it down
As though they did not care.

BLACK WOMAN

Don't knock at my door, little child,
  I cannot let you in,
You know not what a world this is
  Of cruelty and sin.
Wait in the still eternity
  Until I come to you,
The world is cruel, cruel, child,
  I cannot let you in!

Don't knock at my heart, little one,
  I cannot bear the pain
Of turning deaf-ear to your call
  Time and time again!
You do not know the monster men
  Inhabiting the earth,
Be still, be still, my precious child,
  I must not give you birth!

THE HEART OF A WOMAN

The heart of a woman goes forth with the dawn,
As a lone bird, soft winging, so restlessly on,
Afar o'er life's turrets and vales does it roam
In the wake of those echoes the heart calls home.

The heart of a woman falls back with the night,
And enters some alien cage in its plight,
And tries to forget it has dreamed of the stars,
While it breaks, breaks, breaks on the sheltering bars.

I WANT TO DIE WHILE YOU LOVE ME

I want to die while you love me,
    While yet you hold me fair,
While laughter lies upon my lips
    And lights are in my hair.

I want to die while you love me,
    And bear to that still bed,
Your kisses turbulent, unspent,
    To warm me when I'm dead.

I want to die while you love me,
    Oh, who would care to live
Till love has nothing more to ask
    And nothing more to give!

I want to die while you love me
    And never, never see
The glory of this perfect day
    Grow dim or cease to be.

HELENE JOHNSON

HELENE JOHNSON'S POETRY was concerned with the lives of un-sophisticated and poor people, although the language of her verse was distinctly Talented Tenth

MY RACE

Ah my race,
Hungry race,
Throbbing and young—
Ah, my race,
Wonder race,
Sobbing with song—
Ah, my race,
Laughing race,
Careless in mirth—
Ah, my veiled
Unformed race,
Fumbling in birth.

A SOUTHERN ROAD

Yolk-colored tongue
Parched beneath a burning sky,
A lazy little tune

Hummed up the crest of some
Soft sloping hill.
One streaming line of beauty
Flowing by a forest
Pregnant with tears.
A hidden nest for beauty
Idly flung by God
In one lonely lingering hour
Before the Sabbath.
A blue-fruited black gum,
Like a tall predella.

SONNET TO A NEGRO IN HARLEM

You are disdainful and magnificent—
Your perfect body and your pompous gait,

Your dark eyes flashing solemnly with hate,
Small wonder that you are incompetent
To imitate those whom you so despise—
Your shoulders towering high above the throng,
Your head thrown back in rich, barbaric song,
Palm trees and mangoes stretched before your eyes.
Let others toil and sweat for labor's sake
And wring from grasping hands their meed of gold.
Why urge ahead your supercilious feet?
Scorn will efface each footprint that you make.
I love your laughter arrogant and bold.
You are too splendid for this city street.

POEM

Little brown boy,
Slim, dark, big-eyed,
Crooning love songs to your banjo
Down at the Lafayette—
Gee, boy, I love the way you hold your head,

High sort of and a bit to one side,
Like a prince, a jazz prince. And I love
Your eyes flashing, and your hands,
And your patent-leathered feet,
And your shoulders jerking the jig-wa.
And I love your teeth flashing,
And the way your hair shines in the spotlight
Like it was the real stuff.
Gee, brown boy, I loves you all over.
I'm glad I'm a jig. I'm glad I can
understand your dancin' and your
Singin', and feel all the happiness
And joy and don't-care in you.
Gee, boy, when you sing, I can close my ears
And hear tomtoms just as plain.
Listen to me, will you, what do I know
About tomtoms? But I like the word, sort of,
Don't you? It belongs to us.
Gee, boy, I love the way you hold your head,
And the way you sing and dance,
And everything.
Say, I think you're wonderful. You're
All right with me,
You are.

JAMES WELDON JOHNSON

JAMES WELDON JOHNSON, though an agnostic, wrote verse of compelling religious beauty. "Go Down Death," "The Creation," and other poems from God's Trombones *were recited on public occasions, in churches, and in Park Avenue apartments, where they never failed to move listeners to tearful meditation on social injustice and moral deficiency. Johnson and his musician brother, Rosamond, had an unerring knack for the commercial exploitation of "Negro" material, but there was also a strategy for racial uplift behind the dialect poetry and the minstrel music. Johnson was among the first African American intellectuals (along with Du Bois) to assert publicly and before white audiences that Negro spirituals were America's sole cultural contribution. "You sang a race from wood and stone to Christ," he proclaimed in "O Black and Unknown Bards." Implicit in some of Johnson's poetry was the grim judgment (anticipating that of the Greenwich Village revoltes) that white America—"The White Witch"—was materialistic, soulless, and self-devouring: "For in her glance there is a snare,/And in her smile there is a blight." "The Color Sergeant" was a comment on the historic patriotism of African Americans and the historic ingratitude shown them by white Americans.*

THE WHITE WITCH

O brothers mine, take care! Take care!
The great white witch rides out tonight.
Trust not your prowess nor your strength,

Your only safety lies in flight;
For in her glance there is a snare,
And in her smile there is a blight.

The great white witch you have not seen?
Then, younger brothers mine, forsooth,
Like nursery children you have looked
For ancient hag and snaggle-tooth;
But no, not so; the witch appears
In all the glowing charms of youth.

Her lips are like carnations, red,
Her face like new-born lilies, fair,
Her eyes like ocean waters, blue,
She moves with subtle grace and air,
And all about her head there floats
The golden glory of her hair.

But though she always thus appears
In form of youth and mood of mirth,
Unnumbered centuries are hers,
The infant planets saw her birth;
The child of throbbing Life is she,
Twin sister to the greedy earth.

And back behind those smiling lips,
And down within those laughing eyes,
And underneath the soft caress
Of hand and voice and purring sighs,
The shadow of the panther lurks,
The spirit of the vampire lies.

For I have seen the great white witch,
And she has led me to her lair,
And I have kissed her red, red lips
And cruel face so white and fair;
Around me she has twined her arms,
And bound me with her yellow hair.

I felt those red lips burn and sear
My body like a living coal;

Obeyed the power of those eyes
As the needle trembles to the pole;
And did not care although I felt
The strength go ebbing from my soul.

Oh! she has seen your strong young limbs,
And heard your laughter loud and gay,
And in your voices she has caught
The echo of a far-off day,
When man was closer to the earth;
And she has marked you for her prey.

She feels the old Antaean strength
In you, the great dynamic beat
Of primal passions, and she sees
In you the last besieged retreat
Of love relentless, lusty, fierce,
Love fain-ecstatic, cruel-sweet.

O brothers mine, take care! Take care!
The great white witch rides out tonight.
O younger brothers mine, beware!
Look not upon her beauty bright;
For in her glance there is a snare,
And in her smile there is a blight.

THE COLOR SERGEANT
(On an Incident at the Battle of San Juan Hill)

Under a burning tropic sun,
With comrades around him lying,
A trooper of the sable Tenth
Lay wounded, bleeding, dying.

First in the charge up the fort-crowned hill,
His company's guidon bearing,

He had rushed where the leaden hail fell fast,
Not death nor danger fearing.

He fell in the front where the fight grew fierce,
Still faithful in life's last labor;
Black though his skin, yet his heart as true
As the steel of his blood-stained saber.

And while the battle around him rolled,
Like the roar of a sullen breaker,
He closed his eyes on the bloody scene,
And presented arms to his Maker.

There he lay, without honor or rank,
But, still, in a grim-like beauty;
Despised of men for his humble race,
Yet true, in death, to his duty.

O BLACK AND UNKNOWN BARDS

O black and unknown bards of long ago,
How came your lips to touch the sacred fire?
How, in your darkness, did you come to know
The power and beauty of the minstrel's lyre?
Who first from midst his bonds lifted his eyes?
Who first from out the still watch, lone and long,
Feeling the ancient faith of prophets rise
Within his dark-kept soul, burst into song?

Heart of what slave poured out such melody
As "Steal away to Jesus"? On its strains
His spirit must have nightly floated free,
Though still about his hands he felt his chains.
Who heard great "Jordan roll"? Whose starward eye
Saw chariot "swing low"? And who was he
That breathed that comforting, melodic sigh,
"Nobody knows de trouble I see"?

What merely living clod, what captive thing,
Could up toward God through all its darkness grope,
And find within its deadened heart to sing
These songs of sorrow, love and faith, and hope?
How did it catch that subtle undertone,
That note in music heard not with the ears?
How sound the elusive reed so seldom blown,
Which stirs the soul or melts the heart to tears.

Not that great German master in his dream
Of harmonies that thundered amongst the stars
At the creation, ever heard a theme
Nobler than "Go down, Moses." Mark its bars
How like a mighty trumpet-call they stir
The blood. Such are the notes that men have sung
Going to valorous deeds; such tones there were
That helped make history when Time was young.

There is a wide, wide wonder in it all,
That from degraded rest and servile toil
The fiery spirit of the seer should call
These simple children of the sun and soil.
O black slave singers, gone, forgot, unfamed,
You—you alone, of all the long, long line
Of those who've sung untaught, unknown, unnamed,
Have stretched out upward, seeking the divine.

You sang not deeds of heroes or of kings;
No chant of bloody war, no exulting pean
Of arms-won triumphs; but your humble strings
You touched in chord with music empyrean.
You sang far better than you knew; the songs
That for your listeners' hungry hearts sufficed
Still live,—but more than this to you belongs:
You sang a race from wood and stone to Christ.

GO DOWN DEATH
A Funeral Sermon

Weep not, weep not,
She is not dead;
She's resting in the bosom of Jesus.
Heart-broken husband—weep no more;
Grief-stricken son—weep no more;
Left-lonesome daughter—weep no more;
She's only just gone home.

Day before yesterday morning,
God was looking down from his great, high heaven,
Looking down on all his children,
And his eye fell on Sister Caroline,
Tossing on her bed of pain.
And God's big heart was touched with pity,
With the everlasting pity.

And God sat back on his throne,
And he commanded that tall, bright angel standing at his
    right hand:
Call me Death!
And that tall, bright angel cried in a voice
That broke like a clap of thunder:
Call Death!—Call Death!
And the echo sounded down the streets of heaven
Till it reached away back to that shadowy place,
Where Death waits with his pale, white horses.

And Death heard the summons,
And he leaped on his fastest horse,
Pale as a sheet in the moonlight.
Up the golden street Death galloped,
And the hoofs of his horse struck fire from the gold,
But they didn't make no sound.
Up Death rode to the Great White Throne,
And waited for God's command.

And God said: Go down, Death, go down,
Go down to Savannah, Georgia,
Down in Yamacraw,
And find Sister Caroline.
She's borne the burden and heat of the day,
She's labored long in my vineyard,
And she's tired—
She's weary—
Go down, Death, and bring her to me.

And Death didn't say a word,
But he loosed the reins on his pale, white horse,
And he clamped the spurs to his bloodless sides,
And out and down he rode,
Through heaven's pearly gates,
Past suns and moons and stars;
On Death rode,
And the foam from his horse was like a comet in the sky;
On Death rode,
Leaving the lightning's flash behind;
Straight on down he came.

While we were watching round her bed,
She turned her eyes and looked away,
She saw what we couldn't see;
She saw Old Death. She saw Old Death,
Coming like a falling star.
But Death didn't frighten Sister Caroline;
He looked to her like a welcome friend.
And she whispered to us: I'm going home,
And she smiled and closed her eyes.

And Death took her up like a baby,
And she lay in his icy arms,
But she didn't feel no chill.
And Death began to ride again—
Up beyond the evening star,
Out beyond the morning star,
Into the glittering light of glory,
On to the Great White Throne.

And there he laid Sister Caroline
On the loving breast of Jesus.

And Jesus took his own hand and wiped away her tears,
And he smoothed the furrows from her face,
And the angels sang a little song,
And Jesus rocked her in his arms,
And kept a-saying: Take your rest,
Take your rest, take your rest.

Weep not—weep not,
She is not dead;
She's resting in the bosom of Jesus.

THE CREATION

A Negro Sermon

And God stepped out on space,
And He looked around and said,
"I'm lonely
I'll make me a world."

And as far as the eye of God could see
Darkness covered everything,
Blacker than a hundred midnights
Down in a cypress swamp.

Then God smiled,
And the light broke,
And the darkness rolled up on one side,
And the light stood shining on the other,
And God said, *"That's good!"*

Then God reached out and took the light in His hands,
And God rolled the light around in His hands
Until He made the sun;
And He set that sun a-blazing in the heavens.
And the light that was left from making the sun

God gathered it up in a shining ball
And flung it against the darkness,
Spangling the night with the moon and stars.
Then down between
The darkness and the light
He hurled the world;
And God said, *"That's good."*

Then God Himself stepped down—
And the sun was on His right hand
And the moon was on His left;
The stars were clustered about His head,
And the earth was under His feet.
And God walked, and where He trod
His footsteps hollowed the valleys out
And bulged the mountains up.

Then He stopped and looked, and saw
That the earth was hot and barren.
So God stepped over to the edge of the world
And He spat out the seven seas;
He batted His eyes, and the lightnings flashed;
He clapped His hands, and the thunders rolled;
And the waters above the earth came down,
The cooling waters came down.

Then the green grass sprouted,
And the little red flowers blossomed,
The pine tree pointed his finger to the sky,
And the oak spread out his arms,
And the lakes cuddled down in the hollows of the ground,
And the rivers ran to the sea;
And God smiled again,
And the rainbow appeared,
And curled itself around His shoulder.

Then God raised His arm and He waved His hand,
Over the sea and over the land,
And He said, *"Bring forth. Bring forth."*
And quicker than God could drop His hand
Fishes and fowls

And beasts and birds
Swam the rivers and the seas,
Roamed the forests and the woods,
And split the air with their wings.
And God said, *"That's good."*

Then God walked around,
And God looked around
On all that He had made.
He looked at His sun,
And He looked at His moon,
And He looked at His little stars;
He looked on His world,
With all its living things,
And God said, *"I'm lonely still."*

Then God sat down
On the side of a hill where He could think;
By a deep, wide river He sat down;
With His head in His hands,
God thought and thought,
Till He thought, *"I'll make me a man."*

Up from the bed of a river
God scooped the clay;
And by the bank of the river
He kneeled Him down;
And there the great God Almighty
Who lit the sun and fixed it in the sky,
Who flung the stars to the most far corner of the night,
Who rounded the earth in the middle of His hand;
This Great God,
Like a mammy bending over her baby,
Kneeled down in the dust
Toiling over a lump of clay
Till He shaped it in His own image;

Then into it He blew the breath of life,
And man became a living soul.
Amen. Amen.

CLAUDE MCKAY

THE PUBLICATION OF CLAUDE MCKAY's "If We Must Die" gave African Americans a virtual catechism with which to confront the terrible Red Summer of 1919. "Baptism," published in that year, had a similar tonic effect. With the appearance of Harlem Shadows (1922), his first book of poetry in the United States, he became for a time the most famous poet of African descent writing in English. The inspiration of McKay's example was one of the most important factors in making possible the Harlem Renaissance.

McKay regarded the black folk of humble background as the only source worthy of the African American artist. But he was far more dogmatic in his contempt for middle-class values than Langston Hughes. Furthermore, like fellow Jamaican Marcus Garvey, McKay possessed a strong aversion to men and women of racially mixed ancestry. Finally, because he was willing to leave them behind for London, Moscow, and Paris, or Marseilles and Tangiers, McKay surpassed his contemporaries in denouncing the racial hypocrisy of American white people, as in "The White House" and "The Negro's Friend."

The appeal of the pastoral, the natural, the simple, was central to the Harlem Renaissance. The ills and corruption of urban life were inveighed against in the works of James Weldon Johnson, Jean Toomer, Langston Hughes, and Zora Neale Hurston, but none matched the philosophical grandeur McKay achieved in "The Desolate City" or the seminal ambivalence of "When Dawn Comes to the City."

Repelled by what he saw as its intellectual parochialism and petit-bourgeois social agenda, McKay ridiculed the Harlem Renaissance and left in 1922 for the Soviet Union. The two poems

*included here from the post–Harlem period—"St. Isaac's Church,
Petrograd" and "Barcelona"—reflect the range of an African
American artist's concerns outside the crucible of American racism.*

IF WE MUST DIE

>If we must die, let it not be like hogs
>Hunted and penned in an inglorious spot,
>While round us bark the mad and hungry dogs,
>Making their mock at our accursèd lot.
>If we must die, O let us nobly die,
>So that our precious blood may not be shed
>In vain; then even the monsters we defy
>Shall be constrained to honor us though dead!
>O kinsmen! we must meet the common foe!
>Though far outnumbered let us show us brave,
>And for their thousand blows deal one deathblow!
>What though before us lies the open grave?
>Like men we'll face the murderous, cowardly pack,
>Pressed to the wall, dying, but fighting back!

BAPTISM

>Into the furnace let me go alone;
>Stay you without in terror of the heat.
>
>I will go naked in—for thus 'tis sweet—
>Into the weird depths of the hottest zone.
>I will not quiver in the frailest bone,
>You will not note a flicker of defeat;
>My heart shall tremble not its fate to meet,
>Nor mouth give utterance to any moan.
>The yawning oven spits forth fiery spears;
>Red aspish tongues shout wordlessly my name.
>Desire destroys, consumes my mortal fears,
>Transforming me into a shape of flame.
>
>I will come out, back to your world of tears,
>A stronger soul within a finer frame.

THE WHITE HOUSE

Your door is shut against my tightened face,
And I am sharp as steel with discontent;
But I possess the courage and the grace
To bear my anger proudly and unbent.
The pavement slabs burn loose beneath my feet,
A chafing savage, down the decent street;
And passion rends my vitals as I pass,
Where boldly shines your shuttered door of glass.
Oh, I must search for wisdom every hour,
Deep in my wrathful bosom sore and raw,
And find in it the superhuman power
To hold me to the letter of your law!
Oh, I must keep my heart inviolate
Against the potent poison of your hate.

THE NEGRO'S FRIEND

There is no radical the Negro's friend
Who points some other than the classic road
For him to follow, fighting to the end,
Thinking to ease him of one half his load.
What waste of time to cry: "No Segregation!"
When it exists in stark reality,
Both North and South, throughout this total nation,
The state decreed by white authority.

Must fifteen million blacks be gratified,
That one of them can enter as a guest,
A fine white house—the rest of them denied
A place of decent sojourn and a rest?
Oh, Segregation is not the whole sin,
The Negroes need salvation from within.

ON A PRIMITIVE CANOE

Here, passing lonely down this quiet lane,
Before a mud-splashed window long I pause
To gaze and gaze, while through my active brain
Still thoughts are stirred to wakefulness; because
Long, long ago in a dim unknown land,
A massive forest-tree, axe-felled, adze-hewn,
Was deftly done by cunning mortal hand
Into a symbol of the tender moon.
Why does it thrill more than the handsome boat
That bore me o'er the wild Atlantic ways,
And fill me with a rare sense of things remote
From this harsh life of fretful nights and days?
I cannot answer but, whate'er it be,
An old wine has intoxicated me.

THE TROPICS IN NEW YORK

Bananas ripe and green, and ginger-root,
    Cocoa in pods and alligator pears,
And tangerines and mangoes and grape fruit,
    Fit for the highest prize at parish fairs,

Set in the window, bringing memories
    Of fruit-trees laden by low-singing rills,
And dewy dawns, and mystical blue skies
    In benediction over nun-like hills.

My eyes grew dim, and I could no more gaze;
    A wave of longing through my body swept,
And, hungry for the old, familiar ways,
    I turned aside and bowed my head and wept.

WHEN DAWN COMES TO THE CITY

The tired cars go grumbling by,
   The moaning, groaning cars,
And the old milk carts go rumbling by
   Under the same dull stars.
Out of the tenements, cold as stone,
   Dark figures start for work;
I watch them sadly shuffle on,
   'Tis dawn, dawn in New York.

But I would be on the island of the sea,
   In the heart of the island of the sea,
Where the cocks are crowing, crowing, crowing,
   And the hens are cackling in the rose-apple tree,
Where the old draft-horse is neighing, neighing, neighing
    Out on the brown dew-silvered lawn,
   And the tethered cow is lowing, lowing, lowing,
And dear old Ned is braying, braying, braying,
And the shaggy Nannie goat is calling, calling, calling
   From her little trampled corner of the long wide lea
That stretches to the waters of the hill-stream falling
   Sheer upon the flat rocks joyously!
   There, oh there! on the island of the sea,
    There I would be at dawn.

The tired cars go grumbling by,
   The crazy, lazy cars,
And the same milk carts go rumbling by
   Under the dying stars.
A lonely newsboy hurries by,
   Humming a recent ditty;
Red streaks strike through the gray of the sky,
   The dawn comes to the city.

But I would be on the island of the sea,
   In the heart of the island of the sea,
Where the cocks are crowing, crowing, crowing,
   And the hens are cackling in the rose-apple tree,
Where the old draft-horse is neighing, neighing, neighing

Out on the brown dew-silvered lawn,
  And the tethered cow is lowing, lowing, lowing,
And dear old Ned is braying, braying, braying,
And the shaggy Nannie goat is calling, calling, calling
  From her little trampled corner of the long wide lea
That stretches to the waters of the hill-stream falling
    Sheer upon the flat rocks joyously!
      There, oh there! on the island of the sea,
        There I would be at dawn.

THE DESOLATE CITY

My spirit is a pestilential city,
With misery triumphant everywhere,
Glutted with baffled hopes and human pity.
Strange agonies make quiet lodgement there:
Its sewers, bursting, ooze up from below
And spread their loathsome substance through its lanes,
Flooding all areas with their evil flow
And blocking all the motions of its veins:
Its life is sealed to love or hope or pity,
My spirit is a pestilential city.

Above its walls the air is heavy-wet,
Brooding in fever mood and hanging thick
Round empty tower and broken minaret,
Settling upon the tree tops stricken sick
And withered under its contagious breath.
Their leaves are shrivelled silver, parched decay,
Like wilting creepers trailing underneath
The chalky yellow of a tropic way.
Round crumbling tower and leaning minaret,
The air hangs fever-filled and heavy-wet.

And all its many fountains no more spurt;
Within the dammed-up tubes they tide and foam,
Around the drifted sludge and silted dirt,
And weep against the soft and liquid loam.
And so the city's ways are washed no more,

All is neglected and decayed within,
Clean waters beat against its high-walled shore
In furious force, but cannot enter in:
The suffocated fountains cannot spurt,
They foam and rage against the silted dirt.

Beneath the ebon gloom of mounting rocks
The little pools lie poisonously still,
And birds come to the edge in forlorn flocks,
And utter sudden, plaintive notes and shrill,
Pecking at strangely gray-green substances;
But never do they dip their bills and drink.
They twitter, sad beneath the mournful trees,
And fretfully flit to and from the brink,
In little gray-brown, green-and-purple flocks,
Beneath the jet-gloom of the mounting rocks.

And green-eyed moths of curious design,
With gold-black wings and rarely silver-dotted,
On nests of flowers among those rocks recline,
Bold, burning blossoms, strangely leopard-spotted,
But breathing deadly poison from their lips.
And every lovely moth that wanders by,
And from the blossoms fatal nectar sips,
Is doomed to drooping stupor, there to die;
All green-eyed moths of curious design
That on the fiercely-burning blooms recline.

Oh cold as death is all the loveliness,
That breathes out of the strangeness of the scene,
And sickening like a skeleton's caress,
Of clammy clinging fingers, long and lean.
Above it float a host of yellow flies,
Circling in changeless motion in their place,
That came down snow-thick from the freighted skies,
Swarming across the gluey floor of space:
Oh cold as death is all the loveliness,
And sickening like a skeleton's caress.

There was a time when, happy with the birds,
The little children clapped their hands and laughed;

And midst the clouds the glad winds heard their words
And blew down all the merry ways to waft
The music through the scented fields of flowers.
Oh sweet were children's voices in those days,
Before the fall of pestilential showers,
That drove them forth far from the city's ways:
Now never, nevermore their silver words
Will mingle with the golden of the birds.

Gone, gone forever the familiar forms
To which the city once so dearly clung,
Blown worlds beyond by the destroying storms
And lost away like lovely songs unsung.
Yet life still lingers, questioningly strange,
Timid and quivering, naked and alone,
Against the cycle of disruptive change,
Though all the fond familiar forms are gone,
Forever gone, the fond familiar forms;
Blown worlds beyond by the destroying storms.

THE HARLEM DANCER

Applauding youths laughed with young prostitutes
And watched her perfect, half-clothed body sway;
Her voice was like the sound of blended flutes
Blown by black players upon a picnic day.
She sang and danced on gracefully and calm,
The light gauze hanging loose about her form;
To me she seemed a proudly-swaying palm
Grown lovelier for passing through a storm.
Upon her swarthy neck black, shiny curls
Profusely fell; and, tossing coins in praise,
The wine-flushed, bold-eyed boys, and even the girls,
Devoured her with their eager, passionate gaze;
But looking at her falsely-smiling face,
I knew her self was not in that strange place.

SAINT ISAAC'S CHURCH, PETROGRAD

Bow down my soul in worship very low
And in the holy silences be lost.
Bow down before the marble man of woe,
Bow down before the singing angel host.

What jewelled glory fills my spirit's eye!
What golden grandeur moves the depths of me!
The soaring arches lift me up on high
Taking my breath with their rare symmetry.

Bow down my soul and let the wondrous light
Of Beauty bathe thee from her lofty throne
Bow down before the wonder of man's might.
Bow down in worship, humble and alone;
Bow lowly down before the sacred sight
Of man's divinity alive in stone.

BARCELONA

I

In Barcelona city they dance the nights
Along the streets. The folk, erecting stands
Upon the people's pavements, come together
From pueblo, barrio, in families,
Lured by the lilting playing of the bands,
Rejoicing in the balmy summer weather,
In spreading rings they weave fine fantasies
Like rare mosaics of many-colored lights.

Kindled, it glows, the magical Sardana,
And sweeps the city in a glorious blaze.
The garrison, the sailors from the ships,
The workers join and block the city's ways,
Ripe laughter ringing from intriguing lips,
Crescending like a wonderful hosanna.

II

Oh admirable city from every range!
Whether I stand upon your natural towers,—
With your blue carpet spreading to their feet,
Its patterns undulate between the bars,—
Watching until the tender twilight hours,
Its motion cradling soft a silver fleet;
Or far descend from underneath the stars.

Down—to your bottoms sinister and strange:
The nights eccentric of the Barrio Chino,
The creatures of the shadows of the walls,
Gray like the savage caricatures of Goya,
The chulos of the abysmal dancing halls,
And in the garish lights of La Criolla,
The feminine flamenco of El Niño.

III

Oh Barcelona, queen of Europe's cities,
From dulcet thoughts of you my guts are twisted
With bitter pain of longing for your sights,
And for your hills, your picturesque glory singing,
My feet are mutinous, mine eyes are misted.
Upon my happy thoughts your harbor lights
Are shimmering like bells melodious ringing
With sweet cadenzas of flamenco ditties.

I see your movement flashing like a knife,
Reeling my senses, drunk upon the hues
Of motion, the eternal rainbow wheel,
Your passion smouldering like a lighted fuse,
But more than all sensations, oh I feel
Your color flaming in the dance of life.

ANNE SPENCER

ANNE SPENCER, *whose house and garden in Lynchburg, Virginia, served much the same sheltering role as Georgia Johnson's salon (Du Bois and Sterling Brown were regulars), was considered to be one of the most talented poets of the New Negro literacy ferment. Spencer's verse was noble and mildly feminist, if not particularly animated.*

LADY, LADY

Lady, Lady, I saw your face,
Dark as night withholding a star . . .
The chisel fell, or it might have been
You had borne so long the yoke of men.

Lady, Lady, I saw your hands,
Twisted, awry, like crumpled roots,
Bleached poor white in a sudsy tub,
Wrinkled and drawn from your rub-a-dub.

Lady, Lady, I saw your heart,
And altared there in its darksome place
Were the tongues of flame the ancients knew,
Where the good God sits to spangle through.

JEAN TOOMER

JEAN TOOMER *shared with Claude McKay the distinction of early publication in Bohemia's leading little magazines*—Seven Arts, S 4 N, Broom, *and* Liberator. *His connection to Harlem as a place and to the spirit of the Renaissance was tenuous. He seems to have belonged more to the Lost Generation than to the New Negro Arts Movement. Two years after his discovery in 1922 by Jessie Fauset, literary editor of* The Crisis, *Toomer had become the principal spokesman for the mystical Gurdjieff movement in America. A short time thereafter, he professed not to be an African American, claiming, rather, that the aim of art as well as that of the evolution of America lay in transcending categories of race.*

Toomer was deeply influenced by Sherwood Anderson and Waldo Frank, but his first collection of short stories and poems, Cane *(1923), was a unique work of art, evoking from Jean Wagner, among the most judicious students of the Harlem Renaissance, the accolade of being* "*one of the most remarkable in all postwar American literature.*" *After a few summer weeks in Georgia, the Washington-bred Toomer had returned to the genteel poverty of his District of Columbia family home to translate luminously the ethos of the agrarian South. The form of the work continues to escape precise categorization—a prose poem is perhaps the most serviceable label. Although it sold less than five hundred copies for its venturesome publisher, Horace Liveright,* Cane *was a catalyst for the New Negro Arts Movement.*

"Georgia opened me," he wrote in Locke's The New Negro. *"I received my initial impulse to an individual art form from my experience there. . . . There one finds soil . . . the soil every art*

and literature that is to live must be embodied in." Because he soon forgot his own maxim, Toomer lost his extraordinary gift and gradually lapsed into silence. "The Blue Meridian," his virtually forgotten epic poem that appeared in 1929 and is reproduced in part here, was to be his final public word on the themes central to the Harlem Renaissance.

SONG OF THE SON

Pour, O pour that parting soul in song,
O pour it in the saw-dust glow of night,
Into the velvet pine-smoke air to-night,
And let the valley carry it along,
And let the valley carry it along.

O land and soil, red soil and sweet-gum tree,
So scant of grass, so profligate of pines,
Now just before an epoch's sun declines
Thy son, in time, I have returned to thee,
Thy son, I have in time returned to thee.

In time, although the sun is setting on
A song-lit race of slaves, it has not set;
Though late, O soil, it is not too late yet
To catch thy plaintive soul, leaving, soon gone,
Leaving, to catch thy plaintive soul soon gone.

O Negro slaves, dark purple ripened plums,
Squeezed, and bursting in the pine-wood air,
Passing, before they strip the old tree bare
One plum was saved for me, one seed becomes

An everlasting song, a singing tree,
Caroling softly souls of slavery,
What they were, and what they are to me,
Carolling softly souls of slavery.

GEORGIA DUSK

The sky, lazily disdaining to pursue
   The setting sun, too indolent to hold
   A lengthened tournament for flashing gold,
Passively darkens for night's barbecue,

A feast of moon and men and barking hounds,
   An orgy for some genius of the South
   With blood-hot eyes and cane-lipped scented
     mouth,
Surprised in making folk-songs from soul sounds.

The sawmill blows its whistle, buzz-saws stop,
   And silence breaks the bud of knoll and hill,
   Soft settling pollen where ploughed lands fulfill
Their early promise of a bumper crop.

Smoke from the pyramidal sawdust pile
   Curls up, blue ghosts of trees, tarrying low
   Where only chips and stumps are left to show
The solid proof of former domicile.

Meanwhile, the men, with vestiges of pomp,
   Race memories of king and caravan,
   High-priests, an ostrich, and a juju-man,
Go singing through the footpaths of the swamp.

Their voices rise . . . the pine trees are guitars,
   Strumming, pine-needles fall like sheets of rain . . .
   Their voices rise . . . the chorus of the cane
Is carolling a vesper to the stars.

O singers, resinous and soft your songs
   Above the sacred whisper of the pines,
   Give virgin lips to cornfield concubines,
Bring dreams of Christ to dusky cane-lipped throngs.

THE BLUE MERIDIAN

It is a new America,
To be spiritualized by each new American.

Black Meridian, black light,
Dynamic atom-aggregate,
Lay sleeping on an inland lake.

Lift, lift, thou waking forces!
Let us feel the energy of animals,
The force of rumps and bull-bent heads
Crashing the barrier to man.
It must spiral on!
A million million men, or twelve men,
Must crash the barrier to the next higher form.

Beyond plants are animals,
Beyond animals is man,
Beyond man is the universe.

The Big Light,
Let the Big Light in!

O thou, Radiant Incorporeal,
The I of earth and of mankind, hurl
Down these seaboards, across this continent,
The thousand-rayed discus of thy mind,
And above our walking limbs unfurl
Spirit-torsos of exquisite strength!

The Mississippi, sister of the Ganges,
Main artery of earth in the western world,
Is waiting to become
In the spirit of America, a scared river.
Whoever lifts the Mississippi
Lifts himself and all America;

Whoever lifts himself
Makes that great brown river smile.
The blood of earth and the blood of man
Course swifter and rejoice when we spiritualize.

We—priest, clown, scientist, technician,
Artist, rascal, worker, lazybones,
This is the whole—
Individuals and people,
This is the whole that stood with Adam
And has come down to us,
Never to be less,
Whatever side is up, however viewed,
Whatever the vicissitudes,
The needs of evolution that bring
Emphasis upon a part—
Man himself, his total body and soul,
This is the moving whole.

Men of the East, men of the West,
Men in life, men in death,
Americans and all countrymen—
Growth is by admixture from less to more,
Preserving the great granary intact,
Through cycles of death and life,
Each stage a pod,
Perpetuating and perfecting
An essence identical in all,
Obeying the same laws, unto the same goal,
That far-distant objective,
By ways both down and up,
Down years ago, now struggling up.

So lift, lift, thou waking forces!

The old gods, led by an inverted Christ,
A shaved Moses, a blanched Lemur,
And a moulting Thunderbird,
Withdrew into the distance and died,

Their dust and seed drifting down
To fertilize the seven regions of America.

We are waiting for a new God,
For revelation in our day,
For growth towards faceless Deity.

The old peoples—
The great European races sent wave after wave
That washed the forests, the earth's rich loam,
Grew towns with the seeds of giant cities,
Made roads, laid silver rails,
Sang of their swift achievement
And perished, displaced by machines,
Smothered by a world too huge for little men,
Too empty for life to breathe in.
They say that near the end
It was a chaos of crying men and hard women,
A city of goddamn and Jehovah
Baptized in finance
Without benefit of saints,
Of dear defectives
Winnowing their likenesses from synthetic rock
Sold by national organizations of undertakers.

Someone said:
    Blood cannot mix with the stuff upon our boards
    As water with flour to make bread,
    Nor have we yeast, nor have we fire.
    Not iron, not chemicals or money
    Are animate to suffer and rejoice,
    Not what we have become, this angel-dough,
    But slowly die, never attaining birth
    Above the body, above its pain and hungers,
    To beat pavements, stand in lines,
    Fill space and drive motor-cars.

Another cried:
    It is because of thee, O Life,
    That the first prayer ends in the last curse.

Another sang:
> Late minstrels of the restless earth,
> No muteness can be granted thee,
> Lift thy laughing energies
> To that white point which is a star.

The great African races sent a single wave
And singing riplets to sorrow in red fields,
Sing a swan song, to break rocks
And immortalize a hiding water boy.

> I'm leaving the shining ground, brothers,
> I sing because I ache,
> I go because I must,
> I'm leaving the shining ground;
> Don't ask me where,
> I'll meet you there,
> Brothers, I am leaving the shining ground.

> But we must keep keep keep the watermelon—
> He moaned, O Lord, Lord,
> This bale will break me—
> But we must keep keep keep the watermelon.

The great red race was here.
In a land of flaming earth and torrent-rains,
Of red sea-plains and majestic mesas,
At sunset from a purple hill
The Gods came down;
They serpentined into pueblo,
And a white-robed priest
Danced with them five days and nights;
But pueblo, priest, and Shalakos
Sank into the sacred earth
To fertilize the seven regions of America.

> Hé-ya, hé-yo, hé-yo,
> Hé-ya, hé-yo, hé-yo,
> The ghosts of buffaloes,
> A lone eagle feather,
> An untamed Navajo,

Hé-ya, hé-yo, hé-yo
Hé-ya, hé-yo, hé-yo.

We are waiting for a new people,
For the joining of men to men
And man to God.

PART III

FICTION

EUGENE O'NEILL

EUGENE O'NEILL's The Emperor Jones *opened at the Provincetown Playhouse in Greenwich Village in November 1920, with the
African American actor Charles Gilpin in the starring role. The
principal role of Brutus Jones went to novice actor Paul Robeson
when the play was revived in 1924. O'Neill parodies the brilliant,
tragic reign of the Haitian emperor Henri Christophe, creating in
the American escaped convict Jones a Noble Savage type who is
destroyed by his own Jungian atavism as he attempts to escape
from the island kingdom he has plundered. The Emperor Jones set
Robeson solidly on his career path as a powerful if still unskilled
actor and confirmed the mainstream fascination with "primitive"
dramatic and literary themes. African American audiences appreciated the heightened attention to matters racial generated by
O'Neill's play but were not especially pleased by its message of
racial atavism. The following scenes from the play present Brutus
Jones stumbling petrified through the jungle to his death by suicide
as tom-toms beat insistently.*

FROM THE EMPEROR JONES

SCENE VI

THREE O'CLOCK. *A cleared space in the forest. The limbs of
the trees meet over it forming a low ceiling about five feet from
the ground. The interlocked ropes of creepers reaching upward to
entwine the tree trunks give an arched appearance to the sides. The*

space this encloses is like the dark, noisome hold of some ancient vessel. The moonlight is almost completely shut out and only a vague, wan light filters through. The scene is in complete darkness at first. There is the noise of someone approaching from the left, stumbling and crawling through the undergrowth. JONES'S *voice is heard, between chattering moans.*

JONES. Oh, Lawd, what I gwine do now? Ain't got no bullet left on'y de silver one. If mo' o' dem ha'nts come after me, how I gwine skeer dem away? Oh, Lawd, on'y de silver one left— an' I gotta save dat fo' luck. If I shoots dat one I'm a goner sho'! Lawd, it's black heah! Whar's de moon? Oh, Lawd, don't dis night evah come to an end? (*By the sounds, he is feeling his way cautiously forward.*) Dere! Dis feels like a clear space. I gotta lie down an' rest. I don't care if dem niggers does catch me. I gotta rest. (*He is well forward now where his figure can be dimly made out. His pants have been so torn away that what is left of them is no better than a breechcloth. He flings himself full length, face downward on the ground, panting with exhaustion. Gradually it seems to grow lighter in the enclosed space and two rows of seated figures can be seen behind* JONES. *They are sitting in crumpled, despairing attitudes, hunched facing one another with their backs touching the forest walls as if they were shackled to them. All are Negroes, naked save for loin cloths. At first they are silent and motionless. Then they begin to sway slowly forward toward each other and back again in unison, as if they were laxly letting themselves follow the long roll of a ship at sea. At the same time, a low, melancholy murmur rises among them, increasing gradually by rhythmic degrees which seems to be directed and controlled by the throb of the tom-tom in the distance, to a long, tremendous wail of despair that reaches a certain pitch, unbearably acute, then falls by slow gradations of tone into silence and is taken up again.* JONES *starts, looks up, sees the figures, and throws himself down again to shut off the sight. A shudder of terror shakes his whole body as the wail rises up about him again. But the next time, his voice, as if under some uncanny compulsion, starts with the others. As their chorus lifts he rises to a sitting posture similar to the others, swaying back and forth. His voice reaches the highest pitch of sorrow, of desolation. The light fades out, the other voices cease, and only darkness is left.* JONES *can be heard scrambling to his feet and running off, his voice sinking down the scale and receding as he moves farther and farther away in the forest. The tom-tom beats louder, quicker, with a more insistent, triumphant pulsation.)*

SCENE VII

FIVE O'CLOCK. *The foot of a gigantic tree by the edge of a great river. A rough structure of boulders, like an altar, is by the tree. The raised river bank is in the nearer background. Beyond this the surface of the river spreads out, brilliant and unruffled in the moonlight, blotted out and merged with a veil of bluish mist in the distance.* JONES'S *voice is heard from the left rising and falling in the long, despairing wail of the chained slaves, to the rhythmic beat of the tom-tom.—As his voice sinks into silence, he enters the open space.—The expression of his face is fixed and stony, his eyes have an obsessed glare, he moves with a strange deliberation like a sleepwalker or one in a trance. He looks around at the tree, the rough stone altar, the moonlit surface of the river beyond and passes his hand over his head with a vague gesture of puzzled bewilderment. Then, as if in obedience to some obscure impulse, he goes into a kneeling, devotional posture before the altar. Then he seems to come to himself partly, to have an uncertain realization of what he is doing, for he straightens up and stares about him horrifiedly—in an incoherent mumble.*

JONES. What—what is I doin'? What is—dis place? Seems like— seems like I know dat tree—an' dem stones—an' de river. I remember—seems like I been heah befo'. *(Tremblingly)* Oh, gorry, I'se skeered in dis place! I'se skeered! Oh, Lawd, pertect dis sinner! *(Crawling away from the altar, he cowers close to the ground, his face hidden, his shoulders heaving with sobs of hysterical fright. From behind the trunk of the tree, as if he had sprung out of it, the figure of the* CONGO WITCH DOCTOR *appears. He is wizened and old, naked except for the fur of some small animal tied about his waist, its bushy tail hanging down in front like a Highlander's. His body is stained all over a bright red. Antelope horns are on each side of his head, branching upward. In one hand he carries a bone rattle, in the other a charm stick with a bunch of white cockatoo feathers tied to the end. A great number of glass beads and bone or-*

naments are about his neck, ears, wrists, and ankles. He struts noiselessly with a queer prancing step to a position in the clear ground between JONES and the altar. Then with a preliminary, summoning stamp of his foot on the earth, he begins to dance and to chant. As if in response to his summons the beating of the tom-tom grows to a fierce, exultant boom whose throbs seem to fill the air with vibrating rhythm. JONES looks up, starts to spring to his feet, reaches a half-kneeling, half-squatting position and remains rigidly fixed there, paralyzed with awed fascination by this new apparition. The WITCH DOCTOR sways, stamping with his foot, his bone rattle clicking the time. His voice rises and falls in a weird, monotonous croon, without articulate word divisions. Gradually his dance becomes clearly one of a narrative in pantomime, his croon is an incantation, a charm to allay the fierceness of some implacable deity demanding sacrifice. He flees, he is pursued by devils, he hides, he flees again. Ever wilder and wilder becomes his flight, nearer and nearer draws the pursuing evil, more and more the spirit of terror gains possession of him. His croon, rising to intensity, is punctuated by shrill cries. JONES has become completely hypnotized. His voice joins in the incantation, in the cries, he beats time with his hands and sways his body to and fro from the waist. The whole spirit and meaning of the dance has entered into him, has become his spirit. Finally the theme of the pantomime halts, on a howl of despair, and is taken up again in a note of savage hope. There is a salvation. The forces of evil demand sacrifice. They must be appeased. The WITCH DOCTOR points with his wand to the sacred tree, the river beyond, to the altar, and finally to JONES with a ferocious command. JONES seems to sense the meaning of this. It is he who must offer himself for sacrifice. He beats his forehead abjectly to the ground, moaning hysterically.) Mercy, oh, Lawd! Mercy! Mercy on dis po' sinner! (The witch doctor springs to the river bank. He stretches out his arms and calls to some God within its depths. Then he starts backward slowly, his arms remaining out. A huge head of a crocodile appears over the bank and its eyes, glittering greenly, fasten upon JONES. He stares into them fascinatedly. The witch doctor prances up to him, touches him with his wand, motions with hideous command toward the waiting monster. JONES squirms on his belly nearer and nearer, moaning continually.)

Mercy, Lawd! Mercy! (*The crocodile heaves more of his enormous bulk on to the land.* JONES *squirms toward him. The witch doctor's voice shrills out in furious exultation, the tom-tom beats madly.* JONES *cries out in fierce, exhausted spasms of anguished pleading.*) Lawd, save me! Lawd Jesus, heah my prayer! (*Immediately, in answer to his prayer, comes the thought of the one bullet left him. He snatches at his hip, shouting defiantly.*) De silver bullet! Yo' don't git me yit! (*He fires at the green eyes in front of him. The head of the crocodile sinks back behind the river bank, the witch doctor springs behind the sacred tree and disappears.* JONES *lies with his face to the ground, his arms outstretched, whimpering with fear as the throb of the tom-tom fills the silence about him with a somber pulsation, a baffled but revengeful power.*)

SCENE VIII

DAWN. *Same as* SCENE TWO, *the dividing line of forest and plain. The nearest tree trunks are dimly revealed but the forest behind them is still a mass of glooming shadow. The tom-tom seems on the very spot, so loud and continuously vibrating are its beats.* LEM *enters from the left, followed by a small squad of his soldiers, and by the Cockney trader,* SMITHERS. LEM *is a heavy-set, ape-faced old savage of the extreme African type, dressed only in a loin cloth. A revolver and cartridge belt are about his waist. His soldiers are in different degrees of rag-concealed nakedness. All wear broad palm-leaf hats. Each one carries a rifle.* SMITHERS *is the same as in* SCENE ONE. *One of the soldiers, evidently a tracker, is peering about keenly on the ground. He grunts and points to the spot where* JONES *entered the forest.* LEM *and* SMITHERS *come to look.*)

SMITHERS. (*After a glance, turns away in disgust*) That's where 'e went in right enough. Much good it'll do yer. 'E's miles orf by this an' safe to the Coast, damn 'is 'ide! I tole yer yer'd lose 'im, didn't I—wastin' the 'ole bloomin' night beatin' yer bloody drum and castin' yer silly spells! Gawd blimey, wot a pack!

LEM. (*Gutturally*) We cotch him. You see. (*He makes a motion to his soldiers, who squat down on their haunches in a semicircle.*)

SMITHERS. (*Exasperatedly*) Well, ain't yer goin' in an' 'unt 'im in the woods? What the 'ell's the good of waitin'?

LEM. (*Imperturbably—squatting down himself*) We cotch him.

SMITHERS. (*Turning away from him contemptuously*) Aw! Garn! 'E's a better man than the lot o' you put together. I 'ates the sight o' 'im but I'll say that for 'im. (*A sound of snapping twigs comes from the forest. The soldiers jump to their feet, cocking their rifles alertly. LEM remains sitting with an imperturbable expression, but listening intently. He makes a quick signal with his hand. His followers creep quickly into the forest, scattering so that each enters at a different spot.*)

SMITHERS. (*In the silence that follows—in a contemptuous whisper*) You ain't thinkin' that would be 'im, I 'ope?

LEM. (*Calmly*) We cotch him.

SMITHERS. Blarsted fat'eads. (*Then after a second's thought—wonderingly*) Still an' all, it might happen. If 'e lost 'is bloody way in these stinkin' woods 'e'd likely turn in a circle without 'is knowin' it. They all does.

LEM. (*Peremptorily*) Ssshh! (*The reports of several rifles sound from the forest, followed a second later by savage, exultant yells. The beating of the tom-tom abruptly ceases. LEM looks up at the white man with a grin of satisfaction.*) We cotch him. Him dead.

SMITHERS. (*With a snarl*) 'Ow d'yer know it's 'im an' 'ow d'yer know 'e's dead?

LEM. My men's dey got 'um silver bullets. Dey kill him shore.

SMITHERS. (*Astonished*) They got silver bullets?

LEM. Lead bullet no kill him. He got um strong charm. I cook um money, make um silver bullet, make um strong charm, too.

SMITHERS. (*Light breaking upon him*) So that's wot you was up to all night, wot? You was scared to put after 'im till you'd moulded silver bullets, eh?

LEM. (*Simply stating a fact*) Yes. Him got strong charm. Lead no good.

SMITHERS. (*Slapping his thigh and guffawing*) Haw-haw! If yer don't beat all 'ell! (*Then recovering himself—scornfully*) I'll bet you it ain't 'im they shot at all, yer bleedin' looney!

LEM. (*Calmly*) Dey come bring him now. (*The soldiers come out of the forest, carrying JONES's limp body. He is dead. They carry him to LEM, who examines his body with great satisfaction. SMITHERS leans over his shoulder—in a tone of frightened awe.*)

SMITHERS. Well, they did for yer right enough, Jonesy, me lad! Dead as a 'erring! (*Mockingly*) Where's yer 'igh an' mighty airs now, yer bloomin' Majesty? (*Then with a grin*) Silver bullets! Gawd blimey, but yer died in the 'eighth o' style, any'ow!

CURTAIN

JEAN TOOMER

THE FOLLOWING EXCERPTS from Jean Toomer's Cane *(1923) explore the fate of two women of the rural South, "Karintha" and "Fern," the first a black beauty "perfect as dusk when the sun goes down," the second a blend of two races who creates strong, mysterious yearnings in the men who possess her. In "Bona and Paul," Toomer spoke to that racially amalgamated future he believed would be America's salvation. Paul is black, Bona is white. "I came back to tell you, to shake your hand, and tell you that you are wrong," Paul explains to a leering black doorman as they leave the dance hall. "I came back to tell you, brother, that white faces are petals of roses. That dark faces are petals of dusk. That I am going out and gather petals." But Bona is gone from the spot where Paul left her; he has lost her by taking time to explain himself.*

FROM CANE

KARINTHA

> Her skin is like dusk,
> O cant you see it,
> Her skin is like dusk,
> When the sun goes down.

Karintha is a woman. She who carries beauty, perfect as dusk when the sun goes down. She has been married many times. Old men remind her that a few years back they rode her hobbyhorse upon their knees. Karintha smiles, and indulges them when she is in the mood for it. She has contempt for them. Karintha is a woman. Young men run stills to make her money. Young men go to the big cities and run on the road. Young men go away to college. They all want to bring her money. These are the young men who thought that all they had to do was to count time. But Karintha is a woman, and she has had a child. A child fell out of her womb onto a bed of pine-needles in the forest. Pine-needles are smooth and sweet. They are elastic to the feet of rabbits . . . A sawmill was nearby. Its pyramidal sawdust pile smouldered. It is a year before one completely burns. Meanwhile, the smoke curls up and hangs in odd wraiths about the trees, curls up, and spreads itself out over the valley . . . Weeks after Karintha returned home the smoke was so heavy you tasted it in water. Some one made a song:

> Smoke is on the hills. Rise up.
> Smoke is on the hills, O rise
> And take my soul to Jesus.

Karintha is a woman. Men do not know that the soul of her was a growing thing ripened too soon. They will bring their money; they will die not having found it out . . . Karintha at twenty, carrying beauty, perfect as dusk when the sun goes down. Karintha . . .

> Her skin is like dusk on the eastern horizon,
> O cant you see it, O cant you see it,
> Her skin is like dusk on the eastern horizon
> . . . When the sun goes down.

> Goes down . . .

FERN

HER NOSE WAS AQUILINE, Semitic. If you have heard a Jewish cantor sing, if he has touched you and made your own sorrow seem trivial when compared with his, you will know my feeling when I follow the curves of her profile, like mobile rivers, to their common

delta. They were strange eyes. In this, that they sought nothing—
that is, nothing that was obvious and tangible and that one could
see, and they gave the impression that nothing was to be denied.
When a woman seeks, you will have observed, her eyes deny.
Fern's eyes desired nothing that you could give her; there was no
reason why they should withhold. Men saw her eyes and fooled
themselves. Fern's eyes said to them that she was easy. . . .

Anyone, of course, could see her, could see her eyes. If you
walked up the Dixie Pike most any time of day, you'd be most like
to see her resting listless-like on the railing of her porch, back
propped against a post, head tilted a little forward because there
was a nail in the porch post just where her head came which for
some reason or other she never took the trouble to pull out. Her
eyes, if it were sunset, rested idly where the sun, molten and glorious, was pouring down between the fringe of pines. Or maybe
they gazed at the gray cabin on the knoll from which an evening
folk-song was coming. Perhaps they followed a cow that had been
turned loose to roam and feed on cotton-stalks and corn leaves.
Like as not they'd settle on some vague spot above the horizon,
though hardly a trace of wistfulness would come to them. If it were
dusk, then they'd wait for the search-light of the evening train
which you could see miles up the track before it flared across the
Dixie Pike, close to her home. Wherever they looked, you'd follow
them and then waver back. Like her face, the whole countryside
seemed to flow into her eyes. Flowed into them with the soft listless
cadence of Georgia's South. A young Negro, once, was looking at
her, spellbound, from the road. A white man passing in a buggy
had to flick him with his whip if he was to get by without running
him over. I first saw her on her porch. I was passing with a fellow
whose crusty numbness (I was from the North and suspected of
being prejudiced and stuck-up) was melting as he found me warm.
I asked him who she was. "That's Fern," was all that I could get
from him. Some folks already thought that I was given to nosing
around; I let it go at that, so far as questions were concerned. But
at first sight of her I felt as if I heard a Jewish cantor sing. As if
his singing rose above the unheard chorus of a folk-song. And I
felt bound to her. I too had my dreams: something I would do for
her. I have knocked about from town to town too much not to
know the futility of mere change of place. Besides, picture if you
can, this cream-colored solitary girl sitting at a tenement window
looking down on the indifferent throngs of Harlem. Better that she

listen to folk-songs at dusk in Georgia, you would say, and so would I. Or, suppose she came up North and married. Even a doctor or a lawyer, say, one who would be sure to get along— that is, make money. You and I know, who have had experience in such things, that love is not a thing like prejudice which can be bettered by changes of town. Could men in Washington, Chicago, or New York, more than the men of Georgia, bring her something left vacant by the bestowal of their bodies? You and I who know men in these cities will have to say, they could not. See her out and out a prostitute along State Street in Chicago. See her move into a southern town where white men are more aggressive. See her become a white man's concubine . . . Something I must do for her. There was myself. What could I do for her? Talk, of course. Push back the fringe of pines upon new horizons. To what purpose? and what for? Her? Myself? Men in her case seem to lose their selfishness. I lost mine before I touched her. I ask you, friend (it makes no difference if you sit in the Pullman or the Jim Crow as the train crosses her road), what thoughts would come to you —that is, after you'd finished with the thoughts that leap into men's minds at the sight of a pretty woman who will not deny them; what thoughts would come to you, had you seen her in a quick flash, keen and intuitively, as she sat there on her porch when your train thundered by? Would you have got off at the next station and come back for her to take her where? Would you have completely forgotten her as soon as you reached Macon, Atlanta, Augusta, Pasadena, Madison, Chicago, Boston, or New Orleans? Would you tell your wife or sweetheart about a girl you saw? Your thoughts can help me, and I would like to know. Something I would do for her . . .

One evening I walked up the Pike on purpose, and stopped to say hello. Some of her family were about, but they moved away to make room for me. Damn if I knew how to begin. Would you? Mr. and Miss So-and-So, people, the weather, the crops, the new preacher, the frolic, the church benefit, rabbit and possum hunting, the new soft drink they had at old Pap's store, the schedule of the trains, what kind of town Macon was, Negro's migration north, boll-weevils, syrup, the Bible—to all these things she gave a yassur or nassur, without further comment. I began to wonder if perhaps my own emotional sensibility had played one of its tricks on me.

"Lets take a walk," I at last ventured. The suggestion, coming after so long an isolation, was novel enough, I guess, to surprise. But it wasnt that. Something told me that men before me had said just that as a prelude to the offering of their bodies. I tried to tell her with my eyes. I think she understood. The thing from her that made my throat catch, vanished. Its passing left her visible in a way I'd thought, but never seen. We walked down the Pike with people on all the porches gaping at us. "Doesnt it make you mad?" She meant the row of petty gossiping people. She meant the world. Through a canebrake that was ripe for cutting, the branch was reached. Under a sweet-gum tree, and where reddish leaves had dammed the creek a little, we sat down. Dusk, suggesting the almost imperceptible procession of giant trees, settled with a purple haze about the cane. I felt strange, as I always do in Georgia, particularly at dusk. I felt that things unseen to men were tangibly immediate. It would not have surprised me had I had vision. People have them in Georgia more often than you would suppose. A black woman once saw the mother of Christ and drew her in charcoal on the courthouse wall . . . When one is on the soil of one's ancestors, most anything can come to one . . . From force of habit, I suppose, I held Fern in my arms—that is, without at first noticing it. Then my mind came back to her. Her eyes, unusually weird and open, held me. Held God. He flowed in as I've seen the countryside flow in. Seen men. I must have done something—what, I dont know, in the confusion of my emotion. She sprang up. Rushed some distance from me. Fell to her knees, and began swaying, swaying. Her body was tortured with something it could not let out. Like boiling sap it flooded arms and fingers till she shook them as if they burned her. It found her throat, and spattered inarticulately in plaintive, convulsive sounds, mingled with calls to Christ Jesus. And then she sang, brokenly. A Jewish cantor singing with a broken voice. A child's voice, uncertain, or an old man's. Dusk hid her; I could hear only her song. It seemed to me as though she were pounding her head in anguish upon the ground. I rushed to her. She fainted in my arms.

There was talk about her fainting with me in the canefield. And I got one or two ugly looks from town men who'd set themselves up to protect her. In fact, there was talk of making me leave town. But they never did. They kept a watch-out for me, though. Shortly after, I came back North. From the train window I saw her as I crossed her road. Saw her on her porch, head tilted a little forward where the nail was, eyes vaguely focused on the sunset. Saw her face flow into them, the countryside and something that I call God, flowing into them . . . Nothing ever really happened. Nothing ever came to Fern, not even I. Something I would do for her. Some fine unnamed thing . . . And, friend, you? She is still living, I have reason to know. Her name, against the chance that you might happen down that way, is Fernie May Rosen.

BONA AND PAUL

1

ON THE SCHOOL GYMNASIUM FLOOR, young men and women are drilling. They are going to be teachers, and go out into the world . . . thud, thud . . . and give precision to the movements of sick people who all their lives have been drilling. One man is out of step. In step. The teacher glares at him. A girl in bloomers, seated on a mat in the corner because she has told the director that she is sick, sees that the footfalls of the men are rhythmical and syncopated. The dance of his blue-trousered limbs thrills her.

Bona: He is a candle that dances in a grove swung with pale balloons.

Columns of the drillers thud towards her. He is in the front row. He is in no row at all. Bona can look close at him. His red-brown face—

Bona: He is a harvest moon. He is an autumn leaf. He is a nigger. Bona! But dont all the dorm girls say so? And dont you, when you are sane, say so? Thats why I love— Oh, nonsense. You have never loved a man who didnt first love you. Besides—

Columns thud away from her. Come to a halt in line formation. Rigid. The period bell rings, and the teacher dismisses them.

A group collects around Paul. They are choosing sides for basket-ball. Girls against boys. Paul has his. He is limbering up beneath the basket. Bona runs to the girl captain and asks to be chosen. The girls fuss. The director comes to quiet them. He hears what Bona wants.

"But, Miss Hale, you were excused—"

"So I was, Mr. Boynton, but—"

"—you can play basket-ball, but you are too sick to drill."

"If you wish to put it that way."

She swings away from him to the girl captain.

"Helen, I want to play, and you must let me. This is the first time I've asked and I dont see why—"

"Thats just it, Bona. We have our team."

"Well, team or no team, I want to play and thats all there is to it."

She snatches the ball from Helen's hands, and charges down the floor.

Helen shrugs. One of the weaker girls says that she'll drop out. Helen accepts this. The team is formed. The whistle blows. The game starts. Bona, in center, is jumping against Paul. He plays with her. Out-jumps her, makes a quick pass, gets a quick return, and shoots a goal from the middle of the floor. Bona burns crimson. She fights, and tries to guard him. One of her team-mates advises her not to play so hard. Paul shoots his second goal.

Bona begins to feel a little dizzy and all in. She drives on. Almost hugs Paul to guard him. Near the basket, he attempts to shoot, and Bona lunges into his body and tries to beat his arms. His elbow, going up, gives her a sharp crack on the jaw. She whirls. He catches her. Her body stiffens. Then becomes strangely vibrant, and bursts to a swift life within her anger. He is about to give way before her hatred when a new passion flares at him and makes his stomach fall. Bona squeezes him. He suddenly feels stifled, and wonders why in hell the ring of silly gaping faces that's caked about him doesnt make way and give him air. He has a swift illusion that it is himself who has been struck. He looks at Bona. Whir. Whir. They seem to be human distortions spinning tensely in a fog. Spinning . . . dizzy . . . spinning . . . Bona jerks herself free, flushes a startling crimson, breaks through the bewildered teams, and rushes from the hall.

2

Paul is in his room of two windows.

Outside, the South-Side L track cuts them in two.

Bona is one window. One window, Paul.

Hurtling Loop-jammed L trains throw them in swift shadow.

Paul goes to his. Gray slanting roofs of houses are tinted lavender in the setting sun. Paul follows the sun, over the stock-

yards where a fresh stench is just arising, across wheat lands that
are still waving above their stubble, into the sun. Paul follows the
sun to a pine-matted hillock in Georgia. He sees the slanting roofs
of gray unpainted cabins tinted lavender. A Negress chants a lullaby beneath the mate-eyes of a southern planter. Her breasts are
ample for the suckling of a song. She weans it, and sends it, curiously weaving, among lush melodies of cane and corn. Paul follows
the sun into himself in Chicago.

He is at Bona's window.

With his own glow he looks through a dark pane.

Paul's room-mate comes in.

"Say, Paul, I've got a date for you. Come on. Shake a leg, will
you?"

His blonde hair is combed slick. His vest is snug about him.

He is like the electric light which he snaps on.

"Whatdoysay, Paul? Get a wiggle on. Come on. We havent
got much time by the time we eat and dress and everything."

His bustling concentrates on the brushing of his hair.

Art: What in hell's getting into Paul of late, anyway?
Christ, but he's getting moony. Its his blood. Dark blood: moony.
Doesnt get anywhere unless you boost it. You've got to keep it
going—

"Say, Paul!"

—or it'll go to sleep on you. Dark blood; nigger? Thats what
those jealous she-hens say. Not Bona though, or she . . . from the
South . . . wouldnt want me to fix a date for him and her. Hell of
a thing, that Paul's dark: you've got to always be answering
questions.

"Say, Paul, for Christ's sake leave that window, cant you?"

"Whats it, Art?"

"Hell, I've told you about fifty times. Got a date for you.
Come on."

"With who?"

Art: He didnt use to ask; now he does. Getting up in the air.
Getting funny.

"Heres your hat. Want a smoke? Paul! Here. I've got a match.
Now come on and I'll tell you all about it on the way to supper."

Paul: He's going to Life this time. No doubt of that. Quit your
kidding. Some day, dear Art, I'm going to kick the living slats out

of you, and you wont know what I've done it for. And your slats
will bring forth Life . . . beautiful woman . . .

"Bring me some soup with a lot of crackers, understand? And then
a roast-beef dinner. Same for you, eh, Paul? Now as I was saying,
you've got a swell chance with her. And she's game. Best proof:
she dont give a damn what the dorm girls say about you and her
in the gym, or about the funny looks that Boynton gives her, or
about what they say about, well, hell, you know, Paul. And say,
Paul, she's a sweetheart. Tall, not puffy and pretty, more serious
and deep—the kind you like these days. And they say she's got a
car. And say, she's on fire. But you know all about that. She got
Helen to fix it up with me. The four of us—remember the last
party? Crimson Gardens! Boy!"
    Paul's eyes take on a light that Art can settle in.

3

Art has on his patent-leather pumps and fancy vest. A loose fall
coat is swung across his arm. His face has been massaged, and
over a close shave, powdered. It is a healthy pink the blue of evening tints a purple pallor. Art is happy and confident in the good
looks that his mirror gave him. Bubbling over with a joy he must
spend now if the night is to contain it all. His bubbles, too, are
curiously tinted purple as Paul watches them. Paul, contrary to
what he had thought he would be like, is cool like the dusk, and
like the dusk, detached. His dark face is a floating shade in evening's shadow. He sees Art, curiously. Art is a purple fluid, carbon-
charged, that effervesces besides him. He loves Art. But is it not
queer, this pale purple facsimile of a red-blooded Norwegian friend
of his? Perhaps for some reason, white skins are not supposed to
live at night. Surely, enough nights would transform them fantas-
tically, or kill them. And their red passion? Night paled that too,
and made it moony. Moony. Thats what Art thought of him. Bona
didnt, even in the daytime. Bona, would she be pale? Impossible.
Not that red glow. But the conviction did not set his emotion
flowing.
    "Come right in, wont you? The young ladies will be right
down. Oh, Mr. Carlstrom, do play something for us while you are
waiting. We just love to listen to your music. You play so well."

Houses, and dorm sitting-rooms are places where white faces seclude themselves at night. There is a reason . . .

Art sat on the piano and simply tore it down. Jazz. The picture of Our Poets hung perilously.

Paul: I've got to get the kid to play that stuff for me in the daytime. Might be different. More himself. More nigger. Different? There is. Curious, though.

The girls come in. Art stops playing, and almost immediately takes up a petty quarrel, where he had last left it, with Helen.

Bona, black-hair curled staccato, sharply contrasting with Helen's puffy yellow, holds Paul's hand. She squeezes it. Her own emotion supplements the return pressure. And then, for no tangible reason, her spirits drop. Without them, she is nervous, and slightly afraid. She resents this. Paul's eyes are critical. She resents Paul. She flares at him. She flares to poise and security.

"Shall we be on our way?"

"Yes, Bona, certainly."

The Boulevard is sleek in asphalt, and, with arc-lights and limousines, aglow. Dry leaves scamper behind the whir of cars. The scent of exploded gasoline that mingles with them is faintly sweet. Mellow stone mansions overshadow clapboard homes which now resemble Negro shanties in some southern alley. Bona and Paul, and Art and Helen, move along an island-like, far-stretching strip of leaf-soft ground. Above them, worlds of shadow-planes and solids, silently moving. As if on one of these, Paul looks down on Bona. No doubt of it: her face is pale. She is talking. Her words have no feel to them. One sees them. They are pink petals that fall upon velvet cloth. Bona is soft, and pale, and beautiful.

"Paul, tell me something about yourself—or would you rather wait?"

"I'll tell you anything you'd like to know."

"Not what I want to know, Paul; what you want to tell me."

"You have the beauty of a gem fathoms under sea."

"I feel that, but I dont want to be. I want to be near you. Perhaps I will be if I tell you something. Paul, I love you."

The sea casts up its jewel into his hands, and burns them furiously. To tuck her arm under his and hold her hand will ease the burn.

"What can I say to you, brave dear woman—I cant talk love. Love is a dry grain in my mouth unless it is wet with kisses."

"You would dare? right here on the Boulevard? before Arthur and Helen?"

"Before myself? I dare."

"Here then."

Bona, in the slim shadow of a tree trunk, pulls Paul to her. Suddenly she stiffens. Stops.

"But you have not said you love me."

"I cant—yet—Bona."

"Ach, you never will. Youre cold. Cold."

Bona: Colored; cold. Wrong somewhere.

She hurries and catches up with Art and Helen.

4

Crimson Gardens. Hurrah! So one feels. People . . . University of Chicago students, members of the stock exchange, a large Negro in crimson uniform who guards the door . . . had watched them enter. Had leaned towards each other over ash-smeared tablecloths and highballs and whispered: What is he, a Spaniard, an Indian, an Italian, a Mexican, a Hindu, or a Japanese? Art had at first fidgeted under their stares . . . what are *you* looking at, you godam pack of owl-eyed hyenas? . . . but soon settled into his fuss with Helen, and forgot them. A strange thing happened to Paul. Suddenly he knew that he was apart from the people around him. Apart from the pain which they had unconsciously caused. Suddenly he knew that people saw, not attractiveness in his dark skin, but difference. Their stares, giving him to himself, filled something long empty within him, and were like green blades sprouting in his consciousness. There was fullness, and strength and peace about it all. He saw himself, cloudy, but real. He saw the faces of the people at the tables round him. White lights, or as now, the pink lights of the Crimson Gardens gave a glow and immediacy to white faces. The pleasure of it, equal to that of love or dream, of seeing this. Art and Bona and Helen? He'd look. They were wonderfully flushed and beautiful. Not for himself; because they were. Distantly. Who were they, anyway? God, if he knew them. He'd come in with them. Of that he was sure. Come where? Into life? Yes. No. Into the Crimson Gardens. A part of life. A carbon bubble. Would it look purple if he went out into the night and looked at it? His sudden starting to rise almost upset the table.

"What in hell—pardon—whats the matter, Paul?"

"I forgot my cigarettes—"

"Youre smoking one."

"So I am. Pardon me."

The waiter straightens them out. Takes their order.

Art: What in hell's eating Paul? Moony aint the word for it. From bad to worse. And those godam people staring so. Paul's a queer fish. Doesnt seem to mind . . . He's my pal, let me tell you, you horn-rimmed owl-eyed hyena at that table, and a lot better than you whoever you are . . . Queer about him. I could stick up for him if he'd only come out, one way or the other, and tell a feller. Besides, a room-mate has a right to know. Thinks I wont understand. Said so. He's got a swell head when it comes to brains, all right. God, he's a good straight feller, though. Only, moony. Nut. Nuttish. Nuttery. Nutmeg . . . "What'd you say, Helen?"

"I was talking to Bona, thank you."

"Well, its nothing to get spiffy about."

"What? Oh, of course not. Please lets dont start some silly argument all over again."

"Well."

"Well."

"Now thats enough. Say, waiter, whats the matter with our order? Make it snappy, will you?"

Crimson Gardens. Hurrah! So one feels. The drinks come. Four highballs. Art passes cigarettes. A girl dressed like a bare-back rider in flaming pink, makes her way through tables to the dance floor. All lights are dimmed till they seem a lush afterglow of crimson. Spotlights the girl. She sings. "Liza, Little Liza Jane."

Paul is rosy before his window.

He moves, slightly, towards Bona.

With his own glow, he seeks to penetrate a dark pane.

Paul: From the South. What does that mean, precisely, except that you'll love or hate a nigger? Thats a lot. What does it mean except that in Chicago you'll have the courage to neither love or hate. A priori. But it would seem that you have. Queer words, arent these, for a man who wears blue pants on a gym floor in the daytime. Well, never matter. You matter. I'd like to know you whom I look at. Know, not love. Not that knowing is a greater pleasure; but that I have just found the joy of it. You came just a month too late. Even this afternoon I dreamed. To-night, along the Boulevard, you found me cold. Paul Johnson, cold! Thats a good one, eh, Art, you fine old stupid fellow, you! But I feel good! The

color and the music and the song . . . A Negress chants a lullaby
beneath the mate-eyes of a southern planter. O song! . . . And
those flushed faces. Eager brilliant eyes. Hard to imagine them as
unawakened. Your own. Oh, they're awake all right. "And you
know it too, dont you Bona?"

"What, Paul?"

"The truth of what I was thinking."

"I'd like to know I know—something of you."

"You will—before the evening's over. I promise it."

Crimson Gardens. Hurrah! So one feels. The bare-back rider
balances agilely on the applause which is the tail of her song. Or-
chestral instruments warm up for jazz. The flute is a cat that ripples
its fur against the deep-purring saxophone. The drum throws
sticks. The cat jumps on the piano keyboard. Hi diddle, hi diddle,
the cat and the fiddle. Crimson Gardens . . . hurrah! . . . jumps
over the moon. Crimson Gardens! Helen . . . O Eliza . . . rabbit-
eyes sparkling, plays up to, and tries to placate what she con-
siders to be Paul's contempt. She always does that . . . Little Liza
Jane . . . Once home, she burns with the thought of what she's
done. She says all manner of snidy things about him, and swears
that she'll never go out again when he is along. She tries to get Art
to break with him, saying, that if Paul, whom the whole dormitory
calls a nigger, is more to him than she is, well, she's through. She
does not break with Art. She goes out as often as she can with Art
and Paul. She explains this to herself by a piece of information
which a friend of hers had given her: men like him (Paul) can
fascinate. One is not responsible for fascination. Not one girl had
really loved Paul; he fascinated them. Bona didnt; only thought she
did. Time would tell. And of course, *she* didnt. Liza . . . She plays
up to, and tries to placate, Paul.

"Paul is so deep these days, and I'm so glad he's found some
one to interest him."

"I dont believe I do."

The thought escapes from Bona just a moment before her anger at having said it.

Bona: You little puffy cat, I do. I do!

Dont I, Paul? her eyes ask.

Her answer is a crash of jazz from the palm-hidden orchestra.
Crimson Gardens is a body whose blood flows to a clot upon the
dance floor. Art and Helen clot. Soon, Bona and Paul. Paul finds
her a little stiff, and his mind, wandering to Helen (silly little kid

who wants every highball spoon her hands touch, for a souvenir), supple, perfect little dancer, wishes for the next dance when he and Art will exchange.

Bona knows that she must win him to herself.

"Since when have men like you grown cold?"

"The first philosopher."

"I thought you were a poet—or a gym director."

"Hence, your failure to make love."

Bona's eyes flare. Water. Grow red about the rims. She would like to tear away from him and dash across the clotted floor.

"What do you mean?"

"Mental concepts rule you. If they were flush with mine— good. I dont believe they are."

"How do you know, Mr. Philosopher?"

"Mostly a priori."

"You talk well for a gym director."

"And you—"

"I hate you. Ou!"

She presses away. Paul, conscious of the convention in it, pulls her to him. Her body close. Her head still strains away. He nearly crushes her. She tries to pinch him. Then sees people staring, and lets her arms fall. Their eyes meet. Both, contemptuous. The dance takes blood from their minds and packs it, tingling, in the torsos of their swaying bodies. Passionate blood leaps back into their eyes. They are a dizzy blood clot on a gyrating floor. They know that the pink-faced people have no part in what they feel. Their instinct leads them away from Art and Helen, and towards the big uniformed black man who opens and closes the gilded exit door. The cloak-room girl is tolerant of their impatience over such trivial things as wraps. And slightly superior. As the black man swings the door for them, his eyes are knowing. Too many couples have passed out, flushed and fidgety, for him not to know. The chill air is a shock to Paul. A strange thing happens. He sees the Gardens purple, as if he were way off. And a spot is in the purple. The spot comes furiously towards him. Face of the black man. It leers. It smiles sweetly like a child's. Paul leaves Bona and darts back so quickly that he doesnt give the door-man a chance to open. He swings in. Stops. Before the huge bulk of the Negro.

"Youre wrong."

"Yassur."

"Brother, youre wrong.

"I came back to tell you, to shake your hand, and tell you that you are wrong. That something beautiful is going to happen. That the Gardens are purple like a bed of roses would be at dusk. That I came into the Gardens, into life in the Gardens with one whom I did not know. That I danced with her, and did not know her. That I felt passion, contempt and passion for her whom I did not know. That I thought of her. That my thoughts were matches thrown into a dark window. And all the while the Gardens were purple like a bed of roses would be at dusk. I came back to tell you, brother, that white faces are petals of roses. That dark faces are petals of dusk. That I am going out and gather petals. That I am going out and know her whom I brought here with me to these Gardens which are purple like a bed of roses would be at dusk."

Paul and the black man shook hands.

When he reached the spot where they had been standing, Bona was gone.

T. S. STRIBLING

T. S. Stribling's Birthright (1922) was the first work by a white writer since Uncle Tom's Cabin *to feature an African American protagonist. The principal character is a Harvard graduate of impressive (if somewhat wooden) bearing and admirable courage who is destroyed by the savage bigotry of race prejudice in the South. The impact of* Birthright *on the Harlem Renaissance was enormous. Both Jessie Fauset and Walter White set about the task of writing a truer novel about African American life after reading* Birthright.

FROM *BIRTHRIGHT*

At Cairo, Illinois, the Pullman-car conductor asked Peter Siner to take his suitcase and traveling-bag and pass forward into the Jim Crow car. The request came as a sort of surprise to the negro. During Peter Siner's four years in Harvard the segregation of black folk on Southern railroads had become blurred and reminiscent in his mind; now it was fetched back into the sharp distinction of the present instant. With a certain sense of strangeness, Siner picked up his bags, and saw his own form, in the car mirrors, walking down the length of the sleeper. He moved on through the dining-car, where a few hours before he had had dinner and talked with two white men, one an Oregon apple-grower, the other a Wisconsin paper-manufacturer. The Wisconsin man had furnished cigars, and the three had sat and smoked in the drawing-room, indeed, had discussed this very point; and now it was upon him.

At the door of the dining-car stood the porter of his Pullman, a negro like himself, and Peter mechanically gave him fifty cents. The porter accepted it silently, without offering the amenities of his whisk-broom and shoe-brush, and Peter passed on forward.

Beyond the dining-car and Pullmans stretched twelve day-coaches filled with less-opulent white travelers in all degrees of sleepiness and dishabille from having sat up all night. The thirteenth coach was the Jim Crow car. Framed in a conspicuous place beside the entrance of the car was a copy of the Kentucky state ordinance setting this coach apart from the remainder of the train for the purposes therein provided.

The Jim Crow car was not exactly shabby, but it was unkept. It was half filled with travelers of Peter's own color, and these passengers were rather more noisy than those in the white coaches. Conversation was not restrained to the undertones one heard in the other day-coaches or the Pullmans. Near the entrance of the car two negroes in soldiers' uniforms had turned a seat over to face the door, and now they sat talking loudly and laughing the loose laugh of the half intoxicated as they watched the inflow of negro passengers coming out of the white cars.

The windows of the Jim Crow car were shut, and already it had become noisome. The close air was faintly barbed with the peculiar, penetrating odor of dark, sweating skins. For four years Peter Siner had not known that odor. Now it came to him not so much offensively as with a queer quality of intimacy and reminiscence. The tall, carefully tailored negro spread his wide nostrils, vacillating whether to sniff it out with disfavor or to admit it for the sudden mental associations it evoked.

It was a faint, pungent smell that played in the back of his nose and somehow reminded him of his mother, Caroline Siner, a thick-bodied black woman whom he remembered as always bending over a wash-tub. This was only one unit of a complex. The odor was also connected with negro protracted meetings in Hooker's Bend, and the Harvard man remembered a lanky black preacher waving long arms and wailing of hell-fire, to the chanted groans of his dark congregation; and he, Peter Siner, had groaned with the others. Peter had known this odor in the press-room of Tennessee cottongins, over a river packet's boilers, where he and other roustabouts were bedded, in bunk-houses in the woods. It also recalled a certain octoroon girl named Ida May, and an intimacy with her which it still moved and saddened Peter to think of. Indeed, it resurrected innumerable vignettes of his life in the negro village in Hooker's Bend; it was linked with innumerable emotions, this pungent, unforgetable odor that filled the Jim Crow car.

Somehow the odor had a queer effect of appearing to push his conversation with the two white Northern men in the drawing-room back to a distance, an indefinable distance of both space and time.

The negro put his suitcase under the seat, hung his overcoat on the hook, and placed his hand-bag in the rack overhead; then with some difficulty he opened a window and sat down by it.

A stir of travelers in the Cairo station drifted into the car. Against a broad murmur of hurrying feet, moving trucks, and talking there stood out the thin, flat voice of a Southern white girl calling good-by to some one on the train. Peter could see her waving a bright parasol and tiptoeing. A sandwich boy hurried past, shrilling his wares. Siner leaned out, with fifteen cents, and signaled to him. The urchin hesitated, and was about to reach up one of his wrapped parcels, when a peremptory voice shouted at him from a lower car. With a sort of start the lad deserted Siner and went trotting down to his white customer. A moment later the train bell began ringing, and the Dixie Flier puffed deliberately out of the Cairo station and moved across the Ohio bridge into the South.

Half an hour later the blue-grass fields of Kentucky were spinning outside of the window in a vast green whirlpool. The distant trees and houses moved forward with the train, while the foreground, with its telegraph poles, its culverts, section-houses, and shrubbery, rushed backward in a blur. Now and then into the Jim Crow window whipped a blast of coal smoke and hot cinders, for the engine was only two cars ahead.

Peter Siner looked out at the interminable spin of the landscape with a certain wistfulness. He was coming back into the South, into his own country. Here for generations his forebears had toiled endlessly and fruitlessly, yet the fat green fields hurtling past him told with what skill and patience their black hands had labored.

The negro shrugged away such thoughts, and with a certain effort replaced them with the constructive idea that was bringing him South once more. It was a very simple idea. Siner was returning to his native village in Tennessee to teach school. He planned to begin his work with the ordinary public school at Hooker's Bend, but, in the back of his head, he hoped eventually to develop an institution after the plan of Tuskeegee or the Hampton Institute in Virginia.

To do what he had in mind, he must obtain aid from white sources, and now, as he traveled southward, he began conning in his mind the white men and white women he knew in Hooker's Bend. He wanted first of all to secure possession of a small tract of land which he knew adjoined the negro school-house over on the east side of the village.

Before the negro's mind the different villagers passed in review with that peculiar intimacy of vision that servants always have of their masters. Indeed, no white Southerner knows his own village so minutely as does any member of its colored population. The colored villagers see the whites off their guard and just as they are, and that is an attitude in which no one looks his best. The negroes might be called the black recording angels of the South. If what they know should be shouted aloud in any Southern town, its social life would disintegrate. Yet it is a strange fact that gossip seldom penetrates from the one race to the other.

So Peter Siner sat in the Jim Crow car musing over half a dozen villagers in Hooker's Bend. He thought of them in a curious way. Although he was now a B.A. of Harvard University, and although he knew that not a soul in the little river village, unless it was old Captain Renfrew, could construe a line of Greek and that scarcely two had ever traveled farther north than Cincinnati, still, as Peter recalled their names and foibles, he involuntarily felt that he was telling over a roll of the mighty. The white villagers came marching through his mind as beings austere, and the very cranks and quirks of their characters somehow held that austerity. There were the Brownell sisters, two old maids, Molly and Patti, who lived in a big brick house on the hill. Peter remembered that Miss Molly Brownell always doled out to his mother, at Monday's washday dinner, exactly one biscuit less than the old negress wanted to eat, and she always paid her in old clothes. Peter remembered, a dozen times in his life, his mother coming home and wondering in an impersonal way how it was that Miss Molly Brownell could skimp every meal she ate at the big house by exactly one biscuit. It was Miss Brownell's thin-lipped boast that she understood negroes. She had told Peter so several times when, as a lad, he went up to the big house on errands. Peter Siner considered this remembrance without the faintest feeling of humor, and mentally removed Miss Molly Brownell from his list of possible subscribers. Yet, he recalled, the whole Brownell estate had been reared on negro labor.

Then there was Henry Hooker, cashier of the village bank.

Peter knew that the banker subscribed liberally to foreign missions; indeed, at the cashier's behest, the white church of Hooker's Bend kept a paid missionary on the upper Congo. But the banker had sold some village lots to the negroes, and in two instances, where a streak of commercial phosphate had been discovered on the properties, the lots had reverted to the Hooker estate. There had been in the deed something concerning a mineral reservation that the negro purchasers knew nothing about until the phosphate was discovered. The whole matter had been perfectly legal.

A hand shook Siner's shoulder and interrupted his review. Peter turned, and caught an alcoholic breath over his shoulder, and the blurred voice of a Southern negro called out above the rumble of the car and the roar of the engine:

" 'Fo' Gawd, ef dis ain't Peter Siner I's been lookin' at de las' twenty miles, an' not knowin' him wid sich skeniptious clo'es on! Wha you fum, nigger?"

Siner took the enthusiastic hand offered him and studied the heavily set, powerful man bending over the seat. He was in a soldier's uniform, and his broad nutmeg-colored face and hot black eyes brought Peter a vague sense of familiarity; but he never would have identified his impression had he not observed on the breast of the soldier's uniform the Congressional military medal for bravery on the field of battle. Its glint furnished Peter the necessary clew. He remembered his mother's writing him something about Tump Pack going to France and getting "crowned" before the army. He had puzzled a long time over what she meant by "crowned" before he guessed her meaning. Now the medal aided Peter in reconstructing out of this big umber-colored giant the rather spindling Tump Pack he had known in Hooker's Bend.

Siner was greatly surprised, and his heart warmed at the sight of his old playmate.

"What have you been doing to yourself, Tump?" he cried, laughing, and shaking the big hand in sudden warmth. "You used to be the size of a dime in a jewelry store."

"Been in 'e army, nigger, wha I's been fed," said the grinning brown man, delightedly. "I sho is picked up, ain't I?"

"And what are you doing here in Cairo?"

"Tryin' to bridle a lil white mule." Mr. Pack winked a whisky-brightened eye jovially and touched his coat to indicate that some of the "white mule" was in his pocket and had not been drunk.

"How'd you get here?"

"Wucked my way down on de St. Louis packet an' got paid

off at Padjo [Paducah, Kentucky]; 'n 'en I thought I'd come on down heah an' roll some bones. Been hittin' 'em two days now, an' I sho come putty nigh bein' cleaned; but I put up lil Joe heah, an' won 'em all back, 'n 'en some." He touched the medal on his coat, winked again, slapped Siner on the leg, and burst into loud laughter.

Peter was momentarily shocked. He made a place on the seat for his friend to sit. "You don't mean you put up your medal on a crap game, Tump?"

"Sho do, black man." Pack became soberer. "Dat's one o' de great benefits o' bein' dec'rated. Dey ain't a son uv a gun on de river whut kin win lil Joe; dey all tried it."

A moment's reflection told Peter how simple and natural it was for Pack to prize his military medal as a good-luck piece to be used as a last resort in crap games. He watched Tump stroke the face of his medal with his fingers.

"My mother wrote me about your getting it, Tump. I was glad to hear it."

The brown man nodded, and stared down at the bit of gold on his barrel-like chest.

"Yas-suh, dat 'uz guv to me fuh bravery. You know whut a skeery lil nigger I wuz roun' Hooker's Ben'; well, de sahgeant tuk me an' he drill ever' bit o' dat right out 'n me. He gimme a baynit an' learned me to stob dummies wid it over at Camp Oglethorpe, ontil he felt lak I had de heart to stob anything; 'n 'en he sont me acrost. I had to git a new pair breeches ever' three weeks, I growed so fas'." Here he broke out into his big loose laugh again, and renewed the alcoholic scent around Peter.

"And you made good?"

"Sho did, black man, an', 'fo' Gawd, I 'serve a medal ef any man ever did. Dey gimme dish-heah fuh stobbin fo' white men wid a baynit. 'Fo' Gawd, nigger, I never felt so quare in all my born days as when I wuz a-jobbin' de livers o' dem white men lak de sahgeant tol' me to." Tump shook his head, bewildered, and after a moment added, "Yas-suh, I never wuz mo' surprised in all my life dan when I got dis medal fuh stobbin' fo' white men."

Peter Siner looked through the Jim Crow window at the vast rotation of the Kentucky landscape on which his forebears had toiled; presently he added soberly:

"You were fighting for your country, Tump. It was war then; you were fighting for your country."

JESSIE REDMON FAUSET

ALERT TO THE BUILDING INTEREST *in black America among literate white Americans and stimulated by Stribling's* Birthright, *Jessie Redmon Fauset wrote* There Is Confusion *(1924), the first novel (excepting Toomer's eccentric* Cane*) of the Harlem Renaissance. A complex novel of manners in which the well-born, color-conscious Philadelphians Joanna Marshall and Peter Bye, her lover, are parted and finally reunited, Fauset's novel was sociologically instructive and artistically ponderous.*

It was an archetypal Talented Tenth novel, genteel and integrationist. Commenting on the unfortunate anti-white bias Peter falls into through bitterness, one of Fauset's characters sums up the point of her novel: "The time comes when he thinks, 'I might just as well fall back . . . a colored man just can't make any headway in this awful country.' Of course, it's a fallacy. And if a fellow sticks it out he finally gets past it, but not before it has worked considerable confusion in his life."

The excerpts that follow cover the period after Joanna's friend Maggie has saved Philip from death in a field hospital on the Western front at the end of the Great War. Peter, who had fallen in love with Maggie, decides that he loves Joanna after all.

Fauset's second novel, Plum Bun *(1929), continues the author's preoccupation with affluent and very light-skinned African Americans. [The heroine, Angela Murray (called Angele when she "passes" as white), is a talented artist who finds herself in various situations governed by implausible coincidence and sentimental solutions.] Angela's sister, who lives downtown, passes as well. Both have affairs with the same lover (who also passes). The brief excerpt here portrays the high-risk absurdity of the racially ambiguous in America.*

FROM *THERE IS CONFUSION*

CHAPTER XXXV

MAGGIE AND PHILIP had returned from the sanitarium to New York, but Philip undoubtedly was dying. Peter and Harry Portor were at his bedside every day, but not because of their ability to help him. They were simply three friends together. Philip never spoke to Peter of the incident at Des Moines, though it is probable that he thought of it many times, but the young doctor seemed so serenely unaware of any former misunderstanding that Philip, with a deep sense of relief, let the whole incident slide out of his mind.

Joanna, meanwhile, was experiencing a little private purgatory of remorse and grief. As she saw Philip's joy in Maggie, his complete and unbounded satisfaction in her presence, she became more and more overwhelmed with the awfulness of that old unconsidered act of hers, the sending of the letter which had caused Maggie to marry Henderson Neal. Maggie had never told her this, but she was pretty sure that such was the case. The mere fact that Maggie had never spoken about it to Peter, even in the days of their engagement, led her to suspect that her sister-in-law had attached more significance to it than she had cared to show. There was only one thing for her, if she was ever to know any peace, and that was to confess to Philip.

She went to see him in the late October weather. On the way she had passed Morningside Park and the gorgeous autumn sights and colors had brought back to her in a sudden heady rush the memories of the old days,—partings with Peter, concert tours and meetings with Philip, talks, dreams, ambitions, all the activities of her assured, confident, determined youth. If she might only relive a few brief scenes—the night she had dismissed Peter, the time she had spent in writing that cruel letter to Maggie—how different her memories would have been!

Philip was in excellent spirits. He seemed quite reconciled to dying and even spoke of it with a cheerfulness and familiarity that never failed to bring a rush of tears to Joanna's eyes, though this she was careful to conceal. "Just think of the luck I'm in," Philip would say, "I never expected to come home at all. If Maggie hadn't found me there in Chambéry and taken pity on my lonesomeness, I'd probably be lying in a French cemetery this moment with one of those little white crosses standing above me. As it is, I'm seeing you all again and I have Maggie. She has promised to stay with me always. It's all right, Joanna, old girl, I've had a good run for my money and except for Maggie I'm not so sorry to chuck it all. Just think, it might have been my luck never to have found her again at all."

He said something like that to Joanna on this afternoon. Sobbing she fell on her knees beside the bed. "Oh Philip, if it hadn't been for me, you'd have found her long ago."

He was suddenly attentive, his eyes bright and keen in his thin sharpening face as she told him about the letter. With infinite gentleness he let his hand rest on that proud dark head which life had taught so hardly to bow.

"Dear Joanna, dear little sister, don't blame yourself one moment. It was all my fault. If you'd left a hundred letters unwritten, I should hardly have moved any more quickly. In those days I was so taken up with the business of being colored! After I'd adjusted that I thought I'd arrange my life. Ah, Joanna, that's our great mistake. We must learn to look out for life first, then color and limitations. My being colored didn't make me forget to provide myself with food and raiment. I shouldn't have allowed it to make me forget love." His grasp on her hand tightened.

"Learn this, Joanna, and tell the rest of our folks. Our battle is a hard one and for a long time it will seem to be a losing one, but it will never really be that as long as we keep the power of being happy. And happiness has to be deliberately sought for, gained; even that doesn't solve the problem, but it does make it easier for us to fight. Happiness, love, contentment in our own midst, make it possible for us to face those foes without. 'Happy Warriors,' that's the ideal for us. Only I realized it too late."

That was his last long talk with Joanna. Usually he gave all his attention to Maggie who was with him always, supplying and anticipating his wants and radiating an ineffable peace. Her hand was in his when he died.

His father, remembering his intense patriotism as a child, said with a touch of bitter pride: "He died for his country."

"It was what he always wanted to do," Sylvia said gently. But Joanna knew that Philip's real desire envisaged *living* for his country—to save her from something worse than war.

His death diffused a gentle melancholy over the others. It was the first serious rent in the fabric of the Marshall family. Old Joel took to indulging in long, deep reveries. Mrs. Marshall, quite dry-eyed, took out all of Philip's baby things, wrapped them up to send away and quite suddenly put them back in their places. Her interest in Sylvia's children took on an almost feverish intensity. Sylvia herself and Joanna and sometimes Sandy had many talks, wistful with reminiscences.

Maggie alone remained calm and almost cheerful. "Not because she's unfeeling," Joanna explained to Sylvia, "but because she is so satisfied."

Sylvia raised an eyebrow. "Satisfied and Philip dead?"

"Yes, because so easily he might have died without their ever having come together. But they did. Oh, Sylvia, you and Brian have had such a simple, easy, jog-trot time of it, you don't know what it means to have your life all broken up like Maggie's and mine have been, and poor Vera Manning's."

Whatever the cause, Maggie spent her days serenely. Secure not only in the knowledge that she was bulwarked by the Marshall respectability, but also by the resolve which she had made before she saw Philip in Chambéry, she started on the project of her Beauty Parlors.

She said to Joel who, she knew, admired her ability: "See if you can't make me as great a success in business as you've been." They spent many pleasant hours in consultation.

CHAPTER XXXVI

Joanna and Peter married and Peter came at Joel's insistent request to live in the One Hundred and Thirty-eighth Street house. It was marvelous to see how the two old people renewed themselves in the youth of their children. Joel was as proud of Peter as he had been of Joanna. Even Mrs. Marshall's long allegiance to Sylvia wavered a little.

The first child was a boy; "Meriwether," Peter had named him after young Dr. Meriwether Bye. "I'm going to tempt providence," he said to his wife. "I hope he'll not be the sort of Meriwether that my father was. I'll see to it that he isn't. He's going to be all and more than old Isaiah Bye ever dreamed of," and he quoted, to Joanna's mystification: "By *his* fruits shall ye know *me*."

The two possessed happiness; but more than happiness they had found peace. They were united by the very pain which each had caused the other. And the knowledge of how greatly each could suffer created in them a sort of whimsical tolerance. There is nothing like humor to speed the wheels of life.

Joanna, having come to understand the nothingness of that inordinate craving for sheer success, surprised herself by the pleasure which came to her out of what she had always considered the ordinary things of life. Realizing how nearly she had lost the essentials in grasping after the trimmings of existence, she experienced a deep, almost holy joy in the routine of the day. To see about her, her husband and parents, little Meriwether usually in Joel's arms, gave her, she confessed almost shamefacedly to Sylvia, "thoughts that lay too deep for tears." She rarely regretted leaving the stage and although she sang sometimes in churches and concerts and once even went on a brief tour, she almost never danced except in the ordinary way.

Still, as her mentality was essentially creative, she found herself more and more impelled toward the expression of the intense appreciation of living which welled within her. Luckily her training in music offered her some outlet. With her slight knowledge of composition she composed two little songs and glimpsing future possibilities, she began to study that most fascinating of all the sciences—harmony.

The change in Peter was more fundamental than that in Joanna. She at least had always had these possibilities of domesticity. Her desire for greatness had been a sort of superimposed structure which, having been taken off, left her her true self. It was as though her life had expanded on the plan of Holmes' admonition to the Chambered Nautilus:

> Leave thy low vaulted Past—
> Let each new temple,
> Nobler than the last,
> Shut thee from Heaven
> With a dome more vast
> Till thou at length art free,—

Joanna was free.

But Peter had had to undergo a complete metamorphosis. He was a supersensitive colored man living among hosts of indifferent white people. Not only had he to change in every particular his theory of how to maintain such a relationship, but indeed he had to decide what sort of relationship was worth maintaining. At his father's death and during his young manhood he had been absolutely without a notion of the responsibilities which the most average man expects to take upon himself. He looked back with a real shame and chagrin to the many favors which he had accepted without question from his Aunt Susan.

Joanna, clever Joanna, helped him here. She was not only naturally independent, but she was, for all her talent, essentially practical with that clearheadedness which artistic people exhibit sometimes in such unexpected fashion. Perhaps it is wrong to imply that Joanna had lost her ambition. She was still ambitious, only the field of her ambition lay without herself. It was Peter now whom she wished to see succeed. If his success depended ever so little on his achievement of a sense of responsibility, then she meant to develop that sense. To this end, she consulted him, she took his advice, she asked him to arrange about the few recitals which she undertook. In a thousand little ways she deferred to him, and showed him that as a matter of course he was the arbiter of her own and her child's destiny, the *fons et origo* of authority.

So he grew both in the spirit of racial tolerance and in the spirit of responsibility. He wanted to live in America; he wanted to get along with his fellow man, but he no longer proposed to let circumstances shape his career. No one but himself, not even Joanna, should captain his ship. He meant to be a successful surgeon, a responsible husband and father, a self-reliant man.

The memory of Meriwether Bye, never far distant, braced him constantly. The young physician's words and ideas had exercised a singleness of concentration, of influence over Peter such as a friendship of long standing could hardly have hoped to achieve.

For a long time he expected to hear from Meriwether's grandfather. Then as the months and nearly two years rolled by without a sign from Bryn Mawr, Peter decided that the old gentleman wished to spare himself the pain of learning more of the circumstances surrounding his grandson's death.

Sylvia's boy, Roger, captivated by his new soldier-uncle, spent most of his time at Peter's house serving in the purely impressionistic capacity of office-boy. He came up to the sitting room one summer morning bearing a bit of cardboard between his fingers.

"Meriwether Bye," he pronounced, handing the card to Peter. "Ain't it funny he should have the same name as the kid? But he's no relation because he's white and as old as the hills."

"Meriwether's grandfather!" Peter said in astonishment. "Come on down with me, Joanna."

Together they descended to find an old, old man sitting in an absolutely immobile silence in Peter's office. He rose, a tall, straight, white figure and looked at the two young people, still in silence.

"I'm Peter Bye," the young man said, coming forward. "Won't you sit down? Sit here, Joanna."

Together they sat in a strange, strained quiet, Joanna watching Peter in whom she sensed the rising anew of the antagonism of all the years. There they were, she felt, representing the last of the old order and the first of the new, since Peter's generation was the first to escape the effect of the ancient régime, and he personally had not completely escaped it. How many things this ancient, stately personage who sat regarding them with keen though inscrutable eyes could have told them of the circumstances which had combined to make the two of them what they were! For this old man's whole life and fortune had been reared on the institution of slavery.

Out of the puzzling silence he spoke, in the expressionless, brittle tone of extreme old age. "Yes, I know you are a Bye, Isaiah Bye's grandson. And you were with Meriwether at the end. Tell me about it."

Very solemnly, almost pityingly, Peter began the recital of his brief, dream-like acquaintance with Meriwether Bye. "He had quite made up his mind beforehand that he was going to die. Perhaps you knew. So, I'm sure he was quite reconciled to it; I don't think you need grieve for him. And at the very end I was with him. It turned out that we had been fighting just a few yards apart. I think I eased him a little; I'm a doctor, too," said Peter simply. He put his hand in front of his eyes as though trying to shut out the vision of the pitiful, needless death. "His last words were to you, did I tell you, sir? He sat up suddenly against me, his hand on my arm and called out—Oh, I can hear his voice now: 'Grandfather, this is the last of the Byes.'"

They sat again in a deep silence.

"I'm sorry." Peter continued after a long revery, "that he hadn't married, and had no children. It's hard on you, sir, you who are now the last of the Byes."

"Yes," said the old gentleman laconically, "it is. Now, suppose you tell me something about yourself."

But first Peter told him about his father, Meriwether, glossing over the dead man's faults and irresoluteness and dwelling on his ambition. "So you see, I had always had the idea of becoming a doctor before me. But I'm afraid I should never have realized it if it had not been for my wife, here." He smiled gratefully at Joanna, who smiled back at him with a gratitude of another sort. He had uttered no word of complaint nor of the difficulties attendant on being a colored man in America. She was very proud of him. He was so charming, so handsome, growing daily in independence.

"You have a son," said old Meriwether. "I believe you said you had a son, Meriwether? How would you like me to take him and educate him, bring him up away from all he'd have to go through in this country, let him spend his life in Paris and Vienna. Perhaps he would be a doctor, too. When he became a man he could do as he pleased. And probably, probably, I say, I should make him my heir."

Neither Joanna nor Peter had ever thought of wealth. And while neither of them envisaged for a second the possibility of parting from little Meriwether, they were momentarily stunned at such prospects, Joanna especially.

"Why," asked Peter, his old demon of dislike and suspicion flaring up in him, "should you at this late date show interest in a black Bye?"

"Because," said Meriwether Bye, getting up and beginning to pace the floor, "because he *is* my heir. Because he *is* the last of the Byes. Because when my brave boy called out 'this is the last of the Byes,' he meant you, not himself. He had no way of knowing it, but he did know it. That queer sense in him which warned him he was going to die, probably told him.

"You've heard of your grandfather Isaiah, the boy that grew up with me?" Peter nodded. "Well, his father, black Joshua Bye, was my oldest brother; my father—he was Aaron Bye—was his father. Joshua was really his oldest child. His mother was Judy Bye, old Judy Bye, whom I've seen often sitting in Isaiah's house, her eyes straining, straining into the future—perhaps she saw this, who knows?"

"My father," said Peter in a dangerously level voice, "told me and told me often that much of Aaron Bye's prosperity had been due to the loyalty and hard work of Joshua Bye. But he never told me that Aaron was his father. And you knew this, have known it——"

"Not while Isaiah and I were boys. Not for many, many years afterwards. My father," the word seemed strange on this old man's lips, "always meant, I think, to do something for his—his son in his will. But he put it off and finally just before his death he told my brother Elmer—his oldest son by his real wife you know—told him about it. But Elmer was all out of sympathy with the idea, and, although he did not tell my father so, had no notion of acquainting Joshua either with his real parentage or with the fact that he should have been one of Aaron Bye's heirs. Elmer was one of those men with a sharp dislike, amounting to an obsession, almost, for Negroes, for all unfortunate people. I'm free from it personally."

"Yet," said Peter harshly, "your conduct has differed not one whit from his. How long have *you* known this?"

"Since the close of the Civil War. All my brothers had died but Elmer, and all *his* sons were killed in the war. When Elmer was himself about to die, he told me. He thought the loss of his sons was a curse upon him because he had failed to obey my father's wishes. He left their carrying out to me. I was a young man still. I saw no reason for opening up old wounds. Besides, I did not know what had become of Isaiah's son. Isaiah and Joshua were both dead. I could not see that my father had acted differently from other slave-holders—it was the custom of the country—and at least he did not do as many a white man had done, sell his son into deeper and more terrible slavery. . . . I can see now that whatever slavery may have done for other men it has thrown the lives of all the Byes into confusion. Think of the farce my father's religion must have become to him . . . and I shall never forget Elmer. Sometimes I think the shadow of it fell across Meriwether's life—I meant to tell him. I know he would have made restitution. Now I shall do it for him."

He ceased speaking and looked at Peter curiously, wistfully. "I suppose you find it hard to forgive us. I'm afraid I had not thought until very recently what this might have meant to you,—to Isaiah."

Peter ignored this. "If you made my son your heir," he questioned, avoiding Joanna's startled look, "would you be willing to publish to the world that you were doing it because little Meriwether was your blood relation—no matter how distant—or would this be the gift of an eccentric philanthropist?"

The old man's face grew a dull red. "Surely it would not be necessary—think of my father. What good would it do the boy to know that Aaron Bye's blood flowed in his veins?"

"None," said Peter triumphantly. He turned to Joanna. "See,

dear, there is the source of all I used to be. My ingratitude, my inability to adopt responsibility, my very irresoluteness come from that strain of white Bye blood. But I understand it now, I can fight against it. I'm free, Joanna, free."

He walked over to Meriwether Bye, and the two tall straight men—so alike, so different, one young, one very old—gazed for a long time at each other.

"I don't want your gifts," said Peter gently, "nor does my son want them—neither your money nor the acknowledgment of your blood. They come too late." He turned to his wife after Meriwether had left the house. "Thank God, Joanna, they have come too late. Perhaps I might have been like that."

Afterwards the memory of the little black testament returned to him. He found it and showed it to Joanna. "I'll bet that old codger Ceazer knew that Joshua wasn't his son and that's why he scratched his own name out of the book. *He* would have been an ancestor worth having."

Joanna looked at him proudly. "Peter, you are wonderful! Such a man, a great man!"

He sighed a little wistfully. "There spoke the real Joanna. Greatness, even in daily living, will always be your creed, I suppose."

"No," said Joanna, a shameless apostate, "my creed calls for nothing but happiness."

FROM *PLUM BUN*

ANGELA TOOK THE SKETCH of Hetty Daniels to school. "What an interesting type!" said Gertrude Quale, the girl next to her. "Such cosmic and tragic unhappiness in that face. What is she, not an American?"

"Oh yes she is. She's an old coloured woman who's worked in our family for years and she was born right here in Philadelphia."

"Oh coloured! Well, of course I suppose you would call her an American though I never think of darkies as Americans. Coloured,—yes that would account for that unhappiness in her face. I suppose they all mind it awfully."

It was the afternoon for the life class. The model came in, a short, rather slender young woman with a faintly pretty, shrewdish face full of a certain dark, mean character. Angela glanced at her thoughtfully, full of pleasant anticipation. She liked to work for character, preferred it even to beauty. The model caught her eye, looked away and again turned her full gaze upon her with an insistent, slightly incredulous stare. It was Esther Bayliss who had once been in the High School with Angela. She had left not long after Mary Hastings' return to her boarding school.

Angela saw no reason why she should speak to her and presently, engrossed in the portrayal of the round, yet pointed little face, forgot the girl's identity. But Esther kept her eyes fixed on her former school-mate with a sort of intense, angry brooding so absorbing that she forgot her pose and Mr. Shields spoke to her two or three times. On the third occasion he said not unkindly, "You'll have to hold your pose better than this, Miss Bayliss, or we won't be able to keep you on."

"I don't want you to keep me on." She spoke with an amazing vindictiveness. "I haven't got to the point yet where I'm going to lower myself to pose for a coloured girl."

He looked around the room in amazement; no, Miss Henderson wasn't there, she never came to this class he remembered. "Well after that we couldn't keep you anyway. We're not taking orders from our models. But there's no coloured girl here."

"Oh yes there is, unless she's changed her name." She laughed spitefully. "Isn't that Angela Murray over there next to that Jew girl?" In spite of himself, Shields nodded. "Well, she's coloured though she wouldn't let you know. But I know. I went to school with her in North Philadelphia. And I tell you I wouldn't stay to pose for her not if you were to pay me ten times what I'm getting. Sitting there drawing from me just as though she were as good as a white girl!"

Astonished and disconcerted, he told his wife about it. "But I can't think she's really coloured, Mabel. Why she looks and acts just like a white girl. She dresses in better taste than anybody in the room. But that little wretch of a model insisted that she was coloured."

"Well she just can't be. Do you suppose I don't know a coloured woman when I see one? I can tell 'em a mile off."

It seemed to him a vital and yet such a disgraceful matter. "If she is coloured she should have told me. I'd certainly like to know, but hang it all, I can't ask her, for suppose she should be white in spite of what that little beast of a model said?" He found her address in the registry and overcome one afternoon with shamed curiosity drove up to Opal Street and slowly past her house. Jinny was coming in from school and Hetty Daniels on her way to market greeted her on the lower step. Then Virginia put the key in the lock and passed inside. "She is coloured," he told his wife, "for no white girl in her senses would be rooming with coloured people."

"I should say not! Coloured, is she? Well, she shan't come here again, Henry."

Angela approached him after class on Saturday. "How is Mrs. Shields? I can't get out to see her this week but I'll be sure to run in next."

He blurted out miserably, "But, Miss Murray, you never told me that you were coloured."

She felt as though she were rehearsing a well-known part in a play. "Coloured! Of course I never told you that I was coloured. Why should I?"

WALTER WHITE

THE FIRE IN THE FLINT *(1924), by Walter White, was the second novel of the Harlem Renaissance. The author claimed to have written it from start to finish in well under a month. Doran and Company, having already offered White a book contract, decided against publishing the novel after a prominent Southern white reader objected to the manuscript. With the help of H. L. Mencken, White was able to place* The Fire in the Flint *with Alfred A. Knopf. Like Fauset, White had been challenged by Stribling's* Birthright, *and, like Fauset, his concerns were with the "better class" of African Americans. The characters in the novel were largely symbolic, and the action melodramatic, but it sold extremely well.*

The plot concerns the struggles of Kenneth Harper, an African American physician of superlative culture and professional credentials who practices medicine in a small Georgia town. Harper's credo is vintage Talented Tenth: "If he solved his problems and every other Negro did the same, he often thought, then the thing we call the race problem will be solved." Jane Phillips, the love of his life, leads him into moderate militancy and death at the hands of lynchers. Harper had paid an emergency night call to save a pregnant white woman's life. The chapter selected here sets the stage for the novel's barbaric denouement.

FROM *THE FIRE IN THE FLINT*

TO KENNETH, when work grew wearisome or when memories would not down, there came relaxation in literature, an opiate for which he would never cease being grateful to Professor Fuller, his old teacher at Atlanta. It was "Pop" Fuller who, with his benign and paternal manner, his adoration of the best of the world's literature, had sown in Kenneth the seed of that same love. He read and reread *Jean Christophe,* finding in the adventures and particularly in the mental processes of Rolland's hero many of his own reactions towards life. He had read the plays of Bernard Shaw, garnering here and there a morsel of truth though much of Shaw eluded him. Theodore Dreiser's gloominess and sex-obsession he liked though it often repelled him; he admired the man for his honesty and disliked his pessimism or what seemed to him a dolorous outlook on life. He loved the colourful romances of Hergesheimer, considering them of little enduring value but nevertheless admiring his descriptions of affluent life, enjoying it vicariously. Willa Cather's *My Antonia* he delighted in because of its simplicity and power and beauty.

The works of D. H. Lawrence, Kenneth read with conflicting emotions. Mystical, turgid, tortuous phrases, and meaning not always clear. Yet he revelled in Lawrence's clear insight into the bends and backwaters and perplexing twistings of the stream of life. Kenneth liked best of all foreign writers Knut Hamsun. He had read many times *Hunger, Growth of the Soil,* and other novels of the Norwegian writer. He at times was annoyed by their lack of plot, but more often he enjoyed them because they had none, reflecting that life itself is never a smoothly turned and finished work of art, its causes and effects, its tears and joys, its loves and hates neatly dovetailing one into another as writers of fiction would have it. . . .

But perhaps most of all he admired the writing of Du Bois— the fiery, burning philippics of one of his own race against the proscriptions of race prejudice. He read them with a curious sort of detachment—as being something which touched him in a more or less remote way but not as a factor in forming his own opinions as a Negro in a land where democracy often stopped dead at the colour line.

It was in this that Kenneth's attitude towards life was most clearly shown. His was the more philosophic viewpoint on the race question, that problem so close to him. The proscriptions which he and others of his race were forced to endure were inconvenient, yet they were apparently a part of life, one of its annoyances, a thing which had always been and probably would be for all time to come. Therefore, he reasoned, why bother with it any more than one was forced to by sheer necessity? Better it was for him if he attended to his own individual problems, solved them to the best of his ability and as circumstances would permit, and left to those who chose to do it the agitation for the betterment of things in general. If he solved his problems and every other Negro did the same, he often thought, then the thing we call the race problem will be solved. Besides, he reasoned, the whole thing is too big for one man to tackle it, and if he does attack it, more than likely he will go down to defeat in the attempt. And what would be gained? . . .

His office completed, Kenneth began the making of those contacts he needed to secure the patients he knew were coming. In this his mother and Mamie were of invaluable assistance. Everybody knew the Harpers. It was a simple matter for Kenneth to renew acquaintances broken when he had left for school in the North. He joined local lodges of the Grand United Order of Heavenly Reapers and the Exalted Knights of Damon. The affected mysteriousness of his initiation into these fraternal orders, the secret grip, the passwords, the elaborately worded rituals, all of which the other members took so seriously, amused him, but he went through it all with an outwardly solemn demeanour. He knew it was good business to affiliate himself with these often absurd societies which played so large a part in the lives of these simple and illiterate coloured folk. Along with the strenuous emotionalism of their religion, it served as an outlet for their naturally deep feelings.

In spite of the renewal of acquaintances, the careful campaign of winning confidence in his ability as a physician, Kenneth found that the flood of patients did not come as he had hoped. The coloured people of Central City had had impressed upon them by three hundred years of slavery and that which was called freedom after the Emancipation Proclamation was signed, that no Negro doctor, however talented, was quite as good as a white one. This slave mentality, Kenneth now realized, inbred upon generation after generation of coloured folk, is the greatest handicap from which the Negro suffers, destroying as it does that confidence in his own ability which would enable him to meet without fear or apology the test of modern competition.

Kenneth's youthful appearance, too, militated against him. Though twenty-nine years old, he looked not more than a mere twenty-four or twenty-five. "He may know his stuff and be as smart as all outdoors," ran the usual verdict, "but I don't want no boy treating me when I'm sick."

Perhaps the greatest factor contributing to the coloured folks' lack of confidence in physicians of their own race was the inefficiency of Dr. Williams, the only coloured doctor in Central City prior to Kenneth's return. Dr. Williams belonged to the old school and moved on the theory that when he graduated some eighteen years before from a medical school in Alabama, the development of medical knowledge had stopped. He fondly pictured himself as being the most prominent personage of Central City's Negro colony, was pompous, bulbous-eyed, and exceedingly fond of long words, especially of Latin derivation. He made it a rule of his life never to use a word of one syllable if one of two or more would serve as well. Active in fraternal order circles (he was a member of nine lodges), class-leader in Central City's largest Methodist church, arbiter supreme of local affairs in general, he filled the rôle with what he imagined was unsurpassable éclat. His idea of complimenting a hostess was ostentatiously to loosen his belt along about the middle of dinner. Once he had been introduced as the "black William Jennings Bryan," believed it thereafter, and thought it praise of a high order.

He was one of those who say on every possible occasion: "I am kept so terribly busy I never have a minute to myself." Like nine out of ten who say it, Dr. Williams always repeated this stock phrase of those who flatter themselves in this fashion—so necessary to those of small minds who would be thought great—not because it was true, but to enhance his pre-eminence in the eyes of his hearers—and in his own eyes as well.

He always wore coats which resembled morning coats, known in local parlance as "Jim-swingers." He kept his hair straightened, wore it brushed straight back from his forehead like highly polished steel wires, and, with pomades and hair oils liberally applied, it glistened like the patent leather shoes which adorned his ample feet.

His stout form filled the Ford in which he made his professional calls, and it was a sight worth seeing as he majestically rolled through the streets of the town bowing graciously and calling out loud greetings to the acquaintances he espied by the way. Always his bows to white people were twice as low and obsequious as to those of darker skin. Until Kenneth returned, Dr. Williams had had his own way in Central City. Through his fraternal and church connections and lack of competition, he had made a little money, much of it through his position as medical examiner for the lodges to which he belonged. As long as he treated minor ailments—cuts, colic, childbirths, and the like—he had little trouble. But when more serious maladies attacked them, the coloured population sent for the old white physician, Dr. Bennett, instead of for Dr. Williams.

The great amount of time at his disposal irritated Kenneth. He was like a spirited horse, champing at the bit, eager to be off. The patronizing air of his people nettled him—caused him to reflect somewhat bitterly that "a prophet is not without honour save in his own country." And when one has not the gift of prophecy to foretell, or of clairvoyance to see, what the future holds in the way of success, one is not likely to develop a philosophic calm which enables him to await the coming of long-desired results.

He was seated one day in his office reading when his mother entered. Closing his book, he asked the reason for her frown.

"You remember Mrs. Bradley—Mrs. Emma Bradley down on Ashley Street—don't you, Kenneth?" Without waiting for a reply, Mrs. Harper went on: "Well, she's mighty sick. Jim Bradley has had Dr. Bennett in to see what's the matter with her but he don't seem to do her much good."

Kenneth remembered Mrs. Bradley well indeed. The most talkative woman in Central City. It was she who had come to his mother with a long face and dolorous manner when he as a youngster had misbehaved in church. He had learned instinctively to connect Mrs. Bradley's visits with excursions to the little back room accompanied by his mother and a switch cut from the peach-tree in the back yard—a sort of natural cause and effect. Visions of those days rose in his mind and he imagined he could feel the sting of those switches on his legs now.

"What seems to be the trouble with her?" he asked.

"It's some sort of stomach-trouble—she's got an awful pain in her side. She says it can't be her appendix because she had that removed up to Atlanta when she was operated on there for a tumour nearly four years ago. Dr. Bennett gave her some medicine but it doesn't help her any. Won't you run down there to see her?"

"I can't, mamma, until I am called in professionally. Dr. Bennett won't like it. It isn't ethical. Besides, didn't Mrs. Bradley say when I came back that she didn't want any coloured doctor fooling with her?"

"Yes, she did, but you mustn't mind that. Just run in to see her as a social call."

Kenneth rose and instinctively took up his bag. Remembering, he put it down, put on his hat, kissed his mother, and walked down to Mrs. Bradley's. Outside the gate stood Dr. Bennett's mud-splashed buggy, sagging on one side through years of service in carrying its owner's great bulk. Between the shafts stood the old bay horse, its head hung dejectedly as though asleep, which Central City always connected with its driver.

Entering the gate held by one hinge, Kenneth made his way to the little three-room unpainted house which served as home for the Bradleys and their six children. On knocking, the door was opened by Dr. Bennett, who apparently was just leaving. He stood there, his hat on, stained by many storms, its black felt turning a greenish brown through years of service and countless rides through the red dust of the roads leading out of Central City. Dr. Bennett himself was large and flabby. His clothes hung on him in haphazard fashion and looked as though they had never been sub-jected to the indignity of a tailor's iron. A Sherlock Holmes, or even one less gifted, could read on his vest with little difficulty those things which its wearer had eaten for many meals past. Dr. Bennett's face was red through exposure to many suns, and cov-ered with the bristle of a three days' growth of beard. Small eyes set close together, they belied a bluff good humour which Dr. Ben-nett could easily assume when there was occasion for it. The cor-ners of the mouth were stained a deep brown where tobacco juice had run down the folds of the flesh.

Behind him stood Jim Bradley with worried face, his ashy black skin showing the effects of remaining all night by the bedside of his wife.

Dr. Bennett looked at Kenneth inquiringly.

"Don't you remember me, Dr. Bennett? I'm Kenneth Harper."

"Bless my soul, so it is. How're you, Ken? Le's see—it's been nigh on to eight years since you went No'th, ain't it? Heard you was back in town. Hear you goin' to practise here. Come 'round to see me some time. Right glad you're here. I'll be kinder glad to get somebody t' help me treat these niggers for colic or when they get carved up in a crap game. Hope you ain't got none of them No'the'n ideas 'bout social equality while you was up there. Jus' do like your daddy did, and you'll get along all right down here. These niggers who went over to France and ran around with them

Frenchwomen been causin' a lot of trouble 'round here, kickin' up a rumpus, and talkin' 'bout votin' and ridin' in the same car with white folks. But don't you let them get you mixed up in it, 'cause there'll be trouble sho's you born if they don't shut up and git to work. Jus' do like your daddy did, and you'll do a lot to keep the white folks' friendship.''

Dr. Bennett poured forth all this gratuitous advice between asthmatic wheezes without waiting for Kenneth to reply. He then turned to Jim Bradley with a parting word of advice.

"Jim, keep that hot iron on Emma's stomach and give her those pills every hour. 'Tain't nothin' but the belly-ache. She'll be all right in an hour or two.''

Turning without another word, he half ambled, half shuffled out to his buggy, pulled himself up into it with more puffing and wheezing, and drove away.

Jim Bradley took Kenneth's arm and led him back on to the little porch, closing the door behind him.

"I'm pow'ful glad t' see you, Ken. My, but you done growed sence you went up No'th! Befo' you go in dar, I want t' tell you somethin'. Emma's been right po'ly fuh two days. Her stomach's swelled up right sma't and she's been hollering all night. Dis mawning she don't seem jus' right in de haid. I tol' her I was gwine to ast you to come see her, but she said she didn't want no young nigger doctah botherin' with her. But don't you min' her. I wants you to tell me what to do.''

Kenneth smiled.

"I'll do what I can for her, Jim. But what about Dr. Bennett?''

"Dat's a' right. He give her some med'cine but it ain't done her no good. She's too good a woman fuh me to lose her, even if she do talk a li'l' too much. You make out like you jus' drap in to pass the time o' day with her.''

Kenneth entered the dark and ill-smelling room. Opposite the door a fire smouldered in the fire-place, giving fitful spurts of flame that illumined the room and then died down again. There was no grate, the pieces of wood resting on crude andirons, blackened by the smoke of many fires. Over the mantel there hung a cheap charcoal reproduction of Jim and Emma in their wedding-clothes, made by some local "artist" from an old photograph. One or two nondescript chairs worn shiny through years of use stood before the fire. In one corner stood a dresser on which were various bottles of medicine and of "Madame Walker's Hair Grower.'' On the floor a rug, worn through in spots and patched with fragments of other rugs all apparently of different colours, covered the space in front of the bed. The rest of the floor was bare and showed evidences of a recent vigorous scrubbing. The one window was closed tightly and covered over with a cracked shade, long since divorced from its roller, tacked to the upper ledge of the window.

On the bed Mrs. Bradley was rolling and tossing in great pain. Her eyes opened slightly when Kenneth approached the bed and closed again immediately as a new spasm of pain passed through her body. She moaned piteously and held her hands on her side, pressing down hard one hand over the other.

At a sign from Jim, Kenneth started to take her pulse.

"Go way from here and leave me 'lone! Oh, Lawdy, why is I suff'rin' this way? I jus' wish I was daid! Oh—oh—oh!"

This last as she writhed in agony. Kenneth drew back the covers, examined Mrs. Bradley's abdomen, took her pulse. Every sign pointed to an attack of acute appendicitis. He informed Jim of his diagnosis.

"But, Doc, it ain't dat trouble, 'cause Emma says dat was taken out a long time ago."

"I can't help what she says. She's got appendicitis. You go get Dr. Bennett and tell him your wife has got to be operated on right away or she is going to die. Get a move on you now! If it was my case, I would operate within an hour. Stop by my house and tell Bob to bring me an ice bag as quick as he can."

Jim hurried away to catch Dr. Bennett. Kenneth meanwhile did what he could to relieve Mrs. Bradley's suffering. In a few minutes Bob came with the ice bag. Then Jim returned with his face even more doleful than it had been when Kenneth had told him how sick his wife was.

"Doc Bennett says he don't care what you do. He got kinder mad when I told him you said it was 'pendicitis, and tol' me dat if I couldn't take his word, he wouldn't have anything mo' to do with Emma. He seemed kinder mad 'cause you said it was mo' than a stomach-ache. Said he wa'n't goin' to let no young nigger doctor tell him his bus'ness. So, Doc, you'll have t' do what you thinks bes'."

"All right, I'll do it. First thing, I'm going to move your wife over to my office. We can put her up in the spare room. Bob will drive her over in the car. Get something around her and you'd better come on over with her. I'll get Dr. Williams to help me."

Kenneth was jubilant at securing his first surgical case since his return to Central City, though his pleasure was tinged with doubt as to the ethics of the manner in which it had come to him. He did not let that worry him very long, however, but began his preparations for the operation.

First he telephoned to Mrs. Johnson, who, before she married and settled down in Central City, had been a trained nurse at a coloured hospital at Atlanta. She hurried over at once. Neat, quiet, and efficient, she took charge immediately of preparations, sterilizing the array of shiny instruments, preparing wads of absorbent cotton, arranging bandages and catgut and hæmostatics.

Kenneth left all this to Mrs. Johnson, for he knew in her hands it would be well done. He telephoned to Dr. Williams to ask that he give the anæsthesia. In his excitement Kenneth neglected to put in his voice the note of asking a great and unusual favour of Dr. Williams. That eminent physician, eminent in his own eyes, cleared his throat several times before replying, while Kenneth waited at the other end of the line. He realized his absolute dependence on Dr. Williams, for he knew no white doctor would assist a Negro surgeon or even operate with a coloured assistant. There was none other in Central City who could give the ether to Mrs. Bradley. It made him furious that Dr. Williams should hesitate so long. At the same time, he knew he must restrain the hot and burning words that he would have used. The pompous one hinted of the pressure of his own work—work that would keep him busy all day. Into his words he injected the note of affront at being asked—he, *the* coloured physician of Central City—to assist a younger man. Especially on that man's first case. Kenneth swallowed his anger and pride, and pleaded with Dr. Williams at least to come over. Finally, the older physician agreed in a condescending manner to do so.

Hurrying back to his office, Kenneth found Mrs. Bradley arranged on the table ready for the operation. Examining her, he found she was in delirium, her eyes glazed, her abdomen hard and distended, and she had a temperature of 105 degrees. He hastily sterilized his hands and put on his gown and cap. As he finished his preparations, Dr. Williams in leisurely manner strolled into the room with a benevolent and patronizing "Howdy, Kenneth, my boy. I won't be able to help you out after all. I've got to see some patients of my own."

He emphasized "my own," for he had heard of the manner by which Kenneth had obtained the case of Mrs. Bradley. Kenneth, pale with anger, excited over his first real case in Central City, stared at Dr. Williams in amazement at his words.

"But, Dr. Williams, you can't do that! Mrs. Bradley here is dying!"

The older doctor looked around patronizingly at the circle of anxious faces. Jim Bradley, his face lined and seamed with toil, the lines deepened in distress at the agony of his wife and the imminence of losing her, gazed at him with dumb pleading in his eyes, pleading without spoken words with the look of an old, faithful dog beseeching its master. Bob looked with a malevolent glare at his pompous sleekness, as though he would like to spring upon him. Mrs. Johnson plainly showed her contempt of such callousness on the part of one who bore the title, however poorly, of physician. In Kenneth's eyes was a commingling of eagerness and rage and bitterness and anxiety. On Emma Bradley's face there was nothing but the pain and agony of her delirious ravings. Dr. Williams seemed to enjoy thoroughly his little moment of triumph. He delayed speaking in order that it might be prolonged as much as possible. The silence was broken by Jim Bradley.

"Doc, won't you please he'p?" he pleaded. "She's all I got!"

Kenneth could remain silent no longer. He longed to punch that fat face and erase from it the supercilious smirk that adorned it.

"Dr. Williams," he began with cold hatred in his voice, "either you are going to give this anæsthesia or else I'm going to go into every church in Central City and tell exactly what you've done here today."

Dr. Williams turned angrily on Kenneth.

"Young man, I don't allow anybody to talk to me like that— least of all, a young whippersnapper just out of school . . ." he shouted.

By this time Kenneth's patience was at an end. He seized the lapels of the other doctor's coat in one hand and thrust his clenched fist under the nose of the now thoroughly alarmed Dr. Williams.

"Are you going to help—or aren't you?" he demanded.

The situation was becoming too uncomfortable for the older man. He could stand Kenneth's opposition but not the ridicule which would inevitably follow the spreading of the news that he had been beaten up and made ridiculous by Kenneth. He swallowed—a look of indecision passed over his face as he visibly wondered if Kenneth really dared hit him—followed by a look of fear as Kenneth drew back his fist as though to strike. Discretion seemed the better course to pursue—he could wait until a later and more propitious date for his revenge—he agreed to help. A look of relief came over Jim Bradley's face. A grin covered Bob's as he saw his brother showing at last some signs of fighting spirit. Without further words Kenneth prepared to operate. . . .

The patient under the ether, Kenneth with sure, deft strokes made an incision and rapidly removed the appendix. Ten—twelve—fifteen minutes, and the work was done. He found Mrs. Bradley's peritoneum badly inflamed, the appendix swollen and about to burst. A few hours' delay and it would have been too late. . . .

The next morning Mrs. Bradley's temperature had gone down to normal. Two weeks later she was sufficiently recovered to be removed to her home. Three weeks later she was on her feet again. Then Kenneth for the first time in his life had no fault to find with the vigour with which Mrs. Bradley could use her tongue. Glorying as only such a woman can in her temporary fame at escape from death by so narrow a margin, she went up and down the streets of the town telling how Kenneth had saved her life. With each telling of the story it took on more embellishments until eventually the simple operation ranked in importance in her mind with the first sewing-up of the human heart.

Kenneth found his practice growing. His days were filled with his work. One man viewed his growing practice with bitterness. It was Dr. Williams, resentful of the small figure he had cut in the episode in Kenneth's office, which had become known all over Central City. Of a petty and vindictive nature, he bided his time until he could force atonement from the upstart who had so presumptuously insulted and belittled him, the Beau Brummell, the leading physician, the prominent coloured citizen. But Kenneth, if he knew of the hatred in the man's heart, was supremely oblivious of it.

The morning after his operation on Mrs. Bradley, he added another to the list of those who did not wish him well. He had taken the bottle of alcohol containing Mrs. Bradley's appendix to Dr. Bennett to show that worthy that he had been right, after all, in his diagnosis. He found him seated in his office. Dr. Bennett, with little apparent interest, glanced at the bottle.

"Humph!" he ejaculated, aiming at the cuspidor and letting

fly a thin stream of tobacco juice which accurately met its mark. "You never can tell what's wrong with a nigger anyhow. They ain't got nacheral diseases like white folks. A hoss doctor can treat 'em better'n one that treats humans. I always said that a nigger's more animal than human. . . ."

Kenneth had been eager to discuss the case of Mrs. Bradley with his fellow practitioner. He had not even been asked to sit down by Dr. Bennett. He realized for the first time that in spite of the superiority of his medical training to that of Dr. Bennett's, the latter did not recognize him as a qualified physician, but only as a "nigger doctor." Making some excuse, he left the house. Dr. Bennett turned back to the local paper he had been reading when Kenneth entered, took a fresh chew of tobacco from the plug in his hip pocket, grunted, and remarked: "A damned nigger telling me *I* don't know medicine!"

GWENDOLYN BENNETT

GWENDOLYN BENNETT'S SHORT STORY *in the review* Fire!! *was appropriately risqué. Paul Watson, former boxer and African American expatriate, is notorious in the Montmartre quarter of Paris for his hatred of white Americans, whom he instantly pulverizes when they utter the red-flag word "nigger." Burly and basic, Paul Watson uncannily anticipates Claude McKay's protagonist Jake in* Home to Harlem. *Although frequently slipping into stiff turns of phrase—"one always cogitates," "the wont of most bridegrooms"—Bennett's use of streetwise terms represented a significant break with the genteel prose of Fauset and White. Paul feeds and clothes Mary, down on her luck, and falls in love with her, even though she is a white American. The reader is left to reflect on the vagaries of racism as Mary, a prostitute, decides at the last minute not to marry Paul.*

WEDDING DAY

PAUL HAD A WAY about him and seemed to get on with the colored fellows who lived in Montmartre and when the first Negro jazz band played in a tiny Parisian cafe Paul was among them playing the banjo. Those first years were without event so far as Paul was concerned. The members of that first band often say now that they wonder how it was that nothing happened during those first seven years, for it was generally known how great was Paul's hatred for American white people. I suppose the tranquility in the light of what happened afterwards was due to the fact that the cafe in which they worked was one in which mostly French people drank and danced and then too, that was before there were so many Americans visiting Paris. However, everyone had heard Paul speak of his intense hatred of American white folks. It only took two Benedictines to make him start talking about what he would do to the first "Yank" that called him "nigger." But the seven years came to an end and Paul Watson went to work in a larger cafe with a larger band, patronized almost solely by Americans.

I've heard almost every Negro in Montmartre tell about the night that a drunken Kentuckian came into the cafe where Paul was playing and said:

"Look heah, Bruther, what you all doin' ovah heah?"

"None ya bizness. And looka here, I ain't your brother, see?"

"Jack, do you heah that nigger talkin' lak that tah me?"

As he said this, he turned to speak to his companion. I have often wished that I had been there to have seen the thing happen myself. Every tale I have heard about it was different and yet there was something of truth in each of them. Perhaps the nearest one can come to the truth is by saying that Paul beat up about four full-sized white men that night besides doing a great deal of damage to the furniture about the cafe. I couldn't tell you just what did happen. Some of the fellows say that Paul seized the nearest table and mowed down men right and left, others say he took a bottle, then again the story runs that a chair was the instrument of his fury. At any rate, that started Paul Watson on his seige against the American white person who brings his native prejudices into the life of Paris.

It is a verity that Paul was the "black terror." The last syllable of the word, nigger, never passed the lips of a white man without the quick reflex action of Paul's arm and fist to the speaker's jaw. He paid for more glassware and cafe furnishings in the course of the next few years than is easily imaginable. And yet, there was something likable about Paul. Perhaps that's the reason that he stood in so well with the policemen of the neighborhood. Always some divine power seemed to intervene in his behalf and he was excused after the payment of a small fine with advice about his future conduct. Finally, there came the night when in a frenzy he shot the two American sailors.

They had not died from the wounds he had given them hence his sentence had not been one of death but rather a long term of imprisonment. It was a pitiable sight to see Paul sitting in the corner of his cell with his great body hunched almost double. He seldom talked and when he did his words were interspersed with oaths about the lowness of "crackers." Then the World War came.

It seems strange that anything so horrible as that wholesale slaughter could bring about any good and yet there was something of a smoothing quality about even its baseness. There has never been such equality before or since such as that which the World War brought. Rich men fought by the side of paupers; poets swapped yarns with dry-goods salesmen, while Jews and Christians ate corned beef out of the same tin. Along with the general leveling influence came France's pardon of her prisoners in order that they might enter the army. Paul Watson became free and a French soldier. Because he was strong and had innate daring in his heart he was placed in the aerial squad and cited many times for bravery. The close of the war gave him his place in French society as a hero. With only a memory of the war and an ugly scar on his left cheek he took up his old life.

His firm resolutions about American white people still remained intact and many chance encounters that followed the war are told from lip to lip proving that the war and his previous imprisonment had changed him little. He was the same Paul Watson to Montmartre as he shambled up rue Pigalle.

Rue Pigalle in the early evening has a sombre beauty—gray as are most Paris streets and other-worldish. To those who know the district it is the Harlem of Paris and rue Pigalle is its dusky Seventh Avenue. Most of the colored musicians that furnish Parisians and their visitors with entertainment live somewhere in the neighborhood of rue Pigalle. Some time during every day each of these musicians makes a point of passing through rue Pigalle. Little wonder that almost any day will find Paul Watson going his shuffling way up the same street.

He reached the corner of rue de la Bruyere and with sure instinct his feet stopped. Without half thinking he turned into "the Pit." Its full name is The Flea Pit. If you should ask one of the musicians why it was so called, he would answer you to the effect that it was called "the pit" because all the "fleas" hang out there. If you did not get the full import of this explanation, he would go further and say that there were always "spades" in the pit and they were as thick as fleas. Unless you could understand this latter attempt at clarity you could not fully grasp what the Flea-Pit means to the Negro musicians in Montmartre. It is a tiny cafe of the genus that is called *bistro* in France. Here the fiddle players, saxophone blowers, drumbeaters and ivory ticklers gather at four in the afternoon for a porto or a game of billiards. Here the cabaret entertainers and supper musicians meet at one o'clock at night or thereafter for a whiskey and soda, or more billiards. Occasional sandwiches and a "quiet game" also play their parts in the popularity of the place. After a season or two it becomes a settled fact just what time you may catch so-and-so at the famous "Pit."

The musicians were very fond of Paul and took particular delight in teasing him. He was one of the chosen few that all of the musicians conceded as being "regular." It was the pet joke of the habitues of the cafe that Paul never bothered with girls. They always said that he could beat up ten men but was scared to death of one woman.

"Say fellow, when ya goin' a get hooked up?"

"Can't say, Bo. Ain't so much on skirts."

"Man alive, ya don't know what you're missin'—somebody little and cute telling ya sweet things in your ear. Paris is full of women folks."

"I ain't much on 'em all the same. Then too, they're all white."

"What's it to ya? This ain't America."

"Can't help that. Get this—I'm collud, see? I ain't got nothing for no white meat to do. If a woman eva called me nigger I'd have to kill her, that's all!"

"You for it, son. I can't give you a thing on this Mr. Jefferson Lawd way of lookin' at women.

"Oh, tain't that. I guess they're all right for those that wants 'em. Not me!"

"Oh you ain't so forty. You'll fall like all the other spades I've ever seen. Your kind falls hardest."

And so Paul went his way—alone. He smoked and drank with the fellows and sat for hours in the Montmartre cafes and never knew the companionship of a woman. Then one night after his work he was walking along the street in his queer shuffling way when a woman stepped up to his side.

"Voulez vous."

"Naw, gowan away from here."

"Oh, you speak English, don't you?"

"You an 'merican woman?"

"Used to be 'fore I went on the stage and got stranded over here."

"Well, get away from here. I don't like your kind!"

"Aw, Buddy, don't say that. I ain't prejudiced like some fool women."

"You don't know who I am, do you? I'm Paul Watson and I hate American white folks, see?"

He pushed her aside and went on walking alone. He hadn't gone far when she caught up to him and said with sobs in her voice:—

"Oh, Lordy, please don't hate me 'cause I was born white and an American. I ain't got a sou to my name and all the men pass me by cause I ain't spruced up. Now you come along and won't look at me cause I'm white."

Paul strode along with her clinging to his arm. He tried to shake her off several times but there was no use. She clung all the more desperately to him. He looked down at her frail body shaken with sobs, and something caught at his heart. Before he knew what he was doing he had said:—

"Naw, I ain't that mean. I'll get you some grub. Quit your cryin'. Don't like seein' women folks cry."

It was the talk of Montmartre. Paul Watson takes a woman to Gavarnni's every night for dinner. He comes to the Flea Pit less frequently, thus giving the other musicians plenty of opportunity to discuss him.

"How times do change. Paul, the woman-hater, has a Jane now."

"You ain't said nothing, fella. That ain't all. She's white and an 'merican, too."

"That's the way with these spades. They beat up all the white men they can lay their hands on but as soon as a gang of golden hair with blue eyes rubs up close to them they forget all they ever said about hatin' white folks."

"Guess he thinks that skirt's gone on him. Dumb fool!"

"Don' be no chineeman. That old gag don' fit for Paul. He cain't understand it no more'n we can. Says he jess can't help himself, everytime she looks up into his eyes and asks him does he love her. They sure are happy together. Paul's goin' to marry her, too. At first she kept saying that she didn't want to get married cause she wasn't the marrying kind and all that talk. Paul jus' laid down the law to her and told him he never would live with no woman without being married to her. Then she began to tell him all about her past life. He told her he didn't care nothing about what she

used to be jus' so long as they loved each other now. Guess they'll
make it."

"Yeah, Paul told me the same tale last night. He's sure gone
on her all right."

"They're gettin' tied up next Sunday. So glad it's not me.
Don't trust these American dames. Me for the Frenchies."

"She ain't so worse for looks, Bud. Now that he's been fur-
nishing the green for the rags."

"Yeah, but I don't see no reason for the wedding bells. She
was right—she ain't the marrying kind."

. . . and so Montmartre talked. In every cafe where the Negro
musicians congregated Paul Watson was the topic for conversation.
He had suddenly fallen from his place as bronze God to almost
less than the dust.

The morning sun made queer patterns on Paul's sleeping face.
He grimaced several times in his slumber, then finally half-opened
his eyes. After a succession of dream-laden blinks he gave a great
yawn, and rubbing his eyes, looked at the open window through
which the sun shone brightly. His first conscious thought was that
this was the bride's day and that bright sunshine prophesied happiness for the bride throughout her married life. His first impulse
was to settle back into the covers and think drowsily about Mary
and the queer twists life brings about, as is the wont of most
bridegrooms on their last morning of bachelorhood. He put this
impulse aside in favor of dressing quickly and rushing downstairs
to telephone to Mary to say "happy wedding day" to her.

One huge foot slipped into a worn bedroom slipper and then
the other dragged painfully out of the warm bed were the coura-
geous beginnings of his bridal toilette. With a look of triumph he
put on his new grey suit that he had ordered from an English tailor.
He carefully pulled a taffeta tie into place beneath his chin, noting
as he looked at his face in the mirror that the scar he had received
in the army was very ugly—funny, marrying an ugly man like him.

French telephones are such human faults. After trying for
about fifteen minutes to get Central 32.01 he decided that he might
as well walk around to Mary's hotel to give his greeting as to stand
there in the lobby of his own, wasting his time. He debated this in
his mind a great deal. They were to be married at four o'clock. It
was eleven now and it did seem a shame not to let her have a
minute or two by herself. As he went walking down the street
towards her hotel he laughed to think of how one always cogitates

over doing something and finally does the thing he wanted to in the beginning anyway.

Mud on his nice gray suit that the English tailor had made for him. Damn—gray suit—what did he have a gray suit on for, anyway. Folks with black faces shouldn't wear gray suits. Gawd, but it was funny that time when he beat up that cracker at the Periquet. Fool couldn't shut his mouth he was so surprised. Crackers—damn 'em—he was one nigger that wasn't 'fraid of 'em. Wouldn't he have a hell of a time if he went back to America where black was black. Wasn't white nowhere, black wasn't. What was that thought he was trying to get ahold of—bumping around in his head—something he started to think about but couldn't remember it somehow.

The shrill whistle that is typical of the French subway pierced its way into his thoughts. Subway—why was he in the subway— he didn't want to go any place. He heard doors slamming and saw the blue uniforms of the conductors swinging on to the cars as the trains began to pull out of the station. With one or two strides he reached the last coach as it began to move up the platform. A bit out of breath he stood inside the train and looking down at what he had in his hand he saw that it was a tiny pink ticket. A first class ticket in a second class coach. The idea set him to laughing. Everyone in the car turned and eyed him, but that did not bother him. Wonder what stop he'd get off—funny how these French said descend when they meant get off—funny he couldn't pick up French—been here so long. First class ticket in a second class coach!—that was one on him. Wedding day today, and that damn letter from Mary. How'd she say it now, "just couldn't go through with it," white women just don't marry colored men, and she was a street woman, too. Why couldn't she have told him flat that she was just getting back on her feet at his expense. Funny that first class ticket he bought, wish he could see Mary—him a-going there to wish her "happy wedding day," too. Wonder what that French woman was looking at him so hard for? Guess it was the mud.

CLAUDE MCKAY

CLAUDE MCKAY's Home to Harlem *(1928) was a shocking departure from the dominant fiction of the Harlem Renaissance, a fulfillment with a vengeance of Langston Hughes's "Negro Artist and the Racial Mountain" manifesto. It had none of the preciosity and titillating primitivism of Carl Van Vechten's 1926 bombshell novel,* Nigger Heaven. *McKay's characters came from the dives, streets, and, in Du Bois's opinion, the sewers of the cities. Things take a tortured, philosophical turn in "Snowstorm in Pittsburgh," a scene of bedbugs, opium, and grim labor on the railroad. The imperturbably basic Jake teams up with Ray, an intellectual type who is too pensive and alienated for his own good. " 'That theah nigger is dopey from them books o' hisn,' " the dining-car chef snorts to Jake about Ray. "Spring in Harlem" serves up the underbelly of Harlem, a place where sex is central, although, as worldtraveled Jake reminds his friend Billy, " 'The whole wul' is boodycrazy—' "*

Banjo *(1929) transports a less culturally neurotic Ray to Marseilles, where he becomes familiar with Banjo and the human flotsam and jetsam of the "Ditch." Speaking through his characters, McKay greatly intensified his criticism of the African American bourgeoisie, of intellectual solutions to social problems, and of unbridled capitalism.*

In the novel Banana Bottom *(1933), McKay attempts to resolve the dichotomy between the natural and the intellectual in the character of the young Jamaican woman Bita Plant, (soon to be married) who remains true to the culture of Gingertown while yet absorbing "European" learning, courtesy of her British mentor, Squire Gensir. "Perhaps Pascal would have been incredulous if it had been prophesied to him that in future centuries a black girl would have found in his words a golden thread of principle to guide her through the confusion of life," the author concludes significantly.*

FROM *HOME TO HARLEM*

SNOWSTORM IN PITTSBURGH

IN THE MIDDLE of the little bridge built over the railroad crossing he was suddenly enveloped in a thick mass of smoke spouted out by an in-rushing train. That was Jake's first impression of Pittsburgh. He stepped off the bridge into a saloon. From there along a dull-gray street of grocery and fruit shops and piddling South-European children. Then he was on Wiley Avenue, the long, gray, uphill street.

Brawny bronze men in coal-blackened and oil-spotted blue overalls shadowed the doorways of saloons, pool-rooms, and little basement restaurants. The street was animated with dark figures going up, going down. Houses and men, women, and squinting cats and slinking dogs, everything seemed touched with soot and steel dust.

"So this heah is the niggers' run," said Jake. "I don't like its 'pearance, nohow." He walked down the street and remarked a bouncing little chestnut-brown standing smartly in the entrance of a basement eating-joint. She wore a knee-length yellow-patterned muslin frock and a white-dotted blue apron. The apron was a little longer than the frock. Her sleeves were rolled up. Her arms were beautiful, like smooth burnished bars of copper.

Jake stopped and said, "Howdy!"

"Howdy again!" the girl flashed a row of perfect teeth at him.

"Got a bite of anything good?"

"I should say so, Mister Ma-an."

She rolled her eyes and worked her hips into delightful free-and-easy motions. Jake went in. He was not hungry for food. He looked at a large dish half filled with tapioca pudding. He turned to the pie-case on the counter.

"The peach pie is the best," said the girl, her bare elbow on the counter; "it's fresh." She looked straight in his eyes. "All right,

I'll try peach," he said, and, magnetically, his long, shining fingers touched her hand. . . .

In the evening he found the Haytian waiter at the big Wiley Avenue pool-room. Quite different from the pool-rooms in Harlem, it was a sort of social center for the railroad men and the more intelligent black workmen of the quarter. Tobacco, stationery, and odds and ends were sold in the front part of the store. There was a table where customers sat and wrote letters. And there were pretty chocolate dolls and pictures of Negroid types on sale. Curious, pathetic pictures; black Madonna and child; a kinky-haired mulatto angle with African lips and Nordic nose, soaring on a white cloud up to heaven; Jesus blessing a black child and a white one; a black shepherd carrying a white lamb—all queerly reminiscent of the crude prints of the great Christian paintings that are so common in poor religious homes.

"Here he is!" Jake greeted the waiter. "What's the new?"

"Nothing new in Soot-hill; always the same."

The railroad men hated the Pittsburgh run. They hated the town, they hated Wiley Avenue and their wretched free quarters that were in it. . . .

"What're you going to do?"

"Ahm gwine to the colored show with a li'l' brown piece," said Jake.

"You find something already? My me! You're a fast-working one."

"Always the same whenever I hits a new town. Always in cock-tail luck, chappie."

"Which one? Manhattan or Bronx?"

"It's Harlem-Pittsburgh thisanight," Jake grinned. "Wachyu gwine make?"

"Don't know. There's nothing ever in Pittsburgh for me. I'm in no mood for the leg-show tonight, and the colored show is bum. Guess I'll go sleep if I can."

"Awright, I'll see you li'l' later, chappie." Jake gripped his hand. "Say—whyn't you tell a fellow you' name? Youse sure more'n second waiter as Ise more'n third cook. Ev'body calls me Jake. And you?"

"Raymond, but everybody calls me Ray."

Jake heaved off. Ray bought some weekly Negro newspapers:

The Pittsburgh Courier, The Baltimore American, The Negro World, The Chicago Defender. Here he found a big assortment of all the Negro publications that he never could find in Harlem. In a next-door saloon he drank a glass of sherry and started off for the waiters' and cooks' quarters.

It was long after midnight when Jake returned to quarters. He had to pass through the Western men's section to get to the Eastern crews. Nobody was asleep in the Western men's section. No early-morning train was chalked up on their board. The men were grouped off in poker and dice games. Jake hesitated a little by one group, fascinated by a wiry little long-headed finger-snapping black, who with strenuous h'h, h'h, h'h, h'h, was zestfully throwing the bones. Jake almost joined the game but he admonished himself: "You winned five dollars thisaday and you made a nice li'l' brown piece. Wha'more you want?" . . .

He found the beds assigned to the members of his crew. They were double beds, like Pullman berths. Three of the waiters had not come in yet. The second and the fourth cooks were snoring, each a deep frothy bass and a high tenor, and scratching themselves in their sleep. The chef sprawled like the carcass of a rhinoceros, half-naked, mouth wide open. Tormented by bedbugs, he had scratched and tossed in his sleep and hoofed the covers off the bed. Ray was sitting on a lower berth on his Negro newspapers spread out to form a sheet. He had thrown the sheets on the floor, they were so filthy from other men's sleeping. By the thin flame of gas-light he was killing bugs.

"Where is I gwine to sleep?" asked Jake.

"Over me, if you can. I saved the bunk for you," said Ray.

"Some music the niggers am making," remarked Jake, nodding in the direction of the snoring cooks. "But whasmat, chappie, you ain't sleeping?"

"Can't you see?"

"Bugs. Bumbole! This is a hell of a dump for a man to sleep in."

"The place is rocking crazy with them," said Ray. "I hauled the cot away from the wall, but the mattress is just swarming."

Hungry and bold, the bugs crept out of their chinks and hunted for food. They stopped dead-still when disturbed by the slightest shadow, and flattened their bellies against the wall.

"Le's get outa this stinking dump and chase a drink, chappie."

Ray jumped out of his berth, shoved himself into his clothes and went with Jake. The saloon near by the pool-room was still open. They went there. Ray asked for sherry.

"You had better sample some hard liquor if youse gwine back to wrastle with them bugs tonight," Jake suggested.

Ray took his advice. A light-yellow fellow chummed up with the boys and invited them to drink with him. He was as tall as Jake and very thin. There was a vacant, wandering look in his kindly-weak eyes. He was a waiter on another dining-car of the New York-Pittsburg run. Ray mentioned that he had to quit his bed because he couldn't sleep.

"This here town is the rottenest lay-over in the whole railroad field," declared the light-yellow. "I don't never sleep in the quarters here."

"Where do you sleep, then?" asked Ray.

"Oh, I got a sweet baby way up yonder the other side of the hill."

"Oh, ma-ma!" Jake licked his lips. "So youse all fixed up in this heah town?"

"Not going there tonight, though," the light-yellow said in a careless, almost bored tone. "Too far for mine."

He asked Jake and Ray if they would like to go to a little open-all-night place. They were glad to hear of that.

"Any old thing, boh," Jake said, "to get away from that theah Pennsy bug house."

The little place was something of a barrel-house speak-easy, crowded with black steelworkers in overalls and railroad men, and foggy with smoke. They were all drinking hard liquor and playing cards. The boss was a stocky, genial brown man. He knew the light-yellow waiter and shook hands with him and his friends. He moved away some boxes in a corner and squeezed a little table in it, specially for them. They sat down, jammed into the corner, and drank whisky.

"Better here than the Pennsy pigpen," said the light-yellow.

He was slapped on the back by a short, compact young black.

"Hello, you! What you think youse doing theah?"

"Ain't figuring," retorted the light-yellow, "is you?"

"On the red moon gwine around mah haid, yes. How about a li'l' good snow?"

"Now you got mah number down, Happy."

The black lad vanished again through a mysterious back door. The light-yellow said: "He's the biggest hophead I ever seen.

Nobody can sniff like him. Yet he's always the same happy nigger, stout and strong like a bull."

He took another whisky and went like a lean hound after Happy. Jake looked mischievously at the little brown door, remarking: "It's a great life ef youse in on it." . . .

The light-yellow came back with a cold gleam in his eyes, like arsenic shining in the dark. His features were accentuated by a rigid, disturbing tone and he resembled a smiling wax figure.

"Have a li'l' stuff with the bunch?" he asked Jake.

"I ain't got the habit, boh, but I'll try anything once again."

"And you?" The light-yellow turned to Ray.

"No, chief, thank you, but I don't want to."

The waiter went out again with Jake on his heels. Beyond the door, five fellows, kneeling in the sawdust, were rolling the square bones. Others sat together around two tables with a bottle of red liquor and thimble-like glasses before them.

"Oh, boy!" one said. "When I get home tonight it will be some more royal stuff. I ain'ta gwine to work none 'tall tomorrow."

"Shucks!" Another spread away his big mouth. "This heah ain't nothing foh a fellow to turn royal loose on. I remimber when I was gwine with a money gang that hed no use foh nothing but the pipe. That theah time was life, buddy."

"Wha' sorta pipe was that there?" asked Jake.

"The Chinese stuff, old boy."

Instead of deliberately fisting his, like the others, Jake took it up carelessly between his thumb and forefinger and inhaled.

"Say what you wanta about Chinee or any other stuff," said Happy, "but theah ain't nothing can work wicked like snow and whisky. It'll flip you up from hell into heaven befoh you knows it."

Ray looked into the room.

"Who's you li'l' mascot?" Happy asked the light-yellow.

"Tha's mah best pal," Jake answered. "He's got some moh stuff up here," Jake tapped his head.

"Better let's go on back to quarters," said Ray.

"To them bugs?" demanded Jake.

"Yes, I think we'd better."

"Awright, anything you say, chappie. I kain sleep through

worser things." Jake took a few of the little white packets from Happy and gave him some money. "Guess I might need them some day. You never know."

Jake fell asleep as soon as his head touched the dirty pillow. Below him, Ray lay in his bunk, tormented by bugs and the snoring cooks. The low-burning gaslight flickered and flared upon the shadows. The young man lay under the untellable horror of a dead-tired man who wills to sleep and cannot.

In other sections of the big barn building the faint chink of coins touched his ears. Those men gambling the hopeless Pittsburg night away did not disturb him. They were so quiet. It would have been better, perhaps, if they were noisy. He closed his eyes and tried to hypnotize himself to sleep. Sleep . . . sleep . . . sleep . . . sleep . . . sleep. . . . He began counting slowly. His vigil might break and vanish somnolently upon some magic number. He counted a million. Perhaps love would appease this unwavering angel of wakefulness. Oh, but he could not pick up love easily on the street as Jake. . . .

He flung himself, across void and water, back home. Home thoughts, if you can make them soft and sweet and misty-beautiful enough, can sometimes snare sleep. There was the quiet, chalky-dusty street and, jutting out over it, the front of the house that he had lived in. The high staircase built on the outside, and pots of begonias and ferns on the landing. . . .

All the flowering things he loved, red and white and pink hibiscus, mimosas, rhododendrons, a thousand glowing creepers, climbing and spilling their vivid petals everywhere, and bright-buzzing humming-birds and butterflies. All the tropic-warm lilies and roses. Giddy-high erect thatch palms, slender, tall, fur-fronded ferns, majestic cotton trees, stately bamboos creating a green grandeur in the heart of space. . . .

Sleep remained cold and distant. Intermittently the cooks broke their snoring with masticating noises of their fat lips, like animals eating. Ray fixed his eyes on the offensive bug-bitten bulk of the chef. These men claimed kinship with him. They were black like him. Man and nature had put them in the same race. He ought to love them and feel them (if they felt anything). He ought to if he had a shred of social morality in him. They were all chain-ganged together and he was counted as one link. Yet he loathed every soul in that great barrack-room, except Jake. Race. . . . Why should he have and love a race?

Races and nations were things like skunks, whose smells poisoned the air of life. Yet civilized mankind reposed its faith and future in their ancient, silted channels. Great races and big nations! There must be something mighty inspiriting in being the citizen of a great strong nation. To be the white citizen of a nation that can say bold, challenging things like a strong man. Something very different from the keen ecstatic joy a man feels in the romance of being black. Something the black man could never feel nor quite understand.

Ray felt that as he was conscious of being black and impotent, so, correspondingly, each marine down in Hayti must be conscious of being white and powerful. What a unique feeling of confidence about life the typical white youth of his age must have! Knowing that his skin-color was a passport to glory, making him one with ten thousands like himself. All perfect Occidentals and investors in that grand business called civilization. That grand business in whose pits sweated and snored, like the cooks, all the black and brown hybrids and mongrels, simple earth-loving animals, without aspirations toward national unity and racial arrogance.

He remembered when little Hayti was floundering uncontrolled, how proud he was to be the son of a free nation. He used to feel condescendingly sorry for those poor African natives; superior to ten millions of suppressed Yankee "coons." Now he was just one of them and he hated them for being one of them. . . .

But he was not entirely of them, he reflected. He possessed another language and literature that they knew not of. And some day Uncle Sam might let go of his island and he would escape from the clutches of that magnificent monster of civilization and retire behind the natural defenses of his island, where the steam-roller of progress could not reach him. Escape he would. He had faith. He had hope. But, oh, what would become of that great mass of black swine, hunted and cornered by slavering white canaille! Sleep! oh, sleep! Down Thought!

But all his senses were burning wide awake. Thought was not a beautiful and reassuring angel, a thing of soothing music and light laughter and winged images glowing with the rare colors of life. No. It was suffering, horribly real. It seized and worried him from every angle. Pushed him toward the sheer precipice of imagination. It was awful. He was afraid. For thought was a terrible tiger clawing at his small portion of gray substance, throttling, tearing, and tormenting him with pitiless ferocity. Oh, a thousand ideas of life were shrieking at him in a wild orgy of mockery! . . .

He was in the middle of a world suspended in space. A familiar line lit up, like a flame, the vast, crowded, immensity of his vision.

Et l'âme du monde est dans l'air.

A moment's respite. . . .

A loud snore from the half-naked chef brought him back to the filthy fact of the quarters that the richest railroad in the world had provided for its black servitors. Ray looked up at Jake, stretched at full length on his side, his cheek in his right hand, sleeping peacefully, like a tired boy after hard playing, so happy and sweet and handsome. He remembered the neatly-folded white papers in Jake's pocket. Maybe that was the cause of his sleeping so soundly. He reached his hand up to the coat hanging on the nail above his head. It was such an innocent little thing—like a headache powder the paper of which you wipe with your tongue, so that none should be wasted. Apparently the first one had no effect and Ray took the rest.

Sleep capitulated.

Immediately he was back home again. His father's house was a vast forest full of blooming hibiscus and mimosas and giant evergreen trees. And he was a gay humming-bird, fluttering and darting his long needle beak into the heart of a bell-flower. Suddenly he changed into an owl flying by day. . . . Howard University was a prison with white warders. . . . Now he was a young shining chief in a marble palace; slim, naked negresses dancing for his pleasure; courtiers reclining on cushions soft like passionate kisses; gleaming-skinned black boys bearing goblets of wine and obedient eunuchs waiting in the offing. . . .

And the world was a blue paradise. Everything was in gorgeous blue of heaven. Woods and streams were blue, and men and women and animals, and beautiful to see and love. And he was a blue bird in flight and a blue lizard in love. And life was all blue happiness. Taboos and terrors and penalties were transformed into new pagan delights, orgies of Orient-blue carnival, of rare flowers and red fruits, cherubs and seraphs and fetishes and phalli and all the most-high gods. . . .

A thousand pins were pricking Ray's flesh and he was shouting for Jake, but his voice was so faint he could not hear himself. Jake had him in his arms and tried to stand him upon his feet. He crumpled up against the bunk. All his muscles were loose, his cells were cold, and the rhythm of being arrested.

It was high morning and time to go to the train. Jake had picked up the empty little folds of paper from the floor and restored them to his pocket. He knew what had happened to them, and guessed why. He went and called the first and fourth waiters.

The chef bulked big in the room, dressed and ready to go to the railroad yards. He gave a contemptuous glance at Jake looking after Ray and said: "Better leave that theah nigger professor alone and come on 'long to the dining-car with us. That theah nigger is dopey from them books o' hisn. I done said befoh them books would git him yet."

The chef went off with the second and fourth cooks. Jake stayed with Ray. They got his shoes and coat on. The first waiter telephoned the steward, and Ray was taken to the hospital.

"We may all be niggers aw'right, but we ain't nonetall all the same," Jake said as he hurried along to the dining-car, thinking of Ray.

SPRING IN HARLEM

THE LOVELY TREES of Seventh Avenue were a vivid flame-green. Children, lightly clad, skipped on the pavement. Light open coats prevailed and the smooth bare throats of brown girls were a token as charming as the first pussy-willows. Far and high over all, the sky was a grand blue benediction, and beneath it the wonderful air of New York tasted like fine dry champagne.

Jake loitered along Seventh Avenue. Crossing to Lenox, he lazied northward and over the One Hundred and Forty-ninth Street bridge into the near neighborhood of the Bronx. Here, just a step from compactly-built, teeming Harlem, were frame houses and open lots and people digging. A colored couple dawdled by, their arms fondly caressing each other's hips. A white man forking a bit of ground stopped and stared expressively after them.

Jake sat down upon a mound thick-covered with dandelions.

They glittered in the sun away down to the rear of a rusty-gray shack. They filled all the green spaces. Oh, the common little things were glorious there under the sun in the tender spring grass. Oh, sweet to be alive in that sun beneath that sky! And to be in love —even for one hour of such rare hours! One day! One night! Somebody with spring charm, like a dandelion, seasonal and haunting like a lovely dream that never repeats itself. . . . There are hours, there are days, and nights whose sheer beauty overwhelm us with happiness, that we seek to make even more beautiful by comparing them with rare human contacts. . . . It was a day like this we romped in the grass . . . a night as soft and intimate as this on which we forgot the world and ourselves. . . . Hours of pagan abandon, celebrating ourselves. . . .

And Jake felt as all men who love love for love's sake can feel. He thought of the surging of desire in his boy's body and of his curious pure nectarine beginnings, without pain, without disgust, down home in Virginia. Of his adolescent breaking-through when the fever-and-pain of passion gave him a wonderful strange-sweet taste of love that he had never known again. Of rude contacts and swift satisfactions in Norfolk, Baltimore, and other coast ports. . . . Havre. . . . The West India Dock districts of London. . . .

"Only that cute heart-breaking brown of the Baltimore," he mused. "A day like this sure feels like her. Didn't even get her name. O Lawdy! what a night that theah night was. Her and I could sure make a hallelujah picnic outa day like this." . . .

Jake and Billy Biasse, leaving Dixie Red's pool-room together, shuffled into a big excited ring of people at the angle of Fifth Avenue and One Hundred and Thirty-third Street. In the ring three bad actors were staging a rough play—a yellow youth, a chocolate youth, and a brown girl.

The girl had worked herself up to the highest pitch of obscene frenzy and was sicking the dark strutter on to the yellow with all the filthiest phrases at her command. The two fellows pranced round, menacing each other with comic gestures.

"Why, ef it ain't Yaller Prince!" said Jake.

"Him sure enough," responded Billy Biasse. "Guess him done laid off from that black gal why she's shooting her stinking mouth off at him."

"Is she one of his producing goods?"

"She was. But I heard she done beat up anether gal of hisn—a fair-brown that useta hand over moh change than her and Yaller turn' her loose foh it." . . .

"You lowest-down face-artist!" the girl shrieked at Yaller Prince. "I'll bawl it out so all a Harlem kain know what you is." And ravished by the fact that she was humiliating her one-time lover, she gesticulated wildly.

"Hit him, Obadiah!" she yelled to the chocolate chap. "Hit him I tell you. Beat his mug up foh him, beat his mug and bleed his mouf." Over and over again she yelled: "Bleed his mouf!" As if that was the thing in Yaller Prince she had desired most. For it she had given herself up to the most unthinkable acts of degradation. Nothing had been impossible to do. And now she would cut and bruise and bleed that mouth that had once loved her so well so that he should not smile upon her rivals for many a day.

"Two-faced yaller nigger, you does ebery low-down thing, but you nevah done a lick of work in you lifetime. Show him, Obadiah. Beat his face and bleed his mouf."

"Yaller nigger," cried the extremely bandy-legged and grim-faced Obadiah, "Ise gwine kick you pants."

"I ain't scared a you, black buzzard," Yaller Prince replied in a thin, breathless voice, and down he went on his back, no one knowing whether he fell or was tripped up. Obadiah lifted a bottle and swung it down upon his opponent. Yaller Prince moaned and blood bubbled from his nose and his mouth.

"He's a sweet-back, all right, but he ain't a strong one," said some one in the crowd. The police had been conspicuously absent during the fracas, but now a baton tap-tapped upon the pavement and two of them hurried up. The crowd melted away.

Jake had pulled Yaller Prince against the wall and squatted to rest the bleeding head against his knee.

"What's matter here now? What's matter?" the first policeman, with revolver drawn, asked harshly.

"Nigger done beat this one up and gone away from heah, tha's whatsmat," said Billy Biasse.

They carried Yaller Prince into a drugstore for first aid, and the policeman telephoned for an ambulance. . . .

"We gotta look out foh him in hospital. He was a pretty good skate for a sweetman," Billy Biasse said.

"Poor Yaller!" Jake, shaking his head, commented; "it's a bad business."

"He's plumb crazy gwine around without a gun when he's a-playing that theah game," said Billy, "with all these cut-thwoat niggers in Harlem ready to carve up one another foh a li'l' insisnificant humpy."

"It's the same ole life everywhere," responded Jake. "In white man's town or nigger town. Same bloody-sweet life across the pond. I done lived through the same blood-battling foh womens ovah theah in London. Between white and white and between white and black. Done see it in the froggies' country, too. A mess o' fat-headed white soldiers them was knocked off by apaches. Don't tell *me* about cut-thwoat niggers in Harlem. The whole wul' is boody-crazy——"

"But Harlem is the craziest place foh that, I bet you, boh," Billy laughed richly. "The stuff it gives the niggers brain-fevah, so far as I see, and this heah wolf has got a big-long horeezon. Wese too thick together in Harlem. Wese all just lumped together without a chanst to choose and so we nacherally hate one another. It's nothing to wonder that you' buddy Ray done runned away from it. Why, jest the other night I witnessed a nasty stroke. You know that spade prof that's always there on the Avenue handing out the big stuff about niggers and their rights and the wul' and bolschism. . . . He was passing by the pool-room with a bunch o' books when a bad nigger jest lunges out and socks him bif! in the jaw. The poah frightened prof. started picking up his books without a word said, so I ups and asks the boxer what was the meaning o' that pass. He laughed and asked me ef I really wanted to know, and before he could squint I landed him one in the eye and pulled mah gun on him. I chased him off that corner all right. I tell you, boh, Harlem is lousy with crazy-bad niggers, as tough as Hell's Kitchen, and I always travel with mah gun ready."

"And ef all the niggers did as you does," said Jake, "theah'd be a regular gun-toting army of us up here in the haht of the white man's city. . . . Guess ef a man stahts gunning after you and means to git you he will someways——"

"But you might git him fierst, too, boh, ef youse in luck."

"I mean ef you don't know he's gunning after you," said Jake. "I don't carry no weapons nonetall, but mah two long hands."

"Youse a punk customer, then, I tell you," declared Billy Biasse, "and no real buddy o' mine. Ise got a A number one little barker I'll give it to you. You kain't lay you'self wide open lak thataways in this heah burg. No boh!"

Jake went home alone in a mood different from the lyrical

feelings that had fevered his blood among the dandelions. "Niggers fixing to slice one another's throats. Always fighting. Got to fight if youse a man. It ain't because Yaller was a p-i. . . . It coulda been me or anybody else. Wese too close and thick in Harlem. Need some moh fresh air between us. . . . Hitting out at a edjucated nigger minding his own business and without a word said. . . . Guess Billy is right toting his silent dawg around with him. He's gotta, though, when he's running a gambling joint. All the same, I gambles mahself and you nevah know when niggers am gwineta git crazy-mad. Guess I'll take the li'l' dawg offn Billy, all right. It ain't costing me nothing." . . .

In the late afternoon he lingered along Seventh Avenue in a new nigger-brown suit. The fine gray English suit was no longer serviceable for parade. The American suit did not fit him so well. Jake saw and felt it. . . . The only thing he liked better about the American suit was the pantaloons made to wear with a belt. And the two hip pockets. If you have the American habit of carrying your facecloth on the hip instead of sticking it up in your breast pocket like a funny decoration, and if, like Billy Biasse, you're accustomed to toting some steely thing, what is handier than two hip pockets?

Except for that, Jake had learned to prefer the English cut of clothes. Such first-rate tweed stuff, and so cheap and durable compared with American clothes! Jake knew nothing of tariff laws and naïvely wondered why the English did not spread their fine cloth all over the American clothes market. . . . He worked up his shoulders in his nigger-brown coat. It didn't feel right, didn't hang so well. There was something a little too chic in American clothes. Not nearly as awful as French, though, Jake horse-laughed, vividly remembering the popular French styles. Broad-pleated, long-waisted, tight-bottomed pants and close-waisted coats whose breast pockets stick out their little comic signs of color. . . . Better color as a savage wears it, or none at all, instead of the Frenchman's peeking bit. The French must consider the average bantam male killing handsome, and so they make clothes to emphasize all the angular elevated rounded and pendulated parts of the anatomy. . . .

The broad pavements of Seventh Avenue were colorful with promenaders. Brown babies in white carriages pushed by little black brothers wearing nice sailor suits. All the various and varying pigmentation of the human race were assembled there: dim brown,

clear brown, rich brown, chestnut, copper, yellow, near-white, mahogany, and gleaming anthracite. Charming brown matrons,
proud yellow matrons, dark nursemaids pulled a zigzag course by
their restive little charges. . . .

And the elegant strutters in faultless spats; West Indians, carrying canes and wearing trousers of a different pattern from their
coats and vests, drawing sharp comments from their Afro-Yank
rivals.

Jake mentally noted: "A dickty gang sure as Harlem is black,
but——"

The girls passed by in bright batches of color, according to
station and calling. High class, menial class, and the big trading
class, flaunting a front of chiffon-soft colors framed in light coats,
seizing the fashion of the day to stage a lovely leg show and spilling
along the Avenue the perfume of Djer-kiss, Fougère, and Brown
Skin.

"These heah New York gals kain most sartainly wear some
moh clothes," thought Jake, "jest as nifty as them French gals." . . .

Twilight was enveloping the Belt, merging its life into a soft
blue-black symphony. . . . The animation subsided into a moment's
pause, a muffled, tremulous soul-stealing note . . . then electric
lights flared everywhere, flooding the scene with dazzling gold.

Jake went to Aunt Hattie's to feed. Billy Biasse was there and a
gang of longshoremen who had boozed and fed and were boozing
again and, touched by the tender spring night, were swapping love
stories and singing:

"Back home in Dixie is a brown gal there,
Back home in Dixie is a brown gal there,
Back home in Dixie is a brown gal there,
    Back home in Dixie I was bawn in.

"Back home in Dixie is a gal I know,
Back home in Dixie is a gal I know,
Back home in Dixie is a gal I know,
    And I wonder what nigger is saying to her a bootiful good
    mawnin'."

A red-brown West Indian among them volunteered to sing a Port-of-Spain song. It immortalized the drowning of a young black sailor. It was made up by the bawdy colored girls of the port, with whom the deceased had been a favorite, and became very popular among the stevedores and sailors of the island.

> "Ring the bell again,
> Ring the bell again,
> Ring the bell again,
> But the sharks won't puke him up.
> Oh, ring the bell again.
>
> "Empty is you' room,
> Empty is you' room,
> Empty is you' room,
> But you find one in the sea.
> Oh, empty is you' room.
>
> "Ring the bell again,
> Ring the bell again,
> Ring the bell again,
> But we know who feel the pain.
> Oh, ring the bell again."

The song was curious, like so many Negro songs of its kind, for the strange strengthening of its wistful melody by a happy rhythm that was suitable for dancing.

Aunt Hattie, sitting on a low chair, was swaying to the music and licking her lips, her wrinkled features wearing an expression of ecstatic delight. Billy Biasse offered to stand a bottle of gin. Jake said he would also sing a sailor song he had picked up in Limehouse. And so he sang the chanty of Bullocky Bill who went up to town to see a fair young maiden. But he could not remember most of the words, therefore Bullocky Bill cannot be presented here. But Jake was boisterously applauded for the scraps of it that he rendered.

The singing finished, Jake confided to Billy: "I sure don't feel lak spending a lonesome night this heah mahvelous night."

"Ain't nobody evah lonely in Harlem that don't wanta be,"

retorted Billy. "Even yours truly lone Wolf ain't nevah lonesome."

"But I want something as mahvelous as mah feelings."

Billy laughed and fingered his kinks: "Harlem has got the right stuff, boh, for all feelings."

"Youse right enough," Jake agreed, and fell into a reverie of full brown mouth and mischievous brown eyes all composing a perfect whole for his dark-brown delight.

"You wanta take a turn down the Congo?" asked Billy.

"Ah no."

"Rose ain't there no moh."

Rose had stepped up a little higher in her profession and had been engaged to tour the West in a Negro company.

"All the same, I don't feel like the Congo tonight," said Jake. "Le's go to Sheba Palace and jazz around a little."

Sheba Palace was an immense hall that was entirely monopolized for the amusements of the common workaday Negroes of the Belt. Longshoremen, kitchen-workers, laundresses, and W. C. tenders—all gravitated to the Sheba Palace, while the upper class of servitors—bell-boys, butlers, some railroad workers and waiters, waitresses and maids of all sorts—patronized the Casino and those dancings that were given under the auspices of the churches.

The walls of Sheba Palace were painted with garish gold, and tables and chairs were screaming green. There were green benches also lined round the vast dancing space. The music stopped with an abrupt clash just as Jake entered. Couples and groups were drinking at tables. Deftly, quickly the waiters slipped a way through the tables to serve and collect the money before the next dance. . . . Little white-filled glasses, little yellow-filled glasses, general guzzling of gin and whisky. Little saucy brown lips, rouged maroon, sucking up iced crème de menthe through straws, and many were sipping the golden Virginia Dare, in those days the favorite wine of the Belt. On the green benches couples lounged, sprawled, and, with the juicy love of spring and the liquid of Bacchus mingled in fascinating white eyes curious in their dark frames, apparently oblivious of everything outside of themselves, were loving in every way but . . .

The orchestra was tuning up. . . . The first notes fell out like a general clapping for merrymaking and chased the dancers running, sliding, shuffling, trotting to the floor. Little girls energetically chewing Spearmint and showing all their teeth dashed out on the floor and started shivering amorously, itching for their partners to come. Some lads were quickly on their feet, grinning gayly and improvising new steps with snapping of fingers while their girls were sucking up the last of their crème de menthe. The floor was large and smooth enough for anything.

They had a new song-and-dance at the Sheba and the black fellows were playing it with *éclat.*

> Brown gal crying on the corner,
> Yaller gal done stole her candy,
> Buy him spats and feed him cream,
> Keep him strutting fine and dandy.

> Tell me, pa-pa, Ise you' ma-ma,
> Yaller gal can't make you fall,
> For Ise got some loving pa-pa
> Yaller gal ain't got atall.

"Tell me, pa-pa, Ise you' ma-ma." The black players grinned and swayed and let the music go with all their might. The yellow in the music must have stood out in their imagination like a challenge, conveying a sense of that primitive, ancient, eternal, inexplicable antagonism in the color taboo of sex and society. The dark dancers picked up the refrain and jazzed and shouted with delirious joy, "Tell me, pa-pa, Ise you' ma-ma." The handful of yellow dancers in the crowd were even more abandoned to the spirit of the song. "White," "green," or "red" in place of "yaller" might have likewise touched the same deep-sounding, primitive chord. . . .

> Yaller gal sure wants mah pa-pa,
> But mah chocolate turns her down,
> 'Cause he knows there ain't no loving
> Sweeter than his loving brown.

> Tell me, pa-pa, Ise you' ma-ma,
> Yaller gal can't make you fall,
> For Ise got some loving pa-pa
> Yaller gal ain't got atall.

Jake was doing his dog with a tall, shapely quadroon girl when, glancing up at the balcony, he spied the little brown that he had entirely given over as lost. She was sitting at a table while "Tell me pa-pa" was tickling everybody to the uncontrollable point—she was sitting with her legs crossed and well exposed, and, with the aid of the mirror attached to her vanity case, was saucily and nonchalantly powdering her nose.

The quadroon girl nearly fell as Jake, without a word of explanation, dropped her in the midst of a long slide and, dashing across the floor, bounded up the stairs.

"Hello, sweetness! What youse doing here?"

The girl started and knocked over a glass of whisky on the floor: "O my Gawd! it's mah heartbreaking daddy! Where was you all this time?"

Jake drew a chair up beside her, but she jumped up: "Lawdy, no! Let's get outa here quick, 'cause Ise got somebody with me and now I don't want see him no moh."

"Sawright, I kain take care of mahself," said Jake.

"Oh, honey, no! I don't want no trouble and he's a bad actor, that nigger. See, I done break his glass o' whisky and tha's bad luck. Him's just theah in the lav'try. Come quick. I don't want him to ketch us."

And the flustered little brown heart hustled Jake down the stairs and out of the Sheba Palace.

"Tell me, pa-pa, Ise you' ma-ma . . ."

The black shouting chorus pursued them outside.

"There ain't no yaller gal gwine get mah honey daddy thisa-night." She took Jake's arm and cuddled up against his side.

"Aw no, sweetness. I was dogging it with one and jest drops her flat when I seen you."

"And there ain't no nigger in the wul' I wouldn't ditch foh you, daddy. O Lawdy! How Ise been crazy longing to meet you again."

FROM *BANJO*

BANJO'S ACE OF SPADES

RAY TEASED BANJO about going as a seaman to the West Indies so soon after he had turned down a free trip to the United States. He predicted that Banjo would follow his nose to the States in quick time, for he would find the islands too small and sleepy for him.

"I'm gwine along with the gang, pardner, and tha's a different thing from going back with Goosey. This heah is like a big picnic for all of us. If youse wise, you'll join in with us."

The boys scraped, scrubbed, painted. They got only twenty francs a day, although the regular wage for such work was over thirty francs. But they were beach boys and not union men. And the union bosses had no knowledge of what was going on on the little boat. There is sometimes much free-for-all work on the docks. However, the boys did not allow *their* work to push them hard. They made shift to get through it. It would be different when they signed on. Then they would get the union wages of British seamen.

The African Café, The Rendezvous Bar, The bistro-cabaret in the Rue Coin du Reboul—all of them nightly did well with the boys. The Ditch looked at them differently, for they measured up to and above the "leetah" standards.

At last the boat was shipshape and ready to sail. The day came when the boys were called to sign on. Ray could have had an easy place, but he would not take it and he watched Banjo sign a little wistfully. They all had the right, under British Seamen's Regulations, to take part of their month's wages in advance. Each of the boys availed himself of this, that he might buy needful articles. Banjo took a full month's wages.

They cashed their cheques with a seamen's broker in Joliette. That night they had a big celebration. But Banjo was not with them. Nor had he used any of his money to buy new things. He invited Ray to go with him to a quiet little café in Joliette, and there he announced that he was not going to make the trip.

"And Ise gwine beat it outa this burg some convenient time this very night, pardner. Tha's mah ace a spades so sure as Ise a spade. You come along with me?"

Not going on the ship. . . . Beat it. . . . Come along with me.

"But you've signed on and taken a month's wages," protested Ray. "You can't quit now."

"Nix and a zero for what I kain't do. Go looket that book and you won't find mah real name no moh than anybody is gwine find this nigger when I take mahself away from here. I ask you again, Is you going with me?"

Ray did not reply, and after a silence Banjo said: "I know youse thinking it ain't right. But we kain't afford to choose, because we ain't born and growed up like the choosing people. All we can do is grab our chance every time it comes our way."

Ray's thoughts were far and away beyond the right and wrong of the matter. He had been dreaming of what joy it would be to go vagabonding with Banjo. Stopping here and there, staying as long as the feeling held in the ports where black men assembled for the great transport lines, loafing after their labors long enough to laugh and love and jazz and fight.

While Banjo's words brought him back to social morality, they brought him back only to the realization of how thoroughly he was in accord with them. He had associated too closely with the beach boys not to realize that their loose, instinctive way of living was more deeply related to his own self-preservation than all the principles, or social-morality lessons with which he had been inculcated by the wiseacres of the civilized machine.

It seemed a social wrong to him that, in a society rooted and thriving on the principles of the "struggle for existence" and the "survival of the fittest" a black child should be brought up on the same code of social virtues as the white. Especially an American black child.

A Chinese or Indian child could learn the stock virtues without being spiritually harmed by them, because he possessed his own native code from which he could draw, compare, accept, and reject while learning. But the Negro child was a pathetic thing, entirely cut off from its own folk wisdom and earnestly learning the trite moralisms of a society in which he was, as a child and would be as an adult, denied any legitimate place.

Ray was not of the humble tribe of humanity. But he always felt humble when he heard the Senegalese and other West African tribes speaking their own languages with native warmth and feeling.

The Africans gave him a positive feeling of wholesome contact with racial roots. They made him feel that he was not merely an unfortunate accident of birth, but that he belonged definitely to a race weighed, tested, and poised in the universal scheme. They inspired him with confidence in them. Short of extermination by the Europeans, they were a safe people, protected by their own indigenous culture. Even though they stood bewildered before the imposing bigness of white things, apparently unaware of the invaluable worth of their own, they were naturally defended by the richness of their fundamental racial values.

He did not feel that confidence about Aframericans who, long-deracinated, were still rootless among phantoms and pale shadows and enfeebled by self-effacement before condescending patronage, social negativism, and miscegenation. At college in America and among the Negro intelligentsia he had never experienced any of the simple, natural warmth of a people believing in themselves, such as he had felt among the rugged poor and socially backward blacks of his island home. The colored intelligentsia lived its life "to have the white neighbors think well of us," so that it could move more peaceably into nice "white" streets.

Only when he got down among the black and brown working boys and girls of the country did he find something of that raw unconscious and the-devil-with-them pride in being Negro that was his own natural birthright. Down there the ideal skin was brown skin. Boys and girls were proud of their brown, sealskin brown, teasing brown, tantalizing brown, high-brown, low-brown, velvet brown, chocolate brown.

There was the amusing little song they all sang:

> "Black may be evil,
> But Yellow is so low-down;
> White is the devil,
> So glad I'm teasing Brown."

Among them was never any of the hopeless, enervating talk of the chances of "passing white" and the specter of the Future that were the common topics of the colored intelligentsia. Close association with the Jakes and Banjoes had been like participating in a common primitive birthright.

Ray loved to be with them in constant physical contact, keeping warm within. He loved their tricks of language, loved to pick up and feel and taste new words from their rich reservoir of niggerisms. He did not like rotten-egg stock words among rough peo-

ple any more than he liked colorless refined phrases among nice
people. He did not even like to hear cultured people using the
conventional stock words of the uncultured and thinking they were
being free and modern. That sounded vulgar to him.

But he admired the black boys' unconscious artistic capacity
for eliminating the rotten-dead stock words of the proletariat and
replacing them with startling new ones. There were no dots and
dashes in their conversation—nothing that could not be frankly
said and therefore decently—no act or fact of life for which they
could not find a simple passable word. He gained from them finer
nuances of the necromancy of language and the wisdom that any
word may be right and magical in its proper setting.

He loved their natural gusto for living down the past and lifting their kinky heads out of the hot, suffocating ashes, the shadow,
the terror of real sorrow to go on gaily grinning in the present.
Never had Ray guessed from Banjo's general manner that he had
known any deep sorrow. Yet when he heard him tell Goosey that
he had seen his only brother lynched, he was not surprised, he
understood, because right there he had revealed the depths of his
soul and the soul of his race—the true tropical African Negro. No
Victorian-long period of featured grief and sable mourning, no
mechanical-pale graveside face, but a luxuriant living up from it,
like the great jungles growing perennially beautiful and green in
the yellow blaze of the sun over the long life-breaking tragedy of
Africa.

Ray had felt buttressed by the boys with a rough strength and
sureness that gave him spiritual passion and pride to be his human
self in an inhumanly alien world. They lived healthily far beyond
the influence of the colored press whose racial dope was characterized by pungent "bleach-out," "kink-no-more," skin-whitening,
hair-straightening, and innumerable processes for Negro culture,
most of them manufactured by white men's firms in the cracker
states. And thereby they possessed more potential power for racial
salvation than the Negro *litterati*, whose poverty of mind and purpose showed never any signs of enrichment, even though inflated
above the common level and given an appearance of superiority.

From these boys he could learn how to live—how to exist as
a black boy in a white world and rid his conscience of the used-
up hussy of white morality. He could not scrap his intellectual life
and be entirely like them. He did not want or feel any urge to "go
back" that way.

Tolstoy, his great master, had turned his back on the intellect as guide to find himself in Ivan Durak. Ray wanted to hold on to his intellectual acquirements without losing his instinctive gifts. The black gifts of laughter and melody and simple sensuous feelings and responses.

Once when a friend gave him a letter of introduction to a Nordic intellectual, he did not write: I think you will like to meet this young black intellectual; but rather, I think you might like to hear Ray laugh.

His gift! He was of course aware that whether the educated man be white or brown or black, he cannot, if he has more than animal desires, be irresponsibly happy like the ignorant man who lives simply by his instincts and appetites. Any man with an observant and contemplative mind must be aware of that. But a black man, even though educated, was in closer biological kinship to the swell of primitive earth life. And maybe his apparent failing under the organization of the modern world was the real strength that preserved him from becoming the thing that was the common white creature of it.

Ray had found that to be educated, black and his instinctive self was something of a big job to put over. In the large cities of Europe he had often met with educated Negroes out for a good time with heavy literature under their arms. They toted these books to protect themselves from being hailed everywhere as minstrel niggers, coons, funny monkeys for the European audience—because the general European idea of the black man is that he is a public performer. Some of them wore hideous parliamentary clothes as close as ever to the pattern of the most correctly gray respectability. He had remarked wiry students and Negroes doing clerical work wearing glasses that made them sissy-eyed. He learned, on inquiry, that wearing glasses was a mark of scholarship and respectability differentiating them from the common types. . . . (Perhaps the police would respect the glasses.)

No getting away from the public value of clothes, even for you, my black friend. As it was, ages before Carlyle wrote *Sartor Resartus,* so it will be long ages after. And you have reason maybe to be more rigidly formal, as the world seems illogically critical of you since it forced you to discard so recently your convenient fig leaf for its breeches. This civilized society is classified and kept going by clothes and you are now brought by its power to labour and find a place in it.

The more Ray mixed in the rude anarchy of the lives of the black boys—loafing, singing, bumming, playing, dancing, loving, working—and came to a realization of how close-linked he was to them in spirit, the more he felt that they represented more than he or the cultured minority the irrepressible exuberance and legendary vitality of the black race. And the thought kept him wondering how that race would fare under the ever tightening mechanical organization of modern life.

Being sensitively receptive, he had as a boy become interested in and followed with passionate sympathy all the great intellectual and social movements of his age. And with the growth of international feelings and ideas he had dreamed of the association of his race with the social movements of the masses of civilization milling through the civilized machine.

But traveling away from America and visiting many countries, observing and appreciating the differences of human groups, making contact with earthy blacks of tropical Africa, where the great body of his race existed, had stirred in him the fine intellectual prerogative of doubt.

The grand mechanical march of civilization had leveled the world down to the point where it seemed treasonable for an advanced thinker to doubt that what was good for one nation or people was also good for another. But as he was never afraid of testing ideas, so he was not afraid of doubting. All peoples must struggle to live, but just as what was helpful for one man might be injurious to another, so it might be with whole communities of peoples.

For Ray happiness was the highest good, and difference the greatest charm, of life. The hand of progress was robbing his people of many primitive and beautiful qualities. He could not see where they would find greater happiness under the weight of the machine even if progress became left-handed.

Many apologists of a changed and magnified machine system doubted whether the Negro could find a decent place in it. Some did not express their doubts openly, for fear of "giving aid to the enemy." Ray doubted, and openly.

Take, for example, certain Nordic philosophers, as the world was more or less Nordic business: He did not think the blacks would come very happily under the supermechanical Anglo-Saxon-controlled world society of Mr. H. G. Wells. They might shuffle along, but without much happiness in the world of Bernard Shaw.

Perhaps they would have their best chance in a world influenced by the thought of a Bertrand Russell, where brakes were clamped on the machine with a few screws loose and some nuts fallen off. But in this great age of science and super-invention was there any possibility of arresting the thing unless it stopped of its own exhaustion?

"Well, what you say, pardner?" demanded Banjo. "Why you jest sidown theah so long studying ovah nothing at all? You gwine with a man or you ain't?"

"Why didn't you tell me before, so I could have signed on like you and make a getaway mahself?"

"Because I wasn't so certain sure a you. Youse a book fellah and you' mind might tell you to do one thing and them books persweahs you to do another. So I wouldn't take no chances. And maybe it's bettah only one of us do this thing this time. Now wese bettah acquainted, theah's a lotta things befoh us we'll have to make together."

"It would have been a fine thing if we could have taken Latnah along, eh?"

"Don't get soft ovah any one wimmens, pardner. Tha's you' big weakness. A woman is a conjunction. Gawd fixed her different from us in moh ways than one. And theah's things we can git away with all the time and she just kain't. Come on, pardner. Wese got enough between us to beat it a long ways from here."

FROM *BANANA BOTTOM*

THE TIME FIXED FOR THE WEDDING was drawing near. Yoni, who was nursing a plump little baby and was still unmarried, asked Bita if she had any objection to their getting married together. The two young women had become great friends again and Bita thought it would be a pretty thing to have a double wedding. And as Bita's house was larger and better appointed she suggested to Yoni to make one big wedding feast in her house.

Belle Black came from Jubilee to spend a month with Bita and help with the preparations for the wedding. And she and Bita and Yoni went up to the city of Kingston to stay a few days and buy their wedding clothes. When Bita was at Jubilee and visited the city with the Craigs, the party always stayed in a private house with white friends of the Craigs'. But travelling to the chief town independently, she was troubled about finding a decent place to stay in with her friends.

For all the respectable hotels and boarding-houses (most of them owned or managed by light-skinned coloured people) had developed a policy of excluding black or dark-brown guests. For such guests the hotels were either always filled up or if there were vacant rooms they were always reserved. In some quarters it was said that American tourists had determined the policy because they objected to the presence of dark-coloured persons in the hotels in which they stayed. Jamaica was developing a good business in American tourist trade and could not afford to ruin that business by being fair and decent to the people who made up the overwhelming majority of its population.

But the trouble went deeper than that in reality. The social life of the colony was rooted upon shade and colour prejudice. During the epoch of slavery the lighter-skinned offspring of white men and black women had privileges that the black slaves had not. Although the Eurafricans were slaves the majority of them were attached to the masters' households, while the blacks worked in the fields. Many of the Eurafrican children were sent abroad to be educated by their fathers and some in time came into possession of landed property and even became slave-owners themselves. Pretty and elegant Eurafrican girls invariably became the mistresses of white planters and it is recorded that they were even sold at fancy prices by their fathers for that purpose.

With their limited privileges, although they were not free, the Eurafricans constituted a group and looked down with contempt upon the pure-blooded Africans and in time multiplied in numbers to form a distinct middle class between the planter and governing classes and the slaves.

When slavery was abolished in the British West Indies the Eurafricans by their education and experience were in a favourable position to take advantage of the great social change. Many of the abandoned estates finally passed into their hands, the educated ones qualified for the higher professions and were employed in the Government services, and the smaller white-collar jobs such as those of clerks and shopgirls were reserved for the poorer ones. The women were no longer compelled to be the mistresses of white masters and the Eurafricans developed a strong group pride, marrying almost exclusively among themselves and reproducing and rearing their own kind.

But as the Eurafricans developed in wealth and power they also approximated to the social standards and attitudes of the white planters with little sympathy for the freed blacks and their problems, their struggles for social adjustment, and so there had developed between Europeans and Eurafricans on one side a system of social discrimination against the expatriate Africans.

Bita had been advised by Squire Gensir to go to a moderate-priced hotel in which he always stayed when visiting the city. He gave her a note to the owner. Squire Gensir was aware of the discriminations, notably in the city, against black persons, but the owner of that particular hotel happened to be a dark-brown man and he gave Bita a note to him. But this man, according to the general custom, employed as manager a light-coloured woman and he was away in the country when Bita arrived in the city with her friends.

The housekeeper was a haughty woman whose naturally snobbish manner became overbearing when she saw that her would-be guests were black country people who had presumed to think that they could find accommodation at the hotel where she worked. She did not politely say that there were no rooms vacant, but frankly told Bita that that hotel did not accept black persons as guests.

One such rebuff was enough for Bita. She went with Yoni and Belle Black to a cheap unpleasant hotel where decent black persons who could afford to pay for better accommodation were mixed indiscriminately with bad-mannered light-skinned ones and nondescripts who found there their natural element.

Bita wrote to Squire Gensir about her plight and he arrived in the city by the next afternoon's train. The hotel-owner had returned from his visit to the country. Squire Gensir protested to him against the manner in which the young black women were treated and said he was ashamed that such conditions should exist in Jamaica. The hotel-owner apologized, pointing out that he was not at the hotel when the incident occurred, ashamed that in a matter involving Negroes and mulattoes a white man had to intervene to obtain fair treatment for the Negroes. The housekeeper was discharged and Bita, Belle Black and Yoni were given accommodation in the hotel.

Smarting from the insult offered by the yellow woman, Belle Black was in a militant mood and staged a scene when she went with Bita and Yoni to sample the wedding fabrics. They had gone to a large shop in the main business street and as they needed a lot of things the head lady clerk had been assigned to wait upon them.

The head lady clerk was a very gracious, sunny-smiling light-coloured person and seeing that the girls were going to get a wedding trousseau she began exchanging pleasantries with them about marriage.

But while the lady clerk was attending to the girls an octoroon woman, an important customer, entered the shop and addressed herself to her. The woman was accustomed to being served always by that clerk and as she wanted only a small thing the lady clerk excused herself, asking the girls to wait awhile, and went to serve the constant customer.

In a resentful spirit Belle Black interpreted that as a slight towards her and her companions and she turned loose a mitrailleuse of angry protest in the shop.

"Wha' de debbil you mean leabin' us waiting yah fer sarve dat udder woman fust becausen har skin im yaller lak a boil' pumpkin? . . .

"Doan come givin' me any a you' p'lite excuse dem. We was de fust one heah an' we ought to be de fust sarve', becausen we money is as good as anybody elsen money. All unno mulatto niggers am all de same to me. You t'ink youse dat big t'ing dressin' up on six shilling a week, but lemme tell you I cyan't see you. In de country where ah come from you got to show some'n' moh'n a li'l' turn colour to make class. You got to be somet'ing, you got to hab somet'ing.

"Eh, eh! Ku yah though. Ah nebber heah nor seen such a shitination in mi life. Becausen you turn-colour niggers am wearing a standin' collar an' a silk blouse ebery day in de yahr you becomin' to t'inkin' youse de angels demself round' de t'rone of de Lawd Gawd. But lemme tell unno all dat you ain't nuttin' at all but a lotta cans full a somet'ing dat ain't sugar."

The manager of the shop tried to assure Belle Black that it was all a mistake, that he would never countenance any discrimination against black people in his shop because as a group they were his biggest and most important customers, and that the only colour that mattered in his shop was the colour of money.

The manager spoke truly, for prejudices and discriminations

in business can easily stand an economic interpretation and the people who practice them are mean and violently unreasonable because they hate to refuse any kind of money and do so only because acceptance might cause them to lose much more than they receive.

But Belle Black was not appeased and calling Bita and Yoni to follow her she flounced out of the shop.

Came the wedding day. The double wedding. Bita and Jubban, Yoni and Hopping Dick. The marriage ceremonies were to take place at Gingertown. And there was to be a cavalcade. The peasants loved nothing so much as a wedding with many horses, and couples belonging to the same village and who were marrying often preferred to get married away from home at some important place to which they would go riding and return home triumphant on horseback.

Bita also desired to go to Gingertown because she did not want to be married by the Reverend Lambert. The Lamberts had been exceeding tongue-loose about her marriage to Jubban. During a discussion of the matter the Reverend Lambert, accusing Bita of burying her talent and education in the mud, had said that he would be ashamed to perform the marriage ceremony. This was repeated to Bita and irritated her. Also the elder Miss Lambert had said that Bita was a disgrace to all intelligent and high-aiming Negroes. Not only did Bita not want the Reverend Lambert to officiate at the ceremony, but she had not even extended the courtesy of an invitation to any of the family.

Teacher Fearon had pointed out to the Reverend Lambert that Squire Gensir approved of Bita. But that was no recommendation to the Reverend gentleman, who called Squire Gensir a decadent in the literal sense of the word. To the Reverend Lambert Squire Gensir, interested in the collecting of the transplanted African fairy tales and the ditties in dialect of the tea-meetings and of field workers and draymen, was in no sense an inspiring person. Squire Gensir was an unprogressive person, looking backwards, while the minister considered himself a progressive man, forward-looking. He believed in progress for Negroes and preached it according to the lights of his intellect and he could not see any indications of progress in Squire Gensir's work and his atheism nor that they could be beneficial to Negroes in any way.

The marriages were celebrated in the Congregational church

at Gingertown. On the morning of the wedding Jordan Plant's yard, in which the guests had assembled, had the aspect of a horse fair with prancing and neighing stallions and fillies, pawing ponies, stout draught horses and mules.

There were not enough side-saddles in the hill region for the women riders and some who were expert used male saddles, riding sideways. Many used long Indian shawls as riding-habits to cover their frocks. The lovely shawls were much in use among the peasant women as a decorative article of dress.

As Jubban's best man Squire Gensir was among the guests and he was the poorest-dressed man there. While all the young and older men were suited out in broadcloth, serges, tweeds and cutaways and stiff-starched collars, Squire Gensir was at his ease in a brown linen suit and soft shirt, the coolest of them all in that torrid climate.

The cavalcade proceeded in orderly fashion but at a slow enough and almost solemn pace to Gingertown. But it was a great ride back home. The company broke up into cantering and galloping groups along the long level stretches and some matched horses racing.

On the road between Gingertown and Bull's Hoof Bita was galloping along with Teacher Fearon and his wife, Squire Gensir and Jubban, when her horse suddenly bolted down a track leading to a valley. The road there skirted a mountainside and it was a sharp incline down which the horse abruptly started. Bita had a terrible jolt but managed to keep her seat and her head and hold on while the horse raced furiously down the dangerous track. She could not think of controlling him, but only to sit tightly. When the horse reached the gully in the valley he leaped clear of it, but the path turned up a hill and then Bita was able to control him. The men had followed her but were unable to make good headway down the narrow dangerous path. Now they came up alarmed at Bita's state and wondering if she were hurt. But Bita, smiling, demonstrated to them that she was all right by giving the whip to the pony and forcing him to take the hill at full gallop back to the main road.

The wedding feast was served in a vast palm booth erected over Jordan Plant's biggest barbecue. In it were fixed bamboo poles and beams upon which rough boards were laid on which the food was piled. Roast pigs, roast fowls, goat meat, broad dishes of yams, yamies, cocoes and ripe plantains. Fancy loaves of bread. Orange wine, port wine, kola wine, Jamaica rum. Ginger beer for children and teetotallers. And four pyramids of daintily decorated cakes: two for Bita and two for Yoni.

After the cutting of the cake, in which bridesmaids competed, the toasts were proposed with the drinking of the wine. Teacher Fearon was toastmaster and perfectly acted his part. He began by toasting himself first, then the brides and bridegrooms and all Banana Bottom. He called upon Squire Gensir, who made a short speech saying that although he was a bachelor in the bone he could enjoy a happy wedding. Superintendent Delgado also made a speech. But the toast of the toasts was Hopping Dick's. Evidently Hopping Dick thought it was his duty to say something for Jubban too who had waived his right to make a speech.

Hopping Dick spoke facing Bita, Belle Black and Yoni sitting together, and a little ways from them Anty Nommy and Ma Legge bearing in her arms the angel baby. "Ladies and Gen'lemens

"There is no moh wonnerful t'ing in a man life than de day when im get himse'f a wife. A man may go chasing over the wul' lak a tomcat, but de day will come him gwine fin' somet'ing fer hold him down at home. An' it'll be a most happy day ef him get the right pusson de right way. But nobody knows 'bouten dat in de beginning. Ef one yahr pass an' gone any a mi frien's them did tell me ah would be steadyin' mese'f an' hookin' up an' settlin' comfably wid a sweet-lovin' woman I woulda answer him: youse crazy all ways in an' out excepn' none.

"Yet heah I is now hand an' foot an' eberyt'ing in what ah use to say was no man's business. But it's bettah me boys: bettah than runnin' from pillar to post like a mawgar dawg, cracking ebery bone an' always hungry when de dawgs them dat stays at home am growing fat in one place eatin' outa de same ole bowl ebery day, an' a rovin' Rover jest goes on rovin' until him finish up wid gettin' dat tail cut off.

"Yes, ah tell you all, ladies an' gen'lemens, this is one moh mawhvellous mekin' an' turnin' day fer me. An' Ise got fer t'ank Gawd an' de Chu'ch and mi Christian bredderin an' Banana Bottom fer it. And as de udder bridegroom which is de biggest one him refusing fer say anyt'ing but jest contented enough an' nacherally fer gettin' Godsendin' him de most beautiful flowahs in Banana Bottom an' all a Jamaica (an' ah want nobody fer vex cause I say it's de trute) ah wi' jest say fer him dat him is de one luckiest man in de wul'.

"Jest lak a outside horse dat nobody woulda bet on winnin' de race; jest lak a pusson you nebber bliebe could do it walkin' off at de end of de show wid de prize. Yessir, ah got to tek off mi hat again an' mek a low bow to mi frien' de udder bridegroom. An' ah got to admit it him is a bigger affair than mese'f.

"What big-big mens, doctohs an' lawyahs an' teachahs an' preachahs b'en mout'-waterin' fer, beggin' an' beseechin' an' nebber could a get—dat was gived as a free gift to mi breddah bridegroom, Jubban. Ah must gib him de glad hand a congratulations." [Hopping Dick stretched across the festive board and grasped Jubban's hand.] "An' ah want fer declare publicly and graciously fer Jubilee an' all fer hear an' bliebe dat I doan' bear de biggest bridegroom no grudge. An' ah gwine to finish by callin' fer t'ree cheers fer de two bride an' de two bridegroom."

The guests cheered as heartily for the speech as they did for the brides and bridegrooms. After the feasting the boards were removed and the booth cleared for dancing. The dancing went on all the late afternoon until evening, when a great crowd which could not be accommodated at the feast came to Bita's house to dance. All the young village were there and the crowds overflowed the palm booth and the house and spread out on the barbecues.

That evening when the dancing was at its height one group of young men got hold of Hopping Dick and another of Jubban and repaired to the grog-shop proprietor's house. The grog shop was a part of the same building as the proprietor's house and the proprietor let in the company at his back door and served them drinks.

It was a custom to get a young bridegroom away from the bride on the first night of their marriage and fill him up with liquor, and if he got drunk he was locked in and left under the table to sleep all night by himself.

The lads succeeded with Hopping Dick. He drank round after round, mixing the drinks, wine, porter and rum, and regaled the young rustics with lively tales of the small town and its smarter life: of gay parties and drinking bouts, horse-dealing and card-dealing, how the town bucks used to get after the country girls in the market shed in which the girls came to rest and sleep on Friday nights in preparation for the Saturday market.

And while Hopping Dick was laughing with his companions over his jokes one of them shook off his cigar ash into Hopping Dick's glass. There was a saying that tobacco ashes in liquor could get a man drunk quicker than anything. The trick brought an uproarious outburst from those who saw it and Hopping Dick joined in slapping his thigh, thinking that the laughter was because of his joke. The trick was repeated more than once. At last Hopping Dick, weary after a strenuous day's riding and feasting, was swaying sleepy drunk and the fellows laid him out under the table and soon he began snoring.

Jubban had drank nothing but orange wine, refusing to change or mix the drink. He was nice with the fellows, but he was never a man for gay company, and there was something about him that kept them from making as free with him as with Hopping Dick. Now he heaved up, shook himself like a bear, said good-bye to his cheerful companions and strode home.

Late that night or rather before dawn after the dancing was ended, Bita was wakened by subdued singing under her bedroom window. It was the village choir singing the anthem: "Break Forth into Joy." Distinctly she heard Belle Black's treble and recognized Teacher Fearon's voice. She shook Jubban softly out of his heavy sleep so that he too should hear.

That was Teacher Fearon's gift, Bita thought. How beautiful it was, that low singing below her window just before dawn! Oh, it made her happy. Those singing voices were the most beautiful gift of all.

The "Return Thanks" was the closing event of a country wedding. It always took place the Sunday following the wedding, when the married couple and near relatives proceeded in ceremonial fashion to the local church and returned thanks to God for the happy celebration of their union.

As Jubban's best man, Squire Gensir also went to church. And it was the first time he had ever entered a church to sit under a sermon since he became a freethinker. That day he presented his horse to Jubban. He explained to Bita, in making the gift, that riding so hard the day of the wedding had stirred up memories of his fox-hunting days. They were disturbing and he had decided that he did not need a horse any more. No doubt Jubban could make better use of the horse than he.

Bita replied that if the memories were pleasant ones, she thought it was fine to remember them. But Squire Gensir replied that he did not want to be in constant contact with things that reminded him too forcibly of a past he had renounced.

Not long after that the squire announced that he would have to return to England. Bita noticed that he was not his usual quiet composed self. There was a trace of agitation in him. He had been more than twenty years away from England and he did not want to return there. He had always said he wanted to end his days and be buried in the tropical soil of his adopted land.

But a spinster sister to whom he was devoted and who had been ailing a long time had expressed a desire again and again to see him once more. Squire Gensir was conscience-worried, for his relatives thought that the sister was going to die. And so he felt that it was his bounden duty to go.

He went promising to return again. The key of the cottage at Breakneck was left in Bita's care, so that she could avail herself of the use of the piano. The Negro village was sad about the going of Squire Gensir. But he promised to return again. He said that he wanted to come back again to finish his work on the native folk-lore. He had already done three books, but he was planning a larger and more comprehensive one. And besides his work he loved that island and loved its common people as a whole with their good qualities and bad, their earthy common sense and their gentle humour and futile superstitions.

But he never returned. . . .

One twilight Bita and Anty Nommy were startled by a sudden harsh cackling of many fowls and their flying up in the air and over the barbecue like wild birds. Anty Nommy remarked that that was a sure sign of death and began worrying about Bab somewhere in Panama or the United States, from whom she had not had any news for a long time. Bita mocked at Anty Nommy's superstition and said that if people were always sent signs of death one would have been received for the double drowning of Jordan Plant and Malcolm Craig.

But a few weeks later Bita had news of the death of Squire Gensir, and Anty Nommy, figuring up the days, said the death had occurred about the same time the fowls acted so strangely. But Bita was unconvinced.

Squire Gensir had arrived home in the late fall in time to see his sister die. Dreading a long ocean voyage in the winter, he had planned to return to the tropics in the spring. But the northern winter was too hard upon his ageing bones after his long sojourn in the tropics. And so he had succumbed under its rigours.

Bita's sadness was tempered by the knowledge that Squire

Gensir may have had some consolation dying among his own people that he might have missed in his adopted land, the early associations and memories of childhood that cling to the stoic wanderer until the end. He had seemed to her, after all, in spite of his free and easy contacts with the peasants, a lonely man living a lonely life. And although the peasants admired him, his high intellect and acute intelligence precluded him from sinking himself entirely in the austere simplicity of peasant life.

Having the key to the bungalow at Breakneck, Bita continued to go there to play the piano. She had heard nothing definite from the squire's relatives and wondered what would be the ultimate disposal of the house and things. But one day she received a communication from a bank in the city. Squire Gensir had left her the lot of land and the house with everything in it and five hundred pounds in the local bank.

Squire Gensir had always felt that he was instrumental a little for Bita's turning away from the rigid life of the mission, asserting her independence and finally breaking with the Craigs. Touched by the gift and overcome by emotion Bita could not restrain her tears. She shut herself in her room and cried.

She thought of the effect the knowledge of Squire Gensir's bequest would have upon the Lamberts and all her other detractors. They would be sure to find virtue now in the manner in which she had acted. They had talked so much about her irreparable mistake when it became known that Mrs. Craig had given all her money to the Society for the Prevention of Cruelty to Animals. Now she felt that she was amply compensated for whatever material benefit she may have sacrificed by quitting Jubilee.

In the cool of the late afternoon Bita walked over to Breakneck and visited the Hut. The housegirl had been cleaning and dusting it regularly twice a week. Things were in their place just as Squire Gensir had left them: books and magazines, the rough, ink-stained writing-table and the piano.

It gave her an uncanny feeling to think that he would never come back to touch those things again. Never sit down to the piano, and that she would never again hear his voice—that finest thing about his insignificant little body, which had opened the way for him into the deep, obscure heart of the black peasantry.

She sat down to the piano. But she could not perform anything. She could only think of the man. After all, he had been much stranger than she had really imagined. She could see him clearer now. How different his life had been from the life of the other whites. They had come to conquer and explore, govern, trade, preach and educate to their liking, exploit men and material. But this man was the first to enter into the simple life of the island Negroes and proclaim significance and beauty in their transplanted African folk tales and in the words and music of their native dialect songs.

Before him it had been generally said the Negroes were inartistic. But he had found artistry where others saw nothing, because he believed that wherever the imprints of nature and humanity were found, there also were the seeds of creative life, and that above the dreary levels of existence everywhere there were always the radiant, the mysterious, the wonderful, the strange great moments whose magic may be caught by any clairvoyant mind and turned into magical form for the joy of man.

Before dawn on a Sunday Bita was awakened by the sound of the dray passing through the gate. It was Jubban coming home from the far market. The mules snorted hauling the dray round the house to the shed. Bita got up out of bed, wrapped herself in a shawl and went to set Jubban a little cold supper in the dining-room: cold Congo-pea soup with a piece of goat mutton, a slice of yam and a cut of banana pone.

She heard Jubban calling to the boy to wake up. The boy was sleeping in the outroom that had formerly been Jubban's. Now the boy was awake and up and was taking the mules to the paddock. Jubban came round to the back door of the house, outside of which there was a broad wooden bowl. He hauled off the heavy market boots. He washed his hands and face and after he washed his feet. Then he walked into the house and greeted Bita. She kissed him. His clothes smelled strongly of the cane sugar and the perfumed fever grass in which the breadkind for the market was laid.

Jubban sat down to eat and Bita prepared his favourite beverage: crude cane sugar and water with the juice of bitter oranges, while she asked about the market. Jubban answered that it had been good. For the past two years, ever since the hurricane, the market for breadkind had been excellent. He had taken sugar to the market and had sold it as high as five shillings a tin.

He told Bita about the trip to the market and back in a few phrases. He was not voluble. He talked in monosyllables of the dialect. But he expressed himself clearly. Bita appreciated his reticence, which suited her temperament for she was not a talkative woman.

Finishing his supper, Jubban went into the bedroom, took a peep at little Jordan sleeping in his crib and went to sleep. On coming home from the far market he usually slept until midday on Sunday.

Bita never could sleep directly after waking up at that hour. She went into the sitting-room and lay on the sofa and her thoughts flitted in disorder across the world. From Jubban to Jubilee, college days, travelling, Jubilee again, and back to Banana Bottom and Jubban.

Jubban. She was contented with him. She had become used to his kindly-rough gestures and they had adjusted themselves well to each other. The testing-time was over. Three years had passed since the memorable hurricane and flood. Intimate relations with Bita and the mastership of the house had developed in Jubban all the splendid qualities that were latent in him. His sureness and firmness about the things of which he was familiar, such as superintending the clearing of the land, planting, harvesting and marketing and the care and breeding of the live stock.

The land had prospered under Jubban's hand even more than under Jordan Plant's. Bita had purchased from the remnant of the Adair family the crumbling old "'State House" and land that her father had coveted, for less than a hundred pounds, and now there were a few cows feeding upon that fine pasture grass. And Anty Nommy was pleased with the development of the property and as proud of Jubban as Bita.

Thinking of Jubban and how her admiration for him had slowly developed into respect and love, Bita marvelled at the fact that they had never said "I love you" to each other. The thing had become a fact without the declaration.

They lived their life upon a level entirely different from her early romantic conception of love. Once she had thought of love as a kind of mystical force, incomprehensible and uncontrollable. But gradually she had lost all that feeling of the quality of love, for it was a borrowed thing, an exotic imposition, not a real intrinsic thing that had flowered out of the mind of her race.

She had no craving for Jubban to be other than what he was, experienced no hankering for that grace and refinement in him that the local soothsayers said was necessary to an educated person.

She liked to play for him for he had a natural feeling for music and showed appreciation of even the most difficult things. But he was in no way a hindrance to the intellectual side of her life. He accepted with natural grace the fact that she should excel in the things to which she had been educated as he should in the work to which he had been trained.

Her music, her reading, her thinking were the flowers of her intelligence and he the root in the earth upon which she was grafted, both nourished by the same soil.

Reaching her hand out to the bookshelf she drew out her college copy of the *Pensées*. One of the rare pleasures of adult life is returning sometimes to the scriptures of our formal education days and finding new interest and meanings in old passages.

Bita turned the pages of the *Pensées*:

> . . . la vraie morale se moque de la morale; la morale du jugement se moque de la morale de l'esprit.

That was one thought from Pascal that her philosophy teacher had never chosen to expatiate upon as a Christian gem. She had come by it all by herself. Squire Gensir had once said of it that it was more Pagan and Stoic than Christian. A thought like food. Something to live by from day to day. Unbounded by little national and racial lines, but a cosmic thing of all time for all minds.

Perhaps Pascal would have been incredulous if it had been prophesied to him that in future centuries a black girl would have found in his words a golden thread of principle to guide her through the confusion of life. And in a receptive and critical mood Bita turned the familiar pages, picking here and there an outstanding passage at random and thinking how like a risen river overflowing its banks was the man, bigger than the Christian creed in which he was confined.

Alone thinking contemplatively profoundly, the conviction came to her that clear thinking was the most beautiful of all things. Love and music were divine things but none so rare as the pure flight of the mind into the upper realms of thought.

Well, she thought, if my education has been wasted it is a happy waste. They were right perhaps who said it was wasted who believed that the real aims of education were diplomas and degrees and to provide things of snobbery and pretension like a ribbon on the breast and a plume upon the hat to dazzle the multitude.

The *Pensées* fell from her hand. . . . She had fallen asleep.

NELLA LARSEN

NELLA LARSEN'S QUICKSAND *(1928), if not the best novel of the Renaissance, is certainly its most engrossing. McKay's* Home to Harlem *sold more copies, but Larsen's novel won much better critical reviews and one of the Renaissance's newest and most prestigious laurels, the Harmon Foundation's second prize for literature.*

The excerpts here follow the protagonist, Helga Crane, from her faculty position at backwater Naxos College in the Deep South to New York, Denmark, and finally to the South again, where matrimonial bondage and serial pregnancy as the wife of Reverend Pleasant Green flatten her once vibrant, inquisitive personality. Although Larsen's novel has class and color concerns similar to Fauset's and White's, her characters have fuller dimensions. Moreover, Larsen sought to escape the understandable reductionism in most Renaissance fiction by depicting Helga Crane as bedeviled not only by her pale pigment and her racial origins but by her own labile psyche. The quicksand of her novel's title is found not just in the social situations she encounters but in her own inner emptiness. Finally, Helga Crane's dilemma is also a function of gender, of being an intelligent, liberated woman. All the more tragic, then, her desperate plunge into religious revivalism, domestic drudgery, and childbearing in order to extinguish longings and disappointments.

Passing (1929) is one of the four principal Harlem Renaissance novels about the "voluntary" African American—the others being James Weldon Johnson's The Autobiography of an Ex–Colored Man *(1912, 1927), Fauset's* Plum Bun, *and White's* Flight. *Two women, Irene Redfield and Clare Kendry, both white in appearance and childhood friends, follow different paths (Irene as the*

*wife of a successful African American physician, Clare passing as
the white wife of an abusive white businessman) and meet by accident for the first time in many years. Larsen describes Clare,
victimized in adolescence by white relatives because of her racial
origins, as amoral, appealing, and like quicksilver. Irene (who only
passes occasionally) is well adjusted, conventional, and contented
with her Talented Tenth existence. Their lives become entangled
with disastrous consequences as Clare becomes increasingly fascinated by the African American world she has deserted. Irene per-
ceives that her own husband, Brian, is entranced by her friend
Clare's modish vivacity. Larsen ends* Passing *abruptly. Shortly after
a small party gathers to drink and talk in an apartment, Clare's
husband charges noisily up the stairs cursing his wife for deceiving
him about her racial identity. Irene, realizing that the rootless, selfish Clare will now be free to take away her husband, causes Clare
to fall from a window to her death.*

FROM *QUICKSAND*

THREE

ON ONE SIDE OF THE LONG, white, hot sand road that split the flat
green, there was a little shade, for it was bordered with trees. Helga
Crane walked there so that the sun could not so easily get at her.
As she went slowly across the empty campus she was conscious of
a vague tenderness for the scene spread out before her. It was so
incredibly lovely, so appealing, and so facile. The trees in their
spring beauty sent through her restive mind a sharp thrill of pleasure. Seductive, charming, and beckoning as cities were, they had
not this easy unhuman loveliness. The trees, she thought, on city
avenues and boulevards, in city parks and gardens, were tamed,
held prisoners in a surrounding maze of human beings. Here they
were free. It was human beings who were prisoners. It was too
bad. In the midst of all this radiant life. They weren't, she knew,
even conscious of its presence. Perhaps there was too much of it,
and therefore it was less than nothing.

In response to her insistent demand she had been told that Dr.
Anderson could give her twenty minutes at eleven o'clock. Well,
she supposed that she could say all that she had to say in twenty

minutes, though she resented being limited. Twenty minutes. In Naxos, she was as unimportant as that.

He was a new man, this principal, for whom Helga remembered feeling unaccountably sorry, when last September he had first been appointed to Naxos as its head. For some reason she had liked him, although she had seen little of him; he was so frequently away on publicity and money-raising tours. And as yet he had made but few and slight changes in the running of the school. Now she was a little irritated at finding herself wondering just how she was going to tell him of her decision. What did it matter to him? Why should she mind if it did? But there returned to her that indistinct sense of sympathy for the remote silent man with the tired gray eyes, and she wondered again by what fluke of fate such a man, apparently a humane and understanding person, had chanced into the command of this cruel educational machine. Suddenly, her own resolve loomed as an almost direct unkindness. This increased her annoyance and discomfort. A sense of defeat, of being cheated of justification, closed down on her. Absurd!

She arrived at the administration building in a mild rage, as unreasonable as it was futile, but once inside she had a sudden attack of nerves at the prospect of traversing that great outer room which was the workplace of some twenty-odd people. This was a disease from which Helga had suffered at intervals all her life, and it was a point of honor, almost, with her never to give way to it. So, instead of turning away, as she felt inclined, she walked on, outwardly indifferent. Halfway down the long aisle which divided the room, the principal's secretary, a huge black man, surged toward her.

"Good morning, Miss Crane, Dr. Anderson will see you in a few moments. Sit down right here."

She felt the inquiry in the shuttered eyes. For some reason this dissipated her self-consciousness and restored her poise. Thanking him, she seated herself, really careless now of the glances of the stenographers, bookkeepers, clerks. Their curiosity and slightly veiled hostility no longer touched her. Her coming departure had released her from the need for conciliation which had irked her for so long. It was pleasant to Helga Crane to be able to sit calmly looking out of the window onto the smooth lawn, where a few leaves quite prematurely fallen dotted the grass, for once uncaring whether the frock which she wore roused disapproval or envy. . . .

She came back to her own problems. Clothes had been one of her difficulties in Naxos. Helga Crane loved clothes, elaborate ones. Nevertheless, she had tried not to offend. But with small success, for, although she had affected the deceptively simple variety, the hawk eyes of dean and matrons had detected the subtle difference from their own irreproachably conventional garments. Too, they felt that the colors were queer; dark purples, royal blues, rich greens, deep reds, in soft, luxurious woolens or heavy, clinging silks. And the trimmings—when Helga used them at all—seemed to them odd. Old laces, strange embroideries, dim brocades. Her faultless, slim shoes made them uncomfortable and her small plain hats seemed to them positively indecent. Helga smiled inwardly at the thought that whenever there was an evening affair for the faculty the dear ladies probably held their breaths until she had made her appearance. They existed in constant fear that she might turn out in an evening dress. The proper evening wear in Naxos was afternoon attire. And one could, if one wished, garnish the hair with flowers.

Quick, muted footfalls sounded. The secretary had returned. "Dr. Anderson will see you now, Miss Crane."

She rose, followed, and was ushered into the guarded sanctum, without having decided just what she was to say. For a moment she felt behind her the open doorway and then the gentle impact of its closing. Before her at a great desk her eyes picked out the figure of a man, at first blurred slightly in outline in that dimmer light. At his "Miss Crane?" her lips formed for speech, but no sound came. She was aware of inward confusion. For her the situation seemed charged, unaccountably, with strangeness and something very like hysteria. An almost overpowering desire to laugh seized her. Then, miraculously, a complete ease, such as she had never known in Naxos, possessed her. She smiled, nodded in answer to his questioning salutation, and with a gracious "Thank you" dropped into the chair which he indicated. She looked at him frankly now, this man still young, thirty-five perhaps, and found it easy to go on in the vein of a simple statement.

"Dr. Anderson, I'm sorry to have to confess that I've failed in my job here. I've made up my mind to leave. Today."

A short, almost imperceptible silence, then a deep voice of peculiarly pleasing resonance, asking gently: "You don't like Naxos, Miss Crane?"

She evaded. "Naxos, the place? Yes, I like it. Who wouldn't

like it? It's so beautiful. But I—well—I don't seem to fit here."

The man smiled, just a little. "The school? You don't like the school?"

The words burst from her. "No, I don't like it. I hate it!"

"Why?" The question was detached, too detached.

In the girl blazed a desire to wound. There he sat, staring dreamily out of the window, blatantly unconcerned with her or her answer. Well, she'd tell him. She pronounced each word with deliberate slowness.

"Well, for one thing, I hate hypocrisy. I hate cruelty to students, and to teachers who can't fight back. I hate backbiting, and sneaking, and petty jealousy. Naxos? It's hardly a place at all. It's more like some loathsome, venomous disease. Ugh! Everybody spending his time in a malicious hunting for the weaknesses of others, spying, grudging, scratching."

"I see. And you don't think it might help to cure us, to have someone who doesn't approve of these things stay with us? Even just one person, Miss Crane?"

She wondered if this last was irony. She suspected it was humor and so ignored the half-pleading note in his voice.

"No, I don't! It doesn't do the disease any good. Only irritates it. And it makes me unhappy, dissatisfied. It isn't pleasant to be always made to appear in the wrong, even when I know I'm right."

His gaze was on her now, searching. "Queer," she thought, "how some brown people have gray eyes. Gives them a strange, unexpected appearance. A little frightening."

The man said kindly: "Ah, you're unhappy. And for the reasons you've stated?"

"Yes, partly. Then, too, the people here don't like me. They don't think I'm in the spirit of the work. And I'm not, not if it means suppression of individuality and beauty."

"And does it?"

"Well, it seems to work out that way."

"How old are you, Miss Crane?"

She resented this, but she told him, speaking with what curtness she could command only the bare figure: "Twenty-three."

"Twenty-three. I see. Someday you'll learn that lies, injustice, and hypocrisy are a part of every ordinary community. Most people achieve a sort of protective immunity, a kind of callousness, toward them. If they didn't, they couldn't endure. I think there's less of these evils here than in most places, but because we're trying to do such a big thing, to aim so high, the ugly things show more, they irk some of us more. Service is like clean white linen, even the tiniest speck shows." He went on, explaining, amplifying, pleading.

Helga Crane was silent, feeling a mystifying yearning which sang and throbbed in her. She felt again that urge for service, not now for her people, but for this man who was talking so earnestly of his work, his plans, his hopes. An insistent need to be a part of them sprang in her. With compunction tweaking at her heart for even having entertained the notion of deserting him, she resolved not only to remain until June but to return next year. She was shamed yet stirred. It was not sacrifice she felt now, but actual desire to stay, and to come back next year.

He came, at last, to the end of the long speech, only part of which she had heard. "You see, you understand?" he urged.

"Yes, oh yes, I do."

"What we need is more people like you, people with a sense of values, and proportion, an appreciation of the rarer things of life. You have something to give which we badly need here in Naxos. You mustn't desert us, Miss Crane."

She nodded, silent. He had won her. She knew that she would stay. "It's an elusive something," he went on. "Perhaps I can best explain it by the use of that trite phrase, 'You're a lady.' You have dignity and breeding."

At these words turmoil rose again in Helga Crane. The intricate pattern of the rug which she had been studying escaped her. The shamed feeling which had been her penance evaporated. Only a lacerated pride remained. She took firm hold of the chair arms to still the trembling of her fingers.

"If you're speaking of family, Dr. Anderson, why, I haven't any. I was born in a Chicago slum."

The man chose his words—carefully, he thought. "That doesn't at all matter, Miss Crane. Financial, economic circumstances can't destroy tendencies inherited from good stock. You yourself prove that!"

Concerned with her own angry thoughts, which scurried here and there like trapped rats, Helga missed the import of his words. Her own words, her answer, fell like drops of hail.

"The joke is on you, Dr. Anderson. My father was a gambler who deserted my mother, a white immigrant. It is even uncertain that they were married. As I said at first, I don't belong here. I shall be leaving at once. This afternoon. Good morning."

NINE

"To me," asserted Anne Grey, "the most wretched Negro prostitute that walks 135th Street is more than any President of these United States, not excepting Abraham Lincoln." But she turned up her finely carved nose at their lusty churches, their picturesque parades, their naïve clowning on the streets. She would not have desired or even have been willing to live in any section outside the black belt, and she would have refused scornfully, had they been tendered, any invitation from white folk. She hated white people with a deep and burning hatred, with the kind of hatred which, finding itself held in sufficiently numerous groups, was capable someday, on some great provocation, of bursting into dangerously malignant flames.

But she aped their clothes, their manners, and their gracious ways of living. While proclaiming loudly the undiluted good of all things Negro, she yet disliked the songs, the dances, and the softly blurred speech of the race. Toward these things she showed only a disdainful contempt, tinged sometimes with a faint amusement. Like the despised people of the white race, she preferred Pavlova to Florence Mills, John McCormack to Taylor Gordon, Walter Hampden to Paul Robeson. Theoretically, however, she stood for the immediate advancement of all things Negroid, and was in revolt against social inequality.

Helga had been entertained by this racial ardor in one so little affected by racial prejudice as Anne, and by her inconsistencies. But suddenly these things irked her with a great irksomeness and she wanted to be free of this constant prattling of the incongruities, the injustices, the stupidities, the viciousness of white people. It stirred memories, probed hidden wounds, whose poignant ache bred in her surprising oppression and corroded the fabric of her quietism. Sometimes it took all her self-control to keep from tossing sarcastically at Anne Ibsen's remark about there being assuredly something very wrong with the drains, but after all there were other parts of the edifice.

It was at this period of restiveness that Helga met Dr. Anderson again. She had gone, unwillingly, to a meeting, a health meeting, held in a large church—as were most of Harlem's uplift activities—as a substitute for her employer, Mr. Darling. Making her tardy arrival during a tedious discourse by a pompous saffron-hued physician, she was led by the irritated usher, whom she had

roused from a nap in which he had been pleasantly freed from the
intricacies of Negro health statistics, to a very front seat. Complete
silence ensued while she subsided into her chair. The offended doctor looked at the ceiling, at the floor, and accusingly at Helga, and
finally continued his lengthy discourse. When at last he had ended
and Helga had dared to remove her eyes from his sweating face
and look about, she saw with a sudden thrill that Robert Anderson
was among her nearest neighbors. A peculiar, not wholly disagreeable quiver ran down her spine. She felt an odd little faintness.
The blood rushed to her face. She tried to jeer at herself for being
so moved by the encounter.

He, meanwhile, she observed, watched her gravely. And having caught her attention, he smiled a little and nodded.

When all who so desired had spouted to their hearts'
content—if to little purpose—and the meeting was finally over,
Anderson detached himself from the circle of admiring friends and
acquaintances that had gathered around him and caught up with
Helga halfway down the long aisle leading out to fresher air.

"I wondered if you were really going to cut me. I see you
were," he began, with that half-quizzical smile which she remembered so well.

She laughed. "Oh, I didn't think you'd remember me." Then
she added: "Pleasantly, I mean."

The man laughed too. But they couldn't talk yet. People kept
breaking in on them. At last, however, they were at the door, and
then he suggested that they share a taxi "for the sake of a little
breeze." Helga assented.

Constraint fell upon them when they emerged into the hot
street, made seemingly hotter by a low-hanging golden moon and
the hundreds of blazing electric lights. For a moment, before hailing a taxi, they stood together looking at the slow-moving mass of
perspiring human beings. Neither spoke, but Helga was conscious
of the man's steady gaze. The prominent gray eyes were fixed upon
her, studying her, appraising her. Many times since turning her
back on Naxos she had in fancy rehearsed this scene, this re-en-
counter. Now she found that rehearsal helped not at all. It was so
absolutely different from anything that she had imagined.

In the open taxi they talked of impersonal things: books,
places, the fascination of New York, of Harlem. But underneath
the exchange of small talk lay another conversation of which Helga
Crane was sharply aware. She was aware, too, of a strange ill-

defined emotion, a vague yearning rising within her. And she experienced a sensation of consternation and keen regret when with a lurching jerk the cab pulled up before the house in 139th Street. So soon, she thought.

But she held out her hand calmly, coolly. Cordially she asked him to call sometime. "It is," she said, "a pleasure to renew our acquaintance." Was it, she was wondering, merely an acquaintance?

He responded seriously that he too thought it a pleasure, and added: "You haven't changed. You're still seeking for something, I think."

At his speech there dropped from her that vague feeling of yearning, that longing for sympathy and understanding which his presence evoked. She felt a sharp stinging sensation and a recurrence of that anger and defiant desire to hurt which had so seared her on that past morning in Naxos. She searched for a biting remark but, finding none venomous enough, she merely laughed a little rude and scornful laugh and, throwing up her small head, bade him an impatient good night and ran quickly up the steps.

Afterward she lay for long hours without undressing, thinking angry self-accusing thoughts, recalling and reconstructing that other explosive contact. That memory filled her with a sort of aching delirium. A thousand indefinite longings beset her. Eagerly she desired to see him again to right herself in his thoughts. Far into the night she lay planning speeches for their next meeting, so that it was long before drowsiness advanced upon her.

When he did call, Sunday, three days later, she put him off on Anne and went out, pleading an engagement, which until then she had not meant to keep. Until the very moment of his entrance she had had no intention of running away, but something, some imp of contumacy, drove her from his presence, though she longed to stay. Again abruptly had come the uncontrollable wish to wound. Later, with a sense of helplessness and inevitability, she realized that the weapon which she had chosen had been a boomerang, for she herself had felt the keen disappointment of the denial. Better to have stayed and hurled polite sarcasms at him. She might then at least have had the joy of seeing him wince.

In this spirit she made her way to the corner and turned into Seventh Avenue. The warmth of the sun, though gentle on that afternoon, had nevertheless kissed the street into marvelous light and color. Now and then, greeting an acquaintance, or stopping to chat with a friend, Helga was all the time seeing its soft shining brightness on the buildings along its sides or on the gleaming bronze, gold, and copper faces of its promenaders. And another vision, too, came haunting Helga Crane: level gray eyes set down in a brown face which stared out at her, coolly, quizzically, disturbingly. And she was not happy.

The tea to which she had so suddenly made up her mind to go she found boring beyond endurance—insipid drinks, dull conversation, stupid men. The aimless talk glanced from John Wellinger's lawsuit for discrimination because of race against a downtown restaurant and the advantages of living in Europe, especially in France, to the significance, if any, of the Garvey movement. Then it sped to a favorite Negro dancer who had just then secured a foothold on the stage of a current white musical comedy, to other shows, to a new book touching on Negroes. Thence to costumes for a coming masquerade dance, to a new jazz song, to Yvette Dawson's engagement to a Boston lawyer who had seen her one night at a party and proposed to her the next day at noon. Then back again to racial discrimination.

Why, Helga wondered, with unreasoning exasperation, didn't they find something else to talk of? Why must the race problem always creep in? She refused to go on to another gathering. It would, she thought, be simply the same old thing.

On her arrival home she was more disappointed than she cared to admit to find the house in darkness and even Anne gone off somewhere. She would have liked that night to have talked with Anne. Get her opinion of Dr. Anderson.

Anne it was who the next day told her that he had given up his work in Naxos; or rather that Naxos had given him up. He had been too liberal, too lenient, for education as it was inflicted in Naxos. Now he was permanently in New York, employed as welfare worker by some big manufacturing concern, which gave employment to hundreds of Negro men.

"Uplift," sniffed Helga contemptuously, and fled before the onslaught of Anne's harangue on the needs and ills of the race.

TEN

With the waning summer the acute sensitiveness of Helga Crane's frayed nerves grew keener. There were days when the mere sight of the serene tan and brown faces about her stung her like a personal insult. The carefree quality of their laughter roused in her the desire to scream at them: "Fools, fools! Stupid fools!" This passionate and unreasoning protest gained in intensity, swallowing up all else like some dense fog. Life became for her only a hateful place where one lived in intimacy with people one would not have chosen had one been given choice. It was, too, an excruciating agony. She was continually out of temper. Anne, thank the gods! was away, but her nearing return filled Helga with dismay.

Arriving at work one sultry day, hot and dispirited, she found waiting a letter, a letter from Uncle Peter. It had originally been sent to Naxos, and from there it had made the journey back to Chicago to the Young Women's Christian Association, and then to Mrs. Hayes-Rore. That busy woman had at last found time between conventions and lectures to readdress it and had sent it on to New York. Four months, at least, it had been on its travels. Helga felt no curiosity as to its contents, only annoyance at the long delay, as she ripped open the thin edge of the envelope and for a space sat staring at the peculiar foreign script of her uncle.

715 Sheridan Road
Chicago, Ill.

Dear Helga:

It is now over a year since you made your unfortunate call here. It was unfortunate for us all, you, Mrs. Nilssen, and myself. But of course you couldn't know. I blame myself. I should have written you of my marriage.

I have looked for a letter, or some word from you; evidently, with your usual penetration, you understood thoroughly that I must terminate my outward relation with you. You were always a keen one.

Of course I am sorry, but it can't be helped. My wife must be considered, and she feels very strongly about this.

You know, of course, that I wish you the best of luck. But take an old man's advice and don't do as your mother did. Why don't you run over and visit your Aunt Katrina? She always wanted you. Maria Kirkeplads, No. 2, will find her.

I enclose what I intended to leave you at my death. It is better and more convenient that you get it now. I

*wish it were more, but even this little may come in handy
for a rainy day.*
      Best wishes for your luck.

                              Peter Nilssen

Beside the brief, friendly, but none the less final letter there was a
check for five thousand dollars. Helga Crane's first feeling was one
of unreality. This changed almost immediately into one of relief,
of liberation. It was stronger than the mere security from present
financial worry which the check promised. Money as money was
still not very important to Helga. But later, while on an errand in
the big general office of the society, her puzzled bewilderment fled.
Here the inscrutability of the dozen or more brown faces, all cast
from the same indefinite mold, and so like her own, seemed pressing forward against her. Abruptly it flashed upon her that the harrowing irritation of the past weeks was a smoldering hatred. Then
she was overcome by another, so actual, so sharp, so horribly painful, that forever afterwards she preferred to forget it. It was as if
she were shut up, boxed up, with hundreds of her race, closed up
with that something in the racial character which had always been,
to her, inexplicable, alien. Why, she demanded in fierce rebellion,
should she be yoked to these despised black folk?

Back in the privacy of her own cubicle, self-loathing came
upon her. "They're my own people, my own people," she kept
repeating over and over to herself. It was no good. The feeling
would not be routed. "I can't go on like this," she said to herself.
"I simply can't."

There were footsteps. Panic seized her. She'd have to get out.
She terribly needed to. Snatching hat and purse, she hurried to the
narrow door, saying in a forced, steady voice, as it opened to reveal
her employer: "Mr. Darling, I'm sorry, but I've got to go out.
Please, may I be excused?"

At his courteous "Certainly, certainly. And don't hurry. It's
much too hot," Helga Crane had the grace to feel ashamed, but
there was no softening of her determination. The necessity for being alone was too urgent. She hated him and all the others too
much.

Outside, rain had begun to fall. She walked bareheaded, bitter
with self-reproach. But she rejoiced too. She didn't, in spite of her
racial markings, belong to these dark segregated people. She was

different. She felt it. It wasn't merely a matter of color. It was something broader, deeper, that made folk kin.

And now she was free. She would take Uncle Peter's money and advice and revisit her aunt in Copenhagen. Fleeting pleasant memories of her childhood visit there flew through her excited mind. She had been only eight, yet she had enjoyed the interest and the admiration which her unfamiliar color and dark curly hair, strange to those pink, white, and gold people, had evoked. Quite clearly now she recalled that her Aunt Katrina had begged for her to be allowed to remain. Why, she wondered, hadn't her mother consented? To Helga it seemed that it would have been the solution to all their problems, her mother's, her stepfather's, her own.

At home in the cool dimness of the big chintz-hung living room, clad only in a fluttering thing of green chiffon, she gave herself up to daydreams of a happy future in Copenhagen, where there were no Negroes, no problems, no prejudice, until she remembered with perturbation that this was the day of Anne's return from her vacation at the seashore. Worse. There was a dinner party in her honor that very night. Helga sighed. She'd have to go. She couldn't possibly get out of a dinner party for Anne, even though she felt that such an event on a hot night was little short of an outrage. Nothing but a sense of obligation to Anne kept her from pleading a splitting headache as an excuse for remaining quietly at home.

Her mind trailed off to the highly important matter of clothes. What should she wear? White? No, everybody would, because it was hot. Green? She shook her head. Anne would be sure to. The blue thing. Reluctantly she decided against it; she loved it, but she had worn it too often. There was that cobwebby black net touched with orange, which she had bought last spring in a fit of extravagance and never worn, because on getting it home both she and Anne had considered it too décolleté, and too outré. Anne's words: "There's not enough of it, and what there is gives you the air of something about to fly," came back to her, and she smiled as she decided that she would certainly wear the black net. For her it would be a symbol. She was about to fly.

She busied herself with some absurdly expensive roses which she had ordered sent in, spending an interminable time in their arrangement. At last she was satisfied with their appropriateness in some blue Chinese jars of great age. Anne *did* have such lovely things, she thought as she began conscientiously to prepare for her

return, although there was really little to do; Lillie seemed to have
done everything. But Helga dusted the tops of the books, placed
the magazines in ordered carelessness, redressed Anne's bed in
fresh-smelling sheets of cool linen, and laid out her best pale yellow
pajamas of crepe de chine. Finally she set out two tall green glasses
and made a great pitcher of lemonade, leaving only the ginger ale
and claret to be added on Anne's arrival. She was a little con-
science-stricken, so she wanted to be particularly nice to Anne, who
had been so kind to her when first she came to New York, a forlorn
friendless creature. Yes, she was grateful to Anne; but, just the
same, she meant to go. At once.

Her preparations over, she went back to the carved chair from
which the thought of Anne's homecoming had drawn her. Characteristically she writhed at the idea of telling Anne of her impending departure and shirked the problem of evolving a plausible
and inoffensive excuse for its suddenness. "That," she decided lazily, "will have to look out for itself; I can't be bothered just now.
It's too hot."

She began to make plans and to dream delightful dreams of
change, of life somewhere else. Someplace where at last she would
be permanently satisfied. Her anticipatory thoughts waltzed and
eddied about to the sweet silent music of change. With rapture
almost, she let herself drop into the blissful sensation of visualizing
herself in different, strange places, among approving and admiring
people, where she would be appreciated and understood.

ELEVEN

It was night. The dinner party was over, but no one wanted to go
home. Half past eleven was, it seemed, much too early to tumble
into bed on a Saturday night. It was a sulky, humid night, a thick
furry night, through which the electric torches shone like silver
fuzz—an atrocious night for cabareting, Helga insisted, but the
others wanted to go, so she went with them, though half unwillingly. After much consultation and chatter they decided upon a
place and climbed into two patiently waiting taxis, rattling things
which jerked, wiggled, and groaned, and threatened every minute
to collide with others of their kind, or with inattentive pedestrians.
Soon they pulled up before a tawdry doorway in a narrow cross-
town street and stepped out. The night was far from quiet, the

streets far from empty. Clanging trolley bells, quarreling cats, cackling phonographs, raucous laughter, complaining motor horns, low singing, mingled in the familiar medley that is Harlem. Black figures, white figures, little forms, big forms, small groups, large groups, sauntered, or hurried by. It was gay, grotesque, and a little weird. Helga Crane felt singularly apart from it all. Entering the waiting doorway, they descended through a furtive, narrow passage, into a vast subterranean room. Helga smiled, thinking that this was one of those places characterized by the righteous as a hell.

A glare of light struck her eyes, a blare of jazz split her ears. For a moment everything seemed to be spinning round; even she felt that she was circling aimlessly, as she followed with the others the black giant who led them to a small table, where, when they were seated, their knees and elbows touched. Helga wondered that the waiter, indefinitely carved out of ebony, did not smile as he wrote their order: "Four bottles of White Rock, four bottles of ginger ale." Bah! Anne giggled, the others smiled and openly exchanged knowing glances, and under the tables flat glass bottles were extracted from the women's evening scarfs and small silver flasks drawn from the men's hip pockets. In a little moment she grew accustomed to the smoke and din.

They danced, ambling lazily to a crooning melody, or violently twisting their bodies, like whirling leaves, to a sudden streaming rhythm, or shaking themselves ecstatically to a thumping of unseen tomtoms. For the while Helga was oblivious of the reek of flesh, smoke, and alcohol, oblivious of the oblivion of other gyrating pairs, oblivious of the color, the noise, and the grand distorted childishness of it all. She was drugged, lifted, sustained, by the extraordinary music, blown out, ripped out, beaten out, by the joyous, wild, murky orchestra. The essence of life seemed bodily motion. And when suddenly the music died, she dragged herself back to the present with a conscious effort; and a shameful certainty that not only had she been in the jungle, but that she had enjoyed it, began to taunt her. She hardened her determination to get away. She wasn't, she told herself, a jungle creature. She cloaked herself in a faint disgust as she watched the entertainers throw themselves about to the bursts of syncopated jangle, and when the time came again for the patrons to dance, she declined. Her rejected partner excused himself and sought an acquaintance a few tables removed. Helga sat looking curiously about her as the buzz of conversation ceased, strangled by the savage strains of music, and the crowd became a swirling mass. For the hundredth time she marveled at the gradations within this oppressed race of hers. A dozen shades slid by. There was sooty black, shiny black, taupe, mahogany, bronze, copper, gold, orange, yellow, peach, ivory, pinky white, pastry white. There was yellow hair, brown hair, black hair; straight hair, straightened hair, curly hair, crinkly hair, woolly hair. She saw black eyes in white faces, brown eyes in yellow faces, gray eyes in brown faces, blue eyes in tan faces. Africa, Europe, perhaps with a pinch of Asia, in a fantastic motley of ugliness and beauty, semibarbaric, sophisticated, exotic, were here. But she was blind to its charm, purposely aloof and a little contemptuous, and soon her interest in the moving mosaic waned.

She had discovered Dr. Anderson sitting at a table on the far side of the room, with a girl in a shivering apricot frock. Seriously he returned her tiny bow. She met his eyes, gravely smiling, then blushed, furiously, and averted her own. But they went back immediately to the girl beside him, who sat indifferently sipping a colorless liquid from a high glass, or puffing a precariously hanging cigarette. Across dozens of tables, littered with corks, with ashes, with shriveled sandwiches, through slits in the swaying mob, Helga Crane studied her.

She was pale, with a peculiar, almost deathlike pallor. The brilliantly red, softly curving mouth was somehow sorrowful. Her pitch-black eyes, a little aslant, were veiled by long, drooping lashes and surmounted by broad brows, which seemed like black smears. The short dark hair was brushed severely back from the wide forehead. The extreme décolletage of her simple apricot dress showed a skin of unusual color, a delicate, creamy hue, with golden tones. "Almost like an alabaster," thought Helga.

Bang! Again the music died. The moving mass broke, separated. The others returned. Anne had rage in her eyes. Her voice trembled as she took Helga aside to whisper: "There's your Dr. Anderson over there, with Audrey Denney."

"Yes, I saw him. She's lovely. Who is she?"

"She's Audrey Denney, as I said, and she lives downtown. West Twenty-second Street. Hasn't much use for Harlem any more. It's a wonder she hasn't some white man hanging about. The disgusting creature! I wonder how she inveigled Anderson? But that's Audrey! If there is any desirable man about, trust her to attach him. She ought to be ostracized."

"Why?" asked Helga curiously, noting at the same time that three of the men in their own party had deserted and were now congregated about the offending Miss Denney.

"Because she goes about with white people," came Anne's indignant answer, "and they know she's colored."

"I'm afraid I don't quite see, Anne. Would it be all right if they didn't know she was colored?"

"Now don't be nasty, Helga. You know very well what I mean." Anne's voice was shaking. Helga didn't see, and she was greatly interested, but she decided to let it go. She didn't want to quarrel with Anne, not now, when she had that guilty feeling about leaving her. But Anne was off on her favorite subject, race. And it seemed, too, that Audrey Denney was to her particularly obnoxious.

"Why, she gives parties for white and colored people together. And she goes to white people's parties. It's worse than disgusting, it's positively obscene."

"Oh, come, Anne, you haven't been to any of the parties, I know, so how can you be so positive about the matter?"

"No, but I've heard about them. I know people who've been."

"Friends of yours, Anne?"

Anne admitted that they were, some of them.

"Well, then, they can't be so bad. I mean, if your friends sometimes go, can they? Just what goes on that's so terrible?"

"Why, they drink, for one thing. Quantities, they say."

"So do we, at the parties here in Harlem," Helga responded. An idiotic impulse seized her to leave the place, Anne's presence, then, forever. But of course she couldn't. It would be foolish, and so ugly.

"And the white men dance with the colored women. Now you know, Helga Crane, that can mean only one thing." Anne's voice was trembling with cold hatred. As she ended, she made a little clicking noise with her tongue, indicating an abhorrence too great for words.

"Don't the colored men dance with the white women, or do they sit about, impolitely, while the other men dance with their women?" inquired Helga very softly, and with a slowness approaching almost to insolence. Anne's insinuations were too revolting. She had a slightly sickish feeling, and a flash of anger touched her. She mastered it and ignored Anne's inadequate answer.

"It's the principle of the thing that I object to. You can't get round the fact that her behavior is outrageous, treacherous, in fact. That's what's the matter with the Negro race. They won't stick together. She certainly ought to be ostracized. I've nothing but contempt for her, as has every other self-respecting Negro."

The other women and the lone man left to them—Helga's own escort—all seemingly agreed with Anne. At any rate, they didn't protest. Helga gave it up. She felt that it would be useless to tell them that what she felt for the beautiful, calm, cool girl who had the assurance, the courage, so placidly to ignore racial barriers and give her attention to people was not contempt but envious admiration. So she remained silent, watching the girl.

At the next first sound of music Dr. Anderson rose. Languidly the girl followed his movement, a faint smile parting her sorrowful lips at some remark he made. Her long, slender body swayed with an eager pulsing motion. She danced with grace and abandon, gravely, yet with obvious pleasure, her legs, her hips, her back, all swaying gently, swung by that wild music from the heart of the jungle. Helga turned her glance to Dr. Anderson. Her disinterested curiosity passed. While she still felt for the girl envious admiration, that feeling was now augmented by another, a more primitive emotion. She forgot the garish crowded room. She forgot her friends. She saw only two figures, closely clinging. She felt her heart throbbing. She felt the room receding. She went out the door. She climbed endless stairs. At last, panting, confused, but thankful to have escaped, she found herself again out in the dark night alone, a small crumpled thing in a fragile, flying black and gold dress. A taxi drifted toward her, stopped. She stepped into it, feeling cold, unhappy, misunderstood, and forlorn.

FIFTEEN

Well into Helga's second year in Denmark came an indefinite discontent. Not clear, but vague, like a storm gathering far on the horizon. It was long before she would admit that she was less happy than she had been during her first year in Copenhagen, but she knew that it was so. And this subconscious knowledge added to her growing restlessness and little mental insecurity. She desired ardently to combat this wearing down of her satisfaction with her life, with herself. But she didn't know how.

Frankly the question came to this: what was the matter with her? Was there, without her knowing it, some peculiar lack in her? Absurd. But she began to have a feeling of discouragement and hopelessness. Why couldn't she be happy, content, somewhere? Other people managed, somehow, to be. To put it plainly, didn't she know how? Was she incapable of it?

And then on a warm spring day came Anne's letter telling of her coming marriage to Anderson, who retained still his shadowy place in Helga Crane's memory. It added, somehow, to her discontent, and to her growing dissatisfaction with her peacock's life. This, too, annoyed her.

What, she asked herself, was there about that man which had the power always to upset her? She began to think back to her first encounter with him. Perhaps if she hadn't come away—She laughed. Derisively. "Yes, if I hadn't come away, I'd be stuck in Harlem. Working every day of my life. Chattering about the race problem."

Anne, it seemed, wanted her to come back for the wedding. This, Helga had no intention of doing. True, she had liked and admired Anne better than anyone she had ever known, but even for her she wouldn't cross the ocean.

Go back to America, where they hated Negroes! To America, where Negroes were not people. To America, where Negroes were allowed to be beggars only, of life, of happiness, of security. To America, where everything had been taken from those dark ones, liberty, respect, even the labor of their hands. To America, where, if one had Negro blood, one mustn't expect money, education, or, sometimes, even work whereby one might earn bread. Perhaps she was wrong to bother about it now that she was so far away. Helga couldn't, however, help it. Never could she recall the shames and often the absolute horrors of the black man's existence in America without the quickening of her heart's beating and a sensation of disturbing nausea. It was too awful. The sense of dread of it was almost a tangible thing in her throat.

And certainly she wouldn't go back for any such idiotic reason as Anne's getting married to that offensive Robert Anderson. Anne was really too amusing. Just why, she wondered, and how had it come about that he was being married to Anne? And why did Anne, who had so much more than so many others—more than enough—want Anderson too? Why couldn't she— "I think," she told herself, "I'd better stop. It's none of my business. I don't care in the least. Besides," she added irrelevantly, "I hate such nonsensical soul searching."

One night not long after the arrival of Anne's letter with its curious news, Helga went with Olsen and some other young folk to the great Circus, a vaudeville house, in search of amusement on a rare off night. After sitting through several numbers they reluctantly arrived at the conclusion that the whole entertainment was dull, unutterably dull, and apparently without alleviation, and so not to be borne. They were reaching for their wraps when out upon the stage pranced two black men, American Negroes undoubtedly, for as they danced and cavorted they sang in the English of America an old ragtime song that Helga remembered hearing as a child, "Everybody Gives Me Good Advice." At its conclusion the audience applauded with delight. Only Helga Crane was silent, motionless.

More songs, old, all of them old, but new and strange to that audience. And how the singers danced, pounding their thighs, slapping their hands together, twisting their legs, waving their abnormally long arms, throwing their bodies about with a loose ease! And how the enchanted spectators clapped and howled and shouted for more!

Helga Crane was not amused. Instead she was filled with a fierce hatred for the cavorting Negroes on the stage. She felt shamed, betrayed, as if these pale pink and white people among whom she lived had suddenly been invited to look upon something in her which she had hidden away and wanted to forget. And she was shocked at the avidity with which Olsen beside her drank it in.

But later, when she was alone, it became quite clear to her that all along they had divined its presence, had known that in her was something, some characteristic, different from any that they themselves possessed. Else why had they decked her out as they had? Why subtly indicated that she was different? And they hadn't despised it. No, they had admired it, rated it as a precious thing, a thing to be enhanced, preserved. Why? She, Helga Crane, didn't admire it. She suspected that no Negroes, no Americans, did. Else why their constant slavish imitation of traits not their own? Why their constant begging to be considered as exact copies of other people? Even the enlightened, the intelligent ones demanded nothing more. They were all beggars like the motley crowd in the old nursery rhyme:

> Hark! Hark!
> The dogs do bark.
> The beggars are coming to town.
> Some in rags,
> Some in tags,
> And some in velvet gowns.

The incident left her profoundly disquieted. Her old unhappy questioning mood came again upon her, insidiously stealing away more of the contentment from her transformed existence.

But she returned again and again to the Circus, always alone, gazing intently and solemnly at the gesticulating black figures, an ironical and silently speculative spectator. For she knew that into her plan for her life had thrust itself a suspensive conflict in which were fused doubts, rebellion, expediency, and urgent longings.

It was at this time that Axel Olsen asked her to marry him. And now Helga Crane was surprised. It was a thing that at one time she had much wanted, had tried to bring about, and had at last relinquished as impossible of achievement. Not so much because of its apparent hopelessness as because of a feeling, intangible almost, that, excited and pleased as he was with her, her origin a little repelled him, and that, prompted by some impulse of racial antagonism, he had retreated into the fastness of a protecting habit of self-ridicule. A mordantly personal pride and sensitiveness deterred Helga from further efforts at incitation.

True, he had made, one morning, while holding his brush poised for a last, a very last stroke on the portrait, one admirably draped suggestion, speaking seemingly to the pictured face. Had he insinuated marriage, or something less—and easier? Or had he paid her only a rather florid compliment, in somewhat dubious taste? Helga, who had not at the time been quite sure, had remained silent, striving to appear unhearing.

Later, having thought it over, she flayed herself for a fool. It wasn't, she should have known, in the manner of Axel Olsen to pay florid compliments in questionable taste. And had it been marriage that he had meant, he would, of course, have done the proper thing. He wouldn't have stopped—or, rather, have begun—by making his wishes known to her when there was Uncle Poul to be formally consulted. She had been, she told herself, insulted. And a goodly measure of contempt and wariness was added to her interest in the man. She was able, however, to feel a gratifying sense of elation in the remembrance that she had been silent, ostensibly unaware of his utterance, and therefore, as far as he knew, not affronted.

This simplified things. It did away with the quandary in which the confession to the Dahls of such a happening would have involved her, for she couldn't be sure that they, too, might not put it down to the difference of her ancestry. And she could still go attended by him, and envied by others, to openings in Kongens Nytorv, to showings at the Royal Academy or the Charlottenborg. He could still call for her and Aunt Katrina of an afternoon or go with her to Magasin du Nord to select a scarf or a length of silk, of which Uncle Poul could say casually in the presence of interested acquaintances: "Um, pretty scarf"—or "frock"—"you're wearing, Helga. Is that the new one Olsen helped you with?"

Her outward manner toward him changed not at all, save that gradually she became, perhaps, a little more detached and indifferent. But definitely Helga Crane had ceased, even remotely, to consider him other than as someone amusing, desirable, and convenient to have about—if one was careful. She intended, presently, to turn her attention to one of the others. The decorative captain of the Hussars, perhaps. But in the ache of her growing nostalgia, which, try as she might, she could not curb, she no longer thought with any seriousness on either Olsen or Captain Skaargaard. She must, she felt, see America again first. When she returned—

Therefore, where before she would have been pleased and proud at Olsen's proposal, she was now truly surprised. Strangely, she was aware also of a curious feeling of repugnance, as her eyes slid over his face, as smiling, assured, with just the right note of fervor, he made his declaration and request. She was astonished. Was it possible? Was it really this man that she had thought, even wished, she could marry?

He was, it was plain, certain of being accepted, as he was always certain of acceptance, of adulation, in any and every place that he deigned to honor with his presence. Well, Helga was thinking, that wasn't as much his fault as her own, her aunt's, everyone's. He was spoiled, childish almost.

To his words, once she had caught their content and recovered from her surprise, Helga paid not much attention. They would, she knew, be absolutely appropriate ones, and they didn't at all matter. They meant nothing to her—now. She was too amazed to discover suddenly how intensely she disliked him, disliked the shape of his head, the mop of his hair, the line of his nose, the tones of his voice, the nervous grace of his long fingers; disliked even the very look of his irreproachable clothes. And for some inexplicable reason she was a little frightened and embarrassed, so that when he had finished speaking, for a short space there was only stillness in the small room, into which Aunt Katrina had tactfully had him shown. Even Thor, the enormous Persian, curled on the window ledge in the feeble late afternoon sun, had rested for the moment from his incessant purring under Helga's idly stroking fingers.

Helga, her slight agitation vanished, told him that she was surprised. His offer was, she said, unexpected. Quite.

A little sardonically, Olsen interrupted her. He smiled too. "But of course I expected surprise. It is, is it not, the proper thing? And always you are proper, Frøkken Helga, always."

Helga, who had a stripped, naked feeling under his direct glance, drew herself up stiffly. Herr Olsen needn't, she told him, be sarcastic. She *was* surprised. He must understand that she was being quite sincere, quite truthful about that. Really, she hadn't expected him to do her so great an honor.

He made a little impatient gesture. Why, then, had she refused, ignored, his other, earlier suggestion?

At that Helga Crane took a deep indignant breath and was again, this time for an almost imperceptible second, silent. She had, then, been correct in her deduction. Her sensuous, petulant mouth hardened. That he should so frankly—so insolently, it seemed to her—admit his outrageous meaning was too much. She said coldly: "Because, Herr Olsen, in my country the men, of my race, at least, don't make such suggestions to decent girls. And thinking that you were a gentleman, introduced to me by my aunt, I chose to think myself mistaken, to give you the benefit of the doubt."

"Very commendable, my Helga—and wise. Now you have your reward. Now I offer you marriage."

"Thanks," she answered, "thanks, awfully."

"Yes," and he reached for her slim cream hand, now lying quiet on Thor's broad orange and black back. Helga let it lie in his large pink one, noting their contrast. "Yes, because I, poor artist that I am, cannot hold out against the deliberate lure of you. You disturb me. The longing for you does harm to my work. You creep into my brain and madden me," and he kissed the small ivory hand. Quite decorously, Helga thought, for one so maddened that he was driven, against his inclination, to offer her marriage. But

immediately, in extenuation, her mind leapt to the admirable casualness of Aunt Katrina's expressed desire for this very thing, and
recalled the unruffled calm of Uncle Poul under any and all circumstances. It was, as she had long ago decided, security. Balance.

"But," the man before her was saying, "for me it will be an
experience. It may be that with you, Helga, for wife, I will become
great. Immortal. Who knows? I didn't want to love you, but I had
to. That is the truth. I make of myself a present to you. For love."
His voice held a theatrical note. At the same time he moved forward, putting out his arms. His hands touched air. For Helga had
moved back. Instantly he dropped his arms and took a step away,
repelled by something suddenly wild in her face and manner. Sitting down, he passed a hand over his face with a quick, graceful
gesture.

Tameness returned to Helga Crane. Her ironic gaze rested on
the face of Axel Olsen, his leonine head, his broad nose—"broader
than my own"—his bushy eyebrows, surmounting thick, drooping
lids, which hid, she knew, sullen blue eyes. He stirred sharply,
shaking off his momentary disconcertion.

In his assured, despotic way he went on: "You know, Helga,
you are a contradiction. You have been, I suspect, corrupted by
the good Fru Dahl, which is perhaps as well. Who knows? You
have the warm impulsive nature of the women of Africa, but, my
lovely, you have, I fear, the soul of a prostitute. You sell yourself
to the highest buyer. I should of course be happy that it is I. And
I am." He stopped, contemplating her, lost apparently, for the second, in pleasant thoughts of the future.

To Helga he seemed to be the most distant, the most unreal
figure in the world. She suppressed a ridiculous impulse to laugh.
The effort sobered her. Abruptly she was aware that in the end, in
some way, she would pay for this hour. A quick brief fear ran
through her, leaving in its wake a sense of impending calamity. She
wondered if for this she would pay all that she'd had.

And, suddenly, she didn't at all care. She said, lightly but
firmly: "But you see, Herr Olsen, I'm not for sale. Not to you. Not
to any white man. I don't at all care to be owned. Even by you."

The drooping lids lifted. The look in the blue eyes was, Helga
thought, like the surprised stare of a puzzled baby. He hadn't at
all grasped her meaning.

She proceeded, deliberately: "I think you don't understand me.
What I'm trying to say is this: I don't want you. I wouldn't under

any circumstances marry you," and since she was, as she put it, being brutally frank, she added: *"Now."*

He turned a little away from her, his face white but composed, and looked down into the gathering shadows in the little park before the house. At last he spoke, in a queer frozen voice: "You refuse me?"

"Yes," Helga repeated with intentional carelessness. "I refuse you."

The man's full upper lip trembled. He wiped his forehead, where the gold hair was now lying flat and pale and lusterless. His eyes still avoided the girl in the high-backed chair before him. Helga felt a shiver of compunction. For an instant she regretted that she had not been a little kinder. But wasn't it after all the greatest kindness to be cruel? But more gently, less indifferently, she said: "You see, I couldn't marry a white man. I simply couldn't. It isn't just you, not just personal, you understand. It's deeper, broader than that. It's racial. Someday maybe you'll be glad. We can't tell, you know; if we were married, you might come to be ashamed of me, to hate me, to hate all dark people. My mother did that."

"I have offered you marriage, Helga Crane, and you answer me with some strange talk of race and shame. What nonsense is this?"

Helga let that pass because she couldn't, she felt, explain. It would be too difficult, too mortifying. She had no words which could adequately, and without laceration to her pride, convey to him the pitfalls into which very easily they might step. "I might," she said, "have considered it once—when I first came. But you, hoping for a more informal arrangement, waited too long. You missed the moment. I had time to think. Now I couldn't. Nothing is worth the risk. We might come to hate each other. I've been through it, or something like it. I know. I couldn't do it. And I'm glad."

Rising, she held out her hand, relieved that he was still silent. "Good afternoon," she said formally. "It has been a great honor—"

"A tragedy," he corrected, barely touching her hand with his moist fingertips.

"Why?" Helga countered, and for an instant felt as if something sinister and internecine flew back and forth between them like poison.

"I mean," he said, and quite solemnly, "that though I don't entirely understand you, yet in a way I do too. And—" He hesitated. Went on. "I think that my picture of you is, after all, the true Helga Crane. Therefore—a tragedy. For someone. For me? Perhaps."

"Oh, the picture!" Helga lifted her shoulders in a little impatient motion.

Ceremoniously Axel Olsen bowed himself out, leaving her grateful for the urbanity which permitted them to part without too much awkwardness. No other man, she thought, of her acquaintance could have managed it so well—except, perhaps, Robert Anderson.

"I'm glad," she declared to herself in another moment, "that I refused him. And," she added honestly, "I'm glad that I had the chance. He took it awfully well, though—for a tragedy." And she made a tiny frown.

The picture—she had never quite, in spite of her deep interest in him, and her desire for his admiration and approval, forgiven Olsen for that portrait. It wasn't, she contended, herself at all, but some disgusting sensual creature with her features. Herr and Fru Dahl had not exactly liked it either, although collectors, artists, and critics had been unanimous in their praise and it had been hung on the line at an annual exhibition, where it had attracted much flattering attention and many tempting offers.

Now Helga went in and stood for a long time before it, with its creator's parting words in mind: ". . . a tragedy . . . my picture is, after all, the true Helga Crane." Vehemently she shook her head. "It isn't, it isn't at all," she said aloud. Bosh! Pure artistic bosh and conceit. Nothing else. Anyone with half an eye could see that it wasn't at all like her.

"Marie," she called to the maid passing in the hall, "do you think this is a good picture of me?"

Marie blushed. Hesitated. "Of course, Frøkken, I know Herr Olsen is a great artist, but no, I don't like that picture. It looks bad, wicked. Begging your pardon, Frøkken."

"Thanks, Marie, I don't like it either."

Yes, anyone with half an eye could see that it wasn't she.

SIXTEEN

Glad though the Dahls may have been that their niece had had the chance of refusing the hand of Axel Olsen, they were anything but glad that she had taken that chance. Very plainly they said so, and quite firmly they pointed out to her the advisability of retrieving the opportunity, if, indeed, such a thing were possible. But it wasn't, even had Helga been so inclined, for, they were to learn from the columns of *Politikken,* Axel Olsen had gone off suddenly to some queer place in the Balkans. To rest, the newspapers said. To get Frøkken Crane out of his mind, the gossips said.

Life in the Dahl ménage went on, smoothly as before, but not so pleasantly. The combined disappointment and sense of guilt of the Dahls and Helga colored everything. Though she had resolved not to think that they felt that she had, as it were, "let them down," Helga knew that they did. They had not so much expected as hoped that she would bring down Olsen, and so secure the link between the merely fashionable set to which they belonged and the artistic one after which they hankered. It was of course true that there were others, plenty of them. But there was only one Olsen. And Helga, for some idiotic reason connected with race, had refused him. Certainly there was no use in thinking, even, of the others. If she had refused him, she would refuse any and all for the same reason. It was, it seemed, all-embracing.

"It isn't," Uncle Poul had tried to point out to her, "as if there were hundreds of mulattoes here. That, I can understand, might make it a little different. But there's only you. You're unique here, don't you see? Besides, Olsen has money and enviable position. Nobody'd dare to say or even to think anything odd or unkind of you or him. Come now, Helga, it isn't this foolishness about race. Not here in Denmark. You've never spoken of it before. It can't be just that. You're too sensible. It must be something else. I wish you'd try to explain. You don't perhaps like Olsen?"

Helga had been silent, thinking what a severe wrench to Herr Dahl's ideas of decency was this conversation. For he had an almost fanatic regard for reticence, and a peculiar shrinking from what he looked upon as indecent exposure of the emotions.

"Just what is it, Helga?" he asked again, because the pause had grown awkward for him.

"I can't explain any better than I have," she had begun tremulously, "it's just something—something deep down inside of me," and had turned away to hide a face convulsed by threatening tears.

But that, Uncle Poul had remarked with a reasonableness that was wasted on the miserable girl before him, was nonsense, pure nonsense.

With a shaking sigh and a frantic dab at her eyes, in which had come a despairing look, she had agreed that perhaps it was foolish, but she couldn't help it. "Can't you, won't you understand, Uncle Poul?" she begged, with a pleading look at the kindly worldly man who at that moment had been thinking that this strange exotic niece of his wife's was indeed charming. He didn't blame Olsen for taking it rather hard.

The thought passed. She was weeping. With no effort at restraint. Charming, yes. But insufficiently civilized. Impulsive. Imprudent. Selfish.

"Try, Helga, to control yourself," he had urged gently. He detested tears. "If it distresses you so, we won't talk of it again. You, of course, must do as you yourself wish. Both your aunt and I want only that you should be happy." He had wanted to make an end of this fruitless wet conversation.

Helga had made another little dab at her face with the scrap of lace and raised shining eyes to his face. She had said, with sincere regret: "You've been marvelous to me, you and Aunt Katrina. Angelic. I don't want to seem ungrateful. I'd do anything for you, anything in the world but this."

Herr Dahl had shrugged. A little sardonically he had smiled. He had refrained from pointing out that this was the only thing she could do for them, the only thing that they had asked of her. He had been too glad to be through with the uncomfortable discussion.

So life went on. Dinners, coffees, theaters, pictures, music, clothes. More dinners, coffees, theaters, clothes, music. And that nagging aching for America increased. Augmented by the uncomfortableness of Aunt Katrina's and Uncle Poul's disappointment with her, that tormenting nostalgia grew to an unbearable weight. As spring came on with many gracious tokens of following summer, she found her thoughts straying with increasing frequency to Anne's letter and to Harlem, its dirty streets, swollen now, in the warmer weather, with dark, gay humanity.

Until recently she had had no faintest wish ever to see America again. Now she began to welcome the thought of a return. Only a visit, of course. Just to see, to prove to herself that there was nothing there for her. To demonstrate the absurdity of even think-ing that there could be. And to relieve the slight tension here. Maybe when she came back—

Her definite decision to go was arrived at with almost bewil-dering suddenness. It was after a concert at which Dvořák's "New World Symphony" had been wonderfully rendered. Those wailing undertones of "Swing Low, Sweet Chariot" were too poignantly familiar. They struck into her longing heart and cut away her weakening defenses. She knew at least what it was that had lurked formless and undesignated these many weeks in the back of her troubled mind. Incompleteness.

"I'm homesick, not for America, but for Negroes. That's the trouble."

For the first time Helga Crane felt sympathy rather than con-tempt and hatred for that father, whom so often and so angrily she had blamed for his desertion of her mother. She understood, now, his rejection, his repudiation, of the formal calm her mother had represented. She understood his yearning, his intolerable need for the inexhaustible humor and the incessant hope of his own kind, his need for those things, not material, indigenous to all Ne-gro environments. She understood and could sympathize with his facile surrender to the irresistible ties of race, now that they dragged at her own heart. And as she attended parties, the theater, the opera, and mingled with people on the streets, meeting only pale serious faces when she longed for brown laughing ones, she was able to forgive him. Also, it was as if in this understanding and forgiving she had come upon knowledge of almost sacred importance.

Without demur, opposition, or recrimination Herr and Fru Dahl accepted Helga's decision to go back to America. She had expected that they would be glad and relieved. It was agreeable to discover that she had done them less than justice. They were, in spite of their extreme worldliness, very fond of her, and would, as they declared, miss her greatly. And they did want her to come back to them, as they repeatedly insisted. Secretly they felt as she did, that perhaps when she returned—So it was agreed upon that it was only for a brief visit, "for your friend's wedding," and that she was to return in the early fall.

The last day came. The last good-byes were said. Helga began to regret that she was leaving. Why couldn't she have two lives, or why couldn't she be satisfied in one place? Now that she was

actually off, she felt heavy at heart. Already she looked back with
infinite regret at the two years in the country which had given her
so much of pride, of happiness, of wealth, and of beauty.

Bells rang. The gangplank was hoisted. The dark strip of water
widened. The running figures of friends suddenly grown very dear
grew smaller, blurred into a whole, and vanished. Tears rose in
Helga Crane's eyes, fear in her heart.

Good-bye, Denmark! Good-bye. Good-bye!

TWENTY

The day was a rainy one. Helga Crane, stretched out on her bed,
felt herself so broken physically, mentally, that she had given up
thinking. But back and forth in her staggered brain wavering, incoherent thoughts shot shuttlelike. Her pride would have shut out
these humiliating thoughts and painful visions of herself. The effort
was too great. She felt alone, isolated from all other human beings,
separated even from her own anterior existence by the disaster of
yesterday. Over and over, she repeated: "There's nothing left but
to go now." Her anguish seemed unbearable.

For days, for weeks, voluptuous visions had haunted her. Desire had burned in her flesh with uncontrollable violence. The wish
to give herself had been so intense that Dr. Anderson's surprising,
trivial apology loomed as a direct refusal of the offering. Whatever
outcome she had expected, it had been something else than this,
this mortification, this feeling of ridicule and self-loathing, this
knowledge that she had deluded herself. It was all, she told herself,
as unpleasant as possible.

Almost she wished she could die. Not quite. It wasn't that she
was afraid of death, which had, she thought, its picturesque aspects. It was rather that she knew she would not die. And death,
after the debacle, would but intensify its absurdity. Also, it would
reduce her, Helga Crane, to unimportance, to nothingness. Even
in her unhappy present state, that did not appeal to her. Gradually,
reluctantly, she began to know that the blow to her self-esteem,
the certainty of having proved herself a silly fool, was perhaps the
severest hurt which she had suffered. It was her self-assurance that
had gone down in the crash. After all, what Dr. Anderson thought
didn't matter. She could escape from the discomfort of his knowing
gray eyes. But she couldn't escape from sure knowledge that she

had made a fool of herself. This angered her further and she struck the wall with her hands and jumped up and began hastily to dress herself. She couldn't go on with the analysis. It was too hard. Why bother, when she could add nothing to the obvious fact that she had been a fool?

"I can't stay in this room any longer. I must get out or I'll choke." Her self-knowledge had increased her anguish. Distracted, agitated, incapable of containing herself, she tore open drawers and closets, trying desperately to take some interest in the selection of her apparel.

It was evening and still raining. In the streets, unusually deserted, the electric lights cast dull glows. Helga Crane, walking rapidly, aimlessly, could decide on no definite destination. She had not thought to take umbrella or even rubbers. Rain and wind whipped cruelly about her, drenching her garments and chilling her body. Soon the foolish little satin shoes which she wore were sopping wet. Unheeding these physical discomforts, she went on, but at the open corner of 138th Street a sudden more ruthless gust of wind ripped the small hat from her head. In the next minute the black clouds opened wider and spilled their water with unusual fury. The streets became swirling rivers. Helga Crane, forgetting her mental torment, looked about anxiously for a sheltering taxi. A few taxis sped by, but inhabited, so she began desperately to struggle through wind and rain toward one of the buildings, where she could take shelter in a store or a doorway. But another whirl of wind lashed her and, scornful of her slight strength, tossed her into the swollen gutter.

Now she knew beyond all doubt that she had no desire to die, and certainly not there nor then. Not in such a messy wet manner. Death had lost all of its picturesque aspects to the girl lying soaked and soiled in the flooded gutter. So, though she was very tired and very weak, she dragged herself up and succeeded finally in making her way to the store whose blurred light she had marked for her destination.

She had opened the door and had entered before she was aware that, inside, people were singing a song which she was conscious of having heard years ago—hundreds of years, it seemed. Repeated over and over, she made out the words:

> ". . . Showers of blessings,
> Showers of blessings . . ."

She was conscious too of a hundred pairs of eyes upon her as she stood there, drenched and disheveled, at the door of this improvised meeting house.

> ". . . Showers of blessings . . ."

The appropriateness of the song, with its constant reference to showers, the ridiculousness of herself in such surroundings, was too much for Helga Crane's frayed nerves. She sat down on the floor, a dripping heap, and laughed and laughed and laughed.

It was into a shocked silence that she laughed. For at the first hysterical peal the words of the song had died in the singers' throats, and the wheezy organ had lapsed into stillness. But in a moment there were hushed solicitous voices; she was assisted to her feet and led haltingly to a chair near the low platform at the far end of the room. On one side of her a tall angular black woman under a queer hat sat down, on the other a fattish yellow man with huge outstanding ears and long, nervous hands.

The singing began again, this time a low wailing thing:

> "Oh, the bitter shame and sorrow
> That a time could ever be,
> When I let the Savior's pity
> Plead in vain, and proudly answered:
> "All of self and none of Thee,
> All of self and none of Thee."
>
> Yet He found me, I beheld Him,
> Bleeding on the cursed tree;
> Heard Him pray: "Forgive them, Father."
> And my wistful heart said faintly,
> "Some of self and some of Thee,
> Some of self and some of Thee."

There were, it appeared, endless moaning verses. Behind Helga a woman had begun to cry audibly, and soon, somewhere else, another. Outside, the wind still bellowed. The wailing singing went on:

> " '. . . Less of self and more of Thee,
> Less of self and more of Thee.' "

Helga too began to weep, at first silently, softly; then with great racking sobs. Her nerves were so torn, so aching, her body so wet, so cold! It was a relief to cry unrestrainedly, and she gave herself freely to soothing tears, not noticing that the groaning and sobbing of those about her had increased, unaware that the grotesque ebony figure at her side had begun gently to pat her arm to the rhythm of the singing and to croon softly: "Yes, chile, yes, chile." Nor did she notice the furtive glances that the man on her other side cast at her between his fervent shouts of "Amen!" and "Praise God for a sinner!"

She did notice, though, that the tempo, the atmosphere of the place, had changed, and gradually she ceased to weep and gave her attention to what was happening about her. Now they were singing:

". . . Jesus knows all about my troubles . . ."

Men and women were swaying and clapping their hands, shouting and stamping their feet to the frankly irreverent melody of the song. Without warning the woman at her side threw off her hat, leaped to her feet, waved her long arms, and shouted shrilly: "Glory! Hallelujah!" and then in wild, ecstatic fury jumped up and down before Helga, clutching at the girl's soaked coat, and screamed: "Come to Jesus, you pore los' sinner!" Alarmed for the fraction of a second, involuntarily Helga had shrunk from her grasp, wriggling out of the wet coat when she could not loosen the crazed creature's hold. At the sight of the bare arms and neck growing out of the clinging red dress, a shudder shook the swaying man at her right. On the face of the dancing woman before her a disapproving frown gathered. She shrieked: "A scarlet 'oman. Come to Jesus, you pore los' Jezebel!"

At this the short brown man on the platform raised a placating hand and sanctimoniously delivered himself of the words: "Remembah de words of our Mastah: 'Let him that is without sin cast de first stone.' Let us pray for our errin' sistah."

Helga Crane was amused, angry, disdainful, as she sat there, listening to the preacher praying for her soul. But though she was contemptuous, she was being too well entertained to leave. And it was, at least, warm and dry. So she stayed, listening to the fervent exhortation to God to save her and to the zealous shoutings and groanings of the congregation. Particularly she was interested in the writhings and weepings of the feminine portion, which seemed to predominate. Little by little the performance took on an almost Bacchic vehemence. Behind her, before her, beside her, frenzied women gesticulated, screamed, wept, and tottered to the praying of the preacher, which had gradually become a cadenced chant. When at last he ended, another took up the plea in the same moaning chant, and then another. It went on and on without pause with the persistence of some unconquerable faith exalted beyond time and reality.

Fascinated, Helga Crane watched until there crept upon her an indistinct horror of an unknown world. She felt herself in the presence of a nameless people, observing rites of a remote obscure origin. The faces of the men and women took on the aspect of a dim vision. "This," she whispered to herself, "is terrible. I must get out of here." But the horror held her. She remained motionless, watching, as if she lacked the strength to leave the place—foul, vile, and terrible, with its mixture of breaths, its contact of bodies, its concerted convulsions, all in wild appeal for a single soul. Her soul.

And as Helga watched and listened, gradually a curious influence penetrated her; she felt an echo of the weird orgy resound in her own heart; she felt herself possessed by the same madness; she too felt a brutal desire to shout and to sling herself about. Frightened at the strength of the obsession, she gathered herself for one last effort to escape, but vainly. In rising, weakness and nausea from last night's unsuccessful attempt to make herself drunk overcame her. She had eaten nothing since yesterday. She fell forward against the crude railing which enclosed the little platform. For a single moment she remained there in silent stillness, because she was afraid she was going to be sick. And in that moment she was lost—or saved. The yelling figures about her pressed forward, closing her in on all sides. Maddened, she grasped at the railing, and with no previous intention began to yell like one insane, drowning every other clamor, while torrents of tears streamed down her face. She was unconscious of the words she uttered, or their meaning: "Oh, God, mercy, mercy. Have mercy on me!" but she repeated them over and over.

From those about her came a thunderclap of joy. Arms were stretched toward her with savage frenzy. The women dragged themselves upon their knees or crawled over the floor like reptiles, sobbing and pulling their hair and tearing off their clothing. Those who succeeded in getting near to her leaned forward to encourage the unfortunate sister, dropping hot tears and beads of sweat upon her bare arms and neck.

The thing became real. A miraculous calm came upon her. Life seemed to expand and to become very easy. Helga Crane felt within her a supreme aspiration toward the regaining of simple happiness, a happiness unburdened by the complexities of the lives she had known. About her the tumult and the shouting continued, but in a lesser degree. Some of the more exuberant worshipers had fainted into inert masses, the voices of others were almost spent. Gradually the room grew quiet and almost solemn, and to the kneeling girl time seemed to sink back into the mysterious grandeur and holiness of far-off simpler centuries.

TWENTY-ONE

On leaving the mission Helga Crane had started straight back to her room at the hotel. With her had gone the fattish yellow man who had sat beside her. He had introduced himself as the Reverend Mr. Pleasant Green in proffering his escort, for which Helga had been grateful because she had still felt a little dizzy and much exhausted. So great had been this physical weariness that as she had walked beside him, without attention to his verbose information about his own "field," as he called it, she had been seized with a hateful feeling of vertigo and obliged to lay firm hold on his arm to keep herself from falling. The weakness had passed as suddenly as it had come. Silently they had walked on. And gradually Helga had recalled that the man beside her had himself swayed slightly at their close encounter, and that frantically for a fleeting moment he had gripped at a protruding fence railing. That man! Was it possible? As easy as that?

Instantly across her still half-hypnotized consciousness little burning darts of fancy had shot themselves. No. She couldn't. It would be too awful. Just the same, what or who was there to hold her back? Nothing. Simply nothing. Nobody. Nobody at all.

Her searching mind had become in a moment quite clear. She cast at the man a speculative glance, aware that for a tiny space she had looked into his mind, a mind striving to be calm. A mind that was certain that it was secure because it was concerned only with things of the soul, spiritual things, which to him meant religious things. But actually a mind by habit at home amongst the mere material aspect of things, and at that moment consumed by some longing for the ecstasy that might lurk behind the gleam of her cheek, the flying wave of her hair, the pressure of her slim fingers on his heavy arm. An instant's flashing vision it had been and it was gone at once. Escaped in the aching of her own senses and the sudden disturbing fear that she herself had perhaps missed the supreme secret of life.

After all, there was nothing to hold her back. Nobody to care. She stopped sharply, shocked at what she was on the verge of considering. Appalled at where it might lead her.

The man—what was his name?—thinking that she was almost about to fall again, had reached out his arms to her. Helga Crane had deliberately stopped thinking. She had only smiled, a faint provocative smile, and pressed her fingers deep into his arms until a wild look had come into his slightly bloodshot eyes.

The next morning she lay for a long while, scarcely breathing, while she reviewed the happenings of the night before. Curious. She couldn't be sure that it wasn't religion that had made her feel so utterly different from dreadful yesterday. And gradually she became a little sad, because she realized that with every hour she would get a little further away from this soothing haziness, this rest from her long trouble of body and of spirit; back into the clear bareness of her own small life and being, from which happiness and serenity always faded just as they had shaped themselves. And slowly bitterness crept into her soul. Because, she thought, all I've ever had in life has been things—except just this one time. At that she closed her eyes, for even remembrance caused her to shiver a little.

Things, she realized, hadn't been, weren't, enough for her. She'd have to have something else besides. It all came back to that old question of happiness. Surely this was it. Just for a fleeting moment Helga Crane, her eyes watching the wind scattering the gray-white clouds and so clearing a speck of blue sky, questioned her ability to retain, to bear, this happiness at such cost as she must pay for it. There was, she knew, no getting round that. The man's agitation and sincere conviction of sin had been too evident, too illuminating. The question returned in a slightly new form. Was it worth the risk? Could she take it? Was she able? Though what did it matter—now?

And all the while she knew in one small corner of her mind

that such thinking was useless. She had made her decision. Her resolution. It was a chance at stability, at permanent happiness, that she meant to take. She had let so many other things, other chances, escape her. And anyway there was God; He would perhaps make it come out all right. Still confused and not so sure that it wasn't the fact that she was "saved" that had contributed to this after feeling of well-being, she clutched the hope, the desire to believe that now at last she had found some One, some Power, who was interested in her. Would help her.

She meant, however, for once in her life to be practical. So she would make sure of both things, God and man.

Her glance caught the calendar over the little white desk. The tenth of November. The steamer *Oscar II* sailed today. Yesterday she had half thought of sailing with it. Yesterday. How far away!

With the thought of yesterday came the thought of Robert Anderson and a feeling of elation, revenge. She had put herself beyond the need of help from him. She had made it impossible for herself ever again to appeal to him. Instinctively she had the knowledge that he would be shocked. Grieved. Horribly hurt even. Well, let him!

The need to hurry suddenly obsessed her. She must. The morning was almost gone. And she meant, if she could manage it, to be married today. Rising, she was seized with a fear so acute that she had to lie down again. For the thought came to her that she might fail. Might not be able to confront the situation. That would be too dreadful. But she became calm again. How could he, a naïve creature like that, hold out against her? If she pretended to distress? To fear? To remorse? He couldn't. It would be useless for him even to try. She screwed up her face into a little grin, remembering that even if protestations were to fail there were other ways.

And, too, there was God.

TWENTY-TWO

And so in the confusion of seductive repentance Helga Crane was married to the grandiloquent Reverend Mr. Pleasant Green, that rattish yellow man who had so kindly, so unctuously, proffered his escort to her hotel on the memorable night of her conversion. With him she willingly, even eagerly, left the sins and temptations of New York behind her to, as he put it, "labor in the vineyard of the Lord" in the tiny Alabama town where he was pastor to a scattered and primitive flock. And where, as the wife of the preacher, she was a person of relative importance. Only relative.

Helga did not hate him, the town, or the people. No. Not for a long time.

As always, at first the novelty of the thing, the change, fascinated her. There was a recurrence of the feeling that now, at last, she had found a place for herself, that she was really living. And she had her religion, which in her new status as a preacher's wife had of necessity become real to her. She believed in it. Because in its coming it had brought this other thing, this anesthetic satisfaction for her senses. Hers was, she declared to herself, a truly spiritual union. This one time in her life, she was convinced, she had not clutched a shadow and missed the actuality. She felt compensated for all previous humiliations and disappointments and was glad. If she remembered that she had had something like this feeling before, she put the unwelcome memory from her with the thought: "This time I know I'm right. This time it will last."

Eagerly she accepted everything, even that bleak air of poverty which, in some curious way, regards itself as virtuous, for no other reason than that it is poor. And in her first hectic enthusiasm she intended and planned to do much good to her husband's parishioners. Her young joy and zest for the uplifting of her fellow men came back to her. She meant to subdue the cleanly scrubbed ugliness of her own surroundings to soft inoffensive beauty, and to help the other women to do likewise. Too, she would help them with their clothes, tactfully point out that sunbonnets, no matter how gay, and aprons, no matter how frilly, were not quite the proper things for Sunday church wear. There would be a sewing circle. She visualized herself instructing the children, who seemed most of the time to run wild, in ways of gentler deportment. She was anxious to be a true helpmate, for in her heart was a feeling of obligation, of humble gratitude.

In her ardor and sincerity Helga even made some small beginnings. True, she was not very successful in this matter of innovations. When she went about to try to interest the women in what she considered more appropriate clothing and in inexpensive ways of improving their homes according to her ideas of beauty, she was met, always, with smiling agreement and good-natured promises. "Yuh all is right, Mis' Green," and "Ah suttinly will, Mis' Green," fell courteously on her ear at each visit.

She was unaware that afterward they would shake their heads sullenly over their washtubs and ironing boards. And that among themselves they talked with amusement, or with anger, of "dat uppity, meddlin' No'the'nah," and "pore Reve'end," who in their opinion "would 'a done bettah to 'a ma'ied Clementine Richards." Knowing, as she did, nothing of this, Helga was unperturbed. But even had she known, she would not have been disheartened. The fact that it was difficult but increased her eagerness and made the doing of it seem only the more worth while. Sometimes she would smile to think how changed she was.

And she was humble too. Even with Clementine Richards, a strapping black beauty of magnificent Amazon proportions and bold shining eyes of jetlike hardness. A person of awesome appearance. All chains, strings of beads, jingling bracelets, flying ribbons, feathery neckpieces, and flowery hats. Clementine was inclined to treat Helga with an only partially concealed contemptuousness, considering her a poor thing without style, and without proper understanding of the worth and greatness of the man, Clementine's own adored pastor, whom Helga had somehow had the astounding good luck to marry. Clementine's admiration of the Reverend Mr. Pleasant Green was open. Helga was at first astonished. Until she learned that there was really no reason why it should be concealed. Everybody was aware of it. Besides, open adoration was the prerogative, the almost religious duty, of the female portion of the flock. If this unhidden and exaggerated approval contributed to his already oversized pomposity, so much the better. It was what they expected, liked, wanted. The greater his own sense of superiority became, the more flattered they were by his notice and small attentions, the more they cast at him killing glances, the more they hung enraptured on his words.

In the days before her conversion, with its subsequent blurring of her sense of humor, Helga might have amused herself by tracing the relation of this constant ogling and flattering to the proverbially large families of preachers; the often disastrous effect on their wives of this constant stirring of the senses by extraneous women. Now, however, she did not even think of it.

She was too busy. Every minute of the day was full. Necessarily. And to Helga this was a new experience. She was charmed by it. To be mistress in one's own house, to have a garden, and chickens, and a pig; to have a husband—and to be "right with God"—what pleasure did that other world which she had left contain that could surpass these? Here, she had found, she was sure, the intangible thing for which, indefinitely, always she had craved. It had received embodiment.

Everything contributed to her gladness in living. And so for a time she loved everything and everyone. Or thought she did. Even the weather. And it was truly lovely. By day a glittering gold sun was set in an unbelievably bright sky. In the evening silver buds sprouted in a Chinese blue sky, and the warm day was softly soothed by a slight, cool breeze. And night! Night, when a languid moon peeped through the wide-opened windows of her little house, a little mockingly, it may be. Always at night's approach Helga was bewildered by a disturbing medley of feelings. Challenge. Anticipation. And a small fear.

In the morning she was serene again. Peace had returned. And she could go happily, inexpertly, about the humble tasks of her household, cooking, dishwashing, sweeping, dusting, mending, and darning. And there was the garden. When she worked there, she felt that life was utterly filled with the glory and the marvel of God.

Helga did not reason about this feeling, as she did not at that time reason about anything. It was enough that it was there, coloring all her thoughts and acts. It endowed the four rooms of her ugly brown house with a kindly radiance, obliterating the stark bareness of its white plaster walls and the nakedness of its uncovered painted floors. It even softened the choppy lines of the shiny oak furniture and subdued the awesome horribleness of the religious pictures.

And all the other houses and cabins shared in this illumination. And the people. The dark undecorated women unceasingly concerned with the actual business of life, its rounds of births and christenings, of loves and marriages, of deaths and funerals, were to Helga miraculously beautiful. The smallest, dirtiest, brown child, barefooted in the fields or muddy roads, was to her an emblem of the wonder of life, of love, and of God's goodness.

For the preacher, her husband, she had a feeling of gratitude amounting almost to sin. Beyond that, she thought of him not at all. But she was not conscious that she had shut him out from her mind. Besides, what need to think of him? He was there. She was at peace, and secure. Surely their two lives were one, and the companionship in the Lord's grace so perfect that to think about it would be tempting providence. She had done with soul searching.

What did it matter that he consumed his food, even the softest varieties, audibly? What did it matter that, though he did not work with his hands, not even in the garden, his fingernails were always rimmed with black? What did it matter that he failed to wash his fat body, or to shift his clothing, as often as Helga herself did? There were things that more than outweighed these. In the certainty of his goodness, his righteousness, his holiness, Helga somehow overcame her first disgust at the odor of sweat and stale garments. She was even able to be unaware of it. Herself, Helga had come to look upon as a finicky, showy thing of unnecessary prejudices and fripperies. And when she sat in the dreary structure, which had once been a stable belonging to the estate of a wealthy horse-racing man and about which the odor of manure still clung, now the church and social center of the Negroes of the town, and heard him expound with verbal extravagance the gospel of blood and love, of hell and heaven, of fire and gold streets, pounding with clenched fists the frail table before him or shaking those fists in the faces of the congregation like direct personal threats, or pacing wildly back and forth and even sometimes shedding great tears as he besought them to repent, she was, she told herself, proud and gratified that he belonged to her. In some strange way she was able to ignore the atmosphere of self-satisfaction which poured from him like gas from a leaking pipe.

And night came at the end of every day. Emotional, palpitating, amorous, all that was living in her sprang like rank weeds at the tingling thought of night, with a vitality so strong that it devoured all shoots of reason.

TWENTY-THREE

After the first exciting months Helga was too driven, too occupied, and too sick to carry out any of the things for which she had made such enthusiastic plans, or even to care that she had made only slight progress toward their accomplishment. For she, who had never thought of her body save as something on which to hang lovely fabrics, had now constantly to think of it. It had persistently to be pampered to secure from it even a little service. Always she felt extraordinarily and annoyingly ill, having forever to be sinking into chairs. Or, if she was out, to be pausing by the roadside, clinging desperately to some convenient fence or tree, waiting for the horrible nausea and hateful faintness to pass. The light, carefree days of the past, when she had not felt heavy and reluctant or weak and spent, receded more and more with increasing vagueness, like a dream passing from a faulty memory.

The children used her up. There were already three of them, all born within the short space of twenty months. Two great healthy twin boys, whose lovely bodies were to Helga like rare figures carved out of amber, and in whose sleepy and mysterious black eyes all that was puzzling, evasive, and aloof in life seemed to find expression. No matter how often or how long she looked at these two small sons of hers, never did she lose a certain delicious feeling in which were mingled pride, tenderness, and exaltation. And there was a girl, sweet, delicate, and flowerlike. Not so healthy or so loved as the boys, but still miraculously her own proud and cherished possession.

So there was no time for the pursuit of beauty, or for the uplifting of other harassed and teeming women, or for the instruction of their neglected children.

Her husband was still, as he had always been, deferentially kind and incredulously proud of her—and verbally encouraging. Helga tried not to see that he had rather lost any personal interest in her, except for the short spaces between the times when she was preparing for or recovering from childbirth. She shut her eyes to the fact that his encouragement had become a little platitudinous, limited mostly to "The Lord will look out for you," "We must accept what God sends," or "My mother had nine children and was thankful for every one." If she was inclined to wonder a little just how they were to manage with another child on the way, he would point out to her that her doubt and uncertainty were a stupendous ingratitude. Had not the good God saved her soul from hellfire and eternal damnation? Had He not in His great kindness given her three small lives to raise up for His glory? Had He not showered her with numerous other mercies (evidently too numerous to be named separately)?

"You must," the Reverend Mr. Pleasant Green would say unctuously, "trust the Lord more fully, Helga."

This pabulum did not irritate her. Perhaps it was the fact that the preacher was, now, not so much at home that even lent to it a measure of real comfort. For the adoring women of his flock, noting how with increasing frequency their pastor's house went unswept and undusted, his children unwashed, and his wife untidy, took pleasant pity on him and invited him often to tasty orderly meals, specially prepared for him, in their own clean houses.

Helga, looking about in helpless dismay and sick disgust at the disorder around her, the permanent assembly of partly emptied medicine bottles on the clock shelf, the perpetual array of drying baby clothes on the chair backs, the constant debris of broken toys on the floor, the unceasing litter of half-dead flowers on the table, dragged in by the toddling twins from the forlorn garden, failed to blame him for the thoughtless selfishness of these absences. And she was thankful, whenever possible, to be relieved from the ordeal of cooking. There were times when, having had to retreat from the kitchen in lumbering haste with her sensitive nose gripped between tightly squeezing fingers, she had been sure that the greatest kindness that God could ever show to her would be to free her forever from the sight and smell of food.

How, she wondered, did other women, other mothers, manage? Could it be possible that, while presenting such smiling and contented faces, they were all always on the edge of health? All always worn out and apprehensive? Or was it only she, a poor weak city-bred thing, who felt that the strain of what the Reverend Mr. Pleasant Green had so often gently and patiently reminded her was a natural thing, an act of God, was almost unendurable?

One day on her round of visiting—a church duty, to be done no matter how miserable one was—she summoned up sufficient boldness to ask several women how they felt, how they managed. The answers were a resigned shrug, or an amused snort, or an upward rolling of eyeballs with a mention of "de Lawd" looking after us all.

" 'Tain't nothin', nothin' at all, chile," said one, Sary Jones, who, as Helga knew, had had six children in about as many years. "Yuh all takes it too ha'd. Jes' remembah et's natu'al fo' a 'oman to hab chilluns an' don' fret so."

"But," protested Helga, "I'm always so tired and half sick. That can't be natural."

"Laws, chile, we's all ti'ed. An' Ah reckons we's all gwine a be ti'ed till kingdom come. Jes' make de bes' of et, honey. Jes' make de bes' yuh can."

Helga sighed, turning her nose away from the steaming coffee which her hostess had placed for her and against which her squeamish stomach was about to revolt. At the moment the compensations of immortality seemed very shadowy and very far away.

"Jes' remembah," Sary went on, staring sternly into Helga's thin face, "we all gits ouah res' by an' by. In de nex' worl' we's all recompense'. Jes' put yo' trus' in de Sabioah."

Looking at the confident face of the little bronze figure on the opposite side of the immaculately spread table, Helga had a sensation of shame that she should be less than content. Why couldn't she be as trusting and as certain that her troubles would not overwhelm her as Sary Jones was? Sary, who in all likelihood had toiled every day of her life since early childhood except on those days, totaling perhaps sixty, following the birth of her six children. And who by dint of superhuman saving had somehow succeeded in feeding and clothing them and sending them all to school. Before her Helga felt humbled and oppressed by the sense of her own unworthiness and lack of sufficient faith.

"Thanks, Sary," she said, rising in retreat from the coffee, "you've done me a world of good. I'm really going to try to be more patient."

So, though with growing yearning she longed for the great ordinary things of life, hunger, sleep, freedom from pain, she resigned herself to doing without them. The possibility of alleviating her burdens by a greater faith became lodged in her mind. She gave herself up to it. It *did* help. And the beauty of leaning on the wisdom of God, of trusting, gave her a queer sort of satisfaction. Faith was really quite easy. One had only to yield. To ask no questions. The more weary, the more weak, she became, the easier it was. Her religion was to her a kind of protective coloring, shielding her from the cruel light of an unbearable reality.

This utter yielding in faith to what had been sent her found her favor, too, in the eyes of her neighbors. Her husband's flock began to approve and commend this submission and humility to a superior wisdom. The womenfolk spoke more kindly and more affectionately of the preacher's Northern wife. "Pore Mis' Green, wid all dem small chilluns at once. She suah do hab it ha'd. An' she don' nebah complains an' frets no mo'e. Jes' trus' in de Lawd lak de Good Book say. Mighty sweet lil' 'oman too."

Helga didn't bother much about the preparations for the coming child. Actually and metaphorically she bowed her head before God, trusting in Him to see her through. Secretly she was glad that she had not to worry about herself or anything. It was a relief to be able to put the entire responsibility on someone else.

TWENTY-FOUR

It began, this next childbearing, during the morning services of a breathless hot Sunday while the fervent choir soloist was singing: "Ah am freed of mah sorrow," and lasted far into the small hours of Tuesday morning. It seemed, for some reason, not to go off just right. And when, after that long frightfulness, the fourth little dab of amber humanity which Helga had contributed to a despised race was held before her for maternal approval, she failed entirely to respond properly to this sop of consolation for the suffering and horror through which she had passed. There was from her no pleased, proud smile, no loving, possessive gesture, no manifestation of interest in the important matters of sex and weight. Instead she deliberately closed her eyes, mutely shutting out the sickly infant, its smiling father, the soiled midwife, the curious neighbors, and the tousled room.

A week she lay so. Silent and listless. Ignoring food, the clamoring children, the comings and goings of solicitous, kindhearted women, her hovering husband, and all of life about her. The neighbors were puzzled. The Reverend Mr. Pleasant Green was worried. The midwife was frightened.

On the floor, in and out among the furniture and under her bed, the twins played. Eager to help, the churchwomen crowded in and, meeting there others on the same laudable errand, stayed to gossip and to wonder. Anxiously the preacher sat, Bible in hand, beside his wife's bed, or in a nervous half-guilty manner invited the congregated parishioners to join him in prayer for the healing of their sister. Then, kneeling, they would beseech God to stretch out His all-powerful hand on behalf of the afflicted one, softly at first, but with rising vehemence, accompanied by moans and tears, until it seemed that the God to whom they prayed must in mercy to the sufferer grant relief. If only so that she might rise up and escape from the tumult, the heat, and the smell.

Helga, however, was unconcerned, undisturbed by the commotion about her. It was all part of the general unreality. Nothing reached her. Nothing penetrated the kind darkness into which her bruised spirit had retreated. Even that red-letter event, the coming to see her of the old white physician from downtown, who had for a long time stayed talking gravely to her husband, drew from her no interest. Nor for days was she aware that a stranger, a nurse from Mobile, had been added to her household, a brusquely effi-

cient woman who produced order out of chaos and quiet out of
bedlam. Neither did the absence of the children, removed by good
neighbors at Miss Hartley's insistence, impress her. While she had
gone down into that appalling blackness of pain, the ballast of her
brain had got loose and she hovered for a long time somewhere in
that delightful borderland on the edge of unconsciousness, an enchanted and blissful place where peace and incredible quiet encom-
passed her.

After weeks she grew better, returned to earth, set her reluctant feet to the hard path of life again.

"Well, here you are!" announced Miss Hartley in her slightly
harsh voice one afternoon just before the fall of evening. She had
for some time been standing at the bedside gazing down at Helga
with an intent speculative look.

"Yes," Helga agreed in a thin little voice, "I'm back." The
truth was that she had been back for some hours. Purposely she
had lain silent and still, wanting to linger forever in that serene
haven, that effortless calm where nothing was expected of her.
There she could watch the figures of the past drift by. There was
her mother, whom she had loved from a distance and finally so
scornfully blamed, who appeared as she had always remembered
her, unbelievably beautiful, young, and remote. Robert Anderson,
questioning, purposely detached, affecting, as she realized now, her
life in a remarkably cruel degree; for at last she understood clearly
how deeply, how passionately, she must have loved him. Anne,
lovely, secure, wise, selfish. Axel Olsen, conceited, worldly, spoiled.
Audrey Denney, placid, taking quietly and without fuss the things
which she wanted. James Vayle, snobbish, smug, servile. Mrs.
Hayes-Rore, important, kind, determined. The Dahls, rich, correct,
climbing. Flashingly, fragmentarily, other long-forgotten figures,
women in gay fashionable frocks and men in formal black and
white, glided by in bright rooms to distant, vaguely familiar music.

It was refreshingly delicious, this immersion in the past. But
it was finished now. It was over. The words of her husband, the
Reverend Mr. Pleasant Green, who had been standing at the window looking mournfully out at the scorched melon patch, ruined
because Helga had been ill so long and unable to tend it, were
confirmation of that.

"The Lord be praised," he said, and came forward. It was
distinctly disagreeable. It was even more disagreeable to feel his
moist hand on hers. A cold shiver brushed over her. She closed her

eyes. Obstinately and with all her small strength she drew her hand away from him. Hid it far down under the bedcovering, and turned her face away to hide a grimace of unconquerable aversion. She cared nothing, at that moment, for his hurt surprise. She knew only that, in the hideous agony that for interminable hours—no, centuries—she had borne, the luster of religion had vanished; that revulsion had come upon her; that she hated this man. Between them the vastness of the universe had come.

Miss Hartley, all-seeing and instantly aware of a situation, as she had been quite aware that her patient had been conscious for some time before she herself had announced the fact, intervened, saying firmly: "I think it might be better if you didn't try to talk to her now. She's terribly sick and weak yet. She's still got some fever and we mustn't excite her or she's liable to slip back. And we don't want that, do we?"

No, the man, her husband, responded, they didn't want that. Reluctantly he went from the room with a last look at Helga, who was lying on her back with one frail, pale hand under her small head, her curly black hair scattered loose on the pillow. She regarded him from behind dropped lids. The day was hot, her breasts were covered only by a nightgown of filmy crepe, a relic of prematrimonial days, which had slipped from one carved shoulder. He flinched. Helga's petulant lip curled, for she well knew that this fresh reminder of her desirability was like the flick of a whip.

Miss Hartley carefully closed the door after the retreating husband. "It's time," she said, "for your evening treatment, and then you've got to try to sleep for a while. No more visitors tonight."

Helga nodded and tried unsuccessfully to make a little smile. She was glad of Miss Hartley's presence. It would, she felt, protect her from so much. She mustn't, she thought to herself, get well too fast. Since it seemed she was going to get well. In bed she could think, could have a certain amount of quiet. Of aloneness.

In that period of racking pain and calamitous fright Helga had learned what passion and credulity could do to one. In her was born angry bitterness and an enormous disgust. The cruel, unrelieved suffering had beaten down her protective wall of artificial faith in the infinite wisdom, in the mercy, of God. For had she not called in her agony on Him? And He had not heard. Why? Because, she knew now, He wasn't there. Didn't exist. Into that yawning gap of unspeakable brutality had gone, too, her belief in the miracle and wonder of life. Only scorn, resentment, and hate remained—and ridicule. Life wasn't a miracle, a wonder. It was, for Negroes at least, only a great disappointment. Something to be got through with as best one could. No one was interested in them or helped them. God! Bah! And they were only a nuisance to other people.

Everything in her mind was hot and cold, beating and swirling about. Within her emaciated body raged disillusion. Chaotic turmoil. With the obscuring curtain of religion rent, she was able to look about her and see with shocked eyes this thing that she had done to herself. She couldn't, she thought ironically, even blame God for it, now that she knew that He didn't exist. No. No more than she could pray to Him for the death of her husband, the Reverend Mr. Pleasant Green. The white man's God. And His great love for all people regardless of race! What idiotic nonsense she had allowed herself to believe. How could she, how could anyone, have been so deluded? How could ten million black folk credit it when daily before their eyes was enacted its contradiction? Not that she at all cared about the ten million. But herself. Her sons. Her daughter. These would grow to manhood, to womanhood, in this vicious, this hypocritical land. The dark eyes filled with tears.

"I wouldn't," the nurse advised, "do that. You've been dreadfully sick, you know. I can't have you worrying. Time enough for that when you're well. Now you must sleep all you possibly can."

Helga did sleep. She found it surprisingly easy to sleep. Aided by Miss Hartley's rather masterful discernment, she took advantage of the ease with which this blessed enchantment stole over her. From her husband's praisings, prayers, and caresses she sought refuge in sleep, and from the neighbors' gifts, advice, and sympathy.

There was that day on which they told her that the last sickly infant, born of such futile torture and lingering torment, had died after a short week of slight living. Just closed his eyes and died. No vitality. On hearing it Helga too had just closed her eyes. Not to die. She was convinced that before her there were years of living. Perhaps of happiness even. For a new idea had come to her. She had closed her eyes to shut in any telltale gleam of the relief which she felt. One less. And she had gone off into sleep.

And there was that Sunday morning on which the Reverend Mr. Pleasant Green had informed her that they were that day to hold a special thanksgiving service for her recovery. There would, he said, be prayers, special testimonies, and songs. Was there anything particular she would like to have said, to have prayed for, to have sung? Helga had smiled from sheer amusement as she replied that there was nothing. Nothing at all. She only hoped that they would enjoy themselves. And, closing her eyes that he might be discouraged from longer tarrying, she had gone off into sleep.

Waking later to the sound of joyous religious abandon floating in through the opened windows, she had asked a little diffidently that she be allowed to read. Miss Hartley's sketchy brows contracted into a dubious frown. After a judicious pause she had answered: "No, I don't think so." Then, seeing the rebellious tears which had sprung into her patient's eyes, she added kindly: "But I'll read to you a little if you like."

That, Helga replied, would be nice. In the next room on a high-up shelf was a book. She'd forgotten the name, but its author was Anatole France. There was a story, "The Procurator of Judea." Would Miss Hartley read that? "Thanks. Thanks awfully."

" 'Laelius Lamia, born in Italy of illustrious parents,' " began the nurse in her slightly harsh voice.

Helga drank it in.

" '. . . For to this day the women bring down doves to the altar as their victims. . . .' "

Helga closed her eyes.

" '. . . Africa and Asia have already enriched us with a considerable number of gods. . . .' "

Miss Hartley looked up. Helga had slipped into slumber while the superbly ironic ending which she had so desired to hear was yet a long way off. A dull tale, was Miss Hartley's opinion, as she curiously turned the pages to see how it turned out.

" 'Jesus? . . . Jesus—of Nazareth? I cannot call him to mind.' "

"Huh! she muttered, puzzled. "Silly." And closed the book.

TWENTY-FIVE

During the long process of getting well, between the dreamy intervals when she was beset by the insistent craving for sleep, Helga had had too much time to think. At first she had felt only an astonished anger at the quagmire in which she had engulfed herself. She had ruined her life. Made it impossible ever again to do the things that she wanted, have the things that she loved, mingle with the people she liked. She had, to put it as brutally as anyone could, been a fool. The damnedest kind of a fool. And she had paid for it. Enough. More than enough.

Her mind, swaying back to the protection that religion had afforded her, almost she wished that it had not failed her. An illusion. Yes. But better, far better, than this terrible reality. Religion had, after all, its uses. It blunted the perceptions. Robbed life of its crudest truths. Especially it had its uses for the poor—and the blacks.

For the blacks. The Negroes.

And this, Helga decided, was what ailed the whole Negro race in America, this fatuous belief in the white man's God, this childlike trust in full compensation for all woes and privations in "kingdom come." Sary Jones's absolute conviction, "In de nex' worl' we's all recompense'," came back to her. And ten million souls were as sure of it as was Sary. How the white man's God must laugh at the great joke he had played on them! Bound them to slavery, then to poverty and insult, and made them bear it unresistingly, uncomplainingly almost, by sweet promises of mansions in the sky by and by.

"Pie in the sky," Helga said aloud derisively, forgetting for the moment Miss Hartley's brisk presence, and so was a little startled at hearing her voice from the adjoining room saying severely: "My goodness! No! I should say you can't have pie. It's too indigestible. Maybe when you're better—"

"That," assented Helga, "is what I said. Pie—by and by. That's the trouble."

The nurse looked concerned. Was this an approaching relapse? Coming to the bedside, she felt at her patient's pulse while giving her a searching look. No. "You'd better," she admonished, a slight edge to her tone, "try to get a little nap. You haven't had any sleep today, and you can't get too much of it. You've got to get strong, you know."

With this Helga was in full agreement. It seemed hundreds of years since she had been strong. And she would need strength. For in some way she was determined to get herself out of this bog into which she had strayed. Or—she would have to die. She couldn't endure it. Her suffocation and shrinking loathing were too great. Not to be borne. Again. For she had to admit that it wasn't new, this feeling of dissatisfaction, of asphyxiation. Something like it she had experienced before. In Naxos. In New York. In Copenhagen.

This differed only in degree. And it was of the present and therefore seemingly more reasonable. The other revulsions were of the past, and now less explainable.

The thought of her husband roused in her a deep and contemptuous hatred. At his every approach she had forcibly to subdue a furious inclination to scream out in protest. Shame, too, swept over her at every thought of her marriage. Marriage. This sacred thing of which parsons and other Christian folk ranted so sanctimoniously, how immoral—according to their own standards—it could be! But Helga felt also a modicum of pity for him, as for one already abandoned. She meant to leave him. And it was, she had to concede, all of her own doing, this marriage. Nevertheless, she hated him.

The neighbors and church folk came in for their share of her all-embracing hatred. She hated their raucous laughter, their stupid acceptance of all things, and their unfailing trust in "de Lawd." And more than all the rest she hated the jangling Clementine Richards, with her provocative smirkings, because she had not succeeded in marrying the preacher and thus saving her, Helga, from that crowning idiocy.

Of the children Helga tried not to think. She wanted not to leave them—if that were possible. The recollection of her own childhood, lonely, unloved, rose too poignantly before her for her to consider calmly such a solution. Though she forced herself to believe that this was different. There was not the element of race, of white and black. They were all black together. And they would have their father. But to leave them would be a tearing agony, a rending of deepest fibers. She felt that through all the rest of her lifetime she would be hearing their cry of "Mummy, Mummy, Mummy," through sleepless nights. No. She couldn't desert them.

How, then, was she to escape from the oppression, the degradation, that her life had become? It was so difficult. It was terribly difficult. It was almost hopeless. So for a while—for the immediate present, she told herself—she put aside the making of any plan for her going. "I'm still," she reasoned, "too weak, too sick. By and by, when I'm really strong—"

It was so easy and so pleasant to think about freedom and cities, about clothes and books, about the sweet mingled smell of Houbigant and cigarettes in softly lighted rooms filled with inconsequential chatter and laughter and sophisticated tuneless music. It was so hard to think out a feasible way of retrieving all these agreeable, desired things. Just then. Later. When she got up. By and by. She must rest. Get strong. Sleep. Then, afterwards, she could work out some arrangement. So she dozed and dreamed in snatches of sleeping and waking, letting time run on. Away.

And hardly had she left her bed and become able to walk again without pain, hardly had the children returned from the homes of the neighbors, when she began to have her fifth child.

FROM *PASSING*

[FROM PART I, CHAPTER THREE]

THE WAITER CAME WITH CLARE'S CHANGE. Irene reminded herself that she ought immediately to go. But she didn't move.

The truth was, she was curious. There were things that she wanted to ask Clare Kendry. She wished to find out about this hazardous business of "passing," this breaking away from all that was familiar and friendly to take one's chance in another environment, not entirely strange, perhaps, but certainly not entirely friendly. What, for example, one did about background, how one accounted for oneself. And how one felt when one came into contact with other Negroes. But she couldn't. She was unable to think of a single question that in its context or its phrasing was not too frankly curious, if not actually impertinent.

As if aware of her desire and her hesitation, Clare remarked thoughtfully: "You know, 'Rene, I've often wondered why more colored girls, girls like you and Margaret Hammer and Esther Dawson and—oh, lots of others—never 'passed' over. It's such a frightfully easy thing to do. If one's the type, all that's needed is a little nerve."

"What about background? Family, I mean. Surely you can't just drop down on people from nowhere and expect them to receive you with open arms, can you?"

"Almost," Clare asserted. "You'd be surprised, 'Rene, how much easier that is with white people than with us. Maybe because there are so many more of them, or maybe because they are secure and so don't have to bother. I've never quite decided."

Irene was inclined to be incredulous. "You mean that you didn't have to explain where you came from? It seems impossible."

Clare cast a glance of repressed amusement across the table at her. "As a matter of fact, I didn't. Though I suppose under any other circumstances I might have had to provide some plausible tale to account for myself. I've a good imagination, so I'm sure I could have done it quite creditably, and credibly. But it wasn't necessary. There were my aunts, you see, respectable and authentic enough for anything or anybody."

"I see. They were 'passing' too."

"No. They weren't. They were white."

"Oh!" And in the next instant it came back to Irene that she had heard this mentioned before; by her father or, more likely, her mother. They were Bob Kendry's aunts. He had been a son of their brother's, on the left hand. A wild oat.

"They were nice old ladies," Clare explained, "very religious and as poor as church mice. That adored brother of theirs, my grandfather, got through every penny they had after he'd finished his own little bit."

Clare paused in her narrative to light another cigarette. Her smile, her expression, Irene noticed, was faintly resentful.

"Being good Christians," she continued, "when Dad came to his tipsy end, they did their duty and gave me a home of sorts. I was, it was true, expected to earn my keep by doing all the housework and most of the washing. But do you realize, 'Rene, that if it hadn't been for them I shouldn't have had a home in the world?"

Irene's nod and little murmur were comprehensive, understanding.

Clare made a small mischievous grimace and proceeded. "Besides, to their notion, hard labor was good for me. I had Negro blood and they belonged to the generation that had written and read long articles headed: 'Will the Blacks Work?' Too, they weren't quite sure that the good God hadn't intended the sons and daughters of Ham to sweat because he had poked fun at old man Noah once when he had taken a drop too much. I remember the aunts telling me that that old drunkard had cursed Ham and his sons for all time."

Irene laughed. But Clare remained quite serious.

"It was more than a joke, I assure you, 'Rene. It was a hard life for a girl of sixteen. Still, I had a roof over my head, and food, and clothes—such as they were. And there were the Scriptures, and talks on morals and thrift and industry and the loving-kindness of the good Lord."

"Have you ever stopped to think, Clare," Irene demanded, "how much unhappiness and downright cruelty are laid to the loving-kindness of the Lord? And always by His most ardent followers, it seems."

"Have I?" Clare exclaimed. "It, they, made me what I am today. For, of course, I was determined to get away, to be a person and not a charity or a problem, or even a daughter of the indiscreet Ham. Then, too, I wanted things. I knew I wasn't bad-looking and that I could 'pass.' You can't know, 'Rene, how, when I used to go over to the South Side, I used almost to hate all of you. You had all the things I wanted and never had had. It made me all the more determined to get them, and others. Do you, can you understand what I felt?"

She looked up with a pointed and appealing effect, and, evidently finding the sympathetic expression on Irene's face sufficient answer, went on. "The aunts were queer. For all their Bibles and praying and ranting about honesty, they didn't want anyone to know that their darling brother had seduced—ruined, they called it—a Negro girl. They could excuse the ruin, but they couldn't forgive the tar brush. They forbade me to mention Negroes to the neighbors, or even to mention the South Side. You may be sure that I didn't. I'll bet they were good and sorry afterwards."

She laughed and the ringing bells in her laugh had a hard metallic sound.

"When the chance to get away came, that omission was of great value to me. When Jack, a schoolboy acquaintance of some people in the neighborhood, turned up from South America with untold gold, there was no one to tell him that I was colored, and many to tell him about the severity and the religiousness of Aunt Grace and Aunt Edna. You can guess the rest. After he came, I stopped slipping off to the South Side and slipped off to meet him instead. I couldn't manage both. In the end I had no great difficulty in convincing him that it was useless to talk marriage to the aunts. So on the day that I was eighteen we went off and were married. So that's that. Nothing could have been easier."

"Yes, I do see that for you it was easy enough. By the way! I wonder why they didn't tell Father that you were married? He went over to find out about you when you stopped coming over to see us. I'm sure they didn't tell him. Not that you were married."

Clare Kendry's eyes were bright with tears that didn't fall. "Oh, how lovely! To have cared enough about me to do that. The dear sweet man! Well, they couldn't tell him because they didn't know it. I took care of that, for I couldn't be sure that those consciences of theirs wouldn't begin to work on them afterward and make them let the cat out of the bag. The old things probably thought I was living in sin, wherever I was. And it would be about what they expected."

An amused smile lit the lovely face for the smallest fraction of a second. After a little silence she said soberly: "But I'm sorry if they told your father so. That was something I hadn't counted on."

"I'm not sure that they did," Irene told her. "He didn't say so, anyway."

"He wouldn't, 'Rene dear. Not your father."

"Thanks. I'm sure he wouldn't."

"But you've never answered my question. Tell me, honestly, haven't you ever thought of 'passing'?"

Irene answered promptly: "No. Why should I?" And so disdainful was her voice and manner that Clare's face flushed and her eyes glinted. Irene hastened to add: "You see, Clare, I've everything I want. Except, perhaps, a little more money."

At that Clare laughed, her spark of anger vanished as quickly as it had appeared. "Of course," she declared, "that's what everybody wants, just a little more money, even the people who have it. And I must say I don't blame them. Money's awfully nice to have. In fact, all things considered, I think, 'Rene, that it's even worth the price."

Irene could only shrug her shoulders. Her reason partly agreed, her instinct wholly rebelled. And she could not say why. And though conscious that if she didn't hurry away, she was going to be late to dinner, she still lingered. It was as if the woman sitting on the other side of the table, a girl she had known, who had done this rather dangerous and, to Irene Redfield, abhorrent thing successfully and had announced herself well satisfied, had for her a fascination, strange and compelling.

Clare Kendry was still leaning back in the tall chair, her sloping shoulders against the carved top. She sat with an air of indifferent assurance, as if arranged for, desired. About her clung that dim suggestion of polite insolence with which a few women are born and which some acquire with the coming of riches or importance.

Clare, it gave Irene a little prick of satisfaction to recall, hadn't got that by passing herself off as white. She herself had always had it.

Just as she'd always had that pale gold hair, which, unsheared still, was drawn loosely back from a broad brow, partly hidden by the small close hat. Her lips, painted a brilliant geranium red, were sweet and sensitive and a little obstinate. A tempting mouth. The face across the forehead and cheeks was a trifle too wide, but the ivory skin had a peculiar soft luster. And the eyes were magnificent! Dark, sometimes absolutely black, always luminous, and set in long, black lashes. Arresting eyes, slow and mesmeric, and with, for all their warmth, something withdrawn and secret about them.

Ah! Surely! They were Negro eyes! Mysterious and concealing. And set in that ivory face under that bright hair, there was about them something exotic.

Yes, Clare Kendry's loveliness was absolute, beyond challenge, thanks to those eyes which her grandmother and later her mother and father had given her.

Into those eyes there came a smile and over Irene the sense of being petted and caressed. She smiled back.

"Maybe," Clare suggested, "you can come Monday, if you're back. Or, if you're not, then Tuesday."

With a small regretful sigh, Irene informed Clare that she was afraid she wouldn't be back by Monday and that she was sure she had dozens of things for Tuesday, and that she was leaving Wednesday. It might be, however, that she could get out of something Tuesday.

"Oh, do try. Do put somebody else off. The others can see you any time, while I—why, I may never see you again! Think of that, 'Rene! You'll have to come. You'll simply have to! I'll never forgive you if you don't."

At that moment it seemed a dreadful thing to think of never seeing Clare Kendry again. Standing there under the appeal, the caress, of her eyes, Irene had the desire, the hope, that this parting wouldn't be the last.

"I'll try, Clare," she promised gently. "I'll call you—or will you call me?"

"I think, perhaps, I'd better call you. Your father's in the book, I know, and the address is the same. Sixty-four eighteen. Some memory, what? Now remember, I'm going to expect you. You've got to be able to come."

Again that peculiar mellowing smile.

"I'll do my best, Clare."

Irene gathered up her gloves and bag. They stood up. She put out her hand. Clare took and held it.

"It has been nice seeing you again, Clare. How pleased and glad Father'll be to hear about you!"

"Until Tuesday, then," Clare Kendry replied. "I'll spend every minute of the time from now on looking forward to seeing you again. Good-bye, 'Rene dear. My love to your father, and this kiss for him."

The sun had gone from overhead, but the streets were still like fiery furnaces. The languid breeze was still hot. And the scurrying people looked even more wilted than before Irene had fled from their contact.

Crossing the avenue in the heat, far from the coolness of the Drayton's roof, away from the seduction of Clare Kendry's smile, she was aware of a sense of irritation with herself because she had been pleased and a little flattered at the other's obvious gladness at their meeting.

With her perspiring progress homeward this irritation grew, and she began to wonder just what had possessed her to make her promise to find time, in the crowded days that remained of her visit, to spend another afternoon with a woman whose life had so definitely and deliberately diverged from hers; and whom, as had been pointed out, she might never see again.

Why in the world had she made such a promise?

As she went up the steps to her father's house, thinking with what interest and amazement he would listen to her story of the afternoon's encounter, it came to her that Clare had omitted to mention her marriage name. She had referred to her husband as Jack. That was all. Had that, Irene asked herself, been intentional?

Clare had only to pick up the telephone to communicate with her, or to drop her a card, or to jump into a taxi. But she couldn't reach Clare in any way. Nor could anyone else to whom she might speak of their meeting.

"As if I should!"

Her key turned in the lock. She went in. Her father, it seemed, hadn't come in yet.

Irene decided that she wouldn't, after all, say anything to him about Clare Kendry. She had, she told herself, no inclination to speak of a person who held so low an opinion of her loyalty, or her discretion. And certainly she had no desire or intention of making the slightest effort about Tuesday. Nor any other day for that matter.

She was through with Clare Kendry.

[PART III, CHAPTER] ONE

Though, she admitted reluctantly, she herself didn't feel the proper Christmas spirit this year either. But that couldn't be helped, it seemed, any more than the weather. She was weary and depressed. And for all her trying, she couldn't be free of that dull, indefinite misery which with increasing tenaciousness had laid hold of her. The morning's aimless wandering through the teeming Harlem streets, long after she had ordered the flowers which had been her excuse for setting out, was but another effort to tear herself loose from it.

She went up the cream stone steps, into the house, and down to the kitchen. There were to be people in to tea. But that, she found, after a few words with Sadie and Zulena, need give her no concern. She was thankful. She didn't want to be bothered. She went upstairs and took off her things and got into bed. . . .

She wakened to find Brian standing at her bedside looking down at her, an unfathomable expression in his eyes.

She said: "I must have dropped off to sleep," and watched a slender ghost of his old amused smile pass over his face.

"It's getting on to four," he told her, meaning, she knew, that she was going to be late again.

She fought back the quick answer that rose to her lips and said instead: "I'm getting right up. It was good of you to think to call me." She sat up.

He bowed. "Always the attentive husband, you see."

"Yes indeed. Thank goodness, everything's ready."

"Except you. Oh, and Clare's downstairs."

"Clare! What a nuisance! I didn't ask her. Purposely."

"I see. Might a mere man ask why? Or is the reason so subtly feminine that it wouldn't be understood by him?"

A little of his smile had come back. Irene, who was beginning to shake off some of her depression under his familiar banter, said, almost gaily: "Not at all. It just happens that this party happens to be for Hugh, and that Hugh happens not to care a great deal for Clare; therefore I, who happen to be giving the party, didn't happen to ask her. Nothing could be simpler. Could it?"

"Nothing. It's so simple that I can easily see beyond your simple explanation and surmise that Clare, probably, just never happened to pay Hugh the admiring attention that he happens to consider no more than his just due. Simplest thing in the world."

Irene exclaimed in amazement: "Why, I thought you liked Hugh! You don't, you can't, believe anything so idiotic!"

"Well, Hugh does think he's God, you know."

"That," Irene declared, getting out of bed, "is absolutely not true. He thinks ever so much better of himself than that, as you, who know and have read him, ought to be able to guess. If you remember what a low opinion he has of God, you won't make such a silly mistake."

She went into the closet for her things and, coming back, hung her frock over the back of a chair and placed her shoes on the floor beside it. Then she sat down before her dressing table.

Brian didn't speak. He continued to stand beside the bed, seeming to look at nothing in particular. Certainly not at her. True, his gaze was on her, but in it there was some quality that made her feel that at that moment she was no more to him than a pane of glass through which he stared. At what? She didn't know, couldn't guess. And this made her uncomfortable. Piqued her.

She said: "It just happens that Hugh prefers intelligent women."

Plainly he was startled. "D'you mean that you think Clare is stupid?" he asked, regarding her with lifted eyebrows, which emphasized the disbelief of his voice.

She wiped the cold cream from her face before she said: "No, I don't. She isn't stupid. She's intelligent enough in a purely feminine way. Eighteenth-century France would have been a marvelous setting for her, or the old South if she hadn't made the mistake of being born a Negro."

"I see. Intelligent enough to wear a tight bodice and keep bowing swains whispering compliments and retrieving dropped fans. Rather a pretty picture. I take it, though, as slightly feline in its implication."

"Well, then, all I can say is that you take it wrongly. Nobody admires Clare more than I do, for the kind of intelligence she has, as well as for her decorative qualities. But she's not—She isn't—She hasn't—Oh, I can't explain it. Take Bianca, for example, or, to keep to the race, Felise Freeland. Looks *and* brains. Real brains that can hold their own with anybody. Clare has got brains of a sort, the kind that are useful too. Acquisitive, you know. But she'd bore a man like Hugh to suicide. Still, I never thought that even Clare would come to a private party to which she hadn't been asked. But it's like her."

For a minute there was silence. She completed the bright red arch of her full lips. Brian moved towards the door. His hand was on the knob. He said: "I'm sorry, Irene. It's my fault entirely. She seemed so hurt at being left out that I told her I was sure you'd forgotten and to just come along."

Irene cried out: "But, Brian, I—" and stopped, amazed at the fierce anger that had blazed up in her.

Brian's head came round with a jerk. His brows lifted in an odd surprise.

Her voice, she realized, *had* gone queer. But she had an instinctive feeling that it hadn't been the whole cause of his attitude. And that little straightening motion of the shoulders. Hadn't it been like that of a man drawing himself up to receive a blow? Her fright was like a scarlet spear of terror leaping at her heart.

Clare Kendry! So that was it! Impossible. It couldn't be. . . .

TWO

But it did matter. It mattered more than anything had ever mattered before.

What bitterness! That the one fear, the one uncertainty, that she had felt, Brian's ache to go somewhere else, should have dwindled to a childish triviality! And with it the quality of the courage and resolution with which she had met it. From the visions and dangers which she now perceived she shrank away. For them she had no remedy or courage. Desperately she tried to shut out the knowledge from which had risen this turmoil, which she had no power to moderate or still, within her. And half succeeded.

For, she reasoned, what was there, what had there been, to show that she was even half correct in her tormenting notion? Nothing. She had seen nothing, heard nothing. She had no facts or proofs. She was only making herself unutterably wretched by an unfounded suspicion. It had been a case of looking for trouble and finding it in good measure. Merely that.

With this self-assurance that she had no real knowledge, she redoubled her efforts to drive out of her mind the distressing thought of faiths broken and trusts betrayed which every mental vision of Clare, of Brian, brought with them. She could not, she would not, go again through the tearing agony that lay just behind her.

She must, she told herself, be fair. In all their married life she had had no slightest cause to suspect her husband of any infidelity, of any serious flirtation even. If—and she doubted it—he had had his hours of outside erratic conduct, they were unknown to her. Why begin now to assume them? And on nothing more concrete than an idea that had leapt into her mind because he had told her that he had invited a friend, a friend of hers, to a party in his own house. And at a time when she had been, it was likely, more asleep than awake. How could she without anything done or said, or left undone or unsaid, so easily believe him guilty? How be so ready to renounce all confidence in the worth of their life together?

And if, perchance, there were some small something—well, what could it mean? Nothing. There were the boys. There was John Bellew. The thought of these three gave her some slight relief. But she did not look the future in the face. She wanted to feel nothing, to think nothing; simply to believe that it was all silly invention on her part. Yet she could not. Not quite.

Christmas, with its unreality, its hectic rush, its false gaiety, came and went. Irene was thankful for the confused unrest of the season. Its irksomeness, its crowds, its inane and insincere repetitions of genialities, pushed between her and the contemplation of her growing unhappiness.

She was thankful, too, for the continued absence of Clare, who, John Bellew having returned from a long stay in Canada, had withdrawn to that other life of hers, remote and inaccessible. But beating against the walled prison of Irene's thoughts was the shunned fancy that, though absent, Clare Kendry was still present, that she was close.

Brian, too, had withdrawn. The house contained his outward self and his belongings. He came and went with his usual noiseless irregularity. He sat across from her at table. He slept in his room

next to hers at night. But he was remote and inaccessible. No use
pretending that he was happy, that things were the same as they
had always been. He wasn't and they weren't. However, she assured herself, it needn't necessarily be because of anything that
involved Clare. It was, it must be, another manifestation of the old
longing.

But she did wish it were spring, March, so that Clare would
be sailing, out of her life and Brian's. Though she had come almost
to believe that there was nothing but generous friendship between
those two, she was very tired of Clare Kendry. She wanted to be
free of her, and of her furtive comings and goings. If something
would only happen, something that would make John Bellew decide on an earlier departure, or that would remove Clare. Anything. She didn't care what. Not even if it were that Clare's
Margery were ill, or dying. Not even if Bellew should discover—

She drew a quick, sharp breath. And for a long time sat staring
down at the hands in her lap. Strange, she had not before realized
how easily she could put Clare out of her life! She had only to tell
John Bellew that his wife— No. Not that! But if he should somehow learn of these Harlem visits— Why should she hesitate? Why
spare Clare?

But she shrank away from the idea of telling that man, Clare
Kendry's white husband, anything that would lead him to suspect
that his wife was a Negro. Nor could she write it, or telephone it,
or tell it to someone else who would tell him.

She was caught between two allegiances, different, yet the
same. Herself. Her race. Race! The thing that bound and suffocated her. Whatever steps she took, or if she took none at all,
something would be crushed. A person or the race. Clare, herself,
or the race. Or, it might be, all three. Nothing, she imagined, was
ever more completely sardonic.

Sitting alone in the quiet living room in the pleasant firelight,
Irene Redfield wished, for the first time in her life that she had not
been born a Negro. For the first time she suffered and rebelled
because she was unable to disregard the burden of race. It was, she
cried silently, enough to suffer as a woman, an individual, on one's
own account, without having to suffer for the race as well. It was
a brutality, and undeserved. Surely no other people so cursed as
Ham's dark children.

Nevertheless, her weakness, her shrinking, her own inability
to compass the thing, did not prevent her from wishing fervently

that, in some way with which she had no concern, John Bellew would discover, not that his wife had a touch of the tar brush—Irene didn't want that—but that she was spending all the time that he was out of the city in black Harlem. Only that. It would be enough to rid her forever of Clare Kendry.

THREE

As if in answer to her wish, the very next day Irene came face to face with Bellew.

She had gone downtown with Felise Freeland to shop. The day was an exceptionally cold one, with a strong wind that had whipped a dusky red into Felise's smooth golden cheeks and driven moisture into Irene's soft brown eyes.

Clinging to each other, with heads bent against the wind, they turned out of the Avenue into Fifty-seventh Street. A sudden bluster flung them around the corner with unexpected quickness and they collided with a man.

"Pardon," Irene begged laughingly, and looked up into the face of Clare Kendry's husband.

"Mrs. Redfield!"

His hat came off. He held out his hand, smiling genially.

But the smile faded at once. Surprise, incredulity, and—was it understanding?—passed over his features.

He had, Irene knew, become conscious of Felise, golden, with curly black Negro hair, whose arm was still linked in her own. She was sure, now, of the understanding in his face, as he looked at her again and then back at Felise. And displeasure.

He didn't, however, withdraw his outstretched hand. Not at once.

But Irene didn't take it. Instinctively, in the first glance of recognition, her face had become a mask. Now she turned on him a totally uncomprehending look, a bit questioning. Seeing that he still stood with hand outstretched, she gave him the cool appraising stare which she reserved for mashers, and drew Felise on.

Felise drawled: "Aha! Been 'passing,' have you? Well, I've queered that."

"Yes, I'm afraid you have."

"Why, Irene Redfield! You sound as if you cared terribly. I'm sorry."

"I do, but not for the reason you think. I don't believe I've ever gone native in my life except for the sake of convenience, restaurants, theater tickets, and things like that. Never socially I mean, except once. You've just passed the only person that I've ever met disguised as a white woman."

"Awfully sorry. Be sure your sin will find you out and all that. Tell me about it."

"I'd like to. It would amuse you. But I can't."

Felise's laughter was as languidly nonchalant as her cool voice. "Can it be possible that the honest Irene has—Oh, do look at that coat! There. The red one. Isn't it a dream?"

Irene was thinking: "I had my chance and didn't take it. I had only to speak and to introduce him to Felise with the casual remark that he was Clare's husband. Only that. Fool. Fool." That instinctive loyalty to a race. Why couldn't she get free of it? Why should it include Clare? Clare, who'd shown little enough consideration for her and hers. What she felt was not so much resentment as a dull despair because she could not change herself in this respect, could not separate individuals from the race, herself from Clare Kendry.

"Let's go home, Felise. I'm so tired I could drop."

"Why, we haven't done half the things we planned."

"I know, but it's too cold to be running all over town. But you stay down if you want to."

"I think I'll do that, if you don't mind."

And now another problem confronted Irene. She must tell Clare of this meeting. Warn her. But how? She hadn't seen her for days. Writing and telephoning were equally unsafe. And even if it was possible to get in touch with her, what good would it do? If Bellew hadn't concluded that he'd made a mistake, if he was certain of her identity—and he was nobody's fool—telling Clare wouldn't avert the results of the encounter. Besides, it was too late. Whatever was in store for Clare Kendry had already overtaken her.

Irene was conscious of a feeling of relieved thankfulness at the thought that she was probably rid of Clare, and without having lifted a finger or uttered one word.

But she did mean to tell Brian about meeting John Bellew.

But that, it seemed, was impossible. Strange. Something held her back. Each time she was on the verge of saying: "I ran into

Clare's husband on the street downtown today. I'm sure he recognized me, and Felise was with me," she failed to speak. It sounded too much like the warning she wanted it to be. Not even in the presence of the boys at dinner could she make the bare statement.

The evening dragged. At last she said good night and went upstairs, the words unsaid.

She thought: "Why didn't I tell him? Why didn't I? If trouble comes from this, I'll never forgive myself. I'll tell him when he comes up."

She took up a book, but she could not read, so oppressed was she by a nameless foreboding.

What if Bellew should divorce Clare? Could he? There was the Rhinelander case. But in France, in Paris, such things were very easy. If he divorced her—If Clare were free— But of all the things that could happen, that was the one she did not want. She must get her mind away from that possibility. She must.

Then came a thought which she tried to drive away. If Clare should die! Then— Oh, it was vile! To think, yes, to wish that! She felt faint and sick. But the thought stayed with her. She could not get rid of it.

She heard the outer door open. Close. Brian had gone out. She turned her face into her pillow to cry. But no tears came.

She lay there awake, thinking of things past. Of her courtship and marriage and Junior's birth. Of the time they had bought the house in which they had lived so long and so happily. Of the time Ted had passed his pneumonia crisis and they knew he would live. And of other sweet painful memories that would never come again.

Above everything else she had wanted, had striven, to keep undisturbed the pleasant routine of her life. And now Clare Kendry had come into it, and with her the menace of impermanence.

"Dear God," she prayed, "make March come quickly."

By and by she slept.

FOUR

The next morning brought with it a snowstorm that lasted throughout the day.

After a breakfast which had been eaten almost in silence and which she was relieved to have done with, Irene Redfield lingered for a little while in the downstairs hall, looking out at the soft flakes fluttering down. She was watching them immediately fill some ugly irregular gaps left by the feet of hurrying pedestrians when Zulena came to her, saying: "The telephone, Mrs. Redfield. It's Mrs. Bellew."

"Take the message, Zulena, please."

Though she continued to stare out of the window, Irene saw nothing now, stabbed as she was by fear—and hope. Had anything happened between Clare and Bellew? And if so, what? And was she to be freed at last from the aching anxiety of the past weeks? Or was there to be more, and worse? She had a wrestling moment in which it seemed that she must rush after Zulena and hear for herself what it was that Clare had to say. But she waited.

Zulena, when she came back, said: "She says, ma'am, that she'll be able to go to Mrs. Freeland's tonight. She'll be here some-time between eight and nine."

"Thank you, Zulena."

The day dragged on to its end.

At dinner Brian spoke bitterly of a lynching that he had been reading about in the evening paper.

"Dad, why is it that they only lynch colored people?" Ted asked.

"Because they hate 'em, son."

"Brian!" Irene's voice was a plea and a rebuke.

Ted said: "Oh! And why do they hate 'em?"

"Because they are afraid of them."

"But what makes them afraid of 'em?"

"Because—"

"Brian!"

"It seems, son, that is a subject we can't go into at the moment without distressing the ladies of our family," he told the boy with mock seriousness, "but we'll take it up sometime when we're alone together."

Ted nodded in his engaging grave way. "I see. Maybe we can talk about it tomorrow on the way to school."

"That'll be fine."

"Brian!"

"Mother," Junior remarked, "that's the third time you've said 'Brian' like that."

"But not the last, Junior, never you fear," his father told him.

After the boys had gone up to their own floor, Irene said

suavely: "I do wish, Brian, that you wouldn't talk about lynching before Ted and Junior. It was really inexcusable for you to bring up a thing like that at dinner. There'll be time enough for them to learn about such horrible things when they're older."

"You're absolutely wrong! If, as you're so determined, they've got to live in this damned country, they'd better find out what sort of thing they're up against as soon as possible. The earlier they learn it, the better prepared they'll be."

"I don't agree. I want their childhood to be happy and as free from the knowledge of such things as it possibly can be."

"Very laudable," was Brian's sarcastic answer. "Very laudable indeed, all things considered. But can it?"

"Certainly it can. If you'll only do your part."

"Stuff! You know as well as I do, Irene, that it can't. What was the use of our trying to keep them from learning the word 'nigger' and its connotation? They found out, didn't they? And how? Because somebody called Junior a dirty nigger."

"Just the same, you're not to talk to them about the race problem. I won't have it."

They glared at each other.

"I tell you, Irene, they've got to know these things, and it might as well be now as later."

"They do not!" she insisted, forcing back the tears of anger that were threatening to fall.

Brian growled: "I can't understand how anybody as intelligent as you like to think you are can show evidences of such stupidity." He looked at her in a puzzled harassed way.

"Stupid!" she cried. "Is it stupid to want my children to be happy?" Her lips were quivering.

"At the expense of proper preparation for life and their future happiness, yes. And I'd feel I hadn't done my duty by them if I didn't give them some inkling of what's before them. It's the least I can do. I wanted to get them out of this hellish place years ago. You wouldn't let me. I gave up the idea, because you objected. Don't expect me to give up everything."

Under the lash of his words she was silent. Before any answer came to her, he had turned and gone from the room.

Sitting there alone in the forsaken dining room, unconsciously pressing the hands lying in her lap tightly together, she was seized by a convulsion of shivering. For, to her, there had been something ominous in the scene that she had just had with her husband. Over and over in her mind his last words: "Don't expect me to give up everything," repeated themselves. What had they meant? What could they mean? Clare Kendry?

Surely she was going mad with fear and suspicion. She must not work herself up. She must not! Where were all the self-control, the common sense, that she was so proud of? Now, if ever, was the time for it.

Clare would soon be there. She must hurry or she would be late again, and those two would wait for her downstairs together, as they had done so often since that first time, which now seemed so long ago. Had it been really only last October? Why, she felt years, not months, older.

Drearily she rose from her chair and went upstairs to set about the business of dressing to go out when she would far rather have remained at home. During the process she wondered, for the hundredth time, why she hadn't told Brian about herself and Felise running into Bellew the day before, and for the hundredth time she turned away from acknowledging to herself the real reason for keeping back the information.

When Clare arrived, radiant in a shining red gown, Irene had not finished dressing. But her smile scarcely hesitated as she greeted her, saying: "I always seem to keep C. P. time, don't I? We hardly expected you to be able to come. Felise will be pleased. How nice you look."

Clare kissed a bare shoulder, seeming not to notice a slight shrinking.

"I hadn't an idea in the world, myself, that I'd be able to make it; but Jack had to run down to Philadelphia unexpectedly. So here I am."

Irene looked up, a flood of speech on her lips. "Philadelphia. That's not very far, is it? Clare, I—?"

She stopped, one of her hands clutching the side of her stool, the other lying clenched on the dressing table. Why didn't she go on and tell Clare about meeting Bellew? Why couldn't she?

But Clare didn't notice the unfinished sentence. She laughed and said lightly: "It's far enough for me. Anywhere, away from me, is far enough. I'm not particular."

Irene passed a hand over her eyes to shut out the accusing face in the glass before her. With one corner of her mind she wondered how long she had looked like that, drawn and haggard and—yes, frightened. Or was it only imagination?

"Clare," she asked, "have you ever seriously thought what it would mean if he should find you out?"

"Yes."

"Oh! You have! And what you'd do in that case?"

"Yes." And having said it, Clare Kendry smiled quickly, a smile that came and went like a flash, leaving untouched the gravity of her face.

That smile and the quiet resolution of that one word, "Yes," filled Irene with a primitive paralyzing dread. Her hands were numb, her feet like ice, her heart like a stone weight. Even her tongue was like a heavy dying thing. There were long spaces between the words as she asked: "And what should you do?"

Clare, who was sunk in a deep chair, her eyes far away, seemed wrapped in some pleasant impenetrable reflection. To Irene, sitting expectantly upright, it was an interminable time before she dragged herself back to the present to say calmly: "I'd do what I want to do more than anything else right now. I'd come up here to live. Harlem, I mean. Then I'd be able to do as I please, when I please."

Irene leaned forward, cold and tense. "And what about Margery?" Her voice was a strained whisper.

"Margery?" Clare repeated, letting her eyes flutter over Irene's concerned face. "Just this, 'Rene. If it wasn't for her, I'd do it anyway. She's all that holds me back. But if Jack finds out, if our marriage is broken, that lets me out. Doesn't it?"

Her gentle resigned tone, her air of innocent candor, appeared, to her listener, spurious. A conviction that the words were intended as a warning took possession of Irene. She remembered that Clare Kendry had always seemed to know what other people were thinking. Her compressed lips grew firm and obdurate. Well, she wouldn't know this time.

She said: "Do go downstairs and talk to Brian. He's got a mad on."

Though she had determined that Clare should not get at her thoughts and fears, the words had sprung, unthought of, to her lips. It was as if they had come from some outer layer of callousness that had no relation to her tortured heart. And they had been, she realized, precisely the right words for her purpose.

For as Clare got up and went out she saw that that arrangement was as good as her first plan of keeping her waiting up there while she dressed—or better. She would only have hindered and rasped her. And what matter if those two spent one hour, more or less, alone together, one or many, now that everything had happened between them?

Ah! The first time that she had allowed herself to admit to herself that everything had happened, had not forced herself to believe, to hope, that nothing irrevocable had been consummated! Well, it had happened. She knew it, and knew that she knew it.

She was surprised that, having thought the thought, conceded the fact, she was no more hurt, cared no more, than during her previous frenzied endeavors to escape it. And this absence of acute, unbearable pain seemed to her unjust, as if she had been denied some exquisite solace of suffering which the full acknowledgment should have given her.

Was it, perhaps, that she had endured all that a woman could endure of tormenting humiliation and fear? Or was it that she lacked the capacity for the acme of suffering? "No, no!" she denied fiercely. "I'm human like everybody else. It's just that I'm so tired, so worn out, I can't feel any more." But she did not really believe that.

Security. Was it just a word? If not, then was it only by the sacrifice of other things, happiness, love, or some wild ecstasy that she had never known, that it could be obtained? And did too much striving, too much faith in safety and permanence, unfit one for these other things?

Irene didn't know, couldn't decide, though for a long time she sat questioning and trying to understand. Yet all the while, in spite of her searchings and feelings of frustration, she was aware that, to her, security was the most important and desired thing in life. Not for any of the others, or for all of them, would she exchange it. She wanted only to be tranquil. Only, unmolested, to be allowed to direct for their own best good the lives of her sons and her husband.

Now that she had relieved herself of what was almost like a guilty knowledge, admitted that which by some sixth sense she had long known, she could again reach out for plans. Could think again of ways to keep Brian by her side, and in New York. For she would not go to Brazil. She belonged in this land of rising towers. She was an American. She grew from this soil, and she would not be uprooted. Not even because of Clare Kendry, or a hundred Clare Kendrys.

Brian, too, belonged here. His duty was to her and to his boys.

Strange that she couldn't now be sure that she had ever truly known love. Not even for Brian. He was her husband and the father of her sons. But was he anything more? Had she ever wanted or tried for more? In that hour she thought not.

Nevertheless, she meant to keep him. Her freshly painted lips narrowed to a thin straight line. True, she had left off trying to believe that he and Clare loved and yet did not love, but she still intended to hold fast to the outer shell of her marriage, to keep her life fixed, certain. Brought to the edge of distasteful reality, her fastidious nature did not recoil. Better, far better, to share him than to lose him completely. Oh, she could close her eyes, if need be. She could bear it. She could bear anything. And there was March ahead. March and the departure of Clare.

Horribly clear, she could now see the reason for her instinct to withhold—omit, rather—her news of the encounter with Bellew. If Clare was freed, anything might happen.

She paused in her dressing, seeing with perfect clearness that dark truth which she had from that first October afternoon felt about Clare Kendry and of which Clare herself had once warned her—that she got the things she wanted because she met the great condition of conquest, sacrifice. If she wanted Brian, Clare wouldn't revolt from the lack of money or place. It was as she had said, only Margery kept her from throwing all that away. And if things were taken out of her hands— Even if she was only alarmed, only suspected that such a thing was about to occur, anything might happen. Anything.

No! At all costs, Clare was not to know of that meeting with Bellew. Nor was Brian. It would only weaken her own power to keep him.

They would never know from her that he was on his way to suspecting the truth about his wife. And she would do anything, risk anything, to prevent him from finding out that truth. How fortunate that she had obeyed her instinct and omitted to recognize Bellew!

"Ever go up to the sixth floor, Clare?" Brian asked as he stopped the car and got out to open the door for them.

"Why, of course! We're on the seventeenth."

"I mean, did you ever go up by nigger power?"

"That's good!" Clare laughed. "Ask 'Rene. My father was a

janitor, you know, in the good old days before every ramshackle flat had its elevator. But you can't mean we've got to walk up? Not here!"

"Yes, here. And Felise lives at the very top," Irene told her.

"What on earth for?"

"I believe she claims it discourages the casual visitor."

"And she's probably right. Hard on herself, though."

Brian said, "Yes, a bit. But she says she'd rather be dead than bored."

"Oh, a garden! And how lovely with that undisturbed snow!"

"Yes, isn't it? But keep to the walk with those foolish thin shoes. You too, Irene."

Irene walked beside them on the cleared cement path that split the whiteness of the courtyard garden. She felt a something in the air, something that had been between those two and would be again. It was like a live thing pressing against her. In a quick furtive glance she saw Clare clinging to Brian's other arm. She was looking at him with that provocative upward glance of hers, and his eyes were fastened on her face with what seemed to Irene an expression of wistful eagerness.

"It's this entrance, I believe," she informed them in quite her ordinary voice.

"Mind," Brian told Clare, "you don't fall by the wayside before the fourth floor. They absolutely refuse to carry anyone up more than the last two flights."

"Don't be silly!" Irene snapped.

The party began gaily.

Dave Freeland was at his best, brilliant, crystal clear, and sparkling. Felise, too, was amusing, and not so sarcastic as usual, because she liked the dozen or so guests who dotted the long, untidy living room. Brian was witty, though, Irene noted, his remarks were somewhat more barbed than was customary even with him. And there was Ralph Hazelton, throwing nonsensical shining things into the pool of talk, which the others, even Clare, picked up and flung back with fresh adornment.

Only Irene wasn't merry. She sat almost silent, smiling now and then, that she might appear amused.

"What's the matter, Irene?" someone asked. "Taken a vow never to laugh or something? You're as sober as a judge."

"No. It's simply that the rest of you are so clever that I'm speechless, absolutely stunned."

"No wonder," Dave Freeland remarked, "that you're on the verge of tears. You haven't a drink. What'll you take?"

"Thanks. If I must take something, make it a glass of ginger ale and three drops of Scotch. The Scotch first, please. Then the ice, then the ginger ale."

"Heavens! Don't attempt to mix that yourself, Dave darling. Have the butler in," Felise mocked.

"Yes, do. And the footman." Irene laughed a little, then said: "It seems dreadfully warm in here. Mind if I open this window?" With that she pushed open one of the long casement windows of which the Freelands were so proud.

It had stopped snowing some two or three hours back. The moon was just rising, and far behind the tall buildings a few stars were creeping out. Irene finished her cigarette and threw it out, watching the tiny spark drop slowly down to the white ground below.

Someone in the room had turned on the phonograph. Or was it the radio? She didn't know which she disliked more. And nobody was listening to its blare. The talking, the laughter never for a minute ceased. Why must they have more noise?

Dave came with her drink. "You ought not," he told her, "to stand there like that. You'll take cold. Come along and talk to me, or listen to me gabble." Taking her arm, he led her across the room. They had just found seats when the doorbell rang and Felise called over to him to go and answer it.

In the next moment Irene heard his voice in the hall, carelessly polite: "Your wife? Sorry. I'm afraid you're wrong. Perhaps next—"

Then the roar of John Bellew's voice above all the other noises of the room: "I'm *not* wrong! I've been to the Redfields' and I know she's with them. You'd better stand out of my way and save yourself trouble in the end."

"What is it, Dave?" Felise ran out to the door.

And so did Brian. Irene heard him saying: "I'm Redfield. What the devil's the matter with you?"

But Bellew didn't heed him. He pushed past them all into the room and strode towards Clare. They all looked at her as she got up from her chair, backing a little from his approach.

"So you're a nigger, a damned dirty nigger!" His voice was a snarl and a moan, an expression of rage and of pain.

Everything was in confusion. The men had sprung forward. Felise had leapt between them and Bellew. She said quickly: "Careful. You're the only white man here." And the silver chill of her voice, as well as her words, was a warning.

Clare stood at the window, as composed as if everyone were not staring at her in curiosity and wonder, as if the whole structure of her life were not lying in fragments before her. She seemed unaware of any danger or uncaring. There was even a faint smile on her full red lips and in her shining eyes.

It was that smile that maddened Irene. She ran across the room, her terror tinged with ferocity, and laid a hand on Clare's bare arm. One thought possessed her. She couldn't have Clare Kendry cast aside by Bellew. She couldn't have her free.

Before them stood John Bellew, speechless now in his hurt and anger. Beyond them the little huddle of other people, and Brian stepping out from among them.

What happened next, Irene Redfield never afterwards allowed herself to remember. Never clearly.

One moment Clare had been there, a vital glowing thing, like a flame of red and gold. The next she was gone.

There was a gasp of horror, and above it a sound not quite human, like a beast in agony. "Nig! My God! Nig!"

A frenzied rush of feet down long flights of stairs. The slamming of distant doors. Voices.

Irene stayed behind. She sat down and remained quite still, staring at a ridiculous Japanese print on the wall across the room.

Gone! The soft white face, the bright hair, the disturbing scarlet mouth, the dreaming eyes, the caressing smile, the whole torturing loveliness that had been Clare Kendry. That beauty that had torn at Irene's placid life. Gone! The mocking daring, the gallantry of her pose, the ringing bells of her laughter.

Irene wasn't sorry. She was amazed, incredulous almost.

What would the others think? That Clare had fallen? That she had deliberately leaned backward? Certainly one or the other. Not—

But she mustn't, she warned herself, think of that. She was too tired, and too shocked. And, indeed, both were true. She was utterly weary, and she was violently staggered. But her thoughts reeled on. If only she could be as free of mental as she was of bodily vigor; could only put from her memory the vision of her hand on Clare's arm!

"It was an accident, a terrible accident," she muttered fiercely. "It *was*."

People were coming up the stairs. Through the still open door their steps and talk sounded nearer, nearer.

Quickly she stood up and went noiselessly into the bedroom and closed the door softly behind her.

Her thoughts raced. Ought she to have stayed? Should she go back out there to them? But there would be questions. She hadn't thought of them, of afterwards, of this. She had thought of nothing in that sudden moment of action.

It was cold. Icy chills ran up her spine and over her bare neck and shoulders.

In the room outside there were voices. Dave Freeland's and others that she did not recognize.

Should she put on her coat? Felise had rushed down without any wrap. So had all the others. So had Brian. Brian! He mustn't take cold. She took up his coat and left her own. At the door she paused for a moment, listening fearfully. She heard nothing. No voices. No footsteps. Very slowly she opened the door. The room was empty. She went out.

In the hall below she heard dimly the sound of feet going down the steps, of a door being opened and closed, and of voices far away.

Down, down, down, she went, Brian's great coat clutched in her shivering arms and trailing a little on each step behind her.

What was she to say to them when at last she had finished going down those endless stairs? She should have rushed out when they did. What reason could she give for her dallying behind? Even she didn't know why she had done that. And what else would she be asked? There had been her hand reaching out towards Clare. What about that?

In the midst of her wonderings and questionings came a thought so terrifying, so horrible, that she had had to grasp hold of the banister to save herself from pitching downwards. A cold perspiration drenched her shaking body. Her breath came short in sharp and painful gasps.

What if Clare was not dead?

She felt nauseated, as much at the idea of the glorious body mutilated as from fear.

How she managed to make the rest of the journey without fainting she never knew. But at last she was down. Just at the bottom she came on the others, surrounded by a little circle of strangers. They were all speaking in whispers, or in the awed, discreetly lowered tones adapted to the presence of disaster. In the first instant she wanted to turn and rush back up the way she had come. Then a calm desperation came over her. She braced herself, physically and mentally.

"Here's Irene now," Dave Freeland announced, and told her that, having only just missed her, they had concluded that she had fainted or something like that, and were on the way to find out about her. Felise, she saw, was holding on to his arm, all the insolent nonchalance gone out of her, and the golden brown of her handsome face changed to a queer mauve color.

Irene made no indication that she had heard Freeland but went straight to Brian. His face looked aged and altered, and his lips were purple and trembling. She had a great longing to comfort him, to charm away his suffering and horror. But she was helpless, having so completely lost control of his mind and heart.

She stammered: "Is she—is she—?"

It was Felise who answered. "Instantly, we think."

Irene struggled against the sob of thankfulness that rose in her throat. Choked down, it turned to a whimper, like a hurt child's. Someone laid a hand on her shoulder in a soothing gesture. Brian wrapped his coat about her. She began to cry rackingly, her entire body heaving with convulsive sobs. He made a slight perfunctory attempt to comfort her.

"There, there, Irene. You mustn't. You'll make yourself sick. She's—" His voice broke suddenly.

As from a long distance she heard Ralph Hazelton's voice saying: "I was looking right at her. She just tumbled over and was gone before you could say 'Jack Robinson.' Fainted, I guess. Lord! It was quick. Quickest thing I ever saw in all my life."

"It's impossible, I tell you! Absolutely impossible!"

It was Brian who spoke in that frenzied hoarse voice, which Irene had never heard before. Her knees quaked under her.

Dave Freeland said: "Just a minute, Brian. Irene was there beside her. Let's hear what she has to say."

She had a moment of stark craven fear. "Oh, God," she thought, prayed, "help me."

A strange man, official and authoritative, addressed her. "You're sure she fell? Her husband didn't give her a shove or anything like that, as Dr. Redfield seems to think?"

For the first time she was aware that Bellew was not in the little group shivering in the small hallway. What did that mean? As she began to work it out in her numbed mind, she was shaken with another hideous trembling. Not that! Oh, not that!

"No, no!" she protested. "I'm quite certain that he didn't. I was there, too. As close as he was. She just fell, before anybody could stop her. I—"

Her quaking knees gave way under her. She moaned and sank down, moaned again. Through the great heaviness that submerged and drowned her she was dimly conscious of strong arms lifting her up. Then everything was dark.

Centuries after, she heard the strange man saying: "Death by misadventure, I'm inclined to believe. Let's go up and have another look at that window."

ANGELINA WELD GRIMKÉ

ANGELINA WELD GRIMKÉ'S SHORT STORY *"The Closing Door"* appeared in the September–October 1919 issue of the Birth Control Review. *The measure of racial oppression is remarkably illustrated by Grimké, a true aristocrat of color, in this gothic tale of mental sickness and infanticide. Appearing at the time of the Red Summer and in the wake of Southern lynchings and Northern race riots, Grimké's metaphor of the closing door referred both to Agnes Milton's mounting retreat into depression and to the apparent foreclosing of African American citizenship opportunities.*

FROM *THE CLOSING DOOR*

IT WAS THE MOTHER HEART OF AGNES that had yearned over me, had pity upon me, loved me and brought me to live in the only home I have ever known. I have cared for people. I care for Jim; but Agnes Milton is the only person I have ever really loved. I love her still. And before it was too late, I used to pray that in some way I might change places with her and go into that darkness where though, still living, one forgets sun and moon and stars and flowers and winds—and love itself, and existence means dark, foul-smelling cages, hollow clanging doors, hollow monotonous days. But a month ago when Jim and I went to see her, she had changed—she had receded even from us. She seemed—how can I express it?—blank, empty, a grey automaton, a mere shell. No soul looked out at us through her vacant eyes.

We did not utter a word during our long journey homeward. Jim had unlocked the door before I spoke.

"Jim," I said, "they may still have the poor husk of her cooped up there but her soul, thank God, at least for that, is free at last!"

And Jim, I cannot tell of his face, said never a word but turned away and went heavily down the stairs. And I, I went into Agnes Milton's flat and closed the door. You would never have dreamed it was the same place. For a long time I stood amid all the brightness and mockery of her sun-drenched rooms. And I prayed. Night and day I have prayed since, the same prayer—that God, if he knows any pity at all may soon, soon release the poor spent body of hers.

I wish I might show you Agnes Milton of those far off happy days. She wasn't tall and she wasn't short; she wasn't stout and she wasn't thin. Her back was straight and her head high. She was rather graceful, I thought. In coloring she was Spanish or Italian. Her hair was not very long but it was soft and silky and black. Her features were not too sharp, her eyes clear and dark, a warm leaf brown in fact. Her mouth was really beautiful. This doesn't give her I find. It was the shining beauty and gayety of her soul that lighted up her whole body and somehow made her her. And she was generally smiling or chuckling. Her eyes almost closed when she did so and there were the most delightful crinkles all about them. Under her left eye there was a small scar, a reminder of some childhood escapade, that became, when she smiled, the most adorable of dimples. . . .

It was a Tuesday morning about four months, maybe, after my first experience with the closing door. The bell rang three times, the postman's signal when he had left a letter, Agnes came to her feet, her eyes sparkling:

"My letter from Bob," she said and made for the door.

She came back slowly, I noticed, and her face was a little pale and worried. She had an opened and an unopened letter in her hand.

"Well, what does Bob say?" I asked.

"This—this isn't from Bob," she said slowly. "It's only a bill."

"Well, go ahead and open his letter," I said.

"There—there wasn't any, Lucy."

"What!" I exclaimed. I was surprised.

"No. I don't know what it means."

"It will come probably in the second mail," I said. "It has sometimes."

"Yes," she said, I thought rather listlessly.

It didn't come in the second mail nor in the third.

"Agnes," I said. "There's some good explanation. It's not like Bob to fail you."

"No."

"He's busy or got a girl maybe."

She was a little jealous of him and I hoped this last would rouse her, but it didn't.

"Yes, maybe that's it," she said without any life.

"Well, I hope you're not going to let this interfere with your walk," I said.

"I had thought—" she began, but I cut her off.

"You promised Jim you'd go out every single day," I reminded her.

"All right, Agnes Milton's conscience," she said smiling a little. "I'll go then."

She hadn't been gone fifteen minutes when the electric bell began shrilling continuously throughout the flat.

Somehow I knew it meant trouble. My mind immediately flew to Agnes. It took me a second or so to get myself together and then I went to the tube.

"Well," I called. My voice sounded strange and high.

A boy's voice answered:

"Lady here named Mrs. James Milton?"

"Yes." I managed to say.

"Telegram fo' you'se."

It wasn't Agnes, after all. I drew a deep breath. Nothing else seemed to matter for a minute.

"Say!" the voice called up from below. "Wot's de mattah wid you'se up dere?"

"Bring it up," I said at last. "Third floor, front."

I opened the door and waited.

The boy was taking his time and whistling as he came. "Here!" I called out as he reached our floor.

It was inside his cap and he had to take it off to give it to me. I saw him eyeing me rather curiously.

"You Mrs. Milton?" he asked.

"No, but this is her flat. I'll sign for it. She's out. Where do I sign? There? Have you a pencil?"

With the door shut behind me again, I began to think out what I had better do. Jim was not to be home until late that night. Within five minutes I had decided. I tore open the yellow envelope and read the message.

It ran: "Bob died suddenly. Under no circumstances come. Father."

The rest of that day was a nightmare to me. I concealed the telegram in my waist. Agnes came home finally and was so alarmed at my appearance, I pleaded a frightful sick headache and went to bed. When Jim came home late that night Agnes was asleep. I caught him in the hall and gave him the telegram. She had to be told, we decided, because a letter from Mississippi might come at any time. He broke it to her the next morning. We were all hard hit, but Agnes from that time on was a changed woman.

Day after day dragged by and the letter of explanation did not come. It was strange, to say the least.

The Sunday afternoon following, we were all sitting, after dinner, in the little parlor. None of us had been saying much.

Suddenly Agnes said:

"Jim!"

"Yes!"

"Wasn't it strange that father never said how or when Bob died?"

"Would have made the telegram too long and expensive, perhaps," Jim replied.

We were all thinking, in the pause that followed, the same thing, I dare say. Agnes' father was not poor and it did seem he might have done that much.

"And why, do you suppose I was not to come under any circumstances? And why don't they write?"

Just then the bell rang and there was no chance for a reply.

Jim got up in his leisurely way and went to the tube.

Agnes and I both listened—a little tensely, I remember.

"Yes!" we heard Jim say, and then with spaces in between:

"Joe?—Joe who?—I think you must have made a mistake. No, I can't say that I do know anyone called Joe. What? Milton? Yes, that's my name! What? Oh! Brooks. Joe Brooks?—"

But Agnes waited for no more. She rushed by me into the hall.

"Jim! Jim! It's my brother Joe."

"Look here! Are you Agnes' brother, Joe?" Jim called quickly for him. "Great Jehoshaphat! Man! Come up! What a mess I've made of this."

For the first time I saw Jim move quickly. Within a second he was out of the flat and running down the stairs. Agnes followed to the stairhead and waited there. I went back into the little parlor, for I had followed her into the hall, and sat down and waited.

They all came in presently. Joe was older than Agnes but looked very much like her. He was thin, his face really haggard and his hair quite grey. I found out afterward that he was in his early thirties but he appeared much older. He was smiling, but the smile did not reach his eyes. They were strange aloof eyes. They rested on you and yet seemed to see something beyond. You felt as though they had looked upon something that could never be forgotten. When he was not smiling his face was grim, the chin firm and set. He was a man of very few words, I found.

Agnes and Jim were both talking at once and he answered them now and then in monosyllables. Agnes introduced us. He shook hands, I thought in rather a perfunctory way, without saying anything, and we all sat down.

We steered clear quite deliberately from the thoughts uppermost in our minds. We spoke of his journey, when he left Mississippi, the length of time it had taken him to come up and the weather. Suddenly Agnes jumped up:

"Joe, aren't you famished?"

"Well, I wouldn't mind a little something, Agnes," he answered, and then he added: "I'm not as starved as I was traveling in the South, but I have kind of a hollow feeling."

"What do you mean?" she asked.

"Jim-Crow cars," he answered laconically.

"I'd forgotten," she said. "I've been away so long."

He made no reply.

"Aren't conditions any better at all?" she asked after a little.

"No, I can't say as they are."

None of us said anything. She stood there a minute or so, pulling away at the frill on her apron. She stopped suddenly, drew a long breath, and said:

"I wish you all could move away, Joe, and come North."

For one second before he lowered his eyes I saw a strange gleam in them. He seemed to be examining his shoes carefully from all angles. His jaw looked grimmer than ever and I saw a flickering of the muscles in his cheeks.

"That would be nice," he said at last and then added, "but we can't, Agnes. I like my coffee strong, please."

"Joe," she said, going to the door. "I'm sorry, I was forgetting."

I rose at that.

"Agnes, let me go. You stay here."

She hesitated, but Joe spoke up:

"No, Agnes, you go. I know your cooking."

You could have heard a pin drop for a minute. Jim looked queer and so did Agnes for a second and then she tried to laugh it off.

"Don't mind Joe. He doesn't mean anything. He always was like that."

And then she left us.

Well, I was hurt. Joe made no attempt to apologize or anything. He even seemed to have forgotten me. Jim looked at me and smiled, his nice smile, but I was really hurt. I came to understand, however, later. Presently Joe said:

"About Agnes! We hadn't been told anything!"

"Didn't she write about it?"

"No."

"Wanted to surprise you, I guess."

"How long?" Joe asked after a little.

"Before?"

"Yes."

"Four months, I should say."

"That complicates matters some."

I got up to leave. I was so evidently in the way.

Joe looked up quietly and said:

"Oh! don't go! It isn't necessary."

I sat down again.

"No, Lucy, stay." Jim added. "What do you mean 'complicates?' "

Joe examined his shoes for several moments and then looked up suddenly.

"Just where is Agnes?"

"In the kitchen, I guess." Jim looked a trifle surprised.

"Where is that?"

"The other end of the flat near the door."

"She can't possibly hear anything, then?"

"No."

"Well, then, listen Jim, and you, what's your name? Lucy? Well, Lucy, then. Listen carefully, you two, to every single word I am going to say." He frowned a few moments at his shoes and then went on: "Bob went out fishing in the woods near his shack, spent the night there, slept in wet clothes, it had been raining all day, came home, contracted double pneumonia and died in two days time. Have you that?"

We both nodded. "That's the story we are to tell Agnes."

Jim had his mouth open to ask something, when Agnes came in. She had very evidently not heard anything, however, for there was a little color in her face and it was just a little happy again.

"I've been thinking about you, Joe," she said. "What on earth are you getting so grey for?"

"Grey!" he exclaimed. "Am I grey?" There was no doubt about it, his surprise was genuine.

"Didn't you know it?" She chuckled a little. It was the first time in days.

"No, I didn't."

She made him get up, at that, and drew him to the oval glass over the mantel.

"Don't you ever look at yourself, Joe?"

"Not much, that's the truth." I could see his face in the mirror from where I sat. His eyes widened a trifle, I saw, and then he turned away abruptly and sat down again. He made no comment. Agnes broke the rather little silence that followed.

"Joe!"

"Yes!"

"You haven't been sick or anything, have you?"

"No, why?"

"You seem so much thinner. When I last saw you you were almost stout."

"That's some years ago, Agnes."

"Yes, but one ought to get stouter not thinner with age."

Again I caught that strange gleam in his eyes before he lowered them. For a moment he sat perfectly still without answering.

"You can put it down to hard work, if you like, Agnes. Isn't that my coffee I smell boiling over?"

"Yes, I believe it is. I just ran in to tell you I'll be ready for you in about ten minutes."

She went out hastily but took time to pull the portière across the door. I thought it strange at the time and looked at Jim. He didn't seem to notice it, however, but waited, I saw, until he had heard Agnes' heel taps going into the kitchen.

"Now," he said, "what do you mean when you say that is the story we are to tell Agnes?"

"Just that."

"You mean—" he paused "that it isn't true?"

"No, it isn't true."

"Bob didn't die that way?"

"No."

I felt myself stiffening in my chair and my two hands gripping the two arms of my chair tightly. I looked at Jim. I sensed the same tensioning in him. There was a long pause. Joe was examining his shoes again. The flickering in his cheeks I saw was more noticeable.

Finally Jim brought out just one word:

"How?"

"There was a little trouble," he began and then paused so long Jim said:

"You mean he was—injured in some way?"

Joe looked up suddenly at Jim, at that, and then down again. But his expression even in that fleeting glance set me to trembling all over. Jim, I saw, had been affected too. He sat stiffly bent forward. He had been in the act of raising his cigarette to his lips and his arm seemed as though frozen in mid-air.

"Yes," he said, "injured." But the way in which he said "injured" made me tremble all the more.

Again there was a pause and again Jim broke it with his one word:

"How?"

"You don't read the papers, I see," Joe said.

"Yes, I read them."

"It was in all the papers."

"I missed it, then."

"Yes."

It was quiet again for a little.

"Have you ever lived in the South?" Joe asked.

"No."

"Nice civilized place, the South," Joe said.

And again I found myself trembling violently. I had to fight with might and main to keep my teeth from chattering. And yet it was not what he had said but his tone again.

"I hadn't so heard it described," Jim said after a little.

"No?—You didn't know, I suppose, that there is an unwritten law in the South that when a colored and a white person meet on the sidewalk, the colored person must get off into the street until the white one passes?"

"No, I hadn't heard of it."

"Well, it's so. That was the little trouble."

"You mean—"

"Bob refused to get off the sidewalk."

"Well?"

"The white man pushed him off. Bob knocked him down. The white man attempted to teach the 'damned nigger' a lesson." Again he paused.

"Well?"

"The lesson didn't end properly. Bob all but killed him."

It was so still in that room that although Jim was sitting across the room I could hear his watch ticking distinctly in his vest pocket. I had been holding my breath when I was forced to expel it, the sound was so loud they both turned quickly towards me, startled for a second.

"That would have been Bob." It was Jim speaking.

"Yes."

"I suppose it didn't end there?"

"No."

"Go on, Joe." Even Jim's voice sounded strained and strange.

And Joe went on. He never raised his voice, never lowered it. Throughout, his tone was entirely colorless. And yet as though it had been seared into my very soul I remember word for word, everything he said.

"An orderly mob, in an orderly manner, on a Sunday morning—I am quoting the newspapers—broke into the jail, took him out, slung him up to the limb of a tree, riddled his body with bullets, saturated it with coal oil, lighted a fire underneath him, gouged out his eyes with red hot irons, burnt him to a crisp and then sold souvenirs of him, ears, fingers, toes. His teeth brought five dollars each." He ceased for a moment.

"He is still hanging on that tree.—We are not allowed to have even what is left."

There was a roaring in my ears. I seemed to be a long way off. I was sinking into a horrible black vortex that seemed to be sucking me down. I opened my eyes and saw Jim dimly. His nostrils seemed to be two black wide holes. His face was taut, every line set. I saw him draw a great deep breath. The blackness sucked me down still deeper. And then suddenly I found myself on my feet struggling against that hideous darkness and I heard my own voice as from a great distance calling out over and over again, "Oh, my God! Oh, my God! Oh, my God!"

They both came running to me, but I should have fainted for the first and only time in my life but that I heard suddenly above those strange noises in my ears a little choking, strangling sound. It revived me instantly. I broke from them and tried to get to the door.

"Agnes! Agnes!" I called out.

But they were before me. Jim tore the portiere aside. They caught her just as she was falling.

She lay unconscious for hours. When she did come to, she found all three of us about her bed. Her bewildered eyes went from Jim's face to mine and then to Joe's. They paused there, she frowned a little. And then we saw the whole thing slowly come back to her. She groaned and closed her eyes. Joe started to leave the room but she opened her eyes quickly and indicated that he was not to go. He came back. Again she closed her eyes.

And then she began to grow restless.

"Agnes!" I asked, "is there anything you want?"

She quieted a little under my voice.

"No," she said, "No."

Presently she opened her eyes again. They were very bright. She looked at each of us in turn a second time.

Then she said:

"I've had to live all this time to find out."

"Find out what, Agnes?" It was Jim's voice.

"Why I'm here—why I'm here."

"Yes, of course." Jim spoke oh! so gently, humoring her. His hand was smoothing away the damp little curls about her forehead.

"It's no use your making believe you understand, you don't."

It was the first time I had ever heard her speak irritably to Jim. She moved her head away from his hand.

His eyes were a little hurt and he took his hand away.

"No." His voice was as gentle as ever. "I don't understand, then."

There was a pause and then she said abruptly:

"I'm an instrument."

No one answered her.

"That's all—an instrument."

We merely watched her.

"One of the many."

And then Jim in his kindly blundering way made his second mistake.

"Yes, Agnes," he said, "Yes."

But at that, she took even me by surprise. She sat up in bed suddenly, her eyes wild and staring and before we could stop her, began beating her breast.

"Agnes," I said, "Don't! Don't!"

"I shall," she said in a strange high voice.

Well, we let her alone. It would have meant a struggle.

And then amid little sobbing breaths, beating her breast the while, she began to cry out: "Yes!—Yes!—I!—I!—An instrument of reproduction!—another of the many!—a colored woman— doomed!—cursed!—put here!—willing or unwilling! For what?— to bring children here—men children—for the sport—the lust— of possible orderly mobs—who go about things—in an orderly manner—on Sunday mornings!"

"Agnes," I cried out. "Agnes! Your child will be born in the North. He need never go South."

She had listened to me at any rate.

"Yes," she said, "in the North. In the North.—And have there been no lynchings in the North?"

I was silenced.

"The North permits it too," she cried. "The North is silent as well as the South."

And then as she sat there her eyes became less wild but more terrible. They became the eyes of a seeress. When she spoke again she spoke loudly, clearly, slowly:

"There is a time coming—and soon—when no colored man —no colored woman—no colored child, born or unborn—will be safe—in this country."

"Oh Agnes," I cried again, "Sh! sh!"

She turned her terrible eyes upon me.

"There is no more need for silence—in this house. God has found us out."

"Oh Agnes," the tears were frankly running down my cheeks. "We must believe that God is very pitiful. We must. He will find a way."

She waited a moment and said simply:

"Will He?"

"Yes, Agnes! Yes!"

"I will believe you, then. I will give Him one more chance. Then, if He is not pitiful, then if He is not pitiful—" But she did not finish. She fell back upon her pillows. She had fainted again.

Agnes did not die, nor did her child. She had kept her body clean and healthy. She was up and around again, but an Agnes that never smiled, never chuckled any more. She was a grey pathetic shadow of herself. She who had loved joy so much, cared more, it seemed, for solitude than anything else in the world. That was why, when Jim or I went looking for her we found so often only the empty room and that imperceptibly closing, slowly closing, opposite door.

Joe went back to Mississippi and not one of us, ever again, mentioned Bob's name.

And Jim, poor Jim! I wish I could tell you of how beautiful he was those days. How he never complained, never was irritable, but was always so gentle, so full of understanding, that at times, I had to go out of the room for fear he might see my tears.

Only once I saw him when he thought himself alone. I had not known he was in his little den and entered it suddenly. I had made no sound, luckily, and he had not heard me. He was sitting leaning far forward, his head between his hands. I stood there five minutes at least, but not once did I see him stir. I silently stole out and left him.

It was a fortunate thing that Agnes had already done most of her sewing for the little expected stranger, for after Joe's visit, she never touched a thing.

"Agnes!" I said one day, not without fear and trepidation it is true. "Isn't there something I can do?"

"Do?" she repeated rather vaguely.

"Yes. Some sewing?"

"Oh! sewing," she said. "No, I think not, Lucy."

"You've—you've finished? I persisted.

"No."

"Then—" I began.

"I hardly think we shall need any of them." And then she added, "I hope not."

"Agnes!" I cried out.

But she seemed to have forgotten me.

Well, time passed, it always does. And on a Sunday morning early Agnes' child was born. He was a beautiful, very grave baby with her great dark eyes.

As soon as they would let me, I went to her.

She was lying very still and straight, in the quiet, darkened room, her head turned on the pillow towards the wall. Her eyes were closed.

"Agnes!" I said in the barest whisper. "Are you asleep?"

"No," she said. And turned her head towards me and opened

her eyes. I looked into her ravaged face. Agnes Milton had been down into Hell and back again.

Neither of us spoke for some time and then she said:

"Is he dead?"

"Your child?"

"Yes."

"I should say not, he's a perfect darling and so good."

No smile came into her face. It remained as expressionless as before. She paled a trifle more, I thought, if such a thing was possible.

"I'm sorry," she said finally.

"Agnes!" I spoke sharply. I couldn't help it.

But she closed her eyes and made no response.

I sat a long time looking at her. She must have felt my gaze for she slowly lifted her lids and looked at me.

"Well," she said, "what is it, Lucy?"

"Haven't you seen your child, Agnes?"

"No."

"Don't you wish to see it?"

"No."

Again it was wrung out of me:

"Agnes, Agnes, don't tell me you don't love it."

For the first and only time a spasm of pain went over her poor pinched face.

"Ah!" she said, "That's it." And she closed her eyes and her face was as expressionless as ever.

I felt as though my heart were breaking.

Again she opened her eyes.

"Tell me, Lucy," she began.

"What, Agnes?"

"Is he—healthy?"

"Yes."

"Quite strong?"

"Yes."

"You think he will live, then?"

"Yes, Agnes."

She closed her eyes once more. It was very still within the room.

Again she opened her eyes. There was a strange expression in them now.

"Lucy!"

"Yes."

"You were wrong."

"Wrong, Agnes?"

"Yes."

"How?"

"You thought your God was pitiful."

"Agnes, but I do believe it."

After a long silence she said very slowly:

"He—is—not."

This time, when she closed her eyes, she turned her head slowly upon the pillow to the wall. I was dismissed.

And again Agnes did not die. Time passed and again she was up and about the flat. There was a strange, stony stillness upon her, now, I did not like, though. If we only could have understood, Jim and I, what it meant. Her love for solitude, now, had become a passion. And Jim and I knew more and more that empty room and that silently, slowly closing door.

She would have very little to do with her child. For some reason, I saw, she was afraid of it. I was its mother. I did for it, cared for it, loved it.

Twice only during these days I saw that stony stillness of hers broken.

The first time was one night. The baby was fast asleep, and she had stolen in to look at him, when she thought no one would know. I never wish to see such a tortured, hungry face again.

I was in the kitchen, the second time, when I heard strange sounds coming from my room. I rushed to it and there was Agnes, kneeling at the foot of the little crib, her head upon the spread. Great, terrible racking sobs were tearing her. The baby was lying there, all eyes, and beginning to whimper a little.

"Agnes! Oh, my dear! What is it?" The tears were streaming down my cheeks.

"Take him away! Take him away!" she gasped. "He's been cooing, and smiling and holding out his little arms to me. I can't stand it! I can't stand it."

I took him away. That was the only time I ever saw Agnes Milton weep.

The baby slept in my room, Agnes would not have him in hers. He was a restless little sleeper and I had to get up several times during the night to see that he was properly covered.

He was a noisy little sleeper as well. Many a night I have lain awake listening to the sound of his breathing. It is a lovely sound, a beautiful one—the breathing of a little baby in the dark.

This night, I remember, I had been up once and covered him over and had fallen off to sleep for the second time, when, for I had heard absolutely no sound, I awoke suddenly. Thee was upon me an overwhelming utterly paralyzing feeling not of fear but of horror. I thought, at first, I must have been having a nightmare, but strangely instead of diminishing, the longer I lay awake, the more it seemed to increase.

It was a moonlight night and the light came in through the open window in a broad, white, steady stream.

A coldness seemed to settle all about my heart. What was the matter with me? I made a tremendous effort and sat up. Everything seemed peaceful and quiet enough.

The moonlight cut the room in two. It was dark where I was and dark beyond where the baby was.

One brass knob at the foot of my bed shone brilliantly, I remember, in that bright stream and the door that led into the hall stood out fully revealed. I looked at that door and then my heart suddenly seemed to stop beating! I grew deathly cold. The door was closing slowly, imperceptibly, silently. Things were whirling around. I shut my eyes. When I opened them again the door was no longer moving; it had closed.

What had Agnes Milton wanted in my room? And the more I asked myself that question the deeper grew the horror.

And then slowly, by degrees, I began to realize there was something wrong within that room, something terribly wrong. But what was it?

I tried to get out of bed, but I seemed unable to move. I strained my eyes, but I could see nothing—only that bright knob, that stream of light, that closed white door.

I listened. It was quiet, very quiet, too quiet. But why too quiet? And then as though there had been a blinding flash of lightening I knew—the breathing wasn't there.

Agnes Milton had taken a pillow off of my bed and smothered her child.

One last word. Jim received word this morning. The door was finished closing for the last time—Agnes Milton is no more. God, I think, may be pitiful, after all.

DOROTHY WEST

BOSTONIAN DOROTHY WEST was present at the creation of the Harlem Renaissance, "Typewriter" taking second prize in the first Opportunity *magazine contest. West was precocious (seventeen in 1925) but conventional in her fiction. "Typewriter" is significant as one of the early short stories, in the tradition of Dunbar's novella* Sport of the Gods, *depicting the slow, grinding erosion of the lives of many Southern migrants who had sought the main chance in the city.*

THE TYPEWRITER

IT OCCURRED TO HIM, as he eased past the bulging knees of an Irish wash lady and forced an apologetic passage down the aisle of the crowded car, that more than anything in all the world he wanted not to go home. He began to wish passionately that he had never been born, that he had never been married, that he had never been the means of life's coming into the world. He knew quite suddenly that he hated his flat and his family and his friends. And most of all the incessant thing that would "clatter clatter" until every nerve screamed aloud, and the words of the evening paper danced crazily before him, and the insane desire to crush and kill set his fingers twitching.

He shuffled down the street, an abject little man of fifty-odd years, in an ageless overcoat that flapped in the wind. He was cold, and he hated the North, and particularly Boston, and saw suddenly a barefoot pickaninny sitting on a fence in the hot, Southern sun with a piece of steaming corn bread and a piece of fried salt pork in either grimy hand.

He was tired, and he wanted his supper, but he didn't want the beans, and frankfurters, and light bread that Net would undoubtedly have. That Net had had every Monday night since that regrettable moment fifteen years before when he had told her—innocently—that such a supper tasted "right nice. Kinda change from what we always has."

He mounted the four brick steps leading to his door and pulled at the bell, but there was no answering ring. It was broken again, and in a mental flash he saw himself with a multitude of tools and a box of matches shivering in the vestibule after supper. He began to pound lustily on the door and wondered vaguely if his hand would bleed if he smashed the glass. He hated the sight of blood. It sickened him.

Some one was running down the stairs. Daisy probably. Millie would be at that infernal thing, pounding, pounding. . . . He entered. The chill of the house swept him. His child was wrapped in a coat. She whispered solemnly, "Poppa, Miz Hicks an' Miz Berry's orful mad. They gointa move if they can't get more heat. The furnace's birnt out all day. Mama couldn't fix it." He said hurriedly, "I'll go right down. I'll go right down." He hoped Mrs. Hicks wouldn't pull open her door and glare at him. She was large and domineering, and her husband was a bully. If her husband ever struck him it would kill him. He hated life, but he didn't want to die. He was afraid of God, and in his wildest flights of fancy couldn't imagine himself an angel. He went softly down the stairs.

He began to shake the furnace fiercely. And he shook into it every wrong, mumbling softly under his breath. He began to think back over his uneventful years, and it came to him as rather a shock that he had never sworn in all his life. He wondered uneasily if he dared say "damn." It was taken for granted that a man swore when he tended a stubborn furnace. And his strongest interjection was "Great balls of fire!"

The cellar began to warm, and he took off his inadequate overcoat that was streaked with dirt. Well, Net would have to clean that. He'd be damned—! It frightened him and thrilled him. He wanted suddenly to rush upstairs and tell Mrs. Hicks if she didn't like the way he was running things, she could get out. But he heaped another shovelful of coal on the fire and sighed. He would never be able to get away from himself and the routine of years.

He thought of that eager Negro lad of seventeen who had come North to seek his fortune. He had walked jauntily down Boylston Street, and even his own kind had laughed at the incongruity of him. But he had thrown up his head and promised himself: "You'll have an office here some day. With plate-glass windows and a real mahogany desk." But, though he didn't know it then, he was not the progressive type. And he became successively, in the years, bell boy, porter, waiter, cook, and finally janitor in a down town office building.

He had married Net when he was thirty-three and a waiter. He had married her partly because—though he might not have admitted it—there was no one to eat the expensive delicacies the generous cook gave him every night to bring home. And partly because he dared hope there might be a son to fulfill his dreams. But Millie had come, and after her twin girls who had died within two weeks, then Daisy, and it was tacitly understood that Net was done with child-bearing.

Life, though flowing monotonously, had flowed peacefully enough until that sucker of sanity became a sitting-room fixture. Intuitively at the very first he had felt its undesirability. He had suggested hesitatingly that they couldn't afford it. Three dollars: food and fuel. Times were hard, and the twenty dollars apiece the respective husbands of Miz Hicks and Miz Berry irregularly paid was only five dollars more than the thirty-five a month he paid his own Hebraic landlord. And the Lord knew his salary was little enough. At which point Net spoke her piece, her voice rising shrill. "God knows I never complain 'bout nothin'. Ain't no other woman got less than me. I bin wearin' this same dress here five years an' I'll wear it another five. But I don't want nothin'. I ain't never wanted nothin'. An' when I does as', it's only for my children. You're a poor sort of father if you can't give that child jes' three dollars a month to rent that typewriter. Ain't 'nother girl in school ain't got one. An' mos' of 'ems bought an' paid for. You know yourself how Millie is. She wouldn't as' me for it till she had to. An' I ain't going to disappoint her. She's goin' to get that typewriter Saturday, mark my words."

On a Monday then it had been installed. And in the months that followed, night after night he listened to the murderous "tack, tack, tack" that was like a vampire slowly drinking his blood. If only he could escape. Bar a door against the sound of it. But tied hand and foot by the economic fact that "Lord knows we can't afford to have fires burnin' an' lights lit all over the flat. You'all gotta set in one room. An' when y'get tired settin' y' c'n go to bed. Gas bill was somep'n scandalous last month."

He heaped a final shovelful of coal on the fire and watched the first blue flames. Then, his overcoat under his arm, he mounted the cellar stairs. Mrs. Hicks was standing in her kitchen door, arms akimbo. "It's warmin'," she volunteered.

"Yeh," he was conscious of his grime-streaked face and hands, "it's warmin'. I'm sorry 'bout all day."

She folded her arms across her ample bosom. "Tending a furnace ain't a woman's work. I don't blame your wife none 'tall."

Unsuspecting he was grateful. "Yeh, it's pretty hard for a woman. I always look after it 'fore I goes to work, but some days it jes' ac's up."

"Y'oughta have a janitor, that's what y'ought," she flung at him. "The same cullud man that tends them apartments would be willin'. Mr. Taylor has him. It takes a man to run a furnace, and when the man's away all day—"

"I know," he interrupted, embarrassed and hurt, "I know. Tha's right, Miz Hicks tha's right. But I ain't in a position to make no improvements. Times is hard."

She surveyed him critically. "Your wife called down 'bout three times while you was in the cellar. I reckon she wants you for supper."

"Thanks," he mumbled and escaped up the back stairs.

He hung up his overcoat in the closet, telling himself, a little lamely, that it wouldn't take him more'n a minute to clean it up himself after supper. After all Net was tired and prob'bly worried what with Miz Hicks and all. And he hated men who made slaves of their women folk. Good old Net.

He tidied up in the bathroom, washing his face and hands carefully and cleanly so as to leave no—or very little—stain on the roller towel. It was hard enough for Net, God knew.

He entered the kitchen. The last spirals of steam were rising from his supper. One thing about Net she served a full plate. He smiled appreciatively at her unresponsive back, bent over the kitchen sink. There was no one could bake beans just like Net's. And no one who could find a market with frankfurters quite so fat.

He sank down at his place. "Evenin', hon."

He saw her back stiffen. "If your supper's cold, 'tain't my fault. I called and called."

He said hastily, "It's fine, Net, fine. Piping."

She was the usual tired housewife. "Y'oughta et your supper 'fore you fooled with that furnace. I ain't bothered 'bout them niggers. I got all my dishes washed 'cept yours. An' I hate to mess up my kitchen after I once get it straightened up."

He was humble. "I'll give that old furnace an extra lookin' after in the mornin'. It'll las' all day to-morrow, hon."

"An' on top of that," she continued, unheeding him and giving a final wrench to her dish towel, "that confounded bell don't ring. An'—"

"I'll fix it after supper," he interposed hastily.

She hung up her dish towel and came to stand before him looming large and yellow. "An' that old Miz Berry, she claim she was expectin' comp'ny. An' she knows they must 'a' come an' gone while she was in her kitchen an' couldn't be at her winder to watch for 'em. Old liar," she brushed back a lock of naturally straight hair. "She wasn't expectin' nobody."

"Well, you know how some folks are—"

"Fools! Half the world," was her vehement answer. "I'm goin' in the front room an' set down a spell. I bin on my feet all day. Leave them dishes on the table. God knows I'm tired, but I'll come back an' wash 'em." But they both knew, of course, that he, very clumsily, would.

At precisely quarter past nine when he, strained at last to the breaking point, uttering an inhuman, strangled cry, flung down his paper, clutched at his throat and sprang to his feet, Millie's surprised young voice, shocking him to normalcy, heralded the first of that series of great moments that every humble little middle-class man eventually experiences.

"What's the matter, poppa? You sick? I wanted you to help me."

He drew out his handkerchief and wiped his hot hands. "I declare I must 'a' fallen asleep an' had a nightmare. No, I ain't sick. What you want, hon?"

"Dictate me a letter, poppa. I c'n do sixty words a minute.— You know, like a business letter. You know, like those men in your building dictate to their stenographers. Don't you hear 'em sometimes?"

"Oh, sure, I know, hon. Poppa'll help you. Sure. I hear that Mr. Browning—Sure."

Net rose. "Guess I'll put this child to bed. Come on now,

Daisy, without no fuss.—Then I'll run up to pa's. He ain't bin well all week."

When the door closed behind them, he crossed to his daughter, conjured the image of Mr. Browning in the process of dictating, so arranged himself, and coughed importantly.

"Well, Millie—"

"Oh, poppa, is that what you'd call your stenographer?" she teased. "And anyway pretend I'm really one—and you're really my boss, and this letter's real important."

A light crept into his dull eyes. Vigor through his thin blood. In a brief moment the weight of years fell from him like a cloak. Tired, bent, little old man that he was, he smiled, straightened, tapped impressively against his teeth with a toil-stained finger, and became that enviable emblem of American life: a business man.

"You be Miz Hicks, huh, honey? Course we can't both use the same name. I'll be J. Lucius Jones. J. Lucius. All them real big doin' men use their middle names. Jus' kinda looks big doin', doncha think, hon? Looks like money, huh? J. Lucius." He uttered a sound that was like the proud cluck of a strutting hen. "J. Lucius." It rolled like oil from his tongue.

His daughter twisted impatiently. "Now, poppa—I mean Mr. Jones, sir—please begin. I am ready for dictation, sir."

He was in that office on Boylston Street, looking with visioning eyes through its plate-glass windows, tapping with impatient fingers on its real mahogany desk.

"Ah—Beaker Brothers, Park Square Building, Boston, Mass. Ah—Gentlemen: In reply to yours at the seventh instant I would state—"

Every night thereafter in the weeks that followed, with Daisy packed off to bed, and Net "gone up to pa's" or nodding inobtrusively in her corner there was the chamelion change of a Court Street janitor to J. Lucius Jones, dealer in stocks and bonds. He would stand, posturing importantly, flicking imaginary dust from his coat lapel, or, his hands locked behind his back, he would stride up and down, earnestly and seriously debating the advisability of buying copper with the market in such a fluctuating state. Once a week, too, he stopped in at Jerry's, and after a preliminary purchase of cheap cigars, bought the latest trade papers, mumbling an embarrassed explanation: "I got a little money. Think I'll invest it in reliable stock."

The letters Millie typed and subsequently discarded, he rummaged for later, and under cover of writing to his brother in the South, laboriously with a great many fancy flourishes, signed each neatly typed sheet with the exalted J. Lucius Jones.

Later, when he mustered the courage he suggested tentatively to Millie that it might be fun—just fun, of course!—to answer his letters. One night—he laughed a good deal louder and longer than necessary—he'd be J. Lucius Jones, and the next night—here he swallowed hard and looked a little frightened—Rockefeller or Vanderbilt or Morgan—just for fun, y'understand! To which Millie gave consent. It mattered little to her one way or the other. It was practice, and that was what she needed. Very soon now she'd be in the hundred class. Then maybe she could get a job!

He was growing very careful of his English. Occasionally— and must be admitted, ashamedly—he made surreptitious ventures into the dictionary. He had to, of course. J. Lucius Jones would never say "Y'got to" when he meant "It is expedient." And, old brain though he was, he learned quickly and easily, juggling words with amazing facility.

Eventually he bought stamps and envelopes—long, important looking envelopes—and stammered apologetically to Millie, "Honey, poppa thought it'd help you if you learned to type envelopes, too. Reckon you'll have to do that, too, when y'get a job. Poor old man," he swallowed painfully, "came round selling these envelopes. You know how 'tis. So I had to buy 'em." Which was satisfactory to Millie. If she saw through her father, she gave no sign. After all, it was practice, and Mr. Hennessey had said that— though not in just those words.

He had got in the habit of carrying those self-addressed envelopes in his inner pocket where they bulged impressively. And occasionally he would take them out—on the car usually—and smile upon them. This one might be from J. P. Morgan. This one from Henry Ford. And a million-dollar deal involved in each. That narrow, little spinster, who, upon his sitting down, had drawn herself away from his contact, was shunning J. Lucius Jones!

Once, led by some sudden, strange impulse, as an outgoing car rumbled up out of the subway, he got out a letter, darted a quick, shamed glance about him, dropped it in an adjacent box, and swung aboard the car, feeling, dazedly, as if he had committed a crime. And the next night he sat in the sitting-room quite on edge until Net said suddenly, "Look here, a real important letter come to-day for you, pa. Here 'tis. What you s'pose it says," and he reached out a hand that trembled. He made brief explanation. "Advertisement, hon. Thassal."

They came quite frequently after that, and despite the fact that he knew them by heart, he read them slowly and carefully, rustling the sheet, and making inaudible, intelligent comments. He was, in these moments, pathetically earnest.

Monday, as he went about his janitor's duties, he composed in his mind the final letter from J. P. Morgan that would consummate a big business deal. For days now letters had passed between them. J. P. had been at first quite frankly uninterested. He had written tersely and briefly. He wrote glowingly of the advantages of a pact between them. Daringly he argued in terms of billions. And at last J. P. had written his next letter would be decisive. Which next letter, this Monday, as he trailed about the office building, was writing itself on his brain.

That night Millie opened the door for him. Her plain face was transformed. "Poppa—poppa, I got a job! Twelve dollars a week to start with! Isn't that *swell!*"

He was genuinely pleased. "Honey, I'm glad. Right glad," and went up the stairs, unsuspecting.

He ate his supper hastily, went down into the cellar to see about his fire, returned and carefully tidied up, informing his reflection in the bathroom mirror, "Well, J. Lucius, you c'n expect that final letter any day now."

He entered the sitting-room. The phonograph was playing. Daisy was singing lustily. Strange. Net was talking animatedly to —Millie, busy with needle and thread over a neat, little frock. His wild glance darted to the table. The pretty, little centerpiece, the bowl and wax flowers all neatly arranged: the typewriter gone from its accustomed place. It seemed an hour before he could speak. He felt himself trembling. Went hot and cold.

"Millie—your typewriter's—gone!"

She made a deft little in and out movement with her needle. "It's the eighth, you know. When the man came to-day for the money, I sent it back. I won't need it no more—now!—The money's on the mantlepiece, poppa."

"Yeh," he muttered. "All right."

He sank down in his chair, fumbled for the paper, found it.

Net said, "Your poppa wants to read. Stop your noise, Daisy."

She obediently stopped both her noise and the phonograph,

took up her book, and became absorbed. Millie went on with her sewing in placid anticipation of the morrow. Net immediately began to nod, gave a curious snort, slept.

Silence. That crowded in on him, engulfed him. That blurred his vision, dulled his brain. Vast, white, impenetrable. . . . His ears strained for the old, familiar sound. And silence beat upon them. . . . The words of the evening paper jumbled together. He read: J. P. Morgan goes—

It burst upon him. Blinded him. His hands groped for the bulge beneath his coat. Why this—this was the end! The end of those great moments—the end of everything! Bewildering pain tore through him. He clutched at his heart and felt, almost, the jagged edges drive into his hand. A lethargy swept down upon him. He could not move, nor utter a sound. He could not pray, nor curse.

Against the wall of that silence J. Lucius Jones crashed and died.

W. E. B. DU BOIS

THE FOLLOWING EXCERPTS *from* W. E. B. Du Bois's *second novel*,
The Dark Princess *(1928), follow Matthew Towns, the author's
noble, ingenuous protagonist, to Germany, where his quest for a
solution to the race problem brings him into contact with the second compelling woman in his life—the visionary yet competent
Indian princess, Kautilya of Bwodpur. In America, Matthew
Towns had barely escaped being turned from his high purposes by
Sara Andrews, the sophisticated (mulatto) symbol of that country's
corrupt political system. From the princess Matthew learns of a
grand secret design under way to solve the problem of the twentieth century—the color line. They become lovers, are separated,
and Towns returns to America animated by a world perspective
on race.*

*Because the male protagonist (a Hampton Institute graduate)
mainly reacts to the personalities and plans of dynamic women,
Du Bois's sprawling novel is, among other things, one of the first
feminist works of the Harlem Renaissance (his own* Quest of the
Silver Fleece *being a precursor) and a more positive feminist work
than Larsen's* Quicksand. *Du Bois also intended it to serve as an
antidote to the decadent influence of Van Vechten and the "vulgar"
realism of McKay.* The Dark Princess *sought to return Harlem
Renaissance fiction to the redemptive path of civil rights through
arts and letters.*

*With much talk of Debsian socialism, the solidarity of peoples
of color (Japanese, Indians, Africans), conflicts with Garveyites,
and immersion in Chicago politics,* The Dark Princess *ends with
Matthew, Kautilya, and their son, born out of wedlock, reunited
in marriage. That son will become leader of the Great Council of*

Darker Peoples (presently invisible but serving as nucleus for the future interracial World Government). The novel closes with Kautilya holding aloft the baby maharaja and proclaiming him "Messenger and Messiah to all the Darker World."

FROM *THE DARK PRINCESS*

PART I

THE EXILE

August, 1923

Summer is come with bursting flower and promise of perfect fruit. Rain is rolling down Nile and Niger. Summer sings on the sea where giant ships carry busy worlds, while mermaids swarm the shores. Earth is pregnant. Life is big with pain and evil and hope. Summer in blue New York; summer in gray Berlin; summer in the red heart of the world!

They had sat an hour drinking tea in the Tiergarten, that mightiest park in Europe with its lofty trees, its cool dark shade, its sense of withdrawal from the world. He had not meant to be so voluble, so self-revealing. Perhaps the lady had deftly encouraged confidences in her high, but gracious way. Perhaps the mere sight of her smooth brown skin had made Matthew assume sympathy. There was something at once inviting and aloof in the young woman who sat opposite him. She had the air and carriage of one used to homage and yet receiving it indifferently as a right. With all her gentle manner and thoughtfulness, she had a certain faint air of haughtiness and was ever slightly remote.

She was "colored" and yet not at all colored in his intimate sense. Her beauty as he saw it near had seemed even more striking; those thin, smooth fingers moving about the silver had known no work; she was carefully groomed from her purple hair to her slim toe-tips, and yet with few accessories; he could not tell whether she used paint or powder. Her features were regular and delicate, and there was a tiny diamond in one nostril. But quite aside from all details of face and jewels—her pearls, her rings, the old gold bracelet—above and beyond and much more than the sum of them all was the luminous radiance of her complete beauty, her glow of youth and strength behind that screen of a grand yet gracious manner. It was overpowering for Matthew, and yet stimulating. So his story came pouring out before he knew or cared to whom he was speaking. All the loneliness of long, lonely days clamored for speech, all the pent-up resentment choked for words.

The lady listened at first with polite but conscious sympathy; then she bent forward more and more eagerly, but always with restraint, with that mastery of body and soul that never for a moment slipped away, and yet with so evident a sympathy and comprehension that it set Matthew's head swimming. She swept him almost imperiously with her eyes—those great wide orbs of darkening light. His own eyes lifted and fell before them; lifted and fell, until at last he looked past them and talked to the tall green and black oaks.

And yet there was never anything personal in her all-sweeping glance or anything self-conscious in the form that bent toward him. She never seemed in the slightest way conscious of herself. She arranged nothing, glanced at no detail of her dress, smoothed no wisp of hair. She seemed at once unconscious of her beauty and charm, and at the same time assuming it as a fact, but of no especial importance. She had no little feminine ways; she used her eyes apparently only for seeing, yet seemed to see all.

Matthew had the feeling that her steady, full, radiant gaze that enveloped and almost burned him, saw not him but the picture he was painting and the thing that the picture meant. He warmed with such an audience and painted with clean, sure lines. Only once or twice did she interrupt, and when he had ended, she still sat full-faced, flooding him with the startling beauty of her eyes. Her hands clasped and unclasped slowly, her lips were slightly parted, the curve of her young bosom rose and fell.

"And you ran away!" she said musingly. Matthew winced and started to explain, but she continued. "Singular," she said. "How singular that I should meet you; and today." There was no coquetry in her tone. It was evidently not of him, the hero, of whom she was thinking, but of him, the group, the fact, the whole drama.

"And you are two—three millions?" she asked.

"Ten or twelve," he answered.

"You ran away," she repeated, half in meditation.

"What else could I do?" he demanded impulsively. "Cringe and crawl?"

"Of course the Negroes have no hospitals?"

"Of course, they have—many, but not attached to the great schools. What can Howard (rated as our best colored school) do with thousands, when whites have millions? And if we come out poorly taught and half equipped, they sneer at 'nigger' doctors."

"And no Negroes are admitted to the hospitals of New York?"

"O yes—hundreds. But if we colored students are confined to colored patients, we surrender a principle."

"What principle?"

"Equality."

"Oh—equality."

She sat for a full moment, frowning and looking at him. Then she fumbled away at her beads and brought out a tiny jeweled box. Absently she took out a cigarette, lighted it, and offered him one. Matthew took it, but he was a little troubled. White women in his experience smoked of course—but colored women? Well—but it was delicious to see her great, somber eyes veiled in hazy blue.

She sighed at last and said: "I do not quite understand. But at any rate I see that you American Negroes are not a mere amorphous handful. You are a nation! I never dreamed—But I must explain. I want you to dine with me and some friends tomorrow night at my apartment. We represent—indeed I may say frankly, we are—a part of a great committee of the darker peoples; of those who suffer under the arrogance and tyranny of the white world."

Matthew leaned forward with an eager thrill. "And you have plans? Some vast emancipation of the world?"

She did not answer directly, but continued: "We have among us spokesmen of nearly all these groups—of them or for them—except American Negroes. Some of us think these former slaves unready for coöperation, but I just returned from Moscow last week. At our last dinner I was telling of a report I read there from America that astounded me and gave me great pleasure—for I almost alone have insisted that your group was worthy of coöperation. In Russia I heard something, and it happened so curiously that—after sharp discussion about your people but last night (for I will not conceal from you that there is still doubt and opposition in our ranks)—that I should meet you today.

"I had gone up to the Palace to see the exhibition of new paintings—you have not seen it? You must. All the time I was thinking absently of Black America, and one picture there intensified and stirred my thoughts—a weird massing of black shepherds and a star. I dropped into the Viktoria, almost unconsciously, because the tea there is good and the muffins quite unequaled. I know that I should not go there unaccompanied, even in the day; white women may, but brown women seem strangely attractive to white men, especially Americans; and this is the open season for them.

"Twice before I have had to put Americans in their place. I went quite unconsciously and noted nothing in particular until that impossible young man sat down at my table. I did not know he had followed me out. Then you knocked him into the gutter quite beautifully. It had never happened before that a stranger of my own color should offer me protection in Europe. I had a curious sense of some great inner meaning to your act—some world movement. It seemed almost that the Powers of Heaven had bent to give me the knowledge which I was groping for; and so I invited you, that I might hear and know more."

She rose, insisted on paying the bill herself. "You are my guest, you see. It is late, and I must go. Then, tomorrow night at eight. My card and address— Oh, I quite forgot. May I have your name?"

Matthew had no card. But he wrote in her tiny memorandum book with its golden filigree, "Matthew Towns, Exile, Hotel Roter Adler."

She held out her hand, half turning to go. Her slenderness made her look taller than she was. The curved line of her flowed sinuously from neck to ankle. She held her right hand high, palm down, the long fingers drooping, and a ruby flamed dark crimson on her forefinger. Matthew reached up and shook the hand heartily. He had, as he did it, a vague feeling that he took her by surprise. Perhaps he shook hands too hard, for her hand was very little and frail. Perhaps she did not mean to shake hands—but then, what did she mean?

She was gone. He took out her card and read it. There was a little coronet and under it, engraved in flowing script, "H.R.H. the Princess Kautilya of Bwodpur, India." Below was written, "Lützower Ufer, No. 12."

Matthew sat in the dining-room of the Princess on Lützower Ufer. Looking about, his heart swelled. For the first time since he had left New York, he felt himself a man, one of those who could help build a world and guide it. He had no regrets. Medicine seemed a far-off, dry-as-dust thing.

The oak paneling of the room went to the ceiling and there broke softly with carven light against white flowers and into long lucent curves. The table below was sheer with lace and linen, sparkling with silver and crystal. The servants moved deftly, and all of them were white save one who stood behind the Princess' high and crimson chair. At her right sat Matthew himself, hardly realizing until long afterward the honor thus done an almost nameless guest.

Fortunately he had the dinner jacket of year before last with him. It was not new, but it fitted his form perfectly, and his was a form worth fitting. He was a bit shocked to note that all the other men but two were in full evening dress. But he did not let this worry him much.

Ten of them sat at the table. On the Princess' left was a Japanese, faultless in dress and manner, evidently a man of importance, as the deference shown him and the orders on his breast indicated. He was quite yellow, short and stocky, with a face which was a delicately handled but perfect mask. There were two Indians, one a man grave, haughty, and old, dressed richly in turban and embroidered tunic, the other, in conventional dress and turban, a young man, handsome and alert, whose eyes were ever on the Princess. There were two Chinese, a young man and a young woman, he in a plain but becoming Chinese costume of heavy blue silk, she in a pretty dress, half Chinese, half European in effect. An Egyptian and his wife came next, he suave, talkative, and polite—just a shade too talkative and a bit too polite, Matthew thought; his wife a big, handsome, silent woman, elegantly jeweled and gowned, with much bare flesh. Beyond them was a cold and rather stiff Arab who spoke seldom, and then abruptly.

Of the food and wine of such dinners, Matthew had read often but never partaken; and the conversation, now floating, now half submerged, gave baffling glimpses of unknown lands, spiritual and physical. It was all something quite new in his experience, the room, the table, the service, the company.

He could not keep his eyes from continually straying sidewise to his hostess. Never had he seen color in human flesh so regally set: the rich and flowing grace of the dress out of which rose so darkly splendid the jeweled flesh. The black and purple hair was heaped up on her little head, and in its depths gleamed a tiny coronet of gold. Her voice and her poise, her self-possession and air of quiet command, kept Matthew staring almost unmannerly, despite the fact that he somehow sensed a shade of resentment in the young and handsome Indian opposite.

They had eaten some delicious tidbits of meat and vegetables and then were served with a delicate soup when the Princess, turning slightly to her right, said:

"You will note, Mr. Towns, that we represent here much of the Darker World. Indeed, when all our circle is present, we represent all of it, save your world of Black Folk."

"All the darker world except the darkest," said the Egyptian.

"A pretty large omission," said Matthew with a smile.

"I agree," said the Chinaman; but the Arab said something abruptly in French. Matthew had said that he knew "some" French. But his French was of the American variety which one excavates from dictionaries and cements with grammar, like bricks. He was astounded at the ease and the fluency with which most of this company used languages, so easily, without groping or hesitation and with light, sure shading. They talked art in French, literature in Italian, politics in German, and everything in clear English.

"M. Ben Ali suggests," said the Princess, "that even you are not black, Mr. Towns."

"My grandfather was, and my soul is. Black blood with us in America is a matter of spirit and not simply of flesh."

"Ah! mixed blood," said the Egyptian.

"Like all of us, especially me," laughed the Princess.

"But, your Royal Highness—not Negro," said the elder Indian in a tone that hinted a protest.

"Essentially," said the Princess lightly, "as our black and curly-haired Lord Buddha testifies in a hundred places. But"—a bit imperiously—"enough of that. Our point is that Pan-Africa belongs logically with Pan-Asia; and for that reason Mr. Towns is welcomed tonight by you, I am sure, and by me especially. He did me a service as I was returning from the New Palace."

They all looked interested, but the Egyptian broke out:

"Ah, Your Highness, the New Palace, and what is the fad today? What has followed expressionism, cubism, futurism, vorticism? I confess myself at sea. Picasso alarms me. Matisse sets me aflame. But I do not understand them. I prefer the classics."

"The Congo," said the Princess, "is flooding the Acropolis. There is a beautiful Kandinsky on exhibit, and some lovely and startling things by unknown newcomers."

"*Mais*," replied the Egyptian, dropping into French—and they were all off to the discussion, save the silent Egyptian woman and the taciturn Arab.

Here again Matthew was puzzled. These persons easily penetrated worlds where he was a stranger. Frankly, but for the context he would not have known whether Picasso was a man, a city, or a vegetable. He had never heard of Matisse. Lightly, almost carelessly, as he thought, his companions leapt to unknown subjects. Yet they knew. They knew art, books, and literature, politics of all nations, and not newspaper politics merely, but inner currents and whisperings, unpublished facts.

"Ah, pardon," said the Egyptian, returning to English, "I forgot Monsieur Towns speaks only English and does not interest himself in art."

Perhaps Matthew was sensitive and imagined that the Egyptian and the Indian rather often, if not purposely, strayed to French and subjects beyond him.

"Mr. Towns is a scientist?" asked the Japanese.

"He studies medicine," answered the Princess.

"Ah—a high service," said the Japanese. "I was reading only today of the work on cancer by your Peyton Rous in Carrel's laboratory."

Towns was surprised. "What, has he discovered the etiological factor? I had not heard."

"No, not yet, but he's a step nearer."

For a few moments Matthew was talking eagerly, until a babble of unknown tongues interrupted him across the table.

"Proust is dead, that 'snob of humor'—yes, but his *Recherche du Temps Perdu* is finished and will be published in full. I have only glanced at parts of it. Do you know Gasquet's *Hymnes*?"

"Beraud gets the Prix Goncourt this year. Last year it was the Negro, Maran—"

"I have been reading Croce's *Aesthetic* lately—"

"Yes, I saw the Meyerhold theater in Moscow—gaunt realism—*Howl China* was tremendous."

Then easily, after the crisp brown fowl, the Princess tactfully steered them back to the subject which some seemed willing to avoid.

"And so," she said, "the darker peoples who are dissatisfied—"

She looked at the Japanese and paused as though inviting comment. He bowed courteously.

"If I may presume, your Royal Highness, to suggest," he said slowly, "the two categories are not synonymous. We ourselves know no line of color. Some of us are white, some yellow, some black. Rather, is it not, your Highness, that we have from time to time taken council with the oppressed peoples of the world, many of whom by chance are colored?"

"True, true," said the Princess.

"And yet," said the Chinese lady, "it is dominating Europe which has flung this challenge of the color line, and we cannot avoid it."

"And on either count," said Matthew, "whether we be bound by oppression or by color, surely we Negroes belong in the foremost ranks."

There was a slight pause, a sort of hesitation, and it seemed to Matthew as though all expected the Japanese to speak. He did, slowly and gravely:

"It would be unfair to our guest not to explain with some clarity and precision that the whole question of the Negro race both in Africa and in America is for us not simply a question of suffering and compassion. Need we say that for these peoples we have every human sympathy? But for us here and for the larger company we represent, there is a deeper question—that of the ability, qualifications, and real possibilities of the black race in Africa or elsewhere."

Matthew left the piquant salad and laid down his fork slowly. Up to this moment he had been quite happy. Despite the feeling of being out of it now and then, he had assumed that this was his world, his people, from the high and beautiful lady whom he worshiped more and more, even to the Egyptians, Indians, and Arab who seemed slightly, but very slightly, aloof or misunderstanding.

Suddenly now there loomed plain and clear the shadow of a color line within a color line, a prejudice within prejudice, and he and his again the sacrifice. His eyes became somber and did not lighten even when the Princess spoke.

"I cannot see that it makes great difference what ability Negroes have. Oppression is oppression. It is our privilege to relieve it."

"Yes," answered the Japanese, "but who will do it? Who can do it but those superior races whose necks now bear the yoke of the inferior rabble of Europe?"

"This," said the Princess, "I have always believed; but as I have told your Excellency, I have received impressions in Moscow which have given me very serious thought—first as to our judgment of the ability of the Negro race, and second"—she paused in thought—"as to the relative ability of all classes and peoples."

Matthew stared at her, as she continued:

"You see, Moscow has reports—careful reports of the world's masses. And the report on the Negroes of America was astonishing. At the time, I doubted its truth: their education, their work, their property, their organizations; and the odds, the terrible, crushing odds against which, inch by inch and heartbreak by heartbreak, they have forged their unfaltering way upward. If the report is true, they are a nation today, a modern nation worthy to stand beside any nation here."

"But can we put any faith in Moscow?" asked the Egyptian. "Are we not keeping dangerous company and leaning on broken reeds?"

"Well," said Matthew, "if they are as sound in everything as in this report from America, they'll bear listening to."

The young Indian spoke gently and evenly, but with bright eyes.

"Naturally," he said, "one can see Mr. Towns needs must agree with the Bolshevik estimate of the lower classes."

Matthew felt the slight slur and winced. He thought he saw the lips of the Princess tighten ever so little. He started to answer quickly, with aplomb if not actual swagger.

"I reckon," he began—then something changed within him. It was as if he had faced and made a decision, as though some great voice, crying and reverberating within his soul, spoke for him and yet was him. He had started to say, "I reckon there's as much high-born blood among American Negroes as among any people. We've had our kings, presidents, and judges—" He started to say this, but he did not finish. He found himself saying quite calmly and with slightly lifted chin:

"I reckon you're right. We American blacks are very common people. My grandfather was a whipped and driven slave; my father was never really free and died in jail. My mother plows and washes for a living. We come out of the depths—the blood and mud of battle. And from just such depths, I take it, came most of the worth-while things in this old world. If they didn't—God help us."

The table was very still, save for the very faint clink of china as the servants brought in the creamed and iced fruit.

The Princess turned, and he could feel her dark eyes full upon him.

"I wonder—I wonder," she murmured, almost catching her breath.

The Indian frowned. The Japanese smiled, and the Egyptian whispered to the Arab.

"I believe that is true," said the Chinese lady thoughtfully, "and if it is, this world is glorious."

"And if it is not?" asked the Egyptian icily.

"It is perhaps both true and untrue," the Japanese suggested. "Certainly Mr. Towns has expressed a fine and human hope, although I fear that always blood must tell."

"No, it mustn't," cried Matthew, "unless it is allowed to talk. Its speech is accidental today. There is some weak, thin stuff called blood, which not even a crown can make speak intelligently; and at the same time some of the noblest blood God ever made is dumb with chains and poverty."

The elder Indian straightened, with blazing eyes.

"Surely," he said, slowly and calmly, "surely the gentleman does not mean to reflect on royal blood?"

Matthew started, flushed darkly, and glanced quickly at the Princess. She smiled and said lightly, "Certainly not," and then with a pause and a look straight across the table to the turban and tunic, "nor will royal blood offer insult to him." The Indian bowed to the tablecloth and was silent.

As they rose and sauntered out to coffee in the silk and golden drawing-room, there was a discussion, started of course by the Egyptian, first of the style of the elaborate piano case and then of Schönberg's new and unobtrusive transcription of Bach's triumphant choral Prelude, "Komm, Gott, Schöpfer."

The Princess sat down. Matthew could not take his eyes from her. Her fingers idly caressed the keys as her tiny feet sought the pedals. From white, pearl-embroidered slippers, her young limbs, smooth in pale, dull silk, swept up in long, low lines. Even the delicate curving of her knees he saw as she drew aside her drapery and struck the first warm tones. She played the phrase in dispute —great chords of aspiration and vision that melted to soft melody. The Egyptian acknowledged his fault. "Yes—yes, that was the theme I had forgotten."

Again Matthew felt his lack of culture audible, and not simply of his own culture, but of all the culture in white America which he had unconsciously and foolishly, as he now realized, made his norm. Yet withal Matthew was not unhappy. If he was a bit out of it, if he sensed divided counsels and opposition, yet he still felt almost fiercely that that was his world. Here were culture, wealth, and beauty. Here was power, and here he had some recognized part. God! If he could just do his part, any part! And he waited impatiently for the real talk to begin again.

It began and lasted until after midnight. It started on lines so familiar to Matthew that he had to shut his eyes and stare again at their swarthy faces: Superior races—the right to rule—born to command—inferior breeds—the lower classes—the rabble. How the Egyptian rolled off his tongue his contempt for the "r-r-rabble"! How contemptuous was the young Indian of inferior races! But how humorous it was to Matthew to see all tables turned; the rabble now was the white workers of Europe; the inferior races were the ruling whites of Europe and America. The superior races were yellow and brown.

"You see," said the Japanese, "Mr. Towns, we here are all agreed and not agreed. We are agreed that the present white hegemony of the world is nonsense; that the darker peoples are the best—the natural aristocracy, the makers of art, religion, philosophy, life, everything except brazen machines."

"But why?"

"Because of the longer rule of natural aristocracy among us. We count our millenniums of history where Europe counts her centuries. We have our own carefully thought-out philosophy and civilization, while Europe has sought to adopt an ill-fitting mélange of the cultures of the world."

"But does this not all come out the same gate, with the majority of mankind serving the minority? And if this is the only ideal of civilization, does the tint of a skin matter in the question of who leads?" Thus Matthew summed it up.

"Not a whit—it is the natural inborn superiority that matters," said the Japanese, "and it is that which the present color bar of Europe is holding back."

"And what guarantees, in the future more than in the past and with colored more than with white, the wise rule of the gifted and powerful?"

"Self-interest and the inclusion in their ranks of all really superior men of all colors—the best of Asia together with the best of the British aristocracy, of the German Adel, of the French writers and financiers—of the rulers, artists, and poets of all peoples."

"And suppose we found that ability and talent and art is not entirely or even mainly among the reigning aristocrats of Asia and Europe, but buried among millions of men down in the great sodden masses of all men and even in Black Africa?"

"It would come forth."

"Would it?"

"Yes," said the Princess, "it would come forth, but when and how? In slow and tenderly nourished efflorescence, or in wild and bloody upheaval with all that bitter loss?"

"Pah!" blurted the Egyptian—"pardon, Royal Highness—but what art ever came from the canaille!"

The blood rushed to Matthew's face. He threw back his head and closed his eyes, and with the movement he heard again the Great Song. He saw his father in the old log church by the river, leading the moaning singers in the Great Song of Emancipation. Clearly, plainly he heard that mighty voice and saw the rhythmic swing and beat of the thick brown arm. Matthew swung his arm and beat the table; the silver tinkled. Silence dropped on all, and suddenly Matthew found himself singing. His voice full, untrained but mellow, quivered down the first plaintive bar:

"When Israel was in Egypt land—"

Then it gathered depth:

"Let my people go!"

He forgot his audience and saw only the shining river and the bowed and shouting throng:

"Oppressed so hard, they could not stand,
Let my people go."

Then Matthew let go restraint and sang as his people sang in Virginia, twenty years ago. His great voice, gathered in one long deep breath, rolled the Call of God:

"Go down, Moses!
Way down into the Egypt land,

Tell Old Pharaoh
To let my people go!"

He stopped as quickly as he had begun, ashamed, and beads of sweat gathered on his forehead. Still there was silence—silence almost breathless. The voice of the Chinese woman broke it.

"It was an American slave song! I know it. How—how wonderful."

A chorus of approval poured out, led by the Egyptian.

"That," said Matthew, "came out of the black rabble of America." And he trilled his "r." They all smiled as the tension broke.

"You assume then," said the Princess at last, "that the mass of the workers of the world can rule as well as be ruled?"

"Yes—or rather can work as well as be worked, can live as well as be kept alive. America is teaching the world one thing and only one thing of real value, and that is, that ability and capacity for culture is not the hereditary monopoly of a few, but the widespread possibility for the majority of mankind if they only have a decent chance in life."

The Chinaman spoke: "If Mr. Towns' assumption is true, and I believe it is, and recognized, as some time it must be, it will revolutionize the world."

"It will revolutionize the world," smiled the Japanese, "but not—today."

"Nor this *siècle*," growled the Arab.

"Nor the next—and so *in saecula saeculorum*," laughed the Egyptian.

"Well," said the little Chinese lady, "the unexpected happens."

And Matthew added ruefully, "It's about all that does happen!"

He lapsed into blank silence, wondering how he had come to express the astonishing philosophy which had leapt unpremeditated from his lips. Did he himself believe it? As they arose from the table the Princess called him aside.

"I trust you will pardon the interruption at this late hour," said the Japanese. Matthew glanced up in surprise as the Japanese, the two Indians, and the Arab entered his room. "Sure," said he cheerily, "have any seats you can find. Sorry there's so little space."

It was three o'clock in the morning. He was in his shirt sleeves without collar, and he was packing hastily, wondering how on earth all these things had ever come out of his two valises. The little room on the fifth floor of the Roter Adler Hotel did look rather a mess. But his guests smiled and so politely deprecated any excuses or discomfort that he laughed too, and leaned against the window, while they stood about door and bed.

"You had, I believe," continued the Japanese, "an interview with her Royal Highness, the Princess, before you left her home tonight."

"Yes."

"I—er—presume you realize, Mr. Towns, that the Princess of Bwodpur is a lady of very high station—of great wealth and influence."

"I cannot imagine anybody higher."

The elder Indian interrupted. "There are," he said, "of course, some persons of higher hereditary rank than her Royal Highness, but not many. She is of royal blood by many scores of generations of direct descent. She is a ruling potentate in her own right over six millions of loyal subjects and yields to no human being in the ancient splendor of her heritage. Her income, her wealth in treasure and jewels, is uncounted. Sir, there are few people in the world who have the right to touch the hem of her garment." The Indian drew himself to full height and looked at Matthew.

"I'm strongly inclined to agree with you there," said Matthew, smiling genially.

"I had feared," continued the younger Indian, also looking Matthew squarely in the eye, "that perhaps, being American, and unused to the ceremony of countries of rank, you might misunderstand the democratic graciousness of her Royal Highness toward you. We appreciate, sir, more than we can say," and both Indians bowed low, "your inestimable service to the Princess yesterday, in protecting her royal person from insufferable insult. But the very incident illustrates and explains our errand.

"The Princess is young and headstrong. She delights, in her new European independence, to elude her escort, and has given us moments of greatest solicitude and even fright. Meeting her as you did yesterday, it was natural for you to take her graciousness toward you as the camaraderie of an equal, and—quite unconsciously, I am sure—your attitude toward her has caused us grave misgiving."

"You mean that I have not treated the Princess with courtesy?" asked Matthew in consternation. "In what way? Tell me."

"It is nothing—nothing, now that it is past, and since the Princess was gracious enough to allow it. But you may recall that you never addressed her by her rightful title of 'Royal Highness'; you several times interrupted her conversation and addressed her before being addressed; you occupied the seat of honor without even an attempted refusal and actually shook her Highness' hand, which we are taught to regard as unpardonable familiarity."

Matthew grinned cheerfully. "I reckon if the Princess hadn't liked all that she'd have said so—"

The Japanese quickly intervened. "This is, pardon me, beside our main errand," he said. "We realize that you admire and revere the Princess not only as a supremely beautiful woman of high rank, but as one of rare intelligence and high ideals."

"I certainly do."

"And we assume that anything you could do—any way you could coöperate with us for her safety and future, we could count upon your doing?"

"To my very life."

"Good—excellent—you see, my friends," turning to the still disturbed Indians and the silent, sullen Arab, "it is as I rightly divined."

They did not appear wholly convinced, but the Japanese continued:

"In her interview with you she told you a story she had heard in Moscow, of a widespread and carefully planned uprising of the American blacks. She has intrusted you with a letter to the alleged leader of this organization and asked you to report to her your impressions and recommendations; and even to deliver the letter, if you deem it wise.

"Now, my dear Mr. Towns, consider the situation: First of all, our beloved Princess introduces you, a total stranger, into our counsels and tells you some of our general plans. Fortunately, you prove to be a gentleman who can be trusted; and yet you yourself must admit this procedure was not exactly wise. Further than that, through this letter, our reputations, our very lives, are put in danger by this well-meaning but young and undisciplined lady. Her unfortunate visit to Russia has inoculated her with Bolshevism of a mild but dangerous type. The letter contains money to encourage treason. You know perfectly well that the American Negroes will neither rebel nor fight unless put up to it or led like dumb cattle by whites. You have never even heard of the alleged leader, as you acknowledged to the Princess."

"She is evidently well spied upon."

"She is, and will always be, well guarded," answered the elder Indian tensely.

"Except yesterday," said Matthew.

But the Japanese quickly proceeded. "Why then go on this wild goose chase? Why deliver dynamite to children?"

"Thank you."

"I beg your pardon. I may speak harshly, but I speak frankly. You are an exception among your people."

"I've heard that before. Once I believed it. Now I do not."

"You are generous, but you are an exception, and you know you are."

"Most people are exceptions."

"You know that your people are cowards."

"That's a lie; they are the bravest people fighting for justice today."

"I wish it were so, but I do not believe it, and neither do you. Every report from America—and believe me, we have many—contradicts this statement for you. I am not blaming them, poor things, they were slaves and children of slaves. They can not even begin to rise in a century. We Samurai have been lords a thousand years and more; the ancestors of her Royal Highness have ruled for twenty centuries—how can you think to place yourselves beside us as equals? No—no—restrain your natural anger and distaste for such truth. Our situation is too delicate for niceties. We have been almost betrayed by an impulsive woman, high and royal personage though she be. We have come to get that letter and to ask you to write a report now, to be delivered later, thoroughly disenchanting our dear Princess of this black American chimera."

"And if I refuse?"

The Japanese looked pained but patient. The others moved impatiently, and perceptibly narrowed the circle about Matthew. He was thinking rapidly; the letter was in his coat pocket on the bed beyond the Japanese and within easy reach of the Indians if they had known it. If he jumped out the window, he would be dead, and they would eventually secure the letter. If he fought, they were undoubtedly armed, and four to one. The Japanese was elderly and negligible as an opponent, but the young Indian and the Arab were formidable, and the older Indian dangerous. He might perhaps kill one and disable another and raise enough hullabaloo to arouse the hotel, but how would such a course affect the Princess?

The Japanese watched him sadly.

"Why speak of unpleasant things," he said gently, "or contemplate futilities? We are not barbarians. We are men of thought and culture. Be assured our plans have been laid with care. We know the host of this hotel well. Resistance on your part would be absolutely futile. The back stairs opposite your entrance are quite clear and will be kept clear until we go. And when we go, the letter will go with us."

Matthew set his back firmly against the window. His thoughts raced. They were armed, but they would use their arms only as a last resort; pistols were noisy and knives were messy. Oh, they would use them—one look at their hard, set eyes showed that; but not first. Good! Then first, instead of lurching forward to attack as they might expect, he would do a first-base slide and spike the Japanese in the ankles. It was a mean trick, but anything was fair now. He remembered once when they were playing the DeWitt Clinton High— But he jerked his thoughts back. The Japanese was nearest him; the fiery younger Indian just behind him and a bit to the right, bringing him nearer the bed and blocking the aisle. By the door was the elder Indian, and at the foot of the bed, the Arab.

Good! He would, at the very first movement of the young Indian, who, he instinctively knew, would begin the mêlée, slide feet forward into the ankles of the Japanese, catching him a little to the right so that he would fall or lurch between him and the Indian. Then he would with the same movement slide under the low iron bed and rise with the bed as weapon and shield. But he would not keep it. No; he would hurl it sideways and to the left, pinning the young Indian to the wall and the Japanese to the floor. With the same movement he would attempt a football tackle on the Arab. The Arab was a tough customer—tall, sinewy, and hard. If he turned left, got his knife and struck down, quick and sure, Matthew would be done for. But most probably he would, at Matthew's first movement, turn right toward his fellows. If he did, he was done for. He would go down in the heap, knocking the old Indian against the door.

Beside that door was the electric switch. Matthew would turn it and make a last fight for the door. He might get out, and if he did, the stairs were clear. The coat and letter? Leave them, so long as he got his story to the Princess. It was all a last desperate throw. He calculated that he had good chances against the Japanese's shins, about even chances to get under the bed unscathed, and one in two to tackle the Arab. He had not more than one chance in three of making the door unscathed, but this was the only way. If he surrendered without a fight— That was unthinkable. And after all, what had he to lose? Life? Well, his prospects were not brilliant anyhow. And to die for the Princess—silly, of course, but it made his blood race. For the first time he glimpsed the glory of death. Meantime—he said—be sensible! It would not hurt to spar for time.

He pretended to be weighing the matter.

"Suppose you do steal the letter by force, do you think you can make me write a report?"

"No, a voluntary report would be desirable but not necessary. You left with the Princess, you will remember, a page of directions and information about America to guide her in the trip she is preparing to make and from which we hope to dissuade her. You appended your signature and address. From this it will be easy to draft a report in handwriting so similar to yours as to be indistinguishable by ordinary eyes."

"You add forgery to your many accomplishments."

"In the pursuit of our duty, we do not hesitate at theft or forgery."

Still Matthew parried: "Suppose," he said, "I pretended to acquiesce, gave you the letter and reported to the Princess. Suppose even I told the German newspapers of what I have seen and heard tonight."

There was a faraway look in the eyes of the Japanese as he answered slowly: "We must follow Fate, my dear Mr. Towns, even if Fate leads—to murder. We will not let you communicate with the Princess, and you are leaving Berlin tonight."

The Indians gave a low sigh almost like relief.

Matthew straightened and spoke slowly and firmly.

"Very well. I won't surrender that letter to anybody but the Princess—not while I'm alive. And if I go out of here dead I won't be the only corpse."

Every eye was on the Japanese, and Matthew knew his life

was in the balance. The pause was tense; then came the patient voice of the Japanese again.

"You—admire the Princess, do you not?"

"With all my heart."

The Indians winced.

"You would do her a service?"

"To the limit of my strength."

"Very well. Let us assume that I am wrong. Assume that the Negroes are worth freedom and ready to fight for it. Can you not see that the name of this young, beautiful, and high-born lady must under no circumstances be mixed up with them, whether they gain or lose? What would not Great Britain give thus to compromise an Indian ruler?"

"That is for the Princess to decide."

"No! She is a mere woman—an inexperienced girl. You are a man of the world. For the last time, will you rescue her Royal Highness from herself?"

"No. The Princess herself must decide."

"Then—"

"Then," said the Princess' full voice, "the Princess will decide." She stood in the open doorway, the obsequious and scared landlord beside her with his pass-keys. She had thrown an opera cloak over her evening gown, and stood unhatted, white-slippered, and ungloved. She threw one glance at the Indians, and they bowed low with outstretched hands. She stamped her foot angrily, and they went to their knees. She wheeled to the Arab. Without a word, he stalked out. The Japanese alone remained, calm and imperturbable.

"We have failed," he said, with a low bow.

The Princess looked at him.

"You have failed," she said. "I am glad there is no blood on your hands."

"A drop of blood more or less matters little in the great cause for which you and I fight, and if I have incurred your Royal Highness' displeasure tonight, remember that, for the same great cause, I stand ready tomorrow night to repeat the deed and seal it with my life."

The Princess looked at him with troubled eyes. Then she seated herself in the only and rather rickety chair and motioned for her two subjects to arise. Matthew never forgot that scene: he, collarless and in shirt sleeves, with sweat pouring off his face; the room in disorder, mean, narrow, small, and dingy; the Japanese standing in the same place as when he entered, in unruffled evening dress; the Indians on their knees with hidden faces; the Princess, disturbed, yet radiant. She spoke in low tones.

"I may be wrong," she said, "and I know how right, but infinitely and calmly right, you usually are. But some voice within calls me. I have started to fight for the dark and oppressed peoples of the world; now suddenly I have seen a light. A light which illumines the mass of men and not simply its rulers, white and yellow and black. I want to see if this thing is true, if it can possibly be true that wallowing masses often conceal submerged kings. I have decided not simply to send a messenger to America but shortly to sail myself—perhaps this week on the *Gigantic*. I want to see for myself if slaves can become men in a generation. If they can—well, it makes the world new for you and me."

The Japanese started to speak, but she would not pause:

"There is no need for protest or advice. I am going. Mr. Towns will perform his mission as we agreed, if he is still so minded, and as long as he is in Europe, these two gentlemen," she glanced at the Indians, "will bear his safety on their heads, at my command. Go!"

The Indians bowed and walked out slowly, backward. She turned to the Japanese.

"Your Highness, I bid you good night and good-by. I shall write you."

Gravely the Japanese kissed her hand, bowed, and withdrew. The Princess looked at Matthew. He became acutely conscious of his appearance as she looked at him almost a full minute with her great, haunting eyes.

"I thank you, again," she said slowly. "You are a brave man—and loyal." She held out her hand, low, to shake his.

But the tension of the night broke him; he quivered, and taking her hand in both his, kissed it.

She rose quickly, drew herself up, and looked at first almost affronted; then when she saw his swimming eyes, a kind of startled wonder flashed in hers. Slowly she held out her hand again, regally, palm down and the long fingers drooping.

"You are very young," she said.

He was. He was only twenty-five. The Princess was all of twenty-three.

He saw her afar; standing at the gate there at the end of the long path home, and by the old black tree—her tall and slender form like a swaying willow. She was dressed in eastern style, royal in coloring, with no concession to Europe. As he neared, he sensed the flash of great jewels nestling on her neck and arms; a king's ransom lay between the naked beauty of her breasts; blood rubies weighed down her ears, and about the slim brown gold of her waist ran a girdle such as emperors fight for. Slowly all the wealth of silk, gold, and jewels revealed itself as he came near and hesitated for words; then suddenly he sensed a little bundle on her outstretched arms. He dragged his startled eyes down from her face and saw a child—a naked baby that lay upon her hands like a palpitating bubble of gold, asleep.

He swayed against the tall black tree and stood still.

"Thy son and mine!" she whispered. "Oh, my beloved!"

With strangled throat and streaming eyes, he went down upon his knees before her and kissed the sandals of her feet and sobbed:

"Princess—oh, Princess of the wide, wide world!"

Then he arose and took her gently to his breast and folded his arms about her and looked at her long. Through the soft and high-bred comeliness of her lovely face had pierced the sharpness of suffering, and Life had carved deeper strong, set lines of character. An inner spirit, immutable, eternal, glorious, was shadowed behind the pools of her great eyes. The high haughtiness of her mien was still there, but it lay loose like some unlaced garment, and through it shone the flesh of a new humility, of some half-frightened appeal leaping forth to know and prove and beg a self-forgetting love equal to that which she was offering.

He kissed the tendrils of her hair and saw silver threads lurking there; he kissed her forehead and her eyes and lingered on her lips. He hid his head in the hollow of her neck and then lifted his face to the treetops and strained her bosom to his, until she thrilled and gasped and held the child away from harm.

And the child awoke; naked, it cooed and crowed with joy on her soft arm and threw its golden limbs up to the golden sun. Matthew shrank a little and trembled to touch it and only whispered:

"Sweetheart! More than wife! Mother of God and my son!"

At last fearfully he took it in his hands, as slowly, with twined arms, they began to walk toward the cabin, their long bodies and limbs touching in rhythm. At first she said no word, but always in grave and silent happiness looked up into his face. Then as they walked they began to speak in whispers.

"Kautilya, why were you silent? This changes the world!"

"Matthew, the Seal was on my lips. We were parted for all time except your son was born of me. That was my fateful secret."

"Yet when first the babe leapt beneath your heart, still you wrote no word!"

"Still was the Silence sealed, for had it been a girl child, I must have left both babe and you. Bwodpur needs not a princess, but a King."

"And yet even with this our Love Incarnate, you waited an endless month!"

"Oh, silly darling, I waited for all—all; for his birth, for news to India, for your freedom. Do you not see? There had to be a Maharajah in Bwodpur of the blood royal; else brown reaction and white intrigue had made it a footstool of England. If I had not borne your son, I must have gone to prostitute my body to a stranger or lose Bwodpur and Sindrabad; India; and all the Darker World. Oh, Matthew—Matthew, I know the tortures of the damned!"

"And without me and alone you went down into the Valley of the Shadow."

"I arose from the dead. I ascended into heaven with the angel of your child at my breast."

"And now Eternal Life makes us One forever."

"Immortal Mission of the Son of Man."

"And its name?" he asked.

" 'Madhu,' of course; which is 'Matthew' in our softer tongue."

Crimson climbing roses, bursting with radiant bloom, almost covered the black logs of wide twin cabins, one rising higher than the other; the darkness of the low and vine-draped hall between caught and reflected the leaping flames of the kitchen within and beyond. Above and behind the roofs, rose a new round tower and a high hedge; the fields were green and white with cotton and corn; the tall trees were softly singing.

Old stone steps worn to ancient hollows led up to the hall and on them loomed slowly Matthew's mother, straight, immense, white-haired, and darkly brown. She took the baby in one great arm, infinite with tenderness, while the child shivered with delight. She kissed Matthew once and then said slowly with a voice that sternly held back its tears:

"And now, son, we'se gwine to make dis little man an hones' chile.—Preacher!"

A short black man appeared in the door and paused. He looked like incarnate Age; a dish of shining water lay in one hand and a worn book in the other. He was clad in rusty black with snowy linen, and his face was rough and hewn in angry lineaments around the deep and sunken islands of his eyes.

The preacher read in the worn book from the seventh chapter of Revelation:

"After these things I saw four Angels standing on the four corners of the earth"—stumbling over the mighty words with strange accent and pronunciation—"and God shall wipe away all tears from their eyes!"

Then in curious short staccato phrases, with pauses in between, he lined out a hymn. His voice was harsh and strong, and his breath whistled; but the voice of the old mother rose clear and singularly sweet an octave above, while at last the baritone of Matthew and the deep contralto of Kautilya joined to make music under the trees:

> "Shall I—be car—
> ried to-oo—the skies
> on flow-ry be-eds
> of ease!"

Thus in the morning they were married, looking at neither mother nor son, preacher nor shining morning, but deep into each other's hungry eyes. The voice of the child rose in shrill sweet obbligato and drowned here and again the rolling periods:

"—you, Kautilya, take this man . . . love, honor and obey—"

"Yes."

"—Towns, take this woman . . . until death do you part?"

"Yes—yes."

"—God hath joined together; let no man put asunder!"

Then the ancient woman stiffened, closed her eyes, and chanted to her God:

"Jesus, take dis child. Make him a man! Make him a man, Lord Jesus—a leader of his people and a lover of his God!

"Gin him a high heart, God, a strong arm and an understandin' mind. Breathe the holy sperrit on his lips and fill his soul with lovin' kindness. Set his feet on the beautiful mountings of Good Tidings and let my heart sing Hallelujah to the Lamb when he brings my lost and stolen people home to heaven; home to you, my little Jesus and my God!"

She paused abruptly, stiffened, and with rapt face whispered the first words of the old slave song of world revolution:

"I am seekin' for a City—for a City into de Kingdom!"

Then with closed and streaming eyes, she danced with slow and stately step before the Lord. Her voice lifted higher and higher, outstriving her upstretched arms, shrilled the strophe, while the antistrophe rolled in the thick throat of the preacher:

The Woman: "Lord, I don't feel no-ways *tired*—"

The Man: "*Children!* Fight Christ's fury, Hallelu*iah!*"

The Woman: "*I'm*—a gonta shout glory when this world's on *fire!*"

The Man: "*Children!* Shout God's glory, Hallelu!"

There fell a silence, and then out of the gloom of the wood moved a pageant. A score of men clothed in white with shining swords walked slowly forward a space, and from their midst came three old men: one black and shaven and magnificent in raiment; one yellow and turbaned, with a white beard that swept his burning flesh; and the last naked save for a scarf about his loins. They carried dishes of rice and sweetmeats, and they chanted as they came.

One voice said, solemn and low:

"Oh, thou that playest on the flute, standing by the waterghats on the road to Brindaban."

A second voice, still lower, sang:

"Oh, flower of eastern silence, walking in the path of stars, divine, beautiful, whom nothing human makes unclean: bring sunrise, noon and golden night and wordless intercession before the wordless God."

And a third voice rose shrill and clear:

"Oh, Allah, the compassionate, the merciful! who sends his blessing on the Prophet, Our Lord, and on his family and companions and on all to whom he grants salvation."

They gave rice to Matthew and Kautilya, and sweetmeats, and all blessed them as they knelt. Then the Brahmin took the baby from his grandmother and wound a silken turban on its little protesting head—a turban with that mighty ruby that looked like frozen blood. Swaying the babe up and down and east and west, he placed it gently upon Kautilya's outstretched arms. It lay there, a thrill of delight; its little feet, curled petals; its mouth a kiss; its hands like waving prayers. Slowly Kautilya stepped forward and turned her face eastward. She raised her son toward heaven and cried:

"Brahma, Vishnu, and Siva! Lords of Sky and Light and Love! Receive from me, daughter of my fathers back to the hundredth name, his Majesty, Madhu Chandragupta Singh, by the will of God, Maharajah of Bwodpur and Maharajahdhirajah of Sindrabad."

Then from the forest, with faint and silver applause of trumpets:

"King of the Snows of Gaurisankar!"

"Protector of Ganga the Holy!"

"Incarnate Son of the Buddha!"

"Grand Mughal of Utter India!"

"Messenger and Messiah to all the Darker Worlds!"

RUDOLPH FISHER

RUDOLPH FISHER'S THE WALLS OF JERICHO *(1928) avoided* Nigger Heaven's *decadence and* Home to Harlem's *gutter sensationalism, to the immense relief of the senior shepherds of the arts movement. Hero and heroine—burly, profane piano mover Joshua "Shine" Jones and ambitious but undereducated maid Linda Young—were not character types favored by Fauset or White. Fisher's satirical novel belonged to the last phase of the Harlem Renaissance, with its bottom-up optic commended by Langston Hughes and the contributors to* Fire!! *But where McKay reduced the African American upper classes to sterile irrelevancy and Van Vechten made them posture their culture in order to deplore their failure in not being true to their racial selves, Fisher's deft satire was kinder and, in its inclusion of white patrons, broader, and more nuanced.*

The hilarious scene at the annual General Improvement Association Costume Ball burlesques the Civil Rights Establishment as well as archetypal white liberals (Mr. and Mrs. Noel Dunn/Carl and Fania Marinoff Van Vechten, Agatha Cramp/Charlotte Osgood Mason), exposing the cleavages within Afro-America and the curious motives of the Negrotarian allies. "Shine," Jinx, and Bubber meet Linda and her employer, Merrit, Talented Tenth professional, who is passing as white in his recently purchased luxury apartment. Although from vastly different milieux, the piano movers and the light-skinned lawyer are smart enough to realize that they have far more reason to find common ground than to remain fixed in class prejudice.

Fisher's is a social novel with an upbeat ending in which the best elements of Harlem's upper crust ("dickties") eventually col-

laborate with men and women ("rats") normally unwelcome in Talented Tenth salons, in order to combat organized crime, drugs, and other demoralizing forces within the community.

FROM *THE WALLS OF JERICHO*

COURT AVENUE IS A STRAIGHT, thin spinster of a street which even in July is cold. There is about it an air of arched eyebrows, of skirts drawn aside and comments made with a sniff. It is adorned in sparse, lean, scrawny maples, all suffering from malnutrition, and these tend to stress rather than relieve the hardness of dry, level pavements.

The dwellings are all the same pale gray and are all essentially alike, four stories tall, thin to gauntness, droop-eyed with drawn shapes, standing shoulder to shoulder in long, inhospitable rows. Stone stoops, well withdrawn from the sidewalk, lend an air of inaccessibility, and the tiny front yards that might dispel this illusion by only a bit of grass or a flower are instead uniformly laid away beneath slabs of expressionless concrete.

Twice a day, when sunlight touches the windows of this side in the morning and again of that side at night, Court Avenue smiles a chilly, crystalline smile. It is the sort of smile that goes with the words, "My dear! Can you imagine such a thing!" and you might suppose that the street was returning even the sun's genial greeting and warm farewell with a disapproving sneer.

In short, Court Avenue is a snob of a street. Yet it is somewhat to be pitied in its pretense at ignoring the punishment that is at hand: the terribly sure approach of the swiftly spreading Negro colony.

Isaacs' Transportation Company, which is to say old man Isadore Isaacs, would have trusted Joshua Jones with any moving job whatever. It was work that Shine loved because of the challenge it presented to his personal strength and skill. He took charge, accepted responsibility, helped execute the orders he gave. Whenever a staircase or hallway presented a difficult turn or an insufficient dimension, he was at hand to decide just how the problem should be solved. Whenever a valuable piece of ungainly size had to be dismembered, and afterwards reconstructed, his knowledge of the mysterious anatomy of furniture was wholly adequate. Whenever a piano was to be hoisted, he saw to each important item: himself selected and anchored the tackle and guided the instrument through the window that was chosen to admit it.

Pianos indeed, were his particular prey, his almost living archenemies. He personified them, and out of controlling them, handling them, directing them helpless through midair, he derived a satisfaction comparable to that of a tamer of beasts. There was a superstition that a piano would "get" a man one time or another. Jinx and Bubber had both suffered injuries from instruments that slipped from their grips. But Shine laughed at this superstition, not because it was a superstition, but because he knew that he simply couldn't be "had."

Even the four-ton van was to Shine a beloved companion. He called her Bess, and Bess was the only thing on earth that he coveted. She was padded within and especially designed for the moving of things fine and fragile; her engine was responsive and smooth, her treads pneumatic, single in front, double in the rear. She rode like a private ambulance and she could make forty on a level. It was Shine's ambition one day to win her away from old man Isaacs.

The crew was usually made up only of Shine, Jinx, and Bubber, and these three in two years of coöperation had come to work together in a fashion beyond fault-finding, carefully, quickly, punctually, untrailed by patrons' complaints.

This early summer morning Shine swung Bess, loaded with Merrit's possessions, into the chilly Court Avenue atmosphere, and, with deliberate malice, sped up to a roar, then coasted, shifting his spark to make the motor spit.

"That'll wake up somebody," he grinned as Bess bang-banged like an automatic. "Come on you bomb-throwers—do your stuff —let's go!"

"Boy, lemme out this cab," said Bubber. "This darkey done gone crazy."

"Shuh!" complained Jinx. "Ain't go'n' be no rough stuff in this neighborhood. Deader'n Strivers' Row."

They drew up and backed against the curb before number three-thirteen. The door opened and Merrit himself came out to meet them. He wore his usual air of nonchalance and his usual cherubic grin.

"Hello, fellows," he greeted. "Get it all on one load? That's clever."

All three stared. Such cordiality in a dickty was nothing short of astonishing, and it put the suspicious workers immediately on guard.

While Jinx and Bubber unfastened van-doors, Merrit went up to Shine and leaned carelessly against a tree. "What do you think of this?" he said, producing a letter.

Shine accepted the proffered note without enthusiasm. It was without heading or salutation, typewritten, and lacking a signature:

> You are not wanted in this neighborhood.
> If you move in, we'll move you out.

"Where'd you get it?" Shine asked Merrit.

"Found it in the vestibule when I came up to look around yesterday."

"Humph," said Shine. "Jes' let 'em start sump'm while we're here, that's all." And because he disliked dickties and wanted no talk with any one of them, he changed the subject rudely. "Where you want us to put this stuff?"

"Anywhere. Spread it all over the first floor. My house-keeper'll come in from the country-place and have it arranged later."

"Hear that?" Jinx said to Bubber, out of sight at the rear of the van. "Thass what I say 'bout a spade. Spade can't git a little sump'n without stretchin' it. His housekeeper. His country-place. Humph—what's a use lyin' like that——?"

"He ain' lyin', fool. That jasper's got mo' bucks 'n you got freckles. Got a swell place on the upstate Pike, not far out o' town. Throws big parties and raises hell jes' like d' fays. Folks up there didn' know he was a jig till he had a party—and they offered him a million dollars fo' the place jes' to git him out. He wouldn' leave, though."

"Million dollars?"

"Uh-huh."

"And he wouldn' leave?"

"Uh-huh."

"Huh! You lie wuss'n he do."

Merrit's words came to them repeating, "Mrs. Fuller will take care of everything later."

"Thare now," commented Jinx, "y'see?"

"See what?"

"Soon as a old crow gits up in d' world, he got to grab hisse'f some other guy's wife."

Bubber regarded him with pity. "How you figger dat out?"

"*His* name ain't Fuller, is it?"

"No. And yo' name ain' Sherlock. Don't you know what a housekeper is? And ain't you never heard of sech a thing as a widow?"

"Aw man, what you talkin' 'bout?"

"You ought to be a policeman, brother."

"How come?"

" 'Cause you very suspicious and very, very dumb."

These two had been unwrapping carefully covered hindmost pieces of furniture. Shine came around to lend a hand, and Merrit moved along the curb to a position such that he could observe them. Now he indulged in another astonishing speech.

"Don't be too damn careful about these things. Flat didn't have anything but junk in it, anyway. Good stuff's in the country—won't move it in till fall. Just chuck this stuff in and let it lay."

What manner of dickty was this? He greeted you like an equal, casually shared his troubles with you, and did not seem to care in the least what the devil you did with his furniture.

Jinx said sullenly to Bubber. "All he wants is for us to scratch up sump'm, so he kin call the five bucks off."

Bubber said to Jinx, "That ain't it. He's jes' makin' sure o' friends in case d' fays start sump'm."

Shine said to himself, "If this bird wasn't a dickty he'd be o.k. But they never was a dickty worth a damn."

The job was finished and they were throwing by-products into the emptied van—burlap and canvas wrappers, quilting, hemp rope, leather straps. Merrit had just turned the key in his door and was facing about for departure, while Shine was on the point of climbing into the cab. At this juncture, simultaneously, everybody made an observation. It was the only observation that they all would have been likely to make at one time, and it held Merrit at attention on the stoop, rendered Shine motionless with one foot upon the step of his cab, and halted Bubber in the act of throwing a gunnysack over Jinx's head. Along the hitherto empty street a girl was briskly approaching.

You could see that she knew they were staring, so completely did she ignore them, and the ease with which she did so, the queenly unconcern with which she passed, indicated that she was accustomed to being stared at and did not mind it at all.

There was quite obviously no reason why she should have minded it. Certainly her attire invited no criticism—a brief frock of cool black satin, sheer gun-metal hose, and trim patent-leather pumps. Nor did she herself. She was tall and her face was pretty, and her body slenderly invited, though her legs perversely eluded, the persistent caress of the sedulous soft black satin.

Even if this had been all—a pretty girl on that gaunt empty street at this solitary hour, the staring would have been pardonable. But there was in addition an especially extenuating circumstance: the girl was not white.

Before she quite passed beyond earshot Jinx and Bubber were indulging in low enthusiasms:

"Boy, do you see what I see?"

"Law-aw-aw-dy!"

"Mus' be havin' a recess in heaven!"

"No lie. Umh-umh-umh—" Grunts to signify admiration far beyond words.

"Lady, you kin have all my week's pay—ev'y bit of it." Bubber dived elaborately into his empty pockets, while Jinx vowed:

"I'm go'n' get religion and die so I kin go to heaven and meet that angel—yassuh!"

Suddenly comment ceased. Only two doors beyond Merrit's house the girl turned in, traversed the short cement walk, mounted the stoop, unlocked and entered the front door.

Merrit raised his brows in a characteristic little expression of surprise. Shine saw him do so and had a swift interpretation for that expression:

"Figgerin' on a jive already—the doggone dickty hound. Why the hell dickties can't stick to their own women 'thout messin' around honest workin' girls——"

Bubber was rapturizing without restraint, "Man—oh—man! A honey with high yaller laigs! And did you see that walk? That gal walks on ball-bearin's, she do—ev'ything moves at once." He illustrated his idea with head-wobblings, shoulder-rollings, and loose backward protrusions and retractions of buttocks. "See what I mean? Tail-conscious, man, tail-conscious——"

"You jes' a damn liar," came unexpectedly from Shine. "She walks like what she is, a lady—and you talk like what you is, a rat. Come on, it's gettin' late—let's go from here."

Whereupon Jinx looked at Bubber and Bubber looked at Jinx. Here was indeed something new, Shine championing a woman.

"Well, kiss my assorted peanuts!" ejaculated Bubber.

"Guess that's the dynamite," was Jinx's dyspeptic surmise.

Meanwhile Miss Agatha Cramp sat quite overwhelmed at the strangeness of her situation. This was her introduction to the people she planned to uplift. True to her word she had personally investigated the G.I.A. and been welcomed with open arms. Certain members of the executive board knew her and her past works—one or two had been associated with her in other projects—and her experience, resources, and devotion to service were unanimously acclaimed assets. And nobody minded her excessively corrective attitude—all new board members started out revising things. Furthermore, the Costume Ball was at hand and that would be enough to upset anybody's ideas of revision.

Never had Miss Cramp seen so many Negroes in one place at one time. Moreover, never had she dreamed that so many of her own people would for any reason imaginable have descended to mingle with these Negroes. She had prided herself on her own liberality in joining this company to-night. And so it shocked and outraged her to see that most of these fair-skinned visitors were unmistakably enjoying themselves, instead of maintaining the aloof, kindly dignity proper to those who must sacrifice to serve. And of course little did she suspect how many of the fair-skinned ones were not visitors at all but natives.

When she met Nora Byle, for instance, she was first struck with the beauty of her "Latin type." To save her soul she could not help a momentary stiffening when Buckram Byle, who was a jaundice-brown, was presented as Nora's husband: Inter-marriage! She recovered. No. The girl was one of those mulattoes, of course; a conclusion that brought but temporary relief, for the next moment the debonair Tony Nayle had gone off with the "mulatto," both of them flirting disgracefully.

It was all in all a situation which robbed Miss Cramp of words; but she smiled bravely through her distress and found no little relief in sitting beside Fred Merrit, whose perfect manner, cherubic smile and fair skin were highly comforting. She had not yet noticed the significant texture of his hair.

"Well, what do you think of it?" Merrit eventually asked.

"I don't know what to think, really. What do you think?"

"I? Why—it's all too familiar now for me to have thoughts about. I take it for granted."

"Oh—you have worked among Negroes a great deal, then?"

Merrit grinned. "All my life."

"How do you find them?"

That Merrit did not resist temptation and admit his complete identity at this point is easier to explain than to excuse. There was first his admitted joy in discomfiting members of the dominant race. Further, however, there was a special complex of reasons closer at hand.

Merrit was far more outraged by the flirtation between Nora Byle and Tony Nayle than had been even Miss Cramp herself, and with greater cause. His own race prejudice was a bitterer, more deep-seated emotion than was hers, and out of it came an attitude that caused him to look with great suspicion and distrust upon all visitors who came to Harlem "socially." He insisted that the least blameworthy motive that brought them was curiosity, and held that he, for one, was not on exhibition. As for the men who came oftener than once, he felt that they all had but one motive, the pursuit of Harlem women; that their cultivation of Harlem men was a blind and an instrument in achieving this end, and that the end itself was always illicit and therefore reprehensible.

It was with him a terribly serious matter, of which he could see but one side. When Langdon once hinted gently that maybe it was a two-way reaction, he snorted the suggestion away as nonsense. That he should allow it to disturb him so profoundly meant that it went profoundly back into his own life, as it did into the lives of most people of heredity so diverse as his. The everyday difficulty of his own adjustment engendered in him an unforgiving hatred of those past generations responsible for it. Hence every suggestion that history might repeat itself in this particular occasioned revolt. If there could be no fair exchange, said he, let there be no exchange at all.

He knew that no two ardent individuals would ever be concerned with any such formulas, but the very ineffectuality of what seemed to him so just a principle rendered its violation the more irritating. And in the particular case of Tony and Nora—well, he rather liked Nora himself.

And so beneath his pleasant manner, there was a disordered spirit which at this moment almost gleefully accepted the chance to vent itself on Miss Agatha Cramp's ignorance. To admit his identity would have wholly lost him this chance. And as for the fact that she was a woman, that only made the compensation all the more complete, gave it a quality of actual retaliation, of parallel all the more satisfying.

"How do I find Negroes? I like them very much. Ever so much better than white people."

"Oh Mr. Merrit! Really?"

"You see, they have so much more color."

"Yes. I can see that." She gazed upon the mob. "How primitive these people are," she murmured. "So primeval. So unspoiled by civilization."

"Beautiful savages," suggested Merrit.

"Exactly. Just what I was thinking. What abandonment—what unrestraint——"

"Almost as bad as a Yale-Harvard football game, isn't it?" Merrit's eyes twinkled.

"Well," Miss Cramp demurred, "that's really quite a different thing, you know."

"Of course. This unrestraint is the kind that is hostile to society, hostile to civilization. This is the sort of thing that you and I as sociologists must contend with, must wipe out."

"Yes indeed. Quite so. This sort of thing is, as you say, quite unfortunate. We must educate these people out of it. There is so much to be done."

"Listen to that music. Savage too, don't you think?"

"Just what had occurred to me. That music is like the beating of—what do they call 'em?—dum-dums, isn't it?"

"I was just trying to think what it recalled," mused Merrit with great seriousness. "Tom-toms! That's it—of course. How stupid of me. Tom-toms. And the shuffle of feet——"

"Rain," breathed Miss Cramp, who, since her new interest, had deemed it her duty to read some of Langdon's poetry. "Rain falling in a jungle."

"Rain?"

"Rain falling on banana leaves," said the lady. And the gentleman assented, "I know how it is. I once fell on a banana peel myself."

"So primitive." Miss Cramp turned to Mrs. Dunn, who sat behind and above her. "The throb of the jungle," she remarked.

"Marvelous!" exhaled Mrs. Dunn.

"These people—we can do so much for them—we must educate them out of such unrestraint."

Whereupon Tony and Nora appeared laughing and breathless at the box entrance; and Tony, descendant of Cedrics and Cæsars, loudly declared:

"I'm going to get that bump-the-bump dance if it takes me the whole darn night!"

"Bump the what?" Miss Agatha wondered.

"Come on, Gloria," Tony urged Mrs. Dunn. "You ought to know it, long as you've been coming to Harlem. Mrs. Byle gives me up. You try."

Mrs. Dunn smiled and quickly rose. "I'll say I will. Come along. It's perfectly marvelous."

"Furthermore," expounded J. Pennington Potter, "there is a tendency among Negro organizations to incorporate too many words in a single designation with the result that what is intended as mere appellation becomes a detailed description. Take for example the N.O.U.S.E. and the I.N.I.A.W. There can be no excuse for entitlements of such prolixity. They endeavor to encompass a society's past, present and future, embracing as well a description of motive and instrument. There is no call you will agree, no excuse, no justification for delineation, history and prophecy in a single title."

"Quite so, Penny," said Mr. Dunn. "Mrs. Byle, may I have this dance?"

"Certainly," said Nora, smiling a trifle too amusedly.

"We're going home after this one," growled her husband as she passed.

Miss Cramp said in a low voice to Merrit:

"Isn't he a wonderful person?"

"Who?" wondered Merrit.

"Mr. Potter. He talks so beautifully and seems so intelligent."

"He is intelligent, isn't he?" said Merrit, as if the discovery surprised him.

"He must have an awfully good head."

"Unexcelled for certain purposes."

"I had no idea they were ever so cultured. How simple our task would be if they were all like that."

"Like Potter? Heaven forbid!"

"Oh, Mr. Merrit. Really you mustn't let your prejudices prevail. Negroes deserve at least a few leaders like that."

"I don't know what they've ever done to deserve them," he said.

Unable to win him over to her broader viewpoint, she changed the subject.

"Mrs. Byle is very pretty, isn't she?"

"Yes."

"She is so light in complexion for a Negress."

"A what?"

"A Negress. She *is* a Negress, isn't she?"

"Well, I suppose you'd call her that."

"It *is* hard to appreciate, isn't it? It makes one wonder, really. Mrs. Byle is almost as fair as I am, while—well, look at that girl down there. Absolutely black. Yet both——"

"Are Negresses."

"Exactly what I was thinking. I was just thinking—— Now how long have there been Negroes in our country, Mr. Merrit?"

"Longer than most one hundred percent Americans, I believe."

"Really?"

"Since around 1500, I understand. And in numbers since 1619."

"How well informed you are, Mr. Merrit. Imagine knowing dates like that—— Why that's between three and four hundred years ago, isn't it? But of course four hundred years isn't such a long time if you believe in evolution. I consider evolution very important, don't you?"

"Profoundly so."

"But I was just thinking. These people have been out of their native element only three or four hundred years, and just see what it has done to their complexions! It's hard to believe that just three hundred years in our country has brought about such a great variety in the color of the black race."

"Environment is a powerful influence, Miss Cramp," murmured Merrit.

"Yes, of course. Chiefly the climate, I should judge. Don't you think?"

Merrit blinked, then nodded gravely. "Climate undoubtedly. Climate. Changed conditions of heat and moisture and so on."

"Yes, exactly. Remarkable isn't it? Now just consider, Mr. Merrit. The northern peoples are very fair—the Scandinavians, for example. The tropic peoples, on the other hand are very dark—often black like the Negroes in their own country. Isn't that true?"

"Undeniably."

"Now if these very same people here to-night had originally gone to Scandinavia—three or four hundred years ago, you understand—some of them would by now be as fair as the Scandinavians! Why they'd even have blue eyes and yellow hair!"

"No doubt about that," Merrit agreed meditatively. "Oh yes. They'd have them without question."

"Just imagine!" marveled Miss Cramp. "A Negro with skin as fair as your own!"

"M-m. Yes. Just imagine," said he without smiling.

ERIC WALROND

TROPIC DEATH *(1926)* INTRODUCED *one of the most gifted writing talents in the Harlem Renaissance, the Trinidadian novelist Eric Walrond. Walrond belonged to the second phase, having come to the Harlem scene early and serving, along with Charles Johnson and Alain Locke, as one of the movement's advertisers and recruiters. Although, like McKay, he wrote of people on the margins of middle-class society, Walrond's often experimental prose resembled Toomer's in its evocation of the exotic and the mysterious. His Caribbean Gothic tales possessed an elegance entirely lacking in McKay or Wallace Thurman.*

The short stories in Tropic Death *led the senior promoters of the Renaissance to anticipate that Walrond would write the great Renaissance novel. "The Wharf Rats" was a Caribbean Gothic tale of feral jealousy and tragic deception driven by misunderstanding and peradventure. The author experimented with the idiomatic speech of Panamanian Creoles and captured the premodern, polyglot culture of men and women battered by the global backwash of capitalism, in order to present one of the Renaissance's most haunting allegorical reflections about vitality and innocence being toyed with and fatally sucked under by the despoiling forces of modernity.*

"The Yellow One," another Tropic Death *story, pulls the reader in immediately. A baby crying for warm tea in the hold of a rusty steamer, a wastrel husband unwilling to rouse himself to go for hot water, a sensuous mother—"la madurita" ("the Yellow One")—enveloped in mayhem below deck as she returns a second time to the ship's galley for water—"The Yellow One" evokes a steamy surface languor flowing uneasily over a bed of tempestuous*

emotions in a rainbow scene of skin colors and contrasting cultures that is almost palpable.

FROM *TROPIC DEATH*

THE WHARF RATS

AMONG THE MOTLEY CREW recruited to dig the Panama Canal were artisans from the four ends of the earth. Down in the Cut drifted hordes of Italians, Greeks, Chinese, Negroes—a hardy, sun-defying set of white, black and yellow men. But the bulk of the actual brawn for the work was supplied by the dusky peons of those coral isles in the Caribbean ruled by Britain, France and Holland.

At the Atlantic end of the Canal the blacks were herded in box car huts buried in the jungles of "Silver City"; in the murky tenements perilously poised on the narrow banks of Faulke's River; in the low, smelting cabins of Coco Té. The "Silver Quarters" harbored the inky ones, their wives and pickaninnies.

As it grew dark the hewers at the Ditch, exhausted, half-asleep, naked but for wormy singlets, would hum queer creole tunes, play on guitar or piccolo, and jig to the rhythm of the *coombia*. It was a *brujerial* chant, for *obeah*, a heritage of the French colonial, honey-combed the life of the Negro laboring camps. Over smoking pots, on black, death-black nights legends of the bloodiest were recited till they became the essence of a sort of Negro Koran. One refuted them at the price of one's breath. And to question the verity of the *obeah*, to dismiss or reject it as the ungodly rite of some lurid, crack-brained Islander was to be an accursed pale-face, dog of a white. And the *obeah* man, in a fury of rage, would throw a machette at the heretic's head or—worse—burn on his doorstep at night a pyre of Maubé bark or green Ganja weed.

On the banks of a river beyond Cristobal, Coco Té sheltered a colony of Negroes enslaved to the *obeah*. Near a roundhouse, daubed with smoke and coal ash, a river serenely flowed away and into the guava region, at the eastern tip of Monkey Hill. Across the bay from it was a sand bank—a rising out of the sea—where ships stopt for coal.

In the first of the six chinky cabins making up the family quar-

ters of Coco Té lived a stout, pot-bellied St. Lucian, black as the
coal hills he mended, by the name of Jean Baptiste. Like a host of
the native St. Lucian emigrants, Jean Baptiste forgot where the
French in him ended and the English began. His speech was the
petulant *patois* of the unlettered French black. Still, whenever he
lapsed into His Majesty's English, it was with a thick Barbadian
bias.

A coal passer at the Dry Dock, Jean Baptiste was a man of
intense piety. After work, by the glow of a red, setting sun, he
would discard his crusted overalls, get in starched *crocus bag,* aping the Yankee foreman on the other side of the track in the "Gold
Quarters," and loll on his coffee-vined porch. There, dozing in a
bamboo rocker, Celestin, his second wife, a becomingly stout
brown beauty from Martinique, chanted gospel hymns to him.

Three sturdy sons Jean Baptiste's first wife had borne him—
Philip, the eldest, a good-looking, black fellow; Ernest, shifty, cunning; and Sandel, aged eight. Another boy, said to be wayward
and something of a ne'er-do-well, was sometimes spoken of. But
Baptiste, a proud, disdainful man, never once referred to him in
the presence of his children. No vagabond son of his could eat
from his table or sit at his feet unless he went to "meeting." In
brief, Jean Baptiste was a religious man. It was a thrust at the
omnipresent *obeah.* He went to "meeting." He made the boys go,
too. All hands went, not to the Catholic Church, where Celestin
secretly worshiped, but to the English Plymouth Brethren in the
Spanish city of Colon.

Stalking about like a ghost in Jean Baptiste's household was
a girl, a black ominous Trinidad girl. Had Jean Baptiste been a
man given to curiosity about the nature of women, he would have
viewed skeptically Maffi's adoption by Celestin. But Jean Baptiste
was a man of lofty unconcern, and so Maffi remained there, shadowy, obdurate.

And Maffi was such a hardworking *patois* girl. From the break
of day she'd be at the sink, brightening the tinware. It was she who
did the chores which Madame congenitally shirked. And towards
sundown, when the labor trains had emptied, it was she who
scoured the beach for cockles for Jean Baptiste's epicurean palate.

And as night fell, Maffi, a lone, black figure, would disappear
in the dark to dream on top of a canoe hauled up on the mooning
beach. An eternity Maffi'd sprawl there, gazing at the frosting of
the stars and the glitter of the black sea.

A cabin away lived a family of Tortola mulattoes by the name of Boyce. The father was also a man who piously went to "meeting"—gaunt and hollow-cheeked. The eldest boy, Esau, had been a journeyman tailor for ten years; the girl next him, Ora, was plump, dark, freckled; others came—a string of ulcered girls until finally a pretty, opaque one, Maura.

Of the Bantu tribe Maura would have been a person to turn and stare at. Crossing the line into Cristobal or Colon—a city of rarefied gayety—she was often mistaken for a native *señorita* or an urbanized Cholo Indian girl. Her skin was the reddish yellow of old gold and in her eyes there lurked the glint of mother-of-pearl. Her hair, long as a jungle elf's was jettish, untethered. And her teeth were whiter than the full-blooded black Philip's.

Maura was brought up, like the children of Jean Baptiste, in the Plymouth Brethren. But the Plymouth Brethren was a harsh faith to bring hemmed-in peasant children up in, and Maura, besides, was of a gentle romantic nature. Going to the Yankee commissary at the bottom of Eleventh and Front Streets, she usually wore a leghorn hat. With flowers bedecking it, she'd look in it older, much older than she really was. Which was an impression quite flattering to her. For Maura, unknown to Philip, was in love—in love with San Tie, a Chinese half-breed, son of a wealthy canteen proprietor in Colon. But San Tie liked to go fishing and deer hunting up the Monkey Hill lagoon, and the object of his occasional visits to Coco Té was the eldest son of Jean Baptiste. And thus it was through Philip that Maura kept in touch with the young Chinese Maroon.

One afternoon Maura, at her wit's end, flew to the shed roof to Jean Baptiste's kitchen.

"Maffi," she cried, the words smoky on her lips, "Maffi, when Philip come in to-night tell 'im I want fo' see 'im particular, yes?"

"*Sacre gache!* All de time Philip, Philip!" growled the Trinidad girl, as Maura, in heartaching preoccupation, sped towards the lawn. "Why she no le' 'im alone, yes?" And with a spatter she flecked the hunk of lard on Jean Baptiste's stewing okras.

As the others filed up front after dinner that evening Maffi said to Philip, pointing to the cabin across the way, "She—she want fo' see yo'."

Instantly Philip's eyes widened. Ah, he had good news for Maura! San Tie, after an absence of six days, was coming to Coco Té Saturday to hunt on the lagoon. And he'd relish the joy that'd

flood Maura's face as she glimpsed the idol of her heart, the hero
of her dreams! And Philip, a true son of Jean Baptiste, loved to see
others happy, ecstatic.

But Maffi's curious rumination checked him. "All de time,
Maura, Maura, me can't understand it, yes. But no mind, me go
stop it, *oui*, me go stop it, so help me—"

He crept up to her, gently holding her by the shoulders.

"Le' me go, *sacre!*" She shook off his hands bitterly. "Le' me
go—yo' go to yo' Maura." And she fled to her room, locking the
door behind her.

Philip sighed. He was a generous, good-natured sort. But it
was silly to try to enlighten Maffi. It wasn't any use. He could as
well have spoken to the tattered torsos the lazy waves puffed up
on the shores of Coco Té.

"Philip, come on, a ship is in—let's go." Ernest, the wharf rat,
seized him by the arm.

"Come," he said, "let's go before it's too late. I want to get
some money, yes."

Dashing out of the house the two boys made for the wharf.
It was dusk. Already the Hindus in the bachelor quarters were
mixing their *rotie* and the Negroes in their singlets were smoking
and cooling off. Night was rapidly approaching. Sunset, an irides-
cent bit of molten gold, was enriching the stream with its last faint
radiance.

The boys stole across the lawn and made their way to the pier.

"Careful," cried Philip, as Ernest slid between a prong of
oyster-crusted piles to a raft below, "careful, these shells cut wus-
sah'n a knife."

On the raft the boys untied a rowboat they kept stowed away
under the dock, got into it and pushed off. The liner still had two
hours to dock. Tourists crowded its decks. Veering away from the
barnacled piles the boys eased out into the churning ocean.

It was dusk. Night would soon be upon them. Philip took the
oars while Ernest stripped down to loin cloth.

"Come, Philip, let me paddle—" Ernest took the oars. Afar
on the dusky sea a whistle echoed. It was the pilot's signal to the
captain of port. The ship would soon dock.

The passengers on deck glimpsed the boys. It piqued their curiosity to see two black boys in a boat amid stream.

"All right, mistah," cried Ernest, "a penny, mistah."

He sprang at the guilder as it twisted and turned through a streak of silver dust to the bottom of the sea. Only the tips of his crimson toes—a sherbet-like foam—and up he came with the coin between his teeth.

Deep sea gamin, Philip off yonder, his mouth noisy with coppers, gargled, "This way, sah, as far as yo' like, mistah."

An old red-bearded Scot, in spats and mufti, presumably a lover of the exotic in sport, held aloft a sovereign. A sovereign! Already red, and sore by virtue of the leaps and plunges in the briny swirl, Philip's eyes bulged at its yellow gleam.

"Ovah yah, sah—"

Off in a whirlpool the man tossed it. And like a garfish Philip took after it, a falling arrow in the stream. His body, once in the water, tore ahead. For a spell the crowd on the ship held its breath. "Where is he?" "Where is the nigger swimmer gone to?" Even Ernest, driven to the boat by the race for such an ornate prize, cold, shivering, his teeth chattering—even he watched with trembling and anxiety. But Ernest's concern was of a deeper kind. For there, where Philip had leaped, was Deathpool—a spawning place for sharks, for baracoudas!

But Philip rose—a brief gurgling sputter—a ripple on the sea—and the Negro's crinkled head was above the water.

"Hey!" shouted Ernest, "there, Philip! Down!"

And down Philip plunged. One—two—minutes. God, how long they seemed! And Ernest anxiously waited. But the bubble on the water boiled, kept on boiling—a sign that life still lasted! It comforted Ernest.

Suddenly Philip, panting, spitting, pawing, dashed through the water like a streak of lightning.

"Shark!" cried a voice aboard ship. "Shark! There he is, a great big one! Run, boy! Run for your life!"

From the edge of the boat Philip saw the monster as twice, thrice it circled the boat. Several times the shark made a dash for it endeavoring to strike it with its murderous tail.

The boys quietly made off. But the shark still followed the boat. It was a pale green monster. In the glittering dusk it seemed black to Philip. Fattened on the swill of the abattoir nearby and the beef tossed from the decks of countless ships in port it had become used to the taste of flesh and the smell of blood.

"Yo' know, Ernest," said Philip, as he made the boat fast to a raft, "one time I thought he wuz rubbin' 'gainst me belly. He wuz such a big able one. But it wuz wuth it, Ernie, it wuz wuth it—"

In his palm there was a flicker of gold. Ernest emptied his loin cloth and together they counted the money, dressed, and trudged back to the cabin.

On the lawn Philip met Maura. Ernest tipped his cap, left his brother, and went into the house. As he entered Maffi, pretending to be scouring a pan, was flushed and mute as a statue. And Ernest, starved, went in the dining room and for a long time stayed there. Unable to bear it any longer, Maffi sang out, "Ernest, whey Philip dey?"

"Outside—some whey—ah talk to Maura—"

"Yo' sure yo' no lie, Ernest?" she asked, suspended.

"Yes, up cose, I jes' lef' 'im 'tandin' out dey—why?"

"Nutton—"

He suspected nothing. He went on eating while Maffi tiptoed to the shed roof. Yes, confound it, there he was, near the standpipe, talking to Maura!

"Go stop *ee, oui,*" she hissed impishly. "Go 'top ee, yes." . . .

"Oh, Philip," cried Maura, "I am so unhappy. Didn't he ask about me at all? Didn't he say he'd like to visit me—didn't he giv' yo' any message fo' me, Philip?"

The boy toyed with a blade of grass. His eyes were downcast. Sighing heavily he at last spoke. "No, Maura, he didn't ask about you."

"What, he didn't ask about me? Philip? I don't believe it! Oh, my God!"

She clung to Philip, mutely; her face, her breath coming warm and fast.

"I wish to God I'd never seen either of you," cried Philip.

"Ah, but wasn't he your friend, Philip? Didn't yo' tell me that?" And the boy bowed his head sadly.

"Answer me!" she screamed, shaking him. "Weren't you his friend?"

"Yes, Maura—"

"But you lied to me, Philip, you lied to me! You took messages from me—you brought back—lies!" Two *pearls,* large as pigeon's eggs, shone in Maura's burnished face.

"To think," she cried in a hollow sepulchral voice, "that I dreamed about a ghost, a man who didn't exist. Oh, God, why should I suffer like this? Why was I ever born? What did I do, what did my people do, to deserve such misery as this?"

She rose, leaving Philip with his head buried in his hands. She went into the night, tearing her hair, scratching her face, raving.

"Oh, how happy I was! I was a happy girl! I was so young and I had such merry dreams! And I wanted so little! I was carefree—"

Down to the shore of the sea she staggered, the wind behind her, the night obscuring her.

"Maura!" cried Philip, running after her. "Maura! come back!"

Great sheaves of clouds buried the moon, and the wind bearing up from the sea bowed the cypress and palm lining the beach.

"Maura—Maura—"

He bumped into some one, a girl, black, part of the dense pattern of the tropical night.

"Maffi," cried Philip, "have you seen Maura down yondah?"

The girl quietly stared at him. Had Philip lost his mind?

"Talk, no!" he cried, exasperated.

And his quick tones sharpened Maffi's vocal anger. Thrusting him aside, she thundered, "Think I'm she keeper! Go'n look fo' she yo'-self. I is not she keeper! Le' me pass, move!"

Towards the end of the track he found Maura, heartrendingly weeping.

"Oh, don't cry, Maura! Never mind, Maura!"

He helped her to her feet, took her to the stand-pipe on the lawn, bathed her temples and sat soothingly, uninterruptingly, beside her.

At daybreak the next morning Ernest rose and woke Philip.

He yawned, put on the loin cloth, seized a "cracked licker" skillet, and stole cautiously out of the house. Of late Jean Baptiste had put his foot down on his sons' copper-diving proclivities. And he kept at the head of his bed a greased cat-o'-nine-tails which he would use on Philip himself if the occasion warranted.

"Come on, Philip, let's go—"

Yawning and scratching Philip followed. The grass on the lawn was bright and icy with the dew. On the railroad tracks the six o'clock labor trains were coupling. A rosy mist flooded the dawn. Out in the stream the tug *Exotic* snorted in a heavy fog.

On the wharf Philip led the way to the rafters below.

"Look out fo' that *crapeau*, Ernest, don't step on him, he'll spit on you."

The frog splashed into the water. Prickle-backed crabs and oysters and myriad other shells spawned on the rotting piles. The boys paddled the boat. Out in the dawn ahead of them the tug puffed a path through the foggy mist. The water was chilly. Mist glistened on top of it. Far out, beyond the buoys, Philip encountered a placid, untroubled sea. The liner, a German tourist boat, was loaded to the bridge. The water was as still as a lake of ice.

"All right, Ernest, let's hurry—"

Philip drew in the oars. The *Kron Prinz Wilhelm* came near. Huddled in thick European coats, the passengers viewed from their lofty estate the spectacle of two naked Negro boys peeping up at them from a wiggly *bateau*.

"Penny, mistah, penny, mistah!"

Somebody dropped a quarter. Ernest, like a shot, flew after it. Half a foot down he caught it as it twisted and turned in the gleaming sea. Vivified by the icy dip, Ernest was a raving wolf and the folk aboard dealt a lavish hand.

"Ovah, yah, mistah," cried Philip, "ovah, yah."

For a Dutch guilder Philip gave an exhibition of "cork." Under something of a ledge on the side of the boat he had stuck a piece of cork. Now, after his and Ernest's mouths were full of coins, he could afford to be extravagant and treat the Europeans to a game of West Indian "cork."

Roughly ramming the cork down in the water, Philip, after the fifteenth ram or so, let it go, and flew back, upwards, having thus "lost" it. It was Ernest's turn now, as a sort of end-man, to scramble forward to the spot where Philip had dug it down and "find" it; the first one to do so, having the prerogative, which he jealously guarded, of raining on the other a series of thundering leg blows. As boys in the West Indies Philip and Ernest had played it. Of a Sunday the Negro fishermen on the Barbadoes coast made a pagan rite of it. Many a Bluetown dandy got his spine cracked in a game of "cork."

With a passive interest the passengers viewed the proceedings. In a game of "cork," the cork after a succession of "rammings" is likely to drift many feet away whence it was first "lost." One had to be an expert, quick, alert, to spy and promptly seize it as it popped up on the rolling waves. Once Ernest got it and endeavored to make much of the possession. But Philip, besides being two feet taller than he, was slippery as an eel, and Ernest, despite all the artful ingenuity at his command, was able to do no more than ineffectively beat the water about him. Again and again he tried, but to no purpose.

Becoming reckless, he let the cork drift too far away from him and Philip seized it.

He twirled it in the air like a crap shooter, and dug deep down in the water with it, "lost" it, then leaped back, briskly waiting for it to rise.

About them the water, due to the ramming and beating, grew restive. Billows sprang up; soaring, swelling waves sent the skiff nearer the shore. Anxiously Philip and Ernest watched for the cork to make its ascent.

It was all a bit vague to the whites on the deck, and an amused chuckle floated down to the boys.

And still the cork failed to come up.

"I'll go after it," said Philip at last, "I'll go and fetch it." And, from the edge of the boat he leaped, his body long and resplendent in the rising tropic sun.

It was a suction sea, and down in it Philip plunged. And it was lazy, too, and willful—the water. Ebony-black, it tugged and mocked. Old brass staves—junk dumped there by the retiring French—thick, yawping mud, barrel hoops, tons of obsolete brass, a wealth of slimy steel faced him. Did a "rammed" cork ever go that deep?

And the water, stirring, rising, drew a haze over Philip's eyes. Had a cuttlefish, an octopus, a nest of eels been routed? It seemed so to Philip, blindly diving, pawing. And the sea, the tide—touching the roots of Death-pool—tugged and tugged. His gathering hands stuck in mud. Iron staves bruised his shins. It was black down there. Impenetrable.

Suddenly, like a flash of lightning, a vision blew across Philip's brow. It was a soaring shark's belly. Drunk on the nectar of the deep, it soared above Philip—rolling, tumbling, rolling. It had followed the boy's scent with the accuracy of a diver's rope.

Scrambling to the surface, Philip struck out for the boat. But the sea, the depths of it wrested out of an aeon's slumber, had sent it a mile from his diving point. And now, as his strength ebbed, a shark was at his heels.

"Shark! Shark!" was the cry that went up from the ship.

Hewing a lane through the hostile sea Philip forgot the cunning of the doddering beast and swam noisier than he needed to. Faster grew his strokes. His line was a straight, dead one. Fancy strokes and dives—giraffe leaps . . . he summoned into play. He shot out recklessly. One time he suddenly paused—and floated for a stretch. Another time he swam on his back, gazing at the chalky sky. He dived for whole lengths.

But the shark, a bloaty, stone-colored man-killer, took a shorter cut. Circumnavigating the swimmer it bore down upon him with the speed of a hurricane. Within adequate reach it turned, showed its gleaming belly, seizing its prey.

A fiendish gargle—the gnashing of bones—as the sea once more closed its jaws on Philip.

Some one aboard ship screamed. Women fainted. There was talk of a gun. Ernest, an oar upraised, capsized the boat as he tried to inflict a blow on the coursing, chop-licking man-eater.

And again the fish turned. It scraped the waters with its deadly fins.

At Coco Té, at the fledging of the dawn, Maffi, polishing the tinware, hummed an *obeah* melody.

> Trinidad is a damn fine place
> But *obeah* down dey. . . .

Peace had come to her at last.

THE YELLOW ONE

ONCE CATCHING A GLIMPSE OF HER, they swooped down like a brood of starving hawks. But it was the girl's first vision of the sea, and the superstitions of a Honduras peasant heritage tightened her grip on the old rusty canister she was dragging with a frantic effort on to the *Urubamba's* gangplank.

"Le' me help yo', dahtah," said one.

"Go 'way, man, yo' too farrad—'way!"

" 'Im did got de fastiness fi' try fi' jump ahead o' me again, but mahn if yo' t'ink yo' gwine duh me outa a meal yo' is a dam pitty liar!"

"Wha' yo' ah try fi' do, leggo!" cried the girl, slapping the nearest one. But the shock of her words was enough to paralyze them.

They were a harum scarum lot, hucksters, ex-cable divers and thugs of the coast, bare-footed, brown-faced, raggedly—drifting from every cave and creek of the Spanish Main.

They withdrew, shocked, uncertain of their ears, staring at her; at her whom the peons of the lagoon idealized as *la madurita:* the yellow one.

Sensing the hostility, but unable to fathom it, she felt guilty of some untoward act, and guardedly lowered her eyes.

Flushed and hot, she seized the canister by the handle and started resuming the journey. It was heavy. More energy was required to move it than she had bargained on.

In the dilemma rescuing footsteps were heard coming down the gangplank. She was glad to admit she was stumped, and stood back, confronted by one of the crew. He was tall, some six feet and over, and a mestizo like herself. Latin blood bubbled in his veins, and it served at once to establish a ready means of communication between them.

"I'll take it," he said, quietly, "you go aboard—"

"Oh, many thanks," she said, "and do be careful, I've got the baby bottle in there and I wouldn't like to break it." All this in Spanish, a tongue spontaneously springing up between them.

She struggled up the gangplank, dodging a sling drooping tipsily on to the wharf. "Where are the passengers for Kingston station?" she asked.

"Yonder!" he pointed, speeding past her. Amongst a contortion of machinery, cargo, nets and hatch panels he deposited the trunk.

Gazing at his hardy hulk, two emotions seared her. She wanted to be grateful but he wasn't the sort of person she could offer a tip to. And he would readily see through her telling him that Alfred was down the dock changing the money.

But he warmed to her rescue. "Oh, that's all right," he said, quite illogically, "stay here till they close the hatch, then if I am not around, somebody will help you put it where you want it."

Noises beat upon her. Vendors of tropical fruits cluttered the wharf, kept up sensuous cries; stir and clamor and screams rose from every corner of the ship. Men swerved about her, the dock hands, the crew, digging cargo off the pier and spinning it into the yawning hatch.

"Wha' ah lot o' dem," she observed, "an' dem so black and

ugly. R—r—!" Her words had the anti-native quality of her Jamaica spouse's, Alfred St. Xavier Mendez.

The hatch swelled, the bos'n closed it, and the siege commenced. "If Ah did got any sense Ah would Ah wait till dem clean way de rope befo' me mek de sailor boy put down de trunk. Howsomevah, de Lawd will provide, an' all me got fi' do is put me trus' in Him till Halfred come."

With startling alacrity, her prayers were answered, for there suddenly appeared a thin moon-faced decker, a coal-black fellow with a red greasy scarf around his neck, his teeth giddy with an ague he had caught in Puerta Tela and which was destined never to leave him. He seized the trunk by one end and helped her hoist it on the hatch. When he had finished, he didn't wait for her trepid words of thanks but flew to the ship's rail, convulsively shaking.

She grew restive. "Wha' dat Halfred, dey, eh," she cried, "wha' a man can pacify time dough, eh?"

The stream of amassing deckers overran the *Urubamba's* decks. The din of parts being slugged to rights buzzed. An oily strip of canvas screened the hatch. Deckers clamorously crept underneath it.

The sea lay torpid, sizzling. Blue rust flaked off the ship's sides shone upon it. It dazzled you. It was difficult to divine its true color. Sometimes it was so blue it blinded you. Another time it would turn with the cannon roar of the sun, red. Nor was it the red of fire or of youth, of roses or of red tulips. But a sullen, grizzled red. The red of a North Sea rover's icicled beard; the red of a red-headed woman's hair, the red of a red-hot oven. It gave to the water engulfing the ship a dark, copper-colored hue. It left on it jeweled crusts.

A bow-legged old Maroon, with a trunk on his head, explored the deck, smoking a gawky clay pipe of some fiery Jamaica bush and wailing, "Scout bway, scout bway, wha' yo' dey? De old man ah look fa' yo'." The trunk was beardy and fuzzy with the lashes of much-used rope. It was rapidly dusking, and a woman and an amazing brood of children came on. One pulled, screaming, at her skirt, one was astride a hip, another, an unclothed one, tugged enthusiastically at a full, ripened breast. A hoary old black man, in a long black coat, who had taken the Word, no doubt, to the yellow "heathen" of the fever-hot lagoon, shoeless, his hard white crash pants rolled up above his hairy, veiny calves, with a lone yellow pineapple as his sole earthly reward.

A tar-black Jamaica sister, in a gown of some noisy West Indian silk, her face entirely removed by the shadowy girth of a leghorn hat, waltzed grandly up on the deck. The edge of her skirt in one hand, after the manner of the ladies at Wimbledon, in the other a fluttering macaw, she was twittering, "Hawfissah, hawfissah, wear is de hawfissah, he?" Among the battering hordes there were less brusque folk; a native girl,—a flower, a brown flower—was alone, rejecting the opulent offer of a bunk, quietly vowing to pass two nights of sleepful concern until she got to Santiago. And two Costa Rica maidens, white, dainty, resentful and uncommunicative.

He came swaggering at last. La Madurita said, "Wha' yo' been, Halfred, all dis lang time, no?"

"Cho, it wuz de man dem down dey," he replied, "dem keep me back." He gave her the sleeping child, and slipped down to doze on the narrow hatch.

In a mood of selfless bluster he was returning to Kingston. He adored Jamaica. He would go on sprees of work and daring, to the jungles of Changuinola or the Cut at Culebra, but such flights, whether for a duration of one or ten years, were uplifted mainly by the traditional deprivations of Hindu coolies or Polish immigrants—sunless, joyless. Similarly up in Cabello; work, sleep, work; day in and day out for six forest-hewing years. And on Sabbaths a Kentucky evangelist, a red-headed hypochondriac, the murky hue of a British buckra from the beat of the tropic sun, tearfully urged the blacks to embrace the teachings of the Lord Jesus Christ before the wrath of Satan engulfed them. Then, one day, on a tramp to Salamanca, a fancy struck him. It stung, was unexpected. He was unused to the sensations it set going. It related to a vision—something he had surreptitiously encountered. Behind a planter's hut he had seen it. He was slowly walking along the street, shaded by a row of plum trees, and there she was, gloriously unaware of him, bathing her feet in ample view of the sky. She was lovely to behold. Her skin was the ripe red gold of the Honduras halfbreed. It sent the blood streaming to his head. He paused and wiped the sweat from his face. He looked at her, calculating. Five—six—seven-fifty. Yes, that'd do. With seven hundred and fifty pounds, he'd dazzle the foxy folk of Kingston with the mellow *Spanish* beauty of her.

In due time, and by ample means, he had been able to bring round the girl's hitherto *chumbo*-hating folk.

"Him mus' be hungry," she said, gazing intently at the baby's face.

"Cho'," replied Alfred, "leave de picknee alone, le' de gal picknee sleep." He rolled over, face downwards, and folded his arms under his chin. He wore a dirty khaki shirt, made in the States, dark green corduroy pants and big yellow shoes which he seldom took off.

Upright on the trunk, the woman rocked the baby and nursed it. By this time the hatch was overcrowded with deckers.

Down on the dock, oxen were yoked behind wagons of crated bananas. Gnawing on plugs of hard black tobacco and firing reels of spit to every side of them, New Orleans "crackers" swearingly cursed the leisurely lack of native labor. Scaly ragamuffins darted after boxes of stale cheese and crates of sun-sopped iced apples that were dumped in the sea. . . .

Of late he didn't answer her any more. And it was useless to depend upon him. Frantic at the baby's pawing of the clotted air, at the cold dribbling from its twisted mouth, which turned down a trifle at the ends like Alfred's, she began conjecturing on the use to which a decker could put a cup of the precious liquid. Into it one might pour a gill of goat's milk—a Cuban *señora*, a decker of several voyages, had fortified herself with a bucket of it—or melt a sprig of peppermint or a lump of clove or a root of ginger. So many tropical things one could do with a cup of hot water.

The child took on the color of its sweltering environs. It refused to be pacified by sugared words. It was hungry and it wished to eat, to feel coursing down its throat something warm and delicious. It kicked out of its mother's hand the toy engine she locomotioned before it. It cried, it ripped with its naked toes a hole in her blouse. It kept up an irrepressible racket.

The child's agony drove her to reckless alternatives. "If you don't go, then I'll go, yo' lazy t'ing," she said, depositing the baby beside him and disappearing down the galley corridor.

Her bare earth-red feet slid on the hot, sizzling deck. The heat came roaring at her. It swirled, enveloping her. It was a dingy corridor and there were pigmy paneled doors every inch along it. It wasn't clear to her whither she was bound; the vaporing heat dizzied things. But the scent of stewing meat and vegetables lured her on. It sent her scudding in and out of barrels of cold storage, mounds of ash debris of an exotic kind. It shot her into dark twining circles of men, talking. They either paused or grew lecherous at her approach. Some of the doors to the crew's quarters were open and as she passed white men'd stick out their heads and call, pull, tug at her. Grimy, ash-stained faces; leprous, flesh-crazed hands. Onward she fled, into the roaring, fuming galley.

Heat. Hearths aglow. Stoves aglow. Dishes clattering. Engines, donkey-engines, wheezing. Bright-faced and flame-haired Swedes and Bristol cockneys cursing. Half-nude figures of bronze and crimson shouting, spearing, mending the noisy fire. The wet, clean, brick-colored deck danced to the rhythm of the ship. Darky waiters—white shirt bosoms—black bow ties—black, braided uniforms—spat entire menus at the blond cooks.

"Slap it on dey, Dutch, don't starve de man."

"Hey, Hubigon, tightenin' up on any mo' hoss flesh to-day?"

"Come on fellahs, let's go—"

"There's my boy Porto Rico again Hubigon, Ah tell yo' he is a sheik, tryin' to git nex' to dat hot yallah mama."

On entering she had turned, agonized and confused, to a lone yellow figure by the port hole.

"Oh, it's you," she exclaimed, and smiled wanly.

He was sourly sweeping dishes, forks, egg-stained things into a mossy wooden basket which he hoisted and dropped into a cesspool of puttering water.

He paused, blinking uncomprehendingly.

"You," she was catching at mementoes, "you remember—you helped me—my trunk—"

"Oh, yes, I remember," he said slowly. He was a Cuban, mixblooded, soft-haired, and to him, as she stood there, a bare, primitive soul, her beauty and her sex seemed to be in utmost contrast to his mechanical surroundings.

"Can you," she said, in that half-hesitant way of hers, "can you give me some hot watah fo' my baby?"

He was briefly attired; overalls, a dirty, pink singlet. His reddish yellow face, chest and neck shone with the grease and sweat. His face was buttered with it.

"Sure," he replied, seizing an empty date can on the ledge of the port hole and filling it. "Be careful," he cautioned, handing it back to her.

She took it and their eyes meeting, fell.

She started to go, but a burning touch of his hand possessed her.

"Wait," he said, "I almost forgot something." From beneath

the machine he exhumed an old moist gold dust box. Inside it he had pummeled, by some ornate instinct, odds and ends—echoes of the breakfast table. He gave the box to her, saying, "If any one should ask you where you got it, just say Jota Arosemena gave it to you."

"Hey, Porto Rico, wha' the hell yo' git dat stuff at, hotting stuff fo' decks?"

Both of them turned, and the Cuban paled at the jaunty mug of the cook's Negro mate.

"You speak to me?" he said, ice cool.

Hate shone on the black boy's face. "Yo' heard me!" he growled. "Yo' ain't cock-eyed." Ugly, grim, black, his face wore an uneasy leer. He was squat and bleary-eyed.

A son of the Florida Gulf, he hated "Porto Rico" for reasons planted deep in the Latin's past. He envied him the gentle texture of his hair. On mornings in the galley where they both did their toilet he would poke fun at the Cuban's meticulous care in parting it. "Yo' ain't gwine sho'," Hubigon'd growl. "Yo' don't have to dress up like no lady's man." And Jota, failing to comprehend the point of view, would question, "What's the matter with you, mang, you mek too much noise, mang." Hubigon despised him because he was yellow-skinned; one night in Havana he had spied him and the chef cook, a nifty, freckle-faced Carolina "cracker" for whom the cook's mate had no earthly use, and the baker's assistant, a New Orleans creole,—although the Negro waiters aboard were sure he was a "yallah" nigger—drinking *anee* in a high-hat café on the prado which barred jet-black American Negroes. He loathed the Latin for his good looks and once at a port on the Buenaventura River they had gone ashore and met two native girls. One was white, her lips pure as the petals of a water lily; the other was a flaming mulatto. That night, on the steps of an adobe hut, a great, low moon in the sky, both forgot the presence of the cook's mate and pledged tear-stained love to Jota. "An' me standin' right by him, doin' a fadeaway." He envied Jota his Cuban nationality for over and over again he had observed that the Latin was the nearest thing to a white man the *ofay* men aboard had yet met. They'd play cards with him—something they never did with the Negro crew—they'd gang with him in foreign ports, they'd listen in a "natural" sort of way to all the bosh he had to say.

Now all the mate's pent-up wrath came foaming to the front.

He came up, the girl having tarried, a cocky, chesty air about him. He made deft, telling jabs at the vapors enmeshing him. "Yo' can't do that," he said, indicating the victuals, "like hell yo' kin! Who de hell yo' t'ink yo' is anyhow? Yo' ain't bettah'n nobody else. Put it back, big boy, befo' Ah starts whisperin' to de man. Wha' yo' t'ink yo' is at, anyhow, in Porto Rico, where yo' come fum at? Com' handin' out poke chops an' cawn muffins, like yo' is any steward. Yo' cain't do dat, ole man."

It slowly entered the other's brain—all this edgy, snappy, darky talk. But the essence of it was aggressively reflected in the mate's behavior. Hubigon made slow measured steps forward, and the men came flocking to the corner.

"Go to it, Silver King, step on his corns."

"Stick him with a ice pick!"

"Easy fellahs, the steward's comin'."

All of them suddenly fell away. The steward, initiating some fruit baron into the mysteries of the galley, came through, giving them time to speed back to their posts unobserved. The tension subsided, and Jota once more fed the hardware to the dish machine.

As she flew through the corridor all sorts of faces, white ones, black ones, brown ones, leered sensually at her. Like tongues of flame, hands sped after her. Her steps quickened, her heart beat faster and faster till she left behind her the droning of the galley, and safely ascending the hatch, felt on her face the soft, cool breezes of the Caribbean ocean.

Alfred was sitting up, the unpacified baby in his arms.

" 'Im cry all de time yo' went 'way," he said, "wha' yo' t'ink is de mattah wit' 'im, he? Yo' t'ink him tummack a hut 'im?"

"Him is hungry, dat is wha' is de mattah wit' 'im! Move, man! 'Fo Ah knock yo', yah! Giv' me 'im, an' get outa me way! Yo' is only a dyam noosant!"

"Well, what is de mattah, now?" he cried in unfeigned surprise.

"Stid o' gwine fo' de watah yo'self yo' tan' back yah an' giv' hawdahs an' worryin' wha' is de mattah wit' de picknee."

"Cho, keep quiet, woman, an' le' me lie down." Satisfied, he rolled back on the hatch, fatuously staring at the sun sweeping the tropic blue sea.

"T'un ovah, Halfred, an' lif' yo' big able self awf de baby, yo' Ah crush 'im to debt," she said, awake at last. The baby was awake and ravenous before dawn and refused to be quieted by the witty protestations of the Jamaica laborers scrubbing down the deck. But it was only after the sun, stealing a passage through a crack in the canvas, had warmed a spot on the girl's mouth, that she was constrained to respond to his zestful rantings. "Hey, yo' heah de picknee ah bawl all de time an' yo' won't even tek heed—move yah man!" She thrust the sleeping leg aside and drawing the child to her, stuck a breast in his mouth.

The boat had encountered a sultry sea, and was dipping badly. Water flooded her decks. Getting wet, dozing deckers crawled higher on top of each other. The sea was blue as indigo and white reels of foam swirled past as the ship dove ahead.

It was a disgusting spectacle. There was the sea, drumming on the tinsel sides of the ship, and on top of the terror thus resulting rose a wretched wail from the hatch, "Watah! Hot Watah!"

The galley was the Bastille. Questioning none, the Yellow One, giving the baby to Alfred rushed to the door, and flung herself through it. Once in the corridor, the energy of a dynamo possessed her. Heated mist drenched her. She slid on grimy, sticky deck.

He was hanging up the rag on a brace of iron over the port hole. His jaws were firm, grim, together.

The rest of the galley was a foetic blur to her.

He swung around, and his restless eyes met her. He was for the moment paralyzed. His eyes bore into hers. He itched to toss at her words, words, words! He wanted to say, "Oh, why couldn't you stay away—ashore—down there—at the end of the world— anywhere but on this ship."

"Some water," she said with that gentle half-hesitant smile of hers, "can I get some hot water for my little baby?" And she extended the skillet.

He took it to the sink, his eyes still on hers. The water rained into it like bullets and he brought it to her.

But a sound polluted the lovely quiet.

"Hey, Porto Rico, snap into it! Dis ain't no time to git foolin' wit' no monkey jane. Get a move on dey, fellah, an' fill dis pail full o' water."

He was sober, afar, as he swept a pale, tortured face at Hubigon. As if it were the song of a lark, he swung back to the girl, murmuring, "Ah, but you didn't tell me," he said, "you didn't tell me what the baby is, a boy or girl?" For answer, the girl's eyes widened in terror at something slowly forming behind him.

But it was not without a shadow, and Jota swiftly ducked.

The mallet went galloping under the machine. He rose and faced the cook's mate. But Hubigon was not near enough to objectify the jab, sent as fast as the fangs of a striking snake, and Jota fell, cursing, to the hushed cries of the woman. For secretly easing over to the fireplace Hubigon had taken advantage of the opening to grasp a spear and as the other was about to rise brought it thundering down on the tip of his left shoulder. It sent him thudding to the deck in a pool of claret. The cook's mate, his red, red tongue licking his mouth after the manner of a collie in from a strenuous run, pounced on the emaciated figure in the corner, and kicked and kicked it murderously. He kicked him in the head, in the mouth, in the ribs. When he struggled to rise, he sent him back to the floor, dizzy from short, telling jabs with the tip of his boot.

Pale, impassive, the men were prone to take sides. Unconsciously forming a ring, the line was kept taut. Sometimes it surged; once an Atlanta mulatto had to wrest a fiery spear from Foot Works, Hubigon's side kick, and thrust it back in its place. "Keep outa this, if you don't want to get your goddam head mashed in," he said. A woman, a crystal panel in the gray, ugly pattern, tore, fought, had to be kept sane by raw, meaty hands.

Gasping, Hubigon stood by, his eyes shining at the other's languid effort to rise. "Stan' back, fellahs, an' don't interfere. Let 'im come!" With one shoulder jaunty and a jaw risen, claret-drenched, redolent of the stench and grime of Hubigon's boot, parts of it clinging to him, the Cuban rose. A cruel scowl was on his face.

The crowd stood back, and there was sufficient room for them. Hubigon was ripping off his shirt, and licking his red, bleeding lips. He circled the ring like a snarling jungle beast. "Hol' at fuh me, Foot Works, I'm gwine sho' dis monkey when he get off at." He was dancing round, jabbing, tapping at ghosts, awaiting the other's beastly pleasure.

As one cowed he came, his jaw swollen. Then with the vigor of a maniac he straightened, facing the mate. He shot out his left. It had the wings of a dart and juggled the mate on the chin. Hubigon's ears tingled distantly. For the particle of a second he was groggy, and the Cuban moored in with the right, flush on the chin. Down the cook's mate went. Leaping like a tiger cat, Jota was upon him, burying his claws in the other's bared, palpitating throat. His eyes gleamed like a tiger cat's. He held him by the throat and squeezed him till his tongue came out. He racked him till the blood seeped through his ears. Then, in a frenzy of frustration, he lifted him up, and pounded with his head on the bared deck. He pounded till the shirt on his back split into ribbons.

"Jesus, take him awf o' him—he's white or-ready."

"Now, boys, this won't do," cried the baker, a family man. "Come."

And some half dozen of them, running counter to the traditions of the coast, ventured to slug them apart. It was a gruesome job, and Hubigon, once freed, his head and chest smeared with blood, black, was ready to peg at a lancing La Barrie snake.

In the scuffle the woman collapsed, fell under the feet of the milling crew.

"Here," some one cried, "take hold o' her, Butch, she's your kind—she's a decker—hatch four—call the doctor somebody, will ya?"

They took her on a stretcher to the surgeon's room.

The sun had leaped ahead. A sizzling luminosity drenched the sea. Aft the deckers were singing hosannas to Jesus and preparing to walk the gorgeous earth.

Only Alfred St. Xavier Mendez was standing with the baby in his arms, now on its third hunger-nap, gazing with a bewildered look at the deserted door to the galley. "Me wondah wha' mek she 'tan' so lang," he whispered anxiously.

Imperceptibly shedding their drapery of mist, there rose above the prow of the *Urubamba* the dead blue hills of Jamaica.

RICHARD BRUCE NUGENT

RICHARD BRUCE NUGENT'S *"Smoke, Lillies and Jade!"* (1926) was the scandal of the Harlem Renaissance, an impressionistic celebration of androgyny, homosexuality, and drugs. Nugent's Greenwich Village protagonist, Beauty, was a composite of Rudolf Valentino, the artist Miguel Covarrubias, Countee Cullen's male lover Harold Jackman, and Langston Hughes. Du Bois had warned that the diminishing of cultural propaganda in the service of artistic beauty would "turn the Negro renaissance into decadence." Nugent's piece was widely regarded as the quintessential confirmation of that prediction.

SMOKE, LILLIES AND JADE!

HE WANTED to do something . . . to write or draw . . . or something . . . but it was so comfortable to lay there on the bed . . . his shoes off . . . and think . . . think of everything . . . short disconnected thoughts to wonder . . . to remember . . . to think and smoke . . . why wasn't he worried that he had no money . . . he had five cents . . . but he had been hungry . . . he was hungry and still . . . all he wanted to do was . . . lay there comfortably smoking . . . think . . . wishing he were writing . . . or drawing . . . or something . . . something about the things he felt and thought . . . but what did he think . . . he remembered how his mother had awakened him one night . . . ages ago . . . six years ago . . . Alex . . . he had always wondered at the strangeness of it . . . she had seemed so . . . so . . . so just the same . . . Alex . . . I think your father is dead

. . . and it hadn't seemed so strange . . . yet . . . one's mother
didn't say that . . . didn't wake one at midnight every night to say
. . . feel him . . . put your hand on his . . . then whisper with a
catch in her voice . . . I'm afraid . . . she don't wake Lam . . . yet
it hadn't seemed as it should have seemed . . . even when he had
felt his father's cool wet forehead . . . it hadn't been tragic . . . or
weird . . . not at all as one should feel when one's father had died
. . . even his reply of . . . yes he is dead . . . had been commonplace . . . hadn't been dramatic . . . there had been no tears . . .
no sobs . . . not even a sorrow . . . and yet he must have realized
that one's father couldn't smile . . . or sing anymore . . . after he
had died . . . every one remembered his father's voice . . . it had
been a lush voice . . . a promise . . . then that dressing together
. . . his mother and himself . . . in the bathroom . . . why was the
bathroom always the warmest room in the house in the winter . . .
as they had put on their clothes . . . his mother had been telling
him what he must do . . . and cried softly . . . and that had made
him cry too but you mustn't cry Alex . . . remember you have to
be a little man now . . . and that was all . . . didn't other wives
and sons cry more for their dead than that . . . anyway people
never cried for beautiful sunsets . . . or music . . . and those were
the things that hurt . . . the things to sympathize with . . . then
out into the snow and dark of the morning . . . first to the undertaker's . . . no first to Uncle Frank's . . . why did Aunt Lula have
to act like that. . . . to ask again and again . . . but when did he
die. . . . when did he die . . . I just can't believe it . . . poor Minerva
. . . then out into the snow and dark again . . . how had his mother
expected him to find the night bell at the undertaker's . . . he was
the most sensible of them tho . . . all he had said was . . . what
. . . Harry Francis . . . too bad . . . tell mamma I'll be there first
thing in the morning . . . then down the deserted streets again . . .
to grandmother's . . . it was growing light now . . . it must be
terrible to die in daylight . . . grandpa had been sweeping the snow
off the yard . . . he had been glad of that because . . . well he could
tell him better than he could grandma . . . grandpa father's dead
. . . and he hadn't acted strange either . . . books lied . . . he had
just looked at Alex a moment then continued sweeping . . . all he
said was . . . what time did he die . . . she'll want to know . . .
then passing thru the lonesome street toward home . . . Mr. Minnie
Grant was closing a window and spied him . . . hallow Alex and
how's your father this mornin' . . . dead . . . get out . . . tch tch

tch an' I was just around there with a cup a' custard yesterday . . .
Alex puffed contentedly on his cigarette . . . he was hungry and
comfortable . . . and he had an ivory holder inlaid with red jade
and green . . . funny how the smoke seemed to climb up
that ray of sunlight . . . went up the slant just like imagination . . .
was imagination blue . . . or was it because he had spent his last
five cents and couldn't worry . . . anyway it was to lay there and
wonder . . . and remember . . . why was he so different from other
people . . . the only things he remembered of his father's funeral
were the crowded church and the ride in the hack . . . so many
people there in the church . . . and ladies with tears in their eyes
. . . and on their cheeks . . . and some men too . . . why did people
cry . . . vanity that was the reason . . . yet they weren't exactly
hypocrites . . . but . . . it had made him furious . . . all these people
crying . . . it wasn't THEIR father . . . and he wasn't crying . . .
couldn't cry for sorrow although he had loved his father more than
. . . than . . . it had made him so angry that tears had come into
his eyes . . . and he had been ashamed of his mother . . . crying
into a handkerchief . . . so ashamed that tears had run down his
cheeks and he had frowned . . . and someone . . . a woman . . .
had said . . . look at that poor little dear . . . Alex is just like his
father . . . and the tears had run fast . . . because he *wasn't* like
his father . . . he couldn't sing . . . he didn't want to sing . . . he
didn't want to sing . . . Alex blew a cloud of smoke . . . blue smoke
. . . when they had taken his father from the vault three weeks
later . . . he had grown beautiful . . . his nose had become perfect
and clear . . . his turned jet black and silky and glossy . . . and his
skin was a transparent green . . . like the sea only not so deep
. . . and where it was drawn over the cheekbones a pale beautiful
red appeared . . . like a blush . . . why hadn't his father looked
like that always . . . but no . . . to have sung would have broken
the wondrous repose of those lips and maybe that was his beauty
. . . maybe it was wrong to think thoughts like these . . . but they
were nice and pleasant and comfortable . . . when one was smoking a cigarette thru an ivory holder . . . inlaid with red jade and
green . . .

he wondered why he couldn't find work . . . a job . . . when
he had first come to New York he had . . . and he had only been
fourteen then—was it because he was nineteen now that he felt so
idle . . . and contented . . . or because he was an artist . . . but
was he an artist . . . was one an artist before one became known

. . . of course he was an artist . . . and strangely enough so were all his friends . . . he should be ashamed that he didn't work . . . but . . . was it five years in New York . . . or the fact that he was an artist . . . when his mother said she couldn't understand him . . . why did he vaguely pity her instead of being ashamed . . . he should be . . . his mother and all his relatives said so . . . his brother was three years younger than he and yet he had already been away from home a year . . . on the stage . . . making thirty-five dollars a week . . . had three suits of clothes and many clothes and was going to help his mother . . . while he . . . Alex . . . was content to lay and smoke and meet friends at night . . . to argue and read Wilde . . . Freud . . . Boccacio and Schnitzler . . . to attend Gurdjieff meetings and know things . . . Why did they scoff at him for knowing such people as Carl . . . Mencken . . . Toomer . . . Hughes . . . Cullen . . . Wood . . . Cabell . . . oh the whole lot of them . . . was it because it seemed so incongruous to him that he . . . who was so little known . . . should call by first names people they would like to know . . . were they jealous . . . no mothers aren't jealous of their sons . . . they are proud of them . . . why then . . . when these friends accepted him and liked him . . . no matter how he dressed . . . why did mother ask . . . and you went looking like that . . . Langston was a fine fellow . . . he knew there was something in Alex . . . and so did Rene and Borgia . . . and Zora and Clement and Miguel . . . and . . . and . . . and all of them . . . if he went to see mother she would ask . . . how do you feel Alex with nothing in your pockets . . . I don't see how you can be satisfied . . . Really you are a mystery to me . . . I'm sure I don't know . . . none of my brothers were lazy and shiftless . . . I can never remember the time when they weren't sending money home and when your father was your age he was supporting a family . . . where you get your nerve I don't know . . . just because you tried to write one or two little poems that no one understands . . . you seem to think the world owes you a living . . . you should see by now how much is thought of them . . . you can't sell any of them . . . and you won't do anything to make money . . . wake up Alex . . . I don't know what will become of you . . .

it was hard to believe in one's self after that . . . did Wilde's parents or Shelley's or Goya's talk to them like that . . . but it was depressing to think in that vein . . . Alex stretched and yawned . . . Max had died . . . Margaret had died . . . so had Sonia . . . Cynthia . . . Juan-Jose and Harry . . . all people he had loved . . .

loved one by one and together . . . and all had died . . . he never loved a person long before they died . . . in truth he was tragic . . . that was a lovely appellation . . . The Tragic Genius . . . think . . . to go through life known as the Tragic Genius . . . romantic . . . but it was more or less true . . . Alex turned over and blew another cloud of smoke . . . was all life like that . . . smoke . . . blue smoke from an ivory holder . . . he wished he were in New Bedford . . . New Bedford was a nice place . . . snug little houses set complacently behind protecting lawns . . . half open windows showing prim interiors from behind waving cool curtains . . . inviting . . . like precise courtesans winking from behind lace fans . . . and trees . . . many trees . . . casting lacy patterns of shade on the sun dipped sidewalks . . . small stores . . . naively proud of their pseudo grandeur . . . banks . . . called institutions for saving . . . all naive that was it . . . New Bedford was naive . . . after the sophistication of New York it would fan one kikea refreshing breeze . . . and yet he had returned to New York . . . and sophistication . . . was he sophisticated . . . no because he was he was seldom bored . . . seldom bored by anything . . . and weren't the sophisticated continually suffering from ennui . . . on the contrary . . . he was amused . . . amused by the artificiality of sophistication and naivety alike . . . but maybe that in itself was the essence of sophistication or . . . was it cynicism . . . or were the two identical . . . he blew a cloud of smoke . . . it was growing dark now . . . and the smoke no longer had a ladder to climb . . . but soon the moon would rise and then he would clothe the silver moon in blue smoke garments . . . truly smoke was like imagination . . .

Alex sat up . . . pulled on his shoes and went out . . . it was a beautiful night . . . and so large . . . the dusky blue hung like a curtain in an immense arched doorway . . . fastened with silver tacks . . . to wander in the night was wonderful . . . myriads of inquisitive lights . . . curiously prying into the dark . . . and fading unsatisfied . . . he passed a woman . . . she was not beautiful . . . and he was sad because she did not weep that she would never be beautiful . . . was it Wilde who had said . . . a cigarette is the most perfect pleasure because it leaves one unsatisfied . . . the breeze gave to him a perfume stolen from some wandering lady of the evening . . . it pleased him . . . why was it that men wouldn't use perfumes . . . they should . . . each and every one of them liked perfumes . . . the man who denied that was a liar . . . or a coward . . . but if ever he were to voice that thought or express it . . . he

would be misunderstood . . . it made him feel tragic and great
. . . but maybe it would be nicer to be understood . . . but no . . .
no great artist is . . . then again . . . neither were fools . . . they
were strangely akin these two . . . Alex thought of a sketch he
would make . . . a personality sketch of Fania . . . straight classic
features tinted proud purple . . . sensuous fine lips . . . gilded for
truth . . . eyes . . . half opened and lids colored mysterious green
. . . hair black and straight . . . drawn sternly mockingly back from
the false puritanical forehead . . . maybe he would make Edith too
. . . skin a blue . . . infinite like night . . . and eyes . . . slant and
grey . . . very complacent like a cat's . . . Mona Lisa lips . . . red
and seductive as . . . as pomegranate juice . . . in truth it was fine
to be young and hungry and an artist . . . to blow blue smoke
from an ivory holder . . .

here was the cafeteria . . . it was almost as tho it had journeyed
to meet him . . . the night was so blue . . . how does blue feel . . .
or red or gold or any other color . . . if colors could be heard he
would paint most wondrous tunes . . . symphonious . . . think . . .
the dulcet tones of a blue like night . . . of a red like pomegranate
juice . . . like Edith's lips . . . of the fairy tones to be heard in a
sunset . . . like rubies shaken in a crystal cup . . . of the symphony
of Fania . . . and silver . . . and gold . . . he had heard the sound
of gold but they weren't the sounds he wanted to catch . . . no . . .
they must be liquid . . . not so staccato but flowing variations of
the same one caliber . . . there was no one in the cafe as yet . . .
he sat and waited . . . that was a clever idea he had had about the
color music . . . but after all he was a monstrous clever fellow . . .
Jurgen had said that . . . funny how characters in a book said
the things one wanted to say . . . he would like to know Jurgen
. . . how does one go about getting an introduction to the characters in a book . . . go up to the brown cover of the book
and knock gently . . . and say hello . . . then timidly . . . is Duke
Jurgen there . . . or . . . no because if he entered the book in the
beginning Jurgen would only be a pawn broker . . . and one
didn't enter a book in the center . . . but what foolishness . . .
Alex lit a cigarette . . . but Cabell was a master to have written
Jurgen . . . and an artist . . . and a poet . . . Alex blew a cloud of
smoke . . . a few lines of one of Langston's poems came to describe
Jurgen. . . .

> Somewhat like Ariel
> Somewhat like Puck

> Somewhat like a gutter boy
> Who loves to play in muck.
> Somewhat like Bacchus
> Somewhat like Pan
> And a way with women
> Like a sailor man. . . .

Langston must have known Jurgen . . . suppose Jurgen had met people like Tonio Kroeger . . . what a vagrant thought . . . Kroeger . . . Kroeger . . . Kroeger . . . why here was Rene . . . Alex had almost gone to sleep . . . Alex blew a cone of smoke as he took Rene's hand . . . it was nice to have friends like Rene . . . so comfortable . . . Rene was speaking . . . Borgia joined them . . . and de Diego Padro . . . their talk veered to Cabell . . . James Branch Cabell . . . beautiful . . . marvelous . . . Rene had an enchanting accent . . . said sank for thank and souse for south . . . but they couldn't know Cabell's greatness . . . Alex searched the smoke for expression . . . he . . . he . . . well he has created a phantasy mire . . . that's it . . . from clear rich imagery . . . life and silver sands . . . that's nice . . . and silver sands . . . imagine lilies growing in such a mire . . . when they close at night their gilded underside would close and protect . . . but that's not it at all . . . his thoughts just carried and mingled like . . . like odors . . . suggested but never definite . . . Rene was leaving . . . they all were leaving . . . Alex sauntered slowly back . . . the houses all looked sleepy . . . funny . . . made him feel like writing poetry . . . and about death too . . . an elevated crashed by overhead scattering all his thoughts with its noise . . . making them spread . . . in circles . . . then larger circles . . . just like a splash in a calm pool . . . what had he been thinking . . . of . . . a poem about death . . . but he no longer felt that urge . . . just walk and think and wonder . . . think and remember and smoke . . . blow smoke that mixed with his thoughts and the night . . . he would like to live in a large white palace . . . to wear a long black cape . . . very full and lined with vermillion . . . to have many cushions and to lie there among them . . . talking to his friends . . . lie there in a yellow silk shirt and black velvet trousers . . . like music-review artists talking and pouring strange liquors from curiously beautiful bottles . . . bottles with long slender necks . . . he climbed the noisy stairs of the odorous tenement . . . smelled of fish . . . of stale fried fish and dirty milk bottles . . . he rather liked it . . . he liked the acrid smell of horse manure too . . . strong . . . thoughts . . . yes to lie back

among strangely fashioned cushions and sip eastern wines and talk
. . . Alex threw himself on the bed . . . removed his shoes . . .
stretched and relaxed . . . yes and have music waft softly in the
darkened and incensed room . . . he blew a cloud of smoke . . .
oh the joy of being an artist and of blowing blue smoke thru an
ivory holder inlaid with red jade and green. . . .

the street was so long and narrow . . . so long and narrow . . .
and blue . . . in the distance it reached the stars . . . and if he
walked long enough . . . far enough . . . he could reach the stars
too . . . the narrow blue was so empty . . . quiet . . . Alex walked
music . . . it was so nice to walk in the blue after a party . . . Zora
had shone again . . . her stories . . . she always shone . . . and
Monty was glad . . . everyone was glad when Zora shone . . . he
was glad he had gone to Monty's party . . . Monty had a nice place
in the village . . . nice lights . . . and friends and wine . . . mother
would be scandalized that he could think of going to a party . . .
without a copper to his name . . . but then mother had never been
to Monty's . . . and mother had never seen the street seem long
and narrow and blue . . . Alex walked music . . . the click of his
heels kept time with a tune in his mind . . . he glanced into a lighted
cafe window . . . inside were people sipping coffee . . . men . . .
why they sit there in the loud light . . . didn't they know that
outside the street . . . the narrow blue street met the stars . . . that
if they walked long enough . . . far enough . . . Alex walked and
the click of his heels sounded . . . and had an echo . . . sound being
tossed back and forth . . . someone was approaching . . . and their
echoes mingled . . . and gave the sound of castanets . . . Alex liked
the sound of the approaching man's footsteps . . . he walked music
also . . . he knew the beauty of the narrow blue . . . Alex knew
that by the way their echoes mingled . . . he wished he could speak
. . . but strangers don't speak at four o'clock in the morning . . .
at least if they did he couldn't imagine what would be said . . . maybe . . . pardon me but are you walking toward the stars . . .
yes, sir, and if you walk long enough . . . then may I walk with
you I want to reach the stars too . . . perdone me senor tiene vd.
fosforo . . . Alex was glad he had been addressed in Spanish . . .
to have been asked for a match in English . . . or to have been
addressed in English at all . . . would have been blasphemy just
then . . . Alex handed him a match . . . he glanced at his companion

apprehensively in the match glow . . . he was afraid that his appearance would shatter the blue thoughts . . . and stars . . . ah . . . his face was a perfect complement to his voice . . . and the echo of their steps mingled . . . they walked in silence . . . the castanets of their heels clicking perfect accompaniment . . . the stranger inhaled deeply and with a nod of content and a smile . . . blew a cloud of smoke . . . Alex felt like singing . . . the stranger knew the magic of blue smoke also . . . they continued in silence . . . the castanets of their heels clicking rhythmically . . . Alex turned in his doorway . . . up the stairs and the stranger waited for him to light the room . . . no need for words . . . they had always known each other . . . as they undressed by the pale blue dawn . . . Alex knew he had never seen a more perfect human being . . . his body was all symmetry and music . . . and Alex called him Beauty . . . long they lay . . . blowing smoke and exchanging thoughts . . . and Alex swallowed with difficulty . . . he felt a glow of tremor . . . and they talked . . . and . . . slept. . . .

Alex wondered more and more why he liked Adrian so . . . he liked many people . . . Wallie . . . Zora . . . Clement . . . Gloria . . . Langston . . . John . . . Gwenny . . . oh many people . . . and they were friends . . . but Beauty . . . it was different . . . once Alex had admired Beauty's strength . . . and Beauty's eyes had grown soft . . . and he had said . . . I like you more than anyone Dulce . . . Adrian always called him Dulce . . . and Alex had become confused . . . was it that he was so susceptible to beauty that Alex liked Adrian so much . . . but no . . . he knew other people who were beautiful . . . Fania and Gloria . . . Monty and Bunny . . . but he was never confused before them . . . while Beauty . . . Beauty could make him believe in Buddha . . . or imps . . . and no one else could do that . . . that is no one but Melva . . . but then he was in love with Melva . . . and that explained that . . . he would like Beauty to know Melva . . . they were both so perfect . . . such compliments . . . yes he would like Beauty to know Melva because he was in love with both . . . there he had thought it . . . actually dared to think it . . . but Beauty must never know . . . Beauty couldn't understand . . . indeed Alex couldn't understand . . . and it had pained him . . . almost physically . . . and tired his mind . . . Beauty . . . Beauty was in the air . . . the smoke . . . Beauty . . . Melva . . . Beauty . . . Melva . . . Alex slept . . . and dreamed . . .

he was in a field . . . a field of blue smoke and black poppies

. . . and red calla lilies . . . he was searching . . . on his hands and knees . . . searching . . . among black poppies and red calla lilies . . . he was searching . . . pushed aside poppy stems . . . he saw two strong white legs . . . dancer's legs . . . the contours pleased him . . . his eyes wandered . . . on past the muscular hocks to the firm white thighs . . . the rounded buttocks . . . then the lithe narrow waist . . . strong torso and broad deep chest . . . the heavy shoulders . . . the graceful neck . . . squared chin and quizzical lips . . . grecian nose with its temperamental nostrils . . . the brown eyes looking at him . . . like . . . Monty looked at Zora . . . his hair curly black and all tousled . . . and it was Beauty . . . and Beauty smiled and looked at him and smiled . . . said I'll wait Alex . . . and Alex became confused and continued his search . . . on his hands and knees . . . pushing aside poppy stems and lily stems . . . a poppy . . . a black poppy . . . a lilly . . . a red lilly . . . and when he liked back he could no longer see Beauty . . . Alex continued his searched . . . thru poppies . . . lilies . . . poppies and red calla lilies . . . and suddenly he saw . . . two small feet . . . olive-ivory . . . two well turned legs curving gracefully from slender ankles . . . and the contours soothed him . . . he followed them . . . past the narrow hips to the tiny waist . . . the fragile yet firm breasts . . . the graceful slender throat . . . the soft rounded chin . . . slightly parting lips . . . and straight little nose with its slightly flaring nostrils . . . the black eyes with lights in them . . . looking at him . . . the forehead and straight cut black hair . . . and it was Melva . . . and she looked at him and smiled and said . . . I'll wait Alex . . . and Alex became confused and kissed her . . . became confused and continued his search . . . on his hands and knees . . . pushed a poppy stem . . . a black-poppy stem . . . pushed aside a lily stem . . . a red lily stem . . . a poppy a poppy . . . a lily . . . and suddenly he stood erect . . . exultant . . . and in his hand he held . . . an ivory holder inlaid with red jade . . . and green . . .

and Alex awoke . . . Beauty's hair tickled his nose . . . Beauty was smiling in his sleep . . . half his face stained flush color by the sun . . . the other half in shadow . . . blue shadow . . . his eyelashes casting cobwebby blue shadows on his cheek . . . his lips were so beautiful . . . quizzical . . . Alex wondered why he always thought of that passage from Wilde's Salome when he looked at Beauty's lips . . . I would kiss your lips . . . he WOULD like to kiss Beauty's lips . . . Alex flushed warm . . . with shame . . . or was it shame . . . he reached across Beauty for a cigarette . . . Beauty's cheek

felt cool to his arm . . . his hair felt soft . . . Alex lay smoking
. . . such a dream . . . red calla lilies . . . red calla lilies . . . and
. . . what could it all mean . . . did dreams have meanings . . .
Fania said . . . and black poppies . . . thousands . . . millions . . .
Alex put out his cigarette . . . closed his eyes . . . he mustn't see
Beauty yet . . . speak to him . . . his lips were too hot . . . dry
. . . the palms of his hands too cool and moist . . . thru his half
closed eyes he could see Beauty . . . propped . . . cheek in hand
. . . on one elbow . . . looking at him . . . lips smiling quizzically
. . . he wished Beauty wouldn't look so hard . . . Alex was finding
it difficult to breathe . . . breathe normally . . . why MUST Beauty
look so long . . . and smile that way . . . his face seemed nearer
. . . it was . . . Alex could feel Beauty's hair upon his forehead . . .
breathe normally . . . breathe normally . . . could feel Beauty's
breath upon his nostrils and lips . . . and it was clean and faintly
colored with tobacco . . . breathe normally Alex . . . Beauty's lips
were nearer . . . Alex closed his eyes . . . how did none act . . . his
pulse was hammering . . . from wrist to fingertip . . . Beauty's lips
touched his . . . his temples throbbed . . . throbbed . . . his pulse
hammered from wrist to fingertip . . . Beauty's breath came short
now . . . softly staccato . . . breathe normally Alex . . . you are
asleep . . . Beauty's lips touched his . . . breathe normally . . . and
pressed hard . . . hard and cool . . . his body trembled . . . breathe
normally Alex . . . Beauty's lips pressed hard . . . hard and cool
. . . how much pressure does it take to waken one . . . Alex sighed
. . . moved softly . . . how does one act . . . Beauty's hair barely
touched him now . . . his breath was faint on . . . Alex's nostrils
. . . and lips . . . Alex stretched and opened his eyes . . . Beauty
was looking at him . . . propped on one elbow . . . cheek in his
palm . . . Beauty spoke . . . scratch my head please Dulce . . . Alex
was breathing normally now . . . propped against the bed-head
. . . Beauty's head in his lap . . . Beauty spoke . . . I wonder why
I like to look at some things Dulce . . . things like smoke and cats
. . . and . . . you . . . Alex's pulse no longer hammered from wrist
to fingertip . . . wrist to fingertip . . . the rose dusk had become
blue night . . . and soon . . . soon they would go out into the
blue. . . .

LANGSTON HUGHES

HARLEM, APPEARING IN NOVEMBER 1928, *was essentially a reprise of* Fire!! *Langston Hughes's contribution was "Luani of the Jungles," an engrossing piece about a star-crossed interracial romance set in West Africa. A Frenchman of an intellectual bent discovers that the beautiful, sophisticated Nigerian woman he married in Paris, Luani, has put away her European clothes and taken an African lover soon after they reach Lagos. " 'I'm sorry,' she replied with emotion. 'A woman can have two lovers and love them both.' " The European sails four times for France—only to return. The narrator, Hughes himself, encounters the distressed Frenchman sailing to West Africa and his unfaithful wife for the fifth time.*

The excerpt titled "Thursday Afternoon" portrays the yawning chasm between the generations at the heart of Hughes's novel Not Without Laughter, *released by Knopf in 1930. The novel was a huge success, winning the Harmon gold medal, enjoyed alike by white people and black people, by the author's flinty patron, Mrs. R. Osgood Mason, and by the demanding editor of* The Crisis, *W. E. B. Du Bois. Aunt Hager Williams and her family are a microcosm of evolving Afro-America, beleaguered by racism, urban pressures, and changing values. Harriet is Hager's sharp-witted harlot daughter who blasphemes against the church, mocks her mother's pleas for respectability, and becomes a successful blues singer. Annjee, living a day at a time in a Chicago slum, is defeated by the forces of the city. The straitlaced, married, and desperately respectable Tempy (she reads* The Crisis) *raises a family that will take its proud place among the Talented Tenth. The bewildered young boy, Sandy, Annjee's son, studies these women in order to catch a clue, amid the turning-point crises of male adolescence, to his own survival. Intuiting, even when comforted by them, that his grandmother Hager's simple religious ideals (the church that sustained black folk in the past) will be of no more use than a rabbit's foot when he reaches manhood, Sandy, symbol of the race's future, gropes for a formula.*

The collection of fourteen short stories The Ways of White Folks *(1933) contained "Father to Son," an unsentimentalized tale about a suicidally defiant mulatto, Bert, and his caste-ridden white planter father, Colonel Thomas Norwood. Returning home for the summer from college, the Colonel's proud natural son challenges his father to recognize him and disastrously violates the race relations etiquette of the small Southern town. The story was adapted for Broadway as* Mulatto.

In "The Blues I'm Playing," Hughes travestied a thinly disguised Charlotte Osgood Mason ("Godmother"), the patron who had haughtily abandoned him, and the ideologues of the Renaissance. Oceola, a poor young woman from Mobile, Alabama, and something of a musical prodigy, becomes the increasingly unhappy ward of rich, elderly Mrs. Ellsworth. Oceola's simple verdict on the engendering ideology of the Harlem Renaissance spoke for most of the younger artists: " 'And as for the cultured Negroes who were always saying art would break down color lines, art could save the race and prevent lynchings! Bunk!' said Oceola. 'Ma Ma and Pa were both artists when it came to making music, and the white folks ran them out of town for being dressed up in Alabama.' "

LUANI OF THE JUNGLES

"NOT ANOTHER SHILLING," I said. "You must think I'm a millionaire or something. Here I am offering you my best hat, two shirts, and a cigar case, with two shillings besides, and yet you want five shillings more! I wouldn't give five shillings for six monkeys, let alone a mean-looking beast like yours. Come on, let's make a bargain. What do you say?"

But the African, who had come to the wharf on the Niger to sell his monkey remained adamant. "Five shillin' more," he said. "Five shillin'. Him one fine monkey!" However, when he held up the little animal for me to touch, the frightened beast opened his white-toothed mouth viciously and gave a wild scream. "Him no bite," assured the native. "Him good."

"Yes, he's good all right," said Porto Rico sarcastically. "We'll get a monkey at Burutu cheaper, anyhow. It'd take a year to tame this one."

"I won't buy him," I protested to the native. "You want too much."

"But he is a fine monkey," an unknown voice behind us said, and we turned to see a strange, weak-looking little white man standing there. "He is a good monkey," the man went on in a foreign sort of English. "You ought to buy him here. Not often you get a red monkey of this breed. He is rare."

Then the stranger, who seemed to know whereof he spoke, told us that the animal was worth much more than the native asked, and he advised me softly to pay the other five shillings. "He is like a monkey in a poem," the man said. Meanwhile the slender simian clung tightly to the native's shoulder and snarled shrilly whenever I tried to touch him. But the very wildness of the poor captured beast with the wire cord about his hairy neck fascinated me. Given confidence by the stranger, for one old hat, two blue shirts, a broken cigar case, and seven shillings, I bought the animal. Then for fear of being bitten, I wrapped the wild little thing in my coat, carried him up the gangplank of the "West Illana" and put him into an empty prune box standing near the galley door. Porto Rico and the stranger followed and I saw that Porto Rico carried a large valise, so I surmised that the stranger was a new passenger.

The "West Illana," a freight boat from New York to West Africa, seldom carried passengers other than an occasional trader or a few poor missionaries. But when, as now, we were up one of the tributaries of the Niger, where English passenger steamers seldom came, the captain sometimes consented to take on travellers to the coast. The little white man with the queer accent registered for Lagos, a night's journey away. After he had been shown his stateroom he came out on deck and, in a friendly sort of manner, began to tell me about the various methods of taming wild monkeys. Yet there was a vague far-off air about him as though he were not really interested in what he was saying. He took my little beast in his hands and I noticed that the animal did not bite him nor appear particularly alarmed.

It was late afternoon then and all our cargo for that port,— six Fords from Detroit and some electric motors,—had been unloaded. The seamen closed the hatch, the steamer swung slowly away from the wharf with a blast of the whistle and began to glide lazily down the river. Soon we seemed to be floating through the heart of a dense sullen jungle. A tangled mass of trees and vines walled in the sluggish stream and grew out of the very water itself. None of the soil of the river bank could be seen,—only an impenetrable thickness of trees and vines. Nor were there the brilliant jungle trees one likes to imagine in the tropics. They were rather a monotonous grey-green confusion of trunks and leaves with only an occasional cluster of smoldering scarlet flowers or, very seldom, the flash of some bright-winged bird to vary their hopelessness. Once or twice this well of ashey vegetation was broken by a muddy brook or a little river joining the larger stream and giving, along murkey lengths, a glimpse into the further depths of this colorless and forbidding country. Then the river gradually widened and we could smell the sea, but it was almost dinner time before the ship began to roll slowly on the ocean's green and open waters. When I went into the salon to set the officers' table we were still very near the Nigerian coast and the grey vines and dull trees of the delta region.

After dinner I started aft to join Porto Rico and the seamen, but I saw the little white man seated on one of the hawser posts near the handrail so I stopped. It was dusk and the last glow of sunset was fading on the edge of the sea. I was surprised to find this friend of the afternoon seated there because passengers seldom ventured far from the comfortable deck chairs near the salon.

"Good evening," I said.

"Bon soir," answered the little man.

"Vous êtes francais?" I asked, hearing his greeting.

"Non," he replied slowly. "I am not French, but I lived in Paris for a long while." Then he added for seemingly no reason at all. "I am a poet, but I destroy my poems."

The gold streak on the horizon turned to orange.

There was nothing I could logically say except. "Why?"

"I don't know," he said. "I don't know why I destroy my poems. But then there are many things I don't know. . . . I live back in that jungle." He pointed toward the coast. "I don't know why."

The orange in the sunset darkened to blue.

"But why," I asked again stupidly.

"My wife is there," he said. "She is an African."

"Is she?" I could think of nothing other to say.

The blue on the horizon greyed to purple now.

"I'm trying to get away," he went on, paying no attention to my remark. "I'm going down to Lagos now. Maybe I'll forget to come back—back there." And he pointed to the jungles hidden in the distant darkness of the coast. "Maybe I'll forget to come back this time. But I never did before,—not even when I was drunk. I never forgot. I always came back. Yet I hate that woman!"

"What woman?" I asked.

"My wife," he said. "I love her and yet I hate her."

The sea and the sky were uniting in darkness.

"Why?" was again all I could think of saying.

"At Paris," he went on. "I married her at Paris." Then suddenly to me, "Are you a poet, too?"

"Why, yes," I replied.

"Then I can talk to you," he said. "I married her at Paris four years ago when I was a student there in the Sorbonne." As he told his story the night became very black and the stars were warm. "I met her one night at the Bal Bulier,—this woman I love. She was with an African student whom I knew and he told me that she was the daughter of a wealthy native in Nigeria. At once I was fascinated. She seemed to me the most beautiful thing I had ever seen,—dark and wild, exotic and strange,—accustomed as I had been to only pale white women. We sat down at a table and began to talk together in English. She told me she was educated in England but that she lived in Africa. 'With my tribe,' she said. 'When I am home I do not wear clothes like these, nor these things on my fingers.' She touched her evening gown and held out her dark hands sparkling with diamonds. 'Life is simple when I am home,' she said. 'I don't like it here. It is too cold and people wear too many clothes.' She lifted a cigarette holder of platinum and jade to her lips and blew a thin line of smoke into the air. 'Mon dieu!' I thought to myself. 'A child of sophistication and simplicity such as I have never seen!' And suddenly before I knew it, crazy young student that I was, I had leaned across the table and was saying, 'I love you.'

" 'That is what he says, too,' she replied, pointing toward the African student dancing gaily with a blonde girl at the other end of the room. 'You haven't danced with me yet.' We rose. The orchestra played a Spanish waltz full of Gypsy-like nostalgia and the ache of desire. She waltzed as no woman I had ever danced with before could waltz,—her dark body close against my white one, her head on my shoulder, its mass of bushy hair tangled and wild, perfumed with a jungle-scent. I wanted her! I ached for her! She seemed all I had ever dreamed of; all the romance I'd ever found in books; all the lure of the jungle countries; all the passions of the tropic soul.

" 'I need you,' I said. 'I love you.' Her hand pressed mine and our lips met, wedged as we were in the crowd of the Bal Bulier.

" 'I'm sailing from Bordeaux at the end of the month,' she told me as we sat in the Gardens of the Luxemburg at sunset a few days later. 'I'm going back home to the jungle countries and you are coming with me.' "

" 'I know it.' I agreed, as though I had been planning for months to go with her.

" 'You are coming with me back to my people,' she continued. 'You with your whiteness coming to me and my dark land. Maybe I won't love you then. Maybe you won't love me,—but the jungle'll take you and you'll stay there forever.'

" 'It won't be the jungle making me stay,' I protested. 'It'll be you. You'll be the ebony goddess of my heart, the dark princess who saved me from the corrupt tangle of white civilization, who took me away from my books into life, who discovered for me the soul of your dark countries. You'll be the tropic flower of my heart.

"During the following days before our sailing, I made many poems to this black woman I loved and adored. I dropped my courses at the Sorbonne that week and wrote my father in Prague that I would be going on a journey south for my health's sake. I changed my account to a bank in Lagos in West Africa, and paid farewell calls on all my friends in Paris. So much did I love Luani that I had no regrets on taking leave of my classmates nor upon saying adieux to the city of light and joy.

"One night in July we sailed from Bordeaux. We had been married the day before in Paris.

"In August we landed at Lagos and came by river boat to the very wharf where you saw me today. But in the meantime something was lost between us,—something of the first freshness of love that I've never found again. Perhaps it was because of the many days together hour after hour on the boat,—perhaps she saw too much for me. Anyway, when she took off her European clothes at the Liberty Hotel in Lagos to put on the costume of her tribe, and when she sent to the steel safe at the English bank there all of her diamonds and pearls, she seemed to put me away, too, out of her heart, along with the foreign things she had removed from her body. More fascinating than ever in the dress of her people, with the soft cloth of scarlet about her limbs and the little red sandals of buffalo hide on her feet,—more fascinating than ever and yet farther away she seemed, elusive, strange. And she began that day to talk to some of the servants in the language of her land.

"Up to the river town by boat, and then we travelled for days deep into the jungles. After a week we arrived at a high clear space surrounded by bread-fruit, mango, and cocoanut trees. There a hundred or more members of the tribe were waiting to receive her,—beautiful brown-black people whose perfect bodies glistened in the sunlight, bodies that shamed me and the weakness under my European clothing. That night there was a great festival given in honor of Luani's coming,—much beating of drums and wild fantastic dancing beneath the moon,—a festival in which I could take no part for I knew none of their ceremonies, none of their dances. Nor did I understand a word of their language. I could only stand aside and look, or sit in the door of our hut and sip the palm wine they served me. Luani, wilder than any of the others, danced to the drums, laughed and was happy. She seemed to have forgotten me sitting in the doorway of our hut drinking palm wine.

"Weeks passed and months. Luani went hunting and fishing, wandering about for days in the jungles. Sometimes she asked me to go with her, but more often she went with members of the tribe and left me to walk about the village, understanding nobody, able to say almost nothing. No one molested me. I was seemingly respected or at least ignored. Often when Luani was with me she would speak no French or English all day, unless I asked her something. She seemed almost to have forgotten the European languages, to have put them away as she had put away the clothes and customs of the foreigners. Yet she would come when I called and let me kiss her. In a far-off strange sort of way she still seemed to love me. Even then I was happy because I loved her and could hold her body.

"Then one night, trembling from an ugly dream, I suddenly awoke, sat up in bed and discovered in a daze that she was not beside me. A cold sweat broke out on my body. The room was empty. I leaped to the floor and opened the door of the hut. A great streak of moonlight fell across the threshold. A little breeze was blowing and the leaves of the mango trees rustled dryly. The sky was full of stars. I stepped into the grassy village street,—quiet all around. Filled with worry and fear, I called. 'Luani!' As far as I could see the tiny huts were quiet under the moon and no one answered. I was suddenly weak and afraid. The indifference of the silence unnerved me. I called again, 'Luani!' A voice seemed to reply: 'To the palm forest, to the palm forest. Quick, to the palm forest!' And I began to run toward the edge of the village where a great cocoanut grove lay.

"There beneath the trees it was almost as light as day and I sat down to rest against the base of a tall palm, while the leaves in the wind rustled dryly overhead. No other noise disturbed the night and I rested there wide awake remembering Paris and my student days at college. An hour must have passed when, through an aisle of the palm trees. I saw two naked figures walking. Very near me they came and then passed on in the moonlight,—two ebony bodies close together in the moonlight. They were Luani and the chief's young son. Awa Unabo.

"I did not move. Hurt and resentment, anger and weakness filled my veins. Unabo, the strongest and greatest hunter of the tribe, possessed the woman I loved. They were walking together in the moonlight, and weakling that I was, I dared not fight him. He'd break my body as though it were a twig. I could only rage in my futile English and no one except Luani would understand. . . . I went back to the hut. Just before dawn she came, taking leave of her lover at my door.

"Like a delicate statue carved in ebony, a dark halo about her head, she stood before me, beautiful and black like the very soul of the tropics, a woman to write poems about, a woman to go mad over. All the jealous anger died in my heart and only a great hurt remained and a feeling of weakness.

"I am going away, back to Paris," I said.

" 'I'm sorry,' she replied with emotion. 'A woman can have two lovers and love them both.' She put her arms around my neck but I pushed her away. She began to cry then and I cursed her in foreign, futile words. That same day, with two guides and four carriers, I set out through the jungles toward the Niger and the boat for Lagos. She made no effort to keep me back. One word from her and I could not have left the village, I knew. I would have been a prisoner,—but she did not utter that word. Only when I left the clearing she waved to me and said, 'You'll come back.'

"Once in Lagos, I engaged passage for Bordeaux, but when

the time came to sail I could not leave. I thought of her standing before me naked that last morning like a little ebony statue, and I tore up my ticket! I returned to the hotel and began to drink heavily in an effort to forget, but I could not. I remained drunk for weeks, then after some months had passed I boarded a river boat, went back up the Niger, back through the jungles,—back to her.

"Four times that has happened now. Four times I've left her and four times returned. She has borne a child for Awa Unabo. And she tells me that she loves him. But she says she loves me, too. Only one thing I do know,—she drives me mad. Why I stay with her, I do not know any longer. Why her lover tolerates me, I do not know. Luani humiliates me now,—and fascinates me, tortures me and holds me. I love her. I hate her, too. I write poems about her and destroy them. I leave her and come back. I do not know why. I'm like a mad man and she's like the soul of her jungles, quiet and terrible, beautiful and dangerous, fascinating and death-like. I'm leaving her again, but I know I'll come back. . . . I know I'll come back."

Slowly the moon rose out of the sea and the distant coast of Nigeria was like a shadow on the horizon. The "West Illana" rolled languidly through the night. I looked at the little white man, tense and pale, and wondered if he were crazy, or if he were lying.

"We reach Lagos early in the morning, do we not?" he asked. "I must go to sleep. Good night." And the strange passenger went slowly toward the door of the corridor that led to his cabin.

I sat still in the darkness for a few moments, dazed. Then I suddenly came to, heard the chug, chug, of the engines below and the half-audible conversation drifting from the fo'c's'ls, heard the sea lapping at the sides of the ship. Then I got up and went to bed.

FROM *NOT WITHOUT LAUGHTER*

THURSDAY AFTERNOON

HAGER HAD RISEN AT SUNRISE. On Thursdays she did the Reinharts' washing, on Fridays she ironed it, and on Saturdays she sent it home, clean and beautifully white, and received as pay the sum of seventy-five cents. During the winter Hager usually did half a dozen washings a week, but during the hot season her customers had gone away, and only the Reinharts, on account of an invalid grandmother with whom they could not travel, remained in Stanton.

Wednesday afternoon Sandy, with a boy named Jimmy Lane, called at the back door for their soiled clothes. Each child took a handle and between them carried the large wicker basket seven blocks to Aunt Hager's kitchen. For this service Jimmy Lane received five cents a trip, although Sister Lane had repeatedly said to Hager that he needn't be given anything. She wanted him to learn his Christian duties by being useful to old folks. But Jimmy was not inclined to be Christian. On the contrary, he was a very bad little boy of thirteen, who often led Sandy astray. Sometimes they would run with the basket for no reason at all, then stumble and spill the clothes out on the sidewalk—Mrs. Reinhart's summer dresses, and drawers, and Mr. Reinhart's extra-large B. V. D.'s lying generously exposed to the public. Sometimes, if occasion offered, the youngsters would stop to exchange uncouth epithets with strange little white boys who called them "niggers." Or, again, they might neglect their job for a game of marbles, or a quarter-hour of scrub baseball on a vacant lot; or to tease any little colored girl who might tip timidly by with her hair in tight, well-oiled braids —while the basket of garments would be left forlornly in the street without guardian. But when the clothes were safe in Aunt Hager's kitchen, Jimmy would usually buy candy with his nickel and share it with Sandy before he went home.

After soaking all night, the garments were rubbed through the suds in the morning; and in the afternoon the colored articles were on the line while the white pieces were boiling seriously in a large tin boiler on the kitchen-stove.

"They sho had plenty this week," Hager said to her grandson, who sat on the stoop eating a slice of bread and apple butter. "I's mighty late gettin' 'em hung out to dry, too. Had no business stoppin' this mawnin' to go see sick folks, and me here got all I can do maself! Looks like this warm weather old Mis' Reinhart must change ever' piece from her dress to her shimmy three times a day—sendin' me a washin' like this here!" They heard the screen-door at the front of the house open and slam. "It's a good thing they got me to do it fo' 'em! . . . Sandy, see who's that at de do'."

It was Harriett, home from the country club for the afternoon, cool and slender and pretty in her black uniform with its white collar, her smooth black face and neck powdered pearly, and her crinkly hair shining with pomade. She smelled nice and perfumy as Sandy jumped on her like a dog greeting a favorite friend. Harriett kissed him and let him hang to her arm as they went through the bedroom to the kitchen. She carried a brown cardboard suit-case and a wide straw hat in one hand.

"Hello, mama," she said.

Hager poked the boiling clothes with a vigorous splash of her round stick. The steam rose in clouds of soapy vapor.

"I been waitin' for you, madam!" her mother replied in tones that were not calculated to welcome pleasantly an erring daughter. "I wants to know de truth—was you in town last Monday night or not?"

Harriett dropped her suit-case against the wall. "You seem to have the truth," she said carelessly. How'd you get it? . . . Here, Sandy, take this out in the yard and eat it, seed and all." She gave her nephew a plum she had brought in her pocket. "I *was* in town, but I didn't have time to come home. I had to go to Maudel's because she's making me a dress."

"To Maudel's! . . . Unhuh! An' to de Waiters' Ball, besides galavantin' up an' down Pearl Street after ten o'clock! I wouldn't cared so much if you'd told me beforehand, but you said you didn't come in town 'ceptin' Thursday afternoon, an' here I was believing yo' lies."

"It's no lies! I haven't been in town before."

"Who brung you here at night anyhow—an' there ain't no trains runnin'?"

"O, I came in with the cook and some of the boys, mama, that's who! They hired an auto for the dance. What would be the use coming home, when you and Annjee go to bed before dark like chickens?"

"That's all right, madam! Annjee's got sense—savin' her health an' strength!"

Harriett was not impressed. "For what? To spend her life in Mrs. Rice's kitchen?" She shrugged her shoulders.

"What you bring yo' suit-case home fo'?"

"I'm quitting the job Saturday," she said. "I've told them already."

"Quitting!" her mother exclaimed. "What fo'? Lawd, if it ain't one thing, it's another!"

"What for?" Harriett retorted angrily. "There's plenty what for! All that work for five dollars a week with what little tips those pikers give you. And white men insulting you besides, asking you to sleep with 'em. Look at my finger-nails, all broke from scrubbing that dining-room floor." She thrust out her dark slim hands. "Waiting table and cleaning silver, washing and ironing table-linen, and then scrubbing the floor besides—that's too much of a good thing! And only three waitresses on the job. That old steward out there's a regular white folks' nigger. He don't care how hard he works us girls. Well, I'm through with the swell new Stanton Country Club this coming Saturday—I'm telling everybody!" She shrugged her shoulders again.

"What you gonna do then?"

"Maudel says I can get a job with her."

"Maudel? . . . Where?" The old woman had begun to wring the clothes dry and pile them in a large dish-pan.

"At the Banks Hotel, chambermaid, for pretty good pay."

Hager stopped again and turned decisively towards her daughter. "You ain't gonna work in no hotel. You hear me! They's dives o' sin, that's what they is, an' a child o' mine ain't goin' in one. If you was a boy, I wouldn't let you go, much less a girl! They ain't nothin' but strumpets works in hotels."

"Maudel's no strumpet." Harriett's eyes narrowed.

"I don't know if she is or ain't, but I knows I wants you to stop runnin' with her—I done tole you befo'. . . . Her mammy ain't none too straight neither, raisin' them chillen in sin. Look at Sammy in de reform school 'fore he were fifteen for gamblin'. An' de oldest chile, Essie, done gone to Kansas City with that yaller devil she ain't married. An' Maudel runnin' de streets night an' day, with you tryin' to keep up with her! . . . Lawd a mercy! . . . Here, hang up these clothes!"

Her mother pointed to the tin pan on the table filled with damp, twisted, white underwear. Harriett took the pan in both hands. It was heavy and she trembled with anger as she lifted it to her shoulders.

"You can bark at me if you want to, mama, but don't talk about my friends. I don't care what they are! Maudel'd do anything for me. And her brother's a good kid, whether he's been in reform school or not. They oughtn't to put him there just for shooting dice. What's that? I like him, and I like Mrs. Smothers, too. She's not always scolding people for wanting a good time and for being lively and trying to be happy."

Hot tears raced down each cheek, leaving moist lines in the

pink powder. Sandy, playing marbles with Buster under the apple-tree, heard her sniffling as she shook out the clothes and hung them on the line in the yard.

"You Sandy," Aunt Hager called loudly from the kitchen-door. "Come in here an' get me some water an' cut mo' firewood." Her black face was wet with perspiration and drawn from fatigue and worry. "I got to get the rest o' these clothes out yet this evenin'. . . . That chile Harriett's aggravatin' me to death! Help me, Sandy, honey."

They ate supper in silence, for Hager's attempts at conversation with her young daughter were futile. Once the old woman said: "That onery Jimboy's comin' home Saturday," and Harriett's face brightened a moment.

"Gee, I'm glad," she replied, and then her mouth went sullen again. Sandy began uncomfortably to kick the table-leg.

"For Christ's sake!" the girl frowned, and the child stopped, hurt that his favorite aunt should yell at him peevishly for so slight an offense.

"Lawd knows, I wish you'd try an' be mo' like yo' sisters, Annjee an' Tempy," Hager began as she washed the dishes, while Harriett stood near the stove, cloth in hand, waiting to dry them. "Here I is, an old woman, an' you tries ma soul! After all I did to raise you, you don't even hear me when I speak." It was the old theme again, without variation. "Now, there's Annjee, ain't a bet-ter chile livin'—if she warn't crazy 'bout Jimboy. An' Tempy mar-ried an' doin' well, an' respected ever'where. . . . An' you runnin' wild!"

"Tempy?" Harriett sneered suddenly, pricked by this compar-ison. "So respectable you can't touch her with a ten-foot pole, that's Tempy! . . . Annjee's all right, working herself to death at Mrs. Rice's, but don't tell me about Tempy. Just because she's married a mail-clerk with a little property, she won't even see her own family any more. When niggers get up in the world, they act just like white folks—don't pay you no mind. And Tempy's that kind of a nigger—she's up in the world now!"

"Close yo' mouth, talking that way 'bout yo' own sister! I ain't asked her to be always comin' home, is I, if she's satisfied in her own house?"

"No, you aren't asking her, mama, but you're always talking about her being so respectable. . . . Well, I don't want to be re-spectable if I have to be stuck up and dicty like Tempy is. . . . She's

colored and I'm colored and I haven't seen her since before Easter.
. . . It's not being black that matters with her, though, it's being
poor, and that's what we are, you and me and Annjee, working
for white folks and washing clothes and going in back doors, and
taking tips and insults. I'm tired of it, mama! I want to have a
good time once in a while."

"That's 'bout all you does have is a good time," Hager said.
"An' it ain't right, an' it ain't Christian, that's what it ain't! An'
de Lawd is takin' notes on you!" The old woman picked up the
heavy iron skillet and began to wash it inside and out.

"Aw, the church has made a lot of you old Negroes act like
Salvation Army people," the girl returned, throwing the dried
knives and forks on the table. "Afraid to even laugh on Sundays,
afraid for a girl and boy to look at one another, or for people to
go to dances. Your old Jesus is white, I guess, that's why! He's
white and stiff and don't like niggers!"

Hager gasped while Harriett went on excitedly, disregarding
her mother's pain: "Look at Tempy, the highest-class Christian in
the family—Episcopal, and so holy she can't even visit her own
mother. Seems like all the good-time people are bad, and all the
old Uncle Toms and mean, dried-up, long-faced niggers fill the
churches. I don't never intend to join a church if I can help it."

"Have mercy on this chile! Help her an' save her from hell-
fire! Change her heart, Jesus!" the old woman begged, standing in
the middle of the kitchen with uplifted arms. "God have mercy on
ma daughter."

Harriett, her brow wrinkled in a steady frown, put the dishes
away, wiped the table, and emptied the water with a splash
through the kitchen-door. Then she went into the bedroom that
she shared with her mother, and began to undress. Sandy saw,
beneath her thin white underclothes, the soft black skin of her
shapely young body.

"Where you goin'?" Hager asked sharply.

"Out," said the girl.

"Out where?"

"O, to a barbecue at Willow Grove, mama! The boys are coming by in an auto at seven o'clock."

"What boys?"

"Maudel's brother and some fellows."

"You ain't goin' a step!"

A pair of curling-irons swung in the chimney of the lighted

lamp on the dresser. Harriett continued to get ready. She was making bangs over her forehead, and the scent of scorching hair-oil drifted by Sandy's nose.

"Up half de night in town Monday, an' de Lawd knows how late ever' night in de country, an' then you comes home to run out again! . . . You ain't goin'!" continued her mother.

Harriett was pulling on a pair of red silk stockings, bright and shimmering to her hips.

"You quit singin' in de church choir. You say you ain't goin' back to school. You won't keep no job! Now what *is* you gonna do? Yo' pappy said years ago, 'fore he died, you was too purty to 'mount to anything, but I ain't believed him. His last dyin' words was: 'Look out fo' ma baby Harriett.' You was his favorite chile. . . . Now look at you! Runnin' de streets an' wearin' red silk stockings!" Hager trembled. "'Spose yo' pappy was to come back an' see you?"

Harriett powdered her face and neck, pink on ebony, dashed white talcum at each arm-pit, and rubbed her ears with perfume from a thin bottle. Then she slid a light blue dress of many ruffles over her head. The skirt ended midway between the ankle and the knee, and she looked very cute, delicate, and straight, like a black porcelain doll in a Vienna toy shop.

"Some o' Maudel's makin's, that dress—anybody can tell," her mother went on quarrelling. "Short an' shameless as it can be! Regular bad gal's dress, that's what 'tis. . . . What you puttin' it on fo' anyhow, an' I done told you you ain't goin' out? You must think I don't mean ma words. Ain't more'n sixteen last April an' runnin' to barbecues at Willer Grove! De idee! When I was yo' age, wasn't up after eight o'clock, 'ceptin' Sundays in de church house, that's all. . . . Lawd knows where you young ones is headin'. An' me prayin' an' washin' ma fingers to de bone to keep a roof over yo' head."

The sharp honk of an automobile horn sounded from the street. A big red car, full of laughing brown girls gaily dressed, and coatless, slick-headed black boys in green and yellow silk shirts, drew up at the curb. Somebody squeezed the bulb of the horn a second time and another loud and saucy honk! struck the ears.

"You Sandy," Hager commanded. "Run out there an' tell them niggers to leave here, 'cause Harriett ain't goin' no place."

But Sandy did not move, because his young and slender aunt had gripped him firmly by the collar while she searched feverishly in the dresser-drawer for a scarf. She pulled it out, long and flame-colored, with fiery, silky fringe, before she released the little boy.

"You ain't gwine a step this evenin'!" Hager shouted. "Don't you hear me?"

"O, no?" said Harriett coolly in a tone that cut like knives. "You're the one that says I'm not going—*but I am!*"

Then suddenly something happened in the room—the anger fell like a veil from Hager's face, disclosing aged, helpless eyes full of fear and pain.

"Harriett, honey, I wants you to be good," the old woman stammered. The words came pitiful and low—not a command any longer—as she faced her terribly alive young daughter in the ruffled blue dress and the red silk stockings. "I just wants you to grow up decent, chile. I don't want you runnin' to Willer Grove with them boys. It ain't no place fo' you in the night-time—an' you knows it. You's mammy's baby girl. She wants you to be good, honey, and follow Jesus, that's all."

The baritone giggling of the boys in the auto came across the yard as Hager started to put a timid, restraining hand on her daughter's shoulder—but Harriett backed away.

"You old fool!" she cried. "Lemme go! You old Christian fool!"

She ran through the door and across the sidewalk to the waiting car, where the arms of the young men welcomed her eagerly. The big machine sped swiftly down the street and the rapid sput! sput! sput! of its engine grew fainter and fainter. Finally, the auto was only a red tail-light in the summer dusk. Sandy, standing beside his grandmother in the doorway, watched it until it disappeared.

FROM *THE WAYS OF WHITE FOLKS*

FATHER AND SON

COLONEL THOMAS NORWOOD STOOD in his doorway at the Big House looking down the dusty plantation road. Today his youngest son was coming home. A heavy Georgia spring filled the morning air with sunshine and earth-perfumes. It made the old man feel strangely young again. Bert was coming home.

Twenty years ago he had begotten him.

This boy, however, was not his real son, for Colonel Thomas Norwood had no real son, no white and legal heir to carry on the Norwood name; this boy was a son by his Negro mistress, Coralee Lewis, who kept his house and had borne him all his children.

Colonel Norwood never would have admitted, even to himself, that he was standing in his doorway waiting for this half-Negro son to come home. But in truth that is what he was doing. He was curious about this boy. How would he look after all these years away at school? Six or seven surely, for not once in that long time had he been allowed to come back to Big House Plantation. The Colonel had said then that never did he want to see the boy. But in truth he did—for this boy had been, after all, the most beautiful of the lot, the brightest and the baddest of the Colonel's five children, lording it over the other children, and sassing not only his colored mother, but his white father, as well. Handsome and mischievous, favoring too much the Colonel in looks and ways, this boy Bert, at fourteen, had got himself sent off to school to stay. Now a student in college (or what they call a college in Negro terms in Georgia) he was coming home for the summer vacation.

Today his brother, Willie, had been sent to the station to meet him in the new Ford. The ten o'clock train must have reached the Junction by now, thought the Colonel, standing in the door. Soon the Ford would be shooting back down the road in a cloud of dust, curving past the tall white pillars of the front porch, and around to the kitchen stoop where Cora would greet her child.

Thinking thus, Colonel Norwood came inside the house, closed the screen, and pulled at a bell-cord hanging from the wall of the great dark living-room with its dignified but shabby horse hair furniture of the nineties. By and by, an old Negro servant, whose name was Sam and who wore a kind of old-fashioned butler's coat, came and brought the Colonel a drink.

"I'm going in my library where I don't want to be disturbed."

"Yes, suh," said the Negro servant.

"You hear me?"

"Yes, suh," said the servant, knowing that when Colonel Norwood said "library," he meant he did not want to be disturbed.

The Colonel entered the small room where he kept his books and papers of both a literary and a business nature. He closed the door. He did this deliberately, intending to let all the Negroes in the house know that he had no interest whatsoever in the home-coming about to take place. He intended to remain in the library several hours after Bert's arrival. Yet, as he bent over his desk peering at accounts his store-keeper had brought him, his head kept turning toward the window that gave on the yard and the road, kept looking to see if a car were coming in a cloud of dust.

An hour or so later, when shouts of welcome, loud warm Negro-cries, laughter, and the blowing of an auto horn filled the Georgia sunlight outside, the Colonel bent more closely over his ledgers—but he did turn his eyes a little to catch the dust sifting in the sunny air above the road where the car had passed. And his mind went back to that little olive-colored kid he had beaten one day in the stables years ago—the kid grown up now, and just come home.

He had always been a little ashamed of that particular beating he had given the boy. But his temper had got the best of him. That child, Bert, looking almost like a white child (a hell of a lot favoring the Colonel), had come running out to the stables one afternoon when he was showing his horses to some guests from in town. The boy had come up to him crying, "Papa!" (He knew better, right in front of company.) "Papa, Ma says she's got dinner ready."

The Colonel had knocked him down under the feet of the horses right there in front of the guests. And afterwards he had locked him in the stable and beaten him severely. The boy had to learn not to call him papa, and certainly not in front of white people from the town.

But it had been hard to teach Bert anything, the Colonel ruminated. Trouble was, the boy was too smart. There were other unpleasant memories of that same saucy ivory-skinned youngster playing about the front yard, even running through the Big House, in spite of orders that Coralee's children and all other pickaninnies keep to the back of the house, or down in the Quarters. But as a child, Bert had never learned his place.

"He's too damn much like me," the Colonel thought. "Quick as hell. Cora's been telling me he's leading his class at the Institute, and a football captain. . . . H-m-m-m, so they waste their time playing football at these darkie colleges. . . . Well, anyway, he must be a smart darkie. Got my blood in him."

The Colonel had Sam bring some food into the library. He pretended to be extremely busy, and did not give the old Negro, bursting with news, a chance to speak. The Colonel acted as though he were unaware of the presence of the newly arrived boy on the plantation; or if he were aware, completely uninterested, and completely occupied.

But in the late afternoon, the Colonel got up from his desk, went out into the parlor, picked up an old straw hat, and strolled through the front door, across the wide-porticoed porch with its white pillars, and down the road toward the South Field. The Colonel saw the brown backs of his Negroes in the green cotton. He smelt the earth-scent of a day that had been long and hot. He turned off by the edge of a field, went down to the creek, and back toward the house along a path that took him through a grove of pecan trees skirting the old slave quarters, to the back door of the Big House.

Long before he approached the Big House, he could hear Negroes' voices, musical and laughing. Then he could see a small group of dark bare arms and faces about the kitchen stoop. Cora was sitting on a stool in the yard, probably washing fruit for jelly. Livonia, the fat old cook, was on the porch shelling peas for dinner. Seated on the stoop, and on the ground, and standing around, were colored persons the Colonel knew had no good reason to be there at that time of day. Some of them, when they saw the Colonel coming, began to move away, back toward the barns, or whatever work they were doing.

He was aware, too, standing in the midst of this group, of a tall young man in sporty white trousers, black-and-white oxfords, and a blue shirt. He looked very clean and well-dressed, like a white man. The Colonel took this to be his son, and a certain vibration shook him from head to foot. Across the wide dusty yard, their eyes met. The Colonel's brows came together, his shoulders lifted and went back as though faced by an indignity just suffered. His chin went up. And he began to think, on the way toward them, how he would walk through this group like a white man. The Negroes, of course, would be respectful and afraid, as usual. He would say merely, "Good evening, Bert," to this boy, his son, then wait a moment, perhaps, and see what the boy said before passing on into the house.

Laughter died and dripped and trickled away, and talk quieted, and silence fell degree by degree, each step the white man approached. A strange sort of stiffness like steel nearing steel grew and straightened between the colored boy in the black-and-white shoes and the old Colonel who had just come from looking at his fields and his Negroes working.

"Good evening, Bert," the Colonel said.

"Good evening, Colonel Tom," the boy replied quickly, politely, almost eagerly. And then, like a puppet pulled by some perverse string, the boy offered his hand.

The Colonel looked at the strong young near-white hand held out toward him, and made no effort to take it. His eyes lifted to the eyes of the boy, his son, in front of him. The boy's eyes did not fall. But a slow flush reddened the olive of his skin as the old man turned without a word toward the stoop and into the house. The boy's hand went to his side again. A hum of dark voices broke the silence.

This happened between father and son. The mother, sitting there washing plums in a pail, did not understand what had happened. But the water from which she took the plums felt cool to her hands that were suddenly burning hot. . . .

There are people (you've probably noted it also) who have the unconscious faculty of making the world spin around themselves, throb and expand, contract and go dizzy. Then, when they are gone away, you feel sick and lonesome and meaningless.

In the chemistry lab at school, did you ever hold a test tube, pouring in liquids and powders and seeing nothing happen until a *certain* liquid or a *certain* powder is poured in and then everything begins to smoke and fume, bubble and boil, hiss to foam, and sometimes even explode? The tube is suddenly full of action and movement and life. Well, there are people like those certain liquids or powders; at a given moment they come into a room, or into a town, even into a country—and the place is never the same again. Things bubble, boil, change. Sometimes the whole world is changed. Alexander came. Christ. Marconi. A Russian named Lenin.

Not that there is any comparing Bert to Christ or Lenin. But after he returned to the Big House Plantation that summer, life was never the same. From Bert's very first day on the place something was broken, something went dizzy. The world began to spin, to ferment, and move into a new action.

Not to be a *white folks' nigger*—Bert had come home with that idea in his head.

The Colonel sensed it in his out-stretched hand and his tall young body—and had turned his back and walked into the house. Cora with her hands in the cool water where the plums were, suddenly knew in her innermost soul a period of time had closed for her. That first night she prayed, cried in her room, asked the Lord why she had ever let her son come home. In his cabin Willie prayed, too, humble, Lord, humble. The Colonel rocked alone on his front porch sucking a black cigar and cussing bitterly at he knew not what. The hum and laughter of the Negro voices went on as usual on the vast plantation down to the last share-cropper's cabin, but not quite, not *quite* the same as they had been in the morning. And never to be the same again.

"Is you heard about Bert?"

Not to be a *white folks' nigger!*

Bow down and pray in fear and trembling, go way back in the dark afraid; or work harder and harder; or stumble and learn; or raise up your fist and strike—but once the idea comes into your head you'll never be the same again. Oh, test tube of life! Crucible of the South, find the right powder and you'll never be the same again—the cotton will blaze and the cabins will burn and the chains will be broken and men, all of a sudden, will shake hands, black men and white men, like steel meeting steel!

"The bastard," Bert said. "Why couldn't he shake hands with me? I'm a Norwood, too."

"Hush, son," said Cora with the cool water from the plums on her hands.

And the hum of the black voices that afternoon spread to the cabins, to the cotton fields, to the dark streets of the Junction, what Bert had said—Bert with the ivory-yellow skin and the tall proud young body, Bert come home not to be a white folks' nigger.

"Lawd, chile, Bert's come home. . . ."

"Lawd, chile, and he said . . ."

"Lawd, chile, he said . . ."

"Lawd, chile . . ."

"Lawd . . ."

July passed, and August. The hot summer sun marched across the skies. The Colonel ordered Bert to work in the fields. Bert had not done so. Talbot, the white foreman, washed his hands of it, saying that if he had his way, "that nigger would be run off the place."

For the Colonel, the summer was hectic enough, what with cotton prices dropping on the market; share-croppers restless and moving; one black field-hand beaten half to death by Talbot and the store-keeper because he "talked high" to a neighboring white planter; news of the Scottsboro trials and the Camp Hill shootings exciting black labor.

Colonel Norwood ordered the colored rural Baptist minister to start a revival and keep it going until he said stop. Let the Negroes sing and shout their troubles away, as in the past. White folks had always found revivals a useful outlet for sullen overworked darkies. As long as they were singing and praying, they forgot about the troubles of this world. In a frenzy of rhythm and religion, they laid their cross at the feet of Jesus.

Poor over-worked Jesus! Somehow since the War, he hadn't borne that cross so well. Too heavy, it's too heavy! Lately, Negroes seem to sense that it's not Jesus' cross, anyhow, it's their own. Only old people praise King Jesus any more. On the Norwood plantation, Bert's done told the young people to stop being white folks' niggers. More and more, the Colonel felt it was Bert who brought trouble into the Georgia summer. The revival was a failure.

One day he met the boy coming back from the river where he had been swimming. The Colonel lit into him with all the cuss words at his command. He told him in no uncertain language to get down in the South Field to work. He told him there would be no more school at Atlanta for him; that he would show him that just because Cora happened to be his mother, he was no more than any other nigger on the place. God damn him!

Bert stood silent and red in front of his father, looking as the Colonel must have looked forty years ago—except that he was a shade darker. He did not go down to the South Field to work. And all Cora's pleading could not make him go. Yet nothing happened. That was the strange thing about it. The Colonel did nothing—to Bert. But he lit into Cora, nagged and scolded her for days, told her she'd better get some sense into her boy's head if she wanted any skin left on his body.

So the summer passed. Sallie, having worked faithfully in the house throughout the hottest months, went away to school again. Bert remained sullenly behind.

The day that ends our story began like this:

The sun rose burning and blazing, flooding the earth with the heat of early autumn, making even the morning oppressive. Folks

got out of bed feeling like over-ripe fruit. The air of the morning
shimmered with heat and ill-humor. The night before, Colonel
Norwood had been drinking. He got up trembling and shaky, yelling for Cora to bring him something clean to put on. He went
downstairs cussing.

The Colonel did not want to eat. He drank black coffee, and
walked out on the tall-pillared porch to get a breath of air. He was
standing there looking through the trees at his cotton, when the
Ford swept by in a cloud of dust, past the front of the house and
down the highway to town. Bert was driving.

The Colonel cussed out loud, bit his cigar, turned and went
into the house, slamming the door, storming to Cora, calling up
the stairs where she was working, "What the hell does he think he
is, driving off to town in the middle of the morning? Didn't I tell
Bert not to touch that Ford, to stay down yonder in the fields and
work?"

"Yes, suh, Colonel Tom," Cora said. "You sure did."

"Tell him I want to see him soon as he comes back here. Send
him in here. And tell him I'll skin his yellow hide for him." The
Colonel spoke of Bert as though he were still a child.

"Yes, suh, Colonel Tom."

The day grew hotter and hotter. Heat waves rose from the fields.
Sweat dampened the Colonel's body. Sweat dampened the black
bodies of the Negroes in the cotton fields, too, the hard black bodies that had built the Colonel's fortune out of earth and sun and
barehanded labor. Yet the Colonel, in spite of the fact that he lived
on this labor, sat in his shaded house fanning that morning and
wondering what made niggers so contrary—he was thinking of
Bert—as the telephone rang. The fat and testy voice of his old
friend, Mr. Higgins, trembled at the other end of the wire. He was
calling from the Junction.

Accustomed as he was to his friend's voice on the phone, at
first the Colonel could not make out what he was saying. When
he did understand, his neck bulged and the palms of the hands that
held the phone were wet with sweat. Anger and shame made his
tall body stoop and bend like an animal about to spring. Mr. Higgins was talking about Bert.

"That yellow nigger . . ." Mr. Higgins said. "One of your
yard-niggers sassed . . ." Mr. Higgins said. "I thought I'd better

tell you . . ." Mr. Higgins said. "Everybody . . ." Mr. Higgins said.

The whole town was excited about Bert. In the heat of this oven-warm autumn day, the hot heads of the white citizens of the town had suddenly become inflamed about Bert. Mr. Higgins, county politician and Postmaster at the Junction, was well qualified to know. His Office had been the center of the news.

It seemed that Bert had insulted the young white woman who sold stamps and made out money-orders at the Post Office. And Mr. Higgins was telling the Colonel about it on the phone, warning him to get rid of Bert, that people around the Junction were getting sick and tired of seeing him.

At the Post Office this is what happened: a simple argument over change. But the young woman who sold the stamps was not used to arguing with Negroes, or being corrected by them when she made a mistake. Bert said, "I gave you a dollar," holding out the incorrect change. "You gave me back only sixty-four cents."

The young woman said, counting the change, "Yes, but you have eight three-cent stamps. Move on now, there're others waiting." Several white people were in line.

Bert said, "Yes, but eight times three is not thirty-six. You owe me twelve cents more."

The girl looked at the change and realized she was wrong. She looked at Bert—light near-white nigger with grey-blue eyes. You gotta be harder on those kind than you have on the black ones. An educated nigger, too! Besides it was hot and she wasn't feeling well. A light near-white nigger with grey eyes! Instead of correcting the change, she screamed, and let her head fall forward in front of the window.

Two or three white men waiting to buy stamps seized Bert and attempted to throw him out of the Post Office. Bert remembered he'd been a football player—and Colonel Norwood's son—so he fought back. One of the white men got a bloody mouth. Women screamed. Bert walked out of the Post Office, got in the Ford and drove away. By that time, the girl who sold stamps had recovered. She was telling everyone how Bert had insulted her.

"Oh, my God! It was terrible," she said.

"That's one nigger don't know his place, Tom," Mr. Higgins roared over the phone. "And it's your fault he don't—sendin' 'em off to school to be educated." The Colonel listened to his friend at the other end of the wire. "Why that yellow buck comes to my store and if he ain't waited on quick as the white folks are, he walks out. He said last week standin' out on my corner, he wasn't *all* nigger no how; said his name was Norwood—not Lewis, like the rest of Cora's family; said your plantation would be his when you passed out—and all that kind o' stuff, boasting to the niggers listening about you being his father." The Colonel almost dropped the phone. "Now, Tom, you know that stuff don't go 'round these parts o' Georgia. Ruinous to other niggers hearing that sort of talk, too. There ain't been no race trouble in our county for three years—since the Deekins lynching—but I'm telling you, Norwood, folks ain't gonna stand for this. I'm speaking on the quiet, but I see ahead. What happened this morning in the Post Office ain't none too good."

"When I get through with him," said the Colonel hoarsely, "you won't need to worry. Goodbye."

The white man came out of the library, yelled for Sam, shouted for Cora, ordered whisky. Drank and screamed.

"God damn that son of yours! I'm gonna kill him," he said to Cora. "Get out of here," he shouted at Sam, who came back with cigars.

Cora wept. The Colonel raved. A car shot down the road. The Colonel rushed out, brandishing a cane to stop it. It was Bert. He paid no attention to the old man standing on the steps of the pillared porch waving his stick. Ashen with fury, the Colonel came back into the house and fumbled with his keys at an old chest. Finally, a drawer opened and he took out a pistol. He went toward the door as Cora began to howl, but on the porch he became suddenly strengthless and limp. Shaking, the old man sank into a chair holding the gun. He would not speak to Cora.

Late in the afternoon, Colonel Norwood sent Cora for their son. The gun had been put away. At least Cora did not see it.

"I want to talk to that boy," the Colonel said. "Fetch him here." Damned young fool . . . bastard . . . of a nigger. . . .

"What's he gonna do to my boy?" Cora thought. "Son, be careful," as she went across the yard and down toward Willie's cabin to find Bert. "Son, you be careful. I didn't bear you for no white man to kill. Son, you be careful. You ain't white, don't you know that? You be careful. O, Lord God Jesus in heaven! Son, be careful!" Cora was crying when she reached Willie's door, crying all the way back to the Big House with her son.

"To hell with the old man," Bert said. "He ain't no trouble! Old as he is, what can he do to me?"

"Lord have mercy, son, is you crazy? Why don't you be like Willie? He ain't never had no fusses with de Colonel."

"White folks' nigger," Bert said.

"Why don't you talk sense?" Cora begged.

"Why didn't he keep his promise then and let me go back to school in Atlanta, like my sister? You said if I came home this summer he'd lemme go back to the Institute, didn't you? Then why didn't he?"

"Why didn't you act right, son? Oh-o-o!" Cora moaned. "You can't get nothin' from white folks if you don't act right."

"Act like Willie, you mean, and the rest of these cotton pickers? Then I don't want anything."

They had reached the back door now. It was nearly dark in the kitchen where Livonia was making biscuits.

"Don't rile him, Bert, child," Cora said as she took him through the house. "I don't know what he might do to you. He's got a gun."

"Don't worry 'bout me," Bert answered.

The setting sun made long paths of golden light across the parlor floor through the tall windows opening on the West. The air was thick and sultry with autumn heat. The Colonel sat, bent and old, near a table where there were whisky and cigars and a half-open drawer. When Bert entered he suddenly straightened up and the old commanding look came into his eyes. He told Cora to go upstairs to her room.

Of course, he never asked Bert to sit down.

The tall mulatto boy stood before his father, the Colonel. The old white man felt the steel of him standing there, like the steel of himself forty years ago. Steel of the Norwoods darkened now by Africa. The old man got up, straight and tall, too, and suddenly shook his fist in the face of the boy.

"You listen to me," he said, trembling with quiet. "I don't want to have to whip you again like I did when you were a child." He was almost hissing. "The next time I might kill you. I been running this plantation thirty-five years and never had to beat a nigger old as you are. Never had any trouble out of none of Cora's children before either, but you." The old man sat down. "I don't have trouble with my colored folks. They do what I say or what

Talbot says, and that's all there is to it. If they turn in crops, they
get a living. If they work for wages, they get paid. If they spend
their money on licker, or old cars, or fixing up their cabins—they
can do what they choose, long as they know their places and it
don't hinder their work. To Cora's young ones—you hear me,
boy?—I gave all the chances any nigger ever had in these parts.
More'n many a white child's had, too. I sent you off to school. I
gave your brother, Willie, that house he's living in when he got
married, pay him for his work, help him out if he needs it. None
of my darkies suffer. You went off to school. Could have kept on,
would have sent you back this fall, but I don't intend to pay for
no nigger, or white boy either if I had one, that acts the way you
been acting." Colonel Norwood got up again, angrily. "And certainly not for no black fool! I'm talking to *you* like this only because you're Cora's child—but you know damn well it's my habit
to *tell* people what to do, not discuss it with them. I just want to
know what's the matter with you, though—whether you're crazy
or not? And if you're not, you'd better change your ways a damn
sight or it won't be safe for you here, and you know it—venting
your impudence on white women, ruining my niggers, driving like
mad through the Junction, carrying on just as you please. I'm
warning you, boy, God damn it! . . . Now I want you to answer
me, and talk right." The old man sat down in his chair again by
the whisky bottle and the partly opened drawer. He took a drink.

"What do you mean, talk right?" Bert said.

"I mean talk like a nigger should to a white man," the Colonel
snapped.

"Oh, but I'm not a nigger, Colonel Norwood," Bert said, "I'm
your son."

The old man frowned at the boy in front of him. "Cora's son,"
he said.

"Fatherless?" Bert asked.

"Bastard," the old man said.

Bert's hands closed into fists, so the Colonel opened the
drawer where the pistol was. He took it out and laid it on the
table.

"You black bastard," he said.

"I've heard that before." Bert just stood there. "You're talking
about my mother."

"Well," the Colonel answered, his fingers playing over the surface of the gun, "what can you do about it?"

The boy felt his whole body suddenly tighten and pull. The muscles of his forearms rippled.

"Niggers like you are hung to trees," the old man went on.

"I'm not a nigger," Bert said. "Ain't you my father? And a hell of a father you are, too, holding a gun on me."

"I'll break your black neck for you," the Colonel shouted. "Don't talk to me like that!" He jumped up.

"You'll break my neck?" The boy stood his ground as the father came toward him.

"Get out of here!" The Colonel shook with rage. "Get out! Or I'll do more than that if I ever lay eyes on you again." The old man picked up the pistol from the table, yet the boy did not move. "I'll fill you full of bullets if you come back here. Get off this place! Get to hell out of this county! Now, tonight. Go on!" The Colonel motioned with his pistol toward the door that led to the kitchen and the back of the house.

"Not that way," Bert said. "I'm not your servant. You must think I'm scared. Well, you can't drive me out the back way like a dog. You're not going to run me off, like a field hand you can't use any more. I'll go," the boy said, starting toward the front door, "but not out the back—from my own father's house."

"You nigger bastard!" Norwood screamed, springing between his son and the door, but the boy kept calmly on. The steel of the gun was between them, but that didn't matter. Rather, it seemed to pull them together like a magnet.

"Don't you . . . ," Norwood began, for suddenly Bert's hand grasped the Colonel's arm, "dare put your . . . ," and his old bones began to crack, "black hands on . . ."

"Why don't you shoot?" Bert interrupted him, slowly turning his wrist.

". . . me!"

"Why don't you shoot, then?"

The old man twisted and bent in fury and pain, but the gun fell to the floor.

"Why don't you shoot?" Bert said again as his hands sought his father's throat. With furious sureness they took the old white neck in their strong young fingers. "Why don't you shoot then, papa?"

Colonel Norwood clawed the air, breathing hoarsely and loud, his tongue growing stiff and dry, his eyes beginning to burn.

"Shoot—why don't you, then? Huh? Why?"

The chemicals of their two lives exploded. Everything was very black around them. The white man's hands stopped clawing the air. His heart stood still. His blood no longer flowed. He wasn't breathing.

"Why don't you shoot?" Bert said, but there was no answer.

When the boy's eyes cleared, he saw his mother standing at the foot of the stairs, so he let the body drop. It fell with a thud, old and white in a path of red from the setting sun.

"Why didn't he shoot, mama? He didn't want me to live. He was white. Why didn't he shoot then?"

"Tom!" Cora cried, falling across his body. "Colonel Tom! Tom! Tom!"

"He's dead," Bert said. "I'm living though."

"Tom!" Cora screamed, pulling at the dead man. "Colonel Tom!"

Bert bent down and picked up the pistol. "This is what my father wanted to use on me," he said. "He's dead. But I can use it on all the white men in Georgia—they'll be coming to get me now. They never wanted me before, but I know they'll want me now." He stuffed the pistol in his shirt. Cora saw what her son had done.

"Run," she said, rising and going to him. "Run, chile! Out the front way quick, so's they won't see you in the kitchen. Make fo' de swamp, honey. Cross de fields fo' de swamp. Go de crick way. In runnin' water, dogs can't smell no tracks. Hurry, son!"

"Yes, mama," Bert said slowly. "But if I see they gonna get me before I reach the swamp, then I'm coming back here. Let them take me out of my father's house—if they can." He patted the gun inside his shirt, and smiled. "They'll never string me up to some roadside tree for the crackers to laugh at. Not me!"

"Hurry, chile," Cora opened the door and the sunset streamed in like a river of blood. "Hurry, chile."

Bert went out across the wide pillared porch and down the road. He saw Talbot and the storekeeper coming, so he turned off through the trees. And then, because he wanted to live, he began to run. The whole sky was a blaze of color as he ran. Then it began to get dark, and the glow went away.

In the house, Cora started to talk to the dead man on the floor, just as though he were not dead. She pushed and pulled at the body, trying to get him to get up himself. Then she heard the footsteps of Talbot and the storekeeper on the porch. She rose and stood as if petrified in the middle of the floor. A knock, and two men were peering through the screen door into the dusk-dark room. Then Talbot opened the door.

"Hello, Cora," he said. "What's the matter with you, why didn't you let us in? Where's that damn fool boy o' your'n goin', comin' out the front way liked he owned the place? What's the matter with you, woman? Can't you talk? Where's Colonel Norwood?"

"Let's have some light in here," said the storekeeper, turning a button beside the door.

"Great God!" Talbot cried. "Jim, look at this!" The Colonel's body lay huddled on the floor, old and purple-white, at Cora's feet.

"Why, he's blue in the face," the storekeeper said bending over the body. "Oh! Get that nigger we saw walking out the door! That nigger bastard of Cora's. Get that nigger! . . . Why, the Colonel's dead!"

Talbot rushed toward the door. "That nigger," he cried. "He must be running toward the swamps now. . . . We'll get him. Telephone town, Jim, there in the library. Telephone the sheriff. Telephone the Beale family down by the swamp. Get men, white men, after that nigger."

The storekeeper ran into the library and began to call on the phone. Talbot looked at Cora standing in the center of the room. "Where's Norwood's car? In the barn? Talk, you black wench, talk!"

But Cora didn't say a word. She watched the two white men rush out of the house into the yard. In a few minutes, she heard the roar of a motor hurtling down the road. It was dark outside. Night had come.

Cora turned toward the body on the floor. "My boy," she said, "he can't get to de swamp now. They telephoned the white folks down that way to head him off. He'll come back home." She called aloud, "Colonel Tom, why don't you get up from there and help me? You know they're after our boy. You know they got him out there runnin' from de white folks in de night. Runnin' from de hounds and de guns and de ropes and all what they use to kill poor niggers with. . . . Ma boy's out there runnin'. Why don't you help him?" Cora bent over the body. "Colonel Tom, you hear me? You said he was ma boy, ma bastard boy. I heard you. But he's your'n, too—out yonder in de dark runnin'—from your people. Why don't you get up and stop 'em? You know you could. You's a power in Polk County. You's a big man, and yet our son's out there runnin'—runnin' from po' white trash what ain't worth de little finger o' nobody's got your blood in 'em, Tom." Cora shook the dead body fiercely. "Get up from there and stop 'em, Colonel Tom." But the white man did not move.

Gradually Cora stopped shaking him. Then she rose and backed away from this man she had known so long. "You's cruel, Tom," she whispered. "I might a-knowed it—you'd be like that, sendin' ma boy out to die. I might a-knowed it ever since you beat him that time under de feet of de horses. Well, you won't mistreat him no more now. That's finished." She went toward the steps. "I'm gonna make a place for him. Upstairs under ma bed. He's ma chile, and I'll look out for him. And don't you come in ma bed-room while he's up there. Don't you come to my bed either no more a-tall. I calls for you to help me now, Tom, and you just lays there. I calls you to get up now, and you don't move. Whenever you called *me* in de night, I woke up. Whenever you wanted me to love you, I reached out ma arms to you. I bored you five children and now," her voice rose hysterically, "one of 'em's out yonder runnin' from your people. Our youngest boy's out yonder in de dark, runnin'! I 'spects you's out there, too, with de rest of de white folks. Uh-um! Bert's runnin' from *you,* too. You said he warn't your'n—Cora's po' little yellow bastard. But he is your'n, Colonel Tom, and he's runnin' from you. Yes, out yonder in de dark, you, *you* runnin' our chile with a gun in yo' hand, and Talbot followin' behind you with a rope to hang Bert with." She leaned against the wall near the staircase, sobbing violently. Then she went back to-ward the man on the floor. Her sobs gradually ceased as she looked down at his crumpled body. Then she said slowly, "Listen, I been sleepin' with you too long not to know that this ain't you, Tom, layin' down here with yo' eyes shut on de floor. You can't fool me—you ain't never been so still like this before—you's out yonder runnin' ma boy! Colonel Thomas Norwood runnin' ma boy through de fields in de dark, runnin' ma po' little helpless Bert through de fields in de dark for to lynch him and to kill him. . . . God damn you, Tom Norwood!" Cora cried, "God damn you!"

She went upstairs. For a long time the body lay alone on the floor in the parlor. Later Cora heard Sam and Livonia weeping and shouting in the kitchen, and Negro voices outside in the dark, and feet going down the road. She thought she heard the baying of hounds afar off, too, as she prepared a hiding place for Bert in the attic. Then she came down to her room and put the most beautiful quilts she had on her bed. "Maybe he'll just want to rest here first," she thought. "Maybe he'll be awful tired and just want to rest."

Then she heard a loud knock at the door, and white voices talking, and Sam's frightened answers. The doctor and the undertakers had come to take the body away. In a little while she heard them lifting it up and putting it in the dead wagon. And all the time, they kept talking, talking.

". . . 'll be havin' his funeral in town . . . ain't nothin' but niggers left out here . . . didn't have no relatives, did he, Sam? . . . Too bad. . . . Norwood to look after his stuff tonight. Every white man's able to walk's out with the posse . . . that young nigger'll swing before midnight . . . what a neck-tie party! . . . Say, Sam!"

"Yes, sah! Yes, sah!"

". . . that black housekeeper, Cora? . . . murderin' bastard's mother?"

"She's upstairs, I reckon, sah."

". . . like to see how she looks. Get her down here."

"Yes, sah!" Sam's teeth were chattering.

"And how about a little drink before we start back to town?"

"Yes, sah! Cora's got de keys fo' de licker, sah."

"Well, get her down, double quick, then!"

"Yes, sah!" Cora heard Sam coming up for her.

Downstairs, the voices went on. They were talking about her. ". . . lived together . . . ain't been a white woman here overnight since the wife died when I was a kid . . . bad business, though, livin' with a," in drawling cracker tones, "nigger."

As Cora came down the steps, the undertakers looked at her half-grinning. "So you're the black wench that's got these educated darkie children? Hum-m! Well I guess you'll see one of 'em swinging full o' bullet holes before you get up in the morning. . . . Or maybe they'll burn him. How'd you like a roasted darkie for breakfast, girlie?"

Cora stood quite still on the stairs. "Is that all you wanted to say to me?" she asked.

"Now, don't get smart," the doctor said. "Maybe you think there's nobody to boss you now. We're goin' to have a little drink before we go. Get out a bottle."

"I take ma orders from Colonel Norwood, suh," Cora said.

"Well, you'll take no more orders from him," the undertaker

declared. "He's outside in the dead wagon. Get along now and get out a bottle."

"He's out yonder with de mob," Cora said.

"I tell you he's in my wagon, dead as a door nail."

"I tell you he's runnin' with de mob," Cora said.

"I believe this black woman's done gone nuts," the doctor cried. "Sam, you get the licker."

"Yes, sah!" Sam sputtered with fright. "Co-r-r-ra, gimme . . ."

But Cora did not move.

"Ah-a-a-a, Lawd hab mercy!" Sam cried.

"To hell with the licker, Charlie," the undertaker said nervously. "Let's start back to town. We want to get in on some of that excitement, too. They should've found that nigger by now—and I want to see 'em drag him out here."

"All right, Jim," the other agreed. Then, to Cora, "But don't you darkies go to bed until you see the bonfire. You all are gettin' beside yourselves around Polk County. We'll burn a few more of you if you don't watch out."

The men left and the wheels of the wagon turned on the drive. Sam began to cry.

"Hab mercy! Lawd Jesus, hab mercy! Cora, is you a fool? *Is* you? Then why didn't you give de mens de licker, riled as these white folks is? In ma old age, is I gonna be burnt by de crackers? Lawd, is I sinned? Lawd, what has I done?" He looked at Cora. "I sho ain't gonna stay heah tonight. I's gwine."

"Go on," she said. "The Colonel can get his own drinks when he comes back."

"Lawd God Jesus!" Sam, his eyes bucking from their sockets, bolted from the room fast as his old legs could carry him. Cora heard him running blindly through the house, moaning.

She went to the kitchen where pots were still boiling on the stove, but Livonia had fled, the biscuits burnt in the oven. She looked out the back door, but no lights were visible anywhere. The cabins were quiet.

"I reckon they all gone," she said to herself. "Even ma boy, Willie. I reckon he gone, too. You see, Colonel Tom, everybody's scared o' you. They know you done gone with de mob again, like you did that time they hung Luke Jordan and you went to help 'em. Now you's out chasin' ma boy, too. I hears you hollerin'."

And sure enough, all around the Big House in the dark, in a wide far-off circle, men and dog-cries and auto-horns sounded in the night. Nearer they came even as Cora stood at the back door, listening. She closed the door, bolted it, put out the light, and went back to the parlor. "He'll come in by de front," she said. "Back from de swamp way. He won't let 'em stop him from gettin' home to me again, just once. Po' little boy, he ain't got no place to go, no how. Po' boy, what growed up with such pride in his heart. Just like you, Colonel Tom. Spittin' image o' you. . . . Proud! . . . And got no place to go."

Nearer and nearer the man-hunt came, the cries and the horns and the dogs. Headlights began to flash in the dark down the road. Off through the trees, Cora heard men screaming. And suddenly feet running, running, running. Nearer, nearer. She knew it was him. She knew they had seen him, too.

Then there were voices shouting very near the house.

"Don't shoot, men. We want to get him alive."

"Close in on him!"

"He must be in them bushes there by the porch."

"Look!"

And suddenly shots rang out. The door opened. Cora saw flashes of fire spitting into the blackness, and Bert's tall body in the doorway. He was shooting at the voices outside in the dark. The door closed.

"Hello, Ma," he said. "One or two of 'em won't follow me no further."

Cora locked the door as bullets splintered through the wood, shattered the window panes. Then a great volley of shots struck the house, blinding head-lights focused on the porch. Shouts and cries of, "Nigger! Nigger! Get the nigger!" filled the night.

"I was waitin' for you, honey," Cora said. "Quick! Your hidin' place's ready for you, upstairs in de attic. I sawed out a place under de floor. Maybe they won't find you, chile. Hurry, 'fore your father comes."

"No time to hide, Ma," Bert panted. "They're at the door now. They'll be coming in the back way, too. They'll be coming in the windows. They'll be coming in everywhere. I got one bullet left, Ma. It's mine."

"Yes, son, it's your'n. Go upstairs in mama's room and lay down on ma bed and rest. I won't let 'em come up till you're gone. God bless you, chile."

Quickly, they embraced. A moment his head rested on her shoulder.

"I'm awful tired running, Ma. I couldn't get to the swamp. Seems like they been chasing me for hours. Crawling through the cotton a long time, I got to rest now."

Cora pushed him toward the stairs. "Go on, son," she said gently.

At the top, Bert turned and looked back at this little brown woman standing there waiting for the mob. Outside the noise was terrific. Men shouted and screamed, massing for action. All at once they seemed to rush in a great wave for the house. They broke the doors and windows in, and poured into the room—a savage crowd of white men, red and wild-eyed, with guns and knives, sticks and ropes, lanterns and flashlights. They paused at the foot of the stairs where Cora stood looking down at them silently.

"Keep still, men," one of the leaders said. "He's armed. . . . Say where's that yellow bastard of yours, Cora—upstairs?"

"Yes," Cora said. "Wait."

"Wait, hell!" the men cried. "Come on, boys, let's go!"

A shot rang out upstairs, then Cora knew it was all right.

"Go on," she said, stepping aside for the mob.

The next morning when people saw a bloody and unrecognizable body hanging in the public square at the Junction, some said with a certain pleasure, "That's what we do to niggers down here," not realizing Bert had been taken dead, and that all the fun for the mob had been sort of stale at the end.

But others, aware of what had happened, thought, "It'd be a hell of a lot better lynching a live nigger. Say, ain't there nobody else mixed up in this here Norwood murder? Where's that boy's brother, Willie? Heh?"

So the evening papers carried this item in the late editions:

DOUBLE LYNCHING IN GEORGIA

A large mob late this afternoon wrecked vengeance on the second of two Negro field hands, the murderers of Colonel Thomas Norwood, wealthy planter found dead at Big House Plantation. Bert Lewis was lynched last night, and his brother, Willie Lewis, today. The sheriff of the county is unable to identify any members of the mob. Colonel Norwood's funeral has not yet been held. The dead man left no heirs.

THE BLUES I'M PLAYING

THEN BEGAN one of the most interesting periods in Mrs. Ellsworth's whole experience in aiding the arts. The period of Oceola. For the Negro girl, as time went on, began to occupy a greater and greater place in Mrs. Ellsworth's interests, to take up more and more of her time, and to use up more and more of her money. Not that Oceola ever asked for money, but Mrs. Ellsworth herself seemed to keep thinking of so much more Oceola needed.

At first it was hard to get Oceola to need anything. Mrs. Ellsworth had the feeling that the girl mistrusted her generosity, and Oceola did—for she had never met anybody interested in pure art before. Just to be given things for *art's sake* seemed suspicious to Oceola.

That first Tuesday, when the colored girl came back at Mrs. Ellsworth's request, she answered the white woman's questions with a why-look in her eyes.

"Don't think I'm being personal, dear," said Mrs. Ellsworth, "but I must know your background in order to help you. Now, tell me . . ."

Oceola wondered why on earth the woman wanted to help her. However, since Mrs. Ellsworth seemed interested in her life's history, she brought it forth so as not to hinder the progress of the afternoon, for she wanted to get back to Harlem by six o'clock.

Born in Mobile in 1903. Yes, ma'am, she was older than she looked. Papa had a band, that is her stepfather. Used to play for all the lodge turn-outs, picnics, dances, barbecues. You could get the best roast pig in the world in Mobile. Her mother used to play the organ in church, and when the deacons bought a piano after the big revival, her mama played that, too. Oceola played by ear for a long while until her mother taught her notes. Oceola played an organ, also, and a cornet.

"My, my," said Mrs. Ellsworth.

"Yes, ma'am," said Oceola. She had played and practiced on lots of instruments in the South before her step-father died. She always went to band rehearsals with him. . . .

That was some years ago. Eventually art and Mrs. Ellsworth triumphed. Oceola moved out of Harlem. She lived in Gay Street west of Washington Square where she met Genevieve Taggard, and

Ernestine Evans, and two or three sculptors, and a cat-painter who was also a protegee of Mrs. Ellsworth. She spent her days practicing, playing for friends of her patron, going to concerts, and reading books about music. She no longer had pupils or rehearsed the choir, but she still loved to play for Harlem house parties—for nothing—now that she no longer needed the money, out of sheer love of jazz. This rather disturbed Mrs. Ellsworth, who still believed in art of the old school, portraits that really and truly looked like people, poems about nature, music that had soul in it, not syncopation. And she felt the dignity of art. Was it in keeping with genius, she wondered, for Oceola to have a studio full of white and colored people every Saturday night (some of them actually drinking gin *from bottles*) and dancing to the most tom-tom-like music she had ever heard coming out of a grand piano? She wished she could lift Oceola up bodily and take her away from all that, for art's sake.

So in the spring, Mrs. Ellsworth organized weekends in the up-state mountains where she had a little lodge and where Oceola could look from the high places at the stars, and fill her soul with the vastness of the eternal, and forget about jazz. Mrs. Ellsworth really began to hate jazz—especially on a grand piano.

If there were a lot of guests at the lodge, as there sometimes were, Mrs. Ellsworth might share the bed with Oceola. Then she would read aloud Tennyson or Browning before turning out the light, aware all the time of the electric strength of that brown-black body beside her, and of the deep drowsy voice asking what the poems were about. And then Mrs. Ellsworth would feel very motherly toward this dark girl whom she had taken under her wing on the wonderful road of art, to nurture and love until she became a great interpreter of the piano. At such times the elderly white woman was glad her late husband's money, so well invested, furnished her with a large surplus to devote to the needs of her protegees, especially to Oceola, the blackest—and most interesting of all.

Why the most interesting?

Mrs. Ellsworth didn't know, unless it was that Oceola really was talented, terribly alive, and that she looked like nothing Mrs. Ellsworth had ever been near before. Such a rich velvet black, and such a hard young body! The teacher of the piano raved about her strength.

"She can stand a great career," the teacher said. "She has everything for it."

"Yes," agreed Mrs. Ellsworth, thinking, however, of the Pullman porter at Meharry, "but she must learn to sublimate her soul."

So for two years then, Oceola lived abroad at Mrs. Ellsworth's expense. She studied with Philippe, had the little apartment on the Left Bank, and learned about Debussy's African background. She met many black Algerian and French West Indian students, too, and listened to their interminable arguments ranging from Garvey to Picasso to Spengler to Jean Cocteau, and thought they all must be crazy. Why did they or anybody argue so much about life or art? Oceola merely lived—and loved it. Only the Marxian students seemed sound to her for they, at least, wanted people to have enough to eat. That was important, Oceola thought, remembering, as she did, her own sometimes hungry years. But the rest of the controversies, as far as she could fathom, were based on air.

Oceola hated most artists, too, and the word *art* in French or English. If you wanted to play the piano or paint pictures or write books, go ahead! But why talk so much about it? Montparnasse was worse in that respect than the Village. And as for the cultured Negroes who were always saying art would break down color lines, art could save the race and prevent lynchings! "Bunk!" said Oceola. "My ma and pa were both artists when it came to making music, and the white folks ran them out of town for being dressed up in Alabama. And look at the Jews! Every other artist in the world's a Jew, and still folks hate them."

She thought of Mrs. Ellsworth (dear soul in New York), who never made uncomplimentary remarks about Negroes, but frequently did about Jews. Of little Menuhin she would say, for instance, "He's a *genius*—not a Jew," hating to admit his ancestry.

In Paris, Oceola especially loved the West Indian ball rooms where the black colonials danced the beguin. And she liked the entertainers at Bricktop's. Sometimes late at night there, Oceola would take the piano and beat out a blues for Brick and the assembled guests. In her playing of Negro folk music, Oceola never doctored it up, or filled it full of classical runs, or fancy falsities. In the blues she made the bass notes throb like tom-toms, the trebles cry like little flutes, so deep in the earth and so high in the sky that they understood everything. And when the night club crowd would get up and dance to her blues, and Bricktop would yell, "Hey! Hey!" Oceola felt as happy as if she were performing a Chopin étude for the nicely gloved Oh's and Ah-ers in a Crillon salon.

Music, to Oceola, demanded movement and expression, danc-

ing and living to go with it. She liked to teach, when she had the
choir, the singing of those rhythmical Negro spirituals that possessed the power to pull colored folks out of their seats in the amen
corner and make them prance and shout in the aisles for Jesus. She
never liked those fashionable colored churches where shouting and
movement were discouraged and looked down upon, and where
New England hymns instead of spirituals were sung. Oceola's
background was too well-grounded in Mobile, and Billy Kersands'
Minstrels, and the Sanctified churches where religion was a joy, to
stare mystically over the top of a grand piano like white folks and
imagine that Beethoven had nothing to do with life, or that Schu-
bert's love songs were only sublimations.

Whenever Mrs. Ellsworth came to Paris, she and Oceola spent
hours listening to symphonies and string quartets and pianists.
Oceola enjoyed concerts, but seldom felt, like her patron, that she
was floating on clouds of bliss. Mrs. Ellsworth insisted, however,
that Oceola's spirit was too moved for words at such times—therefore she understood why the dear child kept quiet. Mrs. Ellsworth
herself was often too moved for words, but never by pieces like
Ravel's *Bolero* (which Oceola played on the phonograph as a
dance record) or any of the compositions of *les Six*.

What Oceola really enjoyed most with Mrs. Ellsworth was not
going to concerts, but going for trips on the little river boats in the
Seine; or riding out to old chateaux in her patron's hired Renault;
or to Versailles, and listening to the aging white lady talk about
the romantic history of France, the wars and uprisings, the loves
and intrigues of princes and kings and queens, about guillotines
and lace handkerchiefs, snuff boxes and daggers. For Mrs. Ellsworth had loved France as a girl, and had made a study of its life
and lore. Once she used to sing simple little French songs rather
well, too. And she always regretted that her husband never understood the lovely words—or even tried to understand them.

Oceola learned the accompaniments for all the songs Mrs.
Ellsworth knew and sometimes they tried them over together. The
middle-aged white woman loved to sing when the colored girl
played, and she even tried spirituals. Often, when she stayed at the
little Paris apartment, Oceola would go into the kitchen and cook
something good for late supper, maybe an oyster soup, or fried
apples and bacon. And sometimes Oceola had pigs' feet.

"There's nothing quite so good as a pig's foot," said Oceola,
"after playing all day."

"Then you must have pigs' feet," agreed Mrs. Ellsworth.

And all this while Oceola's development at the piano blossomed into perfection. Her tone became a singing wonder and her interpretations warm and individual. She gave a concert in Paris, one in Brussels, and another in Berlin. She got the press notices all pianists crave. She had her picture in lots of European papers. And she came home to New York a year after the stock market crashed and nobody had any money—except folks like Mrs. Ellsworth who had so much it would be hard to ever lose it all.

Oceola's one time Pullman porter, now a coming doctor, was graduating from Meharry that spring. Mrs. Ellsworth saw her dark protegee go South to attend his graduation with tears in her eyes. She thought that by now music would be enough, after all those years under the best teachers, but alas, Oceola was not yet sublimated, even by Philippe. She wanted to see Pete.

Oceola returned North to prepare for her New York concert in the fall. She wrote Mrs. Ellsworth at Bar Harbor that her doctor boy-friend was putting in one more summer on the railroad, then in the autumn he would intern at Atlanta. And Oceola said that he had asked her to marry him. Lord, she was happy!

It was a long time before she heard from Mrs. Ellsworth. When the letter same, it was full of long paragraphs about the beautiful music Oceola had within her power to give the world. Instead, she wanted to marry and be burdened with children! Oh, my dear, my dear!

Oceola, when she read it, thought she had done pretty well knowing Pete this long and not having children. But she wrote back that she didn't see why children and music couldn't go together. Anyway, during the present depression, it was pretty hard for a beginning artist like herself to book a concert tour—so she might just as well be married awhile. Pete, on his last run in from St. Louis, had suggested that they have the wedding Christmas in the South. "And he's impatient, at that. He needs me."

This time Mrs. Ellsworth didn't answer by letter at all. She was back in town in late September. In November, Oceola played at Town Hall. The critics were kind, but they didn't go wild. Mrs. Ellsworth swore it was because of Pete's influence on her protegee.

"But he was in Atlanta," Oceola said.

"His spirit was here," Mrs. Ellsworth insisted. "All the time you were playing on that stage, he was here, the monster! Taking you out of yourself, taking you away from the piano."

"Why, he wasn't," said Oceola. "He was watching an operation in Atlanta."

But from then on, things didn't go well between her and her patron. The white lady grew distinctly cold when she received Oceola in her beautiful drawing room among the jade vases and amber cups worth thousands of dollars. When Oceola would have to wait there for Mrs. Ellsworth, she was afraid to move for fear she might knock something over—that would take ten years of a Harlemite's wages to replace, if broken.

Over the tea cups, the aging Mrs. Ellsworth did not talk any longer about the concert tour she had once thought she might finance for Oceola, if no recognized bureau took it up. Instead, she spoke of that something she believed Oceola's fingers had lost since her return from Europe. And she wondered why any one insisted on living in Harlem.

"I've been away from my own people so long," said the girl, "I want to live right in the middle of them again."

Why, Mrs. Ellsworth wondered farther, did Oceola, at her last concert in a Harlem church, not stick to the classical items listed on the program. Why did she insert one of her own variations on the spirituals, a syncopated variation from the Sanctified Church, that made an old colored lady rise up and cry out from her pew, "Glory to God this evenin'! Yes! Hallelujah! Whooo-oo!" right at the concert? Which seemed most undignified to Mrs. Ellsworth, and unworthy of the teachings of Philippe. And furthermore, why was Pete coming up to New York for Thanksgiving? And who had sent him the money to come?

"Me," said Oceola. "He doesn't make anything interning."

"Well," said Mrs. Ellsworth, "I don't think much of him." But Oceola didn't seem to care what Mrs. Ellsworth thought, for she made no defense.

Thanksgiving evening, in bed, together in a Harlem apartment, Pete and Oceola talked about their wedding to come. They would have a big one in a church with lots of music. And Pete would give her a ring. And she would have on a white dress, light and fluffy, not silk. "I hate silk," she said. "I hate expensive things." (She thought of her mother being buried in a cotton dress, for they were all broke when she died. Mother would have been glad about her marriage.) "Pete," Oceola said, hugging him in the dark, "let's live in Atlanta, where there are lots of colored people, like us."

"What about Mrs. Ellsworth?" Pete asked. "She coming down to Atlanta for our wedding?"

"I don't know," said Oceola.

"I hope not, 'cause if she stops at one of them big hotels. I won't have you going to the back door to see her. That's one thing I hate about the South—where there're white people, you have to go to the back door."

"Maybe she can stay with us," said Oceola. "I wouldn't mind."

"I'll be damned," said Pete. "You want to get lynched?"

But it happened that Mrs. Ellsworth didn't care to attend the wedding, anyway. When she saw how love had triumphed over art, she decided she could no longer influence Oceola's life. The period of Oceola was over. She would send checks, occasionally, if the girl needed them, besides, of course, something beautiful for the wedding, but that would be all. These things she told her the week after Thanksgiving.

"And Oceola, my dear, I've decided to spend the whole winter in Europe. I sail on December eighteenth. Christmas—while you are marrying—I shall be in Paris with my precious Antonio Bas. In January, he has an exhibition of oils in Madrid. And in the spring, a new young poet is coming over whom I want to visit Florence, to really know Florence. A charming white-haired boy from Omaha whose soul has been crushed in the West. I want to try to help him. He, my dear, is one of the few people who live for their art—and nothing else. . . . Ah, such a beautiful life! . . . You will come and play for me once before I sail?"

"Yes, Mrs. Ellsworth," said Oceola, genuinely sorry that the end had come. Why did white folks think you could live on nothing but art? Strange! Too strange! Too strange!

The Persian vases in the music room were filled with long-stemmed lilies that night when Oceola Jones came down from Harlem for the last time to play for Mrs. Dora Ellsworth. Mrs. Ellsworth had on a gown of black velvet, and a collar of pearls about her neck. She was very kind and gentle to Oceola, as one would be to a child who has done a great wrong but doesn't know any better. But to the black girl from Harlem, she looked very cold and white, and her grand piano seemed like the biggest and heaviest in the world—as Oceola sat down to play it with the technique for which Mrs. Ellsworth had paid.

As the rich and aging white woman listened to the great roll of Beethoven sonatas and to the sea and moonlight of the Chopin nocturnes, as she watched the swaying dark strong shoulders of Oceola Jones, she began to reproach the girl aloud for running away from art and music, for burying herself in Atlanta and love —love for a man unworthy of lacing up her boot straps, as Mrs. Ellsworth put it.

"You could shake the stars with your music, Oceola. Depression or no depression, I could make you great. And yet you propose to dig a grave for yourself. Art is bigger than love."

"I believe you, Mrs. Ellsworth," said Oceola, not turning away from the piano. "But being married won't keep me from making tours, or being an artist."

"Yes, it will," said Mrs. Ellsworth. "He'll take all the music out of you."

"No, he won't," said Oceola.

"You don't know, child," said Mrs. Ellsworth, "what men are like."

"Yes, I do," said Oceola simply. And her fingers began to wander slowly up and down the keyboard, flowing into the soft and lazy syncopation of a Negro blues, a blues that deepened and grew into rollicking jazz, then into an earth-throbbing rhythm that shook the lilies in the Persian vases of Mrs. Ellsworth's music room. Louder than the voice of the white woman who cried that Oceola was deserting beauty, deserting her real self, deserting her hope in life, the flood of wild syncopation filled the house, then sank into the slow and singing blues with which it had begun.

The girl at the piano heard the white woman saying, "Is this what I spent thousands of dollars to teach you?"

"No," said Oceola simply. "This is mine. . . . Listen! . . . How sad and gay it is. Blue and happy—laughing and crying. . . . How white like you and black like me. . . . How much like a man. . . . And how like a woman. . . . Warm as Pete's mouth. . . . These are the blues. . . . I'm playing."

Mrs. Ellsworth sat very still in her chair looking at the lilies trembling delicately in the priceless Persian vases, while Oceola made the bass notes throb like tom-toms deep in the earth.

> *O, if I could holler*

sang the blues,

> *Like a mountain jack,*
> *I'd go up on de mountain*

sang the blues,

> *And call my baby back.*

"And I," said Mrs. Ellsworth rising from her chair, "would stand looking at the stars."

WALLACE THURMAN

WALLACE THURMAN'S "CORDELIA THE CRUDE" (in Fire!!) featured a prostitute, in mischievous defiance of the Talented Tenth literary canon. His "Harlem: A Forum of Negro Life," which appeared as an editorial in the two issues to be published of his magazine Harlem, was intended to serve as a manifesto for the new artistic candor and racial realism espoused by the "younger writers, giving them a medium of expression and intelligent criticism."

The title of Thurman's controversial 1929 novel was taken from the folk saying "the blacker the berry, the sweeter the juice." The Blacker the Berry . . . belonged completely to the third phase of the Renaissance, breaking ground (Du Bois had led the way with Zora in The Quest of the Silver Fleece, 1912) by casting as protagonist and tragic heroine a very dark-skinned African American female. The taboo topic within Afro-America of color prejudice was remorselessly exposed. Emma Lou's calvary carries her, as the author's own had, to college in California and anguish in Harlem. Her specific agony—that she is viewed by many African Americans as unattractive because of her dark color, features, and texture of hair—is taken by Thurman as the painful premise for a much broader observation about his racial group. She represents those African Americans in whom respectability extinguishes personality and self-respect—those for whom the least evidence of white influence is esteemed. It was this obsession with respectability, Thurman hammers home, that caused the Harlem Renaissance to misfire, to fail to achieve a breakthrough in the arts—the one place in American life relatively free of racial restraints.

Infants of the Spring (1932) was artistically less successful than Thurman's first novel. The author indulged himself in showy *discussions of decadent French novelists, rehearsed the principal disputes by which Afro-America had been roiled (Booker T. Washington, Garvey, cultural assimilationism versus nationalism), and paraded virtually all of the talents known to Harlem during more than a decade. The novel was melodramatic and much too didactic, its talkative characters caricatures. On the other hand, its disillusionment and searing indictment of the false principles of the Renaissance make Thurman's novel historically and sociologically significant. In this final chapter of* Infants of the Spring, *Paul Arbian (clearly modeled on Thurman's friend Richard Bruce Nugent), is found a suicide in Niggerati Manor by the caustic Raymond (Thurman). His suicide note announces the end of the era.*

CORDELIA THE CRUDE

PHYSICALLY, IF NOT MENTALLY, Cordelia was a potential prostitute, meaning that although she had not yet realized the moral import of her wanton promiscuity nor become mercenary, she had, nevertheless, become quite blasé and bountiful in the matter of bestowing sexual favors upon persuasive and likely young men. Yet, despite her seeming lack of discrimination, Cordelia was quite particular about the type of male to whom she submitted, for numbers do not necessarily denote a lack of taste, and Cordelia had discovered after several months of active observation that one could find the qualities one admires or reacts positively to in a varied hodge-podge of outwardly different individuals.

The scene of Cordelia's activities was The Roosevelt Motion Picture Theatre on Seventh Avenue near 145th Street. Thrice weekly the program changed, and thrice weekly Cordelia would plunk down the necessary twenty-five cents evening admission fee, and saunter gaily into the foul-smelling depths of her favorite cinema shrine. The Roosevelt Theatre presented all of the latest pictures, also, twice weekly, treated its audiences to a vaudeville bill, then too, one could always have the most delightful physical contacts . . . hmm. . . .

Cordelia had not consciously chosen this locale nor had there been any conscious effort upon her part to take advantage of the extra opportunities afforded for physical pleasure. It had just happened that the Roosevelt Theatre was more close to her home than any other neighborhood picture palace, and it had also just happened that Cordelia had become almost immediately initiated into the ways of a Harlem theatre chippie soon after her discovery of the theatre itself.

It is the custom of certain men and boys who frequent these places to idle up and down the aisle until some female is seen sitting alone, to slouch down into a seat beside her, to touch her foot or else press her leg in such a way that it can be construed as accidental if necessary, and then, if the female is wise or else shows signs of willingness to become wise, to make more obvious approaches until, if successful, the approached female will soon be chatting with her baiter about the picture being shown, lolling in his arms, and helping to formulate plans for an after-theatre rendezvous. Cordelia had, you see, shown a willingness to become wise upon her second visit to The Roosevelt. In a short while she had even learned how to squelch the bloated, lewd faced Jews and eager middle aged Negroes who might approach as well as how to inveigle the likeable little yellow or brown half men, embryo avenue sweetbacks, with their well modeled heads, stickily plastered hair, flaming cravats, silken or broadcloth shirts, dirty underwear, low cut vests, form fitting coats, bell-bottom trousers and shiny shoes with metal cornered heels clicking with a brave, brazen rhythm upon the bare concrete floor as their owners angled and searched for prey.

Cordelia, sixteen years old, matronly mature, was an undisciplined, half literate product of rustic South Carolina, and had come to Harlem very much against her will with her parents and her six brothers and sisters. Against her will because she had not been at all anxious to leave the lackadaisical life of the little corn pone settlement where she had been born, to go trooping into the unknown vastness of New York, for she had been in love, passionately in love with one John Stokes who raised pigs, and who, like his father before him, found the raising of pigs so profitable that he could not even consider leaving Lintonville. Cordelia had blankly informed her parents that she would not go with them when they decided to be lured to New York by an older son who had remained there after the demobilization of the war time troops. She had even threatened to run away with John until they should be gone, but of course John could not leave his pigs, and John's mother was not very keen on having Cordelia for a daughter-in-law—those Joneses have bad mixed blood in 'em—so Cordelia had

had to join the Gotham bound caravan and leave her lover to his succulent porkers.

However, the mere moving to Harlem had not doused the rebellious flame. Upon arriving Cordelia had not only refused to go to school and refused to hold even the most easily held job, but had also victoriously defied her harassed parents so frequently when it came to matters of discipline that she soon found herself with a mesmerizing lack of home restraint, for the stress of trying to maintain themselves and their family in the new environment was far too much of a task for Mr. and Mrs. Jones to attend to facilely and at the same time try to control a recalcitrant child. So, when Cordelia had refused either to work or to attend school, Mrs. Jones herself had gone out for day's work, leaving Cordelia at home to take care of their five room railroad flat, the front room of which was rented out to a couple "living together," and to see that the younger children, all of whom were of school age, made their four trips daily between home and the nearby public school —as well as see that they had their greasy, if slim, food rations and an occasional change of clothing. Thus Cordelia's days were full—and so were her nights. The only difference being that the days belonged to the folks at home while the nights (since the folks were too tired or too sleepy to know or care when she came in or went out) belonged to her and to—well—whosoever will, let them come.

Cordelia had been playing this hectic, entrancing game for six months and was widely known among a certain group of young men and girls on the avenue as a fus' class chippie when she and I happened to enter the theatre simultaneously. She had clumped down the aisle before me, her open galoshes swishing noisily, her two arms busy wriggling themselves free from the torn sleeve lining of a shoddy imitation fur coat that one of her mother's wash clients had sent to her. She was of medium height and build, with overly developed legs and bust, and had a clear, keen light brown complexion. Her too slick, too naturally bobbed hair, mussed by the removing of a tight, black turban was of an undecided nature, i.e., it was undecided whether to be kinky or to be kind, and her body, as she sauntered along in the partial light had such a conscious sway of invitation that unthinkingly I followed, slid into the same row of seats and sat down beside her.

Naturally she had noticed my pursuit, and thinking that I was eager to play the game, let me know immediately that she was wise, and not the least bit averse to spooning with me during the evening's performance. Interested, and, I might as well confess, intrigued physically, I too became wise, and played up to her with all the fervor, or so I thought, of an old timer, but Cordelia soon remarked that I was different from mos' of des' sheiks, and when pressed for an explanation brazenly told me in a slightly scandalized and patronizing tone that I had not even felt her legs . . . !

At one o'clock in the morning we strolled through the snowy bleakness of one hundred and forty-fourth street between Lenox and Fifth Avenues to the walk-up tenement flat in which she lived, and after stamping the snow from our feet, pushed through the double outside doors, and followed the dismal hallway to the rear of the building where we began the tedious climbing of the crooked, creaking, inconveniently narrow stairway. Cordelia had informed me earlier in the evening that she lived on the top floor —four flights up east side rear—and on our way we rested at each floor and at each half way landing, rested long enough to mingle the snowy dampness of our respective coats, and to hug clumsily while our lips met in an animal kiss.

Finally only another half flight remained, and instead of proceeding as was usual after our amorous demonstration I abruptly drew away from her, opened my overcoat, plunged my hand into my pants pocket, and drew out two crumpled one dollar bills which I handed to her, and then, while she stared at me foolishly, I muttered good-night, confusedly pecked her on her cold brown cheek, and darted down into the creaking darkness.

Six months later I was taking two friends of mine, lately from the provinces, to a Saturday night house-rent party in a well known whore house on one hundred and thirty-fourth street near Lenox Avenue. The place as we entered seemed to be a chaotic riot of raucous noise and clashing color all rhythmically merging in the red, smoke filled room. And there I saw Cordelia savagely careening in a drunken abortion of the Charleston and surrounded by a perspiring circle of handclapping enthusiasts. Finally fatigued, she whirled into an abrupt finish, and stopped so that she stared directly into my face, but being dizzy from the calisthenic turns and the cauterizing liquor she doubted that her eyes recognized someone out of the past, and, visibly trying to sober herself, languidly began to dance a slow drag with a lean hipped pimply faced yellow man who had walked between her and me. At last he released her, and seeing that she was about to leave the room I rushed forward calling Cordelia?—as if I was not yet sure who it was. Stopping in the doorway, she turned to see who had called, and finally recognizing me said simply, without the least trace of emotion,— 'Lo kid. . . .

And without another word turned her back and walked into the hall to where she joined four girls standing there. Still eager to speak, I followed and heard one of the girls ask: Who's the dicty kid? . . .

And Cordelia answered: The guy who gimme ma' firs' two bucks. . . .

HARLEM: A FORUM OF NEGRO LIFE

IN THE PAST there have been only a few sporadic and inevitably unsuccessful attempts to provide the Negro with an independent magazine of literature and thought. Those magazines which have lived throughout a period of years have been organs of some philanthropic organization whose purpose was to fight the more virulent manifestations of race prejudice. The magazines themselves have been pulpits for alarmed and angry Jeremiahs spouting fire and venom or else weeping and moaning as if they were either predestined or else unable to do anything else. For a while this seemed to be the only feasible course for Negro journalists to take. To the Negro then the most important and most tragic thing in the world was his own problem here in America. He was interested only in making white people realize what dastards they were in denying him equal economic opportunities or in lynching him upon the slightest provocation. This, as has been said, was all right for a certain period, and the journalists of that period are not to be censored for the truly daring and important work they did do. Rather, they are to be blamed for not changing their journalistic methods when time and conditions warranted such a change, and for doing nothing else but preaching and moaning until they completely lost their emotional balance and their sense of true values. Every chord on their publicist instrument had been broken save one, and they continued raucously to twang this, unaware that they were ludicrously out of tune with the other instruments in their environment.

Then came the so-called renaissance and the emergence of the so-called new (in this case meaning widely advertised) Negro. As James Weldon Johnson says in the current issue of *Harper's* magazine: "The Negro has done a great deal thru his folk art creations to change the national attitudes toward him; and now the efforts of the race have been reinforced and magnified by the individual Negro artist, the conscious artist. . . . Overnight, as it were, America became aware that there were Negro artists and that they had something worthwhile to say. This awareness first manifested itself in black America, for, strange as it may seem, Negroes themselves, as a mass, had had little or no consciousness of their own individual artists."

Naturally these new voices had to be given a place in Negro magazines and they were given space that hitherto had been devoted only to propaganda. But the artist was not satisfied to be squeezed between jeremiads or have his work thrown haphazardly upon a page where there was no effort to make it look beautiful as well as sound beautiful. He revolted against shoddy and sloppy publication methods, revolted against the patronizing attitudes his elders assumed toward him, revolted against their editorial astigmatism and their intolerance of new points of view. But revolting left him without a journalistic asylum. True, he could, and did, contribute to the white magazines, but in doing this almost exclusively he felt that he was losing touch with his own group, for he knew just how few Negroes would continually buy white magazines in order to read articles and stories by Negro authors, and he also knew that from a sense of race pride, if nothing more, there were many Negroes who would buy a Negro magazine.

The next step then was for the artist himself to produce this new type of journal. With little money but a plethora of ideas and ambition he proceeded to produce independent art magazines of his own. In New York, *Fire* was the pioneer of the movement. It flamed for one issue and caused a sensation the like of which had never been known in Negro journalism before. Next came *Black Opals* in Philadelphia, a more conservative yet extremely worthwhile venture. Then came *The Quill* in Boston which was to be published whenever its sponsors felt the urge to bring forth a publication of their own works for the benefit of themselves and their friends. And there were other groups of younger Negroes in Chicago, Kansas City and Los Angeles who formed groups to bring out independent magazines which never became actualities.

This last development should have made someone realize that a new type of publication was in order. The old propagandistic journals had served their day and their generation well, but they were emotionally unprepared to serve a new day and a new generation. The art magazines, unsoundly financed as they were, could not last. It was time for someone with vision to found a wholly new type of magazine, one which would give expression to all groups, one which would take into consideration the fact that this was a new day in the history of the American Negro, that this was a new day in the history of the world and that new points of views and new approaches to old problems were necessary and inescapable.

Harlem hopes to fill this new need. It enters the field without any preconceived editorial prejudices, without intolerance, without a reformer's cudgel. It wants merely to be a forum in which all people's opinions may be presented intelligently and from which the Negro can gain some universal idea of what is going on in the world of thought and art. It wants to impress upon the literate members of the thirteen million Negroes in the United States the necessity of becoming "book conscious," the necessity of reading the newer Negro authors, the necessity of realizing that the Negro is not the only, nor the worst mistreated minority group in the world, the necessity of sublimating their inferiority complex and their extreme race sensitiveness and putting the energy, which they have hitherto used in moaning and groaning, into more concrete fields of action.

To this end *Harlem* will solicit articles on current events, essays of the more intimate kind, short stories and poetry from both black and white writers; the only qualification being that they have sufficient literary merit to warrant publication. *Harlem* will also promote debates on both racial and non-racial issues, giving voice to as many sides as there seem to be to the question involved. It will also be a clearing house for the newer Negro literature, striving to aid the younger writers, giving them a medium of expression and intelligent criticism. It also hopes to impress the Negro reading public with the necessity for a more concerted and well-balanced economic and political program. It believes that the commercial and political elements within the race are just as in need of clari-

fication as the literary element and will expend just as much energy
and time in the latter fields as in the former.

This is *Harlem's* program, its excuse for existence. It now remains to be seen whether the Negro public is as ready for such a
publication as the editors and publishers of *Harlem* believe it
to be.

FROM *THE BLACKER THE BERRY . . .*

MORE ACUTELY THAN EVER BEFORE Emma Lou began to feel that
her luscious black complexion was somewhat of a liability, and
that her marked color variation from the other people in her environment was a decided curse. Not that she minded being black,
being a Negro necessitated having a colored skin, but she did mind
being too black. She couldn't understand why such should be the
case, couldn't comprehend the cruelty of the natal attenders who
had allowed her to be dipped, as it were, in indigo ink when there
were so many more pleasing colors on nature's palette. Biologically, it wasn't necessary either; her mother was quite fair, so was
her mother's mother, and her mother's brother, and her mother's
brother's son; but then none of them had had a black man for a
father. Why *had* her mother married a black man? Surely there
had been some eligible brown-skin men around. She didn't particularly desire to have had a "high yaller" father, but for her sake
certainly some more happy medium could have been found.

She wasn't the only person who regretted her darkness either.
It was an acquired family characteristic, this moaning and grieving
over the color of her skin. Everything possible had been done to
alleviate the unhappy condition, every suggested agent had been
employed, but her skin, despite bleachings, scourgings, and pow-
derings, had remained black—fast black—as nature had planned
and effected.

She should have been a boy, then color of skin wouldn't have
mattered so much, for wasn't her mother always saying that a
black boy could get along, but that a black girl would never know
anything but sorrow and disappointment? But she wasn't a boy;
she was a girl, and color did matter, mattered so much that she
would rather have missed receiving her high school diploma than
have to sit as she now sat, the only odd and conspicuous figure on

the auditorium platform of the Boise high school. Why had she allowed them to place her in the center of the first row, and why had they insisted upon her dressing entirely in white so that surrounded as she was by similarly attired pale-faced fellow graduates she resembled, not at all remotely, that comic picture her Uncle Joe had hung in his bedroom? The picture wherein the black, kinky head of a little red-lipped pickaninny lay like a fly in a pan of milk amid a white expanse of bedclothes.

But of course she couldn't have worn blue or black when the call was for the wearing of white, even if white was not complementary to her complexion. She would have been odd-looking anyway no matter what she wore and she would also have been conspicuous, for not only was she the only dark-skinned person on the platform, she was also the only Negro pupil in the entire school, and had been for the past four years. Well, thank goodness, the principal would soon be through with his monotonous farewell address, and she and the other members of her class would advance to the platform center as their names were called and receive the documents which would signify their unconditional release from public school.

As she thought of these things, Emma Lou glanced at those who sat to the right and to the left of her. She envied them their obvious elation, yet felt a strange sense of superiority because of her immunity for the moment from an ephemeral mob emotion. Get a diploma?—What did it mean to her? College?—Perhaps. A job?—Perhaps again. She was going to have a high school diploma, but it would mean nothing to her whatsoever. The tragedy of her life was that she was too black. Her face and not a slender roll of ribbon-bound parchment was to be her future identification tag in society. High school diploma indeed! What she needed was an efficient bleaching agent, a magic cream that would remove this unwelcome black mask from her face and make her more like her fellow men.

"Emma Lou Morgan."

She came to with a start. The principal had called her name and stood smiling down at her benevolently. Some one—she knew it was her Cousin Buddie, stupid imp—applauded, very faintly, very provokingly. Some one else snickered.

"Emma Lou Morgan."

The principal had called her name again, more sharply than before and his smile was less benevolent. The girl who sat to the left of her nudged her. There was nothing else for her to do but to get out of that anchoring chair and march forward to receive her diploma. But why did the people in the audience have to stare so? Didn't they all know that Emma Lou Morgan was Boise high school's only nigger student? Didn't they all know—but what was the use. She had to go get that diploma, so summoning her most insouciant manner, she advanced to the platform center, brought every muscle of her lithe limbs into play, haughtily extended her shiny black arm to receive the proffered diploma, bowed a chilly thanks, then holding her arms stiffly at her sides, insolently returned to her seat in that foreboding white line, insolently returned once more to splotch its pale purity and to mock it with her dark, outlandish difference. . . .

Saturday evening. Alva had urged her to hurry uptown from work. He was going to take her on a party with some friends of his. This was the first time he had ever asked her to go to any sort of social affair with him. She had never met any of his friends save Braxton, who scarcely spoke to her, and never before had Alva suggested taking her to any sort of social gathering either public or semi-public. He often took her to various motion picture theaters, both downtown and in Harlem, and at least three nights a week he would call for her at the theater and escort her to Harlem. On these occasions they often went to Chinese restaurants or to ice cream parlors before going home. But usually they would go to City College Park, find an empty bench in a dark corner where they could sit and spoon before retiring either to her room or to Alva's.

Emma Lou had, long before this, suggested going to a dance or to a party, but Alva had always countered that he never attended such affairs during the summer months, that he stayed away from them for precisely the same reason that he stayed away from work, namely, because it was too hot. Dancing, said he, was a matter of calisthenics, and calisthenics were work. Therefore it, like any sort of physical exercise, was taboo during hot weather.

Alva sensed that sooner or later Emma Lou would become aware of his real reason for not taking her out among his friends. He realized that one as color-conscious as she appeared to be would, at some not so distant date, jump to what for him would be uncomfortable conclusions. He did not wish to risk losing her before the end of summer, but neither could he risk taking her out among his friends, for he knew too well that he would be derided for his unseemly preference for "dark meat," and told publicly without regard for her feelings, that "black cats must go."

Furthermore he always took Geraldine to parties and dances. Geraldine with her olive colored skin and straight black hair. Geraldine, who of all the people he pretended to love, really inspired him emotionally as well as physically, the one person he conquested without thought of monetary gain. Yet he had to do something with Emma Lou, and release from the quandary presented itself from most unexpected quarters.

Quite accidentally, as things of the sort happen in Harlem with its complex but interdependable social structure, he had become acquainted with a young Negro writer, who had asked him to escort a group of young writers and artists to a house-rent party. Though they had heard much of this phenomenon, none had been on the inside of one, and because of their rather polished manners and exteriors, were afraid that they might not be admitted. Proletarian Negroes are as suspicious of their more sophisticated brethren as they are of white men, and resent as keenly their intrusions into their social world. Alva had consented to act as cicerone, and, realizing that these people would be more or less free from the color prejudice exhibited by his other friends, had decided to take Emma Lou along too. He was also aware of her intellectual pretensions, and felt that she would be especially pleased to meet recognized talents and outstanding personalities. She did not have to know that these were not his regular companions, and from then on she would have no reason to feel that he was ashamed to have her meet his friends.

Emma Lou could hardly attend to Arline's change of complexion and clothes between acts and scenes, so anxious was she to get to Alva's house and to the promised party. Her happiness was complete. She was certain now that Alva loved her, certain that he was not ashamed or even aware of her dusky complexion. She had felt from the first that he was superior to such inane truck, now she knew it. Alva loved her for herself alone, and loved her so much that he didn't mind her being a coal scuttle blond.

Sensing something unusual, Arline told Emma that she would remove her own make-up after the performance, and let her have time to get dressed for the party. This she proceeded to do all through the evening, spending much time in front of the mirror at Arline's dressing table, manicuring her nails, marcelling her hair, and applying various creams and cosmetics to her face in order to make her despised darkness less obvious. Finally, she put on one of Arline's less pretentious afternoon frocks, and set out for Alva's house.

As she approached his room door, she heard much talk and laughter, moving her to halt and speculate whether or not she should go in. Even her unusual and high-tensioned jubilance was not powerful enough to overcome immediately her shyness and fears. Suppose these friends of Alva's would not take kindly to her? Suppose they were like Braxton, who invariably curled his lip when he saw her, and seldom spoke even as much as a word of greeting? Suppose they were like the people who used to attend her mother's and grandmother's teas, club meetings and receptions, dismissing her with—"It beats me how this child of yours looks so unlike the rest of you . . . Are you sure it isn't adopted." Or suppose they were like the college youth she had known in Southern California? No, that couldn't be. Alva would never invite her where she would not be welcome. These were his friends. And so was Braxton, but Alva said he was peculiar. There was no danger. Alva had invited her. She was here. Anyway she wasn't so black. Hadn't she artificially lightened her skin about four or five shades until she was almost brown? Certainly it was all right. She needn't be a foolish ninny all her life. Thus, reassured, she knocked on the door, and felt herself trembling with excitement and internal uncertainty as Alva let her in, took her hat and coat, and proceeded to introduce her to the people in the room.

"Miss Morgan, meet Mr. Tony Crews. You've probably seen his book of poems. He's the little jazz boy, you know."

Emma Lou bashfully touched the extended hand of the curly-headed poet. She had not seen or read his book, but she had often noticed his name in the newspapers and magazines. He was all that she had expected him to be except that he had pimples on his face. These didn't fit in with her mental picture.

"Miss Morgan, this is Cora Thurston. Maybe I should'a introduced you ladies first."

"I'm no lady, and I hope you're not either, Miss Morgan." She smiled, shook Emma Lou's hand, then turned away to continue her interrupted conversation with Tony Crews.

"Miss Morgan, meet . . . ," he paused, and addressed a tall, dark yellow youth stretched out on the floor, "What name you going by now?"

The boy looked up and smiled.

"Why, Paul, of course."

"All right then, Miss Morgan, this is Mr. Paul, he changes his name every season."

Emma Lou sought to observe this person more closely, and was shocked to see that his shirt was open at the neck and that he was sadly in need of a haircut and shave.

"Miss Morgan, meet Mr. Walter." A small slender dark youth with an infectious smile and small features. His face was familiar. Where had she seen him before?

"Now that you've met every one, sit down on the bed there beside Truman and have a drink. Go on with your talk folks," he urged as he went over to the dresser to fill a glass with a milk colored liquid. Cora Thurston spoke up in answer to Alva's adjuration:

"Guess there ain't much more to say. Makes me mad to discuss it anyhow."

"No need of getting mad at people like that," said Tony Crews simply and softly. "I think one should laugh at such stupidity."

"And ridicule it, too," came from the luxurious person sprawled over the floor, for he did impress Emma Lou as being luxurious, despite the fact that his suit was unpressed, and that he wore neither socks nor necktie. She noticed the many graceful gestures he made with his hands, but wondered why he kept twisting his lips to one side when he talked. Perhaps he was trying to mask the size of his mouth.

Truman was speaking now, "Ridicule will do no good, nor mere laughing at them. I admit those weapons are about the only ones an intelligent person would use, but one must also admit that they are rather futile."

"Why futile?" Paul queried indolently.

"They are futile," Truman continued, "because, well, those people cannot help being like they are—their environment has made them that way."

Miss Thurston muttered something. It sounded like "hooey," then held out an empty glass. "Give me some more firewater, Alva." Alva hastened across the room and refilled her glass. Emma Lou wondered what they were talking about. Again Cora broke the silence, "You can't tell me they can't help it. They kick about white people, then commit the same crime."

There was a knock on the door, interrupting something Tony Crews was about to say. Alva went to the door.

"Hello, Ray." A tall, blond, fair-skinned youth entered. Ema Lou gasped, and was more bewildered that ever. All of this silly talk and drinking, and now—here was a white man!

"Hy, everybody, Jusas Chraust, I hope you saved me some liquor." Tony Crews held out his empty glass and said quietly, "We've had about umpteen already, so I doubt if there's any more left."

"You can't kid me, bo. I know Alva would save me a dram or two." Having taken off his hat and coat he squatted down on the floor beside Paul.

Truman turned to Emma Lou. "Oh, Ray, meet Miss Morgan. Mr. Jorgenson, Miss Morgan."

"Glad to know you; pardon my not getting up, won't you?" Emma Lou didn't know what to say, and couldn't think of anything appropriate, but since he was smiling, she tried to smile too, and nodded her head.

"What's the big powwow?" he asked. "All of you look so serious. Haven't you had enough liquor, or are you just trying to settle the ills of the universe?"

"Neither," said Paul. "They're just damning our 'pink niggers'."

Emma Lou was aghast. Such extraordinary people—saying "nigger" in front of a white man! Didn't they have any race pride or proper bringing up? Didn't they have any common sense?

"What've they done now?" Ray asked, reaching out to accept the glass Alva was handing him.

"No more than they've always done," Tony Crews answered. "Cora here just felt like being indignant, because she heard of a forthcoming wedding in Brooklyn to which the prospective bride and groom have announced they will *not* invite any dark people."

"Seriously now," Truman began. Ray interrupted him.

"Who in the hell wants to be serious?"

"As I was saying," Truman continued, "you can't blame light Negroes for being prejudiced against dark ones. All of you know that white is the symbol of everything pure and good, whether that everything be concrete or abstract. Ivory Soap is advertised as being ninety-nine and some fraction per cent pure, and Ivory Soap is white. Moreover, virtue and virginity are always represented as being clothed in white garments. Then, too, the God we, or rather most Negroes worship is a patriarchal white man, seated on a white throne, in a spotless white Heaven, radiant with white streets and white-apparelled angels eating white honey and drinking white milk."

"Listen to the boy rave. Give him another drink," Ray shouted, but Truman ignored him and went on, becoming more and more animated.

"We are all living in a totally white world, where all standards are the standards of the white man, and where almost invariably what the white man does is right, and what the black man does is wrong, unless it is precedented by something a white man has done."

"Which," Cora added scornfully, "makes it all right for light Negroes to discriminate against dark ones?"

"Not at all," Truman objected. "It merely explains, not justifies, the evil—or rather, the fact of intraracial segregation. Mulattoes have always been accorded more consideration by white people than their darker brethren. They were made to feel superior even during slave days . . . made to feel proud, as Bud Fisher would say, that they were bastards. It was for the mulatto offspring of white masters and Negro slaves that the first schools for Negroes were organized, and say what you will, it is generally the Negro with a quantity of mixed blood in his veins who finds adaptation to a Nordic environment more easy than one of pure blood, which, of course, you will admit, is, to an American Negro, convenient if not virtuous."

"Does that justify their snobbishness and self-evaluated superiority?"

"No, Cora, it doesn't," returned Truman. "I'm not trying to excuse them. I'm merely trying to give what I believe to be an explanation of this thing. I have never been to Washington and only know what Paul and you have told me about conditions there, but they seem to be just about the same as conditions in Los Angeles, Omaha, Chicago, and other cities in which I have lived or visited. You see, people have to feel superior to something, and there is scant satisfaction in feeling superior to domestic animals or steel machines that one can train or utilize. It is much more pleasing to pick out some individual or some group of individuals on the same plane to feel superior to. This is almost necessary when one is a member of a supposedly despised, mistreated minority group. Then consider that the mulatto is much nearer white than he is black, and is therefore more liable to act like a white man than like a black one, although I cannot say that I see a great deal of difference in any of their actions. They are human beings first and only white or black incidentally."

Ray pursed his lips and whistled.

"But you seem to forget," Tony Crews insisted, "that because a man is dark, it doesn't necessarily mean he is not of mixed blood. Now look at. . . ."

"Yeah, let him look at you or at himself or at Cora," Paul interrupted. "There ain't no unmixed Negroes."

"But I haven't forgotten that," Truman said, ignoring the note of finality in Paul's voice. "I merely took it for granted that we were talking only about those Negroes who were light-skinned."

"But all light-skinned Negroes aren't color struck or color prejudiced," interjected Alva, who, up to this time, like Emma Lou, had remained silent. This was, he thought, a strategic moment for him to say something. He hoped Emma Lou would get the full significance of this statement.

"True enough," Truman began again. "But I also took it for granted that we were only talking about those who were. As I said before, Negroes are, after all, human beings, and they are subject to be influenced and controlled by the same forces and factors that influence and control other human beings. In an environment where there are so many color-prejudiced whites, there are bound to be a number of color-prejudiced blacks. Color prejudice and religion are akin in one respect. Some folks have it and some don't, and the kernel that is responsible for it is present in us all, which is to say, that potentially we are all color-prejudiced as long as we remain in this environment. For, as you know, prejudices are always caused by differences, and the majority group sets the standard. Then, too, since black is the favorite color of vaudeville comedians and jokesters, and conversely, as intimately associated with tragedy, it is no wonder that even the blackest individual will seek out some one more black than himself to laugh at."

"So saith the Lord," Tony answered soberly.

"And the Holy Ghost saith, let's have another drink."

"Happy thought, Ray," returned Cora. "Give us some more ice cream and gin, Alva."

Alva went into the alcove to prepare another concoction.

Tony started the victrola. Truman turned to Emma Lou, who, all this while, had been sitting there with Alva's arm around her, every muscle in her body feeling as if it wanted to twitch, not knowing whether to be sad or to be angry. She couldn't comprehend all of this talk. She couldn't see how these people could sit down and so dispassionately discuss something that seemed particularly tragic to her. This fellow Truman, whom she was certain she knew, with all his hi-faluting talk, disgusted her immeasurably. She wasn't sure that they weren't all poking fun at her. Truman was speaking:

"Miss Morgan, didn't you attend school in Southern California?" Emma Lou at last realized where she had seen him before. So *this* was Truman Walter, the little "cock o' the walk," as they had called him on the campus. She answered him with difficulty, for there was a sob in her throat. "Yes, I did." Before Truman could say more to her, Ray called to him:

"Say, Bozo, what time are we going to the party? It's almost one o'clock now."

"Is it?" Alva seemed surprised. "But Aaron and Alta aren't here yet."

"They've been married just long enough to be late to everything."

"What do you say we go by and ring their bell?" Tony suggested, ignoring Paul's Greenwich Village wit.

" 'Sall right with me." Truman lifted his glass to his lips. "Then on to the house-rent party . . . on to the bawdy bowels of Beale Street!"

They drained their glasses and prepared to leave.

"Ahhhh, sock it." . . . "Ummmm" . . . Piano playing—slow, loud, and discordant, accompanied by the rhythmic sound of shuffling feet. Down a long, dark hallway to an inside room, lit by a solitary red bulb. "Oh, play it you dirty no-gooder." . . . A room full of dancing couples, scarcely moving their feet, arms completely encircling one another's bodies . . . cheeks being warmed by one another's breath . . . eyes closed . . . animal ecstasy agitating their perspiring faces. There was much panting, much hip movement, much shaking of the buttocks. . . . "Do it twice in the same place." . . . "Git off that dime." Now somebody was singing, "I ask you very confidentially. . . ." "Sing it man, sing it." . . . Piano treble moaning, bass rumbling like thunder. A swarm of people, motivating their bodies to express in suggestive movements the ultimate consummation of desire.

The music stopped, the room was suffocatingly hot, and Emma Lou was disturbingly dizzy. She clung fast to Alva, and let the room and its occupants whirl around her. Bodies and faces glided by. Leering faces and lewd bodies. Anxious faces and angular bodies. Sad faces and obese bodies. All mixed up together. She began to wonder how such a small room could hold so many people. "Oh, play it again . . ." She saw the pianist now, silhouetted against the dark mahogany piano, saw him bend his long, slick-haired head, until it hung low on his chest, then lift his hands high in the air, and as quickly let them descend upon the keyboard. There was one moment of cacophony, then the long, supple fingers evolved a slow, tantalizing melody out of the deafening chaos.

Every one began to dance again. Body called to body, and cemented themselves together, limbs lewdly intertwined. A couple there kissing, another couple dipping to the floor, and slowly shimmying, belly to belly, as they came back to an upright position. A slender dark girl with wild eyes and wilder hair stood in the center of the room, supported by the strong, lithe arms of a longshoreman. She bent her trunk backward, until her head hung below her waistline, and all the while she kept the lower portion of her body quivering like jello.

"She whips it to a jelly," the piano player was singing now, and banging on the keys with such might that an empty gin bottle on top of the piano seemed to be seized with the ague. "Oh, play it Mr. Charlie." Emma Lou grew limp in Alva's arms.

"What's the matter, honey, drunk?" She couldn't answer. The music augmented by the general atmosphere of the room and the liquor she had drunk had presumably created another person in her stead. She felt like flying into an emotional frenzy—felt like flinging her arms and legs in insane unison. She had become very fluid, very elastic, and all the while she was giving in more and more to the music and to the liquor and to the physical madness of the moment.

When the music finally stopped, Alva led Emma Lou to a settee by the window which his crowd had appropriated. Every one was exceedingly animated, but they all talked in hushed, almost reverential tones.

"Isn't this marvelous?" Truman's eyes were ablaze with interest and excitement. Even Tony Crews seemed unusually alert.

"It's the greatest I've seen yet," he exclaimed.

Alva seemed the most unemotional one in the crowd. Paul the most detached. "Look at 'em all watching Ray."

"Remember, Bo," Truman counselled him. "Tonight you're 'passing.' Here's a new wrinkle, white man 'passes' for Negro."

"Why not? Enough of you pass for white." They all laughed, then transferred their interest back to the party. Cora was speaking:

"Didya see that little girl in pink—the one with the scar on her face—dancing with that tall, lanky, one-armed man? Wasn't she throwing it up to him?"

"Yeah," Tony admitted, "but she didn't have anything on that little Mexican-looking girl. She musta been born in Cairo."

"Saay, but isn't that one bad looking darkey over there, two chairs to the left; is he gonna smother that woman?" Truman asked excitedly.

"I'd say she kinda liked it," Paul answered, then lit another cigarette.

"Do you know they have corn liquor in the kitchen? They serve it from a coffee pot." Aaron seemed proud of his discovery.

"Yes," said Alva, "and they got hoppin'-john out there too."

"What the hell is hoppin'-john?"

"Ray, I'm ashamed of you. Here you are passing for colored and don't know what hoppin'-john is!"

"Tell him, Cora, I don't know either."

"Another one of these foreigners." Cora looked at Truman disdainfully. "Hoppin'-john is black-eyed peas and rice. Didn't they ever have any out in Salt Lake City?"

"Have they any chitterlings?" Alta asked eagerly.

"No, Alta," Alva replied, dryly. "This isn't Kansas. They have got pig's feet though."

"Lead me to 'em," Aaron and Alta shouted in unison, and led the way to the kitchen. Emma Lou clung to Alva's arm and tried to remain behind. "Alva, I'm afraid."

"Afraid of what? Come on, snap out of it! You need another drink." He pulled her up from the settee and led her through the crowded room down the long narrow dark hallway to the more crowded kitchen.

When they returned to the room, the pianist was just preparing to play again. He was tall and slender, with extra long legs and arms, giving him the appearance of a scarecrow. His pants were tight in the waist and full in the legs. He wore no coat, and a blue silk shirt hung damply to his body. He acted as if he were king of the occasion, ruling all from his piano stool throne. He talked familiarly to every one in the room, called women from other men's arms, demanded drinks from any bottle he happened to see being passed around, laughed uproariously, and made many grotesque and ofttimes obscene gestures.

There were sounds of a scuffle in an adjoining room, and an excited voice exclaimed, "You goddamn son-of-a-bitch, don't you catch my dice no more." The piano player banged on the keys and drowned out the reply, if there was one.

Emma Lou could not keep her eyes off the piano player. He was acting like a maniac, occasionally turning completely around on his stool, grimacing like a witch doctor, and letting his hands dawdle over the keyboard of the piano with an agonizing indolence, when compared to the extreme exertion to which he put the rest of his body. He was improvising. The melody of the piece he had started to play was merely a base for more bawdy variations. His left foot thumped on the floor in time with the music, while his right punished the piano's loud-pedal. Beads of perspiration gathered grease from his slicked-down hair, and rolled oleagenously down his face and neck, spotting the already damp babyblue shirt, and streaking his already greasy black face with more shiny lanes.

A sailor lad suddenly ceased his impassioned hip movement and strode out of the room, pulling his partner behind him, pushing people out of the way as he went. The spontaneous moans and slangy ejaculations of the piano player and of the more articulate dancers became more regular, more like a chanted obligato to the music. This lasted for a couple of hours interrupted only by hectic intermissions. Then the dancers grew less violent in their movements, and though the piano player seemed never to tire there were fewer couples on the floor, and those left seemed less loathe to move their legs.

Eventually, the music stopped for a long interval, and there was a more concerted drive on the kitchen's corn liquor supply. Most of the private flasks and bottles were empty. There were more calls for food, too, and the crap game in the side room annexed more players and more kibitzers. Various men and women had disappeared altogether. Those who remained seemed worn and tired. There was much petty person to person badinage and many whispered consultations in corners. There was an argument in the hallway between the landlord and two couples, who wished to share one room without paying him more than the regulation three dollars required of one couple. Finally, Alva suggested that they leave. Emma Lou had drifted off into a state of semi-consciousness and was too near asleep or drunk to distinguish people or voices. All she knew was that she was being led out of that dreadful place, that the perturbing "pilgrimage to the proletariat's parlor social," as Truman had called it, was ended, and that she was in a taxicab, cuddled up in Alva's arms.

FROM *INFANTS OF THE SPRING*

IT WAS RAYMOND'S LAST NIGHT in Niggeratti Manor. Lucille had spent most of the evening with him, aiding him to pack. The studio was bare and cheerless. The walls had been stripped of the colorful original drawings contributed by Paul and Carl Denny. They were now stark and bare. The book shelves were empty, and yawned hideously in the more shaded corners. The middle of the room was filled with boxes in which his books had been packed, and in the alcove his trunk and suitcases stood at attention in military array. The rest of the house was also in a state of dishevelment. Painters and plasterers had been swarming over the place, leaving undeniable evidence of their presence and handiwork. Niggeratti Manor was almost ready to suffer its transition from a congenial home for Negro artists to a congenial dormitory for bachelor girls.

Amid the gloom and confusion Raymond and Stephen sat, fitfully conversing between frequent drinks which had little effect. There was more bad news. Stephen had been called back to Europe. His mother was dangerously ill. There was little hope of his arriving before she died, but they insisted that he, the eldest son, start for home immediately. He was to sail the next day.

"You know, son, family is a hell of a thing. They should all be dissolved. Of course I'm perturbed at the thought of my mother's death, but I can't stop her from dying, nor can I bring her back to life should she be dead when I arrive. And yet I am dragged across an ocean, expected to display great grief and indulge in all the other tomfoolery human beings indulge themselves in when another human being dies. It's all tommyrot."

"Assuredly," Raymond agreed, "dying is an event, a perversely festive occasion, not so much for the deceased as for his so-called mourners. Let's forget it. You've got to adhere to the traditions of the clan to some degree. Let's drink to the day when a person's death will be the cue for a wild gin party rather than a signal for well meant but purely exhibitionistic grief." He held his glass aloft. "Skip ze gutter." The glasses were drained.

"And after you get in Europe?"

"I will be prevailed upon to stay at home and become a respectable schoolmaster. Now, let's finish the bottle of gin. I've got to go. It's after three and as usual we've been talking for hours and said nothing."

Raymond measured out the remaining liquor.

"O. K., Steve. Here's to the fall of Niggeratti Manor and all within."

Stephen had gone. Raymond quickly prepared himself for bed, and was almost asleep when the telephone began to ring. He cursed, decided not to get up, and turned his face toward the wall. What fool could be calling at this hour of the morning? In the old days it might have been expected, but now Niggeratti Manor was no more. There was nothing left of the old régime except reminiscences and gossip. The telephone continued to ring. Its blaring voice echoed throughout the empty house. Muttering to himself, Raymond finally left his bed, donned his bathrobe and mules, went out into the hallway, and angrily lifted the receiver:

"Hello," he grumbled.

A strange voice answered. "Hello. Is this Raymond Taylor?"

"It is."

"This is Artie Fletcher, Paul's roommate. Can you come down to my house right away? Something terrible has happened."

Raymond was now fully awake. The tone of horror in the voice at the other end of the wire both stimulated and frightened him. He had a vague, eerie premonition of impending tragedy.

"What is it? What's happened?" he queried impatiently.

"Paul's committed suicide."

Raymond almost dropped the receiver. Mechanically he obtained the address, assured Artie Fletcher that he would rush to the scene, and within a very few moments was dressed and on his way.

The subway ride was long and tedious. Only local trains were in operation, local trains which blundered along slowly, stopping at every station, droning noisily: Paul is dead. Paul is dead.

Had Paul the debonair, Paul the poseur, Paul the irresponsible romanticist, finally faced reality and seen himself and the world as they actually were? Or was this merely another act, the final stanza in his drama of beautiful gestures? It was consonant with his character, this committing suicide. He had employed every other conceivable means to make himself stand out from the mob. Wooed the unusual, cultivated artificiality, defied all conventions of dress and conduct. Now perhaps he had decided that there was nothing left for him to do except execute self-murder in some bizarre manner. Raymond found himself not so much interested in the fact that Paul was dead as he was in wanting to know how death had been accomplished. The train trundled along clamoring: What did he do? What did he do? Raymond deplored the fact that he had not had sufficient money to hire a taxi.

The train reached Christopher Street. Raymond rushed out of the subway to the street above. He hesitated a moment to get his bearings, repeated the directions he had been given over the telephone, and plunged into a maze of criss-cross streets. As he neared his goal, a slender white youth fluttered toward him.

"Are you Raymond Taylor?"

"Yes."

"Come this way, please. I was watching for you."

Raymond followed his unknown companion into a malodorous, jerry-built tenement, and climbed four flights of creaky stairs to a rear room, lighted only by burning planks in the fireplace. There were several people in the room, all strangely hushed and pale. A chair was vacated for him near the fireplace. No introductions were made. Raymond lit a cigarette to hide his nervousness. His guide, whom he presumed to be Artie Fletcher, told him the details of Paul's suicide.

Earlier that evening they had gone to a party. It had been a wild revel. There had been liquor and cocaine which everyone had taken in order to experience a new thrill. There had been many people at the party and it had been difficult to keep track of any one person. When the party had come to an end, Paul was nowhere to be found, and his roommate had come home alone.

An hour or so later, he had heard a commotion in the hallway. Several people were congregated outside the bathroom door, grumbling because they had been unable to gain admittance. The bathroom, it seemed, had been occupied for almost two hours and there was no response from within. Finally someone suggested breaking down the door. This had been done. No one had been prepared for the gruesome yet fascinating spectacle which met their eyes.

Paul had evidently come home before the end of the party. On arriving, he had locked himself in the bathroom, donned a crimson mandarin robe, wrapped his head in a batik scarf of his own designing, hung a group of his spirit portraits on the dingy calcimined wall, and carpeted the floor with sheets of paper detached from the notebook in which he had been writing his novel. He had then, it seemed, placed scented joss-sticks in the four corners of the room, lit them, climbed into the bathtub, turned on the water, then slashed his wrists with a highly ornamented Chinese dirk. When they found him, the bathtub had overflowed, and Paul lay crumpled at the bottom, a colorful, inanimate corpse in a crimson streaked tub.

What delightful publicity to precede the posthumous publication of his novel, which novel, however, had been rendered illegible when the overflow of water had inundated the floor, and soaked the sheets strewn over its surface. Paul had not foreseen the possible inundation, nor had he taken into consideration the impermanency of penciled transcriptions.

Artie Fletcher had salvaged as many of the sheets as possible. He handed the sodden mass to Raymond. Ironically enough, only the title sheet and the dedication page were completely legible. The book was entitled:

Wu Sing: The Geisha Man

It had been dedicated:

To
Huysmans' Des Esseintes and Oscar Wilde's Oscar Wilde
Ecstatic Spirits with whom I Cohabit
And whose golden spores of decadent pollen
I shall broadcast and fertilize
It is written
Paul Arbian.

Beneath this inscription, he had drawn a distorted, inky black skyscraper, modeled after Niggeratti Manor, and on which were focused an array of blindingly white beams of light. The foundation of this building was composed of crumbling stone. At first glance it could be ascertained that the skyscraper would soon crumple and fall, leaving the dominating white lights in full possession of the sky.

GEORGE SCHUYLER

NO INSTITUTION OR PERSONALITY *escaped the Juvenalian satire of George Schuyler in his divertingly preposterous* Black No More, *perhaps the most talked about Renaissance novel of 1931. The African American scientist Dr. Junius Crookman invents a process, quickly turned into a commercial bonanza, whereby black people turn themselves into white people. White panic is matched by black consternation, as the National Social Equality League (the NAACP) faces disintegration and the great hair-straightening empire of Madame Sisseretta Blandish (Madame C. J. Walker) totters on the verge of bankruptcy. Santop Licorice (Marcus Garvey) struggles to remain relevant; the KKK stumbles. Du Bois, rendered as Dr. Shakespeare Agamemnon Beard, and Walter White ("his grandfather, it seemed, had been a mulatto") see their life's work in civil rights nullified. The leaders begin to "envision the time when they would no longer be able for the sake of the Negro race to suffer the hardships of lunching on canvasback duck at the Urban Club surrounded by the white dilettante, endure the perils of first-class Transatlantic passage to Save-Dear-Africa Conferences or undergo the excruciating torture of rolling back and forth across the United States in drawing-rooms to hear each lecture upon the Negro problem." The author saves the situation, however, by revealing that the black people who have turned white are slightly whiter than the original white people, thus providing a new basis for a reconstructed racism.*

FROM *BLACK NO MORE*

THE NATIONAL OFFICE of the militant Negro organization, the National Social Equality League, was agog. Telephone bells were ringing, mulatto clerks were hustling excitedly back and forth, messenger boys rushed in and out. Located in the Times Square district of Manhattan, it had for forty years carried on the fight for full social equality for the Negro citizens and the immediate abolition of lynching as a national sport. While this organization had to depend to a large extent upon the charity of white folk for its existence, since the blacks had always been more or less skeptical about the program for liberty and freedom, the efforts of the society were not entirely unprofitable. Vistas of immaculate offices spread in every direction from the elevator and footfalls were muffled in thick imitation-Persian rugs. While the large staff of officials was eager to end all oppression and persecution of the Negro, they were never so happy and excited as when a Negro was barred from a theater or fried to a crisp. Then they would leap for telephones, grab telegraph pads and yell for stenographers; smiling through their simulated indignation at the spectacle of another reason for their continued existence and appeals for funds.

Ever since the first sanitarium of Black-No-More, Incorporated, started turning Negroes into Caucasians, the National Social Equality League's income had been decreasing. No dues had been collected in months and subscriptions to the national mouthpiece, *The Dilemma*, had dwindled to almost nothing. Officials, long since ensconced in palatial apartments, began to grow panic-stricken as pay days got farther apart. They began to envision the time when they would no longer be able for the sake of the Negro race to suffer the hardships of lunching on canvasback duck at the Urban Club surrounded by the white dilettante, endure the perils of first-class Transatlantic passage to stage Save-Dear-Africa Conferences or undergo the excruciating torture of rolling back and forth across the United States in drawing-rooms to hear each other lecture on the Negro problem. On meager salaries of five thousand dollars a year they had fought strenuously and tirelessly to obtain for the Negroes the constitutional rights which only a few thousand rich white folk possessed. And now they saw the work of a lifetime being rapidly destroyed.

Single-handed they felt incapable of organizing an effective opposition to Black-No-More, Incorporated, so they had called a conference of all of the outstanding Negro leaders of the country to assemble at the League's headquarters on December 1, 1933. Getting the Negro leaders together for any purpose except boasting of each other's accomplishments had previously been impossible. As a usual thing they fought each other with a vigor only surpassed by that of their pleas for racial solidarity and unity of action. This situation, however, was unprecedented, so almost all of the representative gentlemen of color to whom invitations had been sent agreed with alacrity to come. To a man they felt that it was time to bury the hatchet before they became too hungry to do any digging.

In a very private inner office of the N. S. E. L. suite, Dr. Shakespeare Agamemnon Beard, founder of the League and a graduate of Harvard, Yale and Copenhagen (whose haughty bearing never failed to impress both Caucasians and Negroes) sat before a glass-topped desk, rubbing now his curly gray head, and now his full spade beard. For a mere six thousand dollars a year, the learned doctor wrote scholarly and biting editorials in *The Dilemma* denouncing the Caucasians whom he secretly admired and lauding the greatness of the Negroes whom he alternately pitied and despised. In limpid prose he told of the sufferings and privations of the downtrodden black workers with whose lives he was totally and thankfully unfamiliar. Like most Negro leaders, he deified the black woman but abstained from employing aught save octoroons. He talked at white banquets about "we of the black race" and admitted in books that he was part-French, part-Russian, part-Indian and part-Negro. He bitterly denounced the Nordics for debauching Negro women while taking care to hire comely yellow stenographers with weak resistance. In a real way, he loved his people. In time of peace he was a Pink Socialist but when the clouds of war gathered he bivouacked at the feet of Mars.

Before the champion of the darker races lay a neatly typed resolution drawn up by him and his staff the day before and addressed to the Attorney General of the United States. The staff had taken this precaution because no member of it believed that the other Negro leaders possessed sufficient education to word the document effectively and grammatically. Dr. Beard re-read the resolution and then placing it in the drawer of the desk, pressed one of a row of buttons. "Tell them to come in," he directed. The mulattress turned and switched out of the room, followed by the appraising and approving eye of the aged scholar. He heaved a regretful sigh as the door closed and his thoughts dwelt on the vigor of his youth.

In three or four minutes the door opened again and several well-dressed blacks, mulattoes and white men entered the large office and took seats around the wall. They greeted each other and the President of the League with usual cordiality but for the first time in their lives they were sincere about it. If anyone could save the day it was Beard. They all admitted that, as did the Doctor himself. They pulled out fat cigars, long slender cigarettes and London briar pipes, lit them and awaited the opening of the conference.

The venerable lover of his race tapped with his knuckle for order, laid aside his six-inch cigarette and rising, said:

"It were quite unseemly for me who lives such a cloistered life and am spared the bane or benefit of many intimate contacts with those of our struggling race who by sheer courage, tenacity and merit have lifted their heads above the mired mass, to deign to take from a more capable individual the unpleasant task of reviewing the combination of unfortunate circumstances that has brought us together, man to man, within the four walls of the office." He shot a foxy glance around the assembly and then went on suavely. "And so, my friends, I beg your august permission to confer upon my able and cultured secretary and confidant, Dr. Napoleon Wellington Jackson, the office of chairman of this temporary body. I need not introduce Dr. Jackson to you. You know of his scholarship, his high sense of duty and his deep love of the suffering black race. You have doubtless had the pleasure of singing some of the many sorrow songs he has written and popularized in the past twenty years, and you must know of his fame as a translator of Latin poets and his authoritative work on the Greek language.

"Before I gratefully yield the floor to Dr. Jackson, however, I want to tell you that our destiny lies in the stars. Ethiopia's fate is in the balance. The Goddess of the Nile weeps bitter tears at the feet of the Great Sphinx. The lowering clouds gather over the Congo and the lightning flashes o'er Togoland. To your tents, O Israel! The hour is at hand."

The president of the N. S. E. L. sat down and the erudite Dr. Jackson, his tall, lanky secretary got up. There was no fear of Dr. Jackson ever winning a beauty contest. He was a sooty black, very broad shouldered, with long, ape-like arms, a diminutive egg-shaped head that sat on his collar like a hen's egg on a demitasse cup and eyes that protruded so far from his head that they seemed about to fall out. He wore pince-nez that were continually slipping from his very flat and oily nose. His chief business in the organization was to write long and indignant letters to public officials and legislators whenever a Negro was mistreated, demanding justice, fair play and other legal guarantees vouchsafed no whites except bloated plutocrats fallen miraculously afoul of the law, and to speak to audiences of sex-starved matrons who yearned to help the Negro stand erect. During his leisure time, which was naturally considerable, he wrote long and learned articles, bristling with references, for the more intellectual magazines, in which he sought to prove conclusively that the plantation shouts of Southern Negro peons were superior to any of Beethoven's symphonies and that the city of Benin was the original site of the Garden of Eden.

"Hhmm! Hu-umn! Now er—ah, gentlemen," began Dr. Jackson, rocking back on his heels, taking off his eye glasses and beginning to polish them with a silk kerchief, "as you know, the Negro race is face to face with a grave crisis. I-ah-presume it is er-ah unnecessary for me to go into any details concerning the-ah activities of Black-No-More, Incorporated. Suffice er-ah umph! ummmmh! to say-ah that it has thrown our society into rather a-ah bally turmoil. Our people are forgetting shamelessly their-ah duty to the-ah organizations that have fought valiantly for them these-ah many years and are now busily engaged chasing a bally-ah will-o-the wisp. Ahem!

"You-ah probably all fully realize that-ah a continuation of the aforementioned activities will prove disastrous to our-ah organizations. You-ah, like us, must feel-uh that something drastic must be done to preserve the integrity of Negro society. Think, gentlemen, what the future will mean to-uh all those who-uh have toiled so hard for Negro society. What-ah, may I ask, will we do when there are no longer any-ah groups to support us? Of course, Dr. Crookman and-ah his associates have a-uh perfect right to-ah engage in any legitimate business, but-ah their present activities cannot-ah be classed under that head, considering the effect on our endeavors. Before we go any further, however, I-ah would like to introduce our research expert Mr. Walter Williams, who will-ah describe the situation in the South."

Mr. Walter Williams, a tall, heavy-set white man with pale blue eyes, wavy auburn hair and a militant, lantern jaw, rose and bowed to the assemblage and proceeded to paint a heartrending picture of the loss of pride and race solidarity among Negroes North and South. There was, he said, not a single local of the N. S. E. L. functioning, dues had dwindled to nothing, he had not been able to hold a meeting anywhere, while many of the stanchest supporters had gone over into the white race.

"Personally," he concluded, "I am very proud to be a Negro and always have been (his great-grandfather, it seemed, had been a mulatto), and I'm willing to sacrifice for the uplift of my race. I cannot understand what has come over our people that they have so quickly forgotten the ancient glories of Ethiopia, Songhay and Dahomey, and their marvelous record of achievement since emancipation." Mr. Williams was known to be a Negro among his friends and acquaintances, but no one else would have suspected it.

Another white man of remote Negro ancestry, Rev. Herbert Gronne of Dunbar University, followed the research expert with a long discourse in which he expressed fear for the future of his institution whose student body had been reduced to sixty-five persons and deplored the catastrophe "that has befallen us black people."

They all listened with respect to Dr. Gronne. He had been in turn a college professor, a social worker and a minister, had received the approval of the white folks and was thus doubly acceptable to the Negroes. Much of his popularity was due to the fact that he very cleverly knew how to make statements that sounded radical to Negroes but sufficiently conservative to satisfy the white trustees of his school. In addition he possessed the asset of looking perpetually earnest and sincere.

Following him came Colonel Mortimer Roberts, principal of the Dusky River Agricultural Institute, Supreme General of the Knights and Daughters of Kingdom Come and president of the Uncle Tom Memorial Association. Colonel Roberts was the acknowledged leader of the conservative Negroes (most of whom had nothing to conserve) who felt at all times that the white folks were in the lead and that Negroes should be careful to guide themselves accordingly.

He was a great mountain of blackness with a head shaped like an upturned bucket, pierced by two pig-like eyes and a cavernous mouth equipped with large tombstone teeth which he almost continually displayed. His speech was a cross between the woofing of a bloodhound and the explosion of an inner tube. It conveyed to most white people an impression of rugged simplicity and sincerity, which was very fortunate since Colonel Roberts maintained his school through their contributions. He spoke as usual about the cordial relations existing between the two races in his native Georgia, the effrontery of Negroes who dared whiten themselves and thus disturb the minds of white people and insinuated alliance with certain militant organizations in the South to stop this whitening business before it went too far. Having spoken his mind and received scant applause, the Colonel (some white man had once called him Colonel and the title stuck) puffing and blowing, sat down.

Mr. Claude Spelling, a scared-looking little brown man with big ears, who held the exalted office of president of the Society of Negro Merchants, added his volume of blues to the discussion. The refrain was that Negro business—always anemic—was about to pass out entirely through lack of patronage. Mr. Spelling had for many years been the leading advocate of the strange doctrine that an underpaid Negro worker should go out of his way to patronize a little dingy Negro store instead of going to a cheaper and cleaner chain store, all for the dubious satisfaction of helping Negro merchants grow wealthy.

The next speaker, Dr. Joseph Bonds, a little rat-faced Negro with protruding teeth stained by countless plugs of chewing tobacco and wearing horn-rimmed spectacles, who headed the Negro Data League, almost cried (which would have been terrible to observe) when he told of the difficulty his workers had encountered in their efforts to persuade retired white capitalists, whose guilty consciences persuaded them to indulge in philanthropy, to give their customary donations to the work. The philanthropists seemed to think, said Dr. Bonds, that since the Negroes were busily solving their difficulties, there was no need for social work among them or any collection of data. He almost sobbed aloud when he described how his collections had fallen from $50,000 a month to less than $1000.

His feeling in the matter could easily be appreciated. He was engaged in a most vital and necessary work: i.e., collecting bales of data to prove satisfactorily to all that more money was needed to collect more data. Most of the data were highly informative, revealing the amazing fact that poor people went to jail oftener than rich ones; that most of the people were not getting enough money for their work; that strangely enough there was some connection between poverty, disease and crime. By establishing these facts with mathematical certitude and illustrating them with elaborate graphs, Dr. Bonds garnered many fat checks. For his people, he said, he wanted work, not charity; but for himself he was always glad to get the charity with as little work as possible. For many years he had succeeded in doing so without any ascertainable benefit accruing to the Negro group.

Dr. Bonds' show of emotion almost brought the others to tears and many of them muttered "Yes, Brother" while he was talking. The conferees were getting stirred up but it took the next speaker to really get them excited.

When he rose an expectant hush fell over the assemblage. They all knew and respected the Right Reverend Bishop Ezekiel Whooper of the Ethiopian True Faith Wash Foot Methodist Church for three reasons: viz., his church was rich (though the parishioners were poor), he had a very loud voice and the white people praised him. He was sixty, corpulent and an expert at the art of making cuckolds.

"Our loyal and devoted clergy," he boomed, "are being forced into manual labor and the Negro church is rapidly dying" and then he launched into a violent tirade against Black-No-More and favored any means to put the corporation out of business. In his excitement he blew saliva, waved his long arms, stamped his feet, pummeled the desk, rolled his eyes, knocked down his chair, almost sat on the rug and generally reverted to the antics of Negro bush preachers.

This exhibition proved contagious. Rev. Herbert Gronne, face flushed and shouting amens, marched from one end of the room to the other; Colonel Roberts, looking like an inebriated black-faced comedian, rocked back and forth clapping his hands; the others began to groan and moan. Dr. Napoleon Wellington Jackson, sensing his opportunity, began to sing a spiritual in his rich soprano voice. The others immediately joined him. The very air seemed charged with emotion.

Bishop Whooper was about to start up again, when Dr. Beard, who had sat cold and disdainful through this outbreak of revivalism, toying with his gold-rimmed fountain pen and gazing at the exhibition through half-closed eyelids, interrupted in sharp metallic tones.

"Let's get down to earth now," he commanded. "We've had

enough of this nonsense. We have a resolution here addressed to the Attorney General of the United States demanding that Dr. Crookman and his associates be arrested and their activities stopped at once for the good of both races. All those in favor of this resolution say aye. Contrary? . . . Very well, the ayes have it . . . Miss Hilton please send off this telegram at once!"

They looked at Dr. Beard and each other in amazement. Several started to meekly protest.

"You gentlemen are all twenty-one, aren't you?" sneered Beard. "Well, then be men enough to stand by your decision."

"But Doctor Beard," objected Rev. Gronne, "isn't this a rather unusual procedure?"

"Rev. Gronne," the great man replied, "it's not near as unusual as Black-No-More. I have probably ruffled your dignity but that's nothing to what Dr. Crookman will do."

"I guess you're right, Beard," the college president agreed.

"I know it," snapped the other.

The Honorable Walter Brybe, who had won his exalted position as Attorney General of the United States because of his long and faithful service helping large corporations to circumvent the federal laws, sat at his desk in Washington, D. C. Before him lay the wired resolution from the conference of Negro leaders. He pursed his lips and reached for his private telephone.

"Gorman?" he inquired softly into the receiver. "Is that you?"

"Nossuh," came the reply, "this heah is Mistah Gay's valet."

"Well, call Mister Gay to the telephone at once."

"Yassuh."

"That you, Gorman," asked the chief legal officer of the nation addressing the National Chairman of his party.

"Yeh, what's up?"

"You heard 'bout this resolution from them niggers in New York, aint you? It's been in all of the papers."

"Yes I read it."

"Well, whaddya think we oughtta do about it?"

"Take it easy, Walter. Give 'em the old run around. You know. They ain't got a thin dime; it's this other crowd that's holding the heavy jack. And 'course you know we gotta clean up our deficit. Just lemme work with that Black-No-More crowd. I can talk business with that Johnson fellow."

"All right, Gorman, I think you're right, but you don't want to forget that there's a whole lot of white sentiment against them coons."

"Needn't worry 'bout that," scoffed Gorman. "There's no money behind it much and besides it's in states we can't carry anyhow. Go ahead; stall them New York niggers off. You're a lawyer, you can always find a reason."

"Thanks for the compliment, Gorman," said the Attorney General, hanging up the receiver.

He pressed a button on his desk and a young girl, armed with pencil and pad, came in.

"Take this letter," he ordered: "To Doctor Shakespeare Agamemnon Beard (what a hell of a name!), Chairman of the Committee for the Preservation of Negro Racial Integrity, 1400 Broadway, New York City.

> "My dear Dr. Beard:
> The Attorney General has received the resolution signed by yourself and others and given it careful consideration.
> Regardless of personal views in the matter (I don't give a damn whether they turn white or not, myself) it is not possible for the Department of Justice to interfere with a legitimate business enterprise so long as its methods are within the law. The corporation in question has violated no federal statute and hence there is not the slightest ground for interfering with its activities.
> Very truly yours,
> Walter Brybe.

"Get that off at once. Give out copies to the press. That's all."

Santop Licorice, founder and leader of the Back-to-Africa Society, read the reply of the Attorney General to the Negro leaders with much malicious satisfaction. He laid aside his morning paper, pulled a fat cigar from a box near by, lit it and blew clouds of smoke above his woolly head. He was always delighted when Dr. Beard met with any sort of rebuff or embarrassment. He was doubly pleased in this instance because he had been overlooked in the sending out of invitations to Negro leaders to join the Committee for the Preservation of Negro Racial Integrity. It was outrageous, after all the talking he had done in favor of Negro racial integrity.

Mr. Licorice for some fifteen years had been very profitably advocating the emigration of all the American Negroes to Africa. He had not, of course, gone there himself and had not the slightest intention of going so far from the fleshpots, but he told the other Negroes to go. Naturally the first step in their going was to join his society by paying five dollars a year for membership, ten dollars for a gold, green and purple robe and silver-colored helmet that together cost two dollars and a half, contributing five dollars to the Santop Licorice Defense Fund (there was a perpetual defense fund because Licorice was perpetually in the courts for fraud of some kind), and buying shares at five dollars each in the Royal Black Steamship Company, for obviously one could not get to Africa without a ship and Negroes ought to travel on Negro-owned and operated ships. The ships were Santop's especial pride. True, they had never been to Africa, had never had but one cargo and that, being gin, was half consumed by the unpaid and thirsty crew before the vessel was saved by the Coast Guard, but they had cost more than anything else the Back-To-Africa Society had purchased even though they were worthless except as scrap iron. Mr. Licorice, who was known by his followers as Provisional President of Africa, Admiral of the African Navy, Field Marshal of the African Army and Knight Commander of the Nile, had a genius for being stuck with junk by crafty salesmen. White men only needed to tell him that he was shrewder than white men and he would immediately reach for a check book.

But there was little reaching for check books in his office nowadays. He had been as hard hit as the other Negroes. Why should anybody in the Negro race want to go back to Africa at a cost of five hundred dollars for passage when they could stay in America and get white for fifty dollars? Mr. Licorice saw the point but instead of scuttling back to Demerara from whence he had come to save his race from oppression, he had hung on in the hope that the activities of Black-No-More, Incorporated, would be stopped. In the meantime, he had continued to attempt to save the Negroes by vigorously attacking all of the other Negro organizations and at the same time preaching racial solidarity and coöperation in his weekly newspaper, "*The African Abroad*," which was printed by white folks and had until a year ago been full of skin-whitening and hair-straightening advertisements.

"How is our treasury?" he yelled back through the dingy suite of offices to his bookkeeper, a pretty mulatto.

"What treasury?" she asked in mock surprise.

"Why, I thought we had seventy-five dollars," he blurted.

"We did, but the Sheriff got most of it yesterday or we wouldn't be in here today."

"Huumn! Well, that's bad. And tomorrow's pay day, isn't it?"

"Why bring that up?" she sneered. "I'd forgotten all about it."

"Haven't we got enough for me to get to Atlanta?" Licorice inquired, anxiously.

"There is if you're gonna hitch-hike."

"Well, of course, I couldn't do that," he smiled deprecatingly.

"I should say not," she retorted surveying his 250-pound, five-feet-six-inches of black blubber.

"Call Western Union," he commanded.

"What with?"

"Over the telephone, of course, Miss Hall," he explained.

"If you can get anything over that telephone you're a better man than I am, Gunga Din."

"Has the service been discontinued, young lady?"

"Try and get a number," she chirped. He gazed ruefully at the telephone.

"Is there anything we can sell?" asked the bewildered Licorice.

"Yeah, if you can get the Sheriff to take off his attachments."

"That's right, I had forgotten."

"You would."

"Please be more respectful, Miss Hall," he snapped. "Somebody might overhear you and tell my wife."

"Which one?" she mocked.

"Shut up," he blurted, touched in a tender spot, "and try to figure out some way for us to get hold of some money."

"You must think I'm Einstein," she said, coming up and perching herself on the edge of his desk.

"Well, if we don't get some operating expenses I won't be able to obtain money to pay your salary," he warned.

"The old songs are the best songs," she wise-cracked.

"Oh, come now, Violet," he remonstrated, pawing her buttock, "let's be serious."

"After all these years!" she declared, switching away.

In desperation, he eased his bulk out of the creaking swivel chair, reached for his hat and overcoat and shuffled out of the office. He walked to the curb to hail a taxicab but reconsidered when he recalled that a worn half-dollar was the extent of his funds. Sighing heavily, he trudged the two blocks to the telegraph office and sent a long day letter to Henry Givens, Imperial Grand Wizard of the Knights of Nordica—collect.

"Well, have you figured it out?" asked Violet when he barged into his office again.

"Yes, I just sent a wire to Givens," he replied.

"But he's a nigger-hater, isn't he?" was her surprised comment.

"You want your salary, don't you?" he inquired archly.

"I have for the past month."

"Well, then, don't ask foolish questions," he snapped.

ARNA BONTEMPS

IN THIS EXCERPT *from Arna Bontemps's first novel,* God Sends Sunday *(1931), the protagonist, Little Augie, heads for Tijuana, once again shambling on to another empty dissipation. Augie was a champion jockey in the days when African Americans dominated that profession. His championship days now in the past, along with his money spent in fast living, Augie's Sundays are less and less heaven-sent. In a flawed novel with tepid character delineation and jumpy plot lines, Bontemps managed, nevertheless, to capture somewhat the sporting life in big towns like New Orleans and St. Louis. Fate was more than kind to* God Sends Sunday. *It was eventually adapted for Broadway as the highly successful musical* St. Louis Woman.*

    Bontemps's Black Thunder *(1936) was the last of the Renaissance novels and one of its few historical ones. Its subject was the 1800 insurrection near Richmond, Virginia, led by the slave Gabriel Prosser. Torrential rains played havoc with the carefully planned conspiracy.*

FROM *GOD SENDS SUNDAY*

IT WAS NEAR CHRISTMAS when Augie reached New Orleans again, and things were sparkling for the Negroes. The eating-places and hang-outs were crowded with country folks who had come to town following the harvests. That portion of the city blacks who worked in sugar refineries or cotton fields during the warm months in order to loaf throughout the winter had returned. Everybody had money;

everybody was nigger-rich. A poker game was not respectable that had less than a hundred dollars in it. Stevedores risked twenty-dollar gold pieces on a single throw of the bones. Certain of the country folks tossed all their nickels and pennies into the gutter in order to keep their pockets from becoming cluttered.

But despite the general affluence, Augie could buy and sell the other blacks by the dozen. His earnings had gone into the thousands. More important than that, his name had risen like a young star; he had become famous.

He and Bad-foot went directly to the barber shop. There they described the St. Louis fancy women to the home-staying fellows. They talked about the Cotton Flower Ball and boasted of Augie's success in taking the cake. Some of the drifters wanted to get tips on horses. Augie assumed an indifference to such questions, but he warned his followers to keep an eye on a young colt named Silver Heels, a recent addition to the Woodbine stables, and a great favorite of Augie's.

The talk switched to other things, and when, a bit later, Mississippi entered the shop, Augie promptly drew him into a corner and asked about Florence.

"I don't know much," Mississippi said. "I ain't got de job no mo'."

"How come dat, Mis'sippi?"

The old frock-tailed Negro seemed embarrassed. "Mistah Woody ain't got Florence now; he done quits."

"Oh! I on'erstand."

"Seems lak his people got wind about it; so he had to duck."

"Lissen, Mis'sippi. You reckon I could ease in *now*?"

"I don't know, Lil Augie. Anuther white man been makin' up to her, but he ain't as fine as Mistah Woody."

"Who he?"

"Gummy, de saloon man."

Augie's lip turned. "Where's yo' rig, Mis'sippi?"

"Down de street a lil piece."

"Come on. Us gonna drive over there."

Half an hour later Augie knocked boldly at Florence's door. Mississippi remained in the high seat. Autumn had touched the leaves of the trees. They kept falling on the old rig, falling like flakes of gold through the transparent golden light. In these fading surroundings, Augie seemed as brilliant as a spring flower. He was dressed in bottle-green with a canary vest and canary spats over pearl-buttoned shoes.

"I jes' come back," he told Florence.

"How you lak St. Louis?"

"There ain't nuthin' there for me. No peace."

"So you come back on account o' dat?"

"De season is done finish," he said. "I'm gonna be heah a long time, an' I wants yo' company, yella gal."

"How you know I don't b'long to somebody else, Lil Augie?"

"If it ain't Mistah Woody, it don't matter," he said.

Florence stood erect between the dark plush curtains of her front room. She was much taller than Little Augie. She was slim and proud-like, and her crimson painted mouth was beautiful against buff-colored skin. Augie's heart leapt as he watched her. His dream seemed so near he could almost put his hands on it.

"You ain't ask me do I love you, Lil Augie."

His diamonds shook nervously. "I ain't askin' a heap, yella gal."

"You is got enough money to ask for de moon. They tells me you got mo' spikes than Carter is got oats, Lil Augie."

"An' I'm fixin' to spend 'em all on you. I'm gonna make you lucky too."

"Is dat truf?"

"Sho, I was borned wid a veil. I'm lucky, an' everybody whut takes up wid me gets lucky."

"We might could be sweet," she said.

When Augie came out of the house a little later he was swollen like a pouter pigeon.

"This heah is gonna be ma house," he told Mississippi. "I done made maself a home. Come back in de mawnin' an' you can have yo' old job back again."

For the next few days Augie and Florence were always together. Florence, the insolent well-kept girl whom young Horace Church-Woodbine had been smitten on, was pointed out all over town with Little Augie, the sparkling nigger-rich jockey. There was something insulting in the match, something humiliating to the friends of the wealthy sportsman. But Augie was unconscious of it. All he knew was that Florence was the yellowest and best-looking gal he had ever seen and that he loved her worse than a horse loves corn.

In the evening she made him sweetened water and kept filling his glass while he pumped the accordion and sang. Florence did not sing. Augie thought that that was just as well; a girl as fine as Florence needed no other talents. Besides, he felt able to supply

enough music for both of them. So he sang for her the new tunes
he had learned on Targee Street, sang them over and over again,
and his heart was so big and swollen with pleasure he thought it
would surely burst.

Wind was coming in from the Gulf with increasing strength,
and all through the cool evening crisp gold leaves fell with a tiny
clang and rattle against the windows and the door. Augie and Florence spent the hours examining new winter velvets that he had
bought her. Recently, money had been short in her house; she had
bought no new clothes in months. It gave Augie pleasure to supply
these; he outdid himself for lavishness. Nothing was too expensive.

Finally, it was arranged for him to move into Florence's
house—the house Mr. Woody had given her. Two full trunks were
sent ahead. His remaining possessions he packed in a new wicker
suitcase. This with the accordion he proposed to carry himself in
the carriage. While Mississippi waited at the door, Augie took
leave of Bad-foot.

"Us ain't gonna bus' up, Bad-foot. Us is always gonna be lak
dis." He held up his first two fingers.

"I gonna miss you jes' de same," Bad-foot said. "You is ma
luck stone, son."

"You is good luck yo' black self," Augie smiled.

"I donno." Bad-foot rubbed his slick head with a hard stubby
hand. "I donno 'bout me."

"I do. An' us gonna stay lak dis—no matter whut!"

Augie moved into Florence's house about midday. About midnight she moved out. The white neighbors, along with Gummy and
other hostile persons, hastily formed a charge of immorality against
the girl as soon as they understood. Florence had been too frankly
a white man's girl. There was nothing to do but go.

So together she and Augie took a simple shack on the far
fringes of the city, a shack behind a thicket on a yellow golden
road near a railroad track. It was too far away from the heart of
town for convenience, but there were trees on the roadside, and
the air was full of birds. In the thickets there were turkeys the color
of gun metal with red enameled heads, and in the road grouse
dusting their wings nervously.

Mississippi had come with them. Each day he drove Augie in
to the city. Often he returned again with both of them in the evening. Most of their time, it seemed, was spent in the carriage. And
Florence did not enjoy it.

All of a sudden bad days came upon Little Augie. An accumulation of bad luck, reserved from many, many days past, fell at once upon his head. For years a successful gambler, he was now unable to draw a single pair from a deck of cards. All the dice that had been so responsive to his cajoling now seemed loaded against him.

In the races his horses stumbled, wrenched their legs, or otherwise failed. Mr. Woody turned spiteful and assigned him to all the impossible mounts. Even Bad-foot, now a trainer and a person of some authority in the stables, seemed distant.

Augie began drinking more than usual. He could not bear to confront his wretched fortunes with a clear mind. He could not bear to look Florence in the face. She had expected so much of him; he had promised so much.

In his misery he returned again and again to the stables; the horses reassured him. As long as he had their mute sympathy, the comfort of their presence, he would never lose hope. Somehow his love of Florence seemed fleeting and unessential, a mere frill on his life, when he was near the horses. As much as he desired to make a fine impression on her, he knew that he would be utterly cast down if he failed. He was no simpering pie-backed nigger who lived by women. He was a race-horse man. A woman was like a fine suit of clothes to him, something to please his vanity, to show him off well in the eyes of his friends.

"Damn 'em all, all de womens! I b'lieve Florence is bad luck to me anyhow."

But that was just mouth-talk. He had hardly spoken the words when he wondered if he were not actually losing his mind about her. How otherwise could he have imagined such an outlandish lie! He sought his accordion.

> Oh, de boat's gone up de river
> An' de tide's gone down. . . .

Augie sat on the edge of his cot, tossing shoes, old shirts, and underclothes into the badly used wicker traveling-bag. It was leaving-time again.

"I thought I was fixed for life," he said. "But I ain't stayed heah no longer'n I stayed anywhere else."

He finished packing and put on the little greasy dirt-colored vest that once had been milk-white with red roses. But he decided

not to wear the coat; so he folded it carefully and laid it across the
other rags in his bag. A moment later he gathered up his luggage,
the bag in one hand, the accordion in the other, and slipped out
beneath the trees of the yard.

Night had fallen, and the moon was up, glimmering white,
remote and sadlike. The garden corn had been shocked and stood
near the fence in little abandoned wigwams. Augie's heart was full
of misery.

"I done carved ole Lissus wid de beet knife," he said. "I done
carved him good an' I'm glad I done it. He over yonder now strug-
glin' in his blood. An' he might be dead. So it's leavin'-time for Lil
Augie. Leavin'-time, an' I ain't comin' back."

He paused a moment, leaning on the gate post, chewing the
stem of his pipe with toothless gums. The dusty road was white in
the moonlight and seemed to curve upward at the end where it
went out of sight. Augie crossed it slowly and began climbing the
railroad embankment. Standing between the tracks, he gazed first
in one direction and then in the other. Both seemed alike from
where he stood. At each end there was a dim shining point. One
way was familiar to Augie—it was the way by which he had come
to Mudtown only a few short weeks earlier. The other way was
new and strange. That was the way he chose to go.

He began walking slowly. Beyond the high weeds, nesting in
a clump of red castor-bean trees, he saw the Clow shack. Farther
away, across the white sandy pasture, was the hut of Lissus and
Tisha. Beulah was in one of those houses. But Augie kept on walking. Behind him on the other side of the road Leah and Terry were
sitting in their tiny kitchen with no idea of what had happened,
no idea that Augie was leaving.

"I done lef' 'em lak a dream," he said. "I'm goin' to Tia Juana,
an' I ain't gonna write no letter."

Suddenly Augie heard footsteps under the low fruit trees on
the Clows' place. He paused a moment and heard his heart thumping. He saw no one. Still the footsteps kept coming. They were
coming toward him.

A moment later Tisha stepped out from the shadows, climbed
the barbed-wire fence, and started up the embankment a distance
behind Augie. Her head was tied in a handkerchief, her skirts were
tucked above her knees, and she was wearing a pair of heavy man's
shoes. She had in her hand the blacksnake with which she drove
the mules, and her cheeks were swollen with chewing-tobacco.

Augie had time to wonder what she was doing on the railroad tracks at that hour—considering the condition of Lissus. But he promptly realized that she was following him. He began to speed his steps. Tisha was after him with the mule whip. She was after him for hitting Lissus with the beet knife. Her steps were steady and deliberate. Yet she seemed to Augie to be drawing closer and closer to him. He was now walking as fast as his legs would carry him. But it wasn't fast enough. He began to run.

Suddenly the wicker bag went off the handle, fell open and tumbled down the side of the embankment. Augie saw at a glance that his rags were scattered among the dry stalks of wild mustard, his Prince Albert was hung on a briar.

"Tha's de las' button on Gabriel's coat," he muttered sadly. "Tha's eve'thing I got."

Tisha was still following, still threatening him with the whip; so he could not stop to regain his possessions. Instead he added speed to his steps.

A moment later, however, a wave of shame passed over him, and he stopped dead still in his tracks.

"Whut done got in me?" he said. "Heah I is breakin' ma neck runnin' from a woman—dat stinkin' black cat Tisha. Dis ain't lak Lil Augie. Dis ain't me."

Tisha had turned back. Augie could see her between the rails. She now seemed tiny and far away in the moonlight.

Augie rubbed his head. His hat too was gone. The night air felt cool on his bald spot. He chewed the stem of his cob pipe and realized that it was dry. The pipe was lost; it had fallen from the stem.

"I ain't nobody. I ain't nuthin'," he said. "I's jes' a po' picked sparrow. I ain't big as a dime, an' I don't worth a nickel."

But there was no need to turn back. He had carved Lissus with the beet knife, and it was leaving-time. He wasn't tired, and he still had his accordion. Tia Juana was somewhere ahead. He had learned that much from the postman. And there, he had been told, there was horse racing and plenty of liquor.

A few moments later a big locomotive headlight rose above the dim horizon and flashed in Augie's face. He left the embankment and got in the middle of the road. As the train drew nearer he could tell by its labored pulling that it was heavily loaded. The whole countryside, a tiny dark world with its near-by horizon, trembled at its approach. The trees rocked; fences swayed.

At a crossroads Augie stopped and waited for the long freighter to pass. While he stood there a large motor truck drove up and stopped beside him.

Some one shouted from the seat, "Where you goin', governor?"

"'Way down de line," Augie said. "To Tia Juana."

"Hop on if you wanna."

"Yes, *suh!*"

When the train finished passing, the truck pulled across the tracks and opened up on the smooth gravel road of the opposite side. Augie stretched out on the floor, resting his head on a pile of sacks, and began limbering up his accordion.

> Oh de boat's gone up de river
> An' de tide's gone down.

The night air whizzed about his head. Trees and houses and hills were flying past him like leaves in a hurricane. A little democrat wagon went by like a mere pasteboard toy. A strangely familiar feeling of exhilaration came to Augie, an illusion that came with speed. When had he felt that thrill before? He recalled Mr. Woody and his fast horses. It had been a good many years. So many indeed that Augie could not remember.

FROM *BLACK THUNDER*

THEY WERE GOING AGAINST RICHMOND with eleven hundred men and one woman. They were gathering like shadows at the Brook Swamp. Through the relentless downpour there went the motley rattle of their scythe-swords and the thump of bludgeons hanging from their belts. The ghostly insurrectionaires raked wet leaves overhead with pikes that stood against their shoulders. They splashed water ankle-deep in the honey-locust grove.

"A little rain won't hurt none," Gabriel said, his back against a sapling.

"No, I reckon it won't," Martin whispered. "Yet and still, it might be a sign, mightn't it?"

"Sign of what?"

"I don't know. Bad hand or something like that, maybe."

"Humph! Whoever heard tell about rain being a sign of a bad hand against you?"

Martin's voice faded into the slosh of water, the swish and thrum in the tree-tops and the rattle of home-made side arms. Bare feet churned the mud. One of the Negroes with an extremely heavy voice had a barking cough on his chest. All of them were restless; they kept plop-plopping like cattle in a bog. Now and again a flash brightened their drenched bodies.

Near Gabriel, beneath the next tree, the thin-waisted girl sat like a statue on the black colt. Her wet hair had tightened into a savage bush. She still wore Marse Prosser's high riding boots, but above her knees her thighs were wet and gleaming. She sat rapt, only the things she had fastened to her ears moving.

"How many's here?" Gabriel asked.

"Near about fo'-hundred."

"Some of them's slow coming."

"The rain's holding them back, I reckon."

"They needs to get a move on. Time ain't waiting and the rain ain't fixing to let up. Leastwise, it don't seem like it is."

"It's getting worser. We going to have a time crossing the branches between here and town if we don't start soon."

"You better go on back with the other womens, gal; you's apt to catch yo' death out in all this water."

"Anybody what's studying about freedom is apt to catch his death, one way or another, ain't he?"

"But it's a men-folks' job just the same. It ain't a fitten way for womens to die."

Thunder broke and a fresh shower began before the old one had diminished. Presently another followed and again another, like waves succeeding waves on a tortured reef. The invisible Negroes milled more and more restlessly in the sloppy grove.

"I don't aim to go back, though."

Gabriel knew how to answer that. He decided to forget the matter.

"Ditcher and his crowd ain't here yet," he said.

"It's the rain, I reckon."

"We got to get started just the same. It ain't good to wait. Some of them'll start talking about signs and one thing and another. We got to keep on the move now we's here. Martin. You Martin!"

The older brother wasn't far away. He came near enough to whisper.

"You 'spect it's too much water tonight, Gabriel?"

"Too much water for what?"

"I's just thinking maybe Ditcher and the country crowd's hemmed in. Them creeks out that a-way might be too deep and swift to cross after all this."

"Well *we's* here. There's near about fo'-hundred of us, and we'll go without the others if they don't come soon. You and Solomon and Blue line them up. Find Criddle and send him here. We got to get a move on. There's creeks for us 'tween here and town, and I bound you there's high water in them too. Hush all the talking and make everyone stand still for orders. Hurry. Get Criddle first."

Martin was gone, splashing a lot of water.

"What line you want me in?" Juba said.

"You can take Ditcher's place till he come. Araby'll be something for the line to follow. That you, Criddle?"

"Yes, this here me."

"You know your first job?"

"H'm. That little old house this side of town."

"That's it. Just stay in the yard till the line pass by. There's a old po' white man there that's apt to jump on his horse and start waking up the town folks do he hear us passing. You stay in the yard till the line get by—on'erstand?"

"H'm. I on'erstands."

"Well, light out then. You's going to wait there for us. If anything happen, you's got yo' blade and you oughta know by now what you got it for. Blue——"

"I'm right here."

"Get my crowd in line. We got to lead the way—hear?"

"They's ready."

"Well and good then. That you, Martin?"

"Yes, this me."

"Why in the nation don't you hurry and get yo' crowd in line?"

"Some of them's thinking maybe all this here thunder and lightning and rain's a sure 'nough bad sign."

"Listen. Listen, all y'-all." Gabriel raised his voice, turning around in excitement. "They ain't a lasting man nowheres ever heard tell of rain being a sign of a bad hand or nothing else. If any one of you's getting afeared, he can tuck his tail and go on back. I'm going to give the word directly, and them what's coming can

come, and them what ain't can talk about signs. Thunder and lightning ain't nothing neither. If it is, I invites it to try me a barrel."
He put out a massive chest, struck it a resounding smack. "Touch
me if you's so bad, Big Man." A huge roar filled the sky. The
lightning snapped bitterly. Gabriel roared with laughter, slapping
his chest again and again. "Sign, hunh! Is y'-all ready to come with
me?"

"We's ready," Blue said.

There was a strong murmur of assent. Then a pause, waiting
for the orders. The colt whinneyed and the thin rider pulled him
around so that his face was away from the force of the rain.

"Remember, we's falling on them like eagles. We's hushing up
everything what opens its mouth—all but the French folks. And
we ain't aiming to miss, neither, but if anything *do* go wrong, there
won't be no turning back. The mountains is the only place for us
then." No one spoke. After a pause he turned to the girl. "Juba, I
reckon you could hurry back and see for sure is Ditcher and his
crowd coming. Tell them we's starting down the creek and they
can meet us at the first crossing place."

Araby wheeled, sloshing water noisily, hastened away. Lightning played on the girl's wet garment. Solomon's voice came out
of a pocket of darkness.

"We's waiting for the word," he said.

"Stay ready," Gabriel told him. "I'm going to give it directly."

Nothing like it had happened before in Virginia. The downpour
came first in swirls; then followed diagonal blasts that bore down
with withering strength. The thirsting earth sucked up as much
water as it could but presently spewed little slobbery streams into
the wrinkles of the ground. Small gullies took their fill with open
mouths and let the rest run out. Rivulets wriggled in the wheel
paths, cascaded over small embankments. The creeks grew fat. Water rose in the swamps and in the low fields, and gradually Henrico
County became a sea with islands and bays, reefs and currents and
atolls.

Cattle, knee-deep in their stalls, set up a vast lamentation. An
old sow, nursing her young in a puddle of slime, let out a sudden
prolonged wail and scampered into a hay mow with her eleven
pigs. Down by a barn fence a lean and sullen mule stood with
lowered head, his hinder parts lashed tender by the storm. A flock

of speckled chickens went down screaming when the wind whipped off a peach bough.

General John Scott stood in a barn door with a lantern in his hand. He wore a frayed overcoat with sleeves that covered his hands and a wet, fallen-down hat with a brim that covered his eyes. His light hollowed out an orange hole in the blackness, and into it rain poured.

"Here I'm is," the old slave muttered, "'tween the earth and the sea and the sky, and how I'm going to get the rest of the way to Richmond to catch the stagecoach is mo'n a nachal man can tell."

The door flew open and a gust like a bucket of water slopped into his face.

Well, suh, if this here storm ain't the beatingest thing yet. Just when everybody was all fixed and fitten to go, here comes a plague of rain to put the whole countryside under water. Now how in the nation is folks going to get together? Lordy, Lordy. Listen, Lordy. You remember about the chillun of Israel, don't you? Well, this here is the very same thing perzactly. . . . The Lord was on their side, sure as you're born, but some of his ways was mysterious plus.

Another bucket of water splashed in the General's face.

"Confound this tarnation door," he said aloud. "It keep on blowing open. This here rain don't let up directly, I'm going to light out walking again anyhow."

In a thicket on the edge of town wind raked the shingles of a small log house. The undersized cabin, hidden in a tangle of wild plum, columbine and honeysuckle, squatted like a hurt thing under a bush. A light burned inside one of the tiny rooms.

Grisselda stood at the window in an outing night dress that covered her feet. She held a lamp so that it would throw a small beam into the yard. Presently the withered voice of her old father came out of the little dark chamber beyond the kitchen.

"You ain't scairt of the wind, air ye, Grisselda?"

"Oh, no. I don't mind the wind, papa."

"Well, why don't you blow the lamp out then?"

"I was just going to blow it out, papa."

She returned to the high bed. In a moment she was again conscious of the old man's snoring. She lay very still, hearing beams groan after the gusts and squalls. Her face must have been flushed; it felt very warm. Suddenly she heard the thing again and the sound brought her bolt upright in the bed. It was a noise the rain could not make, a tearing of twigs that was unlike wind, and Grisselda knew that if it were not a living creature, it was the very beast of ill weather. She waited and heard it rubbing against the house, something heavier than a cat, something with softer feet than a yearling, a more elastic body than a dog. And the girl would have sprung from the bed and rushed into the kitchen screaming, but at that moment the breath was out of her and she could not move.

For many moments she was sitting there imagining the kind of things that might seek a tangled thicket off the big road on a night like this. A panther? A thug? Was the creature hiding or prowling? What would he seek in the cabin of a widowed old man and his young daughter, destitute white folks who were poorer than black slaves?

Grisselda remembered that she was sixteen now; she knew why a young farmer had noticed the color of her hair and why the middle-aged storekeeper had recently pinched her cheek. A lewd word dropped into her thought like a pebble falling into a well. She curled her feet uneasily, but in the next moment she was cold with fear again. The thing seemed to be setting its weight against the door. Grisselda sprang from the bed and ran into the kitchen.

"Papa!"

"Still prowling, air ye?"

"Didn't you hear nothing at all, papa?"

"God bless me, who could help hearing a storm like this, gal?"

"Not that—something in the yard, something against the door?"

"Against the door, hunh?"

She put a hand on the table and felt her own quaking for the first time. The old man murmured something. They waited.

COUNTEE CULLEN

COUNTEE CULLEN'S One Way to Heaven *(1932) was really two novels in one—a story of High Renaissance manners and of working-class life. Despite its publication date, the novel reflected the values of the second phase of the Harlem Renaissance. Unlike McKay, Van Vechten, and Thurman, Cullen explored the cosmopolitan and the unsophisticated in a generous spirit and with a keener sociological eye. The novel respected what it mocked, and so lacked the proletarian grit of* Home to Harlem *and the bitterness of* The Blacker the Berry. . . .*

Constancia Brandon, Radcliffe graduate and socialite wife of Harlem's wealthiest physician, insists that Sam Lucas and Mattie Johnson, her maid, hold their wedding in her home. Amid a roisterous, amusing nuptial at which the full cast of the Harlem Renaissance is present in thin disguise, Cullen attempts to capture High and Low Harlem more fully than had Rudolph Fisher in this somewhat unwieldy and artificial novel, The Walls of Jericho.

FROM ONE WAY TO HEAVEN

"WHAT PLANS HAVE YOU MADE for the wedding?" [Constancia] asked Mattie.

"Oh, we haven't made any plans. Sam is waiting for me at the house. I told him I'd be there as soon as I could get away from here, and then we'd go and get the license together, and come back uptown and have Reverend Drummond marry us."

"Mattie"—Constancia leaned across the table, her gray eyes

kindled with largesse—"you must let me marry you from here. You must let me supervise your wedding."

Mattie demurred, "I don't know how Sam would like it."

"He is only incidental, my dear. This is your wedding. You must let me handle it for you."

As if it were settled, Constancia went on, carried away by the prospect, "Is there anybody you would like to come, any special body?"

"No one but Aunt Mandy."

"Well, I'll send George along with you in the car. He can take you down to get the license, and then bring you and Sam and your Aunt Mandy to the house. I'll arrange with Reverend Drummond and invite the guests, just a few friends of mine, to liven up the proceedings. Tell me, Mattie, how do you feel about miscegenation?"

Mattie, who had been taken unawares, without her dictionary, could only gasp in complete ignorance, "About what, ma'am?"

Constancia was so completely enamored of what the day promised, that she condescended to an explanation.

"I mean, my dear, do you mind if I invite some white people to witness the ceremony?"

"Oh, I don't think I'd like that. I don't care much for white people."

"Well, that's very wrong of you. I had no idea you were prejudiced. Nevertheless, it shall be as you like. You are missing a splendid material opportunity, for Walter Derwent has coined enough money on his articles about us to afford a handsome donation to the gift-table. Now I'll call George and you can go see about the license. We'll set the wedding for five o'clock. But you return as soon as you secure the license, for I want to dress you here. Bring Sam and your aunt along with you, so there will be no danger of his changing his mind. I'll have the minister here. . . . George!"

In answer to Constancia's shrill summons, George lumbered upstairs. "Darling, you will have to divest yourself of that badge of servitude," she said, pointing to the white coat he wore in his office, "and people who can't do any better will just have to die. You are having a holiday today. I am going to give Mattie away; that is I am going to have her married from here. I want you to take her and her husband-to-be down to the license bureau, and then bring them back here. Now run along. No, no, no. (Her negatives were like a dove's cooing, and each one was followed by a peck on George's lips.) No protestations. Run along."

As Mattie and George were leaving, Constancia suddenly remembered something. She ran to the door and poked her head out into the cold January air. Her earrings swung gayly.

"Mattie," she cried, "have we any rice?"

Mattie turned in bewilderment.

"Any rice, child, rice? You can't get married without rice. Oh, it's your wedding. How stupid of me to expect you to know what is needed! George, bring back some rice, about two pounds, superior quality."

Inside again, and seated at her desk, with a small golden pen poised over a white tablet, the telephone at her elbow, Constancia was so filled with plans that even she was at a loss where to begin. She thought it might be best to make certain that the minister was unengaged for the hour agreed upon. She dialed.

"Is this the Mount Hebron Methodist Episcopal Church? . . . Give me Reverend Drummond, please. . . . This *is* Reverend Drummond? How stupid of me! I should have recognized your voice. This is Mrs. Brandon—Mrs. George Brandon. I want to tell you how sorry I was to miss your exquisite revival. I hear it was disconcertingly successful and that sinners were taken in by the hundreds. . . . What? there were only thirty-odd? Well, even that is encouraging. Small commencements sometimes make frightfully large endings. Do let me know when you are having another revival. I have so many friends who might profit by attendance. Now to the point at issue. Can you perform a wedding at my home this afternoon at five? I know you will be interested to learn that the contending parties are two of your converts—my maid Mattie and the one-armed man who discarded his cards and his razor. . . . You will come? . . . How sweet of you. At five, then. Good-by."

She dialed again.

"Mrs. Vanderbilt-Jones? . . . Dear, this is Constancia. I want you to drop everything you are doing and be at my house at five o'clock. Mattie is being married. . . . Who is Mattie? Why, my maid, the one who makes those delicious anchovy sandwiches that you like so well. Yes, you recollect her now? Well, there won't be any anchovy sandwiches today because I can't make them and Mattie is being married. But you will come, won't you? And bring a present, my dear."

She leaned back almost exhausted, but her Spartan courage could not be vanquished. When she had completed her calls she had exacted promises of attendance, with presents, from Lottie Smith, the blues singer; from Lawrence Harper, the poet; from Stanley Bickford, the architect; and from several less-prominent but socially important personalities. For a moment she toyed with the phone as if undecided about something which she very much wanted to do. Finally she yielded to the impulse and dialed.

"Mr. Derwent please. . . . Oh, Walter, this is Constancia. Listen, dear. My maid Mattie is being married today from my house, and I am calling on my friends to donate something to the gift-table. . . . Yes, the lovely little dark thing who serves so nicely, and who slapped your friend's face last time you were here when he attempted to kiss her. Served him right, too. Well, Walter, I want you to send something, something lovely as you always do; you know your taste is so irreproachable. Unfortunately, the child is prejudiced. . . . Yes, that's it, she has race prejudice and simply refuses to have a black-and-tan wedding. So I can't invite you. . . . No, you *couldn't* pass for colored. Don't be pretentious; she has seen you too often. But you will send a present, won't you. . . . That's lovely. And, Walter, if you think it will console you any, you can read all about it in next week's *Tattler*."

When George and Mattie returned, about two hours later, with Aunt Mandy and Sam, Constancia was knee-deep in roses and ferns; six canaries in beribboned cages were doing their infinitesimal best to add to the general derangement, while two extra women, hastily summoned, were busy in the kitchen. Constancia paused long enough to give Sam an appraising and appreciative glance.

"He *is* good-looking," she whispered to Mattie. "Now all of you run up to the top of the house and sleep, play cards, bathe, or do whatever you like, while I finish these nuptial trimmings."

The bell rang. Although it was only one o'clock, Lawrence Harper, who adored Constancia and who had been greatly intrigued by the invitation, had come to see what assistance he might offer. In his hand he held a package tied with blue-and-red ribbon.

"For the bride and groom," he explained, handing the package to Constancia. "May they read and adore them."

"What is it?" asked Constancia.

"My poems, of course! I got them at the author's reduction rate."

"The poet's mite. How sweet of you! Well, just sit down somewhere and write another poem."

A messenger came in holding gingerly a large box which, when

Constancia took it, was much lighter than it looked. Inside were twelve fragile gold-rimmed champagne glasses and Walter Derwent's card, inscribed, "To Mattie with lilacs and geraniums." Constancia held the glasses up to the light, where they sparkled anticipatingly. "Walter must have thought *I* was being married," she commented. "Next time I see him I'll make him supply that for which these glasses were intended."

At three Mrs. Vanderbilt-Jones drove up in suburban dignity, and in a taxi. She had bought a new ear-trumpet which she was clutching violently in one hand while in another she held a fair-sized package.

"Constancia," she complained, "I wouldn't have come for anybody but you. You have no idea how expensive it is to take a taxi from Brooklyn to New York. It's sheer banditry on the part of these taximen. The Subway is cheaper, of course, but so tedious and smelly."

"Have you ever tried the Paris metro, second class?" Constancia inquired.

"I have never tried anything second class—that is, to my knowledge. Here take this present. I hope you like it."

Constancia undid the package and discovered a beautiful porcelain vase. It was so lovely with its blue water and willow trees that she half envied Mattie for it.

"Ravishing," she said. "Is it Sèvres?"

"Certainly not," protested Mrs. Vanderbilt-Jones, petulantly detaching her veil, "It is Ovington's latest.

"Constancia," the old lady continued, settling herself comfortably where she would be most in the way, "come here and sit beside me for a moment. There, that's a dear. I have something of social importance to tell you. I am moving to Harlem. Brooklyn bores me. There is so much life here, and such smart people, and you. I am moving into a very select apartment in that new district known as Sugar Hill. I can't say that I think the name is at all dignified, nothing like *Brooklyn,* you know. But the houses are so lovely. All the white people are moving out, bless them, and only the best colored people are moving in—doctors and lawyers and teachers."

Constancia groaned audibly.

"I have the loveliest apartment," the dowager went on; "seven rooms completely overlooking the city. What a view! And just think, dear, *two bathrooms!*"

Constancia slid to the floor, to busy herself anew twining roses and ferns. Mrs. Vanderbilt-Jones waggled a dropsical finger at Lawrence Harper, but the bard refused to budge. The old lady closed her eyes and fell asleep thinking what temperamental people poets were.

Lottie Smith and Stanley Bickford came together at four. Stanley, tall, indolent, and so Nordic that he spent the major part of his time patiently explaining that he could look as he did and according to American standards be colored at the same time, brought a small parcel which gurgled when Constancia shook it.

"This I shall confiscate, Stanley," she admonished him. "I want these people to enjoy their honeymoon."

Lottie, whose boast was that she could put all the other Smiths to shame with her moaning, was slight, brown, and indescribably chic. She drew fabulous sums and spent them all on clothes; she always looked as if she had come directly from the rue de la Paix. She had burdened herself with two packages; both were circular, but one, wrapped in plain brown paper, was about five times the thickness of the other, which was encased in silver tissue, bound with ribbons of many colors.

Lottie was the only one who made Constancia gasp and stutter. She was so unlike what she ought to be; more like a successful business man's or a doctor's wife in appearance than like a blues singer.

"How Louise Boulanger you look today, Lottie, and how prodigal you are, and how like you to bring two presents!" Constancia complimented her.

"Well," boomed Lottie in that deep contralto voice worshiped from coast to coast, "they are all records—records of the St. Louis blues. These five (pointing to the somber package) are by my rivals. And this (holding up the festively decked disc admiringly) is by me. I want your maid to try these others first, and then I want her to play mine, and see how lousy the others are in comparison."

At this juncture Mrs. Vanderbilt-Jones, having sufficiently refreshed herself, descended upon Lottie to enchant her with the tale of the two bathrooms.

Constancia twined the last rose among the ferns with which she had draped the stairway down which Mattie was to come. She cocked her ear for a moment to see if above the profundity of Lottie's voice pouring into Mrs. Vanderbilt-Jones' trumpet, and over the clatter of a cocktail-shaker which Stanley was manipulating with affectionate and consummate artistry, while Lawrence stood near by, reading "*à haute voix*," his latest poem, she might not discover some coördinated melody in the abandoned rapture of the canaries.

She beamed upon them all, and excused herself.

"Enjoy yourselves in your several ways. I am going up to dress the bride."

Upstairs, she found Sam stretched out stomach down upon a sofa. His face was buried in his arm, while low staccato noises emanating from his direction demonstrated that he was sleeping the sleep of the weary and perhaps of the frightened, if not of the just. Aunt Mandy, arrayed in blue silk, was perched doll-like in a rocker, her small hands spread out on the arms of the chair, her little bird eyes contentedly contemplating her jewelry. The gold hoops were back in her ears. Mattie had drawn a chair up to the sofa, where she sat demure and brooding, keeping happy and guardian watch over Sam.

"Let him sleep," whispered Constancia. "He'll merely have to lave his face afterwards, but you must hurry and get accoutered. You and your aunt come into my room while I transform you into a bride."

"I had planned to be married just as I am, ma'am." Mattie regarded her soberly-cut blue dress as if she found in it all the sartorial excellence necessary.

Constancia merely took her by the arm and drew her along, motioning to Aunt Mandy to follow. "My dear," she said, "this is the one occasion on which you must look your supremest, no matter how dowdy you may become afterwards. One's marriage is not a quotidian affair. I want Sam to be overcome by your loveliness when he sees you, asphixiated, as it were. I want him to think you are a butterfly which has broken its chrysalis and flown straight to him. Men like finery and pretty things on a woman—our men, especially. There's nothing to retain them like a splash of color, or a gold tooth, or some beads around the neck. I have set my heart on having you wear these things. Look!"

She held up the dress; it was cherry-colored; to Mattie's touch it was softer than the stuff of a spider's web. On the floor were a pair of slippers, a darker crimson, with tiny black-velvet bows.

"They're lovely!" Mattie exclaimed. "But I couldn't wear them; they wouldn't go with my color. It's much too red, and I'm too dark."

"Nonsense!" Constancia reassured her. "There's not a lovelier combination than black and red. Just try them on for me."

Mattie allowed herself to be persuaded, and when, after a bit of tucking and pinning to make the dress fit her, she stood before the mirror and looked at herself, and then gazed down to where her little feet peeped out as if half afraid to issue forth in their finery, she was incredulous of her loveliness. Aunt Mandy could only stand off, and then circle her, her hands clasped in admiration, her tongue clucking excitedly as if she were a bantam hen calling her brood.

"Now sit down and compose yourself," Constancia urged Mattie, "while I get dressed."

After Constancia had arrayed herself in a clinging gray dress relieved by a large green brooch, and had changed her swinging gold earrings for others which were longer and which sparkled with small green stones, she descended to see what other arrivals had come while she had been occupied with Mattie.

She found Reverend Drummond in animated conversation with Stanley. "But the church is necessary even to an architect," the minister was saying, while Stanley's childish blue eyes were staring with polite attention but with scant conviction.

Dr. and Mrs. Wilbur Roach had arrived; and Counselor and Mrs. Geoffrey O'Connell, while aloof and to themselves, as if hatching a plot, were the society editors of the *New York Era,* the *Colonial News,* and the *Tattler.* There were two new gifts on the table—a samovar from the Roaches and an envelope from the O'Connells, probably a check, for the slight, monocled lawyer was sure to donate something practical.

"I'm so glad to see you, Reverend." Constancia tendered the pastor a heavily-ringed hand. "We'll be ready in just a moment."

She looked across at Stanley and saw the pleading in his eyes; she had compassion for him. She remembered that he had wanted to be a concert artist before veering off to architecture, and that in his long drink-nervous fingers there still resided a magnetism that could draw harmony from a piano as the magnet draws the nail. "Stanley," she said, in her most improvising tone, "I wish you would play for us, Mendelssohn or Wagner, when Mattie starts down the stairway. You might go over to the piano now and limber your fingers up."

Darting her beams of affectionate gratitude, he scuttled to the piano, where his fingers arabesqued across the keys in the sheerest ecstasy of deliverance.

Reverend Drummond gazed fondly after him.

"A fine young man, a splendid architect, I've been told a real credit to the race," he growled, "but terribly misguided. He has no religious affiliations. I should like to talk to him sometime and put him on the right track."

"I'll bring him to your next revival," promised Constancia. Then raising her voice and addressing them all, "I shall send the groom down now."

She floated upstairs. Sam had washed the sleep from his eyes, and was pacing the room nervously when she entered. George sat moodily in a corner, silently anathematizing Constancia and her mad whims, but letting his devotion for her show all too plainly in his eyes as she rustled into the room.

"It'll soon be over," she consoled Sam. "Take him downstairs, George. They are waiting."

"But where's Mattie?" Sam was not accustomed to pre-marital etiquette, and he had been apprehensive since he woke up to find Mattie gone.

"Oh, she's about," Constancia assured him; "she'll just be fashionably tardy."

As he encountered the unfamiliar faces in the drawing-room, Sam let all the boldness of his gaze go out and affront them. They were not of his world. They had what he hadn't and didn't want —money and schooling; they were society. He eyed them insolently, not bending his head when they bowed to him, raging inwardly as he saw them gaze in astonishment at his lonely arm. What a fool he had been to let this girl drag him here into this marriage.

Lottie Smith, to whom social status was unimportant, in view of the number of Harlem ladies to whom she was *persona non grata,* save when on the stage or when they were seeking a benefit performance for some one of their numerous charity enterprises, went over to Sam. "Let me congratulate you," she said. "Mattie is such a pretty girl."

Mrs. Vanderbilt-Jones, who often disconcerted people by hearing what she was supposed to miss, jerked the blues-singer by the sleeve. "I think you are a bit premature, Lottie," she warned. "Congratulations are due after the ceremony."

Just then Constancia's ivory face appeared at the head of the stairs, thus terminating what might have been a warm argument endangering the friendship of the dowager and the cantatrice. A gem-studded finger was crooked into a signal for Stanley who launched forth into the "Lohengrin Wedding March," while Sam looked up to behold a rapturous vision.

His heart spurted like a fountain within him, sending strong currents beating for release in the palm of his hand, in his ears, and in the somber veins of his temples. Here was the vision which he had seen at the Communion table, but a reality far more ravishing than the dream. Mattie in a bright-red dress, her small dark feet encased in crimson slippers with black-satin bows! Her hair was curled and glossy. A sheaf of roses was in one arm. Her arms made music as she descended the stairs, for as she walked, the thin silver bracelets which Constancia had loaned her jangled and exulted. Her face, enkindled with happiness, rose up above the bouquet like a larger flower for which these others were only a setting, like an animated black tulip, rich and smooth and velvety.

Oh, I will love her and be kind to her and never leave her, Sam promised himself as he thought of his vision and of the black young fellow whose one arm boasted the strength of two. Behind her came Aunt Mandy and Constancia.

Reverend Drummond stood before them with open ritual. George stood at Sam's side, Aunt Mandy at Mattie's, and just in back, jubilant and serene, was Constancia.

"Have you a ring?" the minister asked Sam.

"No." Sam's great shame was in his voice.

"I have a ring," said Mattie. She turned to Sam and gave him her flowers to hold. "It was my mother's." She untied her handkerchief and extracted a plain gold band.

"With this ring I thee wed, and with my worldly goods I thee endow." Sam repeated the words after the minister, feeling small and cheap within himself as he realized their hollow unimportance. He was bringing her nothing but himself, a liar, cheater, professional religionist. But he would make amends. He would be good to her. He would find work and slave, and save, and keep her as the minister had said, "for better, for worse; for richer, for poorer; in sickness and in health," till death should part them.

"I now pronounce you husband and wife. Those whom our God has joined together let no man put asunder."

Forgetful and scornful of his surroundings, Sam encircled Mattie with his arm. Kissing her, he murmured, "Baby, baby!"

while she leaned against him with closed eyes, time and space, guests and surroundings, outdistanced by her happiness.

"Let me congratulate you, Mrs. Lucas." The minister was holding out his hand, stiffly and with ceremony. But Constancia would not have it so. She was gay and happy; the wedding had been a ripping success; she could see the long columns in the *New York Era* and the *Colonial News;* she already saw by faith her picture in the next issue of the *Tattler,* and the caption: "Harlem's most charming and original hostess has magnificent" (the word would certainly be *magnificent*) "wedding for her maid." She was supremely blissful.

"Everybody osculate!" she cried, clapping her hands.

And lest she might not be understood, she leaned over and kissed Sam full on the lips. He stood stiff with rage and resentment, which was not lessened when the minister, after much cajoling by Constancia, pecked Mattie lightly. The women all kissed Sam, with much laughter and coyness, to his infinite disgust and helplessness. Mattie graciously entered into the sport, although it was of no import to her that she was being kissed by one of the famous poets of her race. What mattered was that she would be kissed by Sam over and over again. When Stanley Bickford approached with his blond hair rising in military precision, his fair face flushed, and his blue eyes anticipating the reward of his playing, Mattie drew back from him and looked appealingly at Constancia.

"My dear," said Constancia, with a trace of hurt in her voice, "do you think I would betray you? He's *colored*."

Mattie suffered herself to be kissed.

Reverend Drummond could not be persuaded to remain for the supper. He was wary of these people. He was sure there would be dancing and he felt there were liquors on the table. He had seen Stanley cache the cocktail-shaker as he entered, although it had been too late to conceal the glasses. He drew up the marriage certificate for Mattie. It was a large shiny paper somewhat resembling a diploma, but less severe. On it were roses, and a huge silver bell to ring in all the joys of their matrimonial life. At the bottom there was the picture of a book, open and lined; this was for the signatures of the witnesses. Everybody wanted to sign, and as there weren't lines enough, the names were allowed to spread riotously outside the book.

"It reads like the Social Register of Harlem," commented Constancia as she signed with a flourish.

After he had given Mattie her certificate and had pocketed his fee, the minister left, firmly refusing Constancia's entreaties to "stay for a bit of collation." As the door closed behind him, Stanley rushed to the piano, where he began to play the slow, sorrowful, almost religious strains of a blues. The music invaded Sam until he forgot his alien dislike for these people. He seized Mattie and swung her off into a dance. For a moment it was so blissful to feel his arm about her, and to sense his hot and desirous breath upon her cheeks, while his fine dark eyes unleashed their full power on her, that she allowed herself to float away in his arm. But suddenly she remembered certain mystic symbols tied up in a white handkerchief and hid away; her mind slid back to the white altar with the bowed repentant heads circling it; she thought of the dark, sinful hands faltering out for bread and wine. She stiffened in his arm.

"Sam, Sam," she whispered, "we're church members now. This isn't right. These things don't belong to us any more."

Her protest filled him with doubts and suspicions; small currents of remorse, ever widening and gathering strength, ran through him and shocked him. Had he, after all, chosen the better part? Was his own trickery to come back upon him like a boomerang, separating him from that felicity toward which he had dreamed in taking this woman? Was her religion, rooted and grounded in him, to be a barrier between them?

"Let's don't think of that now," he entreated. "Let's only think of bein' glad and happy; let's only think of lovin' each other." He held her more tightly, laughing at her half-hearted struggles, melting his will and his love into her, striving against the Holy Ghost, and conquering. Her taut body relaxed; she flung her head back until he had to brace his arm to hold her.

"All right," she assented, "let's only think of love tonight and of being happy. Play something fast," she cried to Stanley.

As the music quickened its pace the crimson slippers flashed in and out joyfully, the web-soft, cherry-colored dress whirled and flashed, its folds flaring out like the dress of a ballet-dancer. God! but she was a dancer, Sam thought. Elation filled his breast, and his mind romped ahead to other dances to come. Aunt Mandy, who could find good in cards and fortune-telling, hated dancing and drinking. She sat back in a chair and shut her eyes to blot out the abomination. The other guests formed a cordon around them, urging them on, with clapping hands, time-tapping feet, and those short, spontaneous cries which are the Negro's especially copy-righted expressions of delight. Sam and Mattie broke away from one another; they improvised; they strutted and glided, approached one another and backed away, did as much of the cake-walk as they could remember, and cast in for good measure all the dead-gone and buried steps of Negro dancing which came to mind: they shuffled, balled the jack, eagle-rocked, walked the dog, shimmied and charlestoned, till, breathless and riotously happy, they could only lean panting against each other, in blissful exhaustion.

"*Bravissimo!*" approved Constancia. "Now on to the viands." She threw out her hands and herded them into the dining-room as if she had been a farmer shooing chickens. Constancia was known as a bountiful hostess; the table, loaded with chicken salad, cold ham and tongue, olives, celery, pickles, and hot, buttered rolls, evidenced her decision not to imperil her reputation. Eggnog frothed in a bowl in the center of the table. Mattie caught Aunt Mandy's scandalized eye, and refused to drink, despite Sam's tender entreaties. But when Porter ambled in with iced bottles at the sight of which Mrs. Vanderbilt-Jones forgot her dignity to the extent of exclaiming, incredulously, "Champagne!" Mattie refused to look at her aunt. The pop of the bottles fascinated her, and the sparkling liquid became one final irresistible sin which she would commit on this night of love. She lifted her glass with the rest.

"*Skoal!*" cried Constancia.

"*Buvons!*" exhorted Stanley.

"To Mattie and Sam!" said Lawrence. The liquor had made him prosaic; he had wanted to say something in rhyme, but it wouldn't come.

Mattie tasted her drink and made a wry face; she didn't like it. She set the glass down, but Sam picked it up, kissed the rim where her mouth had been, and drained it.

"How romantic! How perfectly like a lover!" Mrs. Vander-bilt-Jones said, with glistening eyes. "It all takes me back to my marriage with Mr. Vanderbilt-Jones. If he were only living to be here with me now! My dear," she said, turning to Mattie, "you will remember this day when you are like me." Her voice trailed off in revery, her thought sank back into her slightly reeling brain.

But Stanley finished it for her, *sotto voce,* to Lottie, "Yes," he mocked, "with an ear trumpet, and two bathrooms on Sugar Hill. May Heaven forbid!"

Suddenly Constancia remembered something. She rushed up

to Mattie in agitated inquiry. "Where are you honeymooning?"

Mattie laughed. "I hadn't thought of that."

Sam fidgeted uneasily, and cursed Constancia for a meddling fool.

"We're not going away," explained Mattie. "I've got to keep my work, and Sam has to find a job."

"But there must be a honeymoon," insisted Constancia, "of some sort. No wedding is complete without one. Why not go to a theater?"

Sam liked the idea; shows always pleased him.

"Where?" he asked.

"Some place downtown," said Constancia, "to one of the smart revues." She flicked back her sleeve and looked at her watch. "No, time has overruled that suggestion. It's already eight-thirty."

"Well, we could go to a colored show," said Sam. "I'd like it much better, anyhow." He hated to relinquish the idea, and he was anxious to get Mattie away to himself. "The Sable Steppers are at the Lafayette."

"Just the thing, the physician's very prescription," agreed Constancia. "I'll phone for a box for you; you just have time to make the nine-o'clock show. Porter can drive you over and then I'll see that your aunt gets home safely."

As Sam and Mattie were leaving, George came in with a huge pan of rice into which the guests delved; they threw the rice after the departing pair with spirited but inaccurate aim, and with small concern for the cracks and crevices in Constancia's house.

From her doorway Harlem's most ingenious hostess watched her car round the corner. The wedding had been most successful. She stooped and gathered up a few grains of the rice which lay on her brownstone steps like hard snow.

"Hail to Hymen!" she sighed as she sallied back to her guests.

ZORA NEALE HURSTON

ZORA NEALE HURSTON *made her notable debut in the Harlem Renaissance with the prizewinning short story "Drenched in Light," appearing in the December 1924 issue of* Opportunity. *The animating spirit of peasant wit and the deft reproduction of the vernacular of an unspoiled, Deep South adolescence announced one of the great talents of the arts movement. Hurston was viscerally in sync with Langston Hughes's "Negro Artist and the Racial Mountain" ideals well before they appeared in print.*

In Hurston's lively short story, Isis Watts, like Hurston herself in childhood, likes to sit on the gatepost and watch the world go by on the road to Orlando. She is a terrific handful for her grandmother, venerable custodian of the old values in a time of troubling changes. Cavorting with boys, dancing at a cabaret in her grandmother's new red tablecloth, "Isie," an uncontrollable hoyden, is saved from furious corporal punishment when an amused white couple, who stop to ask directions to a nearby hotel, return her to her grandmother. "I want a little of her sunshine to soak into my soul. I need it," says the white woman, expressing a sentiment that underlay the fascination with and patronage of the Harlem Renaissance by many Negrotarians.

Hurston's one-act play "Color Struck" was another remarkable entry in Thurman's controversial Fire!! *Its use of the Deep South vernacular is outstanding. The drama opens in a Jim Crow coach whose occupants are heading for a cakewalk contest and ends in a dance hall in St. Augustine, Florida, where John Turner and Effie Jones win the dance contest in a frenzy of steps. But John's fiancée, Emma, is crazed with jealousy. The attractive Effie, who has come to the contest without her longtime beau, is light-*

skinned, an attribute especially tormenting to Emma. Time passes, some twenty years, and in the final scene John and Emma meet again in Emma's one-room cabin. The melodramatic ending to the play is unsatisfactory, but the emphatic point about the taboo of color prejudice within the racial group is addressed with a candor that foreshadowed Wallace Thurman's heroine, Emma Lou, in The Blacker the Berry . . .

Jonah's Gourd Vine, released by Lippincott in May 1934, was one of the last Renaissance novels. Hurston infuses the folk speech of her characters with a poetic vibrancy that surpasses that of any other African American writer of the period. This first novel was about her immediate family—especially her larger-than-life father—and life in the autonomous African American township of Eatonville, Florida. The plot was vague, the melodrama thick, and the characters verged on the burlesque, but Jonah's Gourd Vine, *as Alain Locke realized immediately, was one of the finest works of the Harlem Renaissance. Hurston's biographer, Robert Hemenway, describes it as "less a narrative than a series of linguistic moments representing the folklife of the black South." As evocative of the souls of black folk as Toomer's* Cane, *Hurston's novel at the end of the era seemed to be authenticity itself.*

DRENCHED IN LIGHT

YOU ISIE WATTS! Git 'own offen dat gate post an' rake up dis yahd!"

The little brown figure perched upon the gate post looked yearningly up the gleaming shell road that led to Orlando, and down the road that led to Sanford and shrugged her thin shoulders. This heaped kindling on Grandma Patts' already burning ire.

"Lawd a-mussy!" she screamed, enraged—"Heah Joel, gimme dat wash stick. Ah'll show dat limb of Satan she kain't shake huh-seff at *me*. If she ain't down by de time Ah gets dere, Ah'll break huh down in de lines" (loins).

"Aw Gran'ma, Ah see Mist' George and Jim Robinson comin' and Ah wanted to wave at 'em," the child said petulantly.

"You jes wave dat rake at dis heah yahd, madame, else Ah'll take you down a button hole lower. You'se too 'oomanish jumpin' up in everybody's face dat pass."

This struck the child in a very sore spot for nothing pleased

her so much as to sit atop of the gate post and hail the passing
vehicles on their way South to Orlando, or North to Sanford. That
white shell road was her great attraction. She raced up and down
the stretch of it that lay before her gate like a round eyed puppy
hailing gleefully all travelers. Everybody in the country, white and
colored, knew little Isis Watts, the joyful. The Robinson brothers,
white cattlemen, were particularly fond of her and always extended
a stirrup for her to climb up behind one of them for a short ride,
or let her try to crack the long bull whips and yee whoo at the
cows.

Grandma Potts went inside and Isis literally waved the rake
at the "chaws" of ribbon cane that lay so bountifully about the
yard in company with the knots and peelings, with a thick sprinkling of peanut hulls.

The herd of cattle in their envelope of gray dust came alongside and Isis dashed out to the nearest stirrup and was lifted up.

"Hello theah Snidlits, I was wonderin' wheah you was," said
Jim Robinson as she snuggled down behind him in the saddle. They
were almost out of the danger zone when Grandma emerged.

"You Isie-s!" she bawled.

The child slid down on the opposite side from the house and
executed a flank movement through the corn patch that brought
her into the yard from behind the privy.

"You lil' hasion you! Wheah you been?"

"Out in de back yahd" Isis lied and did a cart wheel and a
few fancy steps on her way to the front again.

"If you doan git tuh dat yahd, Ah make a mommuk of you!"
Isis observed that Grandma was cutting a fancy assortment of
switches from peach, guana and cherry trees.

She finished the yard by raking everything under the edge of
the porch and began a romp with the dogs, those lean, floppy eared
'coon hounds that all country folks keep. But Grandma vetoed this
also.

"Isie, you set 'own on dat porch! Uh great big 'leben yeah ole
gal racin' an' rompin' lak dat—set 'own!"

Isis impatiently flung herself upon the steps.

"Git up offa dem steps, you aggavatin' limb, 'fore Ah git dem
hick'ries tuh you, an' set yo' seff on a cheah."

Isis petulently arose and sat down as violently as possible in
a chair, but slid down until she all but sat upon her shoulder
blades.

"Now look atcher," Grandma screamed, "Put yo' knees to-

gether, an' git up offen yo' backbone! Lawd, you know dis hellion
is gwine make me stomp huh insides out."

Isis sat bolt upright as if she wore a ramrod down her back
and began to whistle. Now there are certain things that Grandma
Potts felt no one of this female persuasion should do—one was to
sit with the knees separated, "settin' brazen" she called it; another
was whistling, another playing with boys, neither must a lady cross
her legs.

Up she jumped from her seat to get the switches.

"So youse whistlin' in mah face, huh!" She glared till her eyes
were beady and Isis bolted for safety. But the noon hour brought
John Watts, the widowed father, and this excused the child from
sitting for criticism.

Being the only girl in the family, of course she must wash the
dishes, which she did in intervals between frolics with the dogs.
She even gave Jake, the puppy, a swim in the dishpan by holding
him suspended above the water that reeked of "pot likker"—just
high enough so that his feet would be immersed. The deluded
puppy swam and swam without ever crossing the pan, much to his
annoyance. Hearing Grandma she hurriedly dropped him on the
floor, which he tracked up with feet wet with dishwater.

Grandma took her patching and settled down in the front
room to sew. She did this every afternoon, and invariably slept in
the big red rocker with her head lolled back over the back, the
sewing falling from her hand.

Isis had crawled under the center table with its red plush cover
with little round balls for fringe. She was lying on her back imagining herself various personages. She wore trailing robes, golden
slippers with blue bottoms. She rode white horses with flaring pink
nostrils to the horizon, for she still believed that to be land's end.
She was picturing herself gazing over the edge of the world into
the abyss when the spool of cotton fell from Grandma's lap and
rolled away under the whatnot. Isis drew back from her contemplation of the nothingness at the horizon and glanced up at the
sleeping woman. Her head had fallen far back. She breathed with
a regular "snark" intake and soft "poosah" exhaust. But Isis was
a visual minded child. She heard the snores only subconsciously
but she saw straggling beard on Grandma's chin, trembling a little
with every "snark" and "poosah". They were long gray hairs
curled here and there against the dark brown skin. Isis was moved
with pity for her mother's mother.

"Poah Gran-ma needs a shave," she murmured, and set about

it. Just then Joel, next older than Isis, entered with a can of bait.

"Come on Isie, les' we all go fishin'. The perch is bitin' fine in Blue Sink."

"Sh-sh—" cautioned his sister, "Ah got to shave Gran'ma."

"Who say so?" Joel asked, surprised.

"Nobody doan hafta tell me. Look at her chin. No ladies don't weah no whiskers if they kin help it. But Gran'ma gittin' ole an' she doan know how to shave like me."

The conference adjourned to the back porch lest Grandma wake.

"Aw, Isie, you doan know nothin' 'bout shavin' a-tall—but a *man* lak *me*——"

"Ah do so know."

"You don't not. Ah'm goin' shave her mahseff."

"Naw, you won't neither, Smarty. Ah saw her first an' thought it all up first," Isis declared, and ran to the calico covered box on the wall above the wash basin and seized her father's razor. Joel was quick and seized the mug and brush.

"Now!" Isis cried defiantly, "Ah got the razor."

"Goody, goody, goody, pussy cat, Ah got th' brush an' you can't shave 'thout lather—see! Ah know mo' than you," Joel retorted.

"Aw, who don't know dat?" Isis pretended to scorn. But seeing her progress blocked for lack of lather she compromised.

"Ah know! Les' we all shave her. You lather an' Ah shave."

This was agreeable to Joel. He made mountains of lather and anointed his own chin, and the chin of Isis and the dogs, splashed the walls and at last was persuaded to lather Grandma's chin. Not that he was loath but he wanted his new plaything to last as long as possible.

Isis stood on one side of the chair with the razor clutched cleaver fashion. The niceties of razor-handling had passed over her head. The thing with her was to *hold* the razor—sufficient in itself.

Joel splashed on the lather in great gobs and Grandma awoke.

For one bewildered moment she stared at the grinning boy with the brush and mug but sensing another presence, she turned to behold the business face of Isis and the razor-clutching hand. Her jaw dropped and Grandma, forgetting years and rheumatism, bolted from the chair and fled the house, screaming.

"She's gone to tell papa, Isie. You didn't have no business wid

his razor and he's gonna lick yo hide," Joel cried, running to replace mug and brush.

"You too, chuckle-head, you, too," retorted Isis. "You was
playin' wid his brush and put it all over the dogs—Ah seen you
put it on Ned an' Beulah." Isis shaved some slivers from the door
jamb with the razor and replaced it in the box. Joel took his bait
and pole and hurried to Blue Sink. Isis crawled under the house to
brood over the whipping she knew would come. She had meant
well.

But sounding brass and tinkling cymbal drew her forth. The
local lodge of the Grand United Order of Odd Fellows led by a
braying, thudding band, was marching in full regalia down the
road. She had forgotten the barbecue and log-rolling to be held
today for the benefit of the new hall.

Music to Isis meant motion. In a minute razor and whipping
forgotten, she was doing a fair imitation of the Spanish dancer she
had seen in a medicine show some time before. Isis' feet were
gifted—she could dance most anything she saw.

Up, up went her spirits, her brown little feet doing all sorts of
intricate things and her body in rhythm, hand curving above her
head. But the music was growing faint. Grandma nowhere in sight.
She stole out of the gate, running and dancing after the band.

Then she stopped. She couldn't dance at the carnival. Her
dress was torn and dirty. She picked a long stemmed daisy and
thrust it behind her ear. But the dress, no better. Oh, an idea! In
the battered round topped trunk in the bedroom!

She raced back to the house, then, happier, raced down the
white dusty road to the picnic grove, gorgeously clad. People
laughed good naturedly at her, the band played and Isis danced
because she couldn't help it. A crowd of children gather admiringly
about her as she wheeled lightly about, hand on hip, flower between her teeth with the red and white fringe of the table-cloth—
Grandma's new red tablecloth that she wore in lieu of a Spanish
shawl—trailing in the dust. It was too ample for her meager form,
but she wore it like a gipsy. Her brown feet twinkled in and out
of the fringe. Some grown people joined the children about her.
The Grand Exalted Ruler rose to speak; the band was hushed, but
Isis danced on, the crowd clapping their hands for her. No one
listened to the Exalted one, for little by little the multitude had
surrounded the brown dancer.

An automobile drove up to the Crown and halted. Two white

men and a lady got out and pushed into the crowd, suppressing
mirth discreetly behind gloved hands. Isis looked up and waved
them a magnificent hail and went on dancing until—

Grandma had returned to the house and missed Isis and
straightway sought her at the festivities expecting to find her in her
soiled dress, shoeless, gaping at the crowd, but what she saw drove
her frantic. Here was her granddaughter dancing before a gaping
crowd in her brand new red tablecloth, and reeking of lemon ex-
tract, for Isis had added the final touch to her costume. She *must*
have perfume.

Isis saw Grandma and bolted. She heard her cry: "Mah Gawd,
mah brand new table cloth Ah jus' bought f'um O'landah!" as she
fled through the crowd and on into the woods.

She followed the little creek until she came to the ford in a rutty
wagon road that led to Apopka and laid down on the cool grass
at the roadside. The April sun was quite hot.

Misery, misery and woe settled down upon her and the child
wept. She knew another whipping was in store for her.

"Oh, Ah wish Ah could die, then Gran'ma an' papa would be
sorry they beat me so much. Ah b'leeve Ah'll run away an' never
go home no mo'. Ah'm goin' drown mahseff in th' creek!" Her
woe grew attractive.

Isis got up and waded into the water. She routed out a tiny
'gator and a huge bull frog. She splashed and sang, enjoying herself
immensely. The purr of a motor struck her ear and she saw a large,
powerful car jolting along the rutty road toward her. It stopped at
the water's edge.

"Well, I declare, it's our little gypsy," exclaimed the man at
the wheel. "What are you doing here, now?"

"Ah'm killin' mahseff," Isis declared dramatically. "Cause
Gran'ma beats me too much."

There was a hearty burst of laughter from the machine.

"You'll last sometime the way you are going about it. Is this
the way to Maitland? We want to go to the Park Hotel."

Isis saw no longer any reason to die. She came up out of the
water, holding up the dripping fringe of the tablecloth.

"Naw, indeedy. You go to Maitlan' by the shell road—it goes
by mah house—an' turn off at Lake Sebelia to the clay road that
takes you right to the do'."

"Well," went on the driver, smiling furtively. "Could you quit dying long enough to go with us?"

"Yessuh," she said thoughtfully, "Ah wanta go wid you."

The door of the car swung open. She was invited to a seat beside the driver. She had often dreamed of riding in one of these heavenly chariots but never thought she would, actually.

"Jump in then, Madame Tragedy, and show us. We lost ourselves after we left your barbecue."

During the drive Isis explained to the kind lady who smelt faintly of violets and to the indifferent men that she was really a princess. She told them about her trips to the horizon, about the trailing gowns, the gold shoes with blue bottoms—she insisted on the blue bottoms—the white charger, the time when she was Hercules and had slain numerous dragons and sundry giants. At last the car approached her gate over which stood the umbrella Chinaberry tree. The car was abreast of the gate and had all but passed when Grandma spied her glorious tablecloth lying back against the upholstery of the Packard.

"You Isie-e!" she bawled, "You lil' wretch you! Come heah *dis instunt.*"

"That's me," the child confessed, mortified, to the lady on the rear seat.

"Oh, Sewell, stop the car. This is where the child lives. I hate to give her up though."

"Do you wanta keep me?" Isis brightened.

"Oh, I wish I could, you shining little morsel. Wait, I'll try to save you a whipping this time."

She dismounted with the gaudy lemon flavored culprit and advanced to the gate where Grandma stood glowering, switches in hand.

"You're gointuh ketchit f'um yo' haid to yo' heels m'lady. Jes' come in heah."

"Why, good afternoon," she accosted the furious grandparent. "You're not going to whip this poor little thing, are you?" the lady asked in conciliatory tones.

"Yes, Ma'am. She's de wustest lil' limb dat ever drawed bref. Jes' look at mah new table cloth, dat ain't never been washed. She done traipsed all over de woods, uh dancin' an' uh prancin' in it. She done took a razor to me t'day an' Lawd knows whut mo'."

Isis clung to the white hand fearfully.

"Ah wuzn't gointer hurt Gran'ma, miss—Ah wuz jus' gointer shave her whiskers fuh huh 'cause she's old an' can't."

The white hand closed tightly over the little brown one that was quite soiled. She could understand a voluntary act of love even though it miscarried.

"Now, Mrs. er—er—I didn't get the name—how much did your tablecloth cost?"

"One whole big silvah dollar down at O'landah—ain't had it a week yit."

"Now here's five dollars to get another one. The little thing loves laughter. I want her to go on to the hotel and dance in that tablecloth for me. I can stand a little light today—"

"Oh, yessum, yessum." Grandma cut in, "Everything's alright, sho' she kin go, yessum."

The lady went on: "I want brightness and this Isis is joy itself, why she's drenched in light!"

Isis for the first time in her life, felt herself appreciated and danced up and down in an ecstasy of joy for a minute.

"Now, behave yo'seff, Isie, ovah at de hotel wid de white folks," Grandma cautioned, pride in her voice, though she strove to hide it. "Lawd, ma'am, dat gal keeps me so frackshus, Ah doan know mah haid f'um mah feet. Ah orter comb huh haid, too, befo' she go wid you all."

"No, no, don't bother. I like her as she is. I don't think she'd like it either, being combed and scrubbed. Come on, Isis."

Feeling that Grandma had been somewhat squelched did not detract from Isis' spirit at all. She pranced over to the waiting motor and this time seated herself on the rear seat between the sweet, smiling lady and the rather aloof man in gray.

"Ah'm gointer stay wid you all," she said with a great deal of warmth, and snuggled up to her benefactress. "Want me tuh sing a song fuh you?"

"There, Helen, you've been adopted," said the man with a short, harsh laugh.

"Oh, I hope so, Harry." She put her arm about the red draped figure at her side and drew it close until she felt the warm puffs of the child's breath against her side. She looked hungrily ahead of her and spoke into space rather than to anyone in the car. "I want a little of her sunshine to soak into my soul. I need it."

COLOR STRUCK

A Play in Four Scenes

Time: Twenty years ago and present.   *Place: A Southern City.*

PERSONS

JOHN, *A light brown-skinned man*

EMMALINE, *A black woman*

WESLEY, *A boy who plays an accordion*

EMMALINE'S DAUGHTER, *A very white girl*

EFFIE, *A mulatto girl*

A RAILWAY CONDUCTOR   A DOCTOR

Several who play mouth organs, guitars, banjos
Dancers, passengers, etc.

SCENE I

SETTING.—*Early night. The inside of a "Jim Crow" railway coach. The car is parallel to the footlights. The seats on the down stage side of the coach are omitted. There are the luggage racks above the seats. The windows are all open. There are exits in each end of the car—right and left.*

ACTION.—*Before the curtain goes up there is the sound of a locomotive whistle and a stopping engine, loud laughter, many people speaking at once, good-natured shrieks, strumming of stringed instruments, etc. The ascending curtain discovers a happy lot of Negroes boarding the train dressed in the gaudy, tawdry best of 1900. They are mostly in couples—each couple bearing a covered-over market basket which the men hastily deposit in the racks as they scramble for seats. There is a little friendly pushing and shoving. One pair just miss a seat three times, much to the enjoyment of the crowd. Many "plug" silk hats are in evidence, also sun-flowers in button holes. The women are showily dressed in the manner of the time, and quite conscious of their finery. A few seats remain unoccupied.*

Enter Effie (left) above, with a basket. ONE OF THE MEN (*standing, lifting his "plug" in a grand manner*). Howdy do, Miss Effie, you'se lookin' jes lak a rose.

(*Effie blushes and is confused. She looks up and down for a seat.*) Fack is, if you wuzn't walkin' long, ah'd think you *wuz* a rose—(*he looks timidly behind her and the others laugh*). Looka here, where's Sam at?

EFFIE (*tossing her head haughtily*). I don't know an' I don't keer.

THE MAN (*visibly relieved*). Then lemme scorch you to a seat. (*He takes her basket and leads her to a seat center of the car, puts the basket in the rack and seats himself beside her with his hat at a rakish angle.*)

MAN (*sliding his arm along the back of the seat*). How come Sam ain't heah—y'll on a bust?

EFFIE (*angrily*). A man dat don't buy me nothin tuh put in *mah* basket, ain't goin' wid *me* tuh no cake walk. (*The hand on the seat touches her shoulder and she thrusts it away*). Take yo' arms from 'round me, Dinky! Gwan hug yo' Ada!

MAN (*in mock indignation*). Do you think I'd look at Ada when Ah got a chance tuh be wid you? Ah always wuz sweet on you, but you let ole Mullet-head Sam cut me out.

ANOTHER MAN (*with head out of the window*). Just look at de darkies coming! (*With head inside coach.*) Hey, Dinky! Heah come Ada wid a great big basket.

(*Dinky jumps up from beside Effie and rushes to exit right. In a moment they re-enter and take a seat near entrance. Everyone in coach laughs. Dinky's girl turns and calls back to Effie.*)

GIRL. Where's Sam, Effie?

EFFIE. Lawd knows, Ada.

GIRL. Lawd a mussy! Who you gointer walk de cake wid?

EFFIE. Nobody, Ah reckon. John and Emma gointer win it nohow. They's the bestest cake-walkers in dis state.

ADA. You'se better than Emma any day in de week. Cose Sam cain't walk lake John. (*She stands up and scans the coach.*) Looka heah, ain't John an' Emma going? They ain't on heah! (*The locomotive bell begins to ring.*)

EFFIE. Mah Gawd, s'pose dey got left!

MAN (*with head out of window*). Heah they come, nip and tuck

—whoo-ee! They'se gonna make it! (*He waves excitedly.*) Come on Jawn! (*Everybody crowds the windows, encouraging them by gesture and calls. As the whistle blows twice, and the train begins to move, they enter panting and laughing at left. The only seat left is the one directly in front of Effie.*)

DINKY (*standing*). Don't y'all skeer us no mo' lake dat! There couldn't be no cake walk thout y'all. Dem shad-mouf St. Augustine coons would win dat cake and we would have tuh kill 'em all bodaciously.

JOHN. It was Emmaline nearly made us get left. She says I wuz smiling at Effie on the street car and she had to get off and wait for another one.

EMMA (*removing the hatpins from her hat, turns furiously upon him*). You wuz grinning at her and she wuz grinning back jes lake a ole chessy cat!

JOHN (*positively*). I wuzn't.

EMMA (*about to place her hat in rack*). You wuz. I seen you looking jes lake a possum.

JOHN. I wuzn't. I never gits a chance tuh smile at nobody—you won't let me.

EMMA. Jes the same every time you sees a yaller face, you *takes* a chance. (*They sit down in peeved silence for a minute.*)

DINKY. Ada, les we all sample de basket. I bet you got huckleberry pie.

ADA. No I aint, I got peach an' tater pies, but we aint gonna tetch a thing tell we gits tuh de hall.

DINKY (*mock alarm*). Naw, don't do dat! It's all right tuh save the fried chicken, but pies is *always* et on trains.

ADA. Aw shet up! (*He struggles with her for a kiss. She slaps him but finally yields.*)

JOHN (*looking behind him*). Hellow, Effie, where's Sam?

EFFIE. Deed, I don't know.

JOHN. Y'all on a bust?

EMMA. None ah yo' bizness, you got enough tuh mind yo' own self. Turn 'round!

(*She puts up a pouting mouth and he snatches a kiss. She laughs just as he kisses her again and there is a resounding smack which causes the crowd to laugh. And cries of "Oh you kid!" "Salty dog!"*)

(*Enter conductor left calling tickets cheerfully and laughing at the general merriment.*)

CONDUCTOR. I hope somebody from Jacksonville wins this cake.

JOHN. You live in the "Big Jack?"

CONDUCTOR. Sure do. And I wanta taste a piece of that cake on the way back tonight.

JOHN. Jes rest easy—them Augustiners aint gonna smell it. (*Turns to Emma.*) Is they, baby?

EMMA. Not if Ah kin help it.

Somebody with a guitar sings: "Ho babe, mah honey taint no lie."

(*The conductor takes up tickets, passes on and exits right.*)

WESLEY. Look heah, you cake walkers—y'all oughter git up and limber up yo' joints. I heard them folks over to St. Augustine been oiling up wid goose-grease, and over to Ocala they been rubbing down in snake oil.

A WOMAN'S VOICE. You better shut up, Wesley, you just joined de church last month. Somebody's going to tell the pastor on you.

WESLEY. Tell it, tell it, take it up and smell it. Come on out you John and Emma and Effie, and limber up.

JOHN. Naw, we don't wanta do our walking steps—nobody won't wanta see them when we step out at the hall. But we kin do something else just to warm ourselves up.

(*Wesley begins to play "Goo Goo Eyes" on his accordian, the other instruments come in one by one and John and Emma step into the aisle and "parade" up and down the aisle—Emma holding up her skirt, showing the lace on her petticoats. They two-step back to their seat amid much applause.*)

WESLEY. Come on out, Effie! Sam aint heah so you got to hold up his side too. Step on out. (*There is a murmur of applause as she steps into the aisle. Wesley strikes up "I'm gointer live anyhow till I die." It is played quite spiritedly as Effie swings into the pas-me-la*)

WESLEY (*in ecstasy*). Hot stuff I reckon! Hot stuff I reckon! (*The musicians are stamping. Great enthusiasm. Some clap time with hands and feet. She hurls herself into a modified Hoochy Koochy, and finishes up with an ecstatic yell.*)

There is a babble of talk and laughter and exultation.

JOHN (*applauding loudly*). If dat Effie can't step nobody can.

EMMA. Course you'd say so cause it's her. Everything she do is pretty to you.

JOHN (*caressing her*). Now don't say that, Honey. Dancing is danc-

ing no matter who is doing it. But nobody can hold a candle
to you in nothing.

(*Some men are heard tuning up—getting pitch to sing. Four
of them crowd together in one seat and begin the chorus of "Daisies Won't Tell." John and Emma grow quite affectionate.*)

JOHN (*kisses her*). Emma, what makes you always picking a fuss
with me over some yaller girl. What makes you so jealous,
nohow? I don't do nothing.

(*She clings to him, but he turns slightly away. The train whistle blows, there is a slackening of speed. Passengers begin to take
down baskets from their racks.*)

EMMA. John! John, don't you want me to love you, honey?

JOHN (*turns and kisses her slowly*). Yes, I want you to love me,
you know I do. But I don't like to be accused o' ever light
colored girl in the world. It hurts my feeling. I don't want to
be jealous like you are.

(*Enter at right Conductor, crying "St. Augustine, St. Augustine." He exits left. The crowd has congregated at the two exits,
pushing good-naturedly and joking. All except John and Emma.
They are still seated with their arms about each other.*)

EMMA (*sadly*). Then you don't want my love, John, cause I can't
help mahself from being jealous. I loves you so hard, John,
and jealous love is the only kind I got.

(*John kisses her very feelingly.*)

EMMA. Just for myself alone is the only way I knows how to love.

(*They are standing in the aisle with their arms about each
other as the curtain falls.*)

SCENE II

SETTING.—*A weather-board hall. A large room with the joists
bare. The place has been divided by a curtain of sheets stretched
and a rope across from left to right. From behind the curtain there
are occasional sounds of laughter, a note or two on a stringed
instrument or accordion. General stir. That is the dance hall. The
front is the ante-room where the refreshments are being served. A
"plank" seat runs all around the hall, along the walls. The lights
are kerosene lamps with reflectors. They are fixed to the wall. The
lunch-baskets are under the seat. There is a table on either side
upstage with a woman behind each. At one, ice cream is sold, at*

*the other, roasted peanuts and large red-and-white sticks of pep-
permint candy.*

*People come in by twos and three, laughing, joking, horse-plays,
gauchily flowered dresses, small waists, bulging hips and busts,
hats worn far back on the head, etc. People from Ocala greet others from Palatka, Jacksonville, St. Augustine, etc.*

*Some find seats in the ante-room, others pass on into the main
hall.*

Enter the Jacksonville delegation, laughing, pushing proudly.

DINKY. Here we is, folks—here we *is*. Gointer take dat cake on
back tuh Jacksonville where it belongs.

MAN. Gwan! Whut wid you mullet-head Jacksonville Coons know
whut to do wid a cake. It's gointer stay right here in Augustine
where de *good* cake walkers grow.

DINKY. Taint no 'Walkers' never walked till John and Emmaline
prance out—you mighty come a tootin'.

*(Great laughing and joshing as more people come in. John
and Emma are encouraged, urged on to win.)*

EMMA. Let's we git a seat, John, and set down.

JOHN. Sho will—nice one right over there. *(They push over to wall
seat, place basket underneath, and sit. Newcomers shake
hands with them and urge them on to win.)*

*(Enter Joe Clarke and a small group. He is a rotund, expansive
man with a liberal watch chain and charm.)*

DINKY *(slapping Clarke on the back).* If you don't go 'way from
here! Lawdy, if it aint Joe.

CLARKE *(jovially).* Ah thought you had done forgot us people in
Eatonville since you been living up here in Jacksonville.

DINKY. Course Ah aint. *(Turning.)* Looka heah folks! Joe Clarke
oughta be made chairman uh dis meetin'—Ah mean Past
Great-Grand Master of Ceremonies, him being the onliest
mayor of de onliest colored town in de state.

GENERAL CHORUS. Yeah, let him be—thass fine, etc.

Dinky *(setting his hat at a new angle and throwing out his chest).*
And *Ah'll* scorch him to de platform. Ahem!

*(Sprinkling of laughter as Joe Clarke is escorted into next
room by Dinky.)*

*(The musicians are arriving one by one during this time. A
guitar, accordion, mouth organ, banjo, etc. Soon there is a rapping
for order heard inside and the voice of Joe Clarke.)*

JOE CLARKE. Git yo' partners one an' all for de gran' march! Git yo' partners, gent-mens!

A MAN (*drawing basket from under bench*). Let's we all eat first.

(*John and Emma go buy ice-cream. They coquettishly eat from each other's spoons. Old Man Lizzimore crosses to Effie and removes his hat and bows with a great flourish.*)

LIZZIMORE. Sam ain't here t'night, is he, Effie.

EFFIE (*embarrassed*). Naw suh, he aint.

LIZZ. Well, you like chicken? (*Extends arm to her.*) Take a wing!

(*He struts her up to the table amid the laughter of the house. He wears no collar.*)

JOHN (*squeezes Emma's hand*). You certainly is a ever loving mamma—when you aint mad.

EMMA (*smiles sheepishly*). You oughtn't to make me mad then.

JOHN. Ah don't make you! You makes yo'self mad, den blame it on me. Ah keep on tellin' you Ah don't love nobody but you. Ah knows heaps uh half-white girls Ah could git ef Ah wanted to. But (*he squeezes her hard again*) Ah jus' wants *you!* You know what they say! De darker de berry, de sweeter de taste!

EMMA (*pretending to pout.*) Oh, you tries to run over me an' keep it under de cover, but Ah won't let yuh. (*Both laugh.*) Les' we eat our basket!

JOHN. Alright. (*He pulls the basket out and she removes the table cloth. They set the basket on their knees and begin to eat fried chicken.*)

MALE VOICE. Les' everybody eat—motion's done carried. (*Everybody begins to open baskets. All have fried chicken. Very good humor prevails. Delicacies are swapped from one basket to the other. John and Emma offer the man next them some supper. He takes a chicken leg. Effie crosses to John and Emma with two pieces of pie on a plate.*)

EFFIE. Y'll have a piece uh mah blueberry pie—it's mighty nice! (*She proffers it with a timid smile to Emma who "freezes" up instantly.*)

EMMA. Naw! We don't want no pie. We got cocoanut layer-cake.

JOHN. Ah—Ah think ah'd choose a piece uh pie, Effie. (*He takes it.*) Will you set down an' have a snack wid us? (*He slides over to make room.*)

EFFIE (*nervously*). Ah, naw, Ah got to run on back to mah basket, but Ah thought maybe y'll mout' want tuh taste mah pie. (*She turns to go.*)

JOHN. Thank you, Effie. It's mighty good, too. (*He eats it. Effie crosses to her seat. Emma glares at her for a minute, then turns disgustedly away from the basket, John catches her shoulder and faces her around.*)

JOHN (*pleadingly*). Honey, be nice. Don't act lak dat!

EMMA (*jerking free*). Naw, you done ruint mah appetite now, carryin' on wid dat punkin-colored ole gal.

JOHN. Whut kin Ah do? If you had a acted polite Ah wouldn't a had nothin' to say.

EMMA. Naw, youse jus' hog-wile ovah her cause she's half-white! No matter whut Ah say, you keep carryin' on wid her. Act polite? Naw Ah aint gonna be deceitful an' bust mah gizzard fuh nobody! Let her keep her dirty ole pie ovah there where she is!

JOHN (*looking around to see if they are overheard*). Sh-sh! Honey, you mustn't talk so loud.

EMMA (*louder*). Ah-Ah ain't gonna bite mah tongue! If she don't like it she can lump it. Mah back is broad—(*John tries to cover her mouth with his hand*). She calls herself a big cigar, but *I* kin smoke her!

(*The people are laughing and talking for the most part and pay no attention. Effie is laughing and talking to those around her and does not hear the tirade. The eating is over and everyone is going behind the curtain. John and Emma put away their basket like the others, and sit glum. Voice of Master-of-ceremonies can be heard from beyond curtain announcing the pas-me-la contest. The contestants, mostly girls, take the flloor. There is no music except the clapping of hands and the shouts of "Parse-me-lah" in time with the hand-clapping. At the end Master announces winner. Shadows seen on curtain.*)

MASTER. Mathilda Clarke is winner—if she will step forward she will receive a beautiful wook fascinator. (*The girl goes up and receives it with great hand-clapping and good humor.*) And now since the roosters is crowin' foah midnight, an' most of us got to git up an' go to work tomorrow, The Great Cake Walk will begin. Ah wants de floor cleared, cause de representatives of de several cities will be announced an' we wants 'em to take de floor as their names is called. Den we wants 'em to go a gran' promenade roun' de hall. An' they will then commence to walk fuh de biggest cake ever baked in dis state. Ten dozen eggs—ten pounds of flour—ten pounds of butter, and so on and so forth. Now then—(*he strikes a pose*) for St. Augustine—

Miss Lucy Taylor, Mr. Ned Coles.

(*They step out amid applause and stand before stage.*)

For Daytona—

Miss Janie Bradley, Enoch Nixon

(*Same business.*)

For Ocala—

Miss Docia Boger, Mr. Oscar Clarke

(*Same business.*)

For Palatka—

Miss Maggie Lemmons, Mr. Senator Lewis

(*Same business.*)

And for Jacksonville the most popular "walkers" in de state—

Miss Emmaline Beazeby, Mr. John Turner.

(*Tremendous applause. John rises and offers his arm grandiloquently to Emma.*)

EMMA (*pleadingly, and clutching his coat*). John let's we all don't go in there with all them. Let's we all go on home.

JOHN (*amazed*). Why, Emma?

EMMA. Cause, cause all them girls is going to pulling and hauling on you, and—

JOHN (*impatiently*). Shucks! Come on. Don't you hear the people clapping for us and calling our names? Come on!

(*He tries to pull her up—she tries to drag him back.*)

Come on, Emma! Taint no sense in your acting like this. The band is playing for us. Hear 'em? (*He moves feet in a dance step.*)

EMMA. Naw, John, Ah'm skeered. I loves you—I—.

(*He tries to break away from her. She is holding on fiercely.*)

JOHN. I got to go! I been practising almost a year—I—we done come all the way down here. I can walk the cake, Emma— we got to—I got to go in! (*He looks into her face and sees her tremendous fear.*) What you skeered about?

EMMA (*hopefully*). You won't go it—You'll come on go home with me all by ourselves. Come on John. I can't, I just can't go in there and see all them girls—Effie hanging after you—.

JOHN. I got to go in—(*he removes her hand from his coat*)— whether you come with me or not.

EMMA. Oh—them yaller wenchees! How I hate 'em! They gets everything they wants—.

VOICE INSIDE. We are waiting for the couple from Jacksonville—
    Jacksonville! Where is the couple from—.
    (*Wesley parts the curtain and looks out.*)
WESLEY. Here they is out here spooning! You all can't even hear
    your names called. Come on John and Emma.
JOHN. Coming. (*He dashes inside. Wesley stands looking at Emma
    in surprise.*)
WESLEY. What's the matter, Emma? You and John spatting again?
    (*He goes back inside.*)
EMMA (*calmly bitter*). He went and left me. If we is spatting we
    done had our last one. (*She stands and clenches her fists.*) Ah,
    mah God! He's in there with her—Oh, them half whites, they
    gets everything, they gets everything everybody else wants!
    The men, the jobs—everything! The whole world is got a sign
    on it. Wanted: Light colored. Us blacks was made for cobble
    stones. (*She muffles a cry and sinks limp upon the seat.*)
VOICE INSIDE. Miss Effie Jones will walk for Jacksonville with Mr.
    John Turner in place of Miss Emmaline Beazeley.

SCENE III—*Dance Hall*

*Emma springs to her feet and flings the curtains wide open.
She stands staring at the gay scene for a moment defiantly, then
creeps over to a seat along the wall and shrinks into the Spanish
Moss, motionless.*

*Dance hall decorated with palmetto leaves and Spanish
Moss—a flag or two. Orchestra consists of guitar, mandolin,
banjo, accordian, church organ and drum.*

MASTER (*on platform*). Couples take yo' places! Wen de music
    starts, gentlemen parade yo' ladies once round de hall, den de
    walk begins. (*The music begins. Four men come out from be-
    hind the platform bearing a huge chocolate cake. The couples
    are "prancing" in their tracks. The men lead off the procession
    with the cake—the contestants make a grand slam around the
    hall.*)
MASTER. Couples to de floor! Stan' back, ladies an' gentlemen—
    give 'em plenty room.
    (*Music changes to "Way Down in Georgia." Orchestra sings.
Effie takes the arm that John offers her and they parade to the*

other end of the hall. She takes her place. John goes back upstage to the platform, takes off his silk hat in a graceful sweep as he bows deeply to Effie. She lifts her skirts and curtsies to the floor. Both smile broadly. They advance toward each other, meet midway, then, arm in arm, begin to "strut." John falters as he faces her, but recovers promptly and is perfection in his style. (Seven to nine minutes to curtain.) Fervor of spectators grows until all are taking part in some way—either hand-clapping or singing the words. At curtain they have reached frenzy.)

Quick Curtain

(It stays down a few seconds to indicate ending of contest and goes up again on John and Effie being declared winners by Judges.)

MASTER *(on platform, with John and Effie on the floor before him.)* By unanimous decision de cake goes to de couple from Jacksonville! *(Great enthusiasm. The cake is set down in the center of the floor and the winning couple parade around it arm in arm. John and Effie circle the cake happily and triumphantly. The other contestants, and then the entire assembly fall in behind and circle the cake, singing and clapping. The festivities continue. The Jacksonville quartet step upon the platform and sing a verse and chorus of "Daisies won't tell." Cries of "Hurrah for Jacksonville! Glory for the big town," "Hurrah for Big Jack.")*

A MAN *(seeing Emma)*. You're from Jacksonville, aint you? *(He whirls her around and around.)* Aint you happy? Whoopee! *(He releases her and she drops upon a seat. She buries her face in the moss.)*

(Quartet begins on chorus again. People are departing, laughing, humming, with quartet cheering. John, the cake, and Effie being borne away in triumph.)

SCENE IV

Time—present. The interior of a one-room shack in an alley. There is a small window in the rear wall upstage left. There is an enlarged crayon drawing of a man and woman—man sitting cross-legged, woman standing with her hand on his shoulder. A center table, red cover, a low, cheap rocker, two straight chairs, a small kitchen stove at left with a wood-box beside it, a water-bucket on a stand close by. A hand towel and a wash basin. A shelf of dishes above this. There is an ordinary oil lamp on the center table but it is not lighted when the curtain goes up. Some light enters through the window and all falls on the woman seated in the low rocker. The door is center right. A cheap bed is against the upstage wall. Someone is on the bed but is lying so that the back is toward the audience.

ACTION—*As the curtain rises, the woman is seen rocking to and fro in the low rocker. A dead silence except for the sound of the rocker and an occasional groan from the bed. Once a faint voice says "water" and the woman in the rocker arises and carries the tin dipper to the bed.*

WOMAN. No mo' right away—Doctor says not too much. (*Returns dipper to pail.—Pause.*) You got right much fever—I better go git the doctor agin.

(*There comes a knocking at the door and she stands still for a moment, listening. It comes again and she goes to door but does not open it.*)

WOMAN. Who's that?

VOICE OUTSIDE. Does Emma Beasely live here?

EMMA. Yeah—(*pause*)—who is it?

VOICE. It's me—John Turner.

EMMA (*puts hand eagerly on the fastening*). John? did you say John Turner?

VOICE. Yes, Emma, it's me.

(*The door is opened and the man steps inside.*)

EMMA. John! Your hand (*she feels for it and touches it*). John flesh and blood.

JOHN (*laughing awkwardly*). It's me alright, old girl. Just as bright as a basket of chips. Make a light quick so I can see how you look. I'm crazy to see you. Twenty years is a long time wait, Emma.

EMMA (*nervously*). Oh, let's we all just sit in the dark awhile. (*Apologetically.*) I wasn't expecting nobody and my house aint picked up. Sit down. (*She draws up the chair. She sits in rocker.*)

JOHN. Just to think! Emma! Me and Emma sitting down side by each. Know how I found you?

EMMA (*dully*). Naw. How?

JOHN (*brightly*). Soon's I got in town I hunted up Wesley and he told me how to find you. That's who I come to see, you!

EMMA. Where you been all these years, up North somewheres? Nobody round here could find out where you got to.

JOHN. Yes, up North. Philadelphia.

EMMA. Married yet?

JOHN. Oh yes, seventeen years ago. But my wife is dead now and so I came as soon as it was decent to find *you*. I wants to marry you. I couldn't die happy if I didn't. Couldn't get over you—couldn't forget. Forget me, Emma?

EMMA. Naw, John. How could I?

JOHN (*leans over impulsively to catch her hand*). Oh, Emma, I love you so much. Strike a light honey so I can see you—see if you changed much. You was such a handsome girl!

EMMA. We don't exactly need no light, do we, John, tuh jus' set an' talk?

JOHN. Yes, we do, Honey. Gwan, make a light. Ah wanna see you. (*There is a silence.*)

EMMA. Bet you' wife wuz some high-yaller dickty-doo.

JOHN. Naw she wasn't neither. She was jus' as much like you as Ah could get her. Make a light an' Ah'll show you her pictcher. Shucks, ah gotta look at mah old sweetheart. (*He strikes a match and holds it up between their faces and they look intently at each other over it until it burns out.*) You aint changed none atall, Emma, jus' as pretty as a speckled pup yet.

EMMA (*lighter*). Go long, John! (*Short pause*) 'member how you useter bring me magnolias?

JOHN. Do I? Gee, you was sweet! 'Member how Ah useter pull mah necktie loose so you could tie it back for me? Emma, Ah can't see to mah soul how we lived all this time, way from one another. 'Member how you useter make out mah ears had done run down and you useter screw 'em up agin for me? (*They laugh.*)

EMMA. Yeah, Ah useter think you wuz gointer be mah husban' then—but you let dat ole—.

JOHN. Ah aint gonna let you alibi on me lak dat. Light dat lamp! You cain't look me in de eye and say no such. (*He strikes another match and lights the lamp.*) Course, Ah don't wanta look too bossy, but Ah b'lieve you got to marry me tuh git rid of me. That is, if you aint married.

EMMA. Naw, Ah aint. (*She turns the lamp down.*)

JOHN (*looking about the room*). Not so good, Emma. But wait till you see dat little place in Philly! Got a little "Rolls-Rough," too—gointer teach you to drive it, too.

EMMA. Ah been havin' a hard time, John, an' Ah lost you—oh, aint nothin' been right for me! Ah aint never been happy.
(*John takes both of her hands in his.*)

JOHN. You gointer be happy now, Emma. Cause Ah'm gointer make you. Gee Whiz! Ah aint but fortyh-two and you aint forty yet—we got plenty time. (*There is a groan from the bed.*) Gee, what's that?

EMMA (*ill at ease*). Thass mah chile. She's sick. Reckon Ah bettah see 'bout her.

JOHN. You got a chile? Gee, that great! Ah always wanted one, but didn't have no luck. Now we kin start off with a family. Girl or boy?

EMMA (*slowly*). A girl. Comin' tuh see me agin soon, John?

JOHN. Comin' agin? Ah aint gone yet! We aint talked, you aint kissed me an' nothin', and you aint showed me our girl. (*Another groan, more prolonged.*) She must be pretty sick—let's see. (*He turns in his chair and Emma rushes over to the bed and covers the girl securely, tucking her long hair under the covers, too—before he arises. He goes over to the bed and looks down into her face. She is mulatto. Turns to Emma teasingly.*) Talkin' 'bout *me* liking high-yallers—yo husband musta been pretty near *white*.

EMMA (*slowly*). Ah, never wuz married, John.

JOHN. It's alright, Emma. (*Kisses her warmly.*) Everything is going to be O.K. (*Turning back to the bed.*) Our child looks pretty sick, but she's pretty. (*Feels her forehead and cheek.*) Think she oughter have a doctor.

EMMA. Ah done had one. Course Ah cain't git no specialist an' nothin' lak dat. (*She looks about the room and his gaze follows hers.*) Ah aint got a whole lot lake you. Nobody don't git rich in no white-folks' kitchen, nor in de washtub. You know Ah aint no school-teacher an' nothin' lak dat.
(*John puts his arm about her.*)

JOHN. It's all right, Emma. But our daughter is bad off—run out an' git a doctor—she needs one. Ah'd go if Ah knowed where to find one—you kin git one the quickest—hurry, Emma.

EMMA (*looks from John to her daughter and back again.*) She'll be all right, Ah reckon, for a while. John, you love me—you really want me sho' nuff?

JOHN. Sure Ah do—think Ah'd come all de way down here for nothin'? Ah wants to marry agin.

EMMA. Soon, John?

JOHN. Real soon.

EMMA. Ah wuz jus' thinkin', mah folks is away now on a little trip—be home day after tomorrow—we could git married tomorrow.

JOHN. All right. Now run on after the doctor—we must look after our girl. Gee, she's got a full suit of hair! Glad you didn't let her chop it off. (*Looks away from bed and sees Emma standing still.*)

JOHN. Emma, run on after the doctor, honey. (*She goes to the bed and again tucks the long braids of hair in, which are again pouring over the side of the bed by the feverish tossing of the girl.*) What's our daughter's name?

EMMA. Lou Lillian. (*She returns to the rocker uneasily and sits rocking jerkily. He returns to his seat and turns up the light.*)

JOHN. Gee, we're going to be happy—we gointer make up for all them twenty years (*another groan*). Emma, git up an' gwan git dat doctor. You done forgot Ah'm de boss uh dis family now—gwan, while Ah'm here to watch her whilst you're gone. Ah got to git back to mah stoppin'-place after a while.

EMMA. You go git one, John.

JOHN. Whilst Ah'm blunderin' round tryin' to find one, she'll be gettin' worse. She sounds pretty bad (*takes out his wallet and hands her a bill*)—get a taxi if necessary. Hurry!

EMMA (*does not take the money, but tucks her arms and hair in again, and gives the girl a drink*). Reckon Ah better go git a doctor. Don't want nothin' to happen to *her*. After you left, Ah useter have such a hurtin' in heah (*touches bosom*) till she come an' eased it some.

JOHN. Here, take some money and get a good doctor. There must be some good colored ones around here now.

EMMA (*scornfully*). I wouldn't let one of 'em tend my cat if I had one! But let's we don't start a fuss.

(*John caresses her again. When he raises his head he notices the picture on the wall and crosses over to it with her—his arm still about her.*)

JOHN. Why, that's you and me!

EMMA. Yes, I never could part with that. You coming tomorrow morning, John, and we're gointer get married, aint we? Then we can talk over everything.

JOHN. Sure, but I aint gone yet. I don't see how come we can't make all our arrangements now.

(*Groans from bed and feeble movement.*)

Good lord, Emma, go get that doctor!

(*Emma stares at the girl and the bed and seizes a hat from a nail on the wall. She prepares to go but looks from John to bed and back again. She fumbles about the table and lowers the lamp. Goes to door and opens it. John offers the wallet. She refuses it.*)

EMMA. Doctor right around the corner. Guess I'll leave the door open so she can get some air. She won't need nothing while I'm gone, John. (*She crosses and tucks the girl in securely and rushes out, looking backward and pushing the door wide open as she exits. John sits in the chair beside the table. Looks about him—shakes his head. The girl on the bed groans, "Water," "so hot." John looks about him excitely. Gives her a drink. Feels her forehead. Takes a clean handkerchief from his pocket and wets it and places it upon her forehead. She raises her hand to the cool object. Enter Emma running. When she sees John at the bed she is full of fury. She rushes over and jerks his shoulder around. They face each other.*)

EMMA. I knowed it! (*She strikes him.*) A half white skin. (*She rushes at him again. John staggers back and catches her hands.*)

JOHN. Emma!

EMMA (*struggles to free her hands*). Let me go so I can kill you. Come sneaking in here like a pole cat!

JOHN (*slowly, after a long pause*). So this is the woman I've been wearing over my heart like a rose for twenty years! She so despises her own skin that she can't believe any one else could love it!

(*Emma writhes to free herself.*)

JOHN. Twenty years! Twenty years of adoration, of hunger, of worship! (*On the verge of tears he crosses to door and exits quietly, closing the door after him.*)

(*Emma remains standing, looking dully about as if she is half asleep. There comes a knocking at the door. She rushes to open it. It is the doctor. White. She does not step aside so that he can enter.*)

DOCTOR. Well, shall I come in?

EMMA (*stepping aside and laughing a little*). That's right, doctor, come in.

(*Doctor crosses to bed with professional air. Looks at the girl, feels the pulse and draws up the sheet over the face. He turns to her.*)

DOCTOR. Why didn't you come sooner. I told you to let me know of the least change in her condition.

EMMA (*flatly*). I did come—I sent for the doctor.

DOCTOR. Yes, but you waited. An hour more or less is mighty important sometimes. Why didn't you come?

EMMA (*passes hand over face*). Couldn't see.

(*Doctor looks at her curiously, then sympathetically takes out a small box of pills, and hands them to her.*) Here, you're worn out. Take one of these every hour and try to get some sleep. (*He departs.*)

(*She puts the pill-box on the table, takes up the low rocking chair and places it by the head of the bed. She seats herself and rocks monotonously and stares out of the door. A dry sob now and then. The wind from the open door blows out the lamp and she is seen by the little light from the window rocking in an even, monotonous gait, and sobbing.*)

FROM *JONAH'S GOURD VINE*

GOD WAS GRUMBLING his thunder and playing the zig-zag lightning thru his fingers.

Amy Crittenden came to the door of her cabin to spit out a wad of snuff. She looked up at the clouds.

"Ole Massa gwinter scrub floors tuhday," she observed to her husband who sat just outside the door, reared back in a chair. "Better call dem chaps in outa de cotton patch."

" 'Tain't gwine rain," he snorted, "you always talkin' more'n yuh know."

Just then a few heavy drops spattered the hard clay yard. He arose slowly. He was an older middle-age than his years gave him a right to be.

"And eben if hit do rain," Ned Crittenden concluded grudgingly, "ef dey ain't got sense 'nough tuh come in let 'em git wet."

"Yeah, but when us lef' de field, you tole 'em not to come till you call 'em. Go 'head and call 'em 'fo de rain ketch 'em."

Ned ignored Amy and shuffled thru the door with the chair,

and somehow trod on Amy's bare foot. " 'Oman, why don't you git outa de doorway? Jes contrary tuh dat. You needs uh good head stompin', dass whut. You sho is one aggervatin' 'oman."

Amy flashed an angry look, then turned her face again to the sea of wind-whipped cotton, turned hurriedly and took the cow-horn that hung on the wall and placed it to her lips.

"You John Buddy! You Zeke! You Zachariah! Come in!"

From way down in the cotton patch, "Yassum! Us comin'!"

Ned shuffled from one end of the cabin to the other, slamming to the wooden shutter of the window, growling between his gums and his throat the while.

The children came leaping in, racing and tumbling in tense, laughing competition—the three smaller ones getting under the feet of the three larger ones. The oldest boy led the rest, but once inside he stopped short and looked over the heads of the others, back over the way they had come.

"Shet dat door, John!" Ned bellowed, "you ain't got the sense you wuz borned wid."

Amy looked where her big son was looking. "Who dat comin' heah, John?" she asked.

"Some white folks passin' by, mama. Ahm jes' lookin' tuh see whar dey gwine."

"Come out dat do'way and shet it tight, fool! Stand dere gazin' dem white folks right in de face!" Ned gritted at him. "Yo' brazen ways wid dese white folks is gwinter git you lynched one uh dese days."

"Aw 'tain't," Amy differed impatiently, "who can't look at ole Beasley? He ain't no quality no-how."

"Shet dat door, John!" screamed Ned.

"Ah wuznt de last one inside," John said sullenly.

"Don't you gimme no word for word," Ned screamed at him. "You jes' do lak Ah say do and keep yo' mouf shet or Ah'll take uh trace chain tuh yuh. Yo' mammy mought think youse un lump uh gold 'cause you got uh li'l' white folks color in yo' face, but Ah'll stomp yo' guts out and dat quick! Shet dat door!"

He seized a lidard knot from beside the fireplace and limped threateningly towards John.

Amy rose from beside the cook pots like a black lioness.

"Ned Crittenden, you raise dat wood at mah boy, and you gointer make uh bad nigger outa me."

"Dat's right," Ned sneered, "Ah feeds 'im and clothes 'im but Ah ain't tuh do nothin' tuh dat li'l' yaller god cep'n wash 'im up."

"Dat's uh big ole resurrection lie, Ned. Uh slew-foot, drag-leg lie at dat, and Ah dare yuh tuh hit me too. You know Ahm uh fightin' dawg and mah hide is worth money. Hit me if you dare! Ah'll wash *yo'* tub uh 'gator guts and dat quick."

"See dat? Ah ain't fuh no fuss, but you tryin' tuh start uh great big ole ruction 'cause Ah tried tuh chesstize dat youngun."

"Naw, you ain't tried tuh chesstize 'im nothin' uh de kind. Youse tryin' tuh fight 'im on de sly. He is jes' ez obedient tuh you and jes ez humble under yuh, ez he kin be. Yet and still you always washin' his face wid his color and tellin' 'im he's uh bastard. He works harder'n anybody on dis place. You ain't givin' 'im nothin'. He more'n makes whut he gits. Ah don't mind when he needs chesstizin' and you give it tuh 'im, but anytime you tries tuh knock any des chillun 'bout dey head wid sticks and rocks, Ah'll be right dere tuh back dey fallin'. Ahm dey mama."

"And Ahm de pappy uh all but dat one."

"You knowed Ah had 'm fo' yuh married me, and if you didn't want 'im round, whut yuh marry me fuh? Dat ain't whut you said. You washed 'im up jes lak he wuz gold den. You jes took tuh buckin' 'im since you been hangin' round sich ez Beasley and Mimms."

Ned sat down by the crude fireplace where the skillets and spiders (long-legged bread pans with iron cover) sprawled in the ashes.

"Strack uh light, dere, some uh y'all chaps. Hit's dark in heah."

John obediently thrust a piece of lightwood into the embers and the fire blazed up. He retreated as quickly as possible to the farther end of the cabin.

Ned smoked his strong home-grown tobacco twist for a few minutes. Then he thrust out his feet.

"Pour me some water in dat wash-basin, you chaps, and some uh y'all git de washrag."

There was a scurry and bustle to do his bidding, but the drinking-gourd dropped hollowly in the water bucket. Ned heard it.

" 'Tain't no water in dat air water-bucket, Ah'll bound yuh!" He accused the room and glowered all about him, "House full uh younguns fuh me to feed and close, and heah 'tis dust dark and rainin' and not uh drop uh water in de house! Amy, whut kinda 'oman is you nohow?"

Amy said nothing. She sat on the other side of the fireplace and heaped fresh, red coals upon the lid of the spider in which the bread was cooking.

"John!" Ned thundered, "git yo' yaller behind up offa dat floor and go git me some water tuh wash mah foots."

"You been tuh de house longer'n he is," Amy said quietly. "You coulda done been got dat water."

"You think Ah'm gwine take uh 'nother man's youngun and feed 'im and close 'im fuh twelve years and den he too good tuh fetch me uh bucket uh water?" Ned bellowed.

"Iss rainin' out dere, an' rainin' hard," Amy said in the same level tones.

"Dass right," Ned sneered, "John is de housenigger. Ole Marsa always kep' de yaller niggers in de house and give 'em uh job totin' silver dishes and goblets tuh de table. Us black niggers is de ones s'posed tuh ketch de wind and de weather."

"Ah don't want *none* uh mah chilluns pullin' tuh no spring in uh hard rain. Yo' foots kin wait. Come hawg-killin' time Ah been married tuh you twelve years and Ah done seen yuh let 'em wait uh powerful long spell some time. Ah don't want mah chilluns all stove-up wid uh bad cold from proagin' 'round in de rain."

"Ole Marse didn't ast *me* ef hit wuz rainin' uh snowin' uh hot uh col'. When he spoke Ah had tuh move and move quick too, uh git a hick'ry tuh mah back. Dese younguns ain't uh bit better'n me. Let 'em come lak Ah did."

"Naw, Ned, Ah don't want mine tuh come lak yuh come nor neither lak me, and Ahm uh whole heap younger'n you. You growed up in slavery time. When Old Massa wuz drivin' you in de rain and in de col'—he wan't don' it tuh he'p you 'long. He wuz lookin' out for hisself. Course Ah wuz twelve years old when Lee made de big surrender, and dey didn't work me hard, but—but dese heah chillun is diffunt from us."

"How come dey's diffunt? Wese all niggers tuhgether, ain't us? White man don't keer no mo' 'bout one dan he do de other."

"Course dey don't, but we ain't got tuh let de white folks love our chillun fuh us, is us? Dass jest de pint. We black folks don't love our chillun. We couldn't do it when we wuz in slavery. We borned 'em but dat didn't make 'em ourn. Dey b'longed tuh old Massa. 'Twan't no use in treasurin' other folkses property. It wuz liable tuh be took uhway any day. But we's free folks now. De big bell done rung! Us chillun is ourn. Ah doan know, mebbe hit'll take some of us generations, but us got tuh 'gin tuh practise on treasurin' our younguns. Ah loves dese heah already uh whole heap. Ah don't want 'em knocked and 'buked."

Ned raked his stubbly fingers thru his grisly beard in silent hostility. He spat in the fire and tamped his pipe.

"Dey say spare de rod and spile de child, and Gawd knows Ah ain't gwine tuh spile nair one uh dese. Niggers wuz made tuh work and all of 'em gwine work right long wid me. Is dat air supper ready yit?"

"Naw hit ain't. How you speck me tuh work in de field right long side uh you and den have supper ready jis az soon ez Ah git tuh de house? Ah helt uh big-eye hoe in mah hand jes ez long ez you did, Ned."

"Don't you change so many words wid me, 'oman! Ah'll knock yuh dead ez Hector. Shet yo' mouf!"

"Ah change jes ez many words ez Ah durn please! Ahm three times seben and uh button. Ah knows whut's de matter wid *you*. Youse mad cause Beaseley done took dem two bales uh cotton us made las' yeah."

"Youse uh lie!"

"Youse uh nother one, Ned Crittenden! Don't you lak it, don't you take it, heah mah collar come and you shake it! Us wouldn't be in dis fix ef you had uh lissened tuh me. Ah tole you when dey hauled de cotton tuh de gin dat soon ez everything wuz counted up and Beasley give us share for yuh tuh take and haul it straight tuh dis barn. But naw, yuh couldn't lissen tuh me. Beasley told yuh tuh leave hit in *his* barn and being he's uh white man you done whut he told yuh. Now he say he ain't got no cotton uh ourn. Me and you and all de chillun done worked uh whole year. Us done made sixteen bales uh cotton and ain't even got uh cotton seed to show."

"Us et hit up, Major Beasley say. Come to think of it 'tis uh heap uh moufs in one meal barrel."

"No sich uh thing, Ned Crittenden. Fust place us ain't had nothing but meal and sow-belly tuh eat. You mealy-moufin' round cause you skeered tuh talk back tuh Rush Beasley. What us needs tuh do is git offa dis place. Us been heah too long. Ah b'longs on de other side de Big Creek anyhow. Never did lak it over heah. When us gather de crops dis yeah less move."

"Aw, Ah reckon we kin make it heah all right, when us don't have so many moufs in de meal barrel we kin come out ahead. 'Tain't goin' be dat many dis time when Ah goes to de gin house."

"How come?"

"Cause Ah done bound John over tuh Cap'n Mimms. Dat's uh great big ole boy, Amy, sixteen years old and look lak he twenty. He eats uh heap and den you won't let me git de worth uh mah rations out of 'im in work. He could be de finest plowhand in Alabama, but you won't lemme do nothin' wid 'im."

"He don't do nothin'? He's uh better hand wid uh wide sweep plow right now dan you is, and he kin chop mo' cotton dan you, and pick mo' dan ah kin and you knows Ah kin beat you anytime." Then, as if she had just fully heard Ned, "Whut dat you say 'bout boundin' John Buddy over tuh Cap'n Mimms? You ain't uh gonna do no sich uh thing."

"Ah done done it."

In the frenzied silence, Amy noticed that the rain had ceased; that the iron kettle was boiling; that a coon dog struck a trail way down the Creek, and was coming nearer, singing his threat and challenge.

"Ned Crittenden, you know jes ez good ez Ah do dat Cap'n Mimms ain't nothin' but po' white trash, and he useter be de overseer on de plantation dat everybody knowed wuz de wust one in southern Alabama. He done whipped niggers nigh tuh death."

"You call him po' when he got uh thousand acres under de plow and more'n dat in wood lot? Fifty mules."

"Don't keer if he is. How did he git it? When Massa Pinckney got kilt in de war and ole Miss Pinckney didn't had nobody tuh look atter de place she took and married 'im. He wan't nothin' but uh overseer, lived offa clay and black m'lasses. His folks is so po' right now dey can't sit in dey house. Every time you pass dere dey settin' in de yard jes ez barefooted ez uh yard dawg. You ain't gwine put no chile uh mine under no Mimms."

"Ah done done it, and you can't he'p yo'seff. He gwine come git 'im tuhmorrer. He's gwine sleep 'im and feed 'im and effen John Buddy's any account, he say he'll give uh suit uh close come Christmas time."

"Dis heah bindin' over ain't nothin' but uh 'nother way uh puttin' us folks back intuh slavery."

"Amy, you better quit talkin' 'bout de buckra. Some of 'em be outside and hear you and turn over you tuh de patter roller, and dey'll take you outa heah and put uh hun'ed lashes uh raw hide on yo' back. Ah done tole yuh but you won't hear."

The clash and frenzy in the air was almost visible. Something had to happen. Ned stood up and shuffled towards the door.

"Reckon Ahm gwine swill dat sow and feed de mules. Mah vittles better be ready when Ah git back."

He limped on out of the door and left it open.

"John Buddy," Amy said, "you and Zeke go fetch uh bucket full uh water and hurry back tuh yo' supper. De rest uh y'all git yo' plates and come git some uh dese cow-peas and pone bread. Lawd, Lawd, Lawd. Je-sus!"

There was a lively clatter of tin plates and spoons. The largest two boys went after water, Zeke clinging in the darkness to his giant of a brother. Way down in the cotton Zeke gave way to his tears.

"John Buddy, Ah don't want you way from me. John Buddy,—" he grew incoherent. So John Buddy carried him under his arm like a shock of corn and made him laugh. Finally John said, "Sometime Ah jes ez soon be under Mimms ez pappy. One 'bout ez bad as tother. 'Nother thing. Dis ain't slavery time and Ah got two good footses hung onto me." He began to sing lightly.

They returned with the water and were eating supper when Ned got back from the barn. His face was sullen and he carried the raw hide whip in his hand.

Amy stooped over the pot, giving second-helpings to the smaller children. Ned looked about and seeing no plate fixed for him uncoiled the whip and standing tiptoe to give himself more force, brought the whip down across Amy's back.

The pain and anger killed the cry within her. She wheeled to fight. The raw hide again. This time across her head. She charged in with a stick of wood and the fight was on. This had happened many times before. Amy's strength was almost as great as Ned's and she had youth and agility with her. Forced back to the wall by her tigress onslaught, Ned saw that victory for him was possible only by choking Amy. He thrust his knee into her abdomen and exerted a merciless pressure on her throat.

The children screamed in terror and sympathy.

"Help mama, John Buddy," Zeke screamed. John's fist shot out and Ned slid slowly down the wall as if both his legs and his insides were crumbling away.

Ned looked scarcely human on the floor. Almost like an alligator in jeans. His drooling blue lips and snaggled teeth were yellowed by tobacco.

"Lawd, Ah speck you done kilt yo' pappy, John. You didn't mean tuh, and he didn't had no business hittin' me wid dat raw hide and neither chokin' me neither. Jesus, Jesus, Jesus, Jee-sus!''

"He ain't dead, mama. Ah see 'im breathin'.'' Zachariah said, "John Buddy sho is strong! Ah bet he kin whip ev'ry body in Notasulga.''

Ned got up limpingly. He looked around and sat upon the bed.

"Amy, Ahm tellin' yuh, git dat punkin-colored bastard outa dis house. He don't b'long heah wid us nohow.''

"He ain't de onliest yaller chile in de world. Wese uh mingled people.''

Ned limped to the fireplace and Amy piled his plate with corn bread and peas.

"Git dat half-white youngun uh yourn outa heah, Amy. Heah Ah done took 'im since he wus three years ole and done for 'im when he couldn't do for hisseff, and he done raised his hand tuh me. Dis house can't hol' bofe uh us. Yaller niggers ain't no good nohow.''

"Oh yes dey is,'' Amy defended hotly, "yes dey is—jes ez good ez anybody else. You jes started tuh talk dat foolishness since you been hangin' 'round ole Mimms. Monkey see, monkey do.''

"Well, iss de truth. Dese white folks orta know and dey say dese half-white niggers got de worst part uh bofe de white and de black folks.''

"Dey ain't got no call tuh say dat. Is mo' yaller folks on de chain-gang dan black? Naw! Is dey harder tuh learn? Naw! Do dey work and have things lak other folks? Yas. Naw dese po' white folks says dat 'cause dey's jealous uh de yaller ones. How come? Ole Marse got de yaller nigger totin' his silver cup and eatin' Berksher hawg ham outa his kitchin when po' white trash scrab-blin' 'round in de piney woods huntin' up uh razor back. Yaller nigger settin' up drivin' de carriage and de po' white folks got tuh step out de road and leave 'im pass by. And den agin de po' white man got daughters dat don't never eben smell de kitchin at the big house and all dem yaller chillun got mamas, and no black gal ain't never been up tuh de big house and dragged Marse Nobody out. Humph! Talkin' after po' white trash! If Ah wuz ez least ez dey is, Ah speck Ah'd fret mahself tuh death.''

"Aw naw,'' Ned sneered, "de brother in black don't fret tuh death. White man fret and worry and kill hisself. Colored folks fret uh lil' while and gwan tuh sleep. 'Nother thing, Amy, Hagar's chillun don't faint neither when dey fall out, dey jes have uh hard old fit.''

"Dass awright, Ned. You always runnin' yo' race down. We ain't had de same chance dat white folks had. Look lak Ah can't sense you intuh dat."

"Amy, niggers can't faint. Jes ain't in 'em."

"Dass awright. Niggers gwine faint too. May not come in yo' time and it may not come in mine, but way after while, us people is gwine faint jes lak white folks. You watch and see."

"Table dat talk. Dat John is gwine offa dis place effen Ah stay heah. He goes tuh Mimms uh he goes apin' on down de road way from heah. Ah done spoke."

"Naw Ned," Amy began, but John cut her off.

"It's all right, mama, lemme go. Ah don't keer. One place is good ez 'nother one. Leave him do all de plowin' after dis!"

With his mouth full of peas and corn bread, Ned gloated, "De crops is laid by."

"Yeah, but nex' year's crops ain't planted yit," John countered.

So John put on his brass-toed shoes and his clean shirt and was ready to leave. Amy dug out a crumpled and mouldy dollar and gave it to him.

"Where you goin', son?"

"Over de Big Creek, mama. Ah ever wanted tuh cross over."

"Ah'll go piece de way widyuh tuh de Creek, John. Gimme uh li'dud knot, dere, Zeke, so's Ah kin see de way back."

"Good bye, pap," John called from the door. Ned grunted over a full mouth. The children bawled dolefully when John called to them.

Amy threw a rag over her bruised head and closed the door after her. The night was black and starry.

"John, you wuz borned over de Creek."

"You wuz tellin' me dat one day, Ah 'member."

"Dey knows me well, over dere. Maybe Ah kin pint yuh whar some work is at."

"Yassum. Ah wants tuh make money, so's Ah kin come back and git yuh."

"Don't yuh take me tuh heart. Ah kin strain wid Ned. Ah jes been worried 'bout you and him. Youse uh big boy now and you am gwine take and take offa 'im and swaller all his filth lak you been doin' here of late. Ah kin see dat in yo' face. Youse slow, but wid him keerin' on lak he do now, hit takes uh Gawd tuh tell whut gwine happen in dat house. He didn't useter 'buke yuh lak dat. But his old mammy and dat ole cock-eyed sister uh his'n put 'im

up tuh dat. He useter be crazy 'bout yuh. 'Member dat big gol'
watch chain he bought fuh you tuh wear tuh big meetin'? Dey make
lak he love you better'n he do de rest on 'count youse got color in
your face. So he tryin' side wid dem and show 'em he don't. Ahm
kinda glad fuh yuh tuh be 'way from 'round 'im. Massa Alf Pearson,
he got uh big plantation and he's quality white folks. He know me
too. Go in Notasulga and ast fuh 'im. Tell 'im whose boy you is and
maybe he mought put yuh tuh work. And if he do, son, you scuffle
hard so's he'll work yuh reg'lar. Ah hates tuh see yuh knucklin' under 'round heah all de time. G'wan, son, and be keerful uh dat foot-
log 'cross de creek. De Songahatchee is strong water, and look out
under foot so's yuh don't git snake bit."

"Ah done swum dat ole creek, mama—'thout yuh knowin'.
Ah knowed you'd tell me not tuh swim it."

"Dat's how come Ah worries 'bout yuh. Youse always uh runnin' and uh rippin' and clambin' trees and rocks and jumpin', flin-
gin' rocks in creeks and sich like. John, promise me yuh goin'
quit dat."

"Yassum."

"Come tuh see me when yuh kin. G'bye."

Amy was gone back up the rocky path thru the blooming
cotton, across the barren hard clay yard. For a minute she had felt
free and flighty down there as she stood in the open with her tall,
bulky son. Now the welts on her face and body hurt her and the
world was heavy.

John plunged on down to the Creek, singing a new song and
stomping the beats. The Big Creek thundered among its rocks and
whirled on down. So John sat on the foot-log and made some
words to go with the drums of the Creek. Things walked in the
birch woods, creep, creep, creep. The hound dog's lyric crescendo
lifted over and above the tree tops. He was on the foot-log, half
way across the Big Creek where maybe people laughed and maybe
people had lots of daughters. The moon came up. The hunted coon
panted down to the Creek, swam across and proceeded leisurely
up the other side. The tenor-singing hound dog went home. Night
passed. No more Ned, no hurry. No telling how many girls might
be living on the new and shiny side of the Big Creek. John almost
trumpeted exultantly at the new sun. He breathed lustily. He
stripped and carried his clothes across, then recrossed and plunged
into the swift water and breasted strongly over.

ZORA NEALE HURSTON AND
LANGSTON HUGHES

MULE-BONE, *THE ILL-FATED* 1930 *collaboration of Zora Hurston and Langston Hughes, was not to see a stage performance until 1991 at New York's Lincoln Center. Until that time, fragmentary scripts for this interestingly cobbled together three-act comedy remained in boxes on the shelves of several research libraries. The plot, such as it is, has to do with two hunters who quarrel over a turkey until one knocks the other cold with a mule's hock bone. The hunters' quarrel divides their small community down the middle, and what began as a personal matter comes to assume religious (Methodists versus Baptists) and gender (male evasions of family responsibilities) dimensions. The famous Gilpin Players of Cleveland's Karamu House had attempted to perform* Mule-Bone *in January 1931, but the explosive dispute between Hurston and Hughes over authorship forced the cancellation of the production. Their dispute split much of Harlem into two warring camps and led to Hughes being abandoned by Godmother and Locke.*

FROM *MULE-BONE*

SETTING. *A high stretch of railroad track thru a luxurious Florida forest. It is near sundown.*

AT RISE. *When the curtain rises, there is no one on the stage, but there is a tremendous noise and hubbub off-stage right. There are yells of derision and shouts of anger. Part of the mob is trying to keep* JIM *in town, and part is driving him off. After a full minute of this,* JIM *enters with his guitar hanging around his neck and his* coat over his shoulder. The sun is dropping low and red thru the forest. He is looking back angrily and shouting at the mob. A missile is thrown after him. JIM *drops his coat and guitar and picks up a piece of brick, and makes threatening gestures of throwing it.*

(*Running back the way he came and hurling the brick with all his might.*)

JIM. I'll kill some o' you ol' box-ankled fools. (*Grabs up another piece of brick.*)

I'm out o' yo' old town. Now just let some of you ol' half-pint Baptists let yo' wooden God an' Cornstalk Jesus fool you into hittin' me.

(*Threatens to throw again. There are some frightened screams and the mob is heard running back.*)

I'm glad I'm out o' yo' ole town anyhow. I ain't never comin' back no mo', neither. You ole ugly-niggers done ruint de town anyhow.

(*There is complete silence off-stage.* JIM *walks a few steps with his coat and guitar than sits down on the railroad embankment facing the audience. He pulls off one shoe and pours the sand out. He holds the shoe in his hand a moment and looks wistfully back down the railroad track.*)

I never woulda thought people woulda acted like that. (*Laces up the shoe*)

Specially Dave Carter, much as me and him done progue'd 'round together goin' in swimmin' an' playin' ball an' sere-nadin' de girls an' de white folks. (*He sits there gloomily silent for awhile, then looks behind him and picks up his guitar and begins to pick a tune. The music is very sad, but he trails off into,* "YOU MAY LEAVE AN' GO TO HALIMUHFACKS, BUT MY SLOW DRAG WILL BRING YOU BACK." *When he finishes he looks at the sun and picks up his coat.*)

Reckon I better git on down de road and git somewhere. Lawd knows where. (*Stops suddenly in his tracks and turns back toward the village. Takes a step or two.*)

All dat mess and stink for nothin'. Dave know good an' well I didn't mean to hurt him much. (*He takes off his cap and scratches his head thoroughly, then turns again and starts down the road left. Enter* DAISY, *left, walking fast and pant-ing, her head down. They meet.*)

DAISY. Oh, hello, Jim. (*A little surprised and startled*)

JIM (*Not expecting her*). Hello, Daisy. (*Embarrassed silence.*)

DAISY. I was jus' comin' over town to see how you come out.

JIM. You don't have to go way over there to fin' dat out—you and Dave done got me run outa town for nothin'.

DAISY (*Putting her hand on his arm*). Dey didn't run you outa town, did dey?

JIM (*Shaking her hand off*). Whut you reckon I'm countin' Mr. Railroad's ties for—jus' to fin' out how many ties between here and Orlando?

DAISY (*Hand on his arm again*). Dey *cain't* run you off like dat!

JIM. Take yo hands off me, Daisy! How come they cain't run me off wid you an' Dave an—*every*body 'ginst me?

DAISY. I ain't opened my mouf 'gainst you, Jim. I ain't said one word—I wasn't even at de ol' trial. My madame wouldn't let me git off. I wuz jus' comin' to see 'bout you now.

JIM. Aw, go 'head on. You figgered I was gone too long to talk 'bout. You was haulin' it over to town to see Dave—dat's whut you was doin'—after gittin' *me* all messed up.

DAISY (*Making as if to cry*). I wasn't studyin' 'bout no Dave.

JIM (*Hopefully*). Aw, don't tell me. (*Sings*) Ashes to ashes, dust to dust, show me a woman that a man can trust.
(DAISY *is crying now.*)

JIM. Whut you crying for? You know you love Dave. I'm yo' monkey-man. He always could do more wid you than I could.

DAISY. Naw, you ain't no monkey-man neither. I dont' want you to leave town. I didn't want y'all to be fightin' over me, nohow.

JIM. Aw, rock on down de road wid dat stuff. A two-timin' cloaker like you don't keer whut come off. Me and Dave been good frien's ever since we was born till you had to go flouncin' yousef aroun'.

DAISY. What did I do? All I did was to come over town to see you and git a mouf-ful of gum. Next thing I know, y'all is fightin' an' carryin' on.

JIM (*Stands silent for a while*). Did you come over there Sat'day night to see me sho 'nuff, sugar babe?

DAISY. Everybody could see dat but you.

JIM. Jus' like I told you, Daisy, before you *ever* left from 'roun' here and went up North. I could kiss you every day—just as regular as pig-tracks.

DAISY. An' I tole you I could stand it too—just as regular as you could.

JIM (*Catching her by the arm and pulling her down with him onto the rail*). Set down, here, Daisy. Le's talk some chat. You want me sho 'nuff? Hones' to God?

DAISY (*Coyly*). 'Member whut I told you out on de lake last summer?

JIM. Sho 'nuff, Daisy? (DAISY *nods smilingly*)

JIM (*Sadly*). But I got to go 'way. Whut we gointer do 'bout dat?

DAISY. Where you goin', Jim?

JIM (*Looking sadly down the track*). God knows.

(*Off stage from the same direction from which* JIM *entered, comes the sound of whistling and tramping of feet on the ties.*)

JIM (*Brightening*). Dat's Dave! (*Frowning*) Wonder whut he doin' walkin' dis track? (*Looks accusingly at* DAISY) I bet he's goin' to yo' work-place.

DAISY. Whut for?

JIM. He ain't goin' to see de madame—must be goin' to see you.

(*He starts to rise petulantly as* DAVE *comes upon the scene.*

DAISY *rises also.*)

DAVE (*Looks accusingly from one to another*). Whut y'all jumpin' up for? I . . .

JIM. Whut you gut to do wid us business? Tain't none of yo' business if we stand up, set down or fly like a skeeter hawk.

DAVE. Who said I keered? Dis railroad belongs to de *man*—I kin walk it good as you, cain't I?

JIM (*Laughing exultantly*). Oh, yeah, Mr. Do-Dirty! You figgered you had done run me on off so you could git Daisy all by yo' self. You was headin' right for her work-place.

DAVE. I wasn't no such a thing.

JIM. You was. Didn't I hear you coming down de track all whistlin' an' everythin'?

DAVE. Youse a big ole Georgy-somethin'-ain't-so! I done got my belly full of Daisy Sat-day night. She can't snore in my ear no more.

DAISY (*Indignantly*). Whut you come here low-ratin' me for, Dave Carter? I ain't done nothin' to you but treat you white. Who come rubbed yo' ole head for you yestiddy if it wasn't me?

DAVE. Yeah, you rubbed my head all right, and I lakted dat. But everybody say you done toted a pan to Joe Clark's barn for Jim before I see you.

DAISY. Think I was goin' to let Jim lay there 'thout nothin' fitten for a dog to eat?

DAVE. That's all right, Daisy. If you want to pay Jim for knockin' me in de head, all right. But I'm a man in a class—in a class to myself and nobody knows my name.

JIM (*Snatching* DAISY *around to face him*). Was you over to Dave's house yestiddy rubbing his ole head and cloakin 'wid him to run me outa town—and me locked up in dat barn wid de cows and mules?

DAISY (*Sobbing*). All both of y'all hollerin' at me an' fussin' me jus cause I tries to be nice—and neither one of y'all don't keer nothin' bout me.

(*Both boys glare at each other over* DAISY'S *head and both try to hug her at the same time. She violently wrenches herself away from both and makes as if to go on.*)

DAISY. Leave me go! Take yo' rusty pa'ms offen me. I'm goin' on back to my work-place. I jus' got off to see 'bout y'all and look how y'all treat me.

JIM. Wait a minute, Daisy. I love you like God loves Gabriel—an' dat's His bes' angel.

DAVE. Daisy, I love you harder than de thunder can bump a stump—if I don't—God's a gopher.

DAISY (*Brightening*). Dat's de first time you ever said so.

DAVE & JIM. Who?

JIM. Whut you hollerin' "Who" for? You ain't no owl.

DAVE. Speak when you spoken to—come when you called, next fall you'll be my coon houn' dog.

JIM. Table dat discussion. (*Turning to* DAISY) You ain't never give me no chance to talk wid you right.

DAVE. You made *me* feel like you was tryin' to put de Ned book on me all de time. Do you love me sho 'nuff, Daisy?

DAISY (*Blooming again into coquetry*). Aw, y'all better stop dat. You know you don't mean it.

DAVE. Who don't mean it? Lemme tell you somethin', mama, if you was mine, I wouldn't have you countin' no ties wid *yo'* pretty lil toes. Know whut I'd do?

DAISY (*Coyly*). Naw, whut would you do?

DAVE. I'd buy you a whole passenger train—and hire some mens to run it for you.

DAISY (*Happily*). Oo-ooh, Dave!

JIM (*To* DAVE). De wind may blow, de doorway slam
Dat Stuff you shootin' ain't worth a dam.
(*To* DAISY) I'd buy you a great big ole ship—and then, baby, I'd buy you a ocean to sail yo' ship on.

DAISY (*Happily*). Oo-ooh, Jim.

DAVE (*To* JIM). A long train, a short caboose
> Dat lie whut you shootin', ain't no use.

(*To* DAISY) Miss Daisy, know whut I'd do for you?

DAISY. Naw, whut?

DAVE. I'd come down de river ridin' a mud cat and leadin' a minnow.

DAISY. Lawd, Dave, you sho is propaganda.

JIM (*Peevishly*). Naw he ain't—he's jus lyin'—he's a noble liar. Know whut I'd do if you was mine?

DAISY. Naw, Jim.

JIM. I'd make a panther wash yo' dishes and a 'gator chop yo' wood for you.

DAVE. Daisy, how come you let Jim lie lak dat? He's as big a liar as he is a man. But sho 'nuff, now, laying a-side all jokes, Jim there don't even know how to answer you. If you don't b'lieve it—ast him somethin'.

DAISY (*To* JIM). You like me much, Jim?

JIM (*Enthusiastically*). Yeah, Daisy, I sho' do.

DAVE (*Triumphant*). See dat! I tole you he didn't know how to answer nobody like you. If he was talking to some of them ol' funny-lookin' gals over town he'd be answering 'em jus' right. But he got to learn how to answer *you*. Now you ast *me* something and see how I answer you.

DAISY. Do you like me, Dave?

DAVE (*Very properly in a falsetto voice*). *Yes, ma'am!* Dat's de way to answer swell folks like you. Furthermore, less we prove which one of us love you de best right now. (*To* JIM) Jim, how much time would you do on de chain-gang for dis 'oman?

JIM. Twenty years and like it.

DAVE. See dat, Daisy? Dat nigger ain't willin' to do no time for you? I'd *beg* de judge to gimme life. (*Both* JIM *and* DAVE *laugh*)

DAISY. Y'all doin all dis bookooin' out here on de railroad track but I bet y'all crazy 'bout Bootsie and Teets and a whole heap of other gals.

JIM. Cross my feet and hope to die! I'd ruther see all de other wimmen folks in de worl' dead than for you to have de tooth-ache.

DAVE. If I was dead and any other woman come near my coffin de undertaker would have to do his job all over—'cause I'd git right up and walk off. Furthermore, Miss Daisy, ma'am, also ma'am, which would *you* ruther be—a lark a-flyin' or a dove a settin', ma'am, also ma'am?

DAISY. 'Course I'd ruther be a dove.

JIM. Miss Daisy, ma'am, also ma'am . . . if you marry dis nigger over my head, I'm goin' to git me a green hickory club and season it over yo' head.

DAVE. Don't you be skeered, baby . . . papa kin take keer a *you*. (*To* JIM) Countin' from de finger (*Suiting the action to the word*) back to de thumb . . . start anything, I got you some.

JIM. Aw, I don't want no more fight wid you, Dave.

DAVE. Who said anything about fighting? We just provin' who love Daisy de best. (*To* DAISY) Now, which one of us you think love you de best?

DAISY. Deed I don't know, Dave.

DAVE. Baby, I'd walk de water for you—and tote a mountain on my head while I'm walkin'.

JIM. Know whut I'd do, honey babe? If you was a thousand miles from home and you didn't have no ready-made money and you had to walk all de way, walkin' till yo' feet start to rollin', just like a wheel, and I was ridin' way up in de sky, I'd step backwards offa dat airyplane just to walk home wid you.

DAISY (*Falling on* JIM'S *neck*). Jim, when you talk to me like dat, I just can't stand it. Le's us git married right now.

JIM. Now you talkin' like a blue-back speller. Le's go!

DAVE (*Sadly*). You gointer leave me lak dis, Daisy?

DAISY (*Sadly*). I likes you, too, Dave, I sho do. But I can't marry both of y'all at de same time.

JIM. Aw, come on, Daisy—sun's gettin' low. (*He starts off pulling* DAISY)

DAVE. Whut's I'm gointer do? (*Walking after them*)

JIM. Gwan back and dance—you make out you don't need me to play none.

DAVE (*almost tearfully*). Aw, Jim, shucks! Where y'all goin'?
(DAISY *comes to an abrupt halt and stops* JIM)

DAISY. That's right, honey. Where *is* we goin' sho nuff?

JIM (*Sadly*). Deed I don't know, baby. They just sentenced me to go—they didn't say where and I don't know.

DAISY. How we goin' nohow to go when we don't know where we goin'?
(JIM *looks at* DAVE *as if he expects some help but* DAVE *stands*

sadly silent. JIM *takes a few steps forward as if to go on.* DAISY *makes a step or two, unwillingly, then looks behind her and stops.* DAVE *looks as if he will follow them).*

DAISY. Jim! (*He stops and turns*) Wait a minute! Whut we gointer do when we git there?

JIM. Where?

DAISY. Where we goin'?

JIM. I done tole you I don't know where it is.

DAISY. But how we gointer git something to eat and a place to stay?

JIM. Play and dance—jus' like I been doin'.

DAISY. You can't dance and Dave ain't gointer be there.

JIM (*Looks appealing at* DAVE, *then away quickly*). Well, I can't help *dat*, can I?

DAISY (*Brightly*). I tell you whut, Jim! Le's us don't go nowhere. They sentenced you to leave Eatonville and youse more than a mile from de city limits already. Youse in Maitland now. Supposin' you come live on de white folks' place wid me after we git married. Eatonville ain't got nothin' to do wid you livin' in Maitland.

JIM. Dat's a good idea, Daisy.

DAISY (*Jumping into his arms*). And listen, honey, you don't have to be beholden to Dave nor nobody else. You can throw dat ole box away if you want to. I know where you can get a *swell* job.

JIM (*Sheepishly*). Doin' whut? (*Looks lovingly at his guitar*)

DAISY (*Almost dancing*). Yard man. All you have to do is wash windows, and sweep de sidewalk, and scrub off de steps and porch and hoe up de weeds and rake up de leaves and dig a few holes now and then with a spade . . . to plant some trees and things like that. It's a good steady job.

JIM (*After a long deliberation*). You see, Daisy, de Mayor and corporation tol' me to go on off and I oughter go.

DAISY. Well, I'm not goin' tippin' down no railroad track like a Maltese cat. I wasn't brought up knockin' 'round from here to yonder.

JIM. Well, I wasn't brought up wid no spade in my hand—and ain't goin' to start it now.

DAISY. But sweetheart, we got to live, ain't we? We got to git hold of money before we kin do anything. I don't mean to stay in de white folks' kitchen all my days.

JIM. Yeah, all dat's true, but you couldn't buy a flea a waltzin' jacket wid de money *I'm* goin' to make wid a hoe and spade.

DAISY (*Getting tearful*). You don't want me. You don't love me.

JIM. Ye, I do, darlin' I love you. Youse de one lettin' a spade come between us. (*He caresses her*) I loves you and you only. You don't see *me* draggin' a whole gang of farmin' tools into us business, do you?

DAISY (*Stiffly*). Well, I ain't goin' to marry no man that ain't goin' to work and take care of me.

JIM. I don't mind workin' if de job ain't too heavy for me. I ain't goin' to bother wid nothin' in my hands heavier than dis box—and I totes it 'round my neck 'most of de time.

(DAISY *makes a despairing gesture as* JIM *takes a step or two away from her. She turns to* DAVE *finally.*)

DAISY. Well, I reckon you love me the best anyhow. You wouldn't talk to me like Jim did, would you, Dave?

DAVE. Naw, I wouldn't say whut he said a-tall.

DAISY (*Cuddling up to him*). Whut would *you* say, honey?

DAVE. I'd say dat box was too heavy for me to fool wid. I wouldn't tote nothin' heavier than my hat and I feel like I'm 'busin' myself sometime dotin' dat.

DAISY (*Outraged*). Don't you mean to work none?

DAVE. Wouldn't hit a lick at a snake.

DAISY. I don't blame *you*, Dave (*Looking down at his feet*) cause totin' dem feet of yourn is enough to break down your constitution. (*Airily*). That's all right—dem foots done put plenty bread in our moufs.

DAVE. Not by they selves though—wid de help of dat box, Jim. When you gits havin' fits on dat box, boy, my foots has hysterics. Daisy, you marry Jim cause I don't want to come between y'all. He's my buddy.

JIM. Come to think of it, Dave, she was yourn first. You take and handle dat spade for her.

DAVE. You heard her say it's all I can do to lift up dese feets and put 'em down. Where I'm goin' to git any time to wrassle wid any hoes and shovels? You kin git 'round better'n me. You done won Daisy—I give in. I ain't goin' to bite no fren' of mine in de back.

DAISY. Both of you niggers can git yo' hat an' yo' heads and git on down de road. Neither one of y'all don't have to have me. I got a good job and plenty men beggin' for yo' chance.

JIM. Dat's right, Daisy, you go git you one them mens whut don't mind smellin' mules—and beatin' de white folks to de barn every mornin'. I don't wanta be bothered wid nothin' but dis box.

DAVE. An' I can't strain wid nothin' but my feets.

(DAISY *walks slowly away in the direction from which she came. Both watch her a little wistfully for a minute. The sun is setting.*)

DAVE. Guess I better be gittin' on back—it's most dark. Where you goin', Jim?

JIM. I don't know, Dave. Down de road, I reckon.

DAVE. Whyncher come on back to town. 'Tain't no use you proguein' up and down de railroad track when you got a home.

JIM. They done lawed me way from it for hittin' you wid dat bone.

DAVE. Dat ain't nothin'. It was my head you hit. An' if I don't keer whut dem old ugly-rump niggers got to do wid it?

JIM. They might not let me come in town.

DAVE (*Seizing* JIM's *arm and facing him back toward the town*). They better! Look here, Jim, if they try to keep you out dat town we'll go out to dat swamp and git us a mule bone a piece and come into town and boil dat stew down to a low gravy.

JIM. You mean dat, Dave? (DAVE *nods his head eagerly*) Us warn't mad wid one 'nother nohow. (*Belligerently*) Come on, le's go back to town. Dem mullet-heads better leave me be, too. (*Picks up a heavy stick*) I wish Lum would come tellin' me 'bout de law when I got all dis law in *my* hands. And de rest o' dem gator-faced jigs, if they ain't got a whole sto' o' mule bones and a good determination, they better not bring no mess up. Come on, boy.

(*They start back together toward town,* JIM *picking a dance tune on his guitar, and* DAVE *cutting steps on the ties beside him, singing, prancing and happy, they exit, right, as* THE CURTAIN FALLS.)

BIOGRAPHICAL NOTES

BARNES, Albert Coombs (1872–1951), was born in near-poverty in Philadelphia. He completed the three-year medical course at the University of Pennsylvania in 1892. During the late 1890s, and again in 1900, he pursued university studies in chemistry and philosophy in Germany, where he met the gifted research chemist Hermann Hille, who accompanied Barnes back to Philadelphia. Their collaboration and marketing of the hugely successful silver nitrate antiseptic Argyrol and other pharmaceutical products made Barnes and Hille multimillionaires by 1907. After dissolution of the partnership and formation by Barnes of A. C. Barnes Company in 1908, exclusive producer of Argyrol, the almost automatic accumulation of wealth permitted Barnes to return to his early interests in philosophy and painting. The artist William Glackens, a classmate from Barnes's Central High School days, introduced his friend to several of the artists of the Ashcan School, as well as to the French impressionists.

From these beginnings, Barnes would acquire during the next thirty years one of the greatest art collections in private hands in America, including several hundred paintings ranging across the centuries but centered in Renoirs, Manets, Matisses, Gauguins, Degas, Cezannes, Seurats, Soutines, and Modiglianis, and much more from Belle Epoque France. The French art dealer and theorist Paul Guillaume early confirmed Barnes's latent fascination with Africa and Americans of African descent, the result of which was the latter's acquisition over time of sculpture from the African continent, querulous encouragement of the Renaissance undertakings of Alain Locke, Charles Johnson, and Walter White, promotion of the careers of African American artists Gwendolyn Bennett, Aaron

Douglas, and Horace Pippin, as well as abiding interest in Negro spirituals and generous support of the musical program at the Manual Training School for Negroes at Bordentown, New Jersey. He contributed several influential articles to *Opportunity* (May 1924, May 1926, and May 1928) on African influences on European modern art. Barnes died in an automobile accident shortly after conferring upon the trustees of historically black Lincoln University the power to appoint the trustees of the Barnes Foundation, an institution whose eccentric and highly restrictive conditions of public access had become infamous.

BENNETT, Gwendolyn (1902–1981), one of the polymaths of the Renaissance (painter, writer, educator), was the daughter of a Texas lawyer. Her record at Girls High School in Brooklyn, New York, was outstanding. She pursued fine arts studies at Teachers College, Columbia University, and the Pratt Institute. A sorority scholarship enabled Bennett to study art in France in 1925–26. She became an assistant editor of *Opportunity* soon after returning to the United States, performing a talent-scout role on that magazine somewhat similar to that of her friend Jessie Fauset's on *The Crisis*. Her short stories and poems appeared in *American Mercury, The Crisis, The Messenger, Opportunity*, and the scandalous *Fire!!*. Bennett continued to draw and paint. She taught watercolor and design at Howard in the early 1930s, attracting the interest of Albert Barnes. She was the director of the Harlem Community Art Center from 1937 until its suppression in 1940.

BONTEMPS, Arna (1902–1972), novelist, poet, librarian, was born in Alexandria, Louisiana. His family moved to Los Angeles when Bontemps was three. He was educated at San Fernando Academy and Pacific Union College (1923). After Jessie Fauset published his poems in *The Crisis,* Bontemps headed for Harlem, arriving in 1924, where he was welcomed into Talented Tenth circles and struck up a lifelong friendship with Langston Hughes. In 1926, Bontemp's "Golgotha Is a Mountain" won *Opportunity*'s Alexander Pushkin Award for Poetry, and in 1927, the *Crisis* first prize for poetry. After a teaching stint in Alabama, and a position with the Illinois Writers' Project, Bontemps was awarded a Rosenwald Fellowship for travel in the Caribbean. In 1943, he assumed the post of head librarian at Fisk University, enabling Bontemps to support a wife and numerous children. His collaboration with

Countee Cullen in 1943 resulted in the musical adaptation of their dramatic work by Harold Arlen as *St. Louis Woman,* an enormous Broadway success. Bontemps and Hughes collaborated on the anthology *The Poetry of the Negro, 1746–1949* (1949) and *The Book of Negro Folklore* (1951). Bontemps's final years were spent as curator of the James Weldon Johnson Memorial Collection of Negro Arts and Letters at Yale. His *The Harlem Renaissance Remembered* 1972, is an indispensable source.

BROWN, Sterling (1901–1989), poet, critic, folklorist, scholar, teacher, was born in Washington, D.C., where he was educated at the renowned and academically demanding M Street (Dunbar) High School. He won his B.A. and election to Phi Beta Kappa from Williams College (1923). He earned an M.A. in English at Harvard in 1924. After teaching positions at Virginia Seminary and College, Lincoln University (Missouri), and Fisk University, Brown joined the faculty of Howard University in 1929, remaining there until retiring in 1969 after an acclaimed and seminal teaching career. *Southern Road,* his first book of poetry, published in 1932, received considerable critical applause and enjoyed wide popularity. Because of the naturalism he achieved in his verse, Brown is regarded as the folk poet of the Harlem Renaissance. During much of the 1930s, Brown served as literary editor of *Opportunity,* and from 1936 to 1939, he served as Negro Affairs editor for the Federal Writers' Project. His *The Negro in American Fiction* (1937) remains a classic.

COTTER, Joseph Seamon (1861–1949), was the illegitimate son of a prominent white citizen of Louisville, Kentucky. Forced to discontinue his formal education at the age of eight and to take jobs as a rag picker, brick maker, cotton and tobacco picker, the precocious Cotter finally managed to complete his education during an intense ten-month tenure at night school. Eventually, Cotter became the principal of Louisville's Samuel Coleridge–Taylor School. After Paul Laurence Dunbar visited Cotter as his guest and read his poetry in the South for the first time, Cotter was emboldened to publish his own autobiographical, dramatic, and poetry writings. His poetry began to appear in *The Crisis* in 1918, and Cotter won an *Opportunity* prize in 1927 for the poem "The Tragedy of Pete." Countee Cullen included Cotter's verse in *Caroling Dusk.* Cotter's work was highly imitative and soon considered *passé*, although he continued to write and publish until late in life. His far more gifted son, Joseph Cotter, Jr., born in 1895, entered Fisk University in 1911 but was compelled to return home after contracting tuberculosis. A collection of poems, *The Band of Gideon and Other Lyrics*, appeared in 1918. The junior Cotter died the following year.

COTTER, Joseph Seamon Jr. (1895–1919), was born in Louisville, Kentucky. His father was a respected local educator and poet. Paul Laurence Dunbar was a family friend. Cotter entered Fisk University in 1911 but was compelled to return home after contracting tuberculosis. His verse was published in *The Crisis* and the *AME Zion Quarterly Review*. A collection of poems, *The Band of Gideon and Other Lyrics,* appeared in 1918. "Brother, What Shall You Say," included by Countee Cullen in his 1927 *Caroling Dusk* anthology, indicated that Cotter might have gradually turned to protest themes had he not died so young.

CULLEN, Countee Porter (1903–1946), born in Lexington, Kentucky, was the adopted son of Rev. Frederick Asbury Cullen, one of Harlem's leading ministers. He was educated at De Witt Clinton High School, where he edited the weekly newspaper. His first poetry appeared when he was fifteen, in *Modern School Magazine*. Cullen earned his B.A. and a Phi Beta Kappa key at New York University (1925), where he received the Witter Bynner Poetry Prize. His college graduation year also saw the release by Harper & Brothers of *Color,* a collection of new and previously published poems, some of which had been carried in national magazines such as *Century, Harper's, American Mercury,* and *The Nation*. Cullen obtained an M.A. in English at Harvard in 1926, and his precocity was further rewarded with the Harmon Foundation Gold Medal Award, *Opportunity* magazine prizes, and one of the first Guggenheim Fellowships (1928) awarded to an African American. In 1927, Cullen published *Copper Sun,* the *Ballad of a Brown Girl,* and the poetry anthology *Caroling Dusk*. He preferred the genteel genre of poetry, taking John Keats and the English Romantics as models. During most of this period, he was an editor of *Opportunity*. A turbulent, brief marriage to Yolande Du Bois, daughter of the distinguished intellectual and editor of *The Crisis*, W. E. B. Du Bois, ended in divorce in 1930. It was said that his deep friendship with Harold Jackman meant more to Cullen than his marriage. *One Way to Heaven,* the novel that was later adapted in collaboration with Arna Bontemps and Harold Arlen as *St. Louis Woman,* appeared in 1932. Cullen remarried in 1940.

CUNEY, Waring (1906–1975), born into comfortable circumstances in Washington, D.C., was educated at the prestigious M Street (Dunbar) High School and matriculated at Howard University, Lincoln University (Pennsylvania), and the New England Conservatory of Music, with further study in Rome. His poem "No Images" won first prize in the 1926 *Opportunity* contest. Cuney served as art and music columnist for *The Crisis.* His output was slender, although he continued to write poetry until late in life. Most of Cuney's verse consisted of short stanzas and was characterized by aphoristic verve.

DOMINGO, Wilfrid Adolphus (1889–?), a Jamaican-born journalist and racial militant, migrated to the United States in 1910. An archetypal New Negro, he was a founder of the African Blood Brotherhood (1918?), the earliest of the proto-Marxist organizations among African Americans, and he contributed to *Crusader,* the Brotherhood's seminal Harlem journal that combined militant black nationalism with revolutionary socialism. Domingo became one of the earliest and ablest of Marcus Garvey's supporters in the United States, serving as founding editor of the UNIA's principal organ, *The Negro World.* By July 1919, Domingo's commitment to socialism had led him away from Garveyism and into an editorial collaboration on *Messenger* magazine, the militant monthly launched in November 1917 by the African American socialists A. Philip Randolph and Chandler Owen. Domingo's conviction that the UNIA was squandering thousands of its faithful's dollars and that Garvey's extreme racial chauvinism threatened the spread of genuine socialism among African Americans found loud expression in another Harlem journal of brief duration, *The Emancipator.* Domingo's denunciation of Garvey in *Crusader* (October 1921), "Figures Never Lie, But Liars Do Figure," was one of the most damaging pieces of the day. But he was soon distressed by the very success of the "Garvey Must Go" campaign, as it took on increasingly anti–West Indian overtones.

DOUGLAS, Aaron (1898–1979), the most prominent painter of the Harlem Renaissance, was born in Kansas. He received his undergraduate education, majoring in art, at the University of Nebraska. Charles S. Johnson, editor of *Opportunity,* recruited Douglas from a Kansas City high-school teaching position to serve as the painter of the movement. After a period of tutelage under Winold Reiss, Douglas produced canvases, murals, and illustrations for books and magazines distinguished by geometrical motifs depicting the progress from antiquity to modern times of African peoples. He and wife, Alta, knew everyone involved in the Harlem Renaissance, black and white, interesting and influential, destitute and deviant. Their Harlem apartment was one of the principal gathering spots. Douglas's close association with the hugely influential Charles Johnson, as well as his considerable talent, enabled him to obtain a fellowship at the Barnes Foundation, another for study in Paris at the Academie Scandinave, and eventually the chairmanship of the art department of Fisk University. His illustrations appeared in periodicals such as *Theatre Arts, The Crisis, Opportunity, Vanity Fair,* and *American Mercury.* His murals for the Harlem branch of the New York Public Library and the Erastus Milo Cravath Memorial Library of Fisk are considered his finest.

DU BOIS, William Edward Burghardt (1868–1963), historian, sociologist, novelist, essayist, editor, civil rights militant, was born and educated through high school in Great Barrington, Massachusetts. He attended Fisk University with a stipend provided by four New England Congregational churches and graduated in 1888. He entered Harvard College on scholarship as a third-year student and finished cum laude two years later. Du Bois earned an M.A. in history in 1892, then left Harvard for the University of Berlin with a grant from a reluctant Slater Fund. After two years of study in Germany (1892–1894), Du Bois accepted a professorship in classics at Wilberforce University (Ohio). Meanwhile, he completed his Harvard dissertation, "The Suppression of the African Slave Trade to the United States of America, 1638–1870." In 1896, he received the Ph.D., the first awarded to an African American. Two years of research and writing while attached to the University of Pennsylvania produced the monumental *The Philadelphia Negro* (1899), one of the first studies in urban sociology in the United States. From 1899 to 1910, Du Bois held the chair in sociology at Atlanta University and produced the trailblazing series of investigations known internationally as the Atlanta University Studies. In 1903, he published *The Souls of Black Folk,* one of the most moving collections of essays of the twentieth century, in consequence of which he came to assume the role of principal opponent of Booker T. Washington and chief exponent of civil rights for African Americans. From 1910 onward, as founding editor of *The Crisis*, Du Bois's name was synonymous with the new National Association for the Advancement of Colored People (NAACP). His first novel, *The Quest of the Silver Fleece* (1912), encouraged younger African Americans to think of writing as a powerful weapon in the struggle against racism. *Darkwater*, Du Bois's 1920 collection of essays, was significant in stiffening the courage of thinking African Americans in the wake of the infamous Red Summer of 1919. The *Crisis* literary awards created by Du Bois were only slightly less prestigious than the competing ones from *Opportunity*. Du Bois wrote a second novel, *The Dark Princess* (1928), a sprawling saga of the color line in which the high-minded ideals of the early Renaissance were powerfully recapitulated. Du Bois's controversial departure from *The Crisis* in 1934 coincided with the close of the Harlem Renaissance.

FAUSET, Jessie Redmon (1882?–1961), novelist, poet, editor, teacher, was born into a prominent old-line African American family in Philadelphia, Pennsylvania. After public school, Fauset attended Cornell University, graduating with honors and election to Phi Beta Kappa (1905). She earned an M.A. in Romance languages from the University of Pennsylvania and pursued studies at the Sorbonne. From 1906 to 1919, Fauset taught Latin and French at the M Street High School (Dunbar), the elite public school in Washington, D.C. Although her full-time affiliation with *The Crisis* began in 1919, and lasted until 1926, Fauset's editorial and short-story contributions made her presence in the magazine decisive as early as 1912. By 1924, as literary editor, she had begun to identify and publish such coming stars of the Harlem Renaissance as Jean Toomer, Langston Hughes, and Arna Bontemps. Although her personal relations with Alain Locke were problematic, she fully shared his confidence in the power of arts and letters to attenuate racial prejudice. Hers was the first of the Renaissance novels, *There Is Confusion* (1924), appearing several months before her fellow NAACP officer Walter White's *The Fire in the Flint*. Fauset's poetry was undistinguished and of modest output, but she excelled in novel writing, publishing more than any other Renaissance writer: *Plum Bun* (1929), *The Chinaberry Tree* (1931), and *Com-*

edy: American Style (1933). Fauset's novels dealt with the "better classes," the "representative Negroes" she believed could change the chemistry of race relations in the country. She was also abidingly concerned with exploring the pain and paradox of racial intermixture.

FISHER, Rudolph (1897–1934), physician, roentgenologist, musician, novelist, was born in Washington, D.C. His adolescence and early adult years were spent in Providence, Rhode Island, where he graduated from Brown University in 1919 as Phi Beta Kappa. Fisher received his M.D. degree from Howard University Medical School and interned at Freedmen's Hospital. He completed two years of specialized training in biology at Columbia University's College of Physicians and Surgeons. He moved to Harlem in 1925 and began his dual career as physician and novelist. Fisher's short stories and essays appeared from 1925 onward in the *Atlantic Monthly, American Mercury, McClure's, The Crisis,* and *Opportunity*—"City of Refuge" (February 1925), "The Caucasian Storms Harlem" (August 1927), and "Miss Cynthie" (June 1933) being the most notable. "City of Refuge" won the 1925 *Crisis* short-story contest. He also wrote arrangements for Negro spirituals for his friend Paul Robeson. His penetratingly comedic novel *The Walls of Jericho* appeared in 1928, followed in 1932 by the first detective mystery written by an African American, *The Conjure-Man Dies: A Mystery Tale of Dark Harlem*. Fisher died in December 1934, apparently from the effects of chronic exposure to his own X-ray machinery.

FRAZIER, Edward Franklin (1894–1962), educator, sociologist, was born in Baltimore, Maryland. After finishing high school in the city, Frazier entered Howard University, and graduated with honors in 1916. He earned the M.A. degree in sociology at Clark University (1921). In 1931, Frazier received the Ph.D. in sociology from the University of Chicago, under the direction of Robert E. Park. His dissertation, *The Negro in Chicago,* was published in 1932. Frazier taught at Atlanta University (1922–1927) and Fisk University until 1934, when he began his long affiliation with Howard University as chairman of the sociology department. During his tenure at Atlanta University, Frazier's essays and articles appeared in the *Journal of Social Forces, The Nation, The Crisis,* and *Opportunity*. His classic monograph *The Negro in the United*

States appeared in 1939, and his controversial *Black Bourgeoisie* in 1957.

GARVEY, Marcus Mosiah (1887–1940), was born in St. Ann's Bay, Jamaica, the youngest of eleven children. Both parents were of unmixed African descent, and Garvey's stonemason father claimed to be directly descended from the island's fierce Maroons—escaped slaves whose resistance during the seventeenth century forced the British government to grant them a degree of autonomy. With little formal education beyond elementary school, Garvey educated himself through wide reading while mastering the trade of printing. Fired from a foreman's job after joining a printers' strike in Kingston, he left Jamaica in 1907 to work on fruit plantations and newspapers in Central America. Observing labor exploitation firsthand in Panama and Costa Rica, and increasingly appalled by the indifference of British consular officials to the maltreatment of his fellow Jamaicans, Garvey concluded that African peoples must save themselves.

He sailed for Great Britain in 1912, possibly attended the University of London's Birkbeck College, met Africans from the mother continent for the first time, and soon came under the influence of the charismatic Egyptian nationalist Duse Muhammad Ali, on whose newspaper, *Africa Times and Orient Review,* Garvey worked for a time. At about this same time, he read Booker T. Washington's autobiographical *Up from Slavery.* On his return to Jamaica in 1914, Garvey claimed to have experienced an epiphany aboard ship. Henceforth, he believed that he was destined to build the organization and provide the leadership that could empower the African race. Island prejudices of color and class, carefully fanned by British authorities, spelled defeat for Garvey and his ambitious Universal Negro Improvement and Conservation Association and African Communities League (soon shortened to UNIA). Undeterred, he left Jamaica for the United States and Tuskegee Institute in late March 1916, where his hopes of finding material encouragement were aborted by the sudden death two months earlier of Booker Washington.

By January 1918, however, Garvey had realized his long-held dream of establishing a newspaper. *The Negro World,* printed in English, Spanish, and French, began to circulate throughout Latin America and Africa. His travels throughout the United States and evangelizing in Harlem had generated a racial war chest, created an embryonic movement, and catapulted Garvey almost to the front ranks of black leadership. With the extraordinary mass rally and pageant mounted in Harlem and Madison Square Garden in August–September 1920 and acquisition of a freighter and passenger ship for the Black Star Line, Garvey and the UNIA electrified people of African descent throughout the world. Money flowed into the treasury and membership climbed into the tens of thousands in New York and other major American cities. "Africa for the Africans," proclaimed Garvey, as he unveiled his grand Back-to-Africa design to populate a large area of Liberia with his followers.

Poor management, duplicitous subordinates, and mounting opposition by native-born leaders such as W. E. B. Du Bois and A. Philip Randolph to his black separatist ideology and laissez faire economics fatally undermined Garvey's power. Indicted and convicted of mail fraud in 1923 to the cheers of many prominent members of the Talented Tenth (outraged by his public flirtation with the Ku Klux Klan), he was pardoned by President Harding and finally deported to Jamaica in 1927. Garvey's UNIA was the largest mass-based organization among African Americans in the history of the United States.

GRIMKÉ, Angelina Weld (1880–1958), poet, playwright, teacher, was born in Boston, Massachusetts, the only child of the distinguished African American lawyer, journalist, and public servant Archibald H. Grimké, nephew of the abolitionist sisters Angelina and Sarah Grimké. She received a superior education at the Boston Normal School of Gymnastics (1902). Moving to Washington, D.C., Grimké began her long teaching career at the famous M Street High School (Dunbar), which lasted until 1933. Her largely unpublished poetry reflected her concerns for the domestic and social plight of women, as well as a strong lesbian proclivity. Her sentimental drama in three acts about racial injustice, *Rachel*, was performed in Washington in 1916, and later in New York and Boston. Grimké was a member of the lively salon maintained by fellow poet Georgia Douglas Johnson, but as years passed she became increasingly reclusive.

HUGHES, James Langston (1902–1967), author of short stories and works for children, poet, playwright, novelist, anthologist, and historian-popularizer, was born in Joplin, Missouri. Hughes was considered the poet laureate of Harlem. His parents separated when he was a child, and his alienation from his father, a successful expatriate businessman in Mexico, was intense and enduring. Hughes's maternal grandfather was the abolitionist Charles Langston, who fought with John Brown at Harper's Ferry and was half-brother to John Mercer Langston, U.S. congressman from Virginia. Hughes attended elementary school in some seven cities and completed high school in 1919 at Cleveland's Central High School. His literary precociousness won him election as class poet in elementary school and editor of the class yearbook at Central High School. Jessie Fauset published his first short story, "Mexican Games," in *The Brownie's Book* (a children's magazine edited by W. E. B. Du Bois) and his famous poem dedicated to Du Bois, "The Negro Speaks of Rivers," in *The Crisis* that same year (1921). In 1922, Hughes sailed to West Africa, and in 1923 to Europe, as a mess steward on freighters. Returning to the United States in 1924 after odd jobs and wanderings in France and Italy, Hughes was "discovered" by the poet Vachel Lindsay as a "busboy poet" while working in a Washington, D.C., hotel. That same year brought him the second poetry prize and third essay prize in the *Opportunity* contest. Having dropped out of Columbia University in his freshman year (1921), he returned to college in 1926 at Lincoln University (Pennsylvania), with significant financial assistance from Mrs. Amy Spingarn, the wife of the NAACP board chairman, Joel Spingarn, and the imperious Mrs. Charlotte Osgood Mason (the notorious "Godmother"). During this time, Hughes traveled throughout much of the South reading poetry at colleges and universities.

Meanwhile, Hughes had also been discovered by Carl Van Vechten, former music critic for the *New York Times* and intimate advisor to the publishers Alfred and Blanche Knopf. Knopf published Hughes's collection of startling jazz-idiom poems, *The Weary Blues* (1926), and a second volume, *Fine Clothes to the Jew,* in 1927. His novel *Not Without Laughter* appeared in 1931, a year after he graduated from Lincoln. His patron, Charlotte Mason, insisted that Hughes and his bosom friend Zora Neale Hurston buckle down to serious writing in the township of Plainfield, New Jersey, secretarially assisted by Louise Thompson, estranged wife of Wallace Thurman. The controversy with Hurston the following year over authorship of *Mule-Bone,* a dramatic comedy, wrecked their friendship and resulted in Hughes being abandoned by Godmother and Locke. A Harmon Foundation Gold Medal Award for Literature and royalties from sales of his novel *Not Without Laughter* enabled Hughes to escape to Cuba in 1931 and in 1932 to the USSR to take part in a Soviet film about racial supremacy in Alabama. During the balance of the 1930s, under the influence of Louise Thompson and her second husband, William Patterson, Hughes moved far to the left, publishing poetry and plays of a Marxist bent in *New Masses. The Ways of White Folks,* a collection of short stories, was published in 1934. In 1937, he went to Spain as correspondent for the Baltimore *Afro-American* newspaper to cover the civil war. He collaborated with Arna Bontemps on anthologies and childrens' works and founded theater groups in Harlem, Chicago, and Los Angeles.

HURSTON, Zora Neale (1901?–1960), novelist, folklorist, anthropologist, was born in Eatonville, Florida, a small town founded and exclusively populated by African Americans. Although her father eventually abandoned her and her mother died when Hurston was young, she celebrated her handsome father as a commanding figure in two of her novels and frequently recalled the admonition of her mother to "jump at the sun." Hurston attended Morgan Academy (Morgan State University) in Baltimore, Howard University, and Barnard College on scholarship, receiving her B.A. degree in 1927. During her Barnard years, she studied anthropology under Franz Boas and worked as secretary to the novelist Fannie Hurst. Charles S. Johnson had recognized her exceptional abilities in 1921 after Alain Locke called his attention to her short story "John Redding Goes to Sea," appearing in the Howard University *Stylus.* Johnson used his considerable influence to arrange for her relocation to New York in 1925. "Spunk" and "Drenched in Light" won the *Opportunity* second prize for short story in 1924 and 1925, respectively.

Her scholarly article in the *Journal of Negro History* (1927) brought charges of plagiarism, but Hurston stubbornly persevered in her research, generously supported by Mrs. Charlotte Osgood Mason ("Godmother") and a Rosenwald Fellowship in 1934, followed by two Guggenhein fellowships in 1936 and 1937. By then, Hurston had become a fixture in the faded Harlem Renaissance, famous as much for her outspokenness and sometimes crude exhibitionism as for her robust talent. Coining terms such as "Astorperious," "bodacious," "Negrotarian," and "Niggerati," she was one of the driving forces among the younger artists in their breakaway from the self-conscious standards of the Du Boises, Johnsons, and Fausets. Langston Hughes admired her, Carl Van Vechten adored her, Locke promoted her, and Wallace Thurman famously caricatured her as Sweetie May Carr in *Infants of the Spring.* Hurston's novel *Jonah's Gourd Vine* (1934) was a masterpiece in the use of folk idiom, in which the black peasant South was recreated as a place both mythic and palpably real. Her friendship with Hughes ended in dispute in 1931 over authorship of the dramatic comedy *Mule-Bone.*

JOHNSON, Charles S. (1893–1956), social scientist, editor, educator, was born in Bristol, Virginia, the oldest son of a well-read Baptist preacher. Johnson graduated from Wayland Academy and Virginia Union University in Richmond, Virginia, and then earned the Ph.B. degree in sociology from the University of Chicago in 1918. While pursuing his degree, he served as director of research for the Chicago office of the National Urban League. After duty in France as a noncommissioned officer in World War I, Johnson resumed graduate studies under Robert E. Park at the University of Chicago. Because of his outstanding organizational skills, social-science objectivity, and writing ability, Johnson was given the responsibility for producing the classic study in urban sociology issued by the Chicago Commission on Race Relations, *The Negro in Chicago: A Study of Race Relations and a Race Riot* (1919).

In 1921, the newly wed Johnson moved to New York City to direct research for the National Urban League. Two years later, he assumed the editorship of the League's new publication, *Opportunity: A Journal of Negro Life.* Under his guidance, *Opportunity* became the principal organ of the New Negro Arts Movement as Johnson and his able staff (including Ethel Ray Nance) located, recruited, and arranged jobs, scholarships, and patronage for promising artists and writers who became the nucleus of the Harlem Renaissance. Eric Walrond, Zora Neale Hurston, Langston Hughes, Nella Larsen, Aaron Douglas, and Countee Cullen were among those assisted by Johnson. He took the lead in assembling the early network of white philanthropists and publishers (Hurston's "Negrotarians") who made the *Opportunity* prizes possible.

Johnson departed for Fisk University in 1926 to head its department of sociology, but he continued to counsel both Negrotarians and Niggerati from Nashville. The editorial introduction to his prose and poetry anthology *Ebony and Topaz* (1928) was a perceptive and conciliatory appreciation of the insurgent literary and aesthetic ideals espoused by the younger artists. Johnson's major work, *The Negro in American Civilization: A Study of Negro Life and Race Relations in the Light of Social Research,* appeared in 1930. In 1946, Johnson became the first African American president of Fisk University, a factor in making the university a source of employment for Arna Bontemps, James Weldon Johnson, Aaron Douglas, and several other veterans of the Harlem Renaissance.

JOHNSON, Fenton (1888–1958), playwright, poet, editor, was born in Chicago, where he attended the University of Chicago and Northwestern University. Johnson also spent time at the Columbia University School of Journalism. Several of the nineteen-year-old Johnson's plays were performed by the repertory company attached to Chicago's famous Old Pekin Theatre. Johnson spent a year teaching English at Louisville State University in Kentucky. Most of his life was lived in Chicago, where Johnson edited a little magazine called *Correct English* and founded a crusading monthly, *The Champion Magazine* (1916). James Weldon Johnson called Johnson "one of the first Negro revolutionary poets" and included several of his poems in his *The Book of American Negro Poetry* (1922). Fenton Johnson published three volumes of his works: *A Little Dreaming* (1912), *Visions of Dusk* (1915), and *Songs of the Soil* (1916). His verse was more often than not mildly despairing.

JOHNSON, Georgia Douglas (1886–1966), poet, playwright, teacher, was born in Atlanta, Georgia, and educated at Atlanta University and Oberlin Conservatory of Music. She and her Atlanta University–educated husband, Henry Lincoln Johnson, settled in Washington, D.C., where she was employed by the federal government. Her husband was a prominent figure in the Republican party. Johnson's first poetry appeared in 1918 as *The Heart of a Woman,* followed by *Bronze* (1922) and *An Autumn Cycle* (1928). She was the first African American woman to be widely recognized as a poet since Frances E. W. Harper (1825–1911). Johnson's one-act play *Plumes—A Folk Tragedy* won first prize in the 1927 *Opportunity* contest. She was equally famous for the literary club, The Saturday Nighters, over which she presided in her northwest Washington home. Participants included May Miller, Angelina Weld Grimké, Alain Locke, Jean Toomer, Richard

Bruce Nugent, James Weldon Johnson, Du Bois, Jessie Fauset, and Hughes, among others. Johnson's deep devotion to poetry was increasingly frustrated as anthologists and publishers turned away from her work because of its dated sentimentality and gentility. A more kindly reading, however, reveals Johnson's feminist sensibilities to have been surprisingly modern.

JOHNSON, Helene (1907–?), was born in Boston. She attended Boston University and the Columbia University Extension in 1926. Her poems were published in *Opportunity, Vanity Fair,* and *Fire!!.* Locke included her in his *The New Negro.* Johnson's work was distinguished among the early Renaissance participants by its concern with ghetto life. She vanished from the Harlem scene before the end of the Harlem Renaissance.

JOHNSON, James Weldon (1871–1938), poet, novelist, playwright, diplomat, linguist, civil rights leader, was born in Jacksonville, Florida, the son of educated parents who had lived and prospered in the Bahamas. Johnson attended the preparatory school at Atlanta University and earned a B.A. degree in 1894. He returned to Florida to head the segregated African American grammar school in Jacksonville, founded a newspaper, the *Daily American,* and passed the Florida bar examination in 1897. Johnson moved to Manhattan, where he and his brother, Rosamond, in collaboration with the immensely gifted African American musician Bob Cole, wrote light operas, musical comedies, and some two hundred popular songs ("Under the Bamboo Tree," "Oh Didn't He Ramble," and so on), as well as "Lift Every Voice and Sing," known as the "Negro National Anthem." Broadway successes of the Johnson-Cole team were such that they were dubbed "Those Ebony Offenbachs." The musical comedy *The Shoo-Fly Regiment* was a box-office smash on Broadway and a success in London and Paris. At the same time, Johnson studied literature with Columbia University's most famous professor, Brander Matthews.

In 1905, after Johnson wrote lyrics for the campaign song "You're All Right Teddy," Booker T. Washington successfully recommended Johnson's appointment as U.S. consul to Venezuela (1906–1908) and Nicaragua (1909–1912). In 1910, Johnson married Grace Nail, sister of Harlem's major real estate developer, and finished his remarkable novel *The Autobiography of an Ex–Colored Man,* anonymously published in 1912. The presidential victory of the Democrats in 1912 ended Johnson's foreign service career. His patron, Booker Washington, arranged for Johnson to join the editorial staff of the New York newspaper, *Age,* early in 1914. Johnson's widely acclaimed *Fifty Years and Other Poems* appeared in 1917. By then, at the urging of W. E. B. Du Bois and Joel Spingarn, he had become field organizer for the NAACP, a position Johnson discharged with outstanding organizational success. Johnson worked well with the often difficult Du Bois and greatly enhanced the organization's efficiency by recruiting Walter White from Atlanta as assistant executive secretary in 1918.

The publication of *The Book of American Negro Poetry, with an Essay on the Negro's Creative Genius* (1922) was one of the major catalysts of the Harlem Renaissance. Johnson's introduction proclaimed artistic and literary creativity as the measure of an ethnic group's worth and affirmed its potency for improving race relations in the United States. His *God's Trombones: Seven Negro Sermons in Verse* (1927) was immensely popular, its sermons recited on Talented Tenth literary occasions and at the penthouse gatherings of Negrotarians. *Black Manhattan* (1930) was the first history of the African American in New York. He resigned from the NAACP as executive secretary in 1931 to assume the Adam Spence Chair of Literature at Fisk University. His elegantly written and moderately revealing autobiography, *Along This Way* (1933), appeared to enthusiastic reviews. Johnson, who added Weldon to his name for purposes of euphony, was killed in an automobile crash in 1938 as he and his wife returned to Fisk from vacation in New England. Mrs. Johnson survived.

LARSEN, Nella (1891–1963), writer, librarian, nurse, claimed to have been born in Chicago. Her mother was white and of Danish extraction. Her African American father was probably a chauffeur who worked in the same New York City household as Larsen's mother. Larsen claimed to have spent several years before 1911 living with maternal relatives in Denmark. It is certain that she never attended the University of Copenhagen, as she often asserted. She did spend a year as a student at Fisk University. In 1915, Larsen graduated from the Lincoln Hospital Training Program in New York City. She also completed the course at the New York Public Library Training School and served as a children's librarian at the Harlem (135th Street) branch of the New York Public Library from 1922 to 1929. Her unhappy marriage to the prominent

African American physicist and Fisk professor Elmer Imes took place during this time.

Larsen was befriended by Walter White, Carl Van Vechten, Charles S. Johnson, and Alain Locke, all of whom encouraged her obvious writing prowess. In 1928, she published her first novel, *Quicksand,* which won the Harmon Foundation's second prize in literature. *Passing,* her second novel (1929), earned the Harmon Foundation's bronze medal. That same year Larsen won the first Guggenheim Fellowship awarded to an African American woman, but she also suffered traumatic allegations that her short story "Sanctuary," appearing in *Forum,* was plagiarized. Larsen left for Spain to work on her third novel, which she never completed. A widely publicized and bitter divorce (1933) from Professor Imes may have reinforced Larsen's inclination to withdraw from public scrutiny. It was long rumored in Harlem that she lived out the remainder of her life as a white person somewhere in New York. In fact, Larsen worked as a highly respected nurse at Gouverneur Hospital in New York, where her identity as an African American was never in question.

LOCKE, Alain Leroy (1885–1954), critic, philosopher, teacher, was born into a distinguished African American family of impressive Philadelphia pedigree. His father, Pliny Ishmael Locke, held a Howard University Law School degree and taught at the Philadelphia School of Pedagogy. Locke's academic performance from elementary school through Harvard was uniformly brilliant. His health was delicate throughout life due to rheumatic fever damage to his heart in childhood. He graduated from Harvard College in three years as Phi Beta Kappa and magna cum laude (1907) and became the first African American Rhodes scholar (1907–1910). After two years at Oxford, Locke spent academic year 1910–1911 at the University of Berlin and the College de France. He earned a Ph.D. in philosophy from Harvard in 1918. From 1912 until his retirement, he was a towering presence on the Howard University faculty, except for a brief hiatus (1925–1928) when he was suspended from the university for insubordination by the tyrannical white president.

Charles S. Johnson recruited Locke to edit the special Harlem Renaissance edition of *Survey Graphic* (May 1925) and the catalytic anthology for Albert and Charles Boni, *The New Negro* (1926), during his Fisk exile from Howard. Locke's influence in the Harlem Renaissance was unsurpassed. He advanced the careers of Countee Cullen, Zora Neale Hurston, Claude McKay, Richmond Barthe, Aaron Douglas, and Langston Hughes. Locke was untiring and long suffering in his efforts to placate, cajole, and flatter Mainstream influentials into supporting the Harlem Renaissance. He served as virtual chamberlain to the imperious Charlotte Osgood Mason ("Godmother"), whose great wealth was bestowed with Locke's advice upon Hughes, Hurston, Barthe, Douglas, Louise Thompson, and others, on condition that they remain faithful to her notions of black creativity. Locke's role in the Harmon Foundation's decision to support African American painters and sculptors was crucial.

MCKAY, Claude (1889–1948), poet, novelist, was born in the hill country of Jamaica. His older brother and an eccentric British expatriate nurtured an appreciation for literature in him and a strong desire to write poetry. McKay's experimental verse was increasingly acclaimed, and, in 1912, he saw two volumes of his dialect poetry published, *Constab Ballads* and *Songs from Jamaica*. Scholarship assistance from the Jamaican authorities permitted McKay to seek training in agriculture at Tuskegee Institute in Alabama, but he transferred, dissatisfied after two years, to Kansas State College. Poetry not planting attracted McKay. Arriving in New York's Greenwich Village in 1917, he inserted himself into its bohemian and revolutionary circles and impressed Frank Harris and Max and Crystal Eastman. McKay's first poems in America, "Harlem Dancer" and "Invocation," appeared under a pseudonym (Eli Edwards) in *Pearson's* and *Seven Arts* in 1917. "If We Must Die" (1919) gained wide notice and electrified African Americans experiencing the terrible Red Summer of 1919. McKay left for London that year, read the works of Marx and Lenin, and joined the staff of Sylvia Pankhurst's communist newspaper, *The Worker's Dreadnought* (1920).

Returning to New York, McKay saw his first American volume of poetry appear as *Spring in New Hampshire* (1920), followed in 1922 by *Harlem Shadows*. Enjoying unprecedented fame, he assumed the co-editorship with Michael Gold of the Eastmans' *Liberator*. Increasingly disenchanted by American race relations, disappointed with Marcus Garvey's UNIA, and unhappy with editorial politics at *The Liberator*, McKay left for Russia in 1922, not to return to the United States until 1934. He wrote his bombshell bestseller *Home to Harlem* (1928) in France, and *Banjo* (1929) in North Africa. McKay received the Harmon Foundation Gold Medal Prize for literature in 1928, but his sharp, mocking criticism of the senior notables of the Harlem Renaissance was unrelenting. His novels, autobiography (*A Long Way from Home,* 1937), and large correspondence with Alain Locke, James Weldon Johnson, Walter White, William Bullitt, Louise Bryant (Eugene O'Neill's former wife), and Arthur Schomburg displayed paranoia, bitter envy of the socially accomplished, and a robust blend of Rabelais and Zola in celebrating the qualities of the downtrodden.

NUGENT, Richard Bruce (1906–1989?), poet, writer, illustrator, professional Bohemian, was born in Washington, D.C. Educated in the public schools of the city, precocious, handsome, and self-consciously decadent, Nugent (a.k.a. Richard Bruce) was a protégé of Alain Locke and an intimate companion of Langston Hughes, Claude McKay, and Wallace Thurman. He wandered off from his well-connected family, to New York City at age thirteen, surviving as an elevator boy, bellhop, and perhaps mascot of Rudolph Valentino. Nugent went to great lengths to model himself on a composite image of the precious characters in Carl Van Vechten's fiction. He delighted in scandalizing Harlem Renaissance officialdom—W. E. B. Du Bois, Jessie Fauset, Benjamin Brawley, and Walter White—but his reputation as enfant terrible of the Renaissance was secretly approved by most of its members. The impressionistic piece in *Fire!!* (November 1916), "Smoke, Lillies and Jade!" may not have distressed its "representative Negro" readership as much as Nugent hoped. Nugent's creative output was fairly thin—a few poems in Cullen's *Caroling Dusk* anthology, theater reviews in *Opportunity,* a choral drama performed at the Eastman School of Music in 1932—*Sadji*—*An African Ballet*—and mauve decade illustrations for *Fire!!, Harlem,* and numerous fugitive publications of the period.

O'NEILL, Eugene Gladstone (1888–1953), dramatist, was born in New York City. His father, James, was a successful touring actor whose role as the Count of Monte Cristo was famous. After boarding school at Betts Academy in Stamford, Connecticut, O'Neill attended Princeton for one year, then spent six years roving much of the globe. In summer 1916, O'Neill joined a group of artists and playwrights in the fishing village of Provincetown, Massachusetts.

Months later, the group converted a Greenwich Village brownstone into the Provincetown Playhouse. O'Neill's *The Emperor Jones,* starring the brilliant, alcoholic African American actor Charles Gilpin, was performed at the Provincetown Playhouse in 1920. Its 1924 revival saw that role taken by the then untested Paul Robeson. *All God's Chillun Got Wings* (1924) was produced on Broadway amid controversy and threats of violence because of its miscegenation theme. Plays such as *The Hairy Ape* (1922), *Desire Under the Elms* (1924), and *Mourning Becomes Electra* (1931) earned the playwright the Nobel Prize for Literature in 1936.

OVINGTON, Mary White (1865–1951), settlement house activist, writer, civil rights official, was born into an abolitionist family in Brooklyn, New York. Educated at Radcliffe College, Ovington early focused her social concerns on the living conditions of the urban poor and the plight of African Americans. *Half a Man: The Status of the Negro in New York* (1911), her sociological study of the different roles available to black and white working women, remains a classic. Ovington was one of the principal founders of the NAACP, whose institutional history she vividly recapitulated in her autobiographical *The Walls Came Tumbling Down* (1947). Her *Portraits in Color* (1927) was equally lively in describing W. E. B. Du Bois, James Weldon Johnson, Walter White, and other early civil rights leaders, as well as Marcus Garvey. Ovington was a major contributor to and occasional editor of *The Crisis.* She was one of Du Bois's closest collaborators. Her role on the board of directors during the NAACP's first quarter-century was second to none in selection of personnel and formulation of policy.

PATTERSON, Louise Thompson (1901–?), essayist, intellectual, was born in Chicago but grew up in a roving household in the Far West and California. She was educated at the University of California at Berkeley, graduating in 1923 with a degree in economics. Her understanding of racism received a memorable boost when she heard W. E. B. Du Bois lecture on the subject while she was in college. Thompson accepted a teaching position in business administration at Hampton Institute (Virginia) in 1926, an embittering experience to her because of the administration's extreme academic and racial conservatism. Having headed for New York on a National Urban League scholarship to pursue graduate studies, Thompson soon entered Harlem Renaissance circles through her friendship with Aaron and Alta Douglas. She married Wallace Thurman and had not divorced him at the time of his death, although temperamental incompatibility had quickly ended any intimacy between them. Her friendship with Langston Hughes deepened, and she was hired by Charlotte Osgood Mason to serve as secretary to both Hughes and Hurston in their writing haven in Plainfield, New Jersey. The bitter dispute between Hughes and Hurston over authorship of the dramatic comedy *Mule-Bone* may have been influenced by the latter's resentment of Thompson's relationship with Hughes. After she took a position with the Congregational Education Society, Thompson's intellect and efficiency attracted the attention of the leading African American communist James W. Ford. She became increasingly involved in the activities of the American Communist party. She was the driving force behind the ill-fated trip taken by Hughes and some thirty African Americans to Russia in June 1932. In 1933, she married the formidable civil rights lawyer and future African American theoretician of the CPUSA, William Patterson.

ROBESON, Paul (1898–1976), athlete, lawyer, singer, actor, militant socialist, was born in Princeton, New Jersey. His father was a minister. Robeson graduated from Rutgers University in 1919, capping a stellar career as winner of twelve varsity letters and junior-year induction into Phi Beta Kappa. Earning a law degree from Columbia University, he spent a year with a New York law firm. His roles in the 1921 Harlem YMCA revival of Ridgely Torrence's *Simon the Cyrenian* and the 1922 Broadway production of Mary Hoyt Wiborg's *Taboo* led to abandonment of the law. His appearance two years later in Eugene O'Neill's explosive Provincetown Players' drama about miscegenation, *All God's Chillun Got Wings*, fully launched Robeson's acting career.

In 1925 Robeson starred in the Broadway revival of O'Neill's *The Emperor Jones*. Acclaimed roles as Crown in *Porgy* (1928) and Joe in *Showboat* (1928) followed. His appearance in London as Othello (1930) and the following year as Yank in *The Hairy Ape* began a long stretch of memorable portrayals in plays, musicals, and film. Robeson made racial history in the American theater when he starred again in *Othello* opposite Uta Hagen and Jose Ferrer at New York's Shubert Theatre. The production opened in 1943 and ran for a record-breaking 296 performances, followed by a long tour. Robeson also pursued a singing career that combined the folk music of the world with spirituals, opera, popular music, and classical songs. *Ballads for Americans,* a recording of his 1939 national radio broadcast, was an enormous commercial success.

Meanwhile, Robeson's concern for social justice gradually drew him to the left. He made his first visit to the Soviet Union in 1934. His dynamic wife, Eslanda Cardoza Goode (descended from an African American family prominent in Reconstruction South Carolina), encouraged Robeson's political activism. He sang to Welsh coal miners and before Republican troops in the Spanish Civil War. After World War Two, Robeson became a passionate critic of American racism and a tireless advocate for peace between the United States and the Soviet Union. Many perceived his conduct as disloyal to his country and subservient to International Communism. His passport was revoked by the State Department in 1950, not to be restored until 1958, and he remained a virtual un-person in the United States until his death.

ROGERS, Joel Augustus (1880–1966), writer, popular historian, and newspaperman, was born in Negril, Jamaica. Very light-skinned, Rogers experienced little racial prejudice until he settled in the United States in 1906. Self-educated, he turned to writing fiction and pseudo-history in order to expose the fallacies of racial prejudice. His first work was *Man and Superman* (1917), an imaginary dialogue about large racial matters between an educated African American porter and a southern white legislator. Rogers's most influential work was *The World's Greatest Men of African Descent* (1931), a monograph in which he identified numerous putatively white historical figures as descendants of African forebears.

SCHOMBURG, Arthur Alfonso (1874–1938), bibliophile, curator, writer, was born in San Juan, Puerto Rico, where he was educated in the public schools. He attended St. Thomas College in the Virgin Islands. Schomburg came in 1891 to the United States, where he worked for a prominent New York law firm and devoted himself to the cause of Puerto Rican independence from Spain. He began to collect literature and materials on Africa and Africans in the New World and in Europe. In 1911, he and the journalist John E. Bruce ("Bruce Grit") founded the Society for Historical Research, which published Schomburg's bibliographic findings and his influential essay *Racial Integrity: A Plea for the Establishment of a*

Chair of Negro History in Our Schools, Colleges, Etc. (1913). Schomburg was elected president of the American Negro Academy in 1922. In 1926, his collection of more than five thousand books, three thousand manuscripts, and several thousand etchings, drawings, and pamphlets was purchased by the New York Public Library with a ten-thousand-dollar grant from the Carnegie Corporation, for which he served as curator until his untimely death. This purchase served as the nucleus for what was to become the Schomburg Center for Research in Black Culture of the New York Public Library.

SCHUYLER, George Samuel (1895–1977), novelist, journalist, was born in Providence, Rhode Island, and educated in the public schools of Syracuse, New York, until he enlisted in the army in 1912. Schuyler served with the famous 25th U.S. Infantry Regiment for seven years (1912–1919), attaining the rank of first lieutenant. Moving to New York in 1922, he came to the attention of A. Philip Randolph and Chandler Owen, editors of the new radical monthly *The Messenger*. Schuyler served on its editorial staff from 1923 to 1928. He also contributed a popular column ("Views and Reviews") to the African American weekly newspaper the *Pittsburgh Courier* during this time. Schuyler's iconoclasm and abiding integrationism led him to discount much of the cultural and ethnic ideas of Harlem Renaissance writers such as Langston Hughes, Wallace Thurman, and Zora Neale Hurston. His "The Negro-Art Hokum," appearing in *The Nation* (June 16, 1926), sparked a memorable rebuttal from Hughes in the next issue: "The Negro Artist and the Racial Mountain." Schuyler and his wife (an affluent white Texan) were close friends of H. L. Mencken, and Schuyler clearly came to model his writings on those of the acerbic "sage of Baltimore." *Black No More* (1931) lampooned virtually every Harlem Renaissance personality, white as well as black.

SPENCER, Anne (1882–1976), was born in Bramwell, West Virginia, and educated at Virginia Seminary and College in Lynchburg, Virginia. Until her retirement in 1943, she was the librarian at Lynchburg's Dunbar High School. Dutiful wife, devoted mother, and active citizen, Spencer was a kindly disposed and even-tempered person who wrote delicately of her likes and dislikes in verse that was characterized as noble and mildly feminist, if not particularly animated. Her first poem, "Lady, Lady," appeared in

Locke's *The New Negro*. She was considered one of the most talented of the New Negro poets. Her Lynchburg house and garden served much the same sheltering role during segregation as poet Georgia Douglas Johnson's Washington, D.C., salon (Du Bois and Sterling Brown were regulars).

STRIBLING, Thomas Sigismund (1881–1965), novelist, was a Southern white whose fascination with African American life resulted in the novel *Birthright* (1922), the first work of fiction featuring an African American male since Harriet Beecher Stowe's *Uncle Tom's Cabin*. Its impact on the Talented Tenth was profound and was the direct cause of Jessie Fauset and Walter White putting their hand to novel writing.

THURMAN, Wallace (1902–1934), dramatist, journalist, novelist, was born in Salt Lake City, Utah. He graduated from high school and attended the University of Utah briefly (1919–1920). After matriculating at the University of Southern California, Thurman found work alongside Arna Bontemps in the Los Angeles central post office. The first of his several efforts to found and edit a magazine came in Los Angeles with *The Outlet* (1924–1925). After its failure, Thurman moved to New York City, where he worked as editor of the short-lived publication *The Looking Glass* (1924–1925). He was befriended by the astute African American literary and theater critic Theophilus Lewis, who helped Thurman find editorial employment with A. Philip Randolph and Chandler Owen's new radical monthly, *The Messenger*. Thurman became circulation manager of the liberal white monthly *The World Tomorrow* in 1926, one of the first African Americans to secure such work. He became something of a legend in Harlem because of his quicksilver brilliance and his phenomenal reading. A loyal circle of Harlem writers and artists formed around Thurman—Langston Hughes, Richard Bruce, Zora Neale Hurston, Aaron Douglas, John P. Davis, and Gwendolyn Bennett—and joined him in founding and editing the quarterly *Fire!!* (November 1926). Together with Hughes's article in *The Nation,* "The Negro Artist and the Racial Mountain" (June 1926), this single issue of Thurman's magazine sounded the knell of the Talented Tenth Renaissance guided by the NAACP and the Urban League.

In 1927, Thurman's depression due to large debts incurred launching *Fire!!* was attenuated by publication of his essays in *New*

Republic, Bookman, Independent, The World Tomorrow, and *Opportunity.* The following year, he attempted to start a successor to *Fire!! Harlem* (November 1928) was less strenuously shocking and survived for two issues. Employment as a reader at Macaulay's kept Thurman afloat, the first African American holding this position in the New York publishing industry. *Harlem,* the sensationalized Broadway adaptation of his short story in *Fire!!* "Cordelia the Crude," opened in February 1929 and ran for almost a hundred performances before traveling successfully to Chicago and Los Angeles. *The Blacker the Berry . . .* was published later that year, a loquacious but engrossing exploration of color prejudice within Afro-America and the peculiar cultural consequences of racial segregation. Thurman had rent-free use of a house at 267 West 136th Street in Harlem that came to be called "Niggerati manor," a gathering spot for Bruce, Hurston, Hughes, Thompson, Bennett, Dorothy West, and other insurgent younger artists. Thurman's unhappy marriage and costly divorce negotiations with Louise Thompson remained unresolved. His last novels appeared in the same year—*The Interne* and *Infants of the Spring* (1932). Two years later, he returned to Harlem from writing film scenarios in Hollywood, disillusioned that he hadn't written the Great American Novel, convinced of the futility of the arts-and-letters movement, and desperately ill with tuberculosis. His novel *The Interne* was set in City Hospital on Welfare Island, where he would die three days before Christmas, 1934, after violating his physician's orders not to drink.

TOOMER, Nathan Eugene (1894–1967), writer, poet, playwright, born in Washington, D.C., was the grandson of the Reconstruction lieutenant governor of Louisiana and contested U.S. senator Pinckney Benton Stewart Pinchback. Deserted by his father and bereft of his mother at an early age, Toomer was raised by his grandparents and given a laissez-faire introduction to literature by his brilliant uncle, Bismarck. He graduated from Washington's famous M Street High School (Dunbar) and attended briefly a variety of academic institutions: University of Wisconsin (1914), Massachusetts College of Agriculture, a physical training institute in Chicago, and lectures at New York University. He flirted with socialism, worked as a ship fitter in New Jersey, sold cars in Chicago, taught physical education in Milwaukee, and finally became attracted to the intellectual ferment in Greenwich Village. His friendship with Waldo Frank, Sherwood Anderson, Hart Crane, Alfred Stieglitz, and Mabel Dodge Luhan, among others, opened the pages of *Double-Dealer, S 4 N, The Dial, Broom,* and *The Liberator.* Gorham Munson, Allen Tate, Kenneth Burke, and other perceptive critics of the day applauded Toomer's verse and short stories enthusiastically. O'Neill's plays had drawn the public's attention to the richness and perceived exoticism of African American life, but Lost Generation novelists believed that the active voices of the South's mudsill peasantry seemed to speak and sing through Toomer's verse. Frank asked Toomer to take him to South Carolina in 1922 so that he could incorporate the experience in his next novel, *Holiday* (1923).

The next year, the firm of Boni & Liveright published Toomer's *Cane,* an uncategorizable collection of poetry and sketches— a "prose poem"—to good critical reviews but dismal sales. Among African American would-be writers, however, Toomer's book was received as an epiphany. It convinced Jessie Fauset, Walter White, and Charles S. Johnson that an artistic movement could be launched based on African American talent and themes. Meanwhile, Toomer, who had become romantically involved with Frank's wife, sailed for France. When he returned to America, he came as the anointed representative of the mystical Gurdjieff movement. Mabel Dodge Luhan gave Toomer large sums of money to further his work for Gurdjieff. When James Weldon Johnson asked permission to include Toomer's poetry in a new edition of his *The Book of American Negro Poetry,* Toomer informed Johnson that he was no longer a Negro. Toomer continued to write, submitting several manuscripts to major publishers without success, but none reflected the singular promise of his early work.

WALROND, Eric (1898–1956), writer, was born in Georgetown, Guyana. He grew up in Barbados and Panama, educated both in English and Spanish. From 1916 to 1918, Walrond worked as a reporter on the *Panama Star and Herald.* He came to New York in 1918, enrolling in literature and writing courses at City College and Columbia University. Walrond attempted to manage an ethnic newspaper and then joined the staff of Marcus Garvey's international newspaper *The Negro World.* He moved with aplomb in many circles—among racially exclusive Garveyites, sophisticated Downtown whites, and the highest rungs of the Talented Tenth. Charles Johnson and Walter White recognized Walrond's value as a suave agent of the arts-and-letters movement and encouraged him to introduce promising poets and writers to influential whites and influential whites to Harlem. Walrond was business manager for *Opportunity* from 1925 to 1927. His perceptive social and political articles began to appear in the *New Republic, Current History,* and the *Independent.* The publication of *Tropic Death* (1926) marked a milestone in the Renaissance. The collection exuded mystery and danger. It was experimental in its use of dialect, sociologically deft in recreating unfamiliar and marginal Creole cultures, and filled with economic insights enveloped in allegory. Charles S. Johnson expected Walrond to write the great Renaissance novel. Provided with a Guggenheim Fellowship and supplementary funds from the writer Zona Gale, Walrond went abroad in 1928 to write under contract to Boni & Liveright a novel about the Panama Canal. Walrond lived on in obscurity in England without ever again publishing.

WEST, Dorothy (1908–), short-story writer, novelist, poet, was born in Boston and educated in the city's public schools. She attended Boston University and the Columbia School of Journalism. Her first story, "The Typewriter," was published in *Opportunity* when West was eighteen years old. She was among the first class of *Opportunity* talents. West was a close friend of Wallace Thurman, Richard Bruce, Paul Robeson, and Gwendolyn Bennett. She kept faith with the original ideals of the Harlem Renaissance until the end, loath to accept the failure of the arts-and-letters movement to transform the racial culture of America. In 1934, she founded *Challenge* to sustain the Harlem Renaissance. Three years later, West collaborated with Richard Wright to found and edit the more political *New Challenge.*

WHITE, Walter Francis (1893–1955), novelist, civil rights leader, was born in Atlanta, Georgia. White and his parents were "voluntary Negroes," blond and blue-eyed, but the scarifying experience of the 1906 Atlanta Riot irreversibly committed Walter White to the struggle for African American civil rights. After graduating from Atlanta University in 1916, White went to work for the Atlanta Life Insurance Company. In 1918, fellow Atlanta alumnus James Weldon Johnson offered White the position of assistant executive secretary of the NAACP. White was a riveting public speaker and a tireless organizer. During the Red Summer, he infiltrated vigilante and Klan groups in the Deep South in order to obtain evidence of mob violence against African Americans. His article in *The Nation* " 'Massacring Whites' in Arkansas" (Dec. 6, 1919) stunned the country. White was quick to perceive the implications of James Weldon Johnson's ideology of cultural achievement, and he excelled all of the orchestrators of the Harlem Renaissance except Charles S. Johnson in indefatigable lobbying, propagandizing, and socializing to further the goals of civil rights advancement of the race through arts and letters. When T. S. Stribling's *Birthright* appeared (1922), White and Jessie Fauset both agreed that they could write a better novel. White composed *The Fire in the Flint* (1924) in a summer. It was a surprisingly good propaganda novel about white supremacy in the South, which sold well in the United States and was subsequently widely translated. White's second novel, *Flight* (1926), was better developed but less interesting.

Having plunged into the literary life, White began to believe that he had the makings of a gifted writer. Sinclair Lewis was a social friend who offered professional advice, as did H. L. Mencken and Carl Van Vechten. White dropped in sometimes at the Algonquin Hotel to chat with members of the Round Table. Alfred and Blanche Knopf were frequent dinner companions along with Dorothy Parker, Heywood Broun, and the Gershwins. In his turn, White took on the role of agent and senior literary advisor to the painters, poets, singers, and novelists of Harlem. He took credit for persuading Paul Robeson to abandon law for acting. The baritone Jules Bledsoe's contract was renegotiated after White interceded on his behalf with the renowned impresario Sol Hurok. Publishing contracts at Knopf for Nella Larsen and Rudolph Fisher came more readily thanks to him. He gave Claude McKay excellent advice about placing the manuscript for *Home to Harlem,* which McKay ignored. A Guggenheim Fellowship enabled White and his family to settle for a year (1927) in the south of France while he worked on a trilogy set in Georgia. What he actually produced, however, was a study of lynching, *Rope and Faggot* (1930). Although White wrote in the same upper-class tradition as Jessie Fauset, his novels were more political and more robust. He allowed himself to be counted among the contributors to *Harlem* (November 1928), Thurman's successor magazine to *Fire!!*

By 1933, White was increasingly embroiled in NAACP policy disputes with W. E. B. Du Bois and preoccupied with the monopolizing of the Scottsboro Boys case by the CPUSA. His career as a novelist was at an end.

WOODSON, Carter Godwin (1875–1950), the "Father of Negro History," was born to former slaves in New Canton, Virginia, and educated at Berea College and, after a three-year stint of teaching in the Philippines, at the University of Chicago. After earning his B.A. and M.A. degrees at Chicago, Woodson entered Harvard, where he became the second African American to earn a doctorate (1912) from that university. While completing work for the Ph.D. in history, Woodson taught French, Spanish, English, and history at the District of Columbia's elite M Street High School. He organized the Association for the Study of Negro Life and History (ASNLH) in 1915 and founded the *Journal of Negro History* a year later. Five years later, Woodson organized the Associated Publishers to make available textbooks and monographs pertaining to African American subjects. That same year, he also established the influential *Negro History Bulletin* for high-school students. He inaugurated the first of the annual Negro History Weeks (later, Months) in February 1926. Woodson retired from teaching at Howard University and West Virginia State College in 1922 in order to devote his life to writing, editing, and promoting general interest in African American history. His *The Negro in Our History* (1922) was one of the first "scientific" works on the topic.